A TEXT BOOK OF

TRANSPORTATION ENGINEERING

FOR
SEMESTER – I
FINAL YEAR (B.E.) DEGREE COURSE IN CIVIL ENGINEERING

As Per the New Revised Syllabus of Savitribai Phule Pune University
(2012 Pattern)

D.R. PHATAK
Formerly Professor in Civil Engg. Deptt.
Government College of Engineering,
PUNE.

H.K. GITE
Assistant Engineer Grade-1
Water Resource Department, Govt. of Maharashtra
Formerly Assistant Professor, Civil Engg. Department
JSPM's Rajarshi Shahu College of Enginering,
Tathwade, Pune.

N 3688

TRANSPORTATION ENGINEERING (PU)   **ISBN 978-93-5164-690-7**

First Edition	:	**July 2015**
©	:	**Authors**

Published By :   **POLYPLATE**

NIRALI PRAKASHAN

Abhyudaya Pragati, 1312, Shivaji Nagar,
Off J.M. Road, PUNE – 411005
Tel - (020) 25512336/37/39, Fax - (020) 25511379
Email : niralipune@pragationline.com

☞ DISTRIBUTION CENTRES

PUNE

Nirali Prakashan : 119, Budhwar Peth, Jogeshwari Mandir Lane, Pune 411002, Maharashtra
Tel : (020) 2445 2044, 66022708, Fax : (020) 2445 1538
Email : bookorder@pragationline.com, niralilocal@pragationline.com

Nirali Prakashan : S. No. 28/27, Dhyari, Near Pari Company, Pune 411041
Tel : (020) 24690204 Fax : (020) 24690316
Email : dhyari@pragationline.com, bookorder@pragationline.com

MUMBAI

Nirali Prakashan : 385, S.V.P. Road, Rasdhara Co-op. Hsg. Society Ltd.,
Girgaum, Mumbai 400004, Maharashtra
Tel : (022) 2385 6339 / 2386 9976, Fax : (022) 2386 9976
Email : niralimumbai@pragationline.com

☞ DISTRIBUTION BRANCHES

JALGAON

Nirali Prakashan : 34, V. V. Golani Market, Navi Peth, Jalgaon 425001,
Maharashtra, Tel : (0257) 222 0395, Mob : 94234 91860

KOLHAPUR

Nirali Prakashan : New Mahadvar Road, Kedar Plaza, 1st Floor Opp. IDBI Bank
Kolhapur 416 012, Maharashtra. Mob : 9850046155

NAGPUR

Pratibha Book Distributors : Above Maratha Mandir, Shop No. 3, First Floor,
Rani Jhanshi Square, Sitabuldi, Nagpur 440012, Maharashtra
Tel : (0712) 254 7129

DELHI

Nirali Prakashan : 4593/21, Basement, Aggarwal Lane 15, Ansari Road, Daryaganj
Near Times of India Building, New Delhi 110002
Mob : 08505972553

BENGALURU

Pragati Book House : House No. 1, Sanjeevappa Lane, Avenue Road Cross,
Opp. Rice Church, Bengaluru – 560002.
Tel : (080) 64513344, 64513355,Mob : 9880582331, 9845021552
Email:bharatsavla@yahoo.com

CHENNAI

Pragati Books : 9/1, Montieth Road, Behind Taas Mahal, Egmore,
Chennai 600008 Tamil Nadu, Tel : (044) 6518 3535,
Mob : 94440 01782 / 98450 21552 / 98805 82331,
Email : bharatsavla@yahoo.com

niralipune@pragationline.com | www.pragationline.com

Also find us on **f** **www.facebook.com/niralibooks**

PREFACE

It gives us great pleasure in presenting the book on **"Transportation Engineering"**, which is written as per Savitribai Phule Pune University's revised syllabus (2012 course) and in most concised form. The book will also be very useful for the students preparing for Engineering Service Examination and AMIE Examination.

The subject matter is presented in simple and easy form. Sufficient care is taken to present the subject matter in the point wise form in most of the chapters.

Authors are extremely grateful to **Shri P. R. Bhamare**, Executive Director, MERI Nashik, **Shri Vijay Pandare**, Chief Engineer, META Nashik, **Dr. Belsare Sanjay**, Deputy Secretary and Superintending Engineer, WRD Mantralaya, Mumabi, **Shri I. S. Chaudhari**, Superintending Engineer, CDO Nashik, **Shri S. M. Sangle**, Executive Engineer, PH-Division 4, CDO Nashik, **Dr. P. P. Vitkar**, Director JSPM's Pune, **Shri S. L. Bhilare**, Associate Professor Civil Engineering Department RSCOE, Pune, and the entire staff of **CDO, Power House Circle, Nashik** for providing conducive environment and facilities for completing this book.

We are sincerely thankful to **Shri Dineshbhai K. Furia, Shri. Jignesh C. Furia, Mrs. Nirali Verma, Shri. M. P. Munde** and the entire team of Nirali Prakashan who really have taken keen interest and untiring efforts in publishing this text. We are also thankful to Mrs. Deepali Lachake (Co-ordinator) Mrs. Shilpa Kale, Miss. Rani Zinjade for their kind co-operation throughout the work.

Also, it is important to mention invaluable moral support of our beloved family members, who consistently encouraged us for better work.

Despite the best efforts taken by authors, it is possible that some unintentional errors might have taken place. Authors would gratefully acknowledge if any of these are pointed out. Suggestions and comments for further improvement of this book will be gratefully received and acknowledged from the students, teachers and others.

Pune   **Authors**

SYLLABUS

Unit I: Highway Engineering   **(6 hrs)**

Introduction:

Role of transportation, scope of road transportation, highway development in India, necessity of highway planning and development plans e.g. Bombay plan, Lucknow plan.

Classification of road:

Classification of roads, road patterns, planning surveys and preparation of master plan based on saturation system, determination of road length by 3rd road development plan.

Traffic engineering:

Traffic characteristics-road user characteristics, vehicular characteristics (only name and significance) Traffic studies –name of various studies and their uses, accident studies-objectives, causes of accident, condition and collision diagram, and measures for the reduction in accidents. Traffic regulation and control devices-traffic signs, traffic signals (types merits and demerits) road markings. Traffic islands, types of road intersections (sketch merits and demerits). Parking facilities.

Unit II   **(6 hrs)**

Highway alignment:

Basic requirements of an ideal alignment and factors controlling it, engineering survey for highway location, special requirements for hill roads,

Geometric design and traffic engineering:

Design controls and criteria for geometric design, cross sectional elements, sight distance requirements, stopping distance, overtaking sight distance, overtaking zones with IRC recommendations, attainment of super elevation, radius of curves, methods of introduction of extra widening, widening of pavement on horizontal curves, horizontal transition curves- objects, necessity, types of transition curves, length and shift of transition curves. Design of vertical alignment, gradient and its type, IRC recommendations, grade compensation on horizontal curve, vertical curves: - crest and sag curves, types of summit curves, length of summit curve for SSD and OSD. Requirements, types of valley curves, length of valley curve for comfort and head light sight distance criteria.

Highway drainage:

Importance of highway drainage, subsurface and surface drainage systems, scope of arboriculture for highway.

Unit III   **(6 hrs)**

Highway materials:

Importance and properties of sub-grade, pavement component materials. Tests on aggregates. Bitumen: Types--cut back, tar, emulsion and tests, modified binders, bitumen mix design by Marshall Stability test, viscosity based gradation of bitumen

Pavement design:

Objects and requirements, types of pavements structures, functions of pavement components factors affecting pavement design, Design of flexible pavement by C.B.R. Method, IRC 37- guidelines design of rigid pavements, actors affecting design & analysis of stress- wheel load stress & temp. Stress, critical combination of stress, IRC 58- design guidelines, types of joints, requirements of joints.

Construction:
Construction process of WBM, WMM, GSB (Mix design). Introduction to bituminous works such as prime coat, tack coat, seal coat, MPM, AC or BC, BM, DBM and premix carpet.

Unit IV: Airport Engineering (6 hrs)

Introduction:
Advantages and limitations of air transportation. Aeroplane component parts and important technical terms.

Airport planning:
Aircraft characteristics, which influence judicious and scientific planning of airports, Selection of sites, survey and drawings to be prepared for airport planning.

Airport layout:
Characteristics of good layout, runway configuration, airport obstruction, location of terminal buildings, aprons and hangers. Zoning requirements regarding permissible heights of constructions and landing within the airport boundary.

Runways and taxiways:
Runway orientation, wind coverage, use of wind rose diagram, basic runway length, corrections for elevation, temperature and gradient as per ICAO and FAA recommendation. Airport classification by ICAO.

Unit V: Bridege Engineering (6 hrs)

Introduction:
Classification of bridges, components of bridges, preliminary data to be collected during investigation of site for bridges, determination of discharge – empirical formula, direct methods, economical span, afflux, HFL, scour depth and clearance, locations of piers and abutments, factors influencing the choice of bridge super structure, approach roads.

Loads on bridges:
Brief specifications of different loads, forces, stresses coming on bridges, IRC load specification, requirements of traffic in the design of highway bridges

Substructure:
Abutment, Piers, and wing walls with their types based on requirement and suitability.

Unit VI (6 hrs)

Types of bridges
Various types of bridges:
a. Culvert: Definition, waterway of culvert and types.
b. Temporary bridges: Definition, materials used brief general ideas about timber, floating and pantoon bridges.
c. Movable Bridges: Bascule, cut boat, flying, swing, lift, transporter and transverse bridges, their requirement and suitability.
d. Fixed span bridges:
Simple, continuous, cantilever, arch, suspension, bowstring girder type and rigid frame and cable stayed bridges, materials for super structure.

Bearing:
Definition, purpose and importance. Types of bearings with their suitability.

Erection of bridge super structure and maintenance:
Introduction to different techniques of erection of bridge super structure and maintenance of bridges.

CONTENTS

Highway Engineering
Unit - I

Unit - II

Unit - III

Airport Engineering

Unit - IV

Bridge Engineering

Unit - V

Unit - VI

Chapter 1
INTRODUCTION

1.1 MEANING OF TRANSPORT

Transport refers to the activity that facilitates physical movement of goods as well as individuals from one place to another. In business, it is considered as an auxiliary to trade, that means, it supports trade and industry in carrying raw materials to the place of production and distributing finished products for consumption. Individuals or business firms that engage themselves in such activities are called transporters. Generally, transporters carry raw material, finished products, passengers etc. from one place to another. So it removes the distance barrier. Now-a-days goods produced at one place are readily available at distant places. People move freely throughout the world because of transport. It is associated with every step of our life. Without transport, we, as well as business units cannot move a single step. Let us discuss its importance.

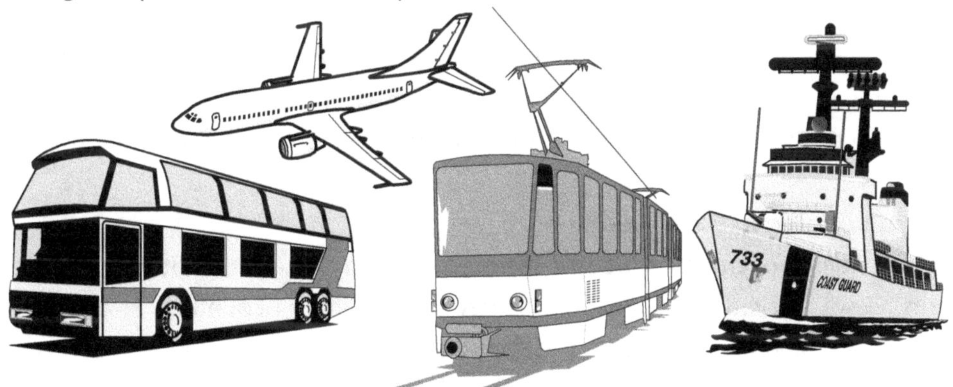

Fig. 1.1

1.1.1 Importance Of Transport

Followings are the points of importance of transport.

(a) Makes Available Raw Materials to Manufacturers or Producers :

Transport makes it possible to carry raw materials from places where they are available, to places where they can be processed and assembled into finished goods.

(b) Makes Available Goods to Customers :

Transport makes possible movement of goods from one place to another with great ease and speed. Thus, consumers spread in different parts of the country have the benefit of consuming goods produced at distant places.

(c) Enhances Standard of Living :

Easy means of transport facilitates large-scale production at low costs. It gives consumers the choice to make use of different quantities of goods at different prices. So it raises the standard of living of the people.

(d) Helps During Emergencies and Natural Calamities :

In times of national crisis, due to war or internal disturbance, transport helps in quick movement of troops and the supplies needed in the operation.

(e) Helps in Creation of Employment :

Transport provides employment opportunity to individuals as drivers, conductors, pilots, cabin crew, captain of the ship etc. who are directly engaged in transport business. It also provides employment to people indirectly in the industries producing various means of transport and other transport equipments. People can also provide repairing and maintenance services by opening service centers at convenient locations.

(f) Helps in Labour Mobility :

Transport helps a lot in providing mobility to workers. You may be aware that people from our country go to foreign countries to work in different industries and factories. Foreingers also come India to work. In India, people also move from one part to another in search of work. Similarly, it is not always possible to have workers near the factory. Most industries have their own transport system to bring the workers from where they reside to the place of work.

(g) Helps in bringing nations together :

Transport facilities movement of people from one country to another. It helps in exchange of cultures, views and practices between the people of different countries. This brings about greater understanding among people and awareness about different countries. Thus, it helps to promote a feeling of international brotherhood.

1.1.2 Modes Of Transport

We fine the basically transport is possible through land, air or water, which are called the different modes of transport. On land we use trucks, tractors etc., to carry goods; train, bus, cars etc. to carry passengers. In air, we find aeroplanes, helicopters to carry passengers as well as goods. Similarly in water we find ships, steamers etc., to carry goods and passengers. All these are known as various means of transport. Let us discuss about various modes of transport. The modes of transport can be broadly divided into three categories.

- Land transport (Road, Railway Pipelines transport, Ropeway transport).
- Water transport (Inland water transport, Ocean transport).
- Air transport.

1.2 HISTORY OF HIGHWAYS IN THE CONTINENT

Civilisation cannot exist without some means of communications. Even sparse human settlements have to communicate with each other and well trodden foot paths may be considered fore - runner of highways. In the Bible too, there is mention to the construction of road between *Egypt and Babylon* about 500 years before the christian era. Roman civilisation which is a founding father of European civilisation had good roads. These roads were primarily made for military conquest and subjugation of colonies. The important road called Via Appia connecting Rome with the Southern tip of Italy could be quoted in this context. These Roman roads were direct in alignment, well drained, well above the general ground level, and sufficiently thick and strong arch bridges spanned the water courses. The roads in the Roman cities were brick on edge pavements to sustain charriot loads. The decline of the Roman empire saw set back in road building in Europe.

Persians under the king Darius 1, are believed to have constructed a road from turkey to the Persian Gulf. This road, called Persian Royal Road was constructed when Persian empire was at it's Zenith.

After the Roman civilisation, the art of road building received a boost in Europe with the coming of Industrial Revolution. Wheeled coaches and animal drawn passenger coaches began to make their appearance in sixteenth century and this gave rise to a demand for good roads.

A french gentleman, who was then the Inspector General of Roads in France, named Pierre Tresaguet, made the road profile slightly higher in the centre and lower towards the shoulder, what we recognise as camber today. He tried for proper maintenance and drainage of roads.

In United Kingdom, around eighteen century, a further development occurred. The art consisted of putting boulders on the ground, compact them and spread gravel as surface layer. For the soft ground, bundles of heather were used as sub-base. This improvement is generally ascribed to John Metcalf. In the early part of nineteenth century, Thomas Telford introduced a innovation in the road building. He used hand picked boulders as foundations for road bases. The original idea was of course due to Met calf but Telford popularised it and constructed many roads with this innovation. In India, many secondary and tertiary roads are constructed with boulder soling as base, the origin of which is Telford construction.

John Macadam, a Scottish engineer must be mentioned here. He propagated two important principles which are valid even now :

(1) All loads are finally carried by mother earth and if the earth on which the road pavement rests is in dry state, heavy loads can be carried without undue settlements.

(2) Instead of big boulder paving, advocated by Telford small angular pieces of aggregate compacted together are better bonded together and thus can provide better hard surface. The size of the stone advocated by Macadam to give practical utility to it, is that it should be possible for the engineer to put it in mouth. The contributions of John Macadam were important. It may be good idea to compare Telford and Macadam construction here.

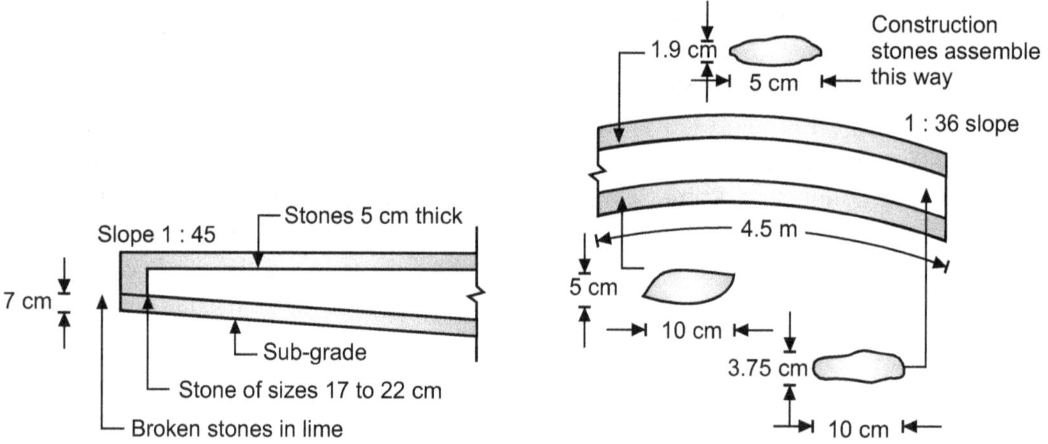

Fig. 1.1 (a): Telford construction **Fig. 1.1 (b): Macadam construction**

Comparison between Telford and Macadom Construction

Telford Construction	Macadam Construction
(1) Gentle slope	(1) Steep slope
(2) Bigger sizes of stones.	(2) Smaller sizes of stones.
(3) Typical assemblage of stones in the standing fashion.	(3) Assemblage in sitting fashion. Therefore better stress distribution.
(4) From the point of view of stress distribution, Telford is inferior.	(4) From the point of view of stress distribution, Macadam is superior.
(5) Requires less stones.	(5) Requires more stones.

The construction features of Roman Roads, Tresaguet, Telford and Macadam are indicated in Fig. 1.2.

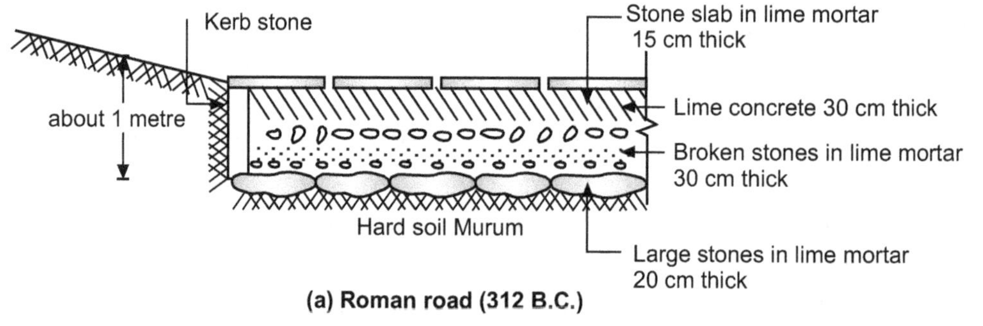

(a) Roman road (312 B.C.)

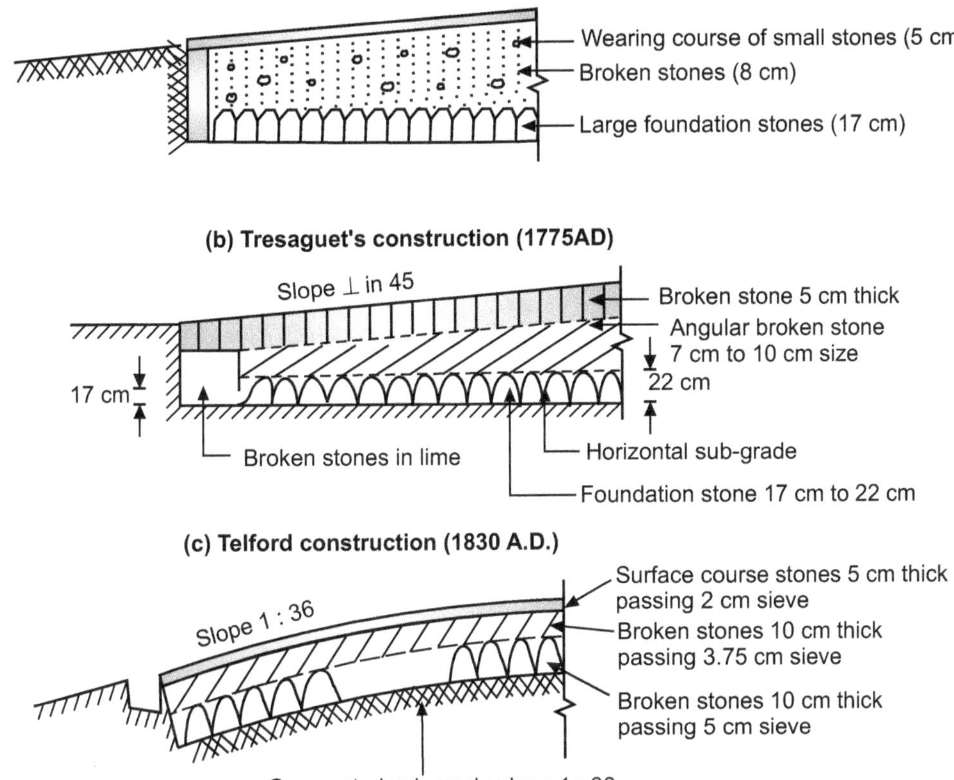

Fig. 1.2 : Early Roads

The use of steam road roller developed by Eveling and Bedford in nineteenth century and use of portland cement in construction in nineteenth century paved the way for modern road construction in Europe. In fact tars and asphalts were being used for road construction in 1830 s. But in fairness it must be said that the basic traffic on road was not much, that need was catered for by Railways. The invention of automobile with pneumatic tyred wheel is vastly responsible for the road development.

Though developed quite early, the automobile had a slow development in the nineteenth century but the first world war of 1914 -18 gave a fantastic boost to it's growth. With the growth in the number of automobiles, the traffic on the roads increased considerably and roads became a permanent and important feature of modern life in Europe. Now, the roads can almost be compared with arteries in human body, which do the basic work of transporting. Without good motorable roads the transportation of material will come to a standstill, and the place of roads is now no more a "stand by" to railways, as more than 40 % of freight is through road and roads have now come to stay as permanent feature of modern life.

1.3 THE HISTORY OF ROADS IN INDIA

Hindu Period in India : During the Aryan period or vedic period, there is no question that a good network of road work existed. Kautilya the great sage and the administrator had laid down standard widths of roads and Megas-thenes, the Greek Ambassador to the Court of Maurya mentions the prevelance of good roads. Patliputra was connected to all important towns by good roads, on which heavy charriots could ply. The roads were lined with trees and provided with wells and rest houses in between. Fa-hein the Chineese traveller had come to India during Gupta (3rd and 4th century) period and his writings indicate presence of good roads. Hiuen-Tsang who visited India during the regime of Harsha testifies it. All this literature tells us that a good trunk road existed connecting Patliputra to Takshashila touching Varanasi, Kausumbhi, Mathura. Indraprastha and Kurukshetra. The excavations carried out at Mohen-Jo-Daro has indicated that good intercity roads existed then - that is in pre-biblic time. However, the art of road making was not converted into a proper text and we can only make a guess as to the material composing the roads. Not only Mohen Jo Daro but recent excavations at Harappan site have also indicated existence of great cities. For example, excavation by the Archaeological Survey of India (ASI) at Dholavira in Gujarat's Kutch border district has unearthed a unique city, probably among the most important Harappan sites discovered yet.

Ever since the discovery of Dholavira in 1967-68 by Jagat Pati Joshi Director-General of ASI this site has aroused the curiosity of archaeologists the world over.

Now a nine-week operation under the direction of ASI superintending archaeologist Ravindra Singh Bisht has revealed part of a magnificant city, indicating earlier surface observations, an official spokesman has said.

The main city, spread over 48 hectares, or even more, was secured by massive mud brick defences. Within these walls, there is evidence of three principal divisions that have been named as the 'Citadel' 'Middle Town', and 'Lower Town', on the basis of their relative location and layout.

While the Citadel and Middle Town have separate but inter-connected fortification systems, the Lower Town has not yet shown any such provision. But all three are within the general fortification and present a perfect example of rectangular town planning.

As in the Harappan site of Kalibangan, the Citadel has two conjoined and fortified sub-divisions the taller of which (in the east) has been named as the 'Castle' and the lower (in the west) as 'Bailey'. The Castle had at least three gates opening in different directions. Of these, the north gate was possibly the grandest and probably used for ceremonial occasions, the excavations indicate.

The gates, at least in the later stage, were designed as ascending terraces with flights of steps, raised platforms, passageways and chambers, all in striking symmetry.

Exposed houses contain rooms, fire places, storage jars, simple or cut stone drains and sullage jars or pits, and some of the houses indicate such specialised craft activity as bead manufacturing or shell work. The principal building material is rubble, hammer-dressed stone blocks pillars, standardised fire bricks and earth.

Apart from town planning, another unique contribution of Dholavira is the find of four members of a stone pillary consisting of an exquisite damru-like base and three pieces of the upward tapering shaft. This kind of pillar has not been found at any other Harappan site so far.

Other important finds include micro-drill bits made out of a hard stone, 13 complete or fragmented seals, eight seal impressions on clay and one bronze figurine of an animal. Seals bear short epigraphs in the Harappan script and many of them are engraved with unicorns.

Among the other finds are beads of semi-precious stones, gold, copper, shell, steatite, faience and clay, copper objects including a pin with two spiral heads, bangles of stone, shell and clay, terracotta models of wheels, animals, games-men and a variety of stone querns, grinders, rubbers, polishers, pestles and mortar used for domestic and manufacturing purposes.

The excavation work underway holds promise of adding new perspectives and colour to the Harappan personality according to archaeologists.

Dholavira is unique in that the striking perfection that underlies the city's layout and construction of gateways does not find a parallel anywhere. Further, the intricately carved pillar members are altogether new items of Harappan architecture. Smaller pillar-like members are also coming up during excavations and their real importance is under investigation.

The excavation may also throw up clues about the locational importance of Dholavira in the settlement network of the Harappans.

There is no question that such a fine city, described as above cannot function without good roads. We as Indians to whatever caste creed and religion we may belong have every reason to take pride in the fact that when most of the rest of the world was moving in sheep skin clothes, our fore-fathers had constructed such good cities and roads.

Islamic Period in India : In northern India, where the, Mughal, Turks, Aphaghan dynasties had a sway over a considerable time, the importance of good roads was immediately felt to subjugate this vast land, where rebellions were but a order of the day. Northern India was essentially a plain country and without the formation of reasonable roads, it was impossible to govern. In fact, one reason why these invaders, which later on became part and parcel of Indian Heritage, could not force their dynasties in the Deccan, Rajastan, the land of the Ahoms - i.e. the Asam, the Chambals, might be that they faced unhospitable country along with the populace. One name which shines in the Islamic period is the Afghan monarch Sher Shah Suri. He adorned the throne of Delhi for a considerable shorter span but he constructed the Grand Trunk Road, more or less on the pattern of the present National Highway from Delhi to Culcutta.

The grand trunk road made by him was paved with Kankar (limestone) and had a sound bed. In fact, he had constructed Sarais (Rest places) and planted trees alongside the road. However, it must be said, that the population in Islamic period was living in sort of ghettos and there was very little interaction between different social economic and ethnic groups, with the result that there must have been very less traffic on roads. With the present day ideas of expecting reasonable return from the road, the roads must have been a "luxury." All the same that the roads existed, may be for the military use, is important.

In general, there were less court historions at the court of Muslim Kings in the Deccan, and as such we have less evidence of recorded building activity, but the excavations at Hampi in Karnataka have indicated high rise wall constructed with two parallel walls along the foundations to remove the thrust of the wall on the main walls. The people whose thinking is so deep must have thought about roads. The ruins of Vijayanagaram clearly indicate that those times also, there was reasonable and efficient road system.

1.4 DEVELOPMENT OF ROADS IN INDIA DURING BRITISH PERIOD

The British when they came to India saw in existing road structure, the possibility of military manoeuvres. William Bentinck constructed the modern Grand Trunk Road from Calcutta to Delhi which was then extended to Peshawar. This particular road had permanent bridges and good stone or Kankar bed. The controversial Dalhousise created the provincial P.W.D. in place of military boards in 1885. Some Engineering Colleges were also started and in general by the end of nineteenth century, there was a good system of trunk roads.

Now, arose a competitor to road industry in the form of Railways. The first railway line was opened in 1853 in Bombay i.e. Mumbai and in the immediate decades to follow the railway network was rapidly extended throughout the length and the breadth of the country. The railways were useful to the British for carrying troops and also raw material and therefore in the British interests only feeder roads that led to and supported the system of railways were constructed. In general, roads received scant attention. The Government of India Act of 1919 made the roads a subject of provincial charge and the Central Government bothered with roads of strategic importance. The lag between the advent of railways and the appearance of motor vehicle in India was nearly fifty years or so and in this time, the road construction took a back seat. Though the development of automobile in Europe and America was faster, the beginning of the twentieth century saw the first motor vehicle on the road which gave impetus to road building as industry. Then came the First World War and partly as it's result, there was a tremendous growth in the number of the motor vehicles.

Jayakar Committee : As a result of this motor vehicle population, there was a demand for better roads, even in the Council of States, then existing. Government of India as a response to this demand, appointed a committee called the Road Development Committee consisting of members from both the houses of central legislature and Mr. M R. Jayakar was appointed chairman of the committee. This committee popularly known as Jayakar committee went into an exercise of finding out

- whether the existing road requires further development and if so
- how this development can be achieved and how finances could be arranged with reference to the distribution of functions between the Central and Provincial Governments in the forms existing then.

The findings of the Jayakar Committee could be summarised as follows :

- It came to the conclusion that the road system existing then was totally inadequate and that it must be developed further so that it can serve specific functions namely (a) as a complement and tributory to the existing railway network (b) for social and political progress of rural population so that they can partake the benefits of motor transport and (c) for better marketing of agricultural produce.

- The committee came to the conclusion that only the resources of state exchequer were not enough for road development and that the Central Government should bear some burden of this task.

- To raise the finances to meet the cost of road development, there should be additional taxation which should include (a) duty on motor spirit (b) vehicle taxation (c) license fee for vehicles plying on the road.

  The additional funds collected from motor spirit duty were to go to the central Revenue as Road Development fund, intended for road development.

- Committee did not consider it worth while to create additional authority in the form of Central Road Board but recommended appointment of road engineer instead.

- Jayakar Committee also recommended holding of periodic Road Conferences to discuss inter alia questions relating to road construction and road development.

Jayakar Committee was possibly the first attempt in the nineteenth century to go into the intricacies involved in the road development and hence is important.

The Government seriously considered the recommendations of the Jayakar Committee. Most of it's findings were accepted. The central road fund was created with the help of additional duty that was then levied on motor fuel i.e. petrol. Ten percent of this fund was detained by the Central Government and the remainder was then distributed amongst the provinces, then existing in the ratio of the consumption of the petrol in that province to the total consumption of India.

As a result of the recommendations of Jayakar Committee, the first conference of highway engineers took place in 1930. These conferences from 1930 – 1934 created greater awareness in the road development and construction and paved the way for establishment of Indian Roads Congress (IRC) in 1934.

1.5 NAGPUR PLAN

The Nagpur Plan was at the initiative of the Central Government then existing in 1943. Then on slaught of Second World War has caused sufficient increase in the traffic and consequent deterioration of the pavements. The Chief Engineers of the then provinces therefore, met at Nagpur at the instance of Central Government to evolve road plan for the next twenty years and is now generally called as the Nagpur plan. The major recommendations of this conference were

- The roads should be divided into four categories viz.

   (a) National Highways : Which would traverse the provinces and would be major arteries of communications and will be of national importance from strategic and other purposes.

   (b) Provincial or State Roads : Which connect major towns in the state or province.

   (c) District Roads : Which would connect important townships in the districts and therefore would take traffic from the national and state roads to the interior of the district. Depending upon the importance they could be further classed as major district roads or other district roads.

   (d) Village Roads : Which would link important villages to the road network.

- National Highways should be the major frame work within which road system of the country should develop. Maintenance and construction of national highways should be liability of Central Government, financially.

- The national, state and major district roads should have durable hard pavement crust, but the other district road, village roads may have an earth surface, but further improvement in this earth surface such as soil-stabilization gravelling should be considered when necessity is felt.

- All national highways, provincial highways, and major district should have permanent bridges - preferably non-submersible bridges and causeways if at all provided should not cause detention of traffic of more than 12 hours at a time or more than six times a year.

- The committee felt that construction of other district road and village roads should not be left to the district boards then existing, and that this role should be assumed by state highway engineers.

- There should be a balanced development of all the roads i.e. all the roads should be developed more or less simultaneously.

1.5.1 Determination of Road Length by Nagpur Plan

The Nagpur plan proposed a formula for calculating the road length of different categories of road, taking into consideration the geographical, agricultural and population conditions.

Length in km of National, State and Major District

$$\text{Roads} = \frac{A}{8} + \frac{B}{32} + 1.6\,N + 8\,T + DJ - R$$

where,
- A = Agricultural Area in km^2.
- B = Non-Agricultural Area in km^2.
- N = Number of towns and villages with population range 2001 to 5000.
- T = Number of towns and villages with population over 5000.
- D = Development allowance, where value will be generally taken as 15 % for agricultural and industrial development.
- R = Existing length of railway track in km.

$$J = \frac{A}{8} + \frac{B}{32} + 1.6\,N + 8\,T$$

The total length of secondary category roads for other district and village roads in km is given by the formula :

$$\text{Mileage of such roads} = 0.32\,V + 0.8\,Q + 1.6\,P + 3.2\,S + DJ$$

where,
- V = Number of villages with population 500 or less.
- Q = Number of villages with population range 501 – 1000
- P = Number of villages with population range 1001 – 2000
- S = Number of villages with population range 2001 – 5000

and
- D = Development allowance generally taken as 15 %.

$$J = 0.32\,V + 0.8\,Q + 1.6\,P + 3.2\,S.$$

The above formula is on the assumption of star and grid pattern of road network.

It must be brought out here that the Nagpur plan strategy gives cumulative lengths i.e. the total length of National highways and total length of secondary roads, but it is not possible to obtain individual road length of state highways or village roads etc. This is it's lacuna.

1.6 BOMBAY PLAN

By the end of second plan, the targets fixed by Nagpur plan were achieved but there was demand for more road to cater for the rapidly growing economy of the country. Estimates committee of the Parliament therefore recommended that draft plan be prepared for the nation's requirement for the next 25 – 30 years. A twenty year draft plan was prepared by the Roads wing of the Government of India and approved by the Chief Engineers in 1959 at Bombay. Hence, it is sometimes called as Bombay Plan.

The Objectives and Features of The Plan : The objectives of the draft plan were :

(1) Provision of good communication network in the rural areas will increase urbanisation and hence every village should be brought near the road. The guidelines were as follows:

- Every village in a developed area should be brought within 6.5 km (4 miles) of a metalled road and 2.4 km (1.5 miles) of any road.

- Every village in semideveloped area should be brought within 13 km (8 miles) of metalled road and 5 km (3 miles) of any road.
- Every village and human settlement in undeveloped and uncultivable area should be bought within 20 km (12 miles) of any road.

(2) The road length should be increased so as to give road density of 32 km per 100 sq. km (52 miles per 100 sq. miles) of area.

(3) There should be overall development road network. Places of pilgrimage, administrative head quarters, ports, railway junctions must be connected by roads and in addition strategic roads should be given due importance.

(4) Express ways should be considered where necessary. In fact the plan envisages 1600 km length of express ways.

(5) While calculating road length in hilly regions, an allowance upto 100 per cent may be made in arriving a road length. Hills with high altitudes above 2300 metres may be ignored in calculating the road length. This is a contradictory recommendation in view of the strategic importance of hill roads.

- The funds for road construction and maintenance should be derived not only from the direct beneficieries (motor vehicle taxation) but also from indirect beneficieries - such as land revenue, tax on diesel oil etc.
- Arterial roads should be bridged and preferably two lane wide.
- Maintenance of roads should be accorded high priority. It was expected that the maintenance expenditure would increase from 30 crores in 1961 to 130 crores in 1981 due to new construction of roads.
- Fresh entrants, who would work as Highway Engineers should be professionally trained.
- Each highway department should have a cell to deal with traffic engineering road standards.
- Some roads such as village roads, panchayat road, zilla parishad roads which are under the superintendence of these authorities, should get guidance from state highway authorities.

Road Way Length Targets

The road lengths for different categories of roads were fixed in miles since km as a unit was not in vogue in 1959. Converted to km these formulas were

(a) National Highway (km)

$$= \left[\frac{A}{64} + \frac{B}{80} + \frac{C}{96}\right] + 32\,K + 8\,M + D\left[\frac{A}{64} + \frac{B}{80} + \frac{C}{96} + 32\,K + 8\,M\right]$$

(b) National Highways + State Highways (km)

$$= \left[\frac{A}{20} + \frac{B}{24} + \frac{C}{32} + 48\,K + 24\,M + 11.2\,N + 1.6\,P\right] \times \left(\frac{100 + D}{100}\right)$$

(c) National Highways + State Highways + Major District Roads (km)

$$= \left[\frac{A}{8} + \frac{B}{16} + \frac{C}{24} + 48K + 24M + 11.2N + 9.6\,P + 6.4\,Q + 2.4R\right] \times \left(\frac{D + 100}{100}\right)$$

(d) National Highway + State Highways + Major District Roads + Other District Roads (km)

$$= \left[\frac{3A}{16} + \frac{3B}{32} + \frac{C}{16} + 48\,K + 24\,M + 11.2\,N + 9.6\,P + 12.8\,Q + 4\,R\right.$$

$$\left. + 0.8\,S + 0.32\,T\right] \times \left(\frac{D + 100}{100}\right)$$

(e) National Highways + State Highways + Major District Roads + Other District Roads + Village Roads

$$= \left[\frac{A}{4} + \frac{B}{8} + \frac{C}{12} + 48\,K + 24\,M + 11.2\,N + 9.6\,P + 12.8\,Q + 5.9\,R\right.$$

$$\left. + 1.6\,S + 0.64\,T + 0.2\,V\right] \times \left(\frac{D + 100}{100}\right)$$

where,

A = Developed and Agricultural Area, km^2

B = Semideveloped Area, km^2

C = Undeveloped Area, km^2

K = Number of towns with population over 1 lakh

M = Number of towns with population between 50000 to 1 lakh

N = Number of towns with population between 20,000 to 50,000

P = Number of towns with population between 10000 to 20000

Q = Number of towns with population between 5000 to 10000

R = Number of towns with population between 2000 to 5000

S = Number of settlements with population between 1000 to 2000

T = Number of settlements with population between 500 to 1000

V = Number of towns with population less than 500

D = Development allowance generally taken as 5 % for the 20 year draft plan period.

1.7 LUCKNOW PLAN

Considering the lessons understood from the first to seventh plan, the Chief Engineers of various states and the Indian Roads Congress formulated a long term plan for India for the period 1981 – 2001. This plan is called as Lucknow Plan. The goals and policies of this road plan are :

- Accessibility to all the villages with a population of above 500 should be provided by the turn of the century.

- Master plan should be prepared, for towns cities, district, state and national level and it should be remembered while making these master plans that the plan should generate employment and industrial growth.

- The national highway length should be so increased as to form square grid of 100 km side.

- Speedy travel may be facilitated by Expressways. The expressways should be constructed on major traffic corridors.

- Environmental standards must be maintained in the construction and maintenance of roads and energy conservation in the form of petrol saving must be given high priority and road safety measures should be undertaken to contain and bring down the accident rates.

- Major District Roads should serve and connect all towns and villages with a population of 1500 and above and other village roads should serve and connect villages with a population of 1000-1500.

- Expressways are recommended on major traffic corridors to promote speedy travel. As traffic develops the widening of roads should be taken-up but care should be taken to see while initial constructing the road that sufficient sideway margin is available for future widening from this point of view, ribbon development should be checked right from the beginning if required by suitable legislative measures.

- Resources crunch may make it difficult to make all rural roads all-weather roads. As a beginning, the roads may be made earthen roads or gravel roads.

- Computer-aided designs of highways and highway parameters, research and development activities and data based on traffic flows and connected fields should be strengthened.

- There should be modernization of road making machinery and strengthened highway contracting industry.

- Additional sources of highway finance such as toll roads and private sector financing should be explored. Where required for special problems, private consulting firms could be contacted without hesitation.

- The lengths of various categories of road as far as twenty year plan is concerned could be calculated as under :

    (a) National Highways, length in km $= \dfrac{\text{Area in sq. km}}{50}$

(b) State Highways, length in km $= \dfrac{\text{Area in sq. km}}{25}$

or

State Highways, length in km $= 62.5 \times \text{Number of Towns} - \dfrac{\text{Area in sq. km}}{50}$

(c) Major District Roads, length in km $= \dfrac{\text{Area in sq. km}}{12.5}$

or

Major District Road length $= 90 \times \text{Number of Towns}$

(d) Total Road length $= 4.74 \times \text{Number of Villages and Towns}$

(e) Rural road length (ODR + Village roads) may be obtained by subtracting the length of SH NH and MDR from the total length. For calculating these road lengths, NH system is supposed to have a grid of 100 km side.

The idea of obtaining State Highway length is that it should be twice the National Highway length. Similarly, it is assumed in the above formula that NH and SH will pass through all towns with population more than 5000. On this basis, on the assumption of 3364 towns, the length of the square grid works out to be

$$\sqrt{\dfrac{\text{Area of the country}}{\text{Number of Towns}}} = \sqrt{\dfrac{3287782}{3364}}$$

$$= 31.25 \text{ km}$$

As such length of NH and SH $= 2 \times 31.25 \times \text{Number of Towns}$

$$= 62.5 \times \text{Number of Towns}$$

The idea behind the formula to work out length of MDR is that it should be twice the length of State Highways, whereas the another formula for MDR is empirical. The total road length in the nation is computed on the assumption that every town and village must be connected by road. Since, there are 583563 villages and towns, the average area per human settlement is

$$= \dfrac{\text{Area of Nation}}{\text{Number of Villages}}$$

$$= \dfrac{3287782}{583563}$$

$$= 5.64 \text{ sq. km}$$

$\therefore$ Length of grid $= \sqrt{5.64} = 2.37 \text{ km}$

$\therefore$ Length of total road $= 2 \times 2.37 \times \text{Number of Villages and Towns}$

$$= 4.74 \times \text{Number of Villages and Towns}$$

The above criteria results in a road density of 0.82 km/sq. km as against 0.46 in 1981.

- Requirement of funds as per 20 year plan (1981 – 2001) is estimated around 64000 crores. The present yearly revenue from the Central and State Governments from motor vehicles is around 5000 crores. Therefore, the expenditure is justified. The overall goal of 20 year plan is indicated in the table below.

Table 1.1

Category of Road	Existing Length km	Target Length km	Additional Length km	Cost in Crores
Express Highway	–	2000	2000	To be met from toll collection
National Highways	31737	66000	34263	16950
State Highways	95491	144000	48509	10664
Major Highways	153000	280000	145000	12759
Rural Roads	912684	2212000	1299316	24879
Total	1192912	2704000	1529088	129774

For calculating road length, formula based on area is preferred. Towns are defined as settlements having at least municipalities.

1.8 THE DEVELOPMENT OF ROADS IN INDEPENDENT INDIA

Speedy economic development and upliftment of masses can be undertaken in India only with efficient road network. The important aspects which road network is going to satisfy in modern India are :

- India with it's about 5,90,000 villages placed in different parts and extreme interior can be connected with good road network thus bringing social uplift health and education of the village population.

- India is a land of many marvels. On one hand we have hilly terrain in Jammu Kashmir, Himachal Pradesh, Sikkim, Assam, Meghalaya, Manipur, Mizoram, Tripura, Nagaland, Arunachal Pradesh, and hilly regions of U. P. and on the other hand we have deserts of Kutch, Rajputana and Swamps of Mand in Punjab. In such unhospitable terrain, only roads can serve as link of mass communication. The roads in such regions are not only serving as arteries of nation but these roads are of strategic importance and serve ideal frame for defence network.

- The roads handle 58 % of goods traffic and about 80 % of passenger traffic. For short hauls of 300 – 350 km cost advantage is with road traffic, high value commodities such as tea, raw cotton are generally transported even for longer hauls. For perishable commodities like fruit and livestock, road transport has an advantage upto about 450 km. Because of this economics, it is generally cheaper to bring agricultural goods to Mandis by road transport. The green revolution in the country owes not a little to roads.

Punjab and Haryana which have connected all their villages by road are examples of agricultural prosperity brought by roads. The collection and processing of surplus milk generated in the villages is possible only because of the road and in that sense even the white revolution owes a lot to the good road network.

- The forest wealth of the country is being exploited mainly because of the roads penetrating into the jungles. Similarly, the development of fisheries along the coast line has been made possible because of the construction of link roads leading to the coast.

- Some of the ancient monuments, religious places, tourist spots are accessible only by roads. Indian tourism has received a big boost because of the motorable road network.

- Road construction in India is still labour intensive. Therefore, it is possible for the road transport sector to give gainful employment to more number of people in the construction, maintenance and in actual transport.

- Presently, India has the smallest ownership rate of car viz 6 per thousand persons as against 668 per thousand in U.S.A. and 320 per thousand in U.K. But India is developing and the growth rate of motor vehicle population is around 10 % per annum (compound). There were about 86 lakhs motor vehicles in India in 1985. Though the growth rate is somewhat smaller, the initial numbers of cars are large (of course due to large population) and therefore number of cars coming every year on road is large, requiring good network.

- This vast land of diverse climate and nature can be brought under one administrative umbrella by efficient network of roads. Law and order and dispensation of justice can not simply be achieved without road network in India. National integration and cohesion has been brought by roads. People go to different parts, understand them and there is a feeling of oneness. Roads have also helped in case of famine and flood operations.

1.9 DEVELOPMENTS OF ROADS IN FIVE YEAR PLANS

After independence, we declared ourselves as socialistic sovereign, state with more or less mixed economy. Systematic planning in public sector and directional planning in private sector started and therefore it is worth while to watch the progress in highways plan wise.

1.9.1 Pre-plan (Period 1943 – 1951)

During the pre-plan period of 1943 – 1951, the Nagpur plan was already there as a model for road development. However, due to partition of our country, there was paucity of fund and Nagpur plan expectations could not be fulfilled.

1.9.2 First Five Year Plan (Period 1951 – 1956)

In this particular plan period, 6.7 % of the total plan expenditure was incurred on roads and this expenditure was about 30.2 per cent of the expenditure on the transport sector. The salient features of road development in the first five year plan could be summarised below.

- **National Highways :** Through the National Highway Act, the national highways became the central subject and the Central Government statutorily took them over. The missing links on N. H. system to the tune of 2000 km were constructed. About 30 major bridges and improvements to nearly 10,000 km of national highway was taken-up. Expenditure to the tune of about Rs. 27 crores was incurred. Some important inter-state reads such as Passi-Badarpur Road in Assam, Assam - Agartala Road connecting Assam with Tripura were taken up. The state sector roads also increased in length. The total road length increased from 399940 km to about 498340 km registering an increase of 25 %.

1.9.3 Second Five Year Plan

About 4.8 % of the total plan expenditure and 20 % of the total transport sector expenditure was incurred on roads. The Central Government sponsored Dhar-Udampur Road and construction of west coast road (Bombay - Kanyakumari Road) which was taken during the first plan was continued. About 40 major bridges were constructed. In line with the activities of the Central Government, the State Governments also formulated different schemes and completed them. As a result, there was an increase in road length from 498340 km to 7012120 km. i.e. about 42 % increase. Thirty three per cent of the roads by this time were surfaced roads.

1.9.4 Third Five Year Plan (Period 1961 – 1966)

The Bombay road plan served as a frame work for the third fourth and fifth five year plans. In fact this plan saw tremendous growth in highway construction activity. The significant developments that took place in this plan period.

- There was the most important and eye opening event of the epoc that is the Chinese external aggression. As a result of this aggression, Border Road Development Board was created under Transport Ministry to deal with problems concerning these roads. Most of these roads were hill roads or desert roads and as such development of hill roads got a boost.

- The system of National Highways was strengthened. Sixty six major bridges were constructed on the national highway system, which included Mahanadi Bridge at Cuttack and Sone Bridge in Bihar.

- In this particular period, there was a bottleneck in the coal transportation and the planners realised the shortcoming of railways as a means of communications. Therefore, they started looking towards road work as a means to transport coal, since coal as a source of energy is very important.

- In general, there was some shift from labour intensive road construction to somewhat mechanised road construction.

- Under the central aided scheme, the lateral road project on the foot - hills of Himalayas from Uttarpradesh to Assam was sanctioned and taken up for construction while the work on West Coast Road already started continued.

- In this plan period, Government of India received credit from the World Bank for construction of selected national highway. An expenditure of about Rs. 440 crores was incurred in this plan period which constituted 22 % of the expenditure on transport sector and 6 % of the overall plan expenditure. The total road length registered a rise of 49 % over the length at the end of the second plan.

1.9.5 The Fourth Plan (Period 1969 – 1974)

In between 1966 - 1969, there was plan holiday and the actual fourth plan commenced in 1969. The salient achievements of this plan were as follows :

- In June, 1971, certain new additions to the highway system were done. These were

  (a) Highway No. NH 44 - connecting Shillong, Passi, Badarpur and Agartala,

  (b) NH 21 Highway connecting Bilaspur, Kulu and Mandi with Chandigarh,

  (c) Highway NH 5A connecting Pardeep port to NH 5 at Haridaspur and

  (d) NH 4 A connecting Belgaum, Phonda and Panaji.

- One important happening in this period was that the Government set-up one - man commission with Mr. H. P. Sinha as chairman to study the condition and possible development of rural roads. This happened in 1967 and the report got published in 1968 just before the plan period. The recommendations of the committee were.

  (a) High-level rural board should be set-up in each state for planning and allocation of funds for the rural roads and there should be a post of chief engineer in the state to look after these roads. This recommendation was not followed.

  (b) It also envisaged that at least third of the rural road construction cost should come from the beneficiaries. In fact the committee made the proposal that if the third road cost is deposited by the people concerned, the state should come forward to spend the rest 2/3 and construct the road.

  (c) The chairman Mr. Sinha favoured a total length of at least 324000 km of village roads and 230,400 km of other district road. Of course the implication of the findings of the committee were felt in fifth plan period.

1.9.6 The Fifth Plan (Period 1974 – 1979)

The significant achievements of this plan period were

- The additions to National Highway network.

- As a part of Minimum Needs Programme (M.N.P.) it was proposed to construct all weather rods so that the villages with a population of more than 1500 are interconnected. This was not totally achieved.

- Expenditure in this plan period including the plan period 1979 - 1980 was around 31 % of the total transport sector and the road length increased from 1393930 km to about 1534200 km. This expenditure includes the cost that went for conversion of single lane widths to two lane widths for certain National Highways.

1.9.7 The Sixth Five Year Plan (Period 1980 – 1985)

Sixth Five Year Plan is characterised by the following achievements :

- Many highways to the tune 2500 km were constructed in the strategic North Eastern Zone.
- The minimum needs programme of the sixth plan was reinforced.
- In general, this plan could be said to be stock checking plan, the deficiencies in the previous plans were made-up, missing links provided, certain inter - state roads of economic importance and border roads were constructed. The sixth plan contained a provision of 3440 crores representing around 29 % of the outlay in the transport sector and around 3.5 % outlay in the total plan.

1.9.8 The Seventh Plan (Period 1985 – 1990)

The main objectives and the achievements of this plan are :

- Proposal to construct expressways i.e. Ahmedabad - Vadodara and Kolkata - Durgapur. These will be first expressways of the country.
- Continued rural road activity so that the minimum needs programme is completed. These rural roads will be constructed if required under Employment Gurantee Scheme or Rural Landless Employment Gurantee Programme (NLEGRP) or National Rural Employment Programme (NREP). Presently out of nearly 6,00,000 villages, about 2,60,000 villages only are connected by all-weather roads. The level of accessibility in respect of villages of 1500 population or above is 86 % and that of 1000 - 1500 is 63%.
- No National Highways as such were proposed and most of the expenditure went in consolidating the gains.
- The system of National Highway was strengthened. The expenditure that is to be in curred on National Highways in this plan as a comparison to other previous plans is indicated in the table 1.1.
- For the first time, provision of new generation of roads along high density corridors with divided carriageway facilities were proposed.
- The seventh plan makes an outlay of Rs. 892 crores for National Highways and Rs. 128 for other centrally sponsored schemes and Rs. 4180 crores for the state sector roads.

1.9.9 Eighth Five Year Plan Roads (Period 1990 - 1995)

- The existing deficiencies in national highways (NH) would require construction of missing links, four laning and two laning of various sections, construction of bridges and by-passes etc. The first priority will be given to complete the ongoing works. For systematic development of the NH system, different strategies will need to be adopted for low, medium and high volume traffic density routes. Capacity augmentation of high density traffic corridors carrying more than 15,000 passenger car units traffic per day, through four laning will need to be taken up during the Eighth Plan. For selected high density corridors, it may be necessary to consider expressway facility for rapid and safe movement of fast traffic. Levy of tolls may be considered for highway users. For national highways carrying medium traffic density, traffic upto 15000 PCUs, strengthening of pavement and widening to two-lanes including reconstruction of bridges, wherever necessary, need to be taken-up. For low traffic density routes carrying traffic upto 5,000 PCUs, widening to two-lanes may be considered only on a selective basis, depending upon the resource availability. However, weak and narrow bridges have to be replaced.

- As regards additions to the National Highways system, it would be necessary to adopt a very selective approach in view of the resource constraints and the need to give priority to removal of deficiencies on the existing NH-system

- Constraints of resources may not permit removal of all the existing deficiencies in the State highways during the Plan period and a selective approach based on economic cost benefit analysis may have to be adopted.

- Rural roads are essential for achieving the objective of integrated rural development. The priority for rural road development in the Eighth Plan would be as under:-

  (a) Linking of all villages with a population of 1000 and above on the basis of 1981 census.

  (b) Special efforts to accelerate village connectivity in respect of backward regions and tribal areas.

- It would be appropriate to integrate rural road construction and maintenance under Minimum Needs Programme (MNP) with local area development planning. State Governments may pool the resources, made available under MNP and special employment programmes and undertake rural road construction under the respective local area development plan.

1.9.10 Ninth Five Year Plan (Period 1995 - 2000)

The following goals and objectives have been kept in view while framing the outline of the Ninth Plan :

- Phased removal of deficiencies in the existing NH network in the tune with traffic needs for 10-15 years with emphasis on high density corridors for four-laning.

- Bring in highway-user oriented project planning in identifying package of projects section-wise rather than isolated stretches.

- Greater attention to rehabilitation and reconstruction of weak/dilapidated bridges for the safety of the traffic.

- Modernization of road construction technology for speedy execution and quality assurance.

- Engineering measures to improve road safety and conservation of energy.

- Continued emphasis on research and development.

- Integrating the development plans with Railways and other modes of transport.

- Providing employment opportunities to the labour force in rural areas.
- Special attention for development of roads in the North-Eastern Region.
- Encouraging private sector participation in development of roads.

1.9.11 Five Year Plan (Period 2001 - 05)

The following broad goals and objectives for road sector development have been set for the Tenth Plan :

- Balanced development of the total road network comprising three functional groups viz. the primary system (National Highways (NH) and expressways), secondary system (State Highways and Major District Roads) and rural roads.
- Development of roads to be considered an integral part of the total transport system supplementing other modes, integrating the development plans with railways and other modes of transport.
- Completion of the National Highways Development Project comprising the Golden Quadrilateral and the North-South and East-West corridors.
- Phased removal of deficiencies in the existing NH network in tune with traffic for the next 10-15 years with emphasis on four-laning of high-density corridors.
- To plan and take preliminary action for expressways to be built in future in those sections where these can be economically justified.
- To make long distance travel safer and faster so as to give a boost to the economy.
- Priority is to be accorded to areas like overloading of trucks, control of encroachments and unplanned ribbon development, energy conservation and environment protection.
- Greater attention to be paid to rehabilitation and reconstruction of weak/dilapidated bridges for traffic safety.
- Special attention is to be paid to the development of roads in the North-Eastern region.
- Particular emphasis needs to be given to the commercialization of highways particularly the National Highways and State Highways and bringing in the concept of user-charges for sustainable financing of the road sector. Further steps must also be taken to encourage private sector participation in the highway sector. It is necessary to implement the policy of levying toll on all four-lane roads on the National Highway network. States must adopt a similar strategy in respect of State Highways etc.
- High-density corridors within the network of National and State Highways and Major District Roads should be identified. Such corridors and major inter-state roads should be developed on a priority basis.
- To improve the quality of life in rural areas and ensure balanced regional development by achieving the PMGSY target of providing connectivity through all-weather roads to all habitations with a population of over 500 persons (as per the 2001 Census).
- To encourage industry and export by providing sufficiently wide roads leading to industrial centres, ports, mining areas and power plants.

- To encourage tourism by improving roads leading to centres of tourist importance.
- To provide wayside amenities along highways.
- To reduce transportation costs by providing better riding surface and popularising the use of containers and multi-axle vehicles in the haulage of goods.
- Utmost attention to the proper upkeep and maintenance of the existing road network.
- To ensure road connectivity where rail link is not available or possible.
- Integrating the development plan with railways and other modes of transport and to:
    (a) Identify feeder roads to important railway routes and undertake needed improvement including periodic maintenance;
    (b) Link minor important ports with minimum two-lane NHs/SHs;
    (c) Link all Inland Container Depots/container freight stations with minimum two-lane NHs / SHs.
- Use of modern management techniques for scientific assessment of maintenance strategies/priorities.
- Development of a road data bank and computerized project monitoring system and promotion of the use of information technology in the highway sector.

1.9.12 Eleventh Five Year Plan (Period 2007 - 2012)

- The Tenth Plan stressed the need for improving mobility and easy accessibility. Accordingly, the National Highway Development Programme (NHDP) consisting of four laning of the Golden Quadrilateral (NHDP I) with a length of 5,846 km and the North-South and East-West Corridor (NHDP II) with a length of 7472 km coupled with Pradhan Mantri Gram Sadak Yojana (PMGSY) for rural roads were taken-up. The PMGSY programme has been recently expanded to achieve the Bharat Nigam target of connecting 1000 + habitation (500 + for hilly and tribal areas) by 2008-09 with all-weather roads. This programme will help bring India's villages into the market economy. It will also help us to tackle social sector problems like illiteracy, high IMR and MMR) which are dragging India down because while roads connect villages to markets, they also connect them to schools and hospitals. The "Special Accelerated Development Road Programme for the North Eastern Region (SARDP-NE)", will help in developing and integrating these regions with the rest of the country.
- The problems of development of our roads network are diverse and future requirements are formidable magnitude. Therefore, the strategy for development of roads would have to vary keeping in view the nature of problem and the development required. It is proposed to undertake an expanded programme for highway development going beyond NHDP I and II to include NHDP III to VII. This programme will involve substantial resources from public private partnership based on build, operate and transfer (BOT) model which has many advantages over the traditional contracts (See *Box* on PPPs). All contracts on provision of road services for high density corridors to be

taken-up under NHDP III onwards would be awarded only on BOT basis, and the traditional construction contracts will be awarded only in specified exceptional cases. A model concession agreement has been developed to facilitate speedy award of contracts. This is a very significant innovation in the areas of public-private partnership. This would leave a substantial part of National Highways network which would also require development during the Eleventh Plan period. These sections are characterised by low density of traffic. Some of these stretches fall in backward and inaccessible areas and others are of strategic importance. The development of these categories of National Highways would be carried out primarily through budgetary resources.

- The present traffic mix consisting of non-motorised and low-powered vehicles   compels low speed Furthermore, most of the National Highways pass through habitations and ribbon development is a perennial problem. It is, therefore, necessary to establish a network of access controlled Expressways across the country for which advance planning would be undertaken during the Eleventh Plan. The actual construction (except for 1000 kms already taken-up) would be undertaken during the Twelth Plan period and would be prioritised according to the density of traffic.

- Vehicular traffic needs more than just the arterial routes to be of world class. Adequate attention has not been given in the past to other roadways, which are the responsibility of the state governments. Priority would be accorded for ensuring integrated development of road networks including State Highways, Major District Roads and Other District Roads. The increased emphasis on rural roads would also continue and a major proportion of the 1.72 lakh unconnected habitations would be connected with all weather roads under the PMGSY.

- The maintenance of roads has not been given adequate importance by the states mainly due to paucity of resources. This has resulted in poor riding quality of the road network which is highly uneconomic. A rupee spend on maintenance saves two to three rupees in vehicle operating costs, besides improving traffic flow. Therefore, there is a need to accord higher priority to the needs of maintenance by providing more allocation or considering it as a part of Plan. In fact, the 12th Finance Commission has recommended additional grants to the States, to the tune of Rs. 15,000 crore for maintenance of roads and bridges for the four-year period 2006-07 to 2009-10.

- The National Highway Authority of India (NHAI) has an enormous task before it to implement a road programme. The Authority is being restructured to give it greater professional skills combined with a measure of autonomy and accountability.

- Indian roads are considered very accident prone and claim a large number of casualties representing an enormous human and economic loss. This problem is compounded by the phenomenal growth in road transport fleet, particularly personalized vehicles and the consequent problems of increase in vehicular pollution and road safety. Steps need to be taken to improve the public transport system and safety of road transport operations.

SOLVED PROBLEMS

Problem 1.1: *A road network is to be planned as per 1961–1981 road plan. The requisite data is as under. Area of District = 25000 km². Developed area = 8000 km². Undeveloped area = 6000 km². Population census is as under.*

Population range	< 500	500 to 1000	1000 to 2000	2000 to 5000	5000 to 10000	10000 to 20000	20000 to 50000	50000 to 1 lakh	> 1 lakh
Nos. of Towns	500	400	1000	400	200	70	30	10	3

There are only 3 towns having more than one lakh population.

Solution: Here,

A = Developed Area, km² = 8000 km²

C = Undeveloped Area = 6000 km²

B = Semideveloped Area = 25000 − 8000 − 6000 = 11000 km²

K = Towns with population > of one lakh = 3

M = Towns with population 50000 to one lakh = 10, D = 5 %

∴ National highway length

$$= \frac{A}{64} + \frac{B}{80} + \frac{C}{96} + (32K + 8M) + D \times Z$$

where $\quad Z = \dfrac{A}{64} + \dfrac{B}{80} + \dfrac{C}{96} + 32K + 8M$

National Highway length $= \dfrac{8000}{64} + \dfrac{11000}{80} + \dfrac{6000}{96} + 32 \times 3 + 8 \times 10 + D \times Z$

$$= 125 + 137.5 + 62.5 + 96 + 80 + \frac{5}{100}[125 + 137.5 + 62.5 + 96 + 80]$$

$$= 501 + \frac{5}{100}(501) = 25.05 + 501$$

$$= 526.05 \text{ say } \textbf{527 km.}$$

Now, N = Towns population 20000 to 50000 = 30

P = Towns with population 10000 to 20000 = 70

(NH + SH) Highways

$$= \left[\frac{A}{24} + \frac{B}{24} + \frac{C}{32} + 48K + 24M + 11.2N + 1.6P\right]\left(\frac{100 + D}{100}\right)$$

$$= \left(\frac{8000}{24} + \frac{11000}{24} + \frac{6000}{32} + 48 \times 3 + 24 \times 10 + 11.2 \times 30 + 1.6 \times 70\right)\left(\frac{100 + 5}{100}\right)$$

$$= (333.3 + 458.3 + 187.5 + 144 + 240 + 336 + 112)\frac{105}{100}$$

$$= 1901.6 \text{ say } \textbf{1902 km}$$

State Highways = 1902 − N. H. = 1902 − 527 = 1375 km

Now, Q = Towns with population 5000 − 10000 = 200

R = Towns with population 2000 − 5000 = 400

S = Towns with population 1000 − 2000 = 1000

$\therefore$ N. H. + State Highways + M. District Roads

$$= \left(\frac{A}{8} + \frac{B}{16} + \frac{C}{24} + 48K + 24M + 11.2N + 9.6P + 6.4Q + 2.4R\right)\left(\frac{D + 100}{100}\right)$$

$$= \left(\frac{8000}{8} + \frac{11000}{16} + \frac{6000}{24} + 48 \times 3 + 24 \times 10 + 11.2 \times 30 + 9.6 \times 70 + 6.4 \times 200 + 2.4 \times 400\right)\frac{105}{100}$$

$$= (1000 + 687.5 + 250 + 144 + 240 + 336 + 672 + 1280 + 960) \times \frac{105}{100}$$

$$= 5847 \text{ km}$$

$\therefore$ Major District Roads = $5847 - (NH + SH) = 5847 - 1902 = 3945$ say **3946 km**

Now   T = Settlements with population 500 – 1000 = 400

   V = Settlements with population < 500 = 500

$\therefore$ NH + SH + M. District Roads + 00R

$$= \left(\frac{3A}{16} + \frac{3B}{32} + \frac{C}{16} + 48K + 24M + 11.2N + 9.6P + 12.8Q + 4R + 0.8S + 32T\right)\left(\frac{100 + D}{100}\right)$$

$$= \left(\frac{3 \times 8000}{16} + \frac{3 \times 11000}{32} + \frac{6000}{16} + 48 \times 3 + 24 \times 10 + 11.2 \times 30\right.$$

$$\left. + 9.6 \times 70 + 12.8 \times 200 + 4 \times 400 + 0.8 \times 1000 + 0.32 \times 400\right) \times \frac{100 + D}{100}$$

$$= (1500 + 1031.2 + 375 + 144 + 240 + 336 + 672 + 2560 + 1600 + 800 + 128)\left(\frac{100 + D}{100}\right)$$

$$= 9855.5 \text{ say } \textbf{9856 km}$$

Other District Roads   = $9856 - 5847 = 4008$ say **4008 km**

NH + SH + M.D.R. + O.D.R. + Village Roads

$$= \left(\frac{A}{4} + \frac{B}{8} + \frac{C}{12} + 48K + 24M + 11.2N + 9.6P + 12.8Q + 5.9R + 1.6S + 0.64T + 0.2V\right)$$

$$\times \left(\frac{D + 100}{100}\right)$$

$$= \left(\frac{8000}{4} + \frac{11000}{8} + \frac{6000}{12} + 48 \times 3 + 24 \times 10 + 11.2 \times 30 + 9.6 \times 70\right.$$

$$\left. + 12.8 \times 200 + 5.9 \times 400 + 1.6 \times 1000 + 0.64 \times 400 + 0.2 \times 500\right) \times \frac{100 + 5}{100}$$

$$= (2000 + 1375 + 500 + 144 + 240 + 336 + 672 + 2560 + 2360 + 1600 + 256 + 200)$$

$$\times \frac{105}{100}$$

$$= 12750$$

$\therefore$ Village Roads = $12750 - 9856 = 2894$ km

Problem 1.2: *A road network is to be planned as per Nagpur plan. The total area of the region is 13000 km² and the agricultural area is 6000 km². The existing track length is about 200 km. The number of towns and villages with population range 2001 to 5000 is 60, whereas towns having population more than 5000 m only 10. The population census indicated the following:*

Population	More than 5000	5000 or less	2001 to 5000	501 to 1000	1001 to 2000
Nos. of Villages	10	500	60	150	150

Determine the length of National, State and Major District roads, and the total length of second category roads such as other district and village roads to be constructed. Development allowance is 15 % and existing road length for National and Secondary roads is 200 and 300 km each. National Roads are metalled and secondary ones are non-metalled.

Solution:

Total length of National, State and Major roads

$$= \frac{A}{8} + \frac{B}{32} + 1.6N + 8T + DJ - R$$

where, A = Agricultural Area = 6000 km²

B = Non-Agricultural Area = (13000 – 6000) = 7000 km²

N = Towns and villages with population range 2001 – 5000 = 60

T = Towns with population more than 5000 = 10

D = Development allowance = 15 %

R = Railway track length = 200 km, as such

$$J = \frac{6000}{8} + \frac{60}{32} + 1.6 \times 60 + 8 \times 10 = 750 + 1.87 + 96 + 80$$

$$= 927.87$$

$$DJ = 927.87 \times \frac{15}{100} = 139.18$$

∴   Length of National, State and Major roads

$$= J + DJ - R = 927.87 + 139.18 - 200$$

$$= 867.05 \text{ say } \textbf{867 km.}$$

Length of secondary category roads (district and village roads)

$$= 0.32\,V + 0.8\,Q + 1.6\,P + 3.2S + DJ$$

where, V = Villages less than 500 = 500

Q = Villages with population range 501 – 1000 = 150

P = Villages with population range 1001 – 2000 = 150

S = Towns with population range 2001 – 5000 = 60

D = 15 % and

$$J = 0.32\,V + 0.8\,Q + 1.6\,P + 3.2\,S$$

$$= 0.32 \times 500 + 0.8 \times 150 + 1.6 \times 150 + 3.2 \times 60$$

$$= 160 + 120 + 90 + 192 = 562$$

$$DJ = 562 \times 0.15 = 84.3$$

Length of secondary roads

$$= J + DJ = 562 + 84.3 = 646.3 \text{ km say } \textbf{640 km}$$

Therefore, additional road network to be constructed. will be

National highways = 867 − 200 = **667 km**

Secondary roads = 640 − 300 = **346 km**.

QUESTIONS

1. What is Nagpur plan? How the roads were classified as per this plan?
2. What factors are considered in finagling 20-year (1961-81) plan?
3. Briefly describe the historical development of roads in India.
4. Highlight the salient features of Bombay road development plan.
5. Highlight the salient features of Nagpur road development plan.
6. Highlight the salient features of Lucknow road development plan.
7. What are the various methods of classification of roads? Briefly explain classification as per Nagpur Road Plan.
8. From the following observations, compute the length of national highways and secondary roads as per Nagpur Plan: Total area 10000 km^2, Developed non - agricultural area = 2800 km^2, Railway track length = 100 km. Population census for the area is as under -

Population	< 500	501 – 1000	1001 – 2000	2001 – 5000	> 5000
Towns or Villages	600	300	100	40	10

9. Determine the road length of different categories of roads in a state in India by the year 2001, using the Third Road development plan formulae for the following data :

    Total Area of the state = 80,000 sq. km.

    Total No. of Towns as per 1981 census = 86

    Overall Road density aimed at = 82 km per 100 sq. km. area.

10. What is the difference between Telford and Macadam construction ?
11. Discuss in details the road development plan of 1981 – 2001.
12. Write notes on:
    (a) Highway planning in India
    (b) Road development in India
    (c) Bombay Plan
    (d) Lucknow Plan

2.1 METHODS OF CLASSIFICATION OF ROAD

2.1.1 Classification Based on the Weather Condition

The different types of road are classified into two categories, depending on whether they can be used during different seasons of the year.

1. All-weather roads
2. Fair-weather roads

All-weather Roads: All-weather roads are those which are negotiable during weather, except at major river crossing where interruption to traffic is permissible upto a certain extent, the road pavement should be negotiable during all weathe.

Fair-weather Roads: Roads which are called fair-weather roads on these, the traffic may be interrupted during monsoon season at causeways where stream may overflow across the road.

2.1.2 Classification Based on the Road Pavement

Based on road pavement, roads are classified as paved roads and unpaved roads.

1. Paved road
2. Unpaved road

Pavement Roads: If they are provided with a hard pavement course which should be at least water bound macadam (WBM) layer.

Unpaved Roads: If they are not provided with a hard pavement course of at least a WBM layer. Thus, earth road and gravel road may be called unpaved roads.

2.1.3 Classification Based on the Pavement Surfacing

Based on the type of pavement surfacing providing, the roads are divided into two categories as:

1. Surfaced road
2. Unsurfaced road

Surfaced Roads: Surface roads which are provided with a bituminous or cement concrete surfacing.

Unsurfaced Roads: Unsurfaced roads which are not provided with bituminous or cement concreting.

2.1.4 Classification Based on the Road Plan

- **Classification of Rural Roads:** (I.R.C-1980)

The road plan classified the roads in India based on location and function into the following categories.

1. Expressways
2. National Highways (NH)
3. State Highways (SH)
4. Major District Roads (MDR)
5. Other District Roads (ODR)
6. Village Roads (VR)

1. Expressways: Expressways are a separate class of highways with superior facilities and design standards and are meant as through routes having very high volume of traffic. The expressways are to be provided with divided carriageways, controlled, grade separations at cross roads and fencing. These highways should permit only fast moving vehicles. Expressways may be owned by Central Government or a State Government, depending on whether the route is a National Highway or State Highway. Example: Mumbai-Pune Expressway.

2. National Highways (NH): National highways are highways running through the length and breadth of India, connecting major ports, foreign highways, capital of large states and large industrial and tourist centres including roads required for strategic movements for the defence of India. Example NH-1 Delhi-Ambala-Amritsar, NH-50 Nasik-Pune.

3. State Highways (SH): State highways are arterial roads of a state, connecting-up with the national highways of the adjacent states, district head quarters and important cities within the state and serving as the main arteries for traffic to and from district roads. The NH and SH have the same design speed and geometric design specifications. Examples:

 SH-61 Belha Pabal Shikrapur Astapur Road

 SH-70 Mahad-Pandharpur Road.

4. Major District Roads (MDR): Major district roads are important roads within a district serving areas of production and markets and connecting those with each other or with the main highways of a district. The MDR has lower speed and geometric design specifications than NH/SH. Example, MDR-2 Kendur Dhamani Hirare Ranjangaon Road.

5. Other District Roads (ODR): Other district roads are roads serving rural areas of production and providing them with outlet to market centres, taluka head quarters, block development head quarters or other main roads. These are of lower design specifications than MDR.

6. Village Roads (VR): Village roads are roads connecting village or groups of villages with each other to the nearest road of a higher category.

 Example. VR-183-Hiware-Jategaon Road

2.1.5 Classification of Urban Roads (I.R.C. - 1977)

The road systems within urban areas are classified as Urban Roads and will form a separate category of roads to be taken care by the respective urban authorities. They are divided into following types.

1. Arterial roads
2. Sub-arterial roads
3. Collector streets and
4. Local streets

1. Arterial Roads: The city roads which are meant for through traffic usually on a continuous route are called arterial streets. Arterial streets are generally spaced at less than 15 km in developed business centres whereas in less important areas, these may be 8 km apart. Arterial roads are also divided highways with fully or partially controlled access. Parking, loading and unloading activities are carefully regulated. Pedestrians are permitted to cross them at intersections only.

2. Sub-Arterial Roads: The city roads which provide lower level of travel mobility than arterial streets are called as sub-arterial streets. Their spacing may vary from 0.5 km in central business districts to 3 to 5 km in sub-urban areas. Loading and unloading are usually restricted. Pedestrians are allowed to cross these highways at intersections.

3. Collector Streets: The city roads which are constructed for collecting and distributing the traffic to and from local streets, and also to provide an access to arterial and sub-arterial streets, are also called collector streets. These are located in residential, business and industrial areas. These roads are accessible from the building along them. Parking restrictions are few that too during peak hours.

4. Local Streets: The city roads which provide an access to residence, business and other building are called local streets. The traffic carried either originates or terminates along the local streets. Depending upon the importance of the adjoining areas, a local street may be residential, commercial or industrial. Along local streets, pedestrians may move freely and parking may be permitted without any restriction.

The road network can be laid in various patterns. These patterns can vary. The patterns in which the road network is laid could be (1) Rectangular or block pattern, (2) Radial or star and block pattern, (3) Radial or star and circular pattern, (4) Radial or star and grid pattern, (5) Hexagonal pattern, (6) Minimum travel pattern. These patterns are illustrated in the next subarticles. The Nagpur road plan formulae were prepared on the assumption of star and grid pattern. Connaught place in New Delhi has radial and circular pattern, whereas Chandigarh has rectangular or block pattern. If the city is being planned from scratch, some pattern can be given. In most of our cities, some of the pattern is already existing and one has to go with them.

2.2 ROAD PATTERNS

Rectangular or Block Pattern: In this pattern, the whole area is divided into rectangular blocks of plots, with streets intersecting at right angles. The main road which passes through the centre of the area should be sufficiently wide and other branch roads may be comparatively narrow. The main road is provided a direct approach to outside the city.

The rectangular plots may be further divided into small rectangular blocks for construction of buildings placed back to back, having roads on their front. The rectangular pattern has been adopted for the city roads of Chandigarh. The construction and maintenance of roads of this pattern is comparatively easier but from traffic point of view, this pattern is not very much convenient because at the intersections, the vehicles face each other.

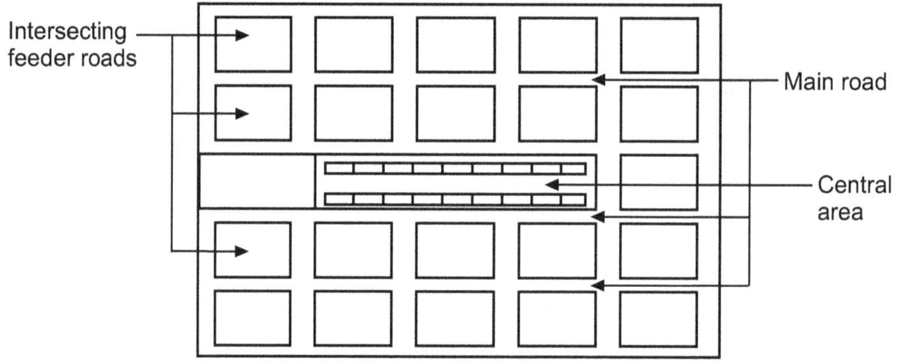

Fig. 2.1: Rectangular or block pattern

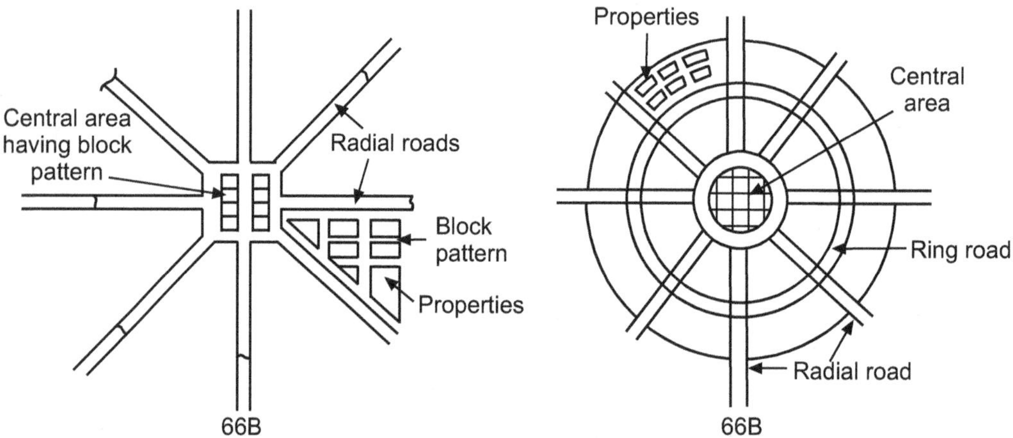

Fig. 2.2: Radial or star and block pattern   **Fig. 2.3: Radial or star and circular pattern**

Radial or Star and Block Pattern: In this pattern, the entire area is divided into a network of roads radiating from the business outwardly. In between radiating main roads, the built-up area may be planned with rectangular blocks.

Radial or Star and Circular Pattern: In this system, the main radial roads radiating from the central business area are connected together with concentric roads. In these areas, boundary by adjacent radial roads and corresponding circular roads, the built-up area is planned with a curved block system. An example of this road pattern is the road network of connaught place in New Delhi.

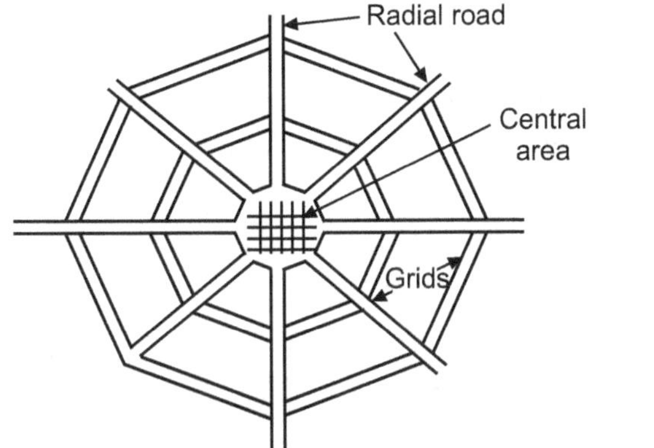

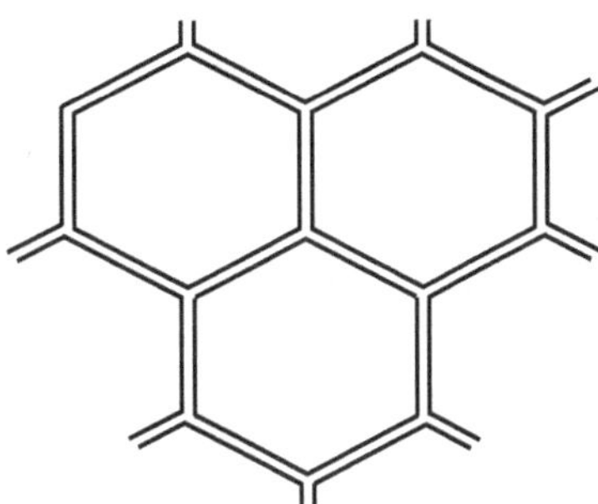

Fig. 2.4: Radial or star and grid pattern　　　**Fig. 2.5: Hexagonal pattern**

Hexagonal Pattern: In this pattern, the entire area is provided with a network of roads forming hexagonal figures. At each corner of the hexagon, three roads meet The built-up area bounded by the sides of the hexagons is further divided in suitable sizes.

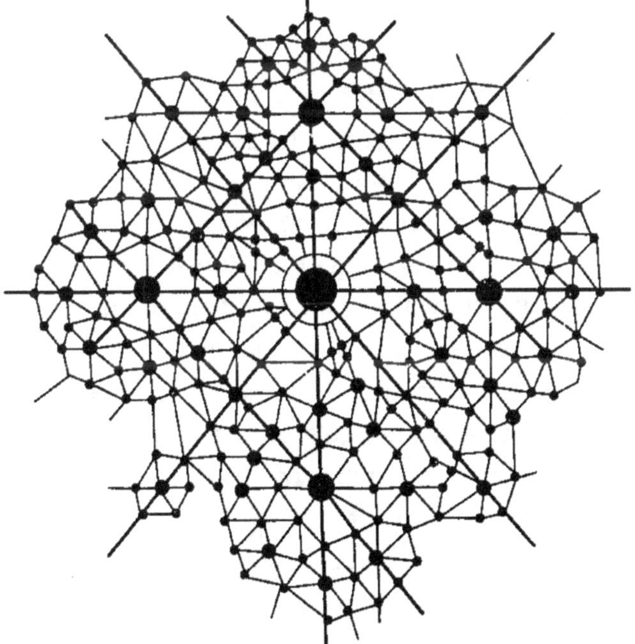

Legend: City centre - encircled dot, Sector centres – •, Suburban centres - •, Neighbourhood centres - •, Representation of a 'Minimum Travel' city (Assumed population of 2 million)

Fig. 2.6

Minimum Travel Pattern: In this road pattern, city (city centre) is contented by sector centres, suburban centres and neighbourhood centres by the road which required minimum to connect the city centre.

2.3 ENGINEERING SURVEYS

Location of the highway alignment is done after carrying out survey of the area; these surveys are called Engineering Surveys. We have to locate an alignment which fulfills the basic requirements like the path must be short, safe, economic, easy and useful. To check all these basic requirements we can carry out the Engineering Surveys in the following phases :

2.3.1 Surveys To Be Conducted

While fixing the alignments, the following types of surveys are conducted.

- Reconnaissance survey.
- Preliminary survey.
- Determination of central line
- Final location survey.
- Traffic survey.
- Soil and material survey.
- Drainage studies.
- Preparation and presentation of Project documents.

Fig. 2.7

2.4 RECONNAISSANCE SURVEY

The main objective of Reconnaissance survey is to examine the general character of the area for the purpose of determining the most feasible route or routes for further detailed investigations. Naturally this type of survey is not required to be carried out where the work consists of improvement to an existing road unless bypasses are involved. The Reconnaissance survey may be conducted in the following sequence.

Study of topographical survey sheets, geological and meteorological maps and photographs if available. Reconnaissance survey begins with the study of all available maps. In India, topographical sheets are available to the scale of one in fifty thousand. After study of the topographical features of the map, a number of alignments feasible in a general way are selected keeping in view the following points.

- Consideration of all control points, i.e. major cities and towns, having shortest length and most economical compatible with the requirements of gradients and curvature in a general way.
- Avoidance as far as possible of marshy ground, steep terrain, unstable hilly features, areas subject to flooding and inundation. Any bridging problems that might arise.

- Important towns and villages should be connected, at the same time, environment should be preserved and ecological balance must be maintained.
- After studying the topographical sheets if required, aerial photography may be arranged for further study in the interests of economy. These may be to a scale 1: 20,000 or 1: 50,000. If stereoscopic techniques are applied, these can yield quantitative data such as significant soil and sub-soil information.
- In addition to aerial photography, an aerial reconnaissance will provide a bird's eye view of the alignments under considerations along with surrounding area. This will help to identify the factors which call for rejection or modification of any of the alignments.

2.4.1 Ground Reconnaissance

The various alternatives located as a result of the map study are further examined in the field by ground reconnaissance. As such, this part of the survey is a very important link in the chain of activities leading to the selection of final route.

Points on which data may be collected during ground reconnaissance.

During ground reconnaissance, certain points should be remembered. These are:

- Topography of the area whether plain, rolling or steep.
- Length of the route along various alternatives and the number and the likely details of bridges on each alternative.
- Existing means of communication between the destinations - such as mule path, jeep, track etc. and right of way available, bringing out the constraints on account of built-up area, monuments and other structures.
- Terrain and the soil conditions and the likely geometrics, such as gradients, curves etc. likely to be met or arranged on each alternative.
- Geology of the area, nature of hill slopes, and the magnitude of the road length passing through different terrain - such as areas subjected to inundation and flooding, areas subjected to avalanches, snow drifts, rocky stretches, steep terrain, desert areas, areas of poor soil drainage, general elevation of the road, indicating maximum and minimum height negotiated by main ascents and descents in hill sections and the total number of ascents and descents in the hill section.
- Climatic conditions enroute such as monthly maximum and minimum temperature, average annual, peak intensity, and monthly distribution of rainfall data and the snowfall data if required, water table and it's variation between maximum and minimum, wind direction and velocities and extent of fog conditions.
- The facilities and the resources available for the proposed alignment: landing and dropping zones in the case of hilly areas, availability of labour, local contractor,

water and the construction material. Value of land acquisition, period required for construction and cost of construction for various alternatives.

- Population that is served by the proposed alignment and the agricultural economic and marketing potential of the area served by the alignment, even future projects, such as dams, hydroelectric projects likely to be taken-up in the area.
- Proposed crossing with rail-lines or highways, necessity of bypasses that are required or that might be required in the future.
- Position of ancient monuments, religious structures etc. and the strategic importance of the route.

Bearing above points in the mind, ground Reconnaissance should be carried. It consists of general examination of the ground by walking or riding along the probable routes and collecting all available information necessary for evaluating the same. In the case of hilly sections, it is advantageous to start Reconnaissance from an obligation point situated close to the top. It is advisable to leave references to facilitate further survey operations. The instrument generally used during ground Reconnaissance will be compass, abeny-level. Pedometer, clinometer, ghat tracer etc. Walkie-Talkie sets are useful for communications. The above instruments are used to measure ground slopes maximum gradient, elevation of critical summits, stream crossings etc.

Based on the information collected during the Reconnaissance survey, a report should be prepared. The report will include a plan to the scale of 1:50000 showing the alternative alignments studied along with their general profiles and rough cost estimates. The information collected should be marked on the map and the different alternatives should be discussed for their merits or otherwise to help the selection of one or more alignments for detailed survey and investigation.

2.5 PRELIMINARY SURVEY

Preliminary survey stage is very important. It is a relatively large-scale instrument survey conducted for the purpose of collecting all the physical information which has the bearing on the proposed location of a new highway or on improvements in existing highway. In the case of new roads, it consists of running an accurate traverse lines along the route previously selected on the basis of Reconnaissance survey. In the case of existing routes where only improvements are proposed, the survey-line is run along the existing alignment. During this phase of survey, topographic features and other features like houses, monuments, places of worship, cremation or burial grounds, utility lines etc. are tied to the traverse line. Longitudinal sections throughout the alignment and cross-sections at regular intervals are taken and bench marks established. The data collected at this stage will form the basis for the determination of the final central line of the road. For this reason, it is essential that every precaution should be taken to maintain a high degree of accuracy. While running a traverse line the information should be collected regarding the following points.

- The character of the embankment foundations, particularly necessary in areas having deep cuts to achieve the grade.
- Any particular construction problem of the area such as high-level water storage across the alignment. Areas prone to land-slide, settlement of the slopes etc.
- The highest subsoil water level and the variation between the maximum and minimum, so also the maximum and minimum rainfall, it's duration and its spacing.
- Nature of the cut sections by ascertaining some trial pits or bore holes.

With the data collected it is generally possible to prepare cost estimates within reasonably, close limits for obtaining administrative approval and for planning further detailed survey and investigation.

- As stated earlier, the preliminary survey consists in running a traverse along the proposed alternative adhering as far as possible to the probable final central line of the road.
- The traverse should consist of a series of straight line, with their distance and intermediate angles measured very carefully.
- It is possible that in a difficult terrain the alignment may have to be negotiated through short chord. The traverse should be done with a theodolite and all angles measured with double reversal method.
- The distances along the traverse line should be measured with metallic tape or chain or tachometer. An accuracy of 1: 2000 is desired in distance measurement.
- The directional changes in the alignment and visibility determine transit stations employed in the survey.
- In any case, these transit stations should be marked by means of stakes and numbered in sequences. They should be protected and preserved till the final location survey.
- Physical features such as building monuments, burial grounds, places of worship, posts, pipelines, existing roads and railwaylines, river crossing, cross drainage structure that are likely to affect the project proposal should be located by means of offsets measured from the traverse line.
- Where survey is for improving or upgrading an existing road, measurements should also be made for existing carriageway, roadway, and location and radius of horizontal curves.
- Generally, the survey should cover the entire right of way of road, with adequate allowance for possible shifting of central line from the traverse line.

Levelling work during the preliminary survey is to be kept to the minimum. Generally, fly level are taken along the traverse line at 50 metre intervals and at all intermediate breaks in the ground. The draw contours of the land survey, cross-sections should be taken at suitable intervals, generally 100 to 250 meters in plain terrain upto 50 meters in rolling terrain, and upto 30 meters in hilly terrain. This is a matter which is largely decided by the site engineer. To facilitate the levelling work, bench marks either temporary or permanent should be established at intervals of 250 to 500 meters.

Based on the Preliminary survey, now maps are to be drawn. Plans and longitudinal sections are referred to for detailed study to determine the final central line of the road. At critical locations like sharp curves, hair-pin bends, bridge crossings the plan should show contour at one to three metre intervals especially for roads in hilly terrain. The scales that are suggested for map preparation are 1: 2500 for horizontal scale and 1: 250 for vertical scale for plain and rolling terrain, and 1: 1000 for horizontal scale and 1: 100 for vertical scale for built-up area and stretches in hilly terrain.

2.6 DETERMINATION OF FINAL CENTRAL LINE IN THE DESIGN OFFICE

This step is actually a fore runners to the final location survey and involves the following operations.

- Making use of the map from the preliminary survey, few alternative alignments for the final Central line of the road are drawn and the one satisfying engineering, aesthetic, and economical requirement is tentatively selected.

- For the selected alignment a trial grade line is drawn, taking into considerations railways crossing, drainage crossings etc. In the case of improvements on existing road, the existing road levels should be kept in view.

- For the selected alignment, a study of the horizontal alignment in conjunction with the profile is carried out and adjustments made in both, for proper co-ordination.

- Horizontal curves are designed and the final central line marked on the map. The vertical curves are also designed and its profile determined. The design office's alignment could be cross checked in the field. Based on the final central line of the road, land acquisition proceedings can be started.

2.7 FINAL LOCATION SURVEY

The purpose of the final location survey is to layout the final centre line of the road in the field based on the alignment selected in the design office. The two operations involved in the survey are the staking out of the final centre line of the road by means of a continuous theodolite survey and detailed levelling. The centre line of the road is then translated on the ground by the continuous survey, angles being measured with a transit theodolite measured with double reversal method. All the curve points namely the beginning of transition curve, beginning of circular curve, end of circular curve and the end of spiral transition should be fixed. The final centre line of the road should be fixed by stakes at 50 m intervals in plain and rolling terrain and 20 m intervals in hilly terrain. The stakes are intended only for short period for taking levels of the ground along the centre line and cross sections with reference there to. In the case of existing reference point, marks may be used instead of the stakes. Distance measurements along the final centre line should be continuous following the horizontal curves where these occur. At road crossing and railway crossings the angle with the intersecting road or railway should be measured by a theodolite.

- Suitable bench marks should be established at intervals of 250 m and at or near all drainages or underpass structures. The reference points for the point of vertical and horizontal intersection could also be used as bench marks.

- All the levels should be tied upto a G.T.S datum. Check level should be run over the entire line back to the first bench mark.

- For series of levels M km. in length the total error should not exceed $\sqrt{m} \times \sqrt{12}$ mm/km. Subject to the maximum error of 5 mm/km.

- Levels along the final centre line should be taken at all the staked stations and at all the breaks in the ground. Cross-section of the ground should be generally taken at 50 to 100 m interval in plan terrain and 50 to 75 m in rolling terrain depending, on the nature of work. Preferred distance for existing roads is around 50 m. The interval might be 20 m in hilly terrain.

- In addition, cross-section should be taken at points of beginning and end of spiral transition curves, and at the beginning, middle and end of circular curves, and at other critical locations.

- All the cross sections should be with reference to the final centre line. These extend normal upto the right of the way limit and show levels at every 2 to 5 m intervals and at all breaks in the profile.

- To connect grades at both ends, centre line profile is normally continued 200 m beyond the limit of the project. Profile along all intersecting roads should be measured upto a distance of 150 m.

- At railway level crossing the level on the top of the rail and in the case of sub-ways the level at the roof should be noted.

- The final location survey is complete when the designer is able to plot the final road profile and prepare the project drawings.

- Clear description of bench marks and reference points is a must so that at the time of construction the centre line and the bench marks could be located in the field without any difficulty at the time of execution. Construction lines will be set out and checked with reference to the final centre line established during the final location survey.

- It is therefore imperative that all the points referencing the centre line should be protected and preserved and so fixed at site that they are not disturbed and removed till the construction is completed.

2.8 TRAFFIC SURVEYS

Information about traffic is important since it forms the basis for the design of the pavement fixing the number of traffic lanes, economical appraisal of the project etc. The traffic survey may be in the nature of traffic counts. On rural highways, 7 days traffic counts once or twice a year for as many years as possible should be gathered. When road is being planned or extensive improvements are to be carried to an existing road, or a by-pass is under consideration it may become necessary to collect information about the origin and destination of traffic passing through the area in which the road is situated. If accident records are maintained they form a good basis for designing the improvements in accident prone locations. Most of this information is the domain of traffic engineering.

2.9 SOIL AND MATERIAL STUDIES

After selection of the final centre line of the road investigation for soil and other material required for constructions should start. This survey is required to ascertain the soil profile for design of embankment and pavements and proper method of handling the soils. If the embankment is to be constructed out of the soil from borrow pit, the borrow pits or borrow areas should be along the roadland at intervals of 200 m. To assess the type of soil in the borrow area test pit 1.5 sq./m should be dug in the borrow area with the depth of the test pit not exceeding the depth of borrow pit by 15 cm. The soil from the test pit should be tested for gradation, liquid limit, plastic limit, optimum moisture content, and deleterious constituents. The results of the laboratory investigations may be summarised in a proforma.

The final selection of the borrow area could then be made in accordance to the norms recommended. For low embankment a soil having a liquid limit of about 40, a plasticity index of 10 and shrinkage limit of more than 10 % is okay. That is the murum soil or sandy soil or stabilized black cotton soil will be alright. However special investigation will be required for the design of high embankments which is dealt with elsewhere. For cut sections the soil properties should be ascertained along the central line of the road as in the case of low embankment. These tests would indicate the land-slide prone areas also. If there is a land-slide prone area, services of a geologist should be requisitioned.

One of the chief problems which the highway engineer has to address himself is the embankment over which the highway is to pass. Generally, problem of embankment construction and design can be divided into three categories:

(1) Routine Cases: In which embankments of low to high heights are constructed over firm or reasonably firm ground, using sand, gravel and other suitable materials.

(2) Special Cases: These cases are generally troublesome stretches of ground extending over limited length of road or the embankment material which is relatively unfavourable, such as silts and clays.

(3) Exceptional Cases: In this category are the embankments that are routed over long distances on marine clays, tidal swamps, peats, creeks etc., where drainage conditions might be critical in causing instability and post construction settlements might assume serious proportions. Whereas for embankments falling under the group routine category, not much vigilance is required in embankment design, when designing highway embankment over difficult foundation condition, the designer could choose one of the several alternatives that are available to him viz.

- Elevated viaduct.
- Embankment fill supported on piles.
- Excavations and replacement of sub soil.
- Sub-soil stabilization.
- Stage construction.
- Construction of embankments with berms.
- Relocation of alignment.
- Displacement of weak soil by surcharge weight or blasting.
- Use of light weight material such as cinder for embankment construction.

Once it is decided to construct the embankment from engineering and economic considerations, detailed calculations should be conducted for the design of embankment, whether the embankment is of low height, medium height, or high embankment. Failure of embankment generally takes place by one of the following modes viz.

- Slip circle failure through the slope or base.
- Block sliding over a weak soil strata in the foundation.
- Plastic squeezing and/or creep of foundation soils.
- Excessive and uneven settlement of embankment and foundation soil and
- Erosion of embankment. No design should be considered complete unless safety against failure by all the above modes is ensured.

Naturally, for a detailed discussion of embankment, the reader is referred to a book on "Soil Engineering."

2.10 DRAINAGE STUDIES

Drainage of highway refers to the disposal of surplus water. The water involved may be precipitation falling on the road, surface run-off from the adjacent land, seepage water moving through sub-surface channels, or moisture rising by capillary action. The main components of drainage study would be fixing the grade line of the road, design of the pavement, and design of the surface and sub-surface drainage system. The main components of the drainage investigation will be to determine highest flood level, pond water, depth of water table, range of tidal levels and amount of surface run-off. The road level should be above the H.F.L. The knowledge of the highest water table is necessary for fixing the sub-grade level, deciding the thickness of the pavement and taking other design measures such as provision of capillary cut-offs, or interceptor drains. The depth of the water table may be measured at open wells along the alignments or at holes specialled bored for this purpose. The observation should be taken at the time of the withdrawal of the monsoon when the water table is likely to be the highest. Such measurements are off course not needed in desert areas. In situations where water stagnates by the road sides for considerable period such as irrigated fields, information about the standing of water should be collected. In cut sections in rolling or hilly terrain, the water may saturate the road bay and it may become necessary to intercept the sub-surface seepage flow. There is generally no problem of surface run-off as for as highway is concerned since such run-off is ultimately laid away from the highway area to the natural drainage channels by means of longitudinal side drains.

The highway alignment is largely influenced by cross drainage works and it's location. This is a matter to be considered in greater detail for which a reference may be made to any book on bridges or aqueducts.

2.11 REALIGNMENT PROJECT

Most of the roads in India have been upgraded from preautomobile era. Naturally, they are lacking in geometric standards, length, widths etc. At least as far as national highways are concerned, it is thought necessary.

- To improve the horizontal alignment such as radius, superelevation, transition curve, site distances.

- To improve vertical alignment like steep gradients, humps and dips.

- Reconstruction of weak and narrow bridges, culverts and construction of over bridges and under bridges at suitable locations across a railway line, in place of level crossings.

- Raising the level of the road so that it is not flooded or water logged and the construction of a bye-pass to avoid the road running into a town or city have been realignment project. But the principles of new highway project and the realignment project are essentially the same, and it is largely a question of economy whether such realignment can be undertaken.

2.12 PREPARATION AND PRESENTATION OF PROJECT DOCUMENTS

The data collected during survey and investigations is to be presented in a proper form, so that the competant authority can take proper decision and funds can be allocated. This is known as complete project document and essentially consists of (1) The project report, (2) Estimate and (3) Drawings.

The Project Report:

The project report should consist of the following:

(1) Preliminary Preamble: Giving the name of the work, authority executing and planning it, the position of the work in the plan/non-plan period, present condition of the road in the case of improvement of road as project, topographical and geological features of the area, rainfall and temperature data such as annual average intensity and distribution during the year, range of temperatures during summer and winter months etc. comes under preliminary preamble.

(2) Road Features: Here the merits and demerits of alternative routes investigated should be discussed and reasons for selecting the proposed route should be given. A tentative idea regarding the effect of the proposed route on the overall transportation pattern of the area should be given. The alignment of the proposed road section with reference to topographical and geological features and obligatory points should be given. Points such as high banks, heavy cuttings, nature of soil along the route should be clearly shown. Similarly, environmental factors, probable acquisition of structures along the roadway, carriageway width should be clearly emphasized and its economic aspect should be discussed. If traffic survey is conducted, the possible traffic that will be plying on new road and the possible future growth should be indicated. For existing roads, where the project is for the improvement, the accident data with special reference to accident prone locations should be given.

(3) Road Design and Specifications: This part should give fixation of grade line, H.F.L. water table level, proposed geometric standards, soil investigation data for the pavement design in a tabular form, deflection data for the existing roads, and tentative pavement design proposals with respective alternative routes, and the economic implications there of. If it is hilly road or high embankment requiring retaining wall, the design for the retaining wall should be given. If the road is having cross drainage works, may be culvert,

hydrological details and the design details of the culverts should be given. The proposed drainage system of the road such as longitudinal side drains, catch water drains, blanket courses etc. should be discussed and relevant design calculations should be appended. This particular part of the project report should clearly bring out material, labour and equipment survey. Borrow area charts, quarry charts, type of equipment required for construction and it's procurement should be detailed. Availability of skilled and non-skilled labour should be given. This part of the project report should also give the schedule of rates that shall be adopted. The construction schedule either in the form of a bar chart or on the basis of critical path method should be developed if the project is big. Even the miscellaneous items, such as temporary worksheds, arrangement for water supply, road side plantations, facilities for tourists such as rest houses etc. should be included in this part of the project report.

Estimate:

This part of the project report is very relevant. The estimate part of the project report will be split-up in two major heads:

(a) General abstract of costs: This part gives the total cost of the scheme, with a general break-up under major heads. (with further sub-divisions as necessary) i.e. land acquisition, site clearance, earth work, sub-bases and bases, bituminous work/cement concrete pavement, cross drainage and other miscellaneous structures, percentage charges for contingencies, work charge establishment, quality control, and other miscellaneous items.

(b) Detailed estimates for each major head: This part of the project report should consist of abstract of cost, estimate of quantities analysis of rates for items not covered by the relevant schedule of rates and material source charts. Where a project work is proposed to be executed in stages, the estimate should be prepared for each stage separately.

2.13 DRAWINGS

The purpose of the drawing is to depict the proposed highway work in relation to the existing feature. It is recommended that the size of the drawing sheet may be 594 mm × 420 mm. On one sheet of this size it should be possible to accommodate the plan and L section of one km length of road, with sufficient overlap on either side, if drawn to the horizontal scale of 1:2500. A wider margin of 40 mm, is kept on the left hand side, so that the drawing sheets could be stitched into a folio. The type of drawings that constitute project report are:

(a) Locality Map Cum Site Plan: The locality map and the site plan could be either on the one sheet, if the length of the road section considered is reasonable. If the length of the section is substantial, the locality map is generally accommodated in one sheet and the site plan in a series of sheets that follow. The locality map also called as a key map is drawn to a scale 1:250,000. It shows the location of the road with respect to important towns, industrial centres etc. In short, it provides a bird's eye view of the project.

The site plan or the index plan shows the proposed project road, its immediate neighbourhood covering the important physical features such as rivers, hill tanks, railway lines etc. The key map shows the kilometrage from the beginning to end and is generally drawn to a scale of 1:50,000. The locality cum site plan should have a legend to explain the abbreviations and symbol used.

(b) Land Acquisition Plans: These maps are required for land acquisition proceedings. Generally, they are prepared on existing village maps, or settlement maps giving details of property and their survey number so that land acquisition proceedings could be smooth. A scale in the range of 1:2000 to 1:8000 depending on available maps will be suitable.

(c) Plan and Longitudinal Section: Plan and longitudinal section for one km length of the road should be shown on a single drawing sheet as far as possible. The plan should be drawn at the top and the longitudinal section at the bottom. The general scale for horizontal length is 1:2500 and for vertical distances 1:250. Naturally for hilly stretches, this scale could be changed. The plan will depict centre line of the road, right of way limits, existing structures, drainage ways intersecting road, and railway lines, electric and telephone cables, location of cross drainage structures, design details of horizontal curves, bench marks and location of cross-sections, contours etc. The longitudinal section should show the profile of the proposed road, and the general ground or the existing road whichever is applicable. It should incorporate details such as gradients, super elevation, details of horizontal alignments, location of drainage crossing and intersecting roads, location and set out data for vertical curves and continuous chainage.

(d) Typical Cross-Section Sheet: In a general highway project, the elements of cross section like width of the carriage way and roadway side slopes, pavement cross fall i.e. camber is likely to remain constant for most of the road length. Therefore only typical cross sections need be drawn. At least one cross section each for road in fill, cut, and curve need be drawn.

(e) Detailed Cross Sections: The cross sections should be drawn serially along the continuous chainage. These cross sections should show existing road level / ground level, and the proposed road level, area of cut and fill involved and type and thickness of different pavement courses.

(f) Drawings for Cross Drainage Structures: A highway is likely to cross many rivulets and streams requiring small and big cross drainage structures. For small cross drainage structures, Standard designs are adopted whereas for bigger cross drainage structures, separate designs are worked out. A separate drawing is given when there is typical and different design for the cross drainage structure. This is largely a part of "Bridge Engineering" for which reader is referred to a text book on "Bridge Engineering".

(g) Road Junction Drawings: A road junction drawing drawn at the initial stages solve many further problems that can crop up later on. The junction drawing should incorporate existing features of the intersecting roads, the proposed improvement and traffic control devices like signs, pavement markings etc. The scale to which these drawings are generally drawn is 1: 500 or 1: 600.

(h) Drawing for Retaining Walls and other Structures: Particularly in hill roads, there are massive retaining walls. Drawings for the retaining wall should accompany the project report, and should show foundation condition and structural details as also the materials proposed to be used.

2.14 CHECK LIST FOR THE HIGHWAY PROJECT REPORT

The items that should be incorporated in complete project document are now summarised below and can form what is termed as check list for the complete project document. The complete project document should consist of

(1)   Preliminaries consisting of:
- Name of the work and it's scope,
- Authority and plan provisions,
- History, Geography, Climate.

(2) Road features consisting of:
- Route selection,
- Alignment,
- Environmental factors,
- Cross-sectional elements,
- Traffic.

(3) Road design specifications consisting of:
- Road design,
- Pavement design,
- Masonry works,
- Specification.

(4) Drainage facilities including cross drainage structures consisting of:
- HFL, water table, seepage flows,
- Surface drainage, catch water drains, longitudinal side drains,
- Sub surface drainage blanket courses, sub drains and
- Cross drainage structures.

(5) Material labour and Equipment consisting of source and transport arrangement for equipment, material and labour.

(6) Rates that is schedule of rates and it's justification.

(7) Construction programming consisting of:

- Working season and
- Schedule of completing the work.

(8) Miscellaneous such as:

- Rest houses,
- Diversions,
- Road side plantations etc.

(9) Estimate consisting of:

- General abstract of work.
- Detailed estimate for each major head which will include abstract of costs, estimates of quantities, analysis of rates and material source charts.

(10) Project drawings consisting of:

- Locality cum site plan.
- Land acquisition plan.
- Plan and L section.
- Typical cross section sheet.
- Detailed cross section.
- Cross drainage drawings.
- Road junction drawings.
- Drawings for retaining wall and other structures.

2.15 THIRD ROAD DEVELOPMENT PLAN

Considering the lessons understood from the first to seventh plan, the Chief Engineers of various states and the Indian Roads Congress formulated a long term plan for India for the period 1981 – 2001. This plan is called as Lucknow Plan. The goals and policies of this road plan are -

- Accessibility to all the villages with a population of above 500 should be provided by the turn of the century.
- Master plan should be prepared, for towns cities, district, state and national level and it should be remembered while making these master plans that the plan should generate employment and industrial growth.

- The national highway length should be so increased so as to form square grid of 100 km side.
- Speedy travel may be facilitated by Expressways. The expressways should be constructed on major traffic corridors.
- Environmental standards must be maintained in the construction and maintenance of roads and energy conservation in the form of petrol saving must be given high priority and road safety measures should be undertaken to contain and bring down the accident rates.
- Major District Roads should serve and connect all towns and villages with a population of 1500 and above and other village roads should serve and connect villages with a population of 1000-1500.
- Expressways are recommended on major traffic corridors to promote speedy travel. As traffic develops the widening of roads should be taken-up but care should be taken to see while initial constructing the road that sufficient sideway margin is available for future widening from this point of view, ribbon development should be checked right from the beginning if required by suitable legislative measures.
- Resources crunch may make it difficult to make all rural roads all-weather roads. As a beginning, the roads may be made earthen roads or gravel roads.
- Computer-aided designs of highways and highway parameters, research and development activities and data based on traffic flows and connected fields should be strengthened.
- There should be modernization of road making machinery and strengthened highway contracting industry.
- Additional sources of highway finance such as toll roads and private sector financing should be explored. Where required for special problems, private consulting firms could be contacted without hesitation.
- The lengths of various categories of road as far as twenty year plan is concerned could be calculated as under:

    (a) National Highways, length in km $= \dfrac{\text{Area in sq. km}}{50}$

    (b) State Highways, length in km $= \dfrac{\text{Area in sq. km}}{25}$

    or

    State Highways, length in km $= 62.5 \times \text{Number of Towns} - \dfrac{\text{Area in sq. km}}{50}$

    (c) Major District Roads, length in km $= \dfrac{\text{Area in sq. km}}{12.5}$

or

Major District Road length $= 90 \times$ Number of Towns

(d) Total Road length $= 4.74 \times$ Number of Villages and Towns

(e) Rural road length (0DR + Village roads) may be obtained by subtracting the length of SH NH and MDR from the total length. For calculating these road lengths, NH system is supposed to have a grid of 100 km side.

The idea of obtaining State Highway length is that it should be twice the National Highway length. Similarly, it is assumed in the above formula that NH and SH will pass through all towns with population more than 5000. On this basis, on the assumption of 3364 towns, the length of the square grid works out to be

$$\sqrt{\frac{\text{Area of the country}}{\text{Number of Towns}}} = \sqrt{\frac{3287782}{3364}}$$

$$= 31.25 \text{ km}$$

As such length of NH and SH $= 2 \times 31.25 \times$ Number of Towns

$$= 62.5 \times \text{Number of Towns}$$

The idea behind the formula to work out length of MDR is that it should be twice the length of State Highways, whereas the another formula for MDR is empirical. The total road length in the nation is computed on the assumption that every town and village must be connected by road. Since, there are 583563 villages and towns, the average area per human settlement is

$$= \frac{\text{Area of Nation}}{\text{Number of Villages}}$$

$$= \frac{3287782}{583563}$$

$$= 5.64 \text{ sq. km}$$

$\therefore$ Length of grid $= \sqrt{5.64} = 2.37$ km

$\therefore$ Length of total road $= 2 \times 2.37 \times$ Number of Villages and Towns

$$= 4.74 \times \text{Number of Villages and Towns}$$

The above criteria results in a road density of 0.82 km/sq. km as against 0.46 in 1981.

- Requirement of funds as per 20 year plan (1981 – 2001) is estimated around 64000 crores. The present yearly revenue from the Central and State Governments from motor vehicles is around 5000 crores. Therefore, the expenditure is justified. The overall goal of 20 year plan is indicated in the table below.

Table 2.1

Category of Road	Existing length km	Target length km	Additional length km	Cost in crores
Express Highway	–	2000	2000	To be met from toll collection
National Highways	31737	66000	34263	16950
State Highways	95491	144000	48509	10664
Major Highways	153000	280000	145000	12759
Rural Roads	912684	2212000	1299316	24879
Total	1192912	2704000	1529088	129774

For calculating road length, formula based on area is preferred. Towns are defined as settlements having at least municipalities.

SOLVED PROBLEMS

Problem 2.1: *Roads are to be planned according to (1981 – 2001) road development plan. Area in sq. kilometres is 25000 km². The number of towns in this area are 200 and villages 1000. Calculate the length of national and state highways and the length of village roads and other district roads.*

Solution:

National highway length

$$= \frac{\text{Area in sq. km}}{50}$$

$$= \frac{25000}{50} = \textbf{500 km}$$

$$\text{State highway length} = \frac{\text{Area in km}^2}{25.0}$$

$$= \frac{25000}{25} = \textbf{1000 km}$$

That is first criteria i.e. state highway length should be double the national highway length.

$$\text{SH} = 1000 \text{ km} = 2 \times \text{National highway length}$$

$$\therefore \quad \text{National highway} = 500 \text{ km}$$

$$\text{Major district roads} = \frac{\text{Area}}{12.5} = \frac{25000}{12.5} = \textbf{2000 km}$$

$$\text{Total road length} = 2 \times 2.37 \times (\text{Towns} + \text{Villages})$$

$$= 2 \times 2.37 (200 + 1000) = 5688$$

Other District Roads and Village Roads

= Total road length – Major District road – State Highways – National Highway length

= 5688 – 2000 – 1000 – 500

= **2188 km.**

Problem 2.2: *The area of one of the district in Maharashtra state is 13,400 sq.km. and there are 12 towns as per 1981 census. Determine the lengths of various categories of Roads to be provided in this district by the method suggested during the 3rd 20 year road development plan period. You may assume any additional data suitably if required. State the assumptions clearly.*

Solution:

(i) Length of NH, km $= \dfrac{13400}{50} = 268$ km.

(ii) Length of SH:

    (a) By area, SH km $= \dfrac{13400}{25} = 536$ km.

    (b) By area and number of towns, SH km $= 62.5 \times 12 - \dfrac{13400}{50} = 482$ km.

       Adopt length or SH (higher of the two criteria) $= 536$ km.

(iii) Length of MDR in the district

    (a) By area MDR, km $= \dfrac{13400}{12.5} = 1072$ km.

    (b) By number of towns, MDR, km $= 90 \times 12 = 1080$ km.

       Provide length of MDR $=$ **1080 km.**

(iv) Total length of all categories of roads may be assumed to provide an overall density of road length equal to 82 km per 100 sq.km. area by the year 2001.

NH + SH + MDR + ODR + VR $= 13400 \times \dfrac{82}{100} = 10988$ km.

    Length of NH + SH + MDR $= 268 + 536 + 1080 = 1884$ km.

Therefore, total length of rural roads consisting of ODR + VR = 10988 – 1884 = 9104 km.

(1) Primary system of NH = 268 km.

(2) Secondary system consisting of SH = 536 and MDR = 1080, total length = 1616 km.

(3) Tertiary system of rural roads consisting of ODR and VR = OR length = 9104 km.

(4) Total road length = 10,988 km.

QUESTIONS

1. With the aid of sketches. Discuss the road patterns which are in use.
2. Write down classification of roads.
3. Outline the main features of various road patterns commonly in use with their diagrams only.

4. Discuss giving suitable sketches various patterns of roads in urban areas. Sate their merits and demerits.
5. Explain how the road length of NH and SH are determined by using the third road plan formula.
6. How do you calculate the lengths of N. H. and S. H. for highway planning based on 3rd and 20th year road development plan ?
7. Differentiate between star and grid system.
8. Discuss how different road patterns are gainfully employed in the metropolitan cities of India.
9. Write a short note on preparation of Master plan.
10. Write an explanatory note on Highway planning Survey's.
11. Determine the length of different categories of roads in a state in India by the year 2001 using the third road development formulae and the following data:
    Total area of the state = 100000 sq. km.
    Total number of towns as per 1981 census = 86.
    Overall road density aimed at = 82 km per 100 sq km area.
12. The area of one of the districts in Maharashtra State is 13,400 sq. km. And there are 12 towns as per 1981 census. Determine the lengths of various categories of roads to be provided in this district by the method suggested during the 3rd and 20th year road development plan period. You may assume any additional data suitably if required. State the assumptions clearly.

Chapter 3

TRAFFIC ENGINEERING

3.1 INTRODUCTION

Traffic engineering is comparatively a new science and it's advent is related to the speedy growth of motor vehicles on the road. Several shades of definition exist for Traffic Engineering. One may say that it is that branch of highway engineering which deals with planning, geometric design of streets and highways and the abutting lands, and with traffic operations thereon, so that convenient and economic transport of men and material can take place on highways.

In order to achieve the above objects, traffic engineering is generally split into further compartments such as

- Traffic characteristics,
- Traffic studies and analysis,
- Traffic operations,
- Planning and analysis,
- Geometric Design,

(6) Administration and management.

These compartments are made so that on one hand we can plan traffic and regulate the traffic generated and on the other hand frame by laws, so that highways are put to maximum efficient use.

3.2 TRAFFIC CHARACTERISTICS

To study the traffic characteristics, we have to know the attributes. i.e. the qualities of elements using the road. These are normally called as road user characteristics and these include the quality of roads also, since road user and the road have to be a contented couple.

Physical Characteristics:

Physical characteristics may be related to road users. For example (1) Vision of the road user: field of clearest and acute vision is within a cone whose angle is about 3°. With eye movement, vision can be satisfactory upto $10^\circ - 20^\circ$ in horizontal plane. This vision element should be used in planning traffic signal. (2) Hearing is a important phenomenon for pedestrian and cyclists but is not considered important for motorist in western countries. In India, honking by motorist and scooter owners is frequent and studies should be conducted in this domain. (3) Strength, Lack of strength for the road can impede traffic flow, especially pot holes and weak spots can cause congestion in the traffic flow. (4) Mental, psychological, and environmental factors. Mental and psychological factors relate to the condition of the mind of the driver: whether he is drunk, fatigued, responsivity of the driver, his anxiousness. These relate to the mind of the driver. To be upright, it should be possible to devise drivers worthyness tests just as air worthyness tests for the pilots, so that the wheel of the vehicle is in safe hands. (5) Environmental factors: These relate to the pattern of traffic flow whether it is mixed, heavy, one way, hilly etc. and the judgement of the driver to such environment. In a way,(4) and (5) are co-related.

3.3 VEHICLE CHARACTERISTICS

Road and the vehicle plying on the road could be considered as a consenting couple. However, a vista of vehicles ply on the road and the static and dynamic characteristics of these vehicles determine certain road elements. For example, the height of the vehicle affects the height of the overbridge. The height of driver seat affects the visibility distance and the height of head light determines the head light sight distance at the valley curve. The length of vehicle can affect the capacity and minimum turning radius. The dynamic characteristics of the vehicle generally refer to its engine weight, its B.H.P., suspension system etc. These factors to a large extent determine the riding comfort. Keeping these considerations in view, IRC has fixed up maximum dimensions of road vehicles and maximum permissible gross weights. These specifications are summarised in the table below.

Table 3.1: Maximum Dimensions of Road Vehicles

Dimensions of Vehicle	Particulars	Maximum Dimensions in Meters (excluding front and rear Bumpers)
Width	All vehicles	2.5
Height	(a) Single decked vehicle for normal application.	3.8
	(b) Double decked vehicle	4.75
Length	(a) Single unit truck with two or more axles (Types 2, 3)	11.0
	(b) Single unit bus with two or more axles (Type 2, 3)	12.0
	(c) Semi-trailer tractor combination (Type 2s1, 2s2, 3s1, 3s2)	16.0
	(d) Tractor and trailer combination (Type 2–2, 3–2, 3–3)	18.0

No combination is allowed to be more than two units and no such combination loaded or otherwise should have overall length exceeding 18 m. The types of road transport vehicles are shown in Fig. 3.1.

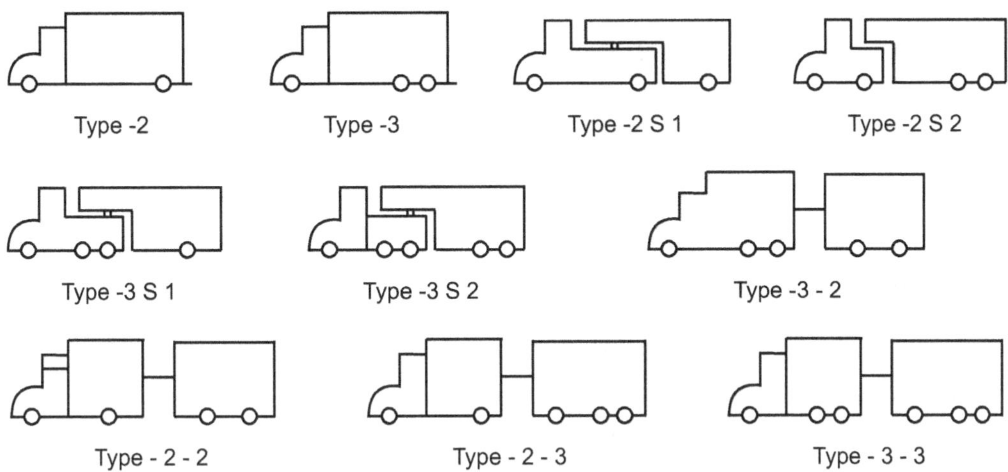

Fig. 3.1

The weights and other details of the vehicle are as shown in Table 3.2.

Table 3.2: Maximum Permissible Gross Weight and Axle Weight of Transport Vehicles

Vehicle Type	Maximum Gross Weight	Maximum Axle weight (tonnes)			
		Truck / Tractor		Trailer	
		FAW	RAW	FAW	RAW
Type 2 (Both Axle single type)	12.0	6	6		
Type 2 (FA single type RA - Duel type)	16.2	6	10.2		
Type 3	24.0	6	18 (TA)	–	
Type 2 S – 1	26.4	6	10.2	–	10.2
Type 2 S – 2	34.2	6	10.2	–	18 TA
Type 3 S – 1	34.2	6	18 (TA)	–	10.2
Type 3 S – 2	42.0	6	18 (TA)	–	18 TA
Type 2 – 2	36.6	6	10.2	10.2	10.2
Type 3 – 2	44.4	6	18 (TA)	10.2	10.2
Type 2 – 3	44.4	6	10.2	10.2	18 TA
Type 3 – 3	52.2	6	18 (TA)	10.2	18 TA

*   FAW – Weight on front axle; RAW – weight on rear axle;

*   TA – Tandem axle fitted with 8 tyres

Braking characteristics of motor vehicles are also very important especially in preventing accidents. Many times a braking test is conducted to assess the condition of braking system. To know whether the brakes are OK or not, a vehicle having initial speed of u m/sec is subjected to full braking for 't' seconds, if the vehicle is brought to stand still position in 'L' meters. Then clearly the braking distance L = $\dfrac{u^2}{2\,g\,f}$ on the assumption of the road being level. This equation can thus yield average skid resistance of the pavement surface.

3.4 TRAFFIC STUDIES

In order to determine the type of traffic which is being accommodated by the road, traffic studies are conducted. These studies are generally divided into (1) Traffic volume studies, (2) Speed studies, (3) Origin and destination study, (4) Traffic flow characteristics, (5) Traffic capacity study, (6) Parking study and (7) Accident studies.

Traffic Volume Study:

This study involves the measurement of the number and the type of vehicles crossing a section of the road per unit time at a selected period. It is similar to determining discharge in a pipe line. To carry such study, naturally, you have to incur considerable cost. But such a study can be beneficial in many respects. For example, (1) Higher the traffic volume, more important is the road. This will aid in not only judicious operation of existing facilities such as signals etc. but it may also tell us, whether road requires widening. (2) Knowing the laden weight of vehicles and their numbers, it should be possible to know whether road cross-section is adequate from the point of view of strength. (3) Traffic volume studies can help in planning regulatory measures such as one way streets intersections, signal timing, whereas pedestrian traffic volume study is used in planning side walks, subways etc. To properly conduct traffic volume study, hourly traffic volume should be known with daily and seasonal variations. Traffic volume studies could be conducted by manual or mechanical counts. In manual methods, the number and type of vehicles passing a cross-section of the road are actually measured by individuals. Naturally this requires a large number of people to be employed for the purpose. And such studies are difficult to conduct for the whole day. In mechanical methods, the mechanical counter which is incorporated in the cross-section of the road records the number of vehicles (weightwise) crossing the section in the desired period. The advantage is one can take observations throughout the day, but the pedestrian traffic is difficult to measure by this method. The traffic volume data so collected in these studies could be expressed in various convenient ways. Some of the ways in which these studies could be expressed are (1) Annual average daily traffic or annual daily traffic. After collecting the data for the year this count can be calculated. Naturally the traffic consists of several type, such as motors, bullock carts, scooters etc. The concept of passenger car unit is employed to convert this traffic in a uniform pattern. (2) Trend charts could be prepared showing volume trends over a period of years. Similarly, variation charts showing hourly, daily or seasonal variations could be prepared. (3) In fact traffic flow maps along the routes could be prepared. To draw such maps the usual method is to consider the thickness of lines representing traffic volume to some derived scale. (4) Traffic flow diagram at any intersection could be prepared. These diagrams will give relative importance of roads and is useful in planning signal timings. A typical flow diagram at an intersection is shown below.

Fig. 3.2 shows that though one arm of the intersection is balanced, the other arm is not balanced. That is the traffic coming in and out is not the same. There is stagnation and the junction requires remedial measures. (5) Thirtieth highest hourly volume: This is defined as the 30th highest hourly volume that will be exceeded only 29 times in a year and all other hourly volumes of the year will be less than this value. This value is generally taken as the hourly volume for the design and will ensure that there will be congestion only during 29 hours in the year. This concept is not as yet popular in India, essentially since it requires amassing large traffic data.

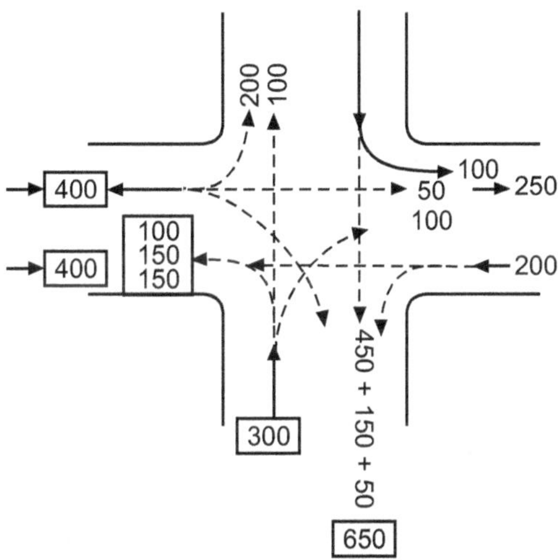

Fig. 3.2

The speed of the vehicle plying on the road can change instant to instant which is a function of geometry of the road and psycological factors related to the driver. The spot speed is the instantaneous speed of the vehicle at a specified location, whereas the average speed is the average of spot speeds of all vehicles passing a given point on the highway. Here again we have space-mean speed and time - mean speed, where the space-mean speed represents the average speed of the vehicle in a certain road of known length at given time, time-mean speed represents the speed distribution of vehicles at a point and it is the average of instantaneous speeds of observed vehicles at the spot. The following table brings out this point.

Table 3.3: Average instantaneous speeds of observed vehicles

Space mean speed	Time mean speed
d = Length of road, in metres n = Number of individual vehicle observation t_1 = Travel time for i^{th} vehicle to travel distance 'd' in seconds then Space mean speed km/hr. $$= \dfrac{3.6\, dn}{\displaystyle\sum_{i=1}^{n} t_1}$$	V_i = Observed instantaneous speed of ith vehicles, km/hr. n = Number of vehicles observed, then Time mean speed $$= \dfrac{\displaystyle\sum_{i=1}^{n} V_i}{n}$$

Generally, space mean speed is slightly lower than time-mean speed especially on Indian rural roads.

Running speed of the vehicle could be obtained by dividing the distance covered by the time during which vehicle was in motion, whereas the overall speed or travel speed is obtained by dividing the total distance between two destinations and time taken to travel between these destinations. Therefore this definition includes the delays and stoppages and the time consumed for them enroute. The speed studies could be further split-up into spot speed studies and speed and delay studies.

Spot speed refers to the speed of the vehicle at the instant. It could be affected by the geometry of the road, gradient, sight distance, the B.H.P. of vehicle etc. At a particular instant the speedometer of the vehicle gives the spot speed. This may be useful for the driver but is not of much use to traffic planner. The traffic planner can get resonably accurate value of spot speed by installing an observer on one side of the road and asking him to start the stop watch when the vehicle crosses him. An enoscope which is just a mirror box supported on tripod is placed away from the observer (say 30 m), so that the image of the vehicle is seen by the observer when the vehicle crosses the section where the enoscope is placed and at that instant the stop-watch is stopped. Thus we know the time required to traverse a particular length and therefore the speed. The method though simple, speedy observations are difficult to take, since spotting a particular vehicle in the stream of vehicles is somewhat cumbersome. There are other methods available such as graphic recorder, radar, photographic methods etc. However for a developing country like ours, these appear to be costly.

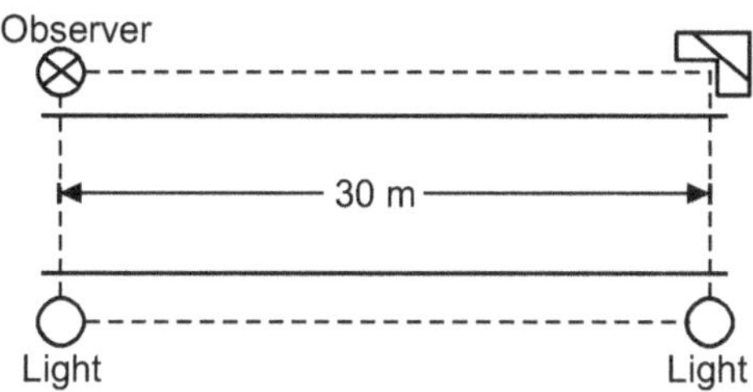

Fig. 3.3

The information from speed studies could be presented as (1) By arranging the data in groups covering various speed ranges and the number of vehicles in that range. Arithmatic mean then gives the average speed. Problem 3.6 explains this concept.

(2) Average value of each speed group can be plotted on X-axis and cumulative percent of vehicles at or below the different speeds can be plotted on Y-axis to generate a graph as shown in Fig. 3.4. From this graph any percentile speed could be obtained. For example, 90th percentile speed is 60 km/hr. This means that only 10 percent of vehicles have speed more than 60 km/hr. Generally 85th percentile speed is considered to be speed limit for that zone. In Fig. 3.4, the 5th percentile speed is around 32 km/hr. For urban roads this is the safe speed limit. On Indian Roads, we do not lower speed limits to avoid congestion on the roads. In many countries, 15th percentile speed represents lower speed limit to avoid bottling of roads.

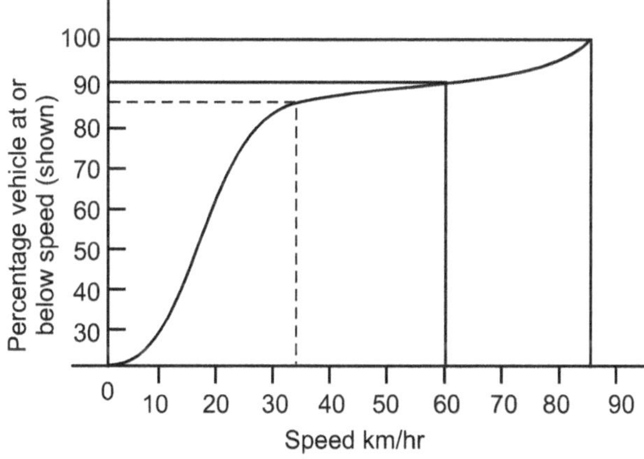

Fig. 3.4: Cumulative speed distribution

(3) Just as we have taken recourse to cumulative speed distribution to know about percentile speeds, we can plot frequency distribution of speeds. Here we plot speed of vehicles or average value of each speed group of vehicles on X-axis and percentage of vehicles in that group on Y-axis to yield speed distribution curve as shown. Such a curve will have a peak value of travel speed across the section, which is generally called as modal speed. The graph helps in determining the speed at which greatest proportion of vehicles

move, which is given by modal speed. The problem 3.7 explains these concepts. The problem 3.8 explains the concept of modal speed.

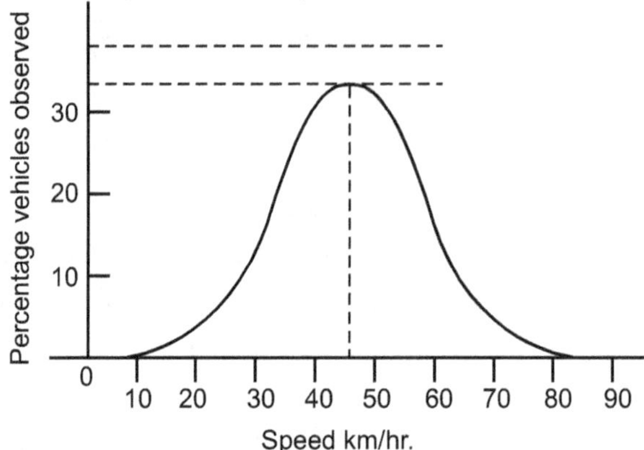

Fig. 3.5: Frequency distribution for spot speeds

Speed and Delay Study:

These studies can give the cause of delay between the two destinations A and B so that spots of congestion could be located and remedial measures undertaken. Travel time so determined can be used in the benefit cost analysis. It is usual to call delays as fixed delays which is due to traffic signals or level crossings whereas the operational delays are there due to traffic movements such as parking and turning, end turning of vehicles etc. Sometimes habitual operational delays can cause change in fixed delays i.e. change in signalling time. The speed and delay study as such can be undertaken by (1) Floating car or Riding check method. (2) Licence plate or vehicle number method. (3) Interview method. (4) Elevated observations and (5) Photographic technique.

The floating car method is generally followed in India. As the name suggests, here we have a car with four observers in it which is floating i.e. which is travelling at approximately the same speed as that of the traffic. The first observer equipped with two stop watches is an observer to record delays. At strategic locations, such as bridges, intersections, roads in vicinity of markets etc., he observes with the help of two stop watches the time required to negotiate these focal points, i.e. he observes the delay time. The second observer in the car notes the cause of this delay either in the tabular form or with vivid descriptions. It is the duty of the third observer seated in the car to find the number of vehicles that this floating car i.e. the test vehicle overtakes or is overtaken by other vehicles in specified time. The fourth observer in the car notes the number of vehicles travelling in opposite direction in each trip. It is possible that in the mixed traffic stream, these four observers are not enough to observe these things and more number of observers may be deployed.

The average journey time for all the vehicles in a traffic stream in the direction of flow q may be given by

$$\bar{t} = t_w - \frac{n_y}{q} \text{ , where } q = \frac{n_a + n_y}{t_a + t_w}$$

n_a = Average number of vehicles counted in the direction of stream when floating/ test vehicle travels in the opposite direction.

n_y = Average number of vehicles overtaking the test vehicle minus the number of vehicles overtaken when the test is in the direction of flow 'q'.

t_w = Average journey time in minutes when the test vehicle is travelling with the stream 'q'.

t_a = Average journey time in minutes when floating / test vehicle is running against the stream.

In the licence plate or vehicle number method, we have observers with synchronised stop watches placed at the entrance and exit of test section. A particular vehicle say MTA/3033 when entering the section, it's time at entry is noted by one observer at entry point and its time at exit is noted by another observer at exit time. These two observations will therefore give journey time. Needless to say that for busy road, you require very large number of observers and of course, duration and reason for delay during journey time is not directly noted. In the interview method, the traffic department interviews the road users and from their experience tries to assess the cause of delay. The method though subjective in nature, sometimes gives very useful information. Elevated observations and photographic technique are excellent but can be used for short test sections such as intersections. The final object of all this study is to evaluate the efficiency and effectiveness of control devices such as signal system, rotary etc. and arrange remedial measures if required.

3.5 ORIGIN AND DESTINATION STUDIES

Origin and destination study means to find out where and why the traffic originates and where and how it is destined. There are many applications and use of such studies. For example,

(1) In any existing highway network, we can know what routes are preferred by users and which are not preferred. We can know where there is congestion on these routes, so that proper one way regulations, bypasses or rescued routes can be introduced. (2) To locate facilities such as bus terminals, bus stops, new bridges, widening of existing bridges, so that the commuters are benefitted to maximum use. (3) Knowing the traffic density, we can check up whether the existing design standards of the road are adequate or otherwise. The origin and destination study can be undertaken by various methods.

License Plate Method: For an area, where origin and destination study is carried out, all the entry and exit points in this area are marked and observers are stationed at all these points and provided with synchronised time pieces. Now these observers note the registration number of the vehicle entering the specified area and the time at which it enters the specified area. Now simultaneously another set of observers may be noting down the registration number of the vehicle exiting this very specified area and the time at which it obtains this exit. Naturally data is collected for allotted time. All junctions have observers. Therefore for a particular vehicle having a given registration number, we can trace its trip direction and time for that trip. Field work is easy in this method but the office work is tedious. We also require large number of observers and hence limited area can be covered.

Return Post-Card Method: It is a sort of modern marketing gimmick. Random road users are provided with reply paid post cards with questionnaire printed on it with a request to return the post-card to the mailbox with the questionnaire properly answered. When sufficient number of such cards are received, traffic planner can deduce proper conclusions from it. The shortcoming of this method is that with general apathy that is prevalent, one may not get sufficient feedback and the whole exercise will be futile. But the method has some promise where traffic density is heavy. In such case distributing points have to been carefully planned. These would be petrol pumps, or road intersections etc.

Tag on Car Method: In this method, in a specified area, a precoded card is struck on the car with requisite information recorded on it. The usual information recorded, is time of entry, its speed etc. When the car leaves the specified area, exit time entry is recorded. The method has been found to be cumbersome to operate in India.

Home Interview Method: In this method, 0.5 to 10 percent of population is first randomly selected. Now trained personnel would visit the residences of these persons and collect from them all the traffic data, which route an individual takes, how much time he takes, what is the cause of delay in his opinion, what are the timings when he uses the road, what suggestion would he likes to make ? etc. The data so collected can give valuable information, if analysed properly.

Work Spot Interview Method: The only difference between home interview method and work spot interview method is that in this method the interviews are being conducted at workplaces, otherwise the method is same.

Road Side Interview Method: In this method, the place of the interview is the road side. Help of administration is sometimes required so that traffic could be diverted to a side lane for interviewing purposes. The commuters may find this procedure irksome, since it might cause delay in going to the office. Very few surveys are undertaken by this method in India. It is true that the data can be collected in short duration and that too from the horse's mouth i.e. the feed back is direct, but the success of the method lies in the co-operation of the commuters which sometimes is not available.

Traffic Flow Characteristics: The traffic study would indicate that there are types of traffic as shown in the figure. In India, due to left hand drives, diverging on the left causes least traffic conflicts, but diverging to the right and also merging from the right can cause traffic conflicts to the traffic moving in the straight path. Naturally, this is due to typical British and Indian pattern of traffic where we stick to left. When the vehicle wants to change the traffic lane, naturally there would be merging and diverging. It is the crossing i.e. the traffic for the

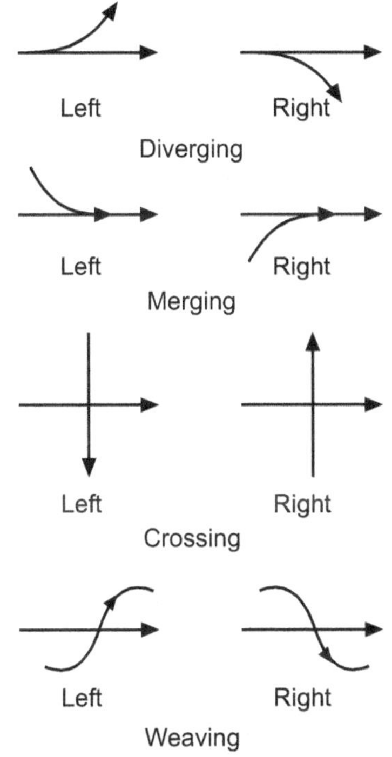

Fig. 3.6

road intersection at level which cause greater problems. In this case, vehicles on one road have to stop, thus allowing the crossing stream of vehicles to cross their path. Traffic capacity is thus greatly reduced at the intersection. Roads could cross at angles also in which case, there is an action of weaving. The most important parameter in the traffic flow is the transverse and longitudinal distribution of vehicles on the road way. As far the longitudinal distribution of vehicles of road way is concerned, the time-interval between the passage of successive vehicles moving in the same lane and measured from head to head as they pass a point on the roadway is termed as time headway. On the other hand the space headway determines the distance between successive vehicles moving in the same line measured from head at any instance. The number of headways per unit of time is a measure of traffic volume.

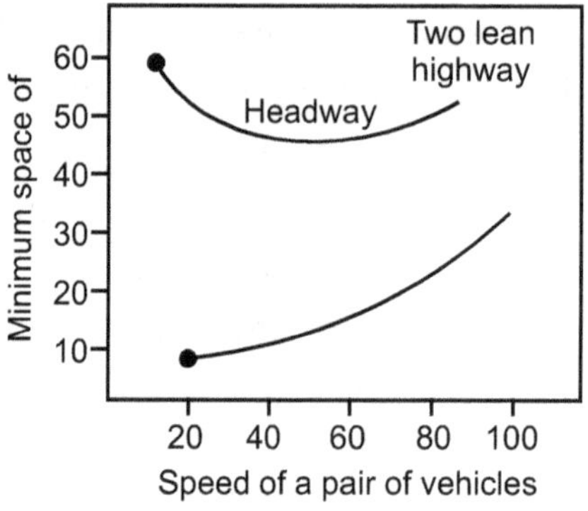

Fig. 3.7

When the vehicles gather speed, the minimum space-headway increases, whereas the minimum time headway would first decrease and after reaching a minimum value at optimum speed on the stream would then increase as shown in Fig. 3.7 for two lane highway. Naturally, maximum capacity would be obtained at this speed when time-headway is minimum.

- One of the important factors in the traffic flow is the problem of lane change. Demand for lane change will be more when the speed range of vehicles and traffic density is high.

- But the problem, as yet has not assumed that importance in India. All these traffic flow studies lead to traffic capacity studies.

- The traffic volume is the number of vehicles moving in a specified direction on a given lane that pass given cross-section during specified unit of time generally expressed as vehicles/hr or vehicles/day.

- Traffic density is the number of vehicles occupying a unit length of lane of roadway at a given instant generally expressed as vehicles/km.

- The third term in traffic flow problems is the traffic capacity. We have already referred to this term. It may be said to be the ability of the roadway to accommodate traffic volume and expressed as the maximum number of vehicles in a lane that can pass a given point in unit time usually an hour.

- Capacity and traffic volume have the same units. But traffic volume is actual rate of flow and depending upon traffic demand it can vary.

- On the other hand, capacity indicates maximum rate of flow that can be accommodated with given service conditions. Thus capacity would depend upon existent roadway and traffic conditions.

- Again this capacity could be thought of as basic capacity, possible capacity and practical capacity, the last being more important. Basic capacity is the theoretical capacity, which we have derived. It refers to the maximum number of cars or vehicles (naturally same type) that can pass on roadway cross-section during one hour under ideal conditions.

- On the other hand, the possible capacity is maximum number of vehicles that can pass roadway cross-section during one hour under prevailing roadways condition. Naturally this is lower than the basic capacity and when there is congestion leading to stagnation of traffic, the possible capacity may even approach zero value.

- On the other hand for the ideal conditions of traffic the possible capacity itself will approach basic capacity. The another term is the practical capacity. It is the maximum number of vehicles that can pass cross-section on the lane or roadway during one hour without causing unreasonable delay, hazard, or accident etc. The practical capacity would depend upon many factors such as

(1) **Lane width:** Decreasing lane, decreasing the capacity.

(2) **Lateral clearances:** Restricted lateral clearances, such as hedging, retaining walls, boundary walls etc. reduce the capacity. A minimum clearance of 1.85 m from the pavement edge to the obstruction is supposed to reflect capacity to its fullness. Reduction in this distance would decrease the practical capacity.

(3) **Commercial vehicles:** Large commercial vehicles such as buses, trucks, trucks with trailer moving with slow speed, occupy greater space and reduce the practical capacity.

(4) **Shoulder widths:** Narrow shoulder widths reduce the effective width of pavement. Vehicle parked on shoulders for some reason or the other would reduce the capacity of road.

(5) **Alignment:** If the alignment and the corresponding stopping distances are not as per specifications, the full exploitation of road section cannot take place, thus telling on capacity.

(6) **Intersections:** It is intersection which causes congestion. Intersection at a grade will have reduced capacity than the intersection on level ground. The best way is to have grade separated intersections. It is very clear from the above discussions, that the practical capacity depends upon many parameters, the definition is subjective in nature and theoretical formulation may be difficult. From this point of view, IRC has made certain recommendations about the practical capacity of roads.

Table 3.4: Capacity of Roads in Rural Areas

Sr. No.	Type of Road	Practical capacity per day (Both directions) p.c.u.
1.	Single lane 3.75 m carriageway and earth shoulders.	1000 p.c.u.
2.	Single lane 3.75 m carriageway 1.0 m hard shoulders.	2500 p.c.u.
3.	Intermediate lanes of width 5.5 m and earth shoulders.	5000 p.c.u.
4.	Two lane roads 3.0 m carriageway and earth shoulders.	10,000 p.c.u.
5.	Four lane divided highway.	20,000 to 30,000 p.c.u.

Table 3.5: Capacity of urban roads

No. of traffic lanes and width	Traffic flow	Capacity pcu/hr. for different traffic roads		
		(i) Roads, no frontage access, very little cross traffic and no standing cars	Roads, frontage, access, high capacity intersections but no standing cars	Roads with free frontage access, parked vehicles and heavy cross-traffic
Two lanes (7.0 – 7.5)	One way	2400	1500	1200
Two lanes (7.0 – 7.5)	Two way	1500	1200	750
Three lanes (10.5 m)	One way	3600	2500	2000
Four lanes (14.0 m)	One way	4800	3000	2400
Four lanes (14.0 m)	Two way	4000	2500	2000
Six lanes (21.0 m)	Two way	6000	4200	3600

The immediate conclusion, if the traffic density is more than the one specified above, then the widening of the road is required.

Origin Destination Study

Data Presentation:

Origin destination data so collected is now to be considered along with existing traffic characteristics. The data could be presented in various forms.

- Desire lines could be plotted. Desire line is a straight line drawn on topo sheet or the map of the area connecting the origin and destination of a particular traffic, width of desire line is drawn proportional to the number of trips in both directions. The existing road pattern may not be always as per desire lines and therefore drawing of desire lines would indicate necessity of new road link, diversion, a bypass or may be a bridge. When desire lines are compared with existing flow pattern, it can tell you the spot of congestion. Therefore desire lines are very helpful.

- Pie charts can be drawn, diameter of circle being proportional to the number of trips.

- Simple tabular forms could be prepared showing trip generation and traffic density. By far, drawing desire lines appear to be a favourite of traffic planners.

3.6 PARKING STUDIES

- In metropolitan cities, parking a vehicle is a great headache. Parked vehicle should cause minimum congestion and disturbance to the free traffic flow. In addition to this, parking facilities provided should be utilizable.

- The initiation of parking studies and for that matter any studies, is, first to assess the demand. One obvious method of knowing parking demand is to find out number of accumulated vehicles in a selected area during designated hour, preferably peak hour.

- Another method may be to find out the number of vehicles actually parked in a specified area in peak hours and duration of their parking time. This will involve large number of observers and field staff.

- Still another obvious method may be to interview the drivers and assess from them the parking demand. After making a reasonable estimate regarding parking demand, we should study existing parking characteristics.

- What are the present frequent places of parking. What is the percentage of two wheelers parked as compared to the four wheelers ? What is the length of parking lot and is the state of affair of kerb parking ? After knowing parking characteristics, we prepare what is known as parking space inventory. The map of specified area showing all places where kerb parking of off-street parking facilities can be provided to meet the parking demand is marked on this map.

- Knowing the parking demand and the existing parking facilities, the engineer has to strike a balance between parking capacity available and the parking demand. It is obvious that the problem is not mathematical but subjective in nature and some give and take is naturally understood.

- A parked vehicle is a necessary evil in an area. A vehicle-that is parked is going to offer some resistance to the traffic flow.

- On the other hand, people cannot transact business unless they park the vehicles. The usual method of parking in India is kerb parking, when you place your vehicle near the kerb, do business and get out. It has the advantage that your vehicle can be lodged near the place where you have work.

The kerb parking can be effected in various ways as shown in Fig. 3.8. For new township, not only wide roads should be provided but adequate parking facility, kerb or otherwise, should be left. For existing roads which are not as yet congested, it is prudent to forecast future traffic problems and make objective provision for the future traffic demand in road with traffic parking etc. It is generally seen that once the road becomes congested, hundred percent solution cannot be found and any solution that is evolved can mitigate partial problems. In order that parking facilities are not misused, these should be controlled by a policeman. It is healthy to collect a fee from the driver of the parked vehicle, so that facility provided is used in a optimum manner. Generally kerb parking is either angle parking or parallel parking. Angle parking is convenient for the motorist than the parallel parking. But this type of parking causes more obstruction to the traffic.

Even accidents have known to have occurred, due to angle parking. Generally 45° as the parking angle has been found to be convenient. In India, we have been preferring parallel parking. It is more effective when the road width and kerb parking space is limited. Parallel parking is difficult to manage, in the sense that for parking and unparking the vehicles, one is required to do forward and reverse movement of vehicle. The drivers generally do not like these movements. Parallel parking may be with equal spacing, facing the same direction or may be two vehicles placed closely with open interval between two car units. The number of scooters in India is also increasing continuously. It is now felt that for optimum use of road width, scooter parking, even when it is kerb parking should have a separate slot other than the car parking.

- The present day, often talked about method of parking, is off-street parking, where the parking is provided at a separate place away from the kerb. This method relieves the traffic congestion but the user has to walk greater distances to do business.

- In the business centre, off-street parking cannot be provided at frequent intervals. Another advantage of off-street parking is that the owner of the vehicle is more certain about the safety of the vehicle in off-street parking than the kerb parking.

- Of course this may be called as mind-set. Off-street parking may be provided in the form of parking lots, when sufficient space is available at low cost.

- This parking lot system can be called as self parking system, when the owner or the driver himself parks the vehicle in the lot or it could be called as attendant parking system, when parking and delivering operations are conducted by the attendants of the parking lot. In both the cases, fees are usually charged for using the parking space.

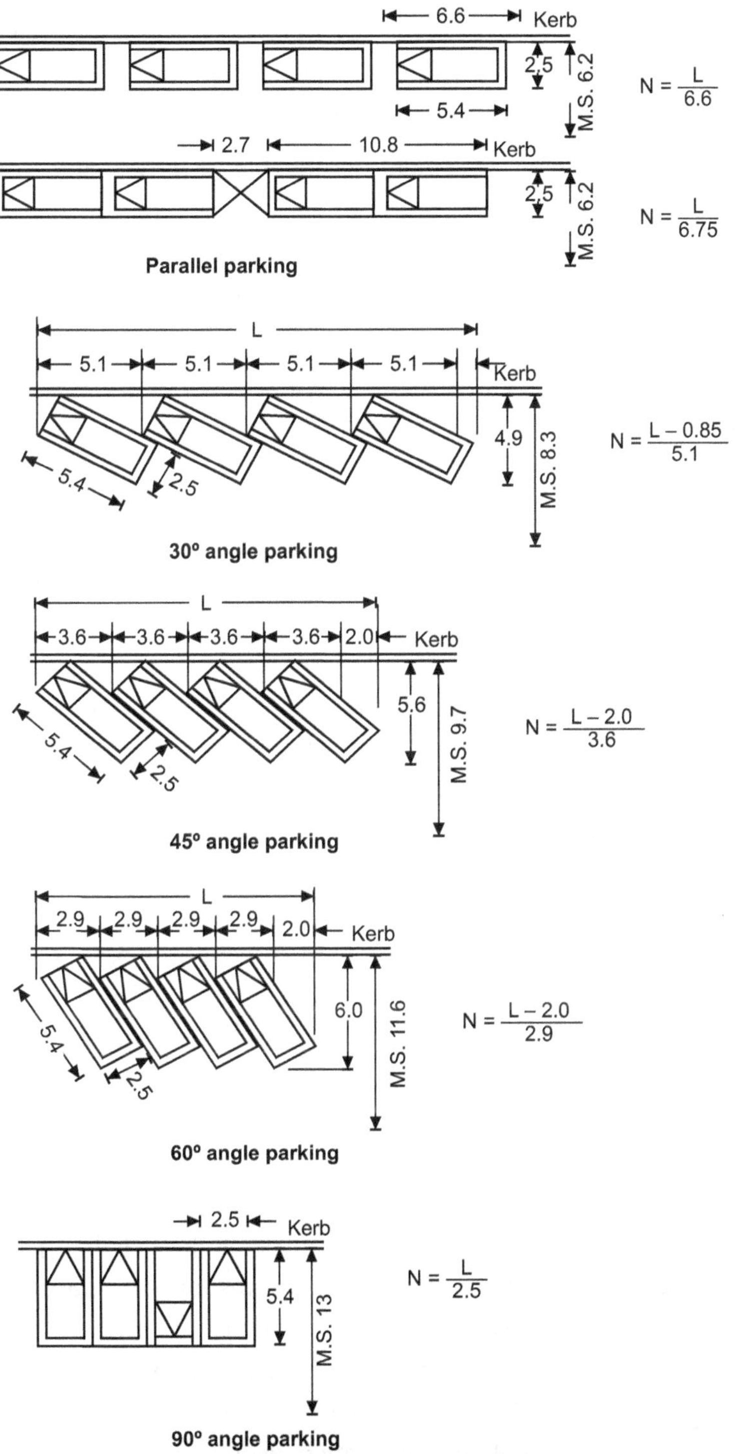

Fig. 3.8: Patterns of kerb parking

- Attendant parking system is not much prevalent in India, though it has some advantages in the sense, that it might lead to optimum utilisation of parking space. If the parking is heavy and space costly, one can resort to multistoreyed parking garages.

- In such multistoreyed garages, it should be possible to provide interfloor travel facility for the vehicles either by elevators or ramps. Ramps need more space, elevators would take less space but would be susceptible to mechanical or power failure. Even multistoreyed parking garage would require some area at the entrance for acceptance and exist of vehicles.

- This space called reservoir area could depend upon arrival and departure rate of cars and the number of attendants for such facilities. In metropolitan cities of India, day is not far off, when multistoreyed parking garages would be required to be provided.

3.7 HIGHWAY LIGHTING

Highway lighting is a very important subject. In view of the fact that most of the accidents have occurred during night times, the subject occupies special importance. Lighting on rural roads has not attained importance due to cost and rather poor percentage of slow traffic that uses rural road during nights. Even on rural roads, lighting has been found to increase safety of travel. On urban roads, intersections, bridge sites, level crossings, places where there is congestion of traffic, proper highway lighting, for obvious reasons is a "must." Driving, with only head light on is not sufficient safe. One common term used by highway engineers is silhoutte. When the brightness of the object is less than that of the background (i.e. highway), the object will appear darker than the road surface, and we have silhoutte effect. When the brightness of the object is more than that of the background, which should be the desired case, the objects above the pavement surface can be better seen by process of reverse silhoutte. Thus night visibility on concrete and other light coloured pavements is better than black top surface. Rough textured surface is the best. Mirror like black top surface, shining wet surfaces are not useful in identifying the objects above the highway pavement. You require more intense highway lighting in these cases. Actually night visibility is a function of many factors which could be (1) Size and brightness of the object on the pavement, (2) Amount and distribution of light flux from highway lighting, (3) Psychology of the driver, time available to him to see the object, his response to glare and (4) Reflecting characteristics of pavement surface. The objective discussion of these parameters is not required at this level. On the other hand, design principle that could govern highway lighting could be listed as (1) Lamps, (2) Distribution of light, (3) Spacing of lighting units, (4) Height and overhang, (5) Lateral placement and (6) Lighting layout.

Lamps and Distribution of light from them: The various types of lamps that could be used are filament, fluorescent, sodium or mercury vapour lamps in the ascending order of preference. It is economical to use large lamp size, thus providing sufficient uniformity of pavement brightness. Lamps should be so provided with covers that high percentage of lamp light is utilized in illuminating the pavement and the adjacent areas. The illumination should preferably cover 3 meter to 5 meter beyond the pavement edge. Average level of illumination on road side could be 20 to 30 lux for important urban roads carrying fast traffic and about 15 lux for main roads carrying mixed and arterial traffic. The Indian standards recommends an average level of illumination of 30 lux on important roads carrying fast traffic and 15 lux on other main roads. The ratio of minimum to average illumination suggested is 0.4.

Spacing, Height and overhang of lighting units: Many times the horizontal spacing of mounting units is not independent. It is a function of electrical distribution poles, road layout, property lines etc. Electrical distribution of pole points are generally the points where highway lighting is arranged. For intersections, bridges, special attention has to be paid. For height and overhang of the mounting the consideration is that of glare. The power of the lamp (i.e. wattage) increases the glare and increased height of mounting decreases the glare. Illumination on the road would increase with the power of the lamp, as such requirements are conflicting with each other. Here the overhang could play an important role.

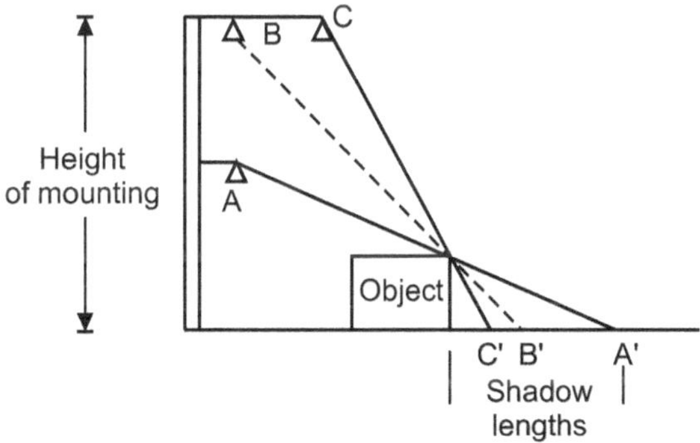

Fig. 3.9

The above figure clearly shows that increased height of mounting and long overhang would decrease shadow lengths, which is good from the point of view of prevention of accidents. It should be interesting to know that minimum vertical clearance for electrical power lines upto 650 volts above the pavement surface is 6 m as per I.R.C. Keeping this in view, usual mounting heights are from 6 metres to 10 metres and the length of overhang is generally the width of foot path on minimum basis. Lateral placement of lighting poles as recommended by I.R.C. is given below.

Table 3.6

	Road specification		Clearance
1.	For roads with raised kerbs (as in urban roads).	1.	Minimum 0.3 metre and desirable 0.6 m from the edge of raised kerb.
2.	Roads without raised kerbs as for rural roads.	2.	Minimum 1.5 m from the edge of carriageway subject to minimum of 5.0 m from the centre line of carriageway.

The clearance mentioned in the table above would also apply to poles carrying electric power and telecommunication lines too. In addition to the above specifications, as a general precaution, poles should not be installed, close to the pavement edge, so that traffic is not obstructed.

Lighting Layouts: Three types of lighting layouts are recognised (1) Single, (2) Staggered, (3) Central. These are shown in the adjoining figure and are self-explanatory. On curves the spacing between light poles is closer and the lights are on the outer side of the curves for better visibility. At vertical summit curves, summit lights have closer intervals. At road intersections, naturally you require more illumination for avoiding conflict of vehicles. For urban area intersection, the illumination could equal to the sum of illumination values for two roads, forming the intersection on a minimum scale. As a rule, lighting unit must be posted near the pedestrian crossing, channeling islands and signs.

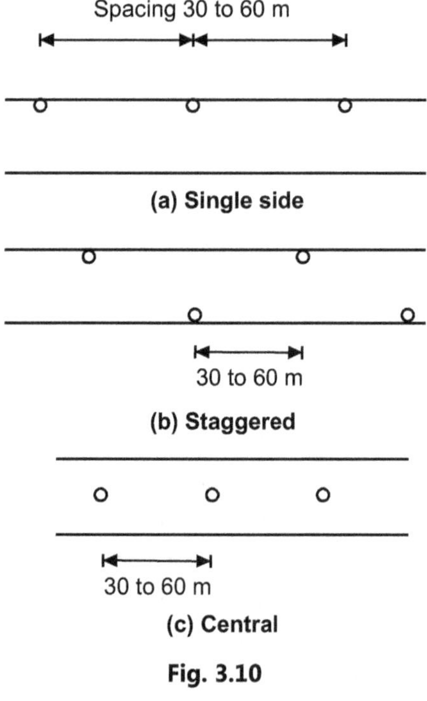

Fig. 3.10

Design of Highway Lighting System:

For approximate design of highway lighting system, you require utilization coefficient chart for determination of average intensity over the pavement surface, when lamp, paved area characteristics and spacing is known. A typical such graph is shown in the adjoining figure which would be used for Indian condition. For computation of spacings, we have,

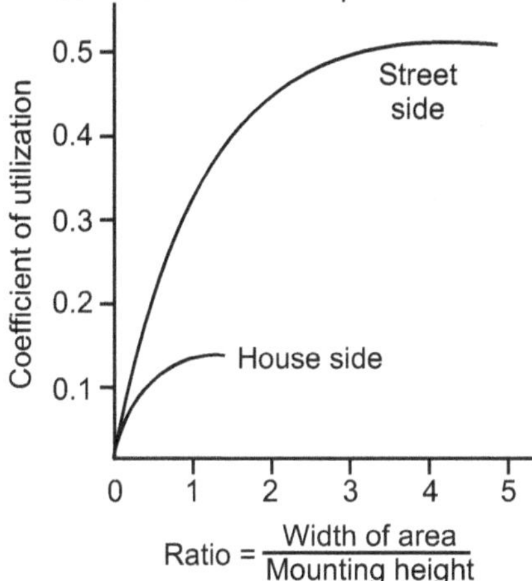

$$\text{Ratio} = \frac{\text{Width of area}}{\text{Mounting height}}$$

Fig. 3.11: Coefficient of utilization

$$\text{Spacings} = \frac{\text{Lamp lumen} \times \text{Coeff. of utilization} \times \text{Maintenance factor}}{\text{Average lux} \times \text{Width of road}}$$

maintenance factor is based on the experience. Problem No. 3.10 illustrates the principle.

3.8 TRAFFIC OPERATIONS

Traffic operations mean, how do we regulate and control the traffic on highways. In order to control flow, regulations have to be exercised. These controls may be:

(1) Driver Controls: Issuing driver's license only after adequate checks and issuing the license in such a way that in case of unforseen circumstances, driver should be traced. In the case of accident, driver has to suffer penal liability and owner civil liability.

(2) Vehicle Controls: This is a job of Regional Transport Office. Inspecting the vehicle for it's driving worthyness on regular basis for passing. Checking the vehicle for it's brake system etc. Motor vehicle act of 1939 generally covers this aspect such as ownership of vehicle, it's lawful transfer to other parties, insurance, vehicle dimensions etc.

(3) Traffic and General Controls: Traffic can be controlled by various signs. There are many signs. For example, the adjoining figure illustrates some signs. What is most important about traffic signs, is the awareness and urgency in the general public to follow these signs. Heavy penalty (financial) should be levied for the drivers who do not abide by these signs. In urban area one of the effective way to control traffic is through traffic signals. At intersections, where two or more roads cross each other the old practice was to post police. He used to show stop signs alternatively at the cross-roads so that one of the traffic streams may be allowed to move, while the cross-traffic is stopped. This used to put extra pressure on traffic police. The present procedure on urban roads is to install automatic signalling and the posting of the traffic police is for the purpose of catching the offenders. Properly designed traffic signals have many advantages. For example,

• There is orderly movement of traffic and increased capacity of intersections along with smooth heavy traffic flow. The pedestrians can cross the road safely.

• Accidents, in our country right angled collisions are reduced.

• Properly co-ordinated signalling system ensures a certain reasonable speed on major roads, but at the same time, traffic plying on minor roads can safely pass the main stream at regular and reasonable interval of time.

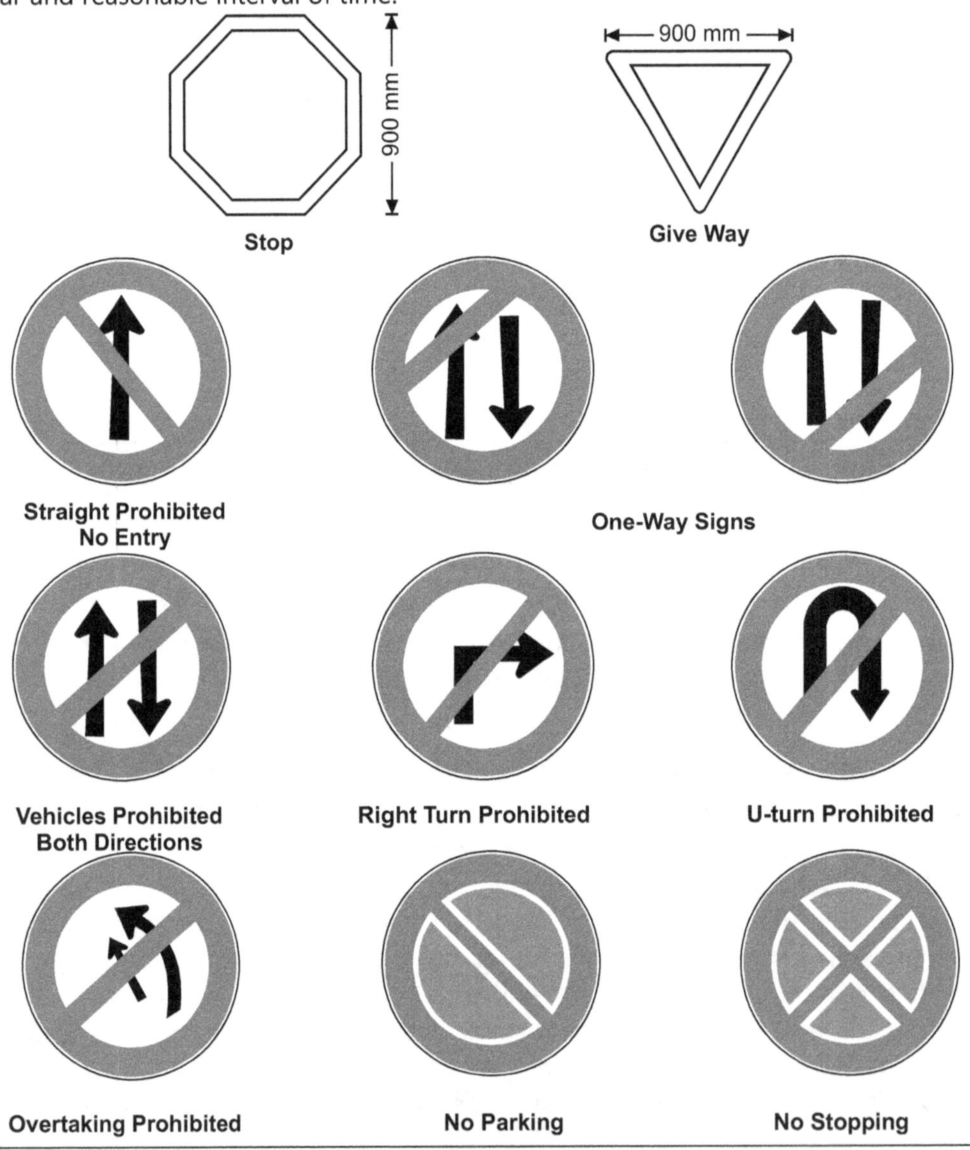

Speed Limit

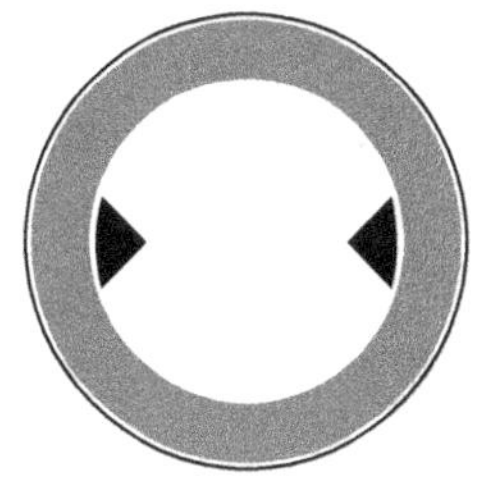

Width Limit

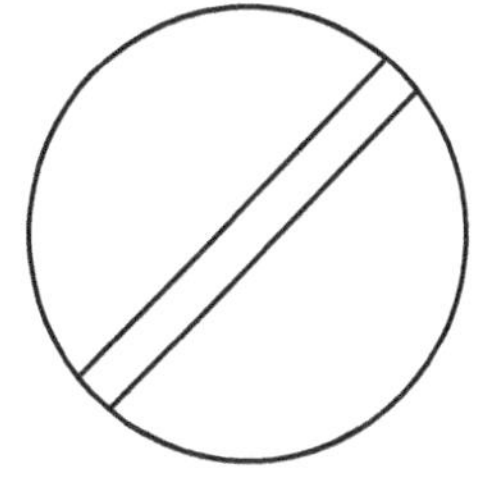

Restriction ends sign

Fig. 3.12

(4) Near the intersection, fitted with signalling, most of the vehicles will move at approximately the same speed, similar to the movement of platoons and thus reducing rate of accidents. That way in final analysis, signalling installation, though costly to start with would prove economical in the longer run. The above discussion may lead to false impression that there are absolutely no shortcomings of signalling as a system. It is not so. Intersections with signalling have tended to increase rear end collisions. Improper design of signalling can increase congestion on that road. Intersections where signalling have been provided, the commuters get used to it. So much so, that electric power failure at such intersections, when it occurs, simply criple such intersections. Such is the force of habit.

In India, traffic control signals have three coloured light glows facing each direction of traffic flow. Whereas the red light signifies stop motion, the green light indicates 'Go' and the amber or yellow light indicates the clearance time for the vehicles which enter the intersection area by the end of green time to clear off. It might be necessary to provide additional green lights for separate movement of turning traffic where necessary. The period of time required for one complete sequence of signal indications is called the **cycle**. That part of the signal cycle where traffic movement is allowed is known as phase and any of the division of signal cycle during which signal indications (i.e. colour) do not change is called as **interval**.

- In India, we have various types of signal procedures. Fixed-time signals or pre-timed signals are set to repeat regularly a cycle of red, amber and green. The timing of each phase of cycle, i.e. duration of time during signal will be red or green or amber is predetermined and managed automatically by electric operation.

- Very simple to install, the only drawback, sometimes when traffic on one road is very heavy and the traffic on the other road almost nil such eventuality cannot be catered by this system. It will continue at predetermined times.

- Traffic actuated signals are those in which signalling time can be changed as per traffic demand. On the other hand, with semiactuated traffic signals, we have detectors installed at the approaches, so that normal green light can be extended for few seconds more, so that few more vehicles approaching closely can be cleared.

- In fully actuated traffic signals, there are detectors and coupled computer which assigns the right of way for various traffic movements on the basis of demand.
- This alternative is somewhat costly and typical, but effective Indian alternative is to assign traffic police at such intersection. It is the job of police, now to assess traffic demand and vary the timing of phase and cycle. This method has proved well.
- When there are series of signals on city road at each intersection with cross-road, signalling system should preferably be operated by one controller. In such road pattern, it should be seen that vehicle moving along main road at normal speed is not required to stop at every signalized intersection at a stretch. Where there are zebra crossing i.e. pathway across the road which can be utilized by the pedestrians for crossing the road, these crossings can also be controlled by proper signaling.

The traffic signal system can be operated in various ways; for example:

(1) Simultaneous system: In a typical system of this type, all signals along a given roadway would show the same colour (indication) at the same time. Thus division of cycle at all intersections is now bound to be same. In general, this system is not preferred.

(2) Alternate system: This system is better than the previous. The principle is alternate signals or group of signals show opposite indications in a route, but at the same time. By reversing the red and green indicator connections at successive signal system, single controller can operate two successive intersections.

(3) Simple progressive system: In this system each signal unit works as a fixed time signal with equal signal cycle length, but the phase and interval at each signal installation may be different. This allows continuous operation of group of vehicles along the main road at moderate reasonable speed. Thus there is predetermined time schedule for "Go" indications along this road.

(4) Flexible progressive system: This is a computerised system and length of cycle, cycle division, time schedule can be altered as per requirements. In addition to these one can use flashing beacons to be carried by traffic police. On seeing this the drivers would stop before entering the nearest cross-walk or at any line which is marked.

Where should traffic signals be installed: Each and every intersection need not and should not have traffic signals. Such general installation of traffic signals infact would cause congestion. Traffic engineering data should justify this installation. The standard recommendations are:

- There should be minimum vehicular traffic. The average traffic volume for eight hours on both approaches should be at least 650 motor vehicles per hour on major street with single lane and 850 vehicles on the streets with two or more lanes. In addition, motor vehicles approaching the intersection on minor street (for one direction only) should be at least 200 vehicles per hour on single lane street and 250 vehicles per hour when there are two or more lanes. The stated requirement could be decreased to 70 percent, when 85th percentile speed or average approach speed on major roads exceeds 60 kmph. Even when the intersection lies within the built-up area, the vehicular volume could be decreased to 70 %.

- Minimum pedestrian traffic of 150 or more per hour should cross the major street with over 600 vehicles per hour on both approaches (1000 vehicles per hour in the case of main street with raised median). Again here also when average approach speed or the 85th percentile speed exceed 60 kmph, 70 % of the stated requirement could be adopted.

- If there is interruption of continuous traffic flow on the major road which carries 1000 to 1200 vehicles per hour or when there is undue delay or hazard to traffic of 100 to 150 vehicles per hour in one direction only during any eight hours on average day, it is a fit case of signalized intersection.

- If there are accidents at the intersections, even 5 or more minor accidents in a year, signalling might help, if designed properly so as not to cause disruption of traffic. Public octroy and public demand are the main cause of installation of signalling in many cases.

3.9 SIGNALIZED INTERSECTION DESIGN

Intersection design objective is to cut short delays and ques and handle high volume of traffic. General principles of design could be listed:

- Red phase of the signal is the sum of either go and clearance intervals or it could be sum of green and amber phases of cross flow. i.e. $G_2 + A_2$ at two phase signal. If turning movements are not permitted, pedestrian crossing time may also be incorporated for the road.

- Towards the end time of red phase, there could be short duration when amber light are put on along with red signal which indicates get set go position. During this red-amber time, vehicles are not supposed to cross the stop line.

- Just after the green but before red, amber phase is provided for the clearance of traffic. This preposition satisfies two requirements (a) It provides stopping time for approaching vehicle to stop at cross line. This is essential when signal changes from green to amber and not to cross the line by the time signal changes to red phase. (b) It can also provide clearance time, which can be utilized by an approaching vehicle travelling at design speed to cross the intersection area. For such a vehicle, it is difficult to stop before the stop line at this stage. For such an operation, 2 to 4 seconds of amber phase is O.K.

- Traffic volume during peak hour and the length of que of vehicles would decide green that is 'go' time.

To design isolated fixed time signal we can resort to trial cycle method, approximate method, Webster's method and I.R.C. method. These methods are now discussed and illustrated in problems 3.11, 3.12 etc. Two phase traffic signals with no turning are considered.

Trial Cycle Method:

Let us suppose that two roads 1 and 2 are crossing each other. Vehicle that ply on these roads during peak hour are n_1 and n_2 during time 't' minutes. Assume first trial cycle of 'C' seconds. Number of cycles in 't' minutes are then $\dfrac{t \times 60}{C}$. Assume time headway be h_1 seconds then green period time $= \dfrac{n_1 \times \text{Time headway}}{\text{No. of cycles in 't' minutes}}$. Amber periods A_1, A_2 could be assumed to be 3 to 4 seconds and cycle length is $(G_1 + G_2 + A_1 + A_2)$ seconds. If the calculated and the assumed cycle length are closer, the exercise is adequate otherwise repeat, till there is reasonable convergence. The method is illustrated in problem 3.11.

Approximate Method: Cross-roads along with pedestrian signals can be designed this way also. Steps are:

- Amber period could be assumed as 2, 3, 4 seconds for low medium and fast approach speeds.
- Clearance for pedestrian time could be considered on the walking speed of   1.2 m/second.
- Pedestrian clearance time plus initial interval for pedestrians to start crossing could be minimum red time. This red time should be equal to minimum green time plus amber time for the cross-road.
- Minimum green time is calculated on the same principle as red time. This minimum green time is equal to red time for cross-roads minus amber period for the cross-road with the provison that (a) Walk period should not be less than 7 seconds, (b) Even when there is no pedestrian signal as such, the walk period of 5 seconds must be left.
- Actual green times may then be increased. For this, one of the green time is considered O.K. and the other increased, with the help of formula

$$\frac{\text{Green time road A}}{\text{Green time road B}} = \frac{\text{Heaviest vol./hr. on road A per lane}}{\text{Heaviest vol./hr on road B per lane}}$$

The cycle length so obtained is adjusted for the next higher 5 second intervals. Extra time so granted could be distributed to green timings in proportion to the approaching volumes of traffic.

These principles are illustrated in problem 3.12.

Webster's Method:

For application of Webster's method we should know: (1) Saturation flow per unit time on each approach of the intersection. (2) Normal flow on each approach during design hour. In case, there is mixed flow, it is to be expressed in terms of passenger car units. Saturation flow should be determined by field studies. In the absence of the data one may assume 160 passenger car units per 0.3 meter width of the approach to be saturation flow. Normal flow has to be determined by field studies conducted during peak or off peak hours. The optimum signal cycle is then $\dfrac{1.5\,L + 5}{1 - Y} = C_o.$

$$\text{where,} \quad L = \text{Total lost time per cycle} = 2n + R.$$
$$n = \text{Number of phase.}$$
$$R = \text{All red time.}$$
$$y = y_1 + y_2$$
$$= \frac{\text{Normal flow on road 1}}{\text{Saturation flow on road 1}} + \frac{\text{Normal flow on road 2}}{\text{Saturation flow on road 2}}$$

$$G_1 = \frac{y_1}{y}\,(C_o - L) \quad \text{and} \quad G_2 = \frac{y_2}{y}\,(C_o - L)$$

Design method as per I.R.C. guidelines:

I.R.C. has formulated certain guidelines based on which signalling can be designed. These guidelines are:

- The green time for pedestrians for major and minor roads to be calculated on the basis of walking speed of 1.2 m/sec and initial walking time of 7.0 seconds. These are considered as minimum green time for vehicular traffic on major and minor roads.
- This minimum green time required for vehicular traffic on the major road is increased in proportion to the traffic on the two approach roads.
- The cycle time is calculated after allowing amber time of 2.0 seconds each. These three steps are similar to the approximate method.
- The minimum green time for the vehicular traffic to clear on any of the approach is 16 seconds. The first vehicle takes 6 seconds to clear and the subsequent vehicles (p.c.u.) in the que are cleared at the rate of 2.0 seconds each.
- The optimum signal time is computed by using Webster formula. For road widths (Kerb to median or centre line) of 3.0, 3.5, 4.0, 4.5, 5.0, 5.5 meter the saturation flows may be considered as 1850, 1890, 1950, 2250, 2550, 2990 pcu/hour. For width more than 5.5 meter, saturation flows could be taken as 525 pcu per hour per metre width in addition to above. The lost time is to be calculated from the amber time, intergreen time and initial delay of 4.0 seconds for the first vehicle on each leg. The signal cycle time and

phases so calculated could be revised keeping in view the optimum cycle length and green time required for clearing the vehicles. The IRC method is compromise between Webster and approximate method. The method is illustrated in problem 3.14.

3.10 PAVEMENT MARKINGS

- In order to regulate the traffic, pavement is sometimes marked by light reflecting paints. Longitudinal line when used as pavement marking should be at least 10 cm thick. Centre lines are the general longitudinal lines. These are used to separate the opposing streams of traffic on undivided two-way roads.

- On national and state highways having two or three lanes, there could be single broken lines of width 0.1 m and length 4.5 segments repeated by 7.5 meter. For horizontal curve and approaches, the gap between the lines could be 3.0 m and 6.0 m respectively.

- For four and six lane highway, two solid continuous parallel lines of 0.1 m width with 0.1 m space in between can be painted. On urban roads upto four traffic lanes, the centre line consists of white broken lines of width 0.10 to 0.15 m, length of segment 3.0 m, and length of gap 4.5 m, to be reduced to 3.0 m, at curves and approaches to intersections.

- For urban undivided roads, where there are two traffic lanes for each direction of traffic flow, the centre line marking should consist of two solid continuous lines.

- Just as we have centre line, we have other lines which indicate the use to which the pavement should be put to.

- There are no passing zone markings to show restriction on overtaking, turn marking which are painted near intersections so that proper lateral placement of vehicles take place turning to the different directions, stop lines which are meant for signalling the drivers to stop near the pedestrian crossing, cross walk lines also called zebra crossing, are places where pedestrians are directed to cross the pavement.

- The width of zebra crossing may be 2.0 to 4.0 m depending upon pedestrian traffic. In addition to these usual lines we have marking for bus-stop.

- The length of kerb or the pavement which is reserved for buses to stop are marked by continuous yellow lines. In this space parking is prohibited. It is better to widen the pavement at the bus-stop point, since later on bus-stop is likely to become focal point of traffic congestion.

- The length and width of pavement reserved for parking should also be marked. Edges of rural roads which have no kerb stones along the edges should be marked by border or edge lines. Route direction arrows should be marked by one or more arrows to guide effectively the traffic lines into correct lanes. Kerb marking could be marking on the kerb and edges of island are marked with alternate black and white lines.

- Similarly obstructions in the pavement way, such as supports for bridge, level crossing gates, culvert head walls should be properly painted. In addition to these markings, to facilitate night driving, we have roadway indicators, hazard markers, and object markers. Roadway indicators are guide posts 0.8 to 1.0 m high painted with black and white strips, preferably reflecting type, to mark the edges of the roadway.

- Hazard markers are about 1.2 m high plates standing on posts either with three red reflectors or markers with black and yellow strips at 45° towards the side of the obstruction.

- This is meant to define obstructions. Object markers are circular red reflectors arranged on triangular or rectangular panels and are used to indicate hazard and obstruction within the path of vehicles like the channelizing islands placed close to the intersections.

3.11 TRAFFIC PLANNING

In India, there is a mixed reaction to traffic planning. The question of traffic planning is very important in urban areas. In India, we have two types of cities. The cities which have been developed and planned such as New Mumbai, New Delhi, Chandigarh etc. In this case the principles of traffic planning can be applied. Since it is a planned city, we know the population present and future which is likely to inhabit particular area, its expanse in sq. km. Shopping arcade, business districts etc. are all fixed, in fact we know the present and approximate future number of cars, therefore traffic planning can be easily done. The problem is acute in existent cities such old Pune, Old Delhi, where population, number of vehicles, pedestrians etc. have increased, whereas the road network is essentially the old one. In this case the problem to be faced is mitigating as far as possible the griefs of the vehicle owners and commuters. The first step in such a case is to estimate trip generation. It means that we have to estimate the trips produced in or attracted to a given zone. Actually the trip has been defined as the one-way movement having single purpose and mode of travel between the point of origin and point of destination. If one can choose zones having less population and estimate the trips, it shall give idea about the type of road network that is required. Knowing the existing network, we can think of measures to better this network. The first step in this case is to develop linear equation connecting total number of trips and the population in the zone. The usual form of equation that is assumed for elementary analysis is

$$y = b_0 + b_1 x_1$$

where, y = Total number of trips in hundred per zone.

x_1 = Population of zone in thousands.

b_0 = Regression constant, and

b_1 = Regression coefficient.

The equation is supplemented by

$$b_1 = \frac{n \sum xy - \sum x \sum y}{n \sum x^2 - (\sum x)^2} \quad \text{and}$$

$$r = \text{correlation coefficient}$$

$$= b_1 \left[\frac{n \sum x^2 - (\sum x)^2}{n \sum y^2 - (\sum y)^2} \right]^{1/2}$$

where, x and y refer respectively to the population of the zone and trips generated in it as a known data. The principle is explained in problem 3.15.

After knowing the generation of trip in a particular zone, we are interested in knowing trips generated between the two zones. For this purpose we use what is known as gravity model. It is based on the principle that the trips generated between any two zones i and j are directly proportional to the number of trips generated in the zone i, the number of trips attracted to zone J and are inversely proportional to some function of distance between the zones or

$$T_{ij} = \frac{G_i \, A_J \, F_{ij}}{\displaystyle\sum_{J=1}^{n} A_J \, F_{iJ}}$$

where, T_{ij} = Number of trips from zone i to zone j.

G_i = Trips generated in zone i.

A_J = Trips attracted to zone J.

F_{iJ} = Friction factor calculated on area-wise basis.

n = Number of zones in the urban area.

Friction factor can be initially assumed and the existing data analysed. If there is discrepancy, friction factor is now modified and the data reworked till tolerance limit is reached. Actual method is beyond the scope of this book. Having known total trips between the zones we can know the trips that are made by cars and how many trips are made by buses. General method to achieve this, between two points, time and cost of travel by car and bus are determined. Then with the help of diversion curves the number of bus trips or car trips, between these two origin destination points can be assessed. This is known as model split. After the work of model split, we can assign the various trips between any two origin-destination pair on different highway routes. This is known as traffic assignment. This is also beyond the graduate studies. The object of traffic planning is to estimate demand so that road network can be planned.

3.12 GEOMETRY OF THE ROAD FOR TRAFFIC PURPOSES

When the traffic on the road increases, we have to construct the "Road Geometry" in a peculiar fashion so that traffic congestion is eased. These are rotaries, round abouts, intersections, etc. We shall now discuss these.

3.12.1 Rotary

See Fig. 3.13. Capacity of the rotary is a function of capacity of weaving section and the capacity of weaving section is a function of percentage of weaving traffic, geometric layout, etc. Without going into intricacies of these details, we may use the following formula recommended by the Transport and Road Research Lab (U.K.).

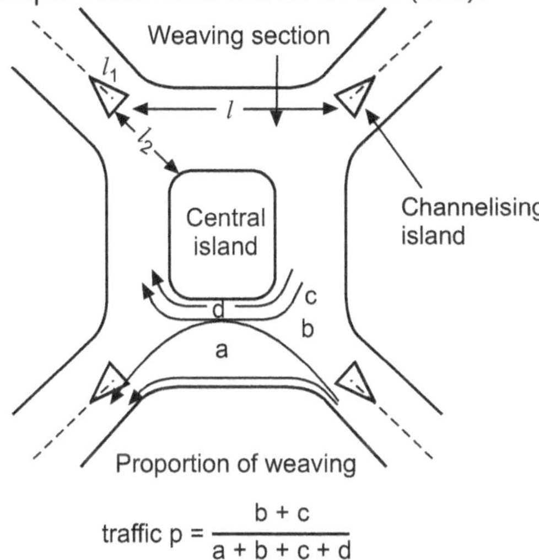

$$\text{traffic } p = \frac{b + c}{a + b + c + d}$$

Fig. 3.13: Relevant dimensions of weaving section and proportion of weaving traffic for use in capacity formula for rotaries

$$Q_p = \frac{280\, w \left(1 + \dfrac{e}{w}\right)\left(1 - \dfrac{p}{3}\right)}{1 + \dfrac{w}{l}}$$

where, Q_p = Capacity of weaving section of rotary.

  w = Width of weaving section in metres (limited from 6 to 18 metres).

  e = Average entry width = $\dfrac{l_1 + l_2}{2}$

  l = Length of weaving sections between ends of channelising islands in metres.

  p = Proportion of the weaving traffic i.e. ratio of sum of crossing streams to the total traffic on the weaving section = $\dfrac{b + c}{a + b + c + d}$

Fig. 3.13 shows the meaning of the symbols. The equivalency factor for passenger car units as recommended by IRC and TRRL are given in Table 3.7.

Table 3.7

Vehicle type	p.c.u. equivalent
Cars, light commercial vehicles, and 3 wheelers, Buses and medium heavy commercial vehicles	1.8
Motor cycles, scooters	0.75
Bicycles	0.5
Animal drawn vehicles	4 to 6

The formula is valid under following condition: (1) No parking vehicles on the approaches, level site and approach gradient not more than 1 in 15. (2) The value of $\dfrac{l}{w}$ is between 0.4 to 1.0 and $\dfrac{w}{l}$ should be between 0.12 and 0.40. (3) p should be between 0.4 and 1.0 and l should be between 18 to 90 meters.

In the above formula, some modifications can be made to cater for geometric layout. These are (a) Where the entry angle is between 0° to 15°, deduct 5 percent from the capacity of the weaving section, and when the entry angle is between 15° and 30°, deduct 2.5 per cent from the capacity of the section. (b) For an exit angle between 60° and 75° and above deduct five percent from the capacity of the weaving section. (c) When the internal angle is greater than 95°, deduct 5 percent from the capacity of weaving section. (d) When the pedestrians cross an exit at the rate equal to or more than 300/hr, deduct 16.7 percent from the capacity of weaving section.

The above recommendations and the design is based on U. K. experience. In India and U. K., traffic pattern is to keep left and hence above recommendation are acceptable.

Miscellaneous Features: Rotary should be located on flat ground, having a slope flatter than 1 in 50. For central islands, and channelising islands, mountable type of kerbs whereas for outer edges of the rotary, a barrier type of kerb may be provided. The later discourages the pedestrians from crossing over.

Increasing the efficiency of Rotary: By adopting traffic signals on the approaches and strictly enforcing "give way to traffic on right" rule, capacity and efficiency of rotary can be increased.

3.12.2 Mini Round Abouts

The rotary, as discussed, suffer from the drawback that once the traffic gets locked into it, the rotary gets jammed and then the police help is required to clear up the traffic. To put it in words, it becomes the case of entering the "Chakravuha" but not finding way out of it. Therefore rotary or round about is not always self regulatary. In U.K., where rotaries are very popular, they introduced "Priority from the right rule" in 1966. This rule reduced weaving and there was a possibility of the central island being cut to size. This rotary with a reduced central island where right rule is strictly followed is called as mini round about. A typical mini round about is shown in Fig. 3.14.

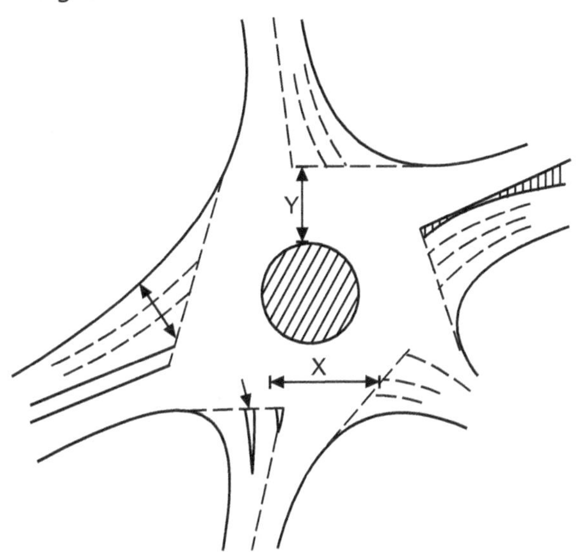

Fig. 3.14: Typical mini round about as per U. K. practice

The basic principles of design of mini round about are (1) A hypothetical circle inscribed within the outer carriage way boundries is drawn. A central island of a diameter $\frac{1}{3}$ of this hypothetical circle can be provided. (2) At the "give way line" i.e. the location where the priority from the right rule is to be enforced, there is additional lane created. (3) A minimum stopping distance between the "give way line" and opposing vehicle from the left is to be provided. This distance is called x in Fig. 3.14 and is generally about 25 meters. The distance between the traffic island and the central island shown x should be equal to or more than the total lane width at the entry (i.e. the distance z). The entry taper (about 1:6) should be twice sharp as the exit taper (1:12). (4) A deflection island shown as B should be installed as as to block straight through movements. (5) The capacity of mini round abouts can be maintained by tapering a single lane approach to three lanes at the junction and two lane approach to four lanes. At the exit, the merge could be from four lanes to two lanes. It is clear that mini round about will work well where there is traffic discipline and priority from the right rule is followed voluntarily and by every person. Given a small percentage of road user not following the rule will result in chaos worse than the chaos when a rotary is blocked. The capacity of a mini round about could be determined by the following formula

$$q = k \left(\sum W + a^{1/2} \right)$$

where,

q = Total entry volume in pcu per hour.

$\sum W$ = Sum of the basic road width (not half widths) used by traffic in both directions to and from the intersection in meters.

a = Area of the junction widening i.e. area within the intersection outline, including the islands which lies outside the area of the basic cross roads in square meters.

k = Efficiency coefficient, whose value would depend upon the number of junctions.

For a three way and four way junctions, the value is 80 and 70 respectively, whereas for 5 and more route junctions, the value is 65. The practical capacity of a mini round about will be 80 % of the theoretical value. The above formula given by Blackmore is applicable to Indian conditions.

Merits and demerits of round about : Where law can be strictly enforced mini round about can accommodate higher volume of traffic, sometimes even higher than the signalized junctions. There is a likelyhood of reduced rate of accidents. The demerits are, the success of the round about revolves around the strict enforcement of priority from the right rule. Similarly a very high standard of pavement markings, great care in the installations of the kerbs, and adequate visibility of approaching drives is necessary. The driver must be in a position to see the approaching drives and then only he can give way to the traffic on the right.

3.12.3 Grade Separated Intersections

Grade separated intersection can very effectively achieve channelization of traffic. The essential principle is that the two intercepting highways or routes are to be provided at different elevations i.e. grades, so that there is no conflict between the crossing streams. In India, provision of grade separated intersections at the railway crossings, specifically in urban area can go a long way in curtailing the accident rates and removing the traffic conjestion. The current Indian practice requires grade separation across streets and highways to be provided based on certain criteria. These criterias are: (1) Grade separation should be provided if the estimated traffic value in the next 5 years is more than the capacity of the intersection. This state of affair requires immediate construction of grade separated intersections, but when traffic estimates show that the traffic in next 20 years is not likely to exceed the capacity of present intersection, grade separated intersection need not be constructed immediately. (2) Intersections of divided rural highways may be provided if the average daily traffic (fast vehicle only) on the cross roads within the next 5 years, exceeds 5 thousand. When there is possibility that this figure is likely to reach with next 20 years, grade separation should be left to the planning stage. The most important grade separation is of course, across the railway lines. IRC recommended that grade separation across the existing railway line should be provided if the product of ADT (fast vehicles only) and the number of trains per day exceeds 50 thousand within the next 5 years. When the facility is planned to relieve the traffic conjestion such as bypasses, grade separation should be provided even when the product of ADT and number of trains per day does not exceed 25 thousands.

3.12.3.1 Types of Grade Separated Intersections

Basically, there are two types of grade separated intersections: (1) Grade separated intersection with interchange: Which is an facility of over-bridge, underpass, or flyover, whereby the traffic at different level ply separately without any interchange between them. (2) In a facility with interchange, though routes at different grades are there, there is a possibility of interchange between them. These facilities can also be classified depending upon the routes involved - such as three leg interchange, four leg interchange etc., and can then be subdivided. The general classification is therefore: (1) Three leg interchange which can be in the form of (a) T interchange, (b) Y interchange or (c) Partial rotary interchange. (2) Four leg interchange, which can be in the form of (a) Diamond interchange, (b) Half clover leaf interchange, (c) Clover leaf interchange, (d) Rotary interchange and (e) Directional interchange. (3) Multi-leg interchange which is generally a rotary interchange.

Types:

The types of interchange mentioned above are now discussed.

Three Leg Interchange:

Fig. 3.15 shows a 'T' interchange, generally called as trumpet, due to it's shape. Junctions of major streets with expressways are suitable locations for this interchange. The drawback is vehicles leaving the major road such as at a in the figure have to negotiate small radius.

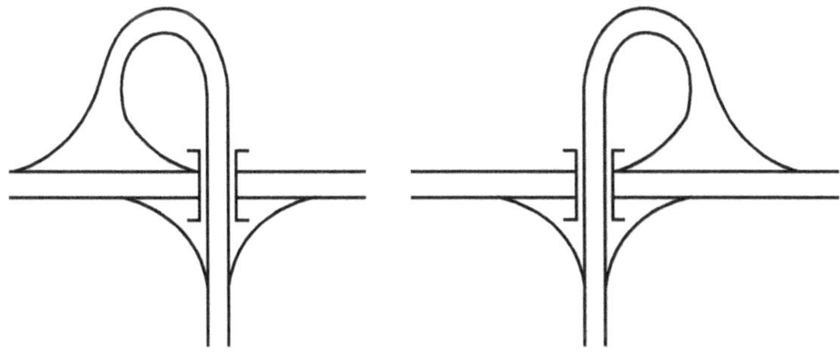

Fig. 3.15: Trumpet interchange

Fig. 3.16 shows Y shaped interchanges which will allow only restricted movements.

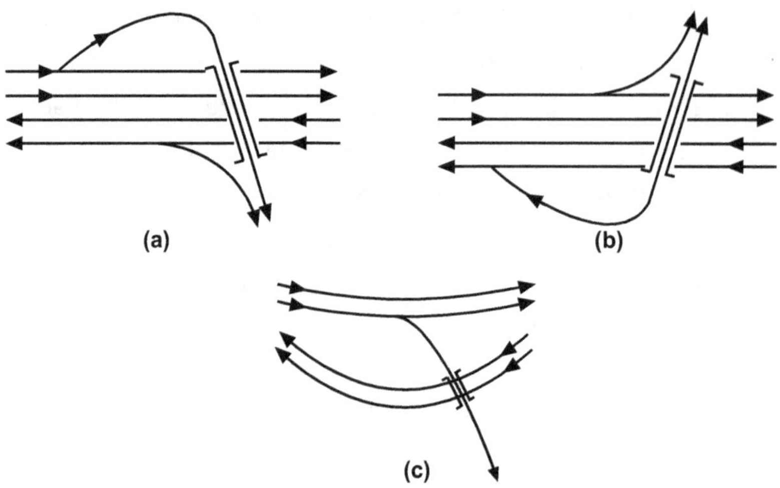

(a)   (b)

(c)

Fig. 3.16: Y - shaped interchanges

Fig. 3.17 is also a three-leg interchange of the Y type. But this can be converted to a full cloverleaf at future date when traffic so demands.

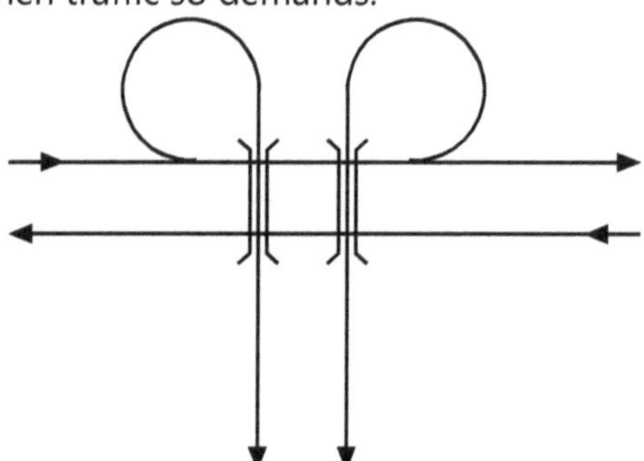

Fig. 3.17: Three-leg interchange which can be converted to a cloverleaf

A partial bridge rotary intersection is shown in Fig. 3.18. It is clear from these figures that overbridge is necessary to work interchange.

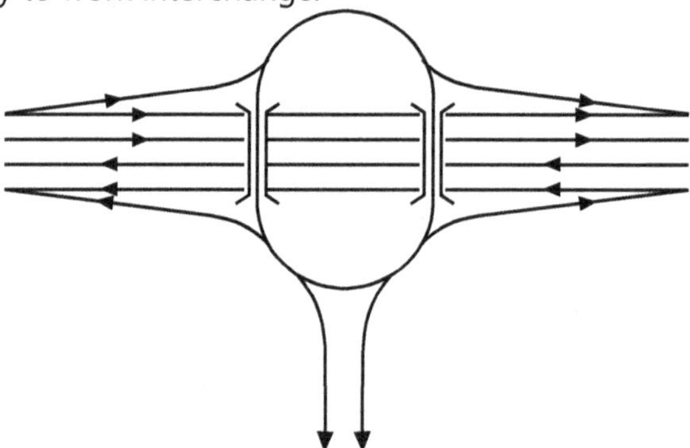

Fig. 3.18: Partial bridged intersection

Four Leg Interchange:

In this the diamond interchange is shown in Fig. 3.19. This is a popular type of interchange for urban sites, for crossing of major and minor roads. The diamond interchange can be of split variety shown in Fig. 3.20, where two parallel cross streets are available as connections to the main road. The half cloverleaf interchange is shown in Fig. 3.20. This interchange is suitable when a major road crosses a minor road with not more than 3 lanes.

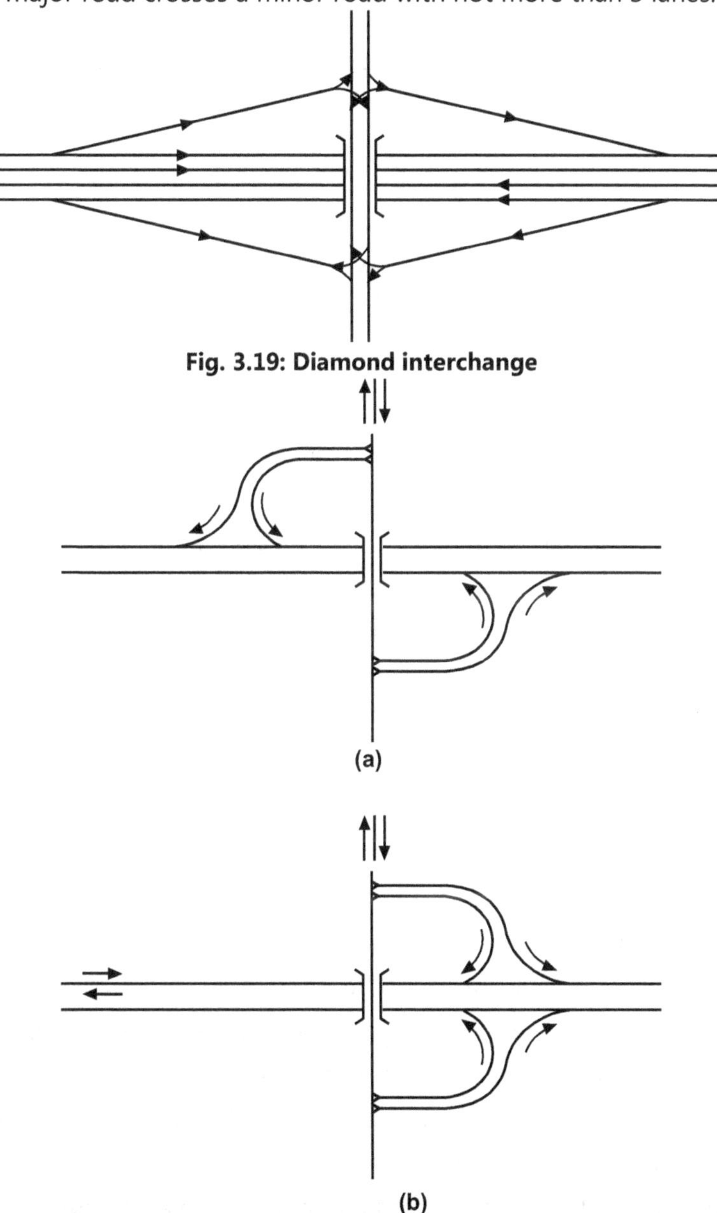

Fig. 3.19: Diamond interchange

(a)

(b)

Fig. 3.20: Partial cloverleaf for major - minor road crossing

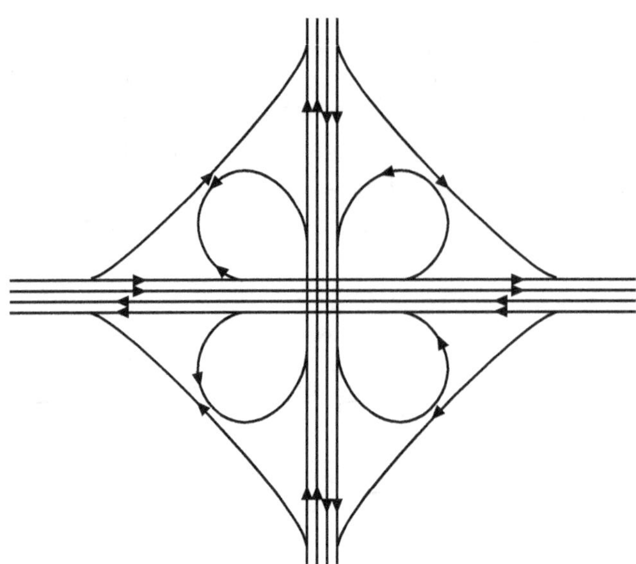

Fig. 3.21: Cloverleaf interchange

Cloverleaf interchange is a four-leg interchange with a single unitary structure. This facility is becoming very popular these days, and is very useful when high volume, high speed vehicle routes such as expressways cross each other. The advantages of the cloverleaf construction are: (1) There is only one unitary structure and left turning traffic has a direct path. (2) There is no impediment to the traffic and it does not confuse the drivers. The disadvantages are: (1) Compared to the rotary intersection, higher carriageway width and more total area is required. (2) The U-turns are long and operationally difficult. (3) The loop design in case you want higher speeds requires very large area is to be acquired. (4) And lastly it is costly to construct the cloverleaf. A typical sketch of cloverleaf interchange is shown in Fig. 3.21.

The rotary interchange is shown in Fig. 3.22. It accommodates rotary and the grade intersection. The advantages are: (1) It requires less area and less carriageway widths. (2) U-turns are comparatively easy. The disadvantages are that the capacity of the rotary interchange is dependant on the capacity of the round about itself. Just as the sketch shows directional interchange with rotary with two levels, 3 level rotary interchange can also be arranged. Directional interchanges are generally complicated structures, but these can give direct or semi-direct connections for the major right turning movements. The trumpet type of interchange can be very useful for expressways with toll plazas. The toll plazas planned on Indian highways are thought somewhat different than toll plazas on bridges. At the entry, the expressway user will only collect the card and pay the toll at the exist. A typical trumpet type interchange with toll plaza is shown in Fig. 3.23.

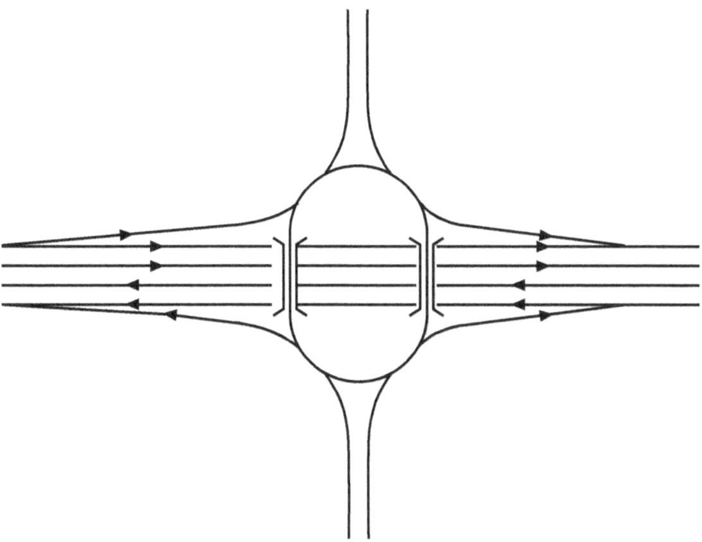

Fig. 3.22: Grade separated interchange

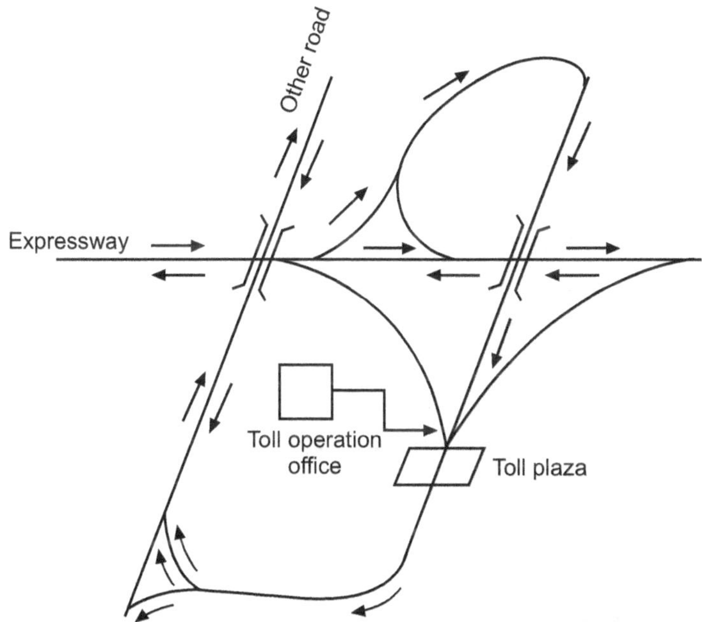

Fig. 3.23: Trumpet type interchange with toll plaza

3.13 CHANNELISATION OF TRAFFIC BY CYCLE TRACKS

As discussed earlier, the cycle tracks can also effectively provide channelisation of traffic, if the cycle traffic is significant. They are generally on both sides of the road but separated from the main carriageway by a berm or verge about 1.0 metre wide. These are clear ways for the cyclists. With approximate design speed of 30 km/hr, the design criteria for cycle tracks are laid down by IRC.

Generally, the cycle track may be provided when the peak hour cycle traffic is 400 or more on routes with a traffic of 100 motor vehicles or more but not more than 200 per hour. When the number of motor vehicles using the route is more than 200 per hour, separate cycle tracks could be justified even if the cycle traffic is only 100 per hour. As a general rule the capacity of cycle track may be taken as given in Table 3.8.

Table 3.8

Width of Cycle Track	Capacity in cycles / day	
	One-Way Traffic	**Two-Way Traffic**
Two lane	2000 to 5000	500 to 2000
Three lane	Over 5000	2000 to 5000
Four lane	–	Over 5000

Cycle track could be classified as *(1) Adjoining cycle tracks:* which completely fit in with the carriageway and are adjacent to and on the same level with it. *(2) Raised cycle track:* These are adjoining the carriageway but are at a higher level. *(3) Free cycle track:* These are separated from the carriageway by a verge and may be at the same level as the carriageway or at a different level.

3.14 ACCIDENT STUDIES

The problem of accident is very acute in highway transportation due to complex flow patterns of vehicular traffic, presence of mixed traffic and pedestrians. Traffic accidents may involve property damage, personal injuries or even causalities. One of the main objectives of traffic engineering is to provide safe traffic movements. Road accidents cannot be totally prevented, but suitable traffic engineering and management measures can decrease the accident rate decreased considerably. Therefore, the traffic engineer has to carry out systematic accident studies to investigate the causes of accidents and to make preventive measure in terms of design and control. It is essential to analyse individual accident and to maintain zone-wise accident records. The statistical analysis of accidents carried out periodically at critical location or road stretches or zones will help to arrive at suitable measures to effectively decrease the accident rates.

Objectives of Accidental Studies:

- To study the causes of accidents and to suggest corrective treatment at potential location.
- To evaluate existing design.
- To support proposed design.
- To carry out before and after studies and to demonstrate the improvement in the problem.

- To make commutations of financial loss.
- To give the economic justification for the improvements suggested by the traffic engineer.

Causes of Accidents:

There are four elements in a traffic accident:

- Road users.
- Vehicles.
- Road and its condition, and
- Environmental factors.

The road user responsible for the accidents may be the driver of one or more vehicles involved, pedestrians or the passengers.

- **Drivers:** Excessive speed and rash driving, carelessness, violation of rules and regulation, failure to see or understand the traffic situation, sign or signal, temporary effects due to fatigue, sleep or alcohol.
- **Pedestrians:** Violating regulation, carelessness in using the carriageway meant for vehicular traffic.
- **Passenger:** Alighting from or getting into moving vehicles.

  Vehicles involved in the accident may be defective.
- **Vehicle Defects:** Failure of breaks, steering system or lighting system, tyre burst and any other defect in the vehicles.

The conditions of road's surface and other existing geometric feature conditions of the road may not be upto the expectation causing an accident.

- **Road Condition:** Slippery or skidding road surface, potholes, ruts and other damaged conditions of the road surface.
- **Road Design:** Defective geometric design like inadequate sight distance, inadequate width of shoulders, improper curve design, improper curve design, improper lighting, and improper traffic control devices.

Environmental Condition: Any environmental conditions of the road may not be upto the expectation causing an accident. To sump-up, an accident may be caused due to a combination of several reasons and seldom due to one particular reason. Hence, it is often not possible to pin point a particular single cause of an accident.

- **Weather:** Unfavourable weather conditions like mist, fog, snow, smoke or heavy rainfall that restrict normal visibility and render driving unsafe.
- **Animals:** Stray animals on the road.
- **Other Causes:** Incorrect signs or signals, gate of level crossing not closed when required, ribbon development, badly located advertisement boards or services station etc.

Accident Studies and Records:

The various steps involved in traffic accident studies are collection of accident date, preparation of reports, location file and diagrams, and application of the above records for suggesting preventive measures.

1. Collection of Accident Data : The collection accident data is the first step in the accident study. Standard forms for collecting the data are prepared, as suggested by the IRC.

The details to be collected are briefly mentioned here.

(a) **General:** Date, time, persons involved in the accident and their particular, classification of accident like fatal, serious, minor etc.

(b) **Location:** Description and details of the location of accidents.

(c) **Details of Vehicles Involved:** Registration number make and description of the vehicles, loading details, vehicular defects.

(d) **Nature of Accidents:** Condition of vehicles involved, details of collision, and pedestrians or objects involved, damages, injuries, causality etc.

(e) **Road and Traffic Conditions:** Details of road geometric, whether the road is straight or curved, surface characteristics such as dry, wet or slippery etc. Traffic condition-type of traffic, traffic density etc.

(f) **Primary Causes of Accidents :** Various possible causes and the primary causes of the accidents.

(g) **Accident Costs:** The total cost of the accidents compound in terms of rupees, of the various involvements like property damages, personal injuries and causalities.

2. Accident Report: The accidents should be reported to police authorities that would take legal actions especially in more serious accidents involving injuries, causalities or severe damages to property. Accident report of the individuals involved may be separately taken. The accidents data should be collected as given above and the report is prepared with all facts, which might be useful in subsequent analysis, claims for compensation.

3. Accident Records: The accident records are maintained giving all particulars of the accidents, location and other details. The records may be maintained by means of location files, spot maps, collision diagrams and condition diagrams.

- **Location Files:** These are useful to keep a check on the location of accident and to identify points of high accident incidences. Location fields should be maintained by each police station for the respective jurisdiction.

- **Spot maps:** Accident location spot maps show accidents by spots, pins or symbols on the map. A map of suitable scale say 1 cm = 40 to 60 meter, may be used for spotting urban accidents. The common legends used for spot maps, are given in Fig. 3.23.

- **Conditional diagram:** A conditional diagram is a drawing to a scale showing all important physical conditions of an accident's location to be studied. The important features generally to be shown in this diagram with suitable dimensions marked there in are roadway limits, curves, kerb lines, bridges, culverts, trees and all details of roadway condition, obstruction to vision, property lines, signs, signal etc. There are standard symbols used in showing various details. The condition and collision diagrams may be combined together in a single sketch, if necessary.

- **Collision Diagram:** These are diagrams showing the approximate path of vehicles and pedestrians involved in the accidents. Collision diagrams are most useful to compare the accident pattern before and after the remedial measures have been taken. A typical collision diagram and symbol are shown in Fig. 3.24.

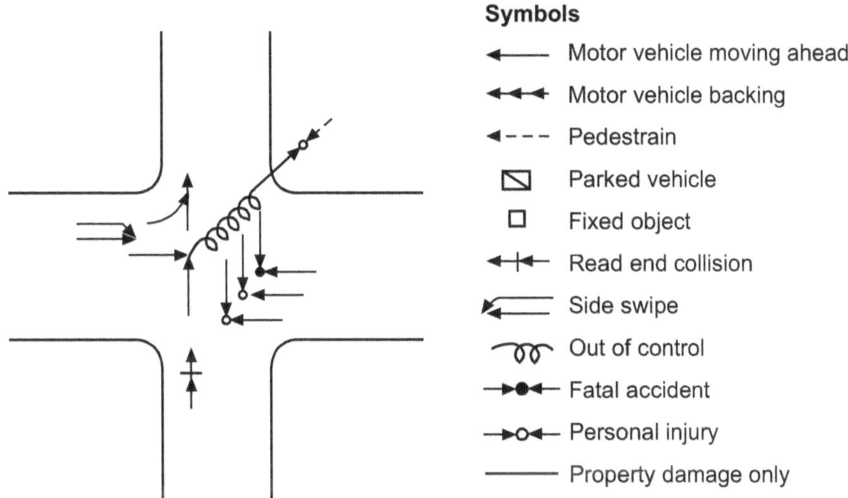

Fig. 3.24

Accident investigations and studies therefore may be carried out scientifically in the following three stages.

- Accident investigations
- Analysis of Individual Accidents
- Statistical Analysis of Accidents

Type of accident	Fatal	Non-Fatal
Motor vehicle-pedestrian	•	•
Other motor vehicle traffic	•	•

The above figure shows legend for spot maps.

3.15 MEASURES FOR THE REDUCTION IN ACCIDENT RATES

The various measures to decrease the accident rates may be divided into three groups:

1. Engineering, 2. Enforcement, 3. Education

These three measures are generally termed "3-Es". The details of these measures are given below.

Engineering Measures:

(a)   **Road Design:** The geometric design features of the road such as sight distances, width of pavement, horizontal and vertical alignment design details and intersection design elements are checked and corrected if necessary. The pavement surface characteristics including the skid resistance values are checked and suitable maintenance steps taken to bring them upto the design standards. Where necessary by-passes may be constructed to separate through traffic from local traffic. To minimize delay and conflicts at the intersections, it may be essential to design and construct grade separated intersections or flyovers.

(b)   **Preventive Maintenance of Vehicles:** The braking system, steering and lighting arrangements of vehicle plying on the roads may be checked at suitable intervals and heavy penalties levied on defective vehicles. These measures are particularly necessary for public carriers.

(c)   **Before and After Studies:** The record of accidents and their patterns for different locations are maintained by means of collision and condition diagrams. After making the necessary improvements in design and enforcing regulation, it is again necessary to collect and maintain the record of accidents "before and after" the introduction of preventive measures to study their efficiency. A typical example of before and after study at an intersection is shown in Fig. 3.25 (a) and (b).

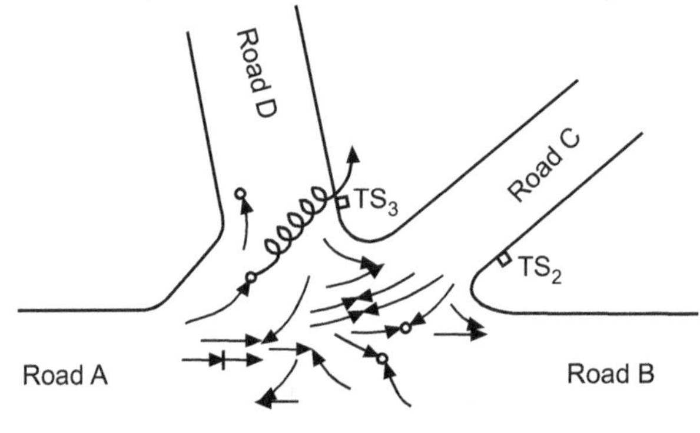

(a) Uncontrolled movements of vehicles and pedestrians
Accident: Twelve in a period of two months

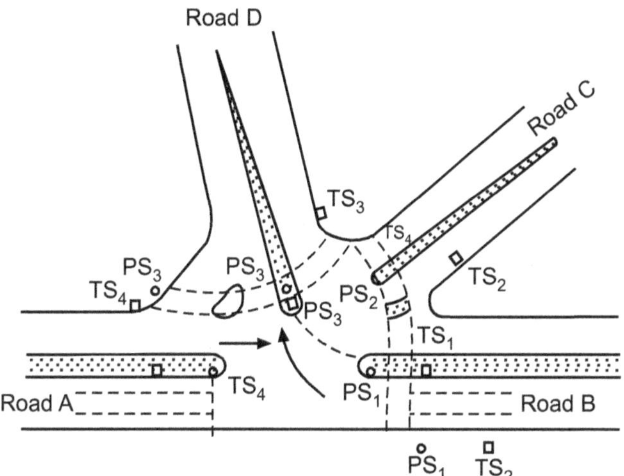

(i)   Additional traffic signals (TS) installed and signal timings re-designed.

(ii)   **Pedestrian signals (PS) installed and pavement markings made for pedestrian crossings and control over other vehicular manoeuvers.**

(iii)   **Divisional islands and channelizing islands provided by widening roads A-B**

        Accident : Only one in a period of two months.

(b)

Fig. 3.25: Typical case of before and after study

(d)   **Road Lighting:** Proper road lighting can decrease the rate of accidents during night, due to poor visibility. Lighting is particularly desirable at intersections, bridge sites and at places where there are restrictions to traffic movements.

Enforcement Measures:

The various measures of enforcement that may be useful to prevent accidents at spots prone to accident are enumerated here. The motor vehicle rules are revised from time to time to make them more comprehensive.

(a)   **Speed Control:** To enable drivers of buses to develop correct speed habits, tachometers may be fitted so as to give record of speeds. Also surprise checks on spot speed of all fast moving vehicles should be done at selected locations and timings and legal actions on those who violate the speed limits should be taken.

(b)   **Traffic Control Devices:** Signals may be designed or signal system be introduced if necessary. Similarly, proper traffic control devices like signs, marking or chennelizing islands may be installed wherever found necessary.

(c)   **Training and Supervision:** The transport authorities should be strict in testing and issuing license to drivers of public service vehicles and taxis. Even the drivers who have passed the requisite tests should be kept under proper supervision and be trained in proper defensive driving.

(d)   **Medical Check:** The drivers should be tested for vision and reaction time at prescribed intervals, say, once in three years.

(e) **Special Precautions for Commercial Vehicles:** It may be insisted on having a conductor or attendant to help and give proper direction to drivers of heavy commercial vehicles.

Educational Measures:

(a) **Education of Road Users:** It is very essential to educate the road user for the various precautionary measures to use the road way facilities with safety. The passengers and measures and pedestrians should be taught the rules of the road, correct manner of crossing etc. This may be possible by introducing necessary instruction in the schools for the children. Posters exhibiting the serious results due to carelessness of road users may also be useful.

(b) **Safety Drives:** Imposing traffic safety week when the road users are properly directed with the help of traffic police and transport staff is a common means of training the public these days. Road users should be impressed on what should documentaries. Training courses may be conducted for drives. The IRC has been organizing Highway safety workshop in different regions of country.

3.16 RELATIONSHIP BETWEEN SPEED, TRAVEL TIME, VOLUME, DENSITY AND CAPACITY

- **Time and Speed:**

The travel time per unit length of road is inversely proportional to the speed. If T is travel time and V is the speed (kmph),

$$T \text{ (min/km)} = \frac{60}{V}$$

or

$$T \text{ (sec./km)} = \frac{3600}{V}$$

Fig. 3.26 shows the relationship between travel time and speed. It is seen that at higher speed, the rate of saving in travel time decreases.

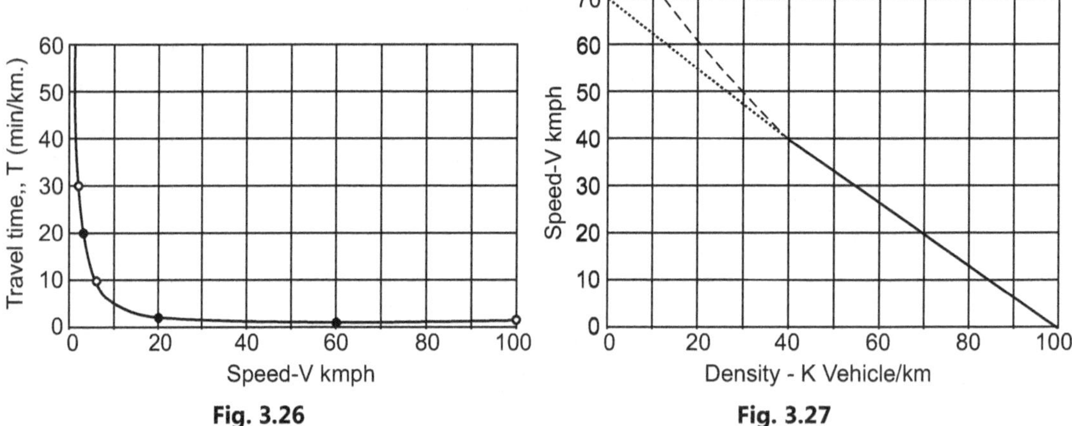

Fig. 3.26   **Fig. 3.27**

The fundamental relationship between traffic volume, density and speed may be given by the general equation of traffic flow:

$$q = K V_s$$

Where, q = The average volume of vehicles passing a point during a specified period of time (vehicle per hour).

K = The average density or number of vehicles occupying a unit length of roadway at a given instant.

V_s = Space-mean speed of vehicles in a unit roadway length (kmph).

With increase in speed of vehicles in a unit roadway length, the average density decreases. It is difficult to measure density directly, in practice. Hence the relationship between volume, density and speed is often used. The value of density K may be obtained by rewriting equation

$$K \text{ (vehicles/km)} = \frac{q}{V}$$

When the speed of the traffic flow decreases and becomes zero, the density attains the maximum value whereas, volume becomes zero. For increasing values of speeds, density decreases, whereas the volume increases upto a certain limit, as shown in Fig. 3.29. At high speeds, the volume starts decreasing and density keeps on further reducing. Eventually, if a hypothetical case is considered when volume approaches zero at very high speeds, the density also approaches zero, as shown in Fig. 3.30. Thus, there is a maximum flow in road corresponding to some optimum values of speed and density.

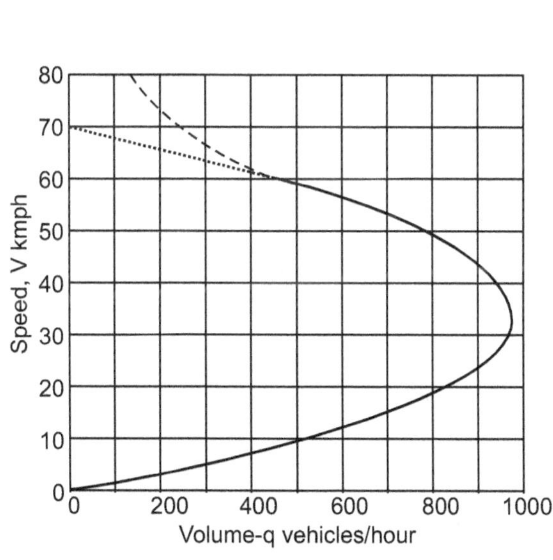

Fig. 3.28

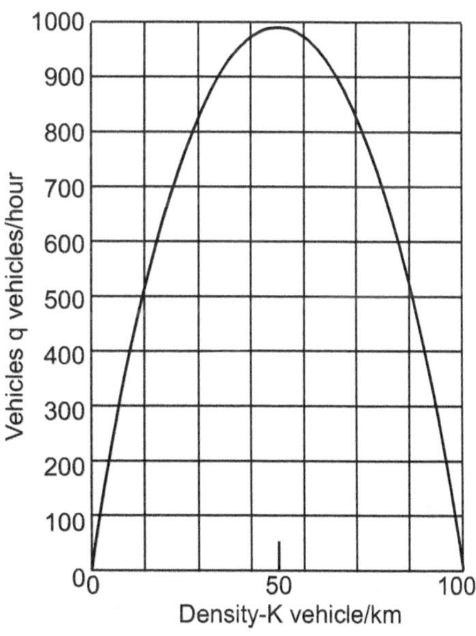

Fig. 3.29

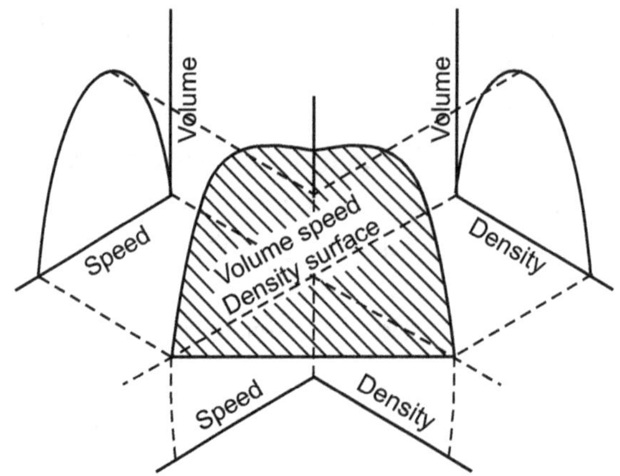

Volume - speed-density surface

Fig. 3.30

SOLVED PROBLEMS

Problem 3.1: *A motor vehicle running at a speed of 30 km/hr was subjected to full loading and was stopped in 5.8 m length. Evaluate average skid resistance of pavement.*

Solution:

$$\text{Initial speed} = \frac{30}{3.6} = 8.33 \text{ m/sec}$$

Since
$$f = \frac{u^2}{2\,gL} = \frac{(8.33)^2}{2 \times 9.81 \times 5.8} = 0.61$$

Problem 3.2: *A motor vehicle running on level road with a speed of 40 km/hr was subjected to braking and the length of skid marks was 10.0 meter. Average skid resistance of the pavement is 0.70. What would be the braking efficiency of this vehicle ?*

Solution:

$$\text{Initial speed} = \frac{40}{3.6} = 11.11 \text{ m/sec.} \qquad L = 10 \text{ m}$$

and $\quad f = 0.70$

$$\text{The developed skid resistance} = f = \frac{u^2}{2\,g\,L} = \frac{(11.11)^2}{2 \times 9.8 \times 10} = 0.629$$

$$\text{Braking efficiency} = \frac{\text{Developed skid resistance}}{\text{Resistance that could be developed}}$$

$$= \frac{0.629}{0.70} = 89.9 \%$$

Problem 3.3 : *Observations were recorded in a 100 meter stretch of the road. The travel time for vehicles to ply this section is as follows:*

Vehicles	Travel time
10	12 seconds
30	15 seconds
7	3 seconds

What would be space mean speed ?

Solution: Space mean speed $= \dfrac{3.6\ dn}{\displaystyle\sum_{i=1}^{n} t_1}$

where, d = length of section meter,

  n = number of vehicles under observation,

  t = corresponding travel time.

Vehicle No.	Travel Time	$\dfrac{3.6\ dn}{t_1}$	Space mean Speed for this Vehicle
1	2	$\dfrac{3.6 \times 10 \times 1}{2}$	= 18
2	3	$\dfrac{3.6 \times 10 \times 1}{3}$	= 12

Space mean speed for the traffic flow

$$= \dfrac{3.6\ dn}{\displaystyle\sum_{i=1}^{n} t_1}$$

$$= \dfrac{3.6 \times 10 \times 2}{2 + 3} = 14.4 \text{ km/h}$$

Instantaneous speed for vehicle 1 $= \dfrac{3.6 \times 10}{2} = 18$ km/hr.

Instantaneous speed for vehicle 2 $= \dfrac{3.6 \times 10}{3} = 12$ km/hr.

$\therefore$ Time mean speed $= \dfrac{18 + 12}{2} = 15$ km/hr.

It should be noted that space mean speed and instantaneous speed would be same if observations are taken for short stretch of road length,

$\therefore$ Space mean speed $= \dfrac{3.6\ [100 \times 10 + 100 \times 30 + 100 \times 7]}{12 \times 10 + 15 \times 30 + 3 \times 7}$

$$= \dfrac{3.6\ [100]\ [47]}{120 + 450 + 21} = \dfrac{16920}{591} = 28.62 \text{ km/hr.}$$

Problem 3.4 : *Observations were recorded in 100 meter stretch and the observed instantaneous speed of the categories of the vehicles are as under.*

Vehicles	Speed
10	20 km/hr.
30	18 km/hr.
7	10 km/hr.

What would be time mean speed ?

Solution:

$$\text{Time mean speed} = \frac{\text{Summation of instantaneous speeds}}{\text{Number of vehicles}}$$

$$= \frac{20 \times 10 + 18 \times 30 + 10 \times 7}{20 + 18 + 7}$$

$$= \frac{200 + 540 + 70}{45}$$

$$= 18 \text{ km/hr.}$$

Problem 3.5: *From the following data, determine the average speed of vehicles on that road.*

Speed range	No. of vehicles
0 – 10 km/hr.	7
10 – 20 km/hr.	20
20 – 40 km/hr.	40
40 – 60 km/hr.	5

Solution:

Vehicles	Average speed
7	5
20	15
40	30
5	50

Average speed on this track

$$= \frac{7 \times 5 + 20 \times 15 + 40 \times 30 + 5 \times 50}{7 + 20 + 40 + 5}$$

$$= \frac{35 + 300 + 1200 + 250}{72}$$

$$= 24.79 \text{ say } 25 \text{ km/hr.}$$

Problem 3.6: *For a certain section of highways, the speed data collected are shown.*

Speed Range, km/hr.	No. of Vehicles Observed	Speed Range, km/hr.	No. of Vehicles Observed
0 – 10	10	50 – 60	250
10 – 20	18	60 – 70	20
20 – 30	70	70 – 80	40
30 – 40	90	80 – 90	30
40 – 50	200	90 – 100	10

Determine (i) Upper and lower values of speed limit for mixed traffic flow, (ii) Design speed.

Solution: We have to prepare cumulative speed distribution table. Total number of vehicles observed

$$= 10 + 18 + 70 + 90 + 200 + 250 + 20 + 40 + 30 + 10$$
$$= 738$$

$\therefore$ Total frequency of vehicles = 738

Plot the graph between speed and cumulative number of vehicles i.e. frequency. Speed corresponding to 85th cumulative frequency i.e. 85th percentile speed is the upper speed limit regulation. The student is advised to plot this graph. He will find this speed limit around 55 km/hr which is the upper speed limit regulation. The lower speed limit regulation to avoid congestion i.e. 15th percentile speed will be around 27th km/hr. For designing geometrical elements, it is traditional to consider 98th percentile speed which is around 85 km/hr.

Speed Range km/hr.	Mid Speed km/hr.	No. of Vehicles or Frequency	Frequency Percentage	Cumulative Frequency
0 – 10	$\dfrac{0 + 10}{2} = 5$	10	$\dfrac{10}{738} = 1.355\ \%$	1.355
10 – 20	$\dfrac{10 + 20}{2} = 15$	18	$\dfrac{18}{738} = 2.439\ \%$	1.355 + 2.439 = 3.794 %
20 – 30	25	70	$\dfrac{70}{738} = 9.485\ \%$	9.485 + 3.794 = 13.27 %
30 – 40	35	90	$\dfrac{90}{738} = 12.19\ \%$	13.27 + 12.19 = 25.46 %
40 – 50	45	200	$\dfrac{200}{738} = 27.10\ \%$	27.10 + 25.46 = 52.56 %
50 – 60	55	250	$\dfrac{250}{738} = 33.87\ \%$	52.56 + 33.87 = 86.43 %
60 – 70	65	20	$\dfrac{20}{738} = 2.60\ \%$	2.6 + 86.43 = 89.03 %

70 – 80	75	40	$\dfrac{40}{738}$ = 5.2 %	5.2 + 89.03 = 94.2 %
80 – 90	85	30	$\dfrac{30}{738}$ = 4.05 %	4.05 + 94.2 = 98.25 %
90 – 100	95	10	$\dfrac{10}{738}$ = 1.35	1.35 + 98.25 = 100 %

Problem 3.7: *Spot speed studies data is given below for a section of the road. Determine the most preferred speed at which maximum proportion of vehicles are travelling.*

Speed Range, km/hr.	No. of Vehicles Observed	Speed Range, km/hr.	No. of Vehicles Observed
0 – 10	0	50 – 60	225
10 – 20	12	60 – 70	70
20 – 30	40	70 – 80	25
30 – 40	100	80 – 90	0
40 – 50	250		

Solution: We need to prepare speed versus percentage of vehicles observed graph i.e. frequency distribution curve for solution of this problem.

Total frequency i.e. total vehicles

$$= 0 + 12 + 40 + 100 + 250 + 225 + 70 + 25 + 0 = 722$$

Speed range, km/hr.	Mean speed	No. of vehicles observed or frequency	Percent frequency
0 – 10	5	0	$\dfrac{0}{722}$ = 0 %
10 – 20	15	12	$\dfrac{12}{722}$ = 1.66 %
20 – 30	25	40	$\dfrac{40}{722}$ = 5.54 %
30 – 40	35	100	$\dfrac{100}{722}$ = 13.85 %
40 – 50	45	250	$\dfrac{250}{722}$ = 34.62 %
50 – 60	55	225	$\dfrac{225}{722}$ = 31.16 %
60 – 70	65	70	$\dfrac{70}{722}$ = 9.69 %
70 – 80	75	25	$\dfrac{25}{722}$ = 3.46 %
80 – 90	85	0	$\dfrac{0}{722}$ = 0 %
			100 %

The modal speed corresponding to the maximum value of percentage frequency when plotted on the graph is 45 km/hr. This is the most preferred speed at which maximum proportion of vehicles would travel.

Problem 3.8: *Speed and delay studies are conducted on a stretch of road measuring 4 km in north-south direction. From this data, determine journey speed, running speed of traffic stream in either direction. Determine average values of volume too.*

Trip No.	Direction	Journey Time		Delay Time		Vehicles Overtaking	Vehicles Overtaken	Vehicles from Opposite Direction
		Min.	Sec.	Min.	Sec.			
1	N – S	6	35	1	30	5	7	250
2	S – N	7	00	1	40	6	3	180
3	N – S	6	50	1	30	5	3	280
4	S – N	7	50	1	30	2	1	200
5	N – S	6	00	1	00	3	4	230
6	S – N	8	15	2	20	2	2	150
7	N – S	6	25	1	30	2	5	300
8	S – N	7	30	1	40	3	2	160

Solution: We first prepare table for speed and delay data.

Trip No.	Direction	Journey time		Delay time		Vehicles overtaking	Vehicles overtaken	Vehicles from opposite direction
		Min.	Sec.	Min.	Sec.			
	N – S	6	35	1	30	5	7	250
		6	50	1	30	5	3	280
		6	00	1	00	3	4	230
		6	25	1	30	2	5	300
Total		25	50	5	30	15	20	1060
mean		6.4	min	1.37	min	7.5	9.75	530
	S – N	7	00	1	40	6	3	180
		7	50	1	30	2	1	200
		8	15	2	20	2	2	150
		7	30	1	40	3	2	160
Total		30.58	min	7.16	min	13	8	690
mean		7.64	min	1.79	min	3.29	2	172.5

We have

(1) North - South Direction:

n_y = Average no. of vehicles overtaking – overtaken

$$= 7.5 - 9.75 = -2.25$$

n_a = Average no. of vehicles in opposite direction i.e. SN = 172.5

t_w = Average journey time = 6.45 minutes = 6mt 27 seconds

t_a = Average journey time in the trip against the stream i.e. SN = 7.64 m = 7 mt 38 sec.

$$q = \text{Average volume} = \frac{n_a + n_y}{t_a + t_w} = \frac{172.5 + (-2.25)}{6.45 + 7.64}$$

$$= 12.083 \text{ veh./min}$$

$$i = \text{Average journey time} = t_w - \frac{n_y}{q} = 6.45 - \frac{-2.25}{12.083} = 6.63 \text{ minutes}$$

$$\text{Average journey speed} = \frac{\text{Journey length}}{\text{Average journey time}} = \frac{4}{6.63} \text{ km/min}$$

$$= \frac{4 \times 60}{6.63} \text{ km/hr.} = 36.19 \text{ km/hr.}$$

Average delay = 1.37 minutes,

$$\text{Average running time} = \text{Average journey time} - \text{Average delay}$$

$$= 6.63 - 1.37 = 5.26 \text{ minutes}$$

$$\text{Average running speed} = \frac{4 \times 60}{5.26} \text{ km/hr.} = 45.62 \text{ km/hr.}$$

(2) South - North direction:

Now, $n_y = 3.25 - 2 = 1.25$, $n_a = 530$, $t_w = 7.64$ minutes, $t_a = 6.45$ minutes

$$q = \frac{n_a + n_y}{t_a + t_w} = \frac{530 + 1.25}{7.64 + 6.45} = 37.704 \text{ veh./minute}$$

$$i = t_w - \frac{n_y}{q} = 7.64 - \frac{1.25}{37.70} = 7.606 \text{ minutes}$$

$$\text{Average journey speed} = \frac{4}{7.606} \text{ km/min.} = \frac{4 \times 60}{7.606} = 31.55 \text{ km/hr.}$$

$$\text{Average delay} = 1.79 \text{ minutes}$$

$$\text{Average running time} = 7.606 - 1.79 = 5.81 \text{ min}$$

$$\text{Average running speed} = \frac{4 \times 60}{5.81} \text{ km/hr,}$$

$$= 41.3 \text{ km/hr}$$

Problem 3.9: *Street lighting system is required to be designed when street width is 15 m and the mounting height is 7.5 m and the lamp size is 7000 lumen. Calculate the spacing between lighting units to produce average lux of 6.0.*

Solution:

$$\frac{\text{Pavement width}}{\text{Mounting height}} = \frac{15}{7.5} = 2$$

From figure, coefficient of utilisation is 0.44.

Maintenance factor relates to the maintenance of system. Let us assume it to be 0.8.

$$\text{Spacing} = \frac{\text{Lamp lumen} \times \text{Coeff. of utilization} \times \text{Maintenance factor}}{\text{Average lux} \times \text{Width of road}}$$

$$= \frac{7000 \times 0.44 \times 0.8}{6.0 \times 15} = 27.7 \text{ meters say } 27 \text{ meters}$$

Problem 3.10: *We observed 15 minute traffic counts on roads 1 and 2, during peak hours to be 180 and 150 vehicles per lane approaching the intersection. Based on approach speeds on roads 1 and 2, the amber time requirement is 3 and 2 seconds respectively. If the time headway is 2.5 seconds, what is total cycle length ?*

Solution: Let

$$C = \text{Assumed trial cycle time} = 50 \text{ seconds}$$

$$t = \text{Duration of traffic count} = 15 \text{ minutes}$$

$$n_1 = \text{No. of cycles} = \frac{t \times 60}{C}$$

$$= \frac{15 \times 60}{50} = 18$$

$$G_1 = \text{Green time for road 1} = \frac{n_1 \times \text{Time headway}}{\text{No. of cycles in 't' minutes}}$$

$$= \frac{2.5 \times 180}{18} = 25 \text{ seconds}$$

$$G_2 = \text{Green time for road 2} = \frac{150 \times 2.5}{18} = 20.8 \text{ seconds}$$

Amber times A_1 and A_2 are 3 and 2 seconds.

Therefore,   cycle length $= 25 + 20.8 + 3 + 2 = 50.8$

This is quite close to the assumed value of 50 seconds. Therefore adopt 50 seconds. Adopt $G_1 = 25$, $G_2 = 20$, $A_1 = 3$ and $A_2 = 2$ seconds respectively. Phase diagram is shown below.

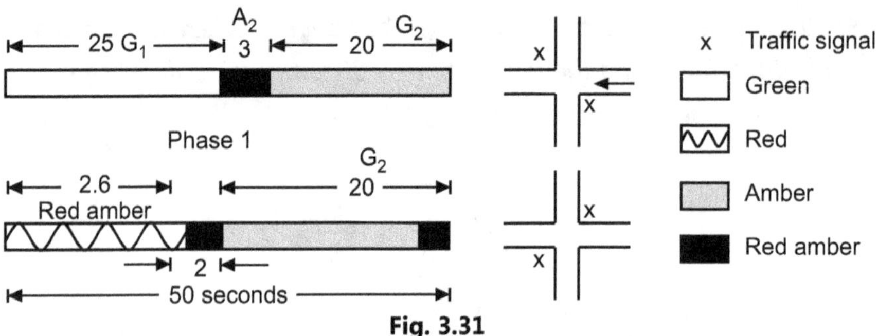

Fig. 3.31

Problem 3.11: *Road A 18 m wide and road B 12 m wide cross each other at right angles. The heaviest volume per hour for each lane of A and B are 300 and 250 respectively. Design pedestrian signal and timings of traffic if approach speeds are 60 and 40 km/hr.*

Solution:

The attack starts with assumption of amber time. Road A has fast approach speed. Road B has medium approach speed. Let us assume amber 4 and 3 seconds for these roads.

$$\text{Pedestrian time for road A} = \frac{\text{Road width}}{\text{Walking speed}} = \frac{18}{1.2} = 15 \text{ seconds}$$

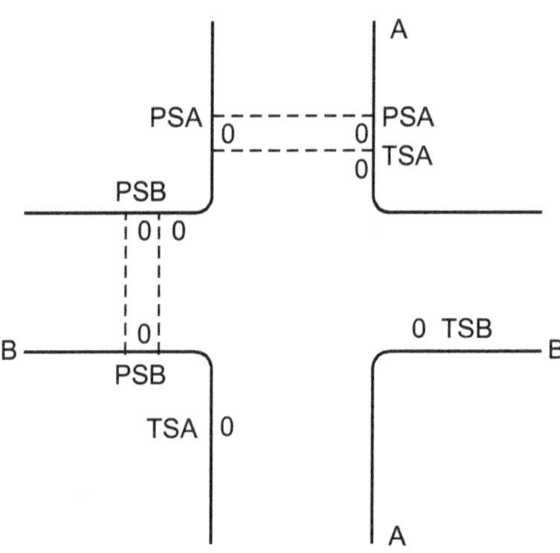

Fig. 3.32

$$\text{For road B, the pedestrian time} = \frac{12}{1.2} = 10 \text{ seconds.}$$

Walk period (min)　= 7 seconds

Pedestrian time for road A　= 15 + 7 = 22 seconds

　= Minimum red time for A

Pedestrian time for road B　= 10 + 7 = 17 seconds

　= Minimum red time for B

Minimum green time for road A　= Red time for B − amber time (B)

$$= (10 + 7) - 4 = 13 \text{ seconds}$$

Minimum green time for road B $= (15 + 7) - 3 = 19$ seconds

Assume green time for road B $= 19$ seconds to be alright. Now

$$\frac{\text{Green time for road A}}{\text{Green time for road B}} = \frac{\text{Heaviest vol./hr/lane of A}}{\text{Heaviest vol./hr./lane of B}}$$

$$\frac{GA}{GB} = \frac{300}{250} = 1.2 \qquad\qquad \therefore GA = 1.2\ GB = 1.2 \times 19$$

$$= 22.8 \text{ seconds}$$

Total cycle length $= GA + \text{Amber times for A and B} + GB$

$$= 22.8 + 4 + 3 + 19 = 48.8 \text{ seconds}$$

Next 5 seconds to be adopted. Adopt 50 seconds.

Additional period $50 - 48.8 = 1.2$ second is distributed to green timings in proportion to approach traffic volume.

Ratio of traffic volume $= \dfrac{300}{250} = 1.2$. Let increments in GA and GB be GA' and GB'.

$$\frac{GA'}{GB'} = \frac{1.2}{1} \quad \text{and} \quad GA' + GB' = 1.2$$

$$1.2\ GB' + GB' = 1.2$$

$$\therefore \qquad GB' = \frac{1.2}{2.2} = 0.54 \text{ second and}$$

$$GA' = 1.2 - 0.54 = 0.68 \text{ seconds}$$

$$\therefore \qquad \text{Actual } GA = 22.8 + 0.68 = 23.48$$

$$GB = 19 + 0.54 = 19.54 \text{ seconds}$$

$$\text{Red amber time } RA = GB + AB = 19.54 + 3 = 22.54 \text{ seconds}$$

$$\text{Red amber time } RB = GA + AB = 23.48 + 4 = 27.48 \text{ seconds}$$

Pedestrian signals

PSA (Don't walk period) = Red amber time for B = 27.48 seconds

PSB (Don't walk period) = Red amber time for A = 22.54 seconds

Pedestrian clearance interval have been calculated to be 15 and 10 seconds respectively

$$\text{For PSA walk time (WA)} = \text{Cycle length} - \left(\text{PSA} + \text{Pedestrian clearance time for A}\right)$$

$$= 50 - (27.48 + 15) = 7.52 \text{ seconds}$$

$$\text{For PSB walk time} = 50 - (22.54 + 10) = 17.46 \text{ seconds}$$

Phase diagram can suitably be drawn.

Problem 3.12: *Average normal flow on roads A and B are 400 and 300 pcu per hour. Saturation flow values on these roads are 1250 and 1000 pcu/hour. The all-red time required for pedestrian crossing is 12 seconds. Using Webster method, design traffic signal on the basis of two phase traffic signal.*

Solution:

$$y_a = \frac{\text{Normal flow on road A}}{\text{Saturation flow on road A}} = \frac{400}{1250} = 0.32$$

$$y_b = \frac{\text{Normal flow on road B}}{\text{Saturation flow on road B}} = \frac{300}{1000} = 0.30$$

$$y = y_a + y_b = 0.32 + 0.30 = 0.62$$

$$L = 2n + R = 2 \times 2 + 12 = 16 \text{ seconds}$$

$$C_o = \frac{1.5\,L + 5}{1 - y} = \frac{1.5 \times 16 + 5}{1 - (0.32 + 0.30)}$$

$$= \frac{29}{0.38} = 76.31 \text{ seconds}$$

$$GA = \frac{y_a}{y}\,(C_o - L)$$

$$= \frac{0.32}{0.62}\,(76.31 - 16) = 31.12 \text{ seconds}$$

$$GB = \frac{y_b}{y}\,(C_o - L)$$

$$= \frac{0.30}{0.62}\,(76.31 - 16) = 29.18 \text{ seconds}$$

All-red time for pedestrian crossing = 12 seconds

$$\text{Total cycle time} = GA + GB + \text{All-red time} + \text{Amber time}$$

$$= 31.12 + 29.18 + 12 + 2 \infty (2) = 76.3 \text{ seconds}$$

Two roads, these 2 × Amber time of 2 seconds.

Problem 3.13: *Road 1 and road 2 are crossing each other at right angles. Road 1 has four lanes and two approaches, has a total width of 12 meters and road 2 having two lanes has total width of 6.6 m. The volume of traffic approaching the intersection during design hour are 900 and 700 pcu/hour on the two approaches of road 1 and 275 and 180 pcu/hour on the two approaches of road 2. Design signal timings as per IRC guidelines.*

Solution:

$$\text{Design traffic on road 1} = \text{higher of the two approach volume}$$

$$= \frac{900}{2} = 450 \text{ pcu/hour}$$

$$\text{Design traffic on road 2} = \frac{275}{2} = 137 \text{ pcu/hour say.}$$

(A) $\text{Pedestrian green time for road 1} = \dfrac{12.0}{1.2} + 7 = 17 \text{ seconds}$

$\text{Pedestrian green time for road 2} = \dfrac{6.6}{1.2} + 7 = 12.5 \text{ seconds}$

Therefore green time for vehicles on road 2 = 17 seconds

$$\text{Green time for road 1} \;=\; 17 \times \frac{450}{275} \;=\; 27.81 \text{ seconds}$$

(B) Let us add 2.0 seconds each towards clearance amber and 2 seconds intergreen period for each phase, therefore total cycle time required = (2 + 17 + 2) + (2 + 27.81 + 2) = 52.81. Since the signal cycle time should be conveniently set in multiples of five seconds, so let us choose the next 5 second phase as such, let the cycle time be 55 seconds. The extra (55 – 52.81 = 2.19 seconds) per cycle may be diverted to the green times of roads 1 and 2. As such, let us make G_1 = 27.81 + 1.2 to be 28 seconds and

$$G_2 \;=\; 17 + 1 \;=\; 18 \text{ seconds.}$$

(C) Vehicle arrivals per lane cycle on road 1 = $\dfrac{450}{55}$ = 8.2 p.c.u.

Minimum green time for clearing vehicles on road 1

$$= 6 + (8.2 - 1.0)\,2 = 20.4 \text{ seconds}$$

Vehicle arrivals per cycle on road 2 = $\dfrac{275}{55}$ = 5 pcu

Minimum green time for clearing vehicles on road 2

$$= 6 + (5 - 2)\,2 = 14 \text{ seconds}$$

Green time provided is more than these values as such above design values are O.K.

(D) Lost time per cycle = (amber time + intergreen time

$$+ \text{ time for initial delay of first vehicle) for two phases}$$

$$= (2 + 2 + 4) \times 2 = 16 \text{ seconds} = L$$

Saturation flow for road 1 $\;= 525 \times 6 = 3150$ pcu/hr.

Saturation flow for road 2 $\;= 1850$ pcu/hr. approximately

$$y_1 = \frac{900}{3150} = 0.286 \quad \text{and} \quad y_2 = \frac{275}{1850} = 0.148$$

$$y = y_1 + y_2 \;=\; 0.286 + 0.148 = 0.434$$

$$\text{Optimum cycle time} \;=\; \frac{1.5\,L + 5}{1 - y} \;=\; \frac{1.5 \times 16 + 5}{1 - 0.434}$$

$$= 51.2 \text{ seconds}$$

Therefore the cycle time of 55 seconds designed earlier is O.K. Cycle time may be shown in the table below.

Road	Green	Amber	Red	Cycle
1	28	2	23 + 2	55
2	18	2	33 + 2	55

Problem 3.14: *Results of transportation survey conducted in a town are given below.*

Traffic zone No.	Population in thousands	Total trips in hundreds
1	25	12
2	28	10
3	30	18
4	35	16
5	20	10
6	30	16
7	20	9
8	25	10

If the population of a particular zone increases to say 50,000, trip generation from that zone is required to be predicted.

Solution: We first prepare the table.

Zone	x	y	xy	x^2	y^2
1	25	12	300	625	144
2	28	10	280	784	100
3	30	18	540	900	324
4	35	16	560	1225	256
5	20	10	200	400	100
6	30	16	480	900	256
7	20	9	180	400	81
8	25	10	250	625	100
$n = 8$	$\sum x = 213$	$\sum y = 101$	$\sum xy = 2790$	$\sum x^2 = 5859$	$\sum y^2 = 1361$

$$b_1 = \frac{n\sum xy - \sum x \sum y}{n\sum x^2 - (\sum x)^2} = \frac{8 \times 2790 - 101 \times 213}{8 \times 5859 - (213)^2}$$

$$= \frac{807}{0.503} = 0.536$$

$$b_0 = y - b_1 x_1 = \frac{\sum y - b \sum x_1}{n}$$

$$= \frac{101 - 0.536 \times 213}{8} = \frac{101 - 114.16}{8} = -1.64$$

Trip model is $\qquad y = -1.64 + 0.536\, x_1 = 0.536\, x_1 - 1.64$

and $\quad r = b_1 \left[\dfrac{n\sum x^2 - (\sum x)^2}{n\sum y^2 - (\sum y)^2}\right]^{1/2} = \left[\dfrac{8 \times 5859 - 213 \times 213}{8 \times 1361 - 101 \times 101}\right]^{1/2} = 1.47$

$$\text{model is } y = 0.536\, x_1 - 1.64$$

Future population of the zone 50,000

$$y = 0.536 \infty 50 - 1.64 = 25.16 \text{ in hundreds}$$

So total trips generated would be 2516.

QUESTIONS

1. What are the traffic characteristics that should be considered while traffic planning ?

2. What are the vehicle characteristics that should be known for traffic planning ?

3. What are traffic volume studies ? How can you find out whether there is congestion at junction ?

4. Describe what is A.A.D.T. and the thirtieth highest hourly volume.

5. What is space-mean speed and time-mean speed ? What are special conditions for a vehicle when their speeds are same numerically ?

6. Calculate - space mean speed for

Vehicle	Road Stretch	Travel Time
30	100	15
40	100	12
10	100	8

(**Ans.** 12.47 km/hr)

7. For the above data calculate time - mean speed.   (**Ans.** 29 – 62 km/hr.)

8. Distinguish between running speed and travel speed.

9. What is percentile speed ? How is it used to determine safe speed limit ?

10. From the following, determine average speed of vehicles on the track.

Speed Range	No. of Vehicles
0 – 10	5
10 – 20	10
20 – 30	30
30 – 40	10

(**Ans.** 24 km/hr.)

11. On the basis of data for spot studies given below, upper and lower speed limit regulation as well as speed for design is to be calculated.

Speed Range	No. of Vehicles Observed	Speed Range	No. of Vehicles Observed
0 – 10	12	50 – 60	255
10 – 20	18	60 – 70	20
20 – 30	68	70 – 80	43
30 – 40	89	80 – 90	33
40 – 50	205	90 – 100	9

(**Ans.**   Upper speed limit for regulation 60 km/hr. Lower speed limit for regulation 30 km/hr. Speed for design = 84 km/hr.)

12. Data of spot speed studies on a section of the road is given. You are required to determine most preferred speed at which maximum proportion of vehicles would travel.

Speed Range	No. of Vehicles	Speed Range	No. of Vehicles
0 – 10	0	50 – 60	216
10 – 20	10	60 – 70	68
20 – 30	30	70 – 80	24
30 – 40	105	80 – 90	0
40 – 50	233		

(**Ans.** Around 47 km/hr.)

13. How origin and destination can be defined ?

14. What are the uses of origin destination study ?

15. Describe how origin destination study can be conducted by "License plate method". What are the uses and limitations of this method ?

16. Fill in the blank and justify the reason for it. In India, diverging on the left would cause problems than diverging to the right.

17. When maximum capacity for a particular speed is obtained on the highway ?

18. Distinguish between traffic volume and traffic capacity.

19. What is possible capacity and when it can approach zero level ?

20. What are desire lines ? What is the exact use for these lines ?

21. Describe the steps that need be taken for parking studies.

22. For an urban road 3.5 km length which runs north-south speed and delay studies were conducted by floating car method, various parameters such as journey speed, running speed, average traffic volume are to be determined.

Trip No.	Direction	Time of Journey		Time of Delay		Overtaking vehicles	Vehicles over Taken	Vehicles from Opposite Direction
		min.	sec.	min.	sec.			
1	NS	6	32	1	40	4	7	268
2	SN	7	14	1	50	5	3	186
3	NS	6	50	1	30	5	3	280
4	SN	7	40	2	00	2	1	200
5	NS	6	10	1	10	3	5	250
6	SN	8	00	2	22	2	2	170
7	NS	6	28	1	40	2	5	290
8	SN	7	30	1	40	3	2	160

(Ans. For NS direction: Av. vol = 13 Veh/min., Speed of Journey = 31.7 km/hr, running speed 31 km/hr.

For SN direction: Av. vol = 19 Veh/min.,

Speed of Journey = 27 km/hr, speed = 27 km/hr.)

23. Describe what is meant by parallel parking and inclined parting. Discuss their merits and demerits.

24. Discuss the need for off-street parting. How it can be arranged ? What are the relative merits and demerits of this system ?

25. Explain the significance of following pavement markings zebra crossing, bus-stop-point, hazard markers, stop lines.

26. What is the use of estimation of trips ? How it is done ?

27. Explain Gravity model and model split.

28. How briefly signalized intersection can be designed ?

29. What are different traffic signal systems ? Explain simple progressive system.

30. What the I.R.C. recommendation that tells you the necessity of traffic signals ?

31. What are the principles of highway lighting ?

32. Explain different highway layouts with their relative merits and demerits.

Chapter 4
HIGHWAY ALIGNMENT

4.1 INTRODUCTION

Once we find that highway is necessary between the two cities or towns A and B, the next question which we should address ourselves is that what route should be taken between A and B, what sort of information should be collected in respect of traffic, soil, drainage etc. to find the most economic and highest return yielding route between A and B? How this information should be gathered and presented in the from of project report so that the authorities can easily come to the conclusion of best alternative? It will be the object of this chapter to know the method of collecting all such information and knowing the process of presenting such information in clear and concise form. The discussion is with reference to the relevant Indian Road Congress Specification.

Basic requirements of an ideal alignment:

The basic requirements of an ideal alignment between two terminal stations are that it should be:

- Short.
- Easy.
- Safe and
- Economical.

Short: It is desirable to have a short alignment between two terminal stations. A straight alignment would be the shortest, though there may be several practical considerations which would cause deviations from the shortest path.

Easy: The alignment should be such that it is easy to construct and maintain the road with minimum problems. Also the alignment should be easy for the operation of vehicles with easy gradients and curves.

Safe: The alignment should be safe enough for the construction and maintenance from the view point of stability of natural hill slopes, embankment and cut slopes and foundation of embankments. Also it should be safe for the traffic operation with safe geometric fractures.

Economical: The road alignment could be considered economical only if the total cost including initial cost, maintenance cost and vehicle operation cost is lowest. All these factors should be given due consideration before working out the economical of each alignment. The alignment should be such that it would offer maximum utility by serving maximum population and products. The utility of a road should be judged from its utility value per unit length of road.

4.2   GUIDING PRINCIPLES OF ROUTE SELECTION AND HIGHWAY LOCATION

The fundamental principle of route selection and highway location is to achieve the least overall cost of transportation which includes the cost of initial construction of highway facility, it's periodic maintenance, and vehicle operation while at the same time satisfying environmental requirements. To achieve this objective it would be necessary to make a detailed investigation before the location is finally decided. The factors that should be kept in view while fixing the road alignment are listed below.

- The highway alignment should be as direct as possible between the towns to be linked resulting in economy in construction and maintenance. As the crow flies is possibly the best alignment, but this alignment should result in minimum interference to agriculture and established industries.

- The location of the highway, should stay clear of obstructions, cemetery burning Ghats, places of worships, archeological and historical monument, public facilities like schools, hospitals playgrounds, fertile lands, and large industrial establishments. The highway can pass near such establishments but the location should be such that the shifting of these establishments is not required since it will involve large compensation.

- The present utility and services like overhead transmission lines, water supply lines should not as far as possible be shifted. The decision between changing the highway alignment or shifting the utility services should be based on relative economics and feasibility.

- The location should as far as possible facilitate easy grades and curvatures with frequent crossing and recrossing of the railway line avoided.

- The site of the river crossing is an important obligatory point in selection of the route.
  If a particular bridge site is better, the highway alignment may be shifted to suit the bridge site, since shifting of the bridge site would generally cause more expenditure. The bridges should not in general be skew and submersible.

- The highway should as far as be located along the edges of properties rather than through their middle so as to cause least interference to cultivation and to avoid the need of frequent crossing of the highway.

- The highway location should be part and parcel of the surrounding landscape. There should be least adverse effects of highway construction on the environment. In this connection, it is better that the highway avoids wooded area so the constant destruction of forest is avoided. Where intrusion into such areas is unavoidable, the highway should be aligned on a curve so as to preserve an unbroken background.

- The location should be close to the sources of embankment and pavement materials so that haulage of these overlong distances is avoided and the cost minimised. An highway alignment if possible should permit balancing of the cost of cut and fill for the formation. This is illustrated in Fig. 4.1.

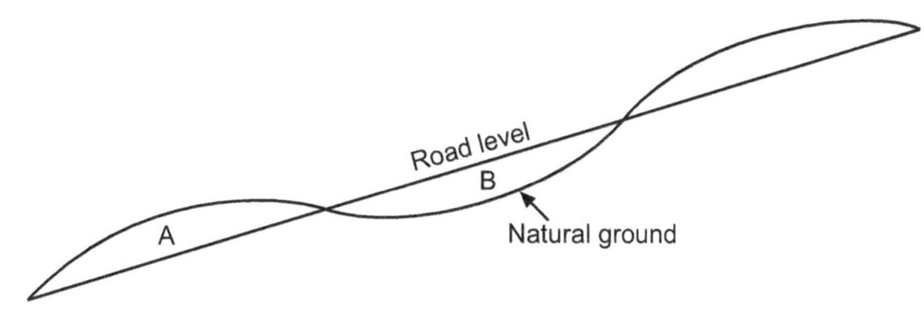

A - Cut portion
B - Earth filling
$\Sigma A = \Sigma B$

Fig. 4.1

- Marshy and low lying land areas having poor drainage and having very poor embankment material, areas liable to flooding, areas susceptible to subsidence due to mining operation should as far as possible be avoided and a preferred location is one which pass through areas having better type of soil. For example for the roads which passes through desert areas, location where sand is loose and unstable should be avoided, and the alignment selected along ridges having vegetation. For roads in desert areas preference should be given to areas having coarse sand against areas having fine wind blown sand. Similarly, in locating a road in this particular area, having longitudinal sand dunes, the best location is at the top of ridge or in the interdunal space. Location along the face of the longitudinal dunes should be avoided.

- Highway through villages and towns increase traffic hazard and cause delay and congestion. Where a serious problem of this nature is featured, it will be advisable to bypass the builtup area, staying clear of the limits upto which the town or village is anticipated to grow in the future.

- If the hill is to be surmounted for on highway alignment, there are special problems and considerations of location of highways in hilly areas, which should be looked into.

4.3 FACTORS CONTROLLING THE ALIGNMENT OF ROADS

The various factors, which control the highway alignment, in general may be listed as:

- Obligatory points
- Traffic
- Geometric design
- Economics
- Other considerations

(a) Obligatory Points :

These control points may be divided in to two categories:

(i) Points through which the alignment is to pass

(ii) Points through which the alignment should not pass.

1. Obligatory points through which the road alignment has to pass may cause the alignment to often deviate from the shortest (or) easiest path.

In Fig. 4.2 (a) shows how the straight alignment AB is deviated along the hillside pass, thus avoiding a tunnel (or) heavy cutting.

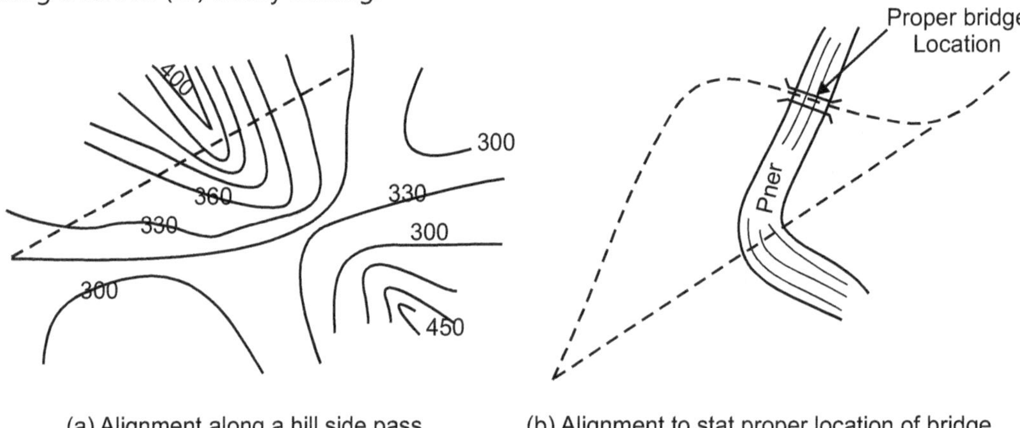

(a) Alignment along a hill side pass   (b) Alignment to stat proper location of bridge

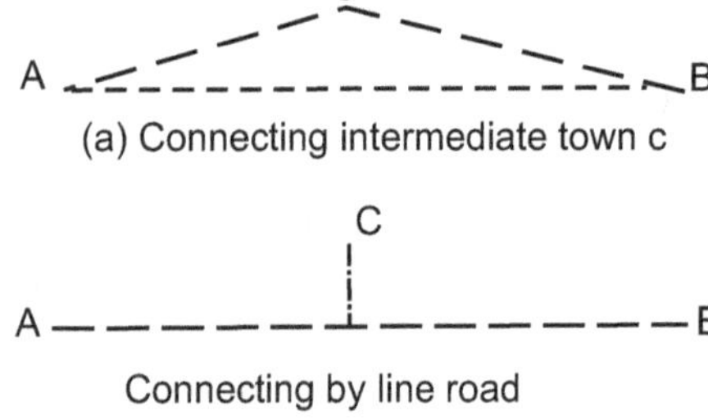

(a) Connecting intermediate town c

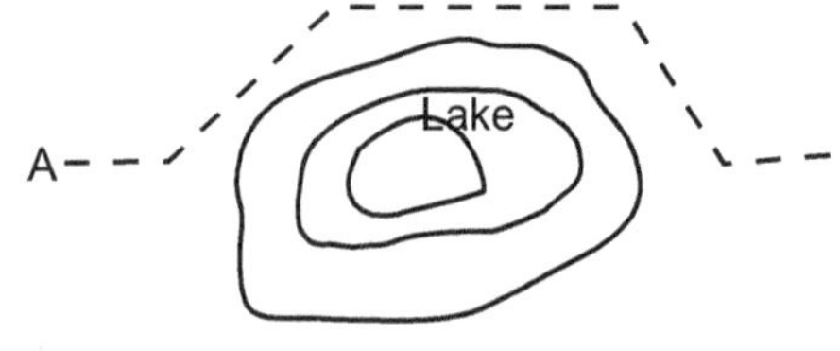

C

A ———————————— B

Connecting by line road

(c) Alignment to connect intermediate town   (d) Alignment avoiding an rmemediate area

Fig. 4.2 : Obligatory points controlling alignment of roads

In Fig. 4.2 (b) .shows that the straight alignment between stations A and B which passes across the river band is to be deviated along the path shown in order to cross the river at a proper bridge location.

(ii) Obligatory points through which the road should not pass also may make it necessary to deviate from the proposed shortest alignment.

• The obligatory points, which should be avoided while aligning a road, include religious places, very costly structures.

• However if there is no alternative and the alignment has to be taken across such an area, the construction and maintenance costs are likely to be very high.

(b) Traffic:

The alignment should suit traffic requirements origin and destination study should be carried out in the area and the desire lines be drawn showing the trend of traffic flow.

(c) Geometric Design:

• Geometric design factors such as gradient, radius of curve and sight distance also would govern the final alignment of the highway.

• The absolute minimum sight distance, which should invariably be available in every section of the road, is the safe stopping distance for the fast moving vehicles.

(d) Economy:

• The alignment finalized based on the above factors should also be economical.

• The initial coast of construction can be decreased if high embankments and deep cuttings are avoided and the alignment is choosing in a manner to balance the cutting and filling.

(e) Other Considerations:

• Various other factors, which may govern the alignment, are drainage considerations, hydrological factors, political considerations and monotony.

• The vertical alignment is often guided by drainage considerations.

• In a flat terrain it is possible to have a very long stretch of road, absolutely straight without horizontal curves.

(f) Special Considerations:

Stability:

While aligning hill roads, special care should be taken to align the road along the side as the hill, which is stable. The cutting and filling of earth to construct roads on hillside causes steepening of existing slopes and affect its stability.

Drainage:

Numerous hillside drains should be provided for adequate drainage facility across the road. But the cross drainage structures being costly, attempts should be made to align the road.

4.4 SPECIAL CONSIDERATIONS FOR ALIGNMENT OF HILL ROADS

The main factors to be considered while deciding the alignment of hill roads are as discussed.

*   **Length:** The cost of construction of hill road per kilometer length is comparatively very high. It should therefore be ensured that length of the road connecting two stations should be minimum possible, adopting gradients along its most of the length.

*   **Altitude of the Road:** At lower altitudes, large numbers of cross drainage works are required to be constructed. Whereas at higher altitudes, the road pavement may witness snowfall during winter. This is why the alignment of hill roads should preferably be provided at an altitude between 900 m to 1500 m above M.S.L. At higher altitude, the alignment, if found necessary, should be provided on the hill slopes exposed to sun. The hill slopes which are subjected to high winds should never be selected unless and until there is no other alternative. In northern hemisphere, southern slopes of the hills are more suitable than northern slopes which remain in shades and are usually subjected to high winds. (See Fig. 4.3)

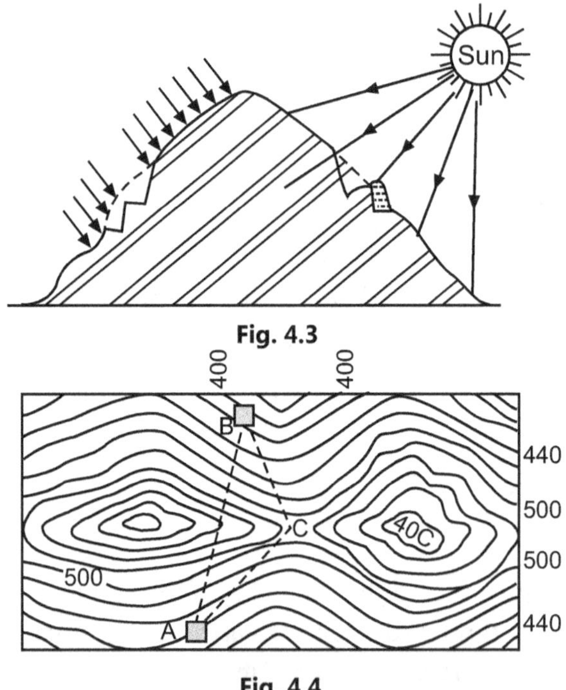

Fig. 4.3

Fig. 4.4

- **Saddles or Passes:** While locating the counter gradient of the proposed alignment of a hill road on a contour map, it should cross the hill range through saddles. Though length of the road is increased, the heavy cost of cutting through rocks is avoided. Due to increased length, ruling gradients can be suitably adjusted. (See Fig. 4.4)

- **Geology of Hill Slope:** Cutting through solid hard rocks is very expensive. The alignments of roads may be suitably deviated to avoid such areas.

- **Tunnels:** Drilling of tunnels is very expensive. The long tunnels need ventilation as well as lighting arrangements. As far as possible, tunnels should be avoided and resorted to only if other suitable alternative is not possible.

- **Valleys:** While deciding the alignment for crossing a river valley, due consideration should be given to avoid construction of a number of bridges on its tributaries.

- **Geometric Standards:** The alignments of the hill roads should be selected on the hill slopes which easily provide recommended geometric standards i.e. gradients, curves, sight distance etc. Hairpin bends on roads should be avoided and if found necessary, these should be on gentle, stable and slopes. To have proper geometric standards, it might be necessary to change the alignment at number of places.

- **Camping Sites:** At intermittent distance, the alignment of the hill road should pass through gentle slopes where suitable camping sites could be developed for military in case of necessity.

- **Stability of Hill Slopes:** While deciding the alignment of hill roads, it should be ensured that the slopes are stable and not very steep. The area is not prone to land slides and settlements. This factor is of special importance in hills having sedimentary rocks.

QUESTIONS

1. What guiding principles should be kept in mind while making a route selection for highway?

2. What is meant by alignment of roads? What are the points to be kept in mind while aligning a road?

3. Discuss the special care to be taken while aligning hill roads.

4. Write note on

   (a) Basic requirement of an ideal alignment of highway

   (b) Factor controlling alignment of highway

   (c) Special alignment requirement of hill road

Chapter 5

GEOMETRIC DESIGN

5.1 INTRODUCTION

The first question that creeps up in the mind of the engineer is regarding meaning of the term geometry of highway. By geometry, we mean the physical proportion of highway, it's breadth, it's configuration on curves, it's cross-section, it's slope in cut and fill sections etc. This geometry of the highway regulates the capacity of the way - meaning thereby the number of road users that can safely and efficiently ply on the roads. For example, if we fix the breadth and cross-section of a highway in a level terrain, it will fix up the number of automobiles that use this way efficiently. It is a very common observation in India and to a certain extent in any developing country that the facility created is not generally adequate for the future. This is true of highways also. A highway which may be created for 100 vehicles/day may not have sufficient traffic to start with. It is possible that only 30 vehicles/day may pass on it. But as the time progresses and people realise the benefits that acquire from the roadway, they start using it. It is very natural that after 3 - 4 years, the highway may become inadequate for the traffic. Highway engineer must have therefore capacity to peep into the future and estimate the future traffic conditions.

5.2 PASSENGER CAR UNIT

In India, traffic is not, in general, segregated. For example, you will find a bullock cart plying on the same road, which is being used by automobile. Except for the future expressway, this scene is likely to continue for the forseeable future. If on the same road, four trucks, three bullock carts and one cycle rikshaw is plying, how do we fix-up the capacity of road. For this purpose, it is necessary to convert the heterogeneous traffic into standard passenger car unit. Indian Roads Congress has suggested for rural conditions the following P.C.U. factors.

Now, if a particular road is being utilized by 50 cycle rikshaw, 10 cars, 2 trucks and 1 bullock cart per hour, then the equivalent passenger car unit which are plying on this road would be [1.5 × 50 + 1 × 10 + 8 × 2] i.e. 75 + 10 + 16 i.e. 101 passenger car units are plying on this road per hour.

Traffic on Indian Roads is of heterogeneous character. It consists of not only fast moving motorized vehicles but also of primitive modes such as animal drawn vehicle and human driven ones like cycle and cycle - rikshaw.

Table 5.1

Sr. No.	Vehicle type	P.C.U. factor
1.	Passenger car, Auto rikshaw	1
2.	Cycle, Motor cycle or Scooter	0.5
3.	Truck, Bus or Agricultural tractor trailor unit	3.0
4.	Cycle Rikshaw	1.5
5.	Horse-drawn vehicle	4
6.	Bullock - cart	8

On Indian roads, these vehicles share the same space without physical segregation creating traffic problems. One way of accounting in configurations and characteristics of vehicles is to convert all vehicles into a common unit, and the most accepted unit for such purpose is passenger car unit (P.C.U.). Various agencies in India and abroad have recommended P.C.U. factors for different categories of vehicles. This is not very correct. For example, traffic stream with 10 bicycles may have more than 10 times detrimental effect on capacity than when there is only one bicycle. P.C.U. values should therefore depend upon factors like composition of traffic stream, total traffic volume on the road, the flow characteristics, etc. In India, IRC 106 - 1990 has provided P.C.U. factors for about 10 types of vehicles found on Indian Road, without considering these details. Chandrakumar and Sikdar have tried to study the effect of these traffic factors on P.C.U. and have tried to evolve a concept of dynamic P.C.U. It is seen that capacity of given facility is about 60 % overestimated with the use of static P.C.U. values as suggested by I.R.C. In a way it is a conservative approach. However, studies should be carried out to extend the concept of dynamic P.C.U. to roads so that some equation should result to calculate P.C.U. for a given vehicle in set of traffic conditions. Passenger car units/hour help us to determine width of road, number of lanes, traffic junctions, etc.

5.3 DESIGN VEHICLE

The next question that naturally will come up to anybody's mind is regarding standard design vehicle. The vehicles that ply on road are of various configurations and just as we had converted the haphazard vehicles into a typical passenger car unit, we might as well decide about standard design vehicle that should ply on the road. The design vehicle could be considered as a selected motor vehicle having standard specifications such as weight, dimensions, and operating conditions. These parameters would influence highway geometric aspects such as width of pavement, clearances, radii of curve, etc. The Indian Roads Congress vide IRC - 3-1984 have fixed up these dimensions as follows:

Table 5.2 (a) : Dimensions

| Authority | Maximum Width | Maximum Height | Maximum Length | | Semi Trailer | Truck Trailer | Single Unit bus |
			Passenger Car	Single Unit Truck			
I.R.C. (1984)	2.5 metre	3.8 to 4.2	–	11.0 metre	16.0 metre	18.0 metre	12.0 metre

Table 5.2 (b): Weights

Authority	Single Axle	Double Axle
I.R.C. (1984)	10.2 metric tonnes	18.0 metric tonnes

There are two things to be remembered regarding design vehicles. The first thing is that choosing of design vehicle is dependent upon type and volume of traffic on the road. For example, super-express highway may have largest design vehicle. The second thing, that the concept of design vehicle is hypothetical in nature. Actual dimensions of vehicle may not tally with the configuration of design vehicle. It is a concept to determine pavement width radii of curve etc. Generally, the design vehicle is conservative in nature i.e. the parameter such as radii and width of pavements deduced on the basis of the concept of design vehicle are on safer side and hence the concept is accepted.

5.4 SPEED

The vehicles that ply on the road will have different speeds. Design speed is the maximum safe speed that can be maintained over a specified section of the highway when conditions are so favourable that the design features of the highway are the governing factors.

Table 5.3: Suggested design speeds in India for Rural Highway (All values in K.P.H.)

| Classification | Plain Terrain | | Rolling Terrain | | Mountainous Terrain | | Steep Terrain | |
	Ruling	Minimum	Ruling	Minimum	Ruling	Minimum	Ruling	Minimum
National Highways and State Highways	100	80	80	65	50	40	40	30
Major District Roads	80	65	65	50	40	30	30	20
Other District Roads	65	50	50	40	30	25	25	20
Village Roads	50	40	40	35	25	20	25	20

Table 5.4: Suggested design speeds for Urban Roads as per I.R.C.

Classification of Roads	Speed in kilometer / hour
Arterial	80
Sub-arterial	60
Collector street	50
Local street	30

A design speed of 120 km/hour has been adopted for the expressway under construction between Ahmedabad and Vadodara. The design speed itself could be subdivided into two categories: (a) Ruling Design Speed and (b) Minimum Design Speed. The word ruling has the same meaning as that of governing. It therefore denotes the maximum Speed within which the designer attempts to design the highway. It therefore shows the upper limit of speed for design purposes. The Indian Roads Congress has also suggested minimum design speed. This suggestion of I.R.C. in the opinion of the author of the book is redundant. If a highway can cater for the ruling design speed, it will automatically cater for minimum design speed for most of the cases. It is therefore un-necessary to suggest minimum design speed.

The design speed is a function of the grade or incline of the road and the type of pavement. Depending upon cross-slope, the terrain have been classified as follows:

Terrain Name	Cross slope of ground in %
Plain	0 – 10
Rolling	10 – 25
Mountainous	25 – 60
Steep	> 60

Now, depending upon road classification which would generally determine the type of pavement surface and terrain classification, design speeds have been suggested for rural roads as follows:

Table 5.5: Design speed on Rural Highways

Road Classi-fication	Design Speed, km/hour for Different Terrain							
	Plain		Rolling		Mountainous		Steep	
	Ruling	Min.	Ruling	Min.	Ruling	Min.	Ruling	Min.
National and State highway	100	80	80	65	50	40	40	30
Major District Roads	80	65	65	50	40	30	30	20

Other District Roads	65	50	50	40	30	25	25	20
Village Roads	50	40	40	35	25	20	25	20

It has already been stated that fixing up of minimum design speed has no relevance if the road has already been designed for either maximum or ruling design speed.

5.5 GRADIENT

Gradient is the rise or fall given to the road pavement in it's longitudinal section. If two points A and B to be connected by road has a difference in elevation of say 100 metres and the distance between the two points A and B is say 10 km, then the road section between A and B should have a gradient of $\dfrac{100}{10 \times 1000} = \dfrac{1}{100}$. Depending upon the topography i.e. geographical features between points A and B, gradients have to be given so that this difference in elevation between points A and B is finally met. If the road between the points C and D is inclined to the horizontal by an angle α, then $\angle DCE = \alpha$. And then the gradient $= \tan \alpha = \dfrac{DE}{CE}$. This fraction $\dfrac{DE}{CE}$ could be expressed 1 in p i.e. $\dfrac{DE}{CE} = \dfrac{1}{p}$. It could also be expressed as n percentage, then $\dfrac{DE}{CE} = \dfrac{n}{100}$. Generally, ascending gradients are given positive sign and descending gradients are given negative sign. For example, the road CFE' between it's journey CF can have ascending gradient say $+ n_1$ percentage and FE' can have descending gradient say $-n_1$ percentage. Then the deviation angle between the roads CF and FE' is angle $D\hat{F}E' = D\hat{C}E + \angle F\hat{E'}C = n_1 + n_2$ in a quantitative way.

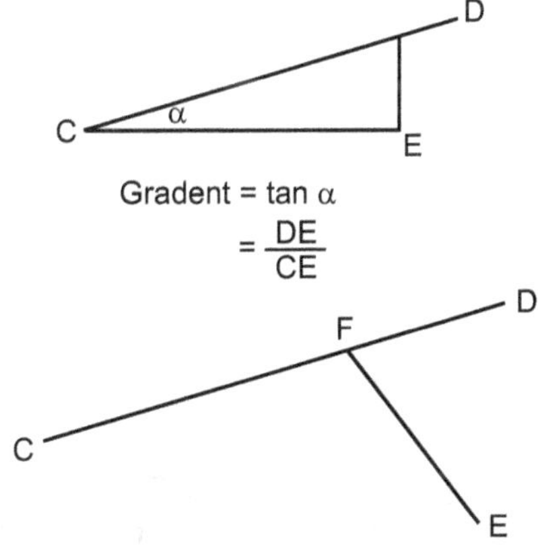

Fig. 5.1

Gradient which is a part of and parcel of vertical alignments can be classified as

(i) Minimum gradient, (ii) Ruling gradient, (iii) Limiting gradient and (iv) Exceptional gradient.

Minimum Gradient: Suppose there is no difference in elevation between the points A and B, then theoretically, the road should be laid between points A and B in a level stretch i.e. no gradient i.e. zero gradient should be given between the points A and B. But this is just theoretical. In practice, even for such a road, gradient has to be given from the point of view of drainage of the road.

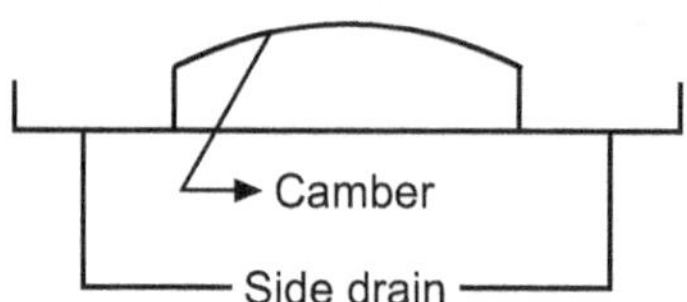

Fig. 5.2

If the road pavement has gradient in it's cross-section, it has camber, then the rain will be collected in side drains. If the road pavement has no gradient, and it's level road, then the rain water that is being collected in side drains have to be let off to natural drain such as nala etc. For this purpose, the side drain will have to be given longitudinal fall even though the road pavement has no longitudinal fall. In order that the water has perceptible velocity, this slope is estimated to be 1 in 300. That is in such case even though the road pavement has no gradient, downstream end of side drain will have to be deepened by 3 meters for every one km of road. This is not welcome from construction point of view and the desirable thing is that road pavement be given some longitudinal gradient so that the water that is collected in side drain shall have some initial force, and the slope to the side drain is gentle. Some sort of minimum ascending or descending gradient is always given to the road. This is called as **minimum gradient**. Naturally minimum gradient would depend upon rainfall run off, type of soil and other site conditions of side drains. The following table gives some guidance in this respect.

Table 5.6

Type of Side Drain	Minimum Gradient
Concrete drains or gutter	1 in 500
Inferior drains, brick drain, slate drains	1 in 200
Kutcha drains i.e soil drains	1 in 100

Grade Compensation: If the road is laid on horizontal curve that has gradient, then auto that plies on such road will have to exert tractive effort on two counts, (a) tractive effort on account of horizontal curve, (b) tractive effort on account of gradient. Sometimes this tractive effort is too much for the vehicle causing discomfort to the passengers. For the horizontal curves which are laid on sharp permissible gradient (ruling gradient), it is customary to reduce the gradient so that passengers do not feel discomfort. This is called as

grade compensation. The grade compensation in percentage is given by $\dfrac{30 + R}{R}$ subjected to a maximum value 75/R, where R is the radius of curve in meters. According to Indian Roads Congress specifications, the grade compensation is not required for gradients flatter than 4 %.

Ruling Gradient: Ruling gradient can also be called as design gradient, since it is defined as the maximum gradient that is available at the disposal of the highway designer for designing the vertical profile of the road. Theoretically, the ruling gradient is a function of automobile horse power. Suppose the vehicle is negotiating an upgrade with a design speed. Then the maximum grade that could be given on this stretch will be such that power developed by the engine is utilized to overcome the resistance generated due to grade. This then is the ruling gradient for this stretch. However, the problem is quite complex and not soluble mathematically in view of the diversity of the road vehicles, differing in tractive efforts, and I.R.C. has therefore recommended certain values.

Limiting gradient and exceptional gradient: If the topography is hilly and you want to adopt ruling gradients only, then this would involve large excavations and fills involving high cost. To prohibit this high cost we adopt gradients which are higher than ruling gradients. These are called as **limiting gradients**. In other words, these are ruling gradients for rolling terrain and hill roads. Such stretches of limiting gradient should be provided with level or easier grade before and after the start of such grade.

Exceptional Gradient: In extra-ordinary circumstances, especially in hill roads, one can provide gradients steeper than the limiting gradients. These are called as **exceptional gradients**. However, exceptional gradients should be limited for a road length of 100 meter at a stretch. The guidelines for these gradients as suggested by I.R.C. are summarised below.

Table 5.7: Guidelines for gradients

Terrain		Ruling Gradient	Limiting Gradient	Exceptional Gradient
(a)	Plain or rolling	3.3 % or 1 in 30	5 % or 1 in 20	6.7 % or 1 in 15
(b)	Mountainous or steep terrain at an elevation of 3000 meters and above the mean sea level	5 % or 1 in 20	6 % or 1 in 16.7	7 % or 1 in 14.3
(c)	Steep terrain upto 3000 m. height above mean sea level	6 % or 1 in 16.7	7 % or 1 in 14.3	8 % or 1 in 12.5

Critical Length of Grade: When a truck negotiates a grade, there is fall in speed. The reduction in speed by about 25 km/hour is considered as reasonable limit and the length of grade at which this reduction in speed occurs is **critical length** of grade. Naturally this length would depend upon initial speed at the start of grade, type of vehicle, it's B.H.P., it's tractive effort, minimum speed that the vehicle can have at the end of the grade so that this particular vehicle does not cause interference with the movement of the other vehicles at the end of grade. Many of these factors are not quantifiable, hence, there are no recommendations regarding critical length of grade by I.R.C.

5.6 CROSS-SLOPE OR CAMBER

Camber is the slope given to road pavement in cross-section. It's use is to drain out rainwater into side drains so that the pavement is free of water. Parabolic or elliptic shape is preferred for fast moving vehicles, since they are likely to cross the crown frequently in overtaking operations. The camber is generally left intact by pneumatic tyred vehicles. It is the animal drawn vehicles that cause serious damage to the camber. These vehicles do not have full and uniform contact with the pavement surface resulting in high stresses and subsequent denudation of pavement. Amount of camber is a function of type of pavement surface, which determines its draining capacity and the amount of rainfall in that region.

The following table recommended by the relevant Indian Roads Congress can be considered as a guide.

Table 5.8: Recommended Values of Camber

Sr. No.	Type of Pavement	Range of Camber in Areas of Rainfall Range		
		Heavy	to	Light
1.	Cement concrete or high grade bituminous	1 in 50	to	1 in 60
2.	Thin bituminous	1 in 40	to	1 in 50
3.	Water bound Macadam	1 in 33	to	1 in 40
4.	Earth	1 in 25	to	1 in 33

The cross-slope of the shoulder could be 0.5 % steeper than the cross-slope of adjoining pavement subject to a minimum of 3.0 % (and a maximum value of 5.0 % for earth slopes).

Providing camber in the field:

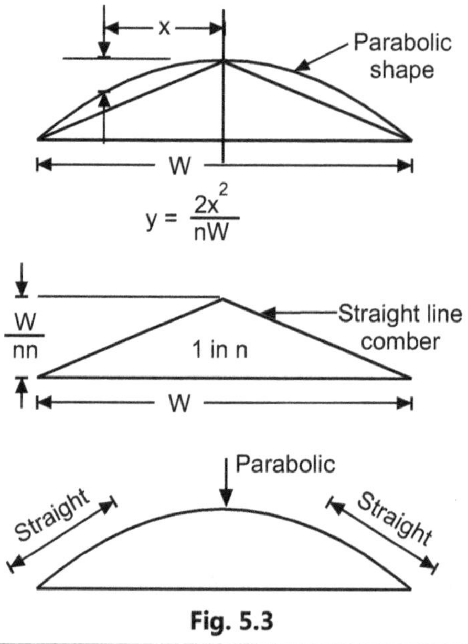

Fig. 5.3

As we know, camber is cross-slope. This cross-slope could be obtained by various curves. Some usual methods are indicated in Fig. 5.3.

The general method in construction to achieve camber is by preparing camber plate which are many times called as camber - boards to check the lateral profile of finished pavement. The camber can be achieved during construction by levelling operations also.

5.7 RIGHT OF WAY

As the name indicates, this is the land width over which highway engineers have authority. In fact, it is the area of land acquired for road construction and for it's future development. It is always better to have more land than the minimum specified by I.R.C. standards. Highway construction gives a fillip to the cost of land and land adjoining highway appreciates. It becomes difficult to acquire it then. This land width to be acquired depends on various factors such as: (i) Category of highway, width of pavement and road margins. (ii) Height of embankment and depth of cutting and the side slopes of those. (iii) Dimensions of side drainage system. (iv) For horizontal curves, there is a widening of pavement and consequently more strip of load is to be acquired. (v) Depending about spurt in the business that the highway is likely to bring, you have to reserve and acquire additional land in addition to above. The table below is indicative at right of way.

Table 5.9: Recommended Land with for Rural Roads

Sr. No	Type of Road	Plain & Rolling Terrain				Steep & mountain Terrain			
		Open area		Built-up area		Open area		Built-up area	
		Normal	Range	Normal	Range	Normal	Range	Normal	Range
1.	National & State Highway	45	30 – 60	30	30 – 60	24	No range specified	20	No range specified
2.	Major District Roads	25	25 – 30	20	15 – 25	18		15	
3.	Other District Roads	15	15 – 25	15	15 – 20	15		12	
4.	Village Roads	12	12 – 18	10	10 – 15	9		9	

The another concept that must be understood at this juncture is the concept regarding building lines and control lines for urban roads. After the land width acquired as right of way, there is building line and no building activity is allowed in between the building line and right of way line as shown in Fig. 5.4. It should be remembered that, though no building activity is allowed in this zone, another activity say even farming, gardening can be allowed. It should be remembered that this space is not owned by the Government or Corporation. It only disallows building activity here. Beyond the building line, there is control line. For the space between control line and building line, the Government exercises control on the type of building to be constructed. For Government may disallow permit bar for reasons of discipline. This space is also not owned by the Government. It exercises control on type of building. Table below indicates recommended standards as per I.R.C.

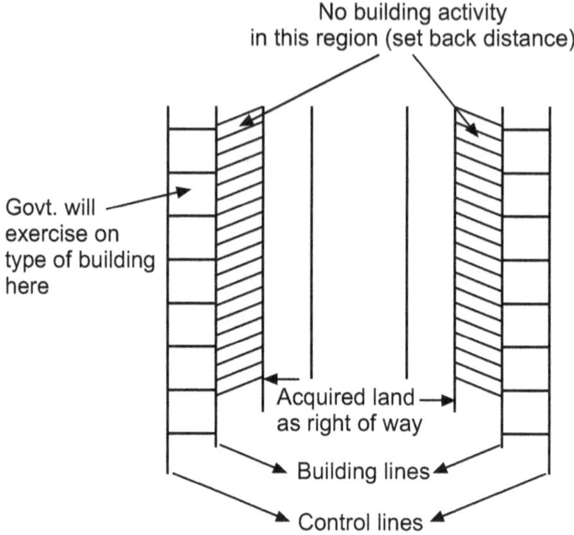

Fig. 5.4

Table 5.10: Recommended standards for building lines and control lines

Road Classification	Plain and Rolling Region			Steep & Hilly Region Distance between Building Line and Road Boundary (Set Back Distance) in m	
	Open Area		Built-up Area		
	Width between Building Lines (m)	Width between Control Lines (m)	Distance between Building Line and Road Boundary (Set Back)	Open Area	Built-up Area
NH & SH	80	150	3 to 6	3 to 5	3 to 5
M. D. R.	50	100	3 to 5	3 to 5	3 to 5
O. D. R.	25 – 30	35	3 to 5	3 to 5	3 to 5
V. R.	25	30	3 to 5	3 to 5	3 to 5

It should be remembered that the above table is indicative practice but certain variations are possible. For urban road, recommended land widths as right of way are 50 to 60 m for arterial roads, 30 - 40 m for sub-arterial roads, 20 to 30 m for collector streets and 10 to 20 m for local streets. Again this is no hard and fast rule because the problem is essentially of land cost and acquisition cost.

5.8 WIDTH OF PAVEMENT OR CARRIAGEWAY

The carriageway for one line of traffic movement is called the traffic lane and width of pavement in this traffic lane is essentially a function of vehicle width and clearances between traffic streams. If side clearance is more, the pavement can accommodate more traffic, that is it's capacity is increased. IRC says that maximum width of vehicle would be 2.50 metres. For this width, single and two lane pavement with requisite clearances is shown below in the figure. This pictorization is without consideration of kerbs or medians when no kerbs or traffic separators are provided. IRC recommendations in this respect are summarised below.

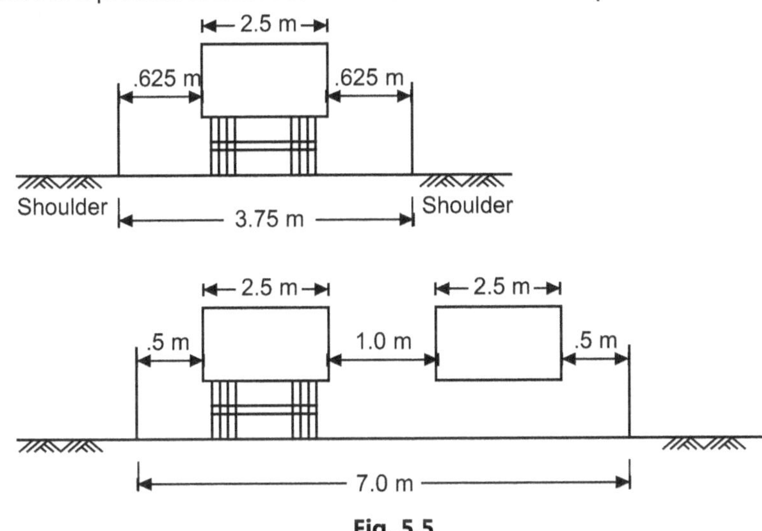

Fig. 5.5

Table 5.11: Width of carriageway

Class of Road	Width of Carriageway	Remarks
(1) Single lane	3.75 m	Single lane, village road could be 3.0 m
(2) Two lanes without raised Kerbs	7.0 m	Single lane urban roads without Kerbs
(3) Two lanes with raised Kerbs	7.5 m	could be 3.5 m and access roads could be 3.0 m
(4) Intermediate carriageway	5.5 m	Minimum width for kerbed urban road is
(5) Multilane pavement	3.5 m/lane	5.5 m

5.9 TRAFFIC SEPARATORS AND KERBS

Traffic separators and Kerbs are shown in Fig. 5.6. Traffic separators also called as medians are provided to prevent head on collision of opposing moving traffic. Their job is to (i) channelize the traffic; (ii) segregate slow traffic and protect the pedestrians. In emergency, pedestrian can at least seek refuse on medians; (iii) helping in turning the traffic. Traffic separators could have width of 8 to 15 m width. The I.R.C. recommends a minimum desirable width of 5.0 m for rural highways, which could be lessened to 3.0 m when land is costly, for urban roads. The minimum width of medians is 1.2 m and the desirable minimum width is 5.0 m for urban roads at intersection, the minimum width for pedestrian refuge is 1.2 m, 4.0 m and 7.5 m for protection of vehicles making right turn and 9.0 to 12.m for protection of vehicles crossing at grade. It should be remembered that the recommendations are not obligatory in nature, since it is largely a question of cost of acquisition of land. The job of the kerbs is to keep the vehicle in it's own stream, but the kerb allow the driver to enter shoulder area in times of difficulty with less bother.

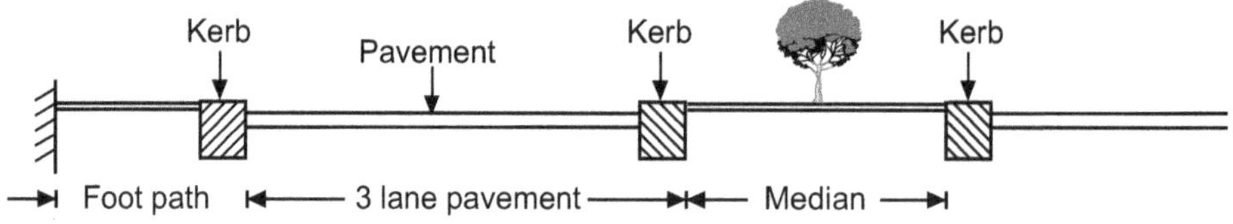

Fig. 5.6

Kerb can be:

(1) Low or mountable type: In this case, kerb is around 10 cm above the pavement edge with a batter for easy mounting of vehicles. Such kerbs are frequent for channelization of traffic scheme and useful for longitudinal drainage system.

(2) Semibarrier type: This type has a height of some 15 cm, above pavement edge with a batter of 1: 1 on top 7.5 cm. This kerb prevents encroachment of parking vehicles and are therefore good when pedestrian traffic is dense.

(3) Barrier type: Such kerb stone height is about 20 cm above pavement edge with a steep batter of 1.0 vertical to 0.25 horizontal. It protects pedestrian traffic and mounting of vehicles on shoulders is difficult.

5.10 ROAD MARGINS

Margins are traditionally provided in the right of way for specific purposes. For example, shoulders are provided along road edge so that, vehicles in times of emergency could use it. It is also a space provided as service lanes for vehicles that have broken down. The minimum width of shoulder as per I.R.C. is 2.5 m. Shoulders should have reserve bearing capacity to support truck load even in wet weather and the surface of the shoulder should be rough so that in general vehicles do not use it. Below is given the typical section with road margin.

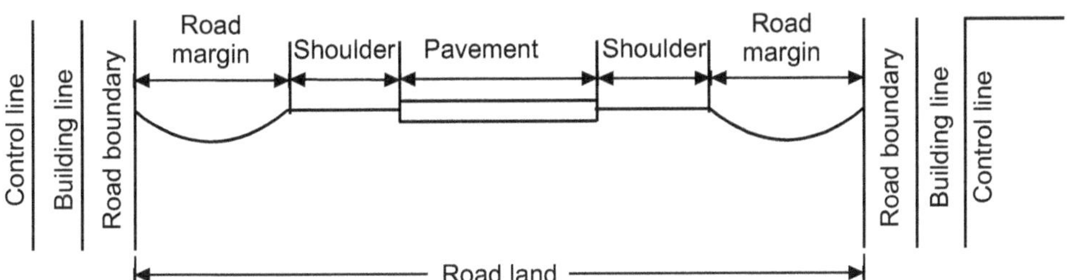

Fig. 5.7

Parking lanes: Whereas shoulders are to be provided for all roads, parking lanes are provided on urban roads for kerb parking. Parking should have width of 3.0 meter and should be marked.

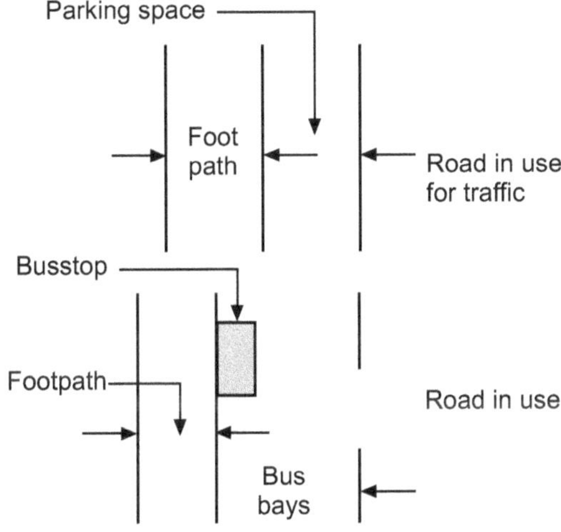

Fig. 5.8

Bus bays are provided to avoid conflict with moving traffic. It's positioning is shown in the figure. Foot-paths are spaces provided for pedestrians to walk whereas the width of foot path depends upon the pedestrian traffic. Slope given to the footpath should generally be 2 to 3 %. Fig. 5.9 shows the typical sections of divided highways on urban areas.

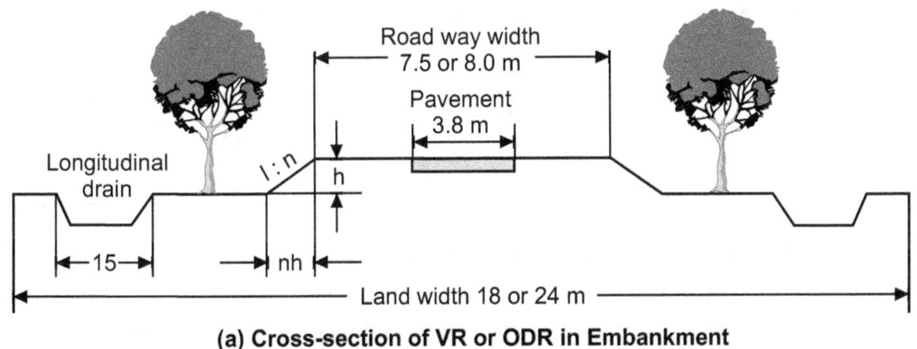

(a) Cross-section of VR or ODR in Embankment

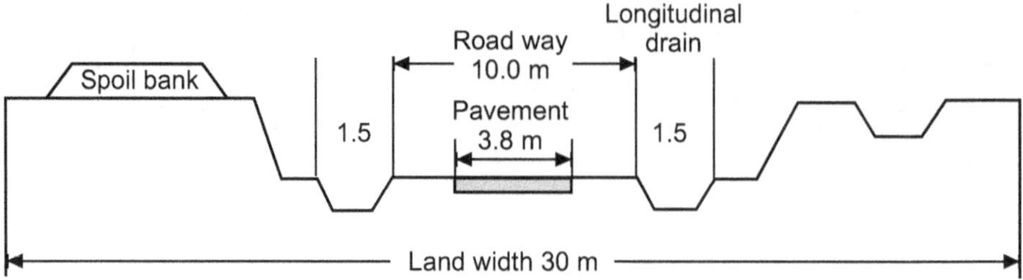

(b) Cross-section of Major district road in cutting

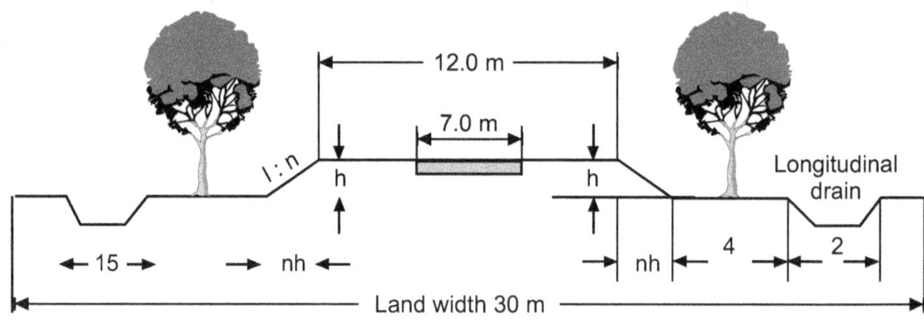

(c) Cross-section of National or S.H. in rural area

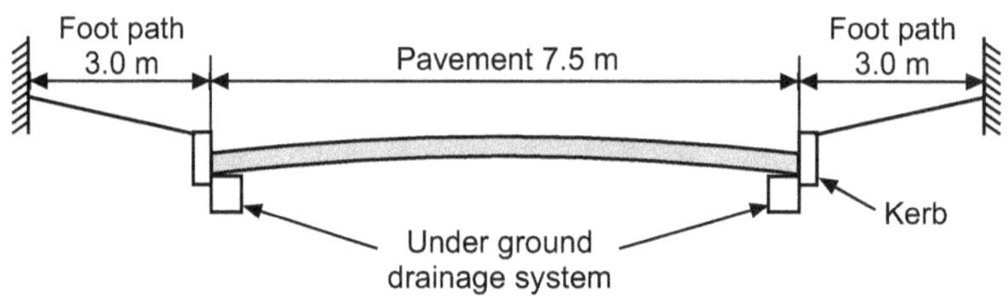

(d) Cross-section of two-line city road in built up area

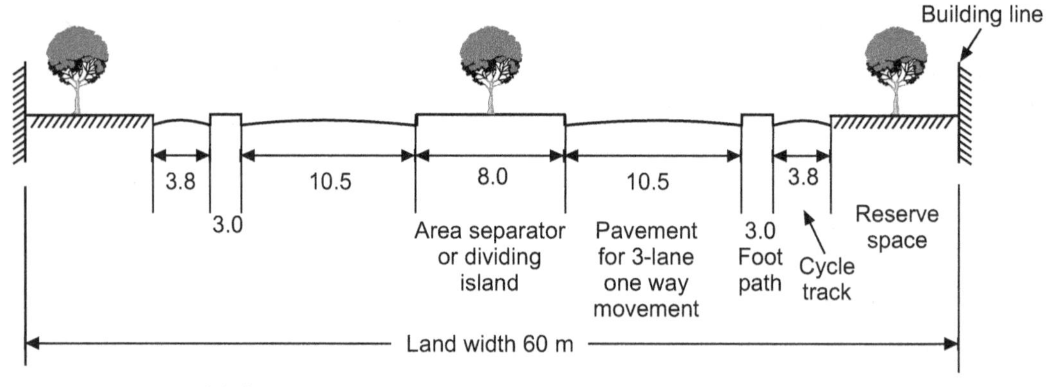

(e) Cross-section of divided Highway in Urban area

Fig. 5.9: Typical sections of divided highways on urban areas

5.11 CAPACITY OF THE ROADS

Capacity of highway has been defined as the safe number of vehicles that can be accommodated on a highway per hour per lane. Naturally, capacity would depend upon the type of vehicles plying on the roads. In the case of Indian Highways, where there is no segregation of traffic, capacity can not be that way determined. In case the road has only one kind of traffic,

Capacity of roads = C

$$C = \frac{1000\ V}{S}$$

where, V = Speed in kilometer per hour.

S = Average spacing in meters between successive moving vehicles called headway.

The headway distance can be determined by actual observations. It could be called as distance travelled by vehicle when the driver of the vehicle sees the on-going vehicle in stream, sees the danger, applies the brake and the distance travelled by the vehicle during braking and the length of vehicle itself. Therefore,

S = Length of vehicle + Distance travelled in perception brake reaction time

+ Braking distance

Perception and Brake Reaction Time: Perception brake reaction time could be split up as summation of reaction time of the driver and brake reaction time. Reaction time of the driver is the time taken from the instant the object is visible to the driver to the instant the brakes are effectively applied. Whereas the perception time depends upon the psychology of the driver, his mental and physical condition and environmental conditions such as the light on road etc. The brake reaction time would depend on the skill of driver and the condition of the vehicle. The total reaction time could be split up into four parts: *(i) Perception time:* Which is the time required to perceive the object. *(ii) Intellection time:* This is the time required by the brain to understand the situation. *(iii) Emotion time:* After understanding the situation, the brain takes certain time to overcome certain human inadequacies such as fear, anger etc. *(iv) Volution time:* The brain takes certain time to arrive at a decision and then gives command which is called as volution time. Therefore, the total reaction time is the summation of these four types of times, and perceiving the total reaction time in this manner is petly called PIEV Theory. In any case, the total reaction time of an average driver may vary from 0.5 seconds to as much as 3 to 4 seconds for complex situations. If V is the design speed in m/sec and 't' the total reaction time in seconds, then the distance travelled by the vehicle during reaction time, which is often called as lag distance, is Vt meters. If V is expressed in kilometer per hour, then the lag distance is V $\times$

$$\frac{1000}{60 \times 60}\ t = 0.278\ V\ t\ \text{metres}$$

Braking distance: Braking distance depends upon the fact whether the vehicle is plying a flat road or is ascending or descending. Let us suppose that the vehicle is plying ascending grade + n percentage. Then the component of gravity adds to the braking action and braking distance is decreased. In this case, component of gravity parallel to road is equal to $W \tan \alpha = \dfrac{Wn}{100}$ approximately, where n is percentage grade. If 'f' is the friction between road surface and vehicle and 'W' is the weight of vehicle, then 'fW' is the component of force due to the weight of vehicle parallel to road surface. Therefore, total force parallel to road surface is $\left(fW + \dfrac{Wn}{100} \right)$. If the braking distance is 'l', then work done is $\left(fW + \dfrac{Wn}{100} \right) \times l$. This should be equated to the kinetic energy of the vehicle during stopping. If 'V' is the speed, then corresponding kinetic energy is $\dfrac{1}{2} mV^2 = \dfrac{1}{2} \times \dfrac{W}{g} \times V^2$. Equating these,

$$\left(fW + \frac{Wn}{100} \right) \times l = \frac{1}{2} \frac{W}{g} \times V^2$$

$$\therefore \qquad l = \frac{V^2}{2 g \left(f + \dfrac{n}{100} \right)}$$

If 'V' is expressed in km/hr.

$$l = \frac{\left(\dfrac{V}{1000 \times 60 \times 60} \right)^2}{2 g \left(f + \dfrac{n}{100} \right)}$$

$$= \frac{V^2}{254 (f + 0.01\, n)}$$

Therefore,

Distance travelled during perception/ brake reaction time

$$= \frac{V^2}{254 (f + 0.01\, n)}$$

Therefore,

$$S = \text{Length of vehicle + Distance travelled in perception brake time + Braking distance.}$$

$$= L + 0.278\, Vt + \frac{V^2}{254 (f + 0.01\, n)} \quad \text{on ascending grade}$$

Obviously,

$$S = L + 0.278\, Vt + \frac{V^2}{254 (f - 0.01\, n)} \quad \text{on descending grade}$$

$$S = L + 0.278\, Vt + \frac{V^2}{254\, f} \quad \text{on flat grade}$$

and

$$C = \frac{1000\ V}{S}$$

The fraction $0.278\ Vt + \dfrac{V^2}{254\ (f \pm 0.01n)}$ is actually the stopping sight distance. Therefore, one can say that

$\quad$ S $\quad$ = L + stopping sight distance in metres

This stopping sight distance which is the distance travelled during perception/brake reaction time theoretically is actually the stopping sight distance. The minimum stopping distance provided on curves, bends on roads is double this distance. The standards recommended by I.R.C. in this connection are as follows:

When there are two distant lanes one need not multiply by two, but when there is only one lane and two way traffic, multiplying by constant of two is essential. Many times the stopping sight distance is called as head light sight distance.

Table 5.12: Stopping Sight Distance

Design Speed, km/hr	20	25	30	40	50	60	65	80	100
Safe Stopping Sight Distance, m.	20	25	30	45	60	80	90	120	180

5.12 CONCEPT OF CAPACITY LEVEL OF SERVICE AND DESIGN VOLUME

The capacity of pavement essentially depends upon the speed. The ideal speed volume relationship is parabola having maximum volume at a value of speed equal to half the speed at free flow conditions (free speed). See the following figure.

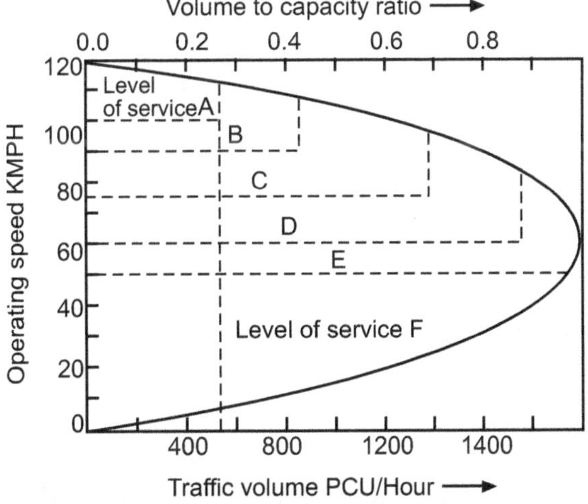

Fig. 5.10: General concept of level of service

The American Highway Capacity manual recognises six levels of service A, B, C, D, E, F as shown in Fig. 5.10. For example, the level of service 'A' means that the volume of traffic to capacity of road is so low that majority of individual vehicles can travel at their design speed and can overtake the slower vehicles at their will. With increase in the volume, the operating speeds of faster vehicles and their opportunities to overtake slower vehicles decrease. In other words, the level of the service, which the highway is giving is decreasing. The Indian practice is to consider level of service B desirable for rural highways. At this level, the volume of traffic will be around 0.5 times the maximum capacity. This could be taken as the design service volume for purpose of determining road width in the design year. The design service volumes recommended by IRC for roads with various pavement widths in plain terrain are given in the table below.

The IRC guidelines give the design service volume for the design year. Thus, if a road is to be constructed, the design year traffic can be estimated knowing the present traffic and traffic growth rate. If the projected traffic is below the designed service volume, the pavement width provided is adequate. If not, higher pavement width is required. These guidelines can be used for determining the road section which have already reached the design service volume and need widening.

Table 5.13: Suggested Design Service Volumes for Rural Highways in Plain Terrain as per IRC

Pavement Type	Pavement Definition	Design Service Volume PCU / Day
Single lane	Narrowest pavement. Traffics in both directions. Width 3 to 3.75 m. Low volume traffic and less overtaking instances. To improve matters paved shoulders 0.75 - 1.0 m on either side could be provided.	1900 – 2000 pcu/day
Intermediate lane	Via media between single lane and two lane pavement 5 - 6 m width. To improve the function paved shoulders 0.75 - 1 m width can be provided. Not favoured on National Highway. In India, it is a common widening option from single lane.	5800 – 6000
Two lanes with earth shoulders	One lane of 7 m for each direction. Even our National Highways carrying 1/3 National traffic do not have this.	12500 – 15000
Two lanes with paved shoulder	Rare. Only urban roads.	14500 – 17250

Shortcomings of this Method:

The limitations of the design service volume concept arise from the fact that it is based on an acceptable level of service with attendant speed and overtaking possibilities and not on any economic criteria such as losses suffered due to higher vehicle operating costs on narrow roads. The design service volume concept cannot provide basis for justifying investments on widening the pavements when costs are weighed against the benefits from widening. One such study conducted by Kadiyali shows (1994) that when you consider these parameters, widening is generally justified at values slightly lower than given by IRC guidelines. This study conducted on the basis of 1994 costs and certain other inputs such as cost of vehicles, cost of tyres, cost of petrol, grease etc. has to be modified on year to year basis but could be used as data base for the next 7 years or so. One of the side advantage of this study is the evolution of equation for determining Internal Rate of return (percentage) that can result from widening options. These equations are summarised in the table below.

Table 5.14

Sr. No.	Widening Option	Equation
1.	Widening single lane to intermediate lane	I. R. R. $= -1.97 - 0.32\,C + 0.014\,pcu + 0.116\,(pcu/C)$
2.	Widening single lane to two lanes	I. R. R. $= 5.42 - 0.167\,C + 0.0094\,pcu + 0.208\,(pcu/C)$
3.	Widening Intermediate lane to two lanes	I. R. R. $= -2.15 - 0.117\,C + 133.98/C + 0.00648\,pcu + 0.08\,pcu/C$
4.	Widening two lanes to four lanes	I. R. R. $= -4.08 - 0.04\,C + 0.0025\,pcu - 3.93 \times 10^{-8}\,(pcu)^2 + 0.093\,(pcu/C)$

Where, C = cost of widening in lakhs/km.

5.13 OVERTAKING SIGHT DISTANCE

The road pavement is occupied by slow and fast moving vehicle. It should be possible for fast moving vehicle to overtake the slow moving vehicle. The overtaking distance is therefore the distance which should be available to overtake another vehicle safely and comfortably without interfering the speed of incoming vehicle travelling at the design speed should it come into view after the overtaking manoeuvre is started. Overtaking sight distance can, of course theoretically calculated by making certain assumptions. In the opinion of the author, places should be provided as a bypass in the road architecture where overtaking should be allowed as shown in the adjoining figure. Overtaking is a problem when speed of vehicles plying the road is not very much. Generally, it is easy to overtake a very slow moving vehicle. Indian Roads Congress has recommended certain safe overtaking sight distances as below –

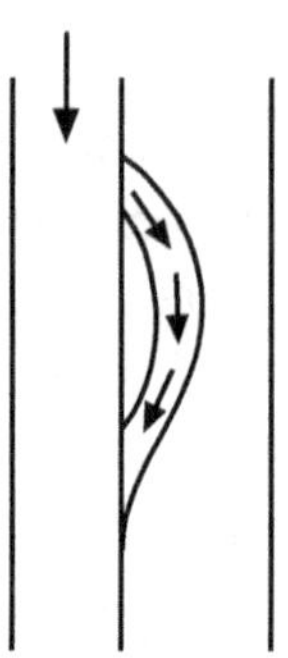

Fig. 5.11

Table 5.15: Overtaking sight distance

Speed, km/hr	Safe Overtaking Sight Distance (Metres)
40	165
50	235
60	300
65	340
80	470
100	640

Sometimes instead of bypass as shown above, road pavement is widened where overtaking is permitted. See the adjoining figure. This is called as overtaking zone.

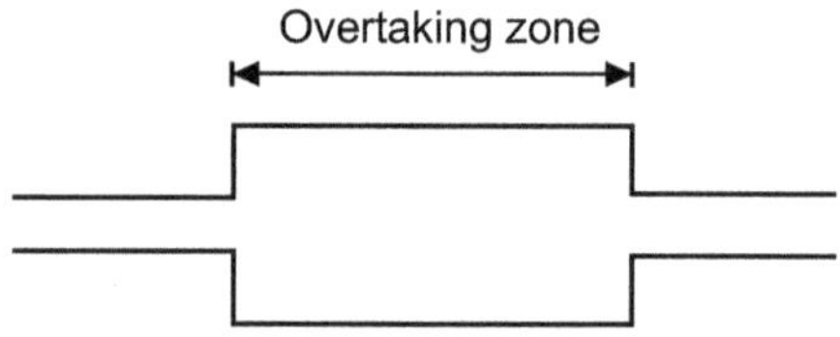

Fig. 5.12

Some of the important factors on which the minimum overtaking sight distance depends, are

- speeds of the overtaking, overtaken and the vehicle coming from opposite direction.
- spacing between vehicles.
- skill and reaction time of the driver.
- rate of acceleration of overtaking vehicle.
- slope of the road.

Analysis of Overtaking Sight Distance:

Fig. 5.13 shows the overtaking manoeuvre of vehicle A travelling at design speed, and another slow vehicle B on a two-lane road. Third vehicle C comes from the opposite direction. The overtaking manoeuvre may be split-up into three operations, thus dividing the overtaking sight distance into three parts d_1, d_2 and d_3.

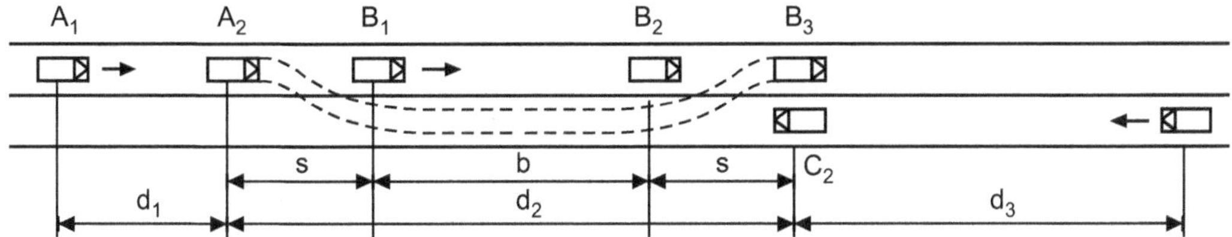

Fig. 5.13: Overtaking manoeuvre

- d_1 is the distance travelled by overtaking vehicle A during the reaction time from position A_1 to A_2.
- d_2 is the distance travelled by the vehicle A from A_2 to A_3 during the actual overtaking operation.
- d_3 is the distance travelled by on-coming vehicle C from C_1 to C_2 during the overtaking operation of A.

Certain assumptions are made in order to calculate the values of d_1, d_2 and d_3. In Fig. 5.13, A is the overtaking vehicle originally travelling at design speed v m/sec or V kmph; B is the overtaken or slow moving vehicle moving with uniform speed or v_b m/sec or V_b kmph; C is a vehicle coming from opposite direction at the design speed v m/sec or V kmph. In a two-lane road, the opportunity to overtake depends on the frequency of vehicles from the opposite direction and the overtaking sight distance available at any instant.

(i) It may be assumed that the vehicle A is forced to reduce its speed to the speed of the slow vehicle B and moves behind it during the reaction time, till there is an opportunity for safe overtaking operation. The distance travelled by the vehicle A during this reaction time is d_1 and is between the positions A_1 and A_2. This distance will be equal to $v_b \times t$ metre, where, 't' is the reaction time of the driver in seconds. This reaction time 't' of the drivers may be taken as 2 seconds as an average value, as the aim of the driver is only to find an opportunity to overtake. Thus,

$$d_1 = v_b t = 2 v_b \text{ metres.}$$

(ii) From position A_2, the vehicle A starts accelerating, shifts to the adjoining lane, overtakes the vehicle B, and shifts back to its original lane ahead of B in position A_3. The straight distance between positions A_2 and A_3 is taken as d_2. The minimum distance between positions A_2 and B_1 may be taken as the minimum spacing 's' of the two vehicles while moving with the speed v_b m/sec. The spacing between vehicles depends on their speed and is given by empirical formula:

$$s = (0.7 v_b + 6) \text{ metres.}$$

The minimum distance between B_3 and A_2 may also be assumed equal to s as mentioned above. Let the time taken by vehicle A for the overtaking operation from position A_2 to A_3 be

T seconds. Then the distance covered by the slow vehicle B travelling at a speed of v_b m/sec in time T sec.

$$= b = v_b\, T \text{ metres}$$

Thus, the distance $d_2 = (b + 2s)$ metres.

Now, the time T depends on speed of overtaken vehicle B and the acceleration of overtaking vehicle A. This time T may be calculated by equating the distance d_2 to $\left(v_b\, T + \dfrac{1}{2}\, a\, T^2\right)$, using the general formula for the distance travelled by an uniformly accelerating body with initial speed v_b m/sec and 'a' is the acceleration in m/sec^2.

$$d_2 \;=\; (b + 2s) \;=\; \left(v_b\, T + \frac{aT^2}{2}\right)$$

Hence, $\qquad b \;=\; v_b,\ T$, and therefore $2s = \dfrac{aT^2}{2}$

Therefore, $\qquad T \;=\; \sqrt{\dfrac{4s}{a}}$ secs, where, $s = (0.7\, v_b + 6)$

Hence, $\qquad d_2 \;=\; (v_b \cdot T + 2s)$ metres

(iii) The distance travelled by vehicle C moving at design speed v m/sec during the overtaking operation of vehicle A i.e., during time T is the distance d_3 between positions C_1 to C_2.

Hence, $\qquad d_3 \;=\; v \times T$

Thus, the overtaking sight distance,

$$OSD \;=\; (d_1 + d_2 + d_3)$$
$$\;=\; (v_b\, t + v_b\, T + 2s + vT)$$

In kmph units, above equation works out as:

$$OSD \;=\; 0.28\, V_b t + 0.28\, V_b T + 2s + 0.28V\, T$$

Here, $\qquad V_b$ = speed of overtaken vehicle, kmph

$\qquad t$ = reaction time of driver = 2 secs

$\qquad V$ = speed of overtaking vehicle or design speed, kmph

$$T \;=\; \sqrt{\frac{4 \times 3.6s}{A}} \;=\; \sqrt{\frac{14.4s}{A}}$$

$\qquad s$ = spacing of vehicles = $(0.2\, V_b + 6)$

$\qquad A$ = acceleration, kmph/sec.

In case the speed of overtaken vehicle V_b is not given, the same may be assumed as $(V - 16)$ kmph, where V is the design speed in kmph or $v_b = (v - 4.5)$ m/sec and v is the design speed in m/sec.

The acceleration of the overtaking vehicle is to be specified. Usually this depends on the make of the vehicle, load and the speed. As a general guide, Table 5.16 may be used for finding the maximum acceleration of vehicles at different speeds. The average rate of acceleration during overtaking manoeuvre may be taken corresponding to the design speed.

Table 5.16: Maximum Overtaking Acceleration at Different Speeds

Speed		Maximum Overtaking Acceleration	
V kmph	v m/sec	A kmph/sec	a m/sec^3
25	6.93	5.00	1.41
30	8.34	4.80	1.30
40	11.10	4.45	1.24
50	13.86	4.00	1.11
65	18.00	3.28	0.92
80	22.20	2.56	0.72
100	27.80	1.92	0.53

At overtaking sections, the minimum overtaking distance should be ($d_1 + d_2 + d_3$) when two-way traffic exists. On divided highway, the overtaking distance need be only ($d_1 + d_2$) as in one-way movement and no vehicle is expected from the opposite direction. On divided highways with four or more lanes, IRC suggests that it is not necessary to provide the usual OSD; however the sight distance in such highways should be more than the SSD.

Effect of Grade in Overtaking Sight Distance:

Appreciable grades in the road, both the descending as well as ascending, increase the sight distance required for safe overtaking. In down grades though it is easier for the overtaking vehicles to accelerate and pass, the overtaking vehicle may also accelerate and cover a greater distance 'b' during the overtaking time.

On up grades, the acceleration of the overtaking vehicle will be less and hence passing will be difficult; but the overtaken vehicle like heavily loaded trucks may also decelerate in steep ascends and compensate to some extent the passing sight distance requirement. Therefore the OSD at both ascending and descending grades are taken as equal to that at level stretch. However, at grades the overtaking sight distance should be greater than the minimum overtaking distance required at level.

The IRC has specified the safe values of overtaking sight distance required for various design speeds between 40 and 100 kmph. These values have been suggested based on the observation that 9 to 14 seconds are required by the overtaking vehicle for the actual overtaking manoeuvre depending on the design speed. This overtaking time may be increased by about two-thirds to take into account the distance covered by the vehicle from the opposing direction in the case of two-way traffic road, during the overtaking operation.

Sight Distance at Intersection:

Another important part of Highway Geometrics is sight distance that should be provided at intersection. Clear view should be available across the corners so as to avoid collision and properties should not be constructed in the sight triangle as shown in the adjoining figure. This is all the more important at unmanned intersections. The sight distance and the sides at sight triangle can again be theoretically calculated. The parameters that are taken into account for this purpose are reaction time for the driver, design speed, widths of road etc. However, I.R.C. has recommended a minimum visibility distance of 15 m along minor road and a distance of 220 meters, 180, 145 and 110 meters along the major road for corresponding design speeds of 100, 85, 65 and 50 km/hr.

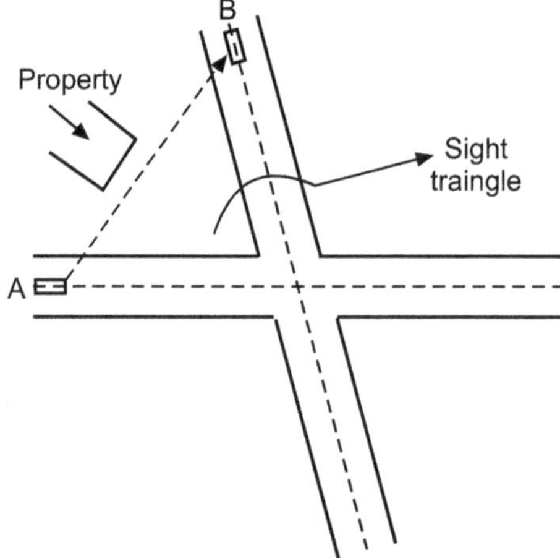

Fig. 5.14

5.14 HORIZONTAL ALIGNMENT

When there is a change of alignment as shown in Fig. 5.15, curves have to be introduced. When such curves are introduced, one shoulder of the pavement is to be raised as compared to the other shoulder. This is called as super-elevation. This is one part. The another part is that the curve cannot start at B'. Some sort of soothing curve has to be given at B' say FB' for the comfort of passengers. This curve is called as transition curve. We shall discuss these aspects now.

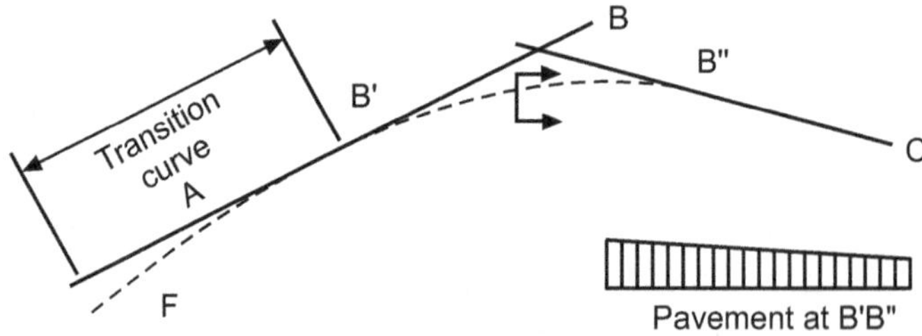

Fig. 5.15

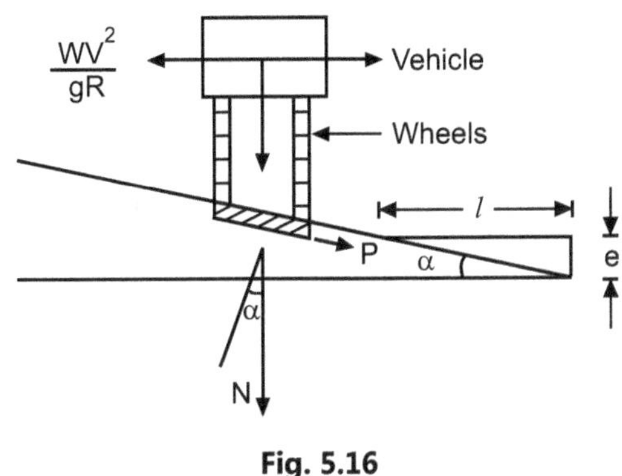

Fig. 5.16

Let,

w	=	Weight of vehicle
V	=	It's speed in m/sec
R	=	Radius of curve
γ	=	Side friction
N	=	Normal force
μ	=	Coefficient of lateral friction
e	=	Super-elevation expressed as 1 in e
α	=	Angle of super-elevation

When the vehicle is negotiating a curve, it experiences a centrifugal force. In order that vehicle body remains perpendicular to the road pavement for the passenger comfort, we have to raise one shoulder. Let that angle be α. For conditions of equilibrium,

$$\frac{W}{g}\frac{V^2}{R}\cos\alpha = W\sin\alpha + P$$

$$= W\sin\alpha + N\mu$$

But,

$$N = P = W\cos\alpha + \frac{W}{g}\frac{V^2}{R}\sin\alpha$$

Therefore,

$$\frac{W}{g}\frac{V^2}{R}\cos\alpha = W\sin\alpha + \mu\left(W\cos\alpha + \frac{W}{g}\frac{V^2}{R}\sin\alpha\right)$$

$$\frac{V^2}{gR} = \tan\alpha + \mu + \frac{\mu V^2}{gR}\tan\alpha$$

$\dfrac{V^2}{gR} \times \tan\alpha$ being very small, is neglected and

$$\frac{V^2}{gR} = \tan\alpha + \mu$$

If V is in km/hr, we have

$$\frac{V^2}{127\,R} = \tan\alpha + \mu$$

This is the basic equation which relates the speed of vehicle, radius of the curve, the super-elevation and coefficient of lateral friction. The value of coefficient of lateral friction depends upon many factors, the condition of tyres, the condition of the road, even wind etc. I.R.C. has recommended a uniform value of μ to be 0.15. Though super-elevation is a necessary evil, it is not asthetic. I.R.C. has therefore recommended certain maximum values of super-elevation that could be given. Super-elevation expressed as 1 in e is limited to 0.07 for hill roads when the area is snow bound. If the hill road area is not snow bound, one can adopt e = 0.1. In general, a value of 0.07 is considered maximum.

Minimum radii for curves

Since, $R = \dfrac{V^2}{127\,(e + \mu)}$ and maximum value of e is fixed, we get the minimum radii for curves as follows:

$R = 0.0357\ V^2$ for plain and rolling terrain.

$R = 0.0315\ V^2$ for hill roads that are snow bound.

$R = 0.0357\ V^2$ for hill roads which are not snow bound.

In the above formula, V is design speed. But the current IRC gives two values of design speed (i.e. ruling and minimum). The above formulae would yield two values for radius, the ruling radius and the absolute minimum radius. One can of course calculate these values knowing V. Alternatively, recourse could be made to the table where these values have been tabulated by I.R.C. See Table 5.17.

The idea behind giving super-elevation is to counterpart of the centrifugal force, the remaining part being resisted by lateral friction. It also lessens skiding and unequal pressure on tyres. But super-elevation can be provided so that complete centrifugal force is catered for (In this case, μ is considered zero) or it can be provided to cater fixed proportion of centrifugal force. If we design that super-elevation is to take all the centrifugal force, it would result in sharp curves and high super-elevation (i.e. more than 1 in 15 also). But IRC has limited the values of super-elevation to 0.07 and 0.1. Therefore in that case, friction (i.e. lateral friction) would be called into play for very sharp curves. On the other hand, when the vehicle is negotiating a flat curve, friction would not be developed to the maximum. As a compromise, super-elevation should be such that moderate amount of friction should be developed in the case, of flat curves, but when negotiating sharp curves, very large friction should not be developed, since that is also not good for passenger comfort. This balance is struck by IRC by stating that super-elevation be calculated on the assumption that it should counteract the centrifugal force developed at three fourth the design speed. That is $e = \dfrac{(0.75\ V)^2}{127\ R} = \dfrac{V^2}{225\ R}$. This super-elevation is now restricted to 0.07 and 0.1 as per IRC.

Radii for Which no Super-Elevation Required:

The normal cambered section of the highway can be continued on the curve, where super-elevation calculated is less than the camber $e = \dfrac{V^2}{225\ R}$ i.e. $R = \dfrac{V^2}{225\ e}$.

If in this equation, e is substituted by allowed camber, we get the minimum radius beyond which no super-elevation is required. Though calculation may prove this point, IRC has prepared a table for the guidance of highway engineers. However, where the radii is more than the one given in the table, it would be desirable to remove the adverse crown in the outer half of the carriage way and super-elevate at the normal crown slope.

Table 5.17 : Minimum Radii of horizontal curve

Classification of Road	Plain Terrain		Rolling Terrain		Mountains Terrain				Steep Terrain			
					Areas not affected by snow		Snow bound area		Areas not affected by snow		Snow bound area	
	Ruling Min.	Abs. Min.	Ruling Min.	Abs. Min.	Ruling Min.	Abs. Min.	Ruling Min.	Abs. Min.	Ruling Min.	Abs. Min.	Ruling Min.	Abs. Min.
1. National Highways and State highways	360	230	230	155	80	50	90	60	50	30	60	33
2. Major District Roads	230	155	105	90	50	30	60	33	30	14	33	16
3. Other District Roads	155	90	98	60	30	20	23	23	20	14	23	15
4. Village Roads	90	60	60	45	20	14	23	15	20	14	23	15

Table 5.18: Radii Beyond Which Super-Elevation is Not Essential for Different Cambers and Speeds (Indian Practice)

Design speed	Radius in Metres beyond Which No Super-Elevation is Required for Values of Camber				
km/hr	4 %	3 %	2.5 %	2 %	1.7 %
20	50	60	70	90	100
25	70	90	110	140	150
30	100	130	160	200	240
35	140	180	220	270	320
40	180	240	280	350	420
50	280	370	450	550	650
65	470	620	750	950	1100
80	700	960	1100	1400	1700
100	1100	1500	1800	2200	2600

Methods of Attaining Super-Elevation: Fig. 5.17 indicates the ways in which super-elevation can be attained. The figures are self explanatory.

- First stage attaining super-elevation by super-elevation equal to camber.
- The surface of the road is rotated about the inner edge, raising the centre and the outer edge.
- The surface of the road is rotated about the outer edge depressing the centre and the inner edge.

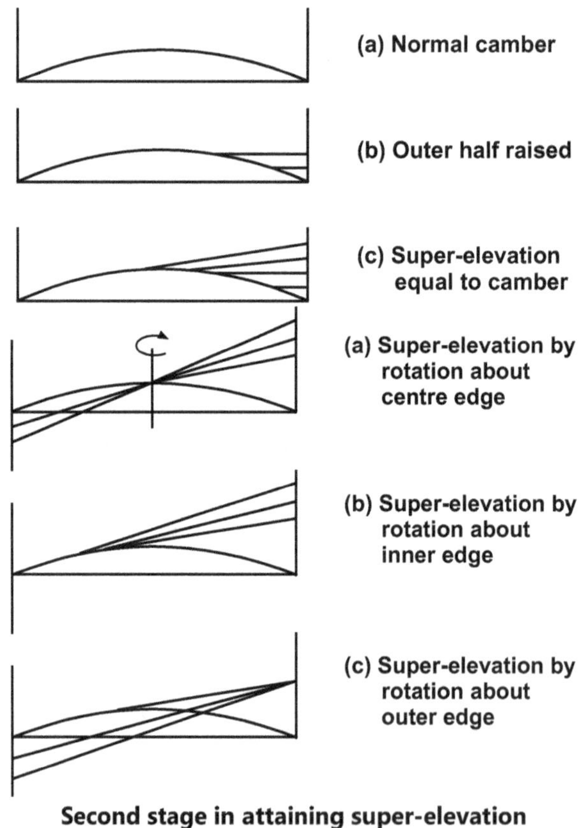

Second stage in attaining super-elevation

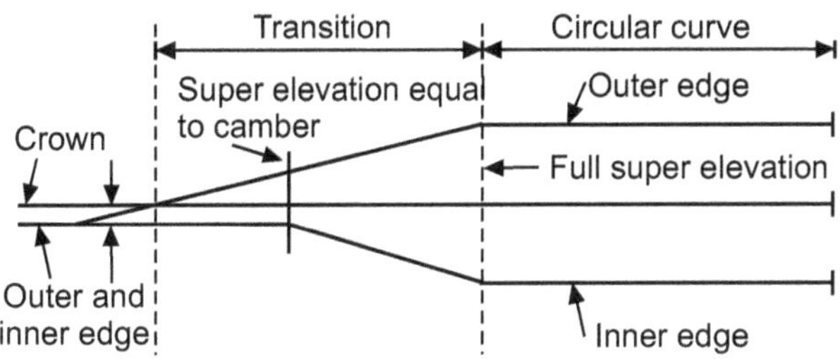

Attaining super-elevation by revolving about the centre line

Fig. 5.17

5.15 TRANSITION CURVES

If a curve is given to a straight road, the vehicle is subjected to sudden centrifugal force causing discomfort to the passengers. This can be avoided by giving a curve such that its radius, where it meets straight section, is infinity and where it meets the designated circular curve, its radius is that of the circular curve. Such a curve is known as **transition curve**. It's function is

- gradual application of centrifugal force,
- gradual application of super-elevation, and
- to ease the driving stress and cause comfort to the passengers.

The curve that could satisfy all such criteria, is ideal transition curve. One curve will not satisfy all the criteria. Many such transition curves are in vogue the most commonly used being spiral. As highway engineers we have already studied how to set out spiral in "Survey", we are only interested as highway engineers as how should we determine the length of this spiral. The length of transition curve is determined from two considerations.

(i) Rate of change of acceleration in negotiating a transition should be tolerable.

Let R be the radius of circular curve and V design speed. Then centrifugal acceleration encountered is $\dfrac{V^2}{R}$ as maximum. If L_s is the length of transition curve, then to transverse this transition curve, the time taken by vehicle is $\dfrac{L_s}{V}$, and rate of change of acceleration

$$= \frac{\text{Acceleration}}{\text{Time for this acceleration to take place}}$$

$$C = \frac{V^2}{R} \div \frac{L_s}{V} = \frac{V^3}{RL}$$

The comfortable rate of change of acceleration is $\dfrac{80}{75 + V}$ (subject to a maximum of 0.8 and minimum of 0.5) as per IRC.

Therefore length of transition curve is determined by

$$C = \frac{80}{75 + V} = \frac{V^3}{RL}$$

where, V is m/sec, R and L in metres. If V is in km/hr and R and L are in meters then

$$L = \frac{0.0215 \, V^3}{CR}$$

(ii) As the transition curve progresses, there is change in super-elevation. At point where it meets straight, super-elevation is zero and where it meets the circular curve, the super-elevation has the designated value. This rate of change of super-elevation should not cause higher gradient and unsightly appearance. Recommendations are 1 in 150 for roads in plain and rolling terrain and 1 in 60 for hilly terrain. Depending upon the way, the super-elevation is given (rotation about centre line, inner edge, outer edge) length of transition will alter. Widening of pavement at curves should be taken into account for calculation of length of transition. Higher of the values given by the above two methods should be adopted.

Widening on Curves:

Curves are a necessary part of horizontal alignment and whenever, there is a curve laid out, the pavement has to be widened at that location. This is necessary since, (1) On curves vehicles are likely to occupy greater width. This is because rear wheels track inside the front wheel. (2) On curves, it becomes difficult for the drivers, psychologically to keep to the centreline of the lane. (3) Similarly, the driver has psychological inhibition to drive close to the edge of the pavement.

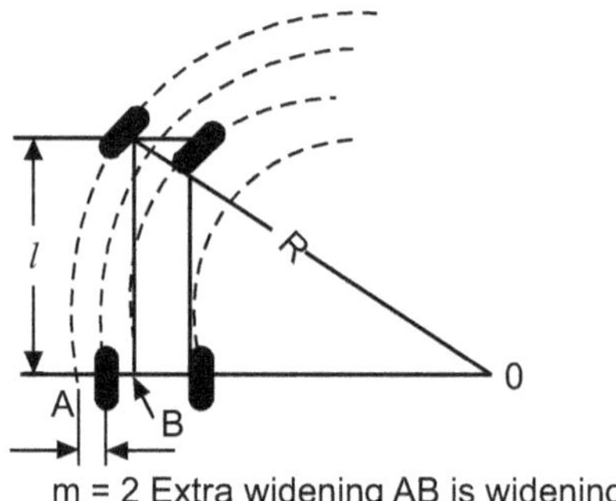

Fig. 5.18: Widening on curves

From Fig. 5.18, and by simple geometry, we have

$$l^2 = AB \times (2 \, AO - AB) = 2 \, Rm - m^2.$$

Widening required being small, we may neglect, square of it. In that case,

$$m = \frac{l^2}{2 \, R}$$

Most of the times, the wheel base is 6 metres and m = $\dfrac{18}{R}$ metres, if R is in metres.

If there are n lanes, then total widening = nm = $\dfrac{n l^2}{2\,R}$.

In addition to this widening, which is required because of vehicle geometry, we have to provide widening to cater for the psychology of the driver. This widening to cater for the psychology of the driver is $0.1\,\dfrac{V}{\sqrt{R}}$, where, V is speed in kilometer/hr and R is radius in metres.

Therefore, total widening = $n\,\dfrac{l^2}{2\,R} + 0.1\,\dfrac{V}{\sqrt{R}}$

Total widening for pavements where width is excess of 2 lanes is total widening

$$= n\,\dfrac{18}{R} + 0.1\,\dfrac{18}{\sqrt{R}}\;.$$

For single and two lane pavement, the widening that is recommended is given below.

Table 5.19: Widening of single lane and two lane pavement

Radius in metres	upto 20	21 to 40	41 to 60	61 to 100	101 to 300	Above 300
Extra width:						
Two lane	1.5	1.5	1.2	0.9	0.6	Nil
Single lane	0.9	0.6	0.6	Nil	Nil	Nil

As expected, when the curve becomes flatter, i.e. when it's radius is large, less and less widening is required.

5.16 GENERAL PRINCIPLES OF HORIZONTAL ALIGNMENT

We can now sum-up general principles of horizontal alignment involving curves. These are:

- Alignment should confirm topography and natural contours.
- It should be our attempt to limit the number of curves especially abrupt cuts. Short curves should be avoided. These locations are invitations to the accidents.
- Large radius curves should be preferred even when costly. For a deflection angle of 5°, curve radius should be minimum 150 metre and for every degree increase in deflection angle, curve radius may be increased by at least 30 metres.
- For high hills, sharp curves be avoided. If there are no shrubs and trees at the roadway perimeter, drivers find it difficult to estimate the extent of curvature. These should be planted.
- Curves in same direction but separated by short tangents called broken back curves should be avoided. These are not good asthetically.

- It is recommended that abrupt reversal in curvature be avoided. On hilly terrain, this is impossible. In that case long transitional curves should be inserted for super-elevation run-off.

- When single circular curve cannot be fit in, we may use compound curve as an exceptional measure. When such two curves are employed, the radius of the flater curve should not be disproportional to the radius of sharper curve. A ratio of 2:1 or preferably 1.5:1 may be adopted.

5.17 VERTICAL ALIGNMENT

Gradient is an important part of vertical alignment. Grade affects the speed of the vehicle and capacity of roads. In Indian context, where there is no segregation of traffic, the problem is more severe. Once the vertical profile is given, up-gradation is difficult since it will involve considerable investment. Therefore grade should be so selected so as to have uniform operation of most of the traffic. Table 5.20 gives Indian practice for maximum gradient.

Table 5.20: Grades for different terrains

Sr. No.	Terrain	Ruling Gradient %	Limiting Gradient %	Exceptional Gradient %
1.	Plain	3.3 (1 in 30)	5 (1 in 20)	6.7 (1 in 15) For short distance not exceeding 100 m
2.	Rolling	3.3 (1 in 30)	4 (1 in 20)	6.7 (1 in 15) For short distance not exceeding 100 m
3.	Mountainous	5 (1 in 20)	6 (1 in 16.7)	7 (1 in 14.3) For a distance not more than 100 m at stretch
4.	Steep (a) Upto 3000 m above m.s.l.	5 (1 in 20)	6 (1 in 16.7)	7 (1 in 14.3) For a distance not more than 100 m
	(b) Above 3000 m (m.s.l.)	6 (1 in 16.7)	7 (1 in 14.3)	8 (1 in 12.5) For a distance not more than 100 m

To use this table, ruling gradient could be used as a matter of routine in the design. Limiting gradient is a gradient where the topography compels it to use it. That is, if one uses gentle gradient, heavy costs are involved, whereas the exceptional gradients are for exceptional circumstances. Even where these are used, these gradients should be separated by a minimum length of 100 meters of gentle gradient which may be even limiting gradient. When one uses exceptional gradients, rise in elevation over a length of 2 km should not exceed 100 metre for mountainous terrain and 120 metres in steep terrain.

Minimum gradient for Drainage:

Drainage of the pavement is affected by camber and longitudinal slope. We have noted that even in flat terrain, same longitudinal slope is necessary.

Grade Compensation in Curves:

For horizontal curves on hill roads, the vehicle has to exert extra effort to negotiate the curve. In order to mitigate the suffering of the vehicle, it is usual to reduce the longitudinal gradient. This is known as **grade compensation**. Grade compensation in percentage is $\dfrac{30 + R}{R}$. Subject to a maximum of $\dfrac{75}{R}$, where R is the radius of the curve in metres.

Vertical Curves:

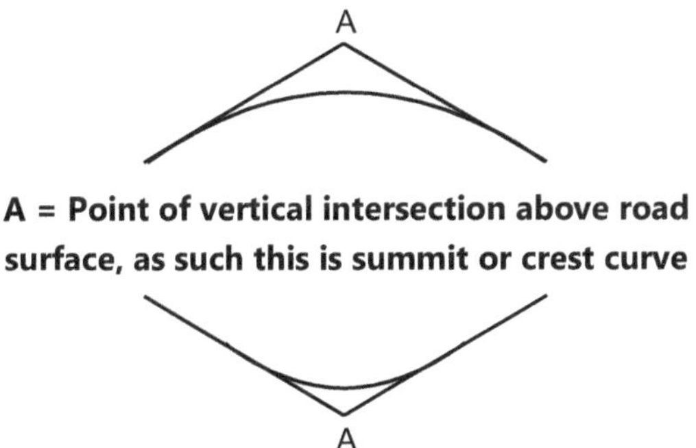

A = Point of vertical intersection above road surface, as such this is summit or crest curve

A = Point of intersection below road surface, as such this is sag curve

Fig. 5.19

Where there is change of grade, vertical curve is provided to see that change is not sudden. It can serve many purposes such as (1) The driver of the vehicle will undergo change of grade without discomfort, (2) For stopping and overtaking, visibility is assured and (3) humps and troughs are avoided. These curves are shown in the figure. If the total change of gradient does not exceed 0.5 %, one need not provide vertical curves. Road engineers have preferred parabola to be a preferred vertical curve. Though, when grade change is small, vertical curve, could be dispensed with, it is also a function of speed. That is for speedy vehicle you do require some curve. The minimum length of such vertical curves is given in Table 5.21.

Table 5.21: Minimum length of vertical curves (sag or summit)

Design Speed, km/hr.	Maximum Grade Change (Percentage) Not Requiring a Vertical Curve	Minimum Length of Vertical Curve (Meters)
upto 35	1.5	15
40	1.2	20
50	1.0	30
65	0.8	40
80	0.6	50
100	0.5	60

Length of vertical apex curve when sight distance 'S' is less than the length of curve 'L'.

To demonstrate this distance, assume h_1 and h_2 to be the height of drivers eye above the curve and height of object on the curve. Let S_1, S_2 be the horizontal distance between the driver and apex of the curve and S_2 be the horizontal distance between the object and the apex. Clearly $(S_1 + S_2)$ is 'S' the stopping sight distance. Let the grades $+ N_1$ and $- N_2$ intersect at point 'O'.

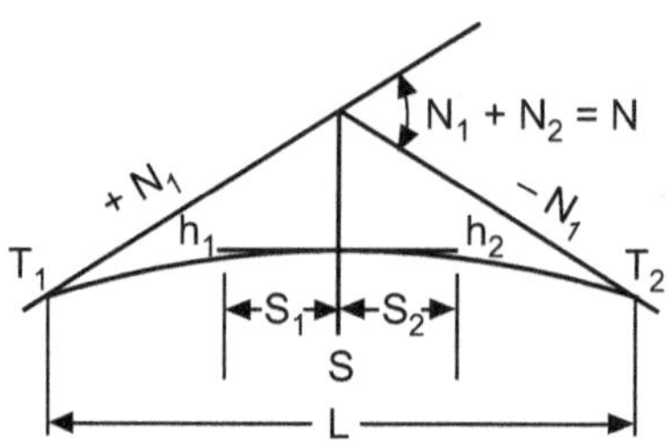

Summit curve when S is less than L

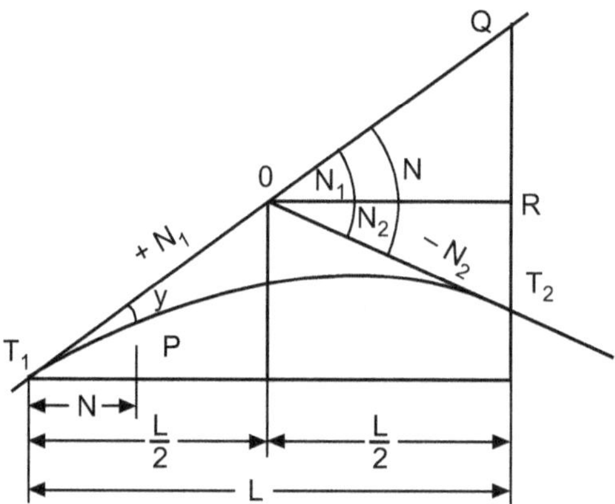

Fig. 5.20: Details of summit curve

Then from Fig. 5.20, we have,

$$h_1 = \frac{S_1^2}{C} \qquad\qquad S_1^2 = \sqrt{Ch_1}$$

$$h_2 = \frac{S_2^2}{C} \qquad\qquad S_2^2 = \sqrt{Ch_2}$$

These equations assume the apex curve to be a parabola.

$$S = S_1 + S_2 = \sqrt{C}\left(\sqrt{h_1} + \sqrt{h_2}\right)$$

To get the value of 'C' we make recourse to the figure and find that for any point 'P' on the parabola,

$$y = \frac{x^2}{C}$$

And geometry demands,

$$QT_2 = QR + RT_2$$

$$= N_1 \frac{L}{2} + N_2 \frac{L}{2} = \frac{L}{2}(N_1 + N_2) = \frac{L}{2} N$$

At the end point of the curve i.e. at T_2,

$$y = \frac{LN}{2} \text{ and } x = L$$

$$\frac{LN}{2} = \frac{L^2}{C} \qquad \therefore C = \frac{2L}{N}$$

Back substituting,

$$S = \sqrt{\frac{2L}{N}} \left(\sqrt{h_1} + \sqrt{h_2}\right)$$

$$= \sqrt{\frac{L}{N}} \left(\sqrt{2h_1} + \sqrt{2h_2}\right)$$

$$\therefore \qquad L = \frac{NS^2}{\left(\sqrt{2h_1} + \sqrt{2h_2}\right)^2}$$

General values of h_1 and h_2 are 1.2 m and 0.15 m as per I. R. C.

$$\therefore \qquad L = \frac{NS^2}{\left(\sqrt{2h_1} + \sqrt{2h_2}\right)^2} = \frac{NS^2}{4.4}$$

and if gradient is in percentage

$$L = \frac{NS^2}{440}$$

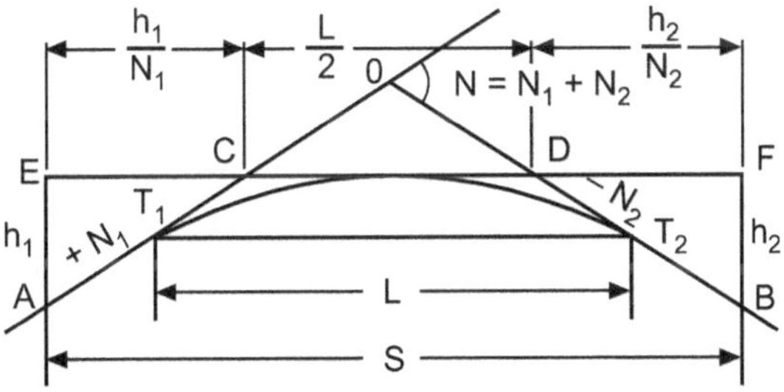

Fig. 5.21

For summit curve where S is greater than L, we take recourse to Fig. 5.21 and state that

$$S = CD + DF + EC$$

$$= \frac{L}{2} + \frac{h_2}{N_2} + \frac{h_1}{N_1}$$

$$= \frac{L}{2} + \frac{h_1}{N_1} + \frac{h_2}{N - N_1}$$

For minimum S,

$$\frac{dS}{dN_1} = 0 = -\frac{h_1}{N_1} + \frac{h_2}{(N - N_1)^2}$$

$$\therefore \quad h_1 (N - N_1)^2 = h_2 N_1^2 \quad \text{or}$$

$$N_1^2 (h_2 - h_1) + 2 N N_1 h_1 - h_1 N^2 = 0$$

which is quadratic in N_1

$$N_1 = \frac{- N h_1 + N \sqrt{h_1 h_2}}{(h_2 - h_1)}$$

When we substitute the above value of N_1 in equation for S, we get,

$$S = \frac{L}{2} + \frac{\left(\sqrt{h_1} + \sqrt{h_2}\right)^2}{N}$$

and,

$$L = 2S - \frac{2\left(\sqrt{h_1} + \sqrt{h_2}\right)^2}{N}$$

It should be noted that for brevity, intermediate steps are ommited. The students are however advised to perform these steps to gain confidence.

If we assume $h_1 = 1.2$ m and $h_2 = 0.15$ m we get

$$L = 2S - \frac{4.4}{N} \quad \text{and if N is expressed in percentage,} \quad L = 2S - \frac{440}{N}$$

Sometimes the values h_1 and h_2 are each taken to be 1.2 m. In that case, the equations are reduced to

$$L > S; \quad L = \frac{NS^2}{9.6}$$

$$L < S; \quad L = 2S - \frac{9.6}{N}$$

This case is sometimes referred as intermediate or overtaking sight distance case. In the case of summit curves, where there is ascending gradient on one side and descending gradient on the other side, effect of gradients on S i.e. stopping sight distance is neglected.

Sag Curves (Valley Curves):

Factors that determine length of valley curves are: (1) Drainage control. i.e. water should not get stagnated at sag point. (2) Vehicle head light sight distance.

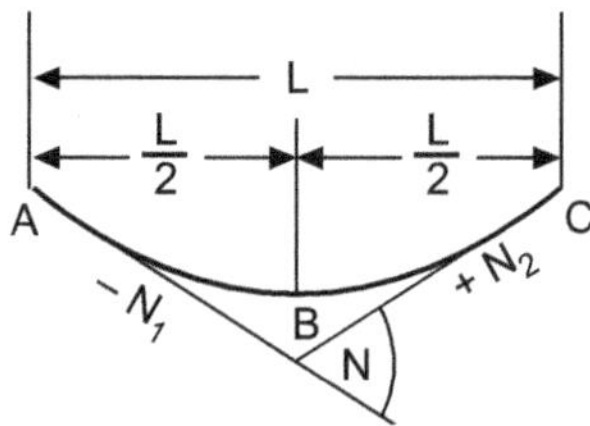

Fig. 5.22

The driver of the vehicle should clearly detect the head light of the oncoming vehicle. (3) Rider comfort I.R.C. has given more credance to the third factor, i.e. the rider comfort.

Let L be the length of total valley curve. Here the assumption is that L is made-up of two transition curves i.e.

$$AC = AB + BC$$
$$= L_s + L_s$$

Vertical radial acceleration at A = 0

Vertical radial acceleration at B $= \dfrac{V^2}{R}$

This change in radial acceleration $\left(\dfrac{V^2}{R} - 0 = \dfrac{V^2}{R}\right)$ occurs in a distance L i.e. AB.

Time to travel $\quad AB = \dfrac{AB}{V} = \dfrac{L_s}{V}$

Rate of change of vertical radial acceleration

$$= \dfrac{V^2}{R} + \dfrac{L_s}{V} = \dfrac{V^2}{R} \times \dfrac{V}{L_s} = \dfrac{V^3}{L_s\,R} = C$$

$L_s = \dfrac{V^3}{CR}$ where, C is recommended value of rate of vertical radical acceleration. I.R.C. says, C = 0.6 m/sec^2

Value of R at $\quad L_s = \dfrac{L_s}{N}$ where, N is deviation angle.

$\therefore \qquad L_s = \dfrac{V^3}{C \times \dfrac{L_s}{N}}$

$\therefore \qquad L_s^2 = \dfrac{NV^3}{C}$

$\therefore \qquad L_s = \left[\dfrac{NV^3}{C}\right]^{1/2}$

Therefore, length of sag curve = L = 2 L$_s$ = $2\left[\dfrac{NV^3}{C}\right]^{1/2}$

But V km/hr $= \dfrac{V}{3.6}$ m/sec. L$_s$ = 0.19 [NV^3]$^{1/2}$

$\therefore$ L = 0.38 [NV^3]$^{1/2}$ where N = Deviation angle in radian approximately equal to tangent of deviation angle.

Length of sag curve on the consideration of head light sight distance.

Two conditions arise (1) length of curve more than stopping sight distance, (2) length of curve less than stopping sight distance.

(i) L > S.S.D.

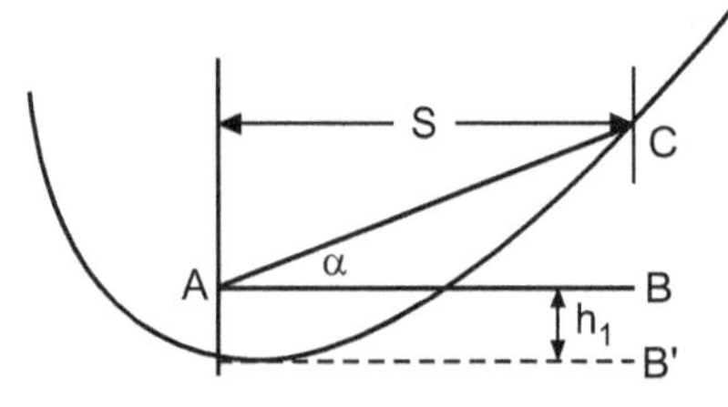

Fig. 5.23

Let head light be located at h_1 above road level and, it focus it's beam α angle upwards. The sight distance available is minimum when the vehicle is at sag point. Let sag curve be parabolic with an equation $y = aX^2$

$$\therefore y = B'C = BB' + BC$$

$$= h_1 + s \tan \alpha = aX^2$$

If the sag curve is cubic parabola,

$$y = h_1 + s \tan \alpha = aX^2 = \frac{N}{2L} \times S^2$$

$$\therefore \quad L = \frac{NS^2}{(2h_1 + 2 s \tan \alpha)} \text{, where S is stopping sight distance}$$

(ii) L < S.S.D.

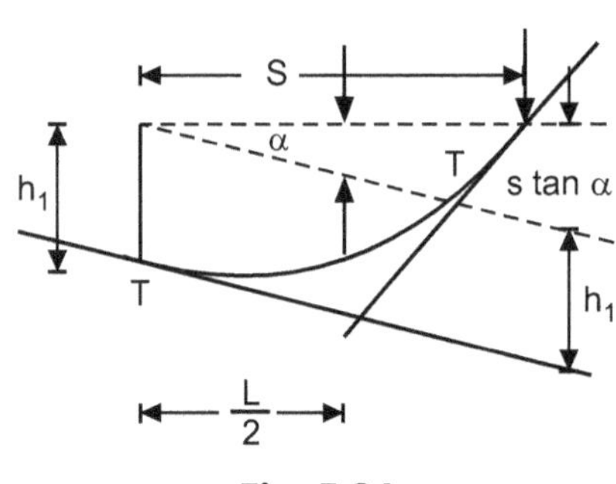

Fig. 5.24

In this case,

$$h_1 + s \tan \alpha = \left(S - \frac{L}{2}\right) N$$

$$\therefore L = 2S - \frac{(2h_1 + 2s \tan \alpha)}{N}$$

The lowest point on sag curve will be on the bisector of grades if equal. If grades are unequal, this point is on a flatter grade at a distance $L \sqrt{N_1/2N}$. Generally the valley curve is given by $y = \frac{2W}{3L^2} X^3$ which is practically a spiral transition.

I.R.C. practice: IRC practice is to take $h_1 = 0.75$ metres and beam angle $\alpha = 1°$ then two cases arise.

When L > SSD, $$L = \frac{NS^2}{(2 h_1 + 2 s \tan \alpha)} = \frac{NS^2}{(1.5 + 0.0355)} \text{ and}$$

When L < SSD, $$L = 2S - \frac{(2 h_1 + 2 s \tan \alpha)}{N} = 2S - \frac{(1.5 + 0.0355)}{N}$$

SOLVED PROBLEMS

Problem 5.1: *For a hill road with a ruling gradient of 8 % with horizontal curve of 100 metres, what could be the compensation of gradient at this curve?*

Solution:

$$\text{Grade compensation} = \frac{30 + R}{R}$$

$$= \frac{30 + 100}{100}$$

$$= 1.3\ \%$$

Max. limit of grade compensation

$$= \frac{75}{R} = \frac{75}{100}$$

$$= 0.75\ \%$$

That is the grade compensation (max.) could be 0.75 % where the ruling gradient is 8 %.

Therefore compensated gradient = 8 % − 0.75 % = 7.25 %.

That is the curve on this stretch shall have a gradient 7.25 % instead of 8 %.

Problem 5.2: *For a hill road with ruling gradient 4 % with horizontal curves of 100 metres, what would be grade compensation?*

Solution: Ruling gradient = 4 %.

Therefore no grade compensation. Gradient need not be eased beyond 4%.

Problem 5.3: *What would be radius of horizontal curve, for which you would recommend no gradient i.e. laying of road on level ground?*

Solution: In this case,

Grade compensation = Max. limit of grade compensation

$$\frac{30 + R}{R} = \frac{75}{R}$$

$$\therefore \qquad R = 75 - 30 = 45.$$

That is for horizontal curves of 45 metres and below, they better be laid on flat ground. That is as far as possible.

Problem 5.4: *Minimum sight distance between two approaching cars at 100 and 50 km/hr is wanted to avoid collision. One can assume reaction time of 3 seconds, coefficient of friction between road and vehicle 0.7 and brake efficiency of 0.8 and flat country. What should be the sight distance to avoid collision?*

Solution: Stopping sight distance for the first car,

$$= 0.278\ Vt + \frac{V^2}{254\ f}$$

$$= 0.278 \times 100 \times 3 + \frac{(100)^2}{254 \times (0.5 \times 0.7)}$$

$$= 83.4 + 112.48 = 195.88 \text{ say } 196 \text{ meter}$$

We have halved, the coefficient of friction here for brake efficiency.

$$\text{S.S.D. for 2nd car} = 0.278 \times 50 \times 3 + \frac{(50)^2}{254 \times (0.5 \times 0.7)}$$

$$= 41.7 + 28.12$$

$$= 69.82 \text{ say } 70 \text{ meter}$$

Sight distance to avoid collision

$$= SD_1 + SD_2 = 196 + 70$$

$$= 266 \text{ metres.}$$

Problem 5.5: *Stopping sight distance is 60 metres for two lane traffic. What would be stopping sight distance when there is only one lane and two way traffic?*

Solution: Two way traffic and one lane, as such the stopping sight distance shall double the farmer i.e. $2 \times 60 = 120$ metres.

Problem 5.6 : *Calculate the grade at which the braking distance is infinite for a speed of 50 km/hr if coefficient of friction between road surface and vehicle is 0.6. Grade is descending.*

Solution: Braking distance on grade $= \dfrac{V^2}{254 \, (f \pm 0.01 \, n)}$

For braking distance to be infinite

$f - 0.01\, n$ should be zero i.e $0.6 = 0.01\, n$

$$n = \frac{0.6}{0.01} = \frac{6}{10} \times \frac{100}{1}$$

$$= 60 \text{ percent}$$

That is if the grade is more than 60 % for this friction coefficient, it is difficult to stop the vehicle. The alternative is to reduce the descending grade.

Problem 5.7: *Calculate the grade at which braking distance is zero. For a speed of 50 km/hr., if coefficient of friction between road surface and vehicle is 0.6 . Grade is ascending.*

Solution: Braking distance on ascending grade

$$= \frac{V^2}{254 \, (f + 0.01 \, n)}$$

In order that this be zero, $f + 0.01\, n$ should be infinite or V should be zero. Both possibilities being improbable, braking distance cannot be zero.

Problem 5.8: *Two major roads intersect at 90° and the design speed is 50 km/hr. If the sight distance at intersection allowed is 110 metres, sketch the triangle at intersection in which properties should not be constructed. Reaction time for the driver is 3 seconds.*

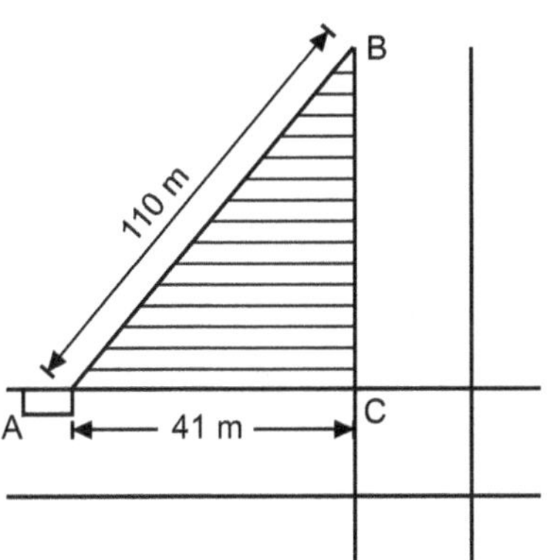

Fig. 5.25

Solution: Reaction distance $= 3 \times \dfrac{50 \times 1000}{60 \times 60} = 41$ metre

That is if the vehicle is A, distance AC must be 41 metres so that driver can take some action. Since sight distance allowed for this junction is 110 metres, AB is 110 metres and

$$BC = \sqrt{AB^2 - AC^2}\ .$$
$$BC = \sqrt{110^2 - 41^2} = \sqrt{12100 - 1681}$$
$$\therefore \qquad BC = \sqrt{10419} = 102 \text{ met.}$$

Therefore, $\triangle ABC$ sides 110, 41 and 102 metre at the intersection as shown, is the approximate area where properties should not be constructed.

Problem 5.9: *For a vehicle traversing a curve of radius 100 metre with a design speed of 80 km/hr, indicate the amount of super-elevation that you would provide. Country is hilly and is non-snow bound.*

Solution: $\qquad e = \dfrac{V^2}{225\,R} = \dfrac{(80)^2}{225 \times 100} = 0.28.$

But the max. value of super-elevation recommended is 0.1 and hence that should be given.

Problem 5.10: *For plain terrain, and national highway, calculate ruling, minimum and absolute minimum radii.*

Solution: Let us assume

Design speed (Ruling)   = 100 km/hr.

Design speed (minimum)   = 80 km/hr.

Maximum super-elevation   = 0.07 (as per IRC recommendations)

Coefficient of lateral friction= μ = 0.15

$$R = \dfrac{V^2}{127\,(e + \mu)} = \dfrac{(100)^2}{127\,(0.07 + 0.15)} = 360 \text{ metres}$$

which is ruling radius.

Minimum design speed = 80

$$\therefore \qquad R = \frac{(80)^2}{127\,(0.07 + 0.15)} = 230 \text{ m.}$$

which is absolute minimum radius.

Problem 5.11: *Horizontal curve radius is 300 metres, design speed of 80 km/hr. and plain terrain. Find super-elevation. What could be coefficient of lateral friction mobilized if super-elevation is restricted to 0.07 ?*

Solution: As per IRC practice,

$$e = \frac{(0.75\,V)^2}{127\,R} = \frac{V^2}{225\,R} = \frac{(80)^2}{225 \times 300} = 0.0999 = 0.1 \text{ say.}$$

As per IRC, maximum super-elevation = 0.07

Therefore balance centrifugal force will be catered by friction that is mobilized.

$$\therefore \quad (e + \mu) = 0.1, \ \mu = 0.1 - e = 0.1 - 0.07 = 0.03$$

which is below the recommended value of 0.15.

Problem 5.12: *There is two lane pavement on national highway. Radius of curve is 300 metres. Ruling design speed is 100 km/hr. Maximum super-elevation is 0.07. Super-elevation is to be given by rotation about centre. Allowable rate of attainment of super-elevation is 1 in 150. Find length of transition curve if pavement is 7 metre.*

Solution: ***Criterion A:***

Satisfactory rate of change of acceleration

$$= \frac{80}{75 + V} = \frac{80}{75 + 100} = 0.46$$

Consider minimum of 0.5

$$L_s = \frac{V^3}{CR} = \frac{0.0215 \times (100)^3}{0.5 \times 300} = 145 \text{ metre}$$

Criterion B:

Super-elevation allowed $= e = \dfrac{(0.75\,V)^2}{127 \times R} = \dfrac{(0.75 \times 100)^2}{127 \times 300}$

$$\therefore \qquad e = 0.147$$

But this is high value and should be 0.07 only.

Since radius is 300 m, widening of pavement on curve is not necessary.

$\therefore$ Raising of pavement due to super-elevation

$$= 0.07 \times 7 = 0.49 \text{ m}$$

Assuming rotation of super-elevation about centre, raising of outer edge

$$= \frac{0.49}{2} = 0.245 \text{ metre.}$$

And length of transition $= 0.245 \times 150 = 36.8$ m

Higher of the two values i.e.145 metres is chosen.

Problem 5.13: *For a curve of radius 50 metres, design speed is 40 km/hr. Determine length of transition curve on the following assumptions:*

(1) *Hilly terrain snow bound.*

(2) *Allowed super-elevation = 0.07*

(3) *Rate of attainment of super-elevation = 1 in 60*

(4) $C = \dfrac{80}{75 + V}$ *with maximum and minimum of 0.8 and 0.5*

(5) *Rotation about pavement centre.*

Solution: *Criterion A:*

$$C \;=\; \frac{80}{75 + V} \;=\; \frac{80}{75 + 40} \;=\; 0.727$$

C is in the range of 0.8 and 0.5

$$L \;=\; \frac{0.0215\, V^3}{CR}$$

$$=\; \frac{0.0215\,(40)^3}{0.72 \times 50} \;=\; 38.2 \text{ metre}$$

Criterion B :

$$e \;=\; \frac{(0.75\,V)^2}{127\,R} \;=\; \frac{(0.75 \times 40)^2}{127 \times 50}$$

$$=\; 0.141 \text{ high value.}$$

Let e = 0.07

Extra-widening on curve

$$=\; n\frac{18}{R} + 0.1\frac{V}{\sqrt{R}} \;=\; 2 \times \frac{18}{50} + 0.1 \times \frac{40}{\sqrt{50}} \;=\; 0.72 + 0.56 = 1.28$$

Pavement width $= 7 + 1.427 = 8.427$ metres

Raising of pavement $= 0.07 \times 8.427 = 0.589$ say 0.6 metre

Assuming rotation about centre line,

Length of transition $= \dfrac{0.6}{2} \times R = 0.3 \times 50 = 15.0$ metre

Higher of the two values i.e. 38.2 metres be adopted.

Problem 5.14: *Radius of curve is 300 metre, super-elevation is 0.07. Is the curve as per standards for major district roads and plain terrain? If the super-elevation is to be provided by rotation about the crown, how much the pavement edge be raised or depressed? Assume pavement width of 7m.*

Solution:

Allowable $\mu = 0.15$

$$\therefore \quad R = \frac{V^2}{127\,(e + \mu)}$$

$$\therefore \quad V^2 = 127\,(e + \mu)\,R = 127\,(0.07 + 0.15)\,300$$

$$\therefore \quad V = \sqrt{127 \times 0.22 \times 300} = 91.55 \text{ km/hour}$$

Ruling design speed for M.D.R. and plain terrain = 80 km/hr. and the absolute minimum design speed is 65 km/hr. These criterions are not met.

Total super-elevation = $0.07 \times 7 = 0.49$ m.

Half of this (0.245 m) to be provided by depressing the inner edge and balance (0.245 m) by raising the outer edge.

Problem 5.15: *For a national highway, plain terrain and high bituminous road has a curve of radius 3000 metres. What should be super-elevation?*

Solution: For this highway, design speed = 100 km/hr.

I.R.C. practice,

$$e = \frac{(0.75\,V)^2}{127\,R} = \frac{(0.75 \times 100)^2}{127 \times 3000} = 0.0147$$

i.e. 1 in 66.

Minimum camber for this type of highway is 1 in 50 to 1 in 60.

Better option would be to give camber of 1 in 66 or more and continue normal cambered section of highway.

Problem 5.16: *Vehicle is negotiating a curve of radius 100 metres with a design speed of 70 km/hr. The wheel base is 8 metres and it is two lane pavement. Calculate the extra widening that is required.*

Solution: Extra widening,

$$= n\frac{l^2}{2\,R} + 0.1\frac{V}{\sqrt{R}}$$

$$= 2 \times \frac{(8)^2}{2 \times 100} + 0.1\frac{70}{\sqrt{100}}$$

$$= 0.64 + 0.7 = 1.71 \text{ metres.}$$

Problem 5.17: *Two grades one 1 in 200 and the other 1 in 200 are meeting at an apex. Stopping sight distance is 175 metre and height of driver and that of the object above roadway could be assumed to be 1.2 metre and 0.15 metre. Find length of apex curve.*

Solution: Assume $S < L$

$$\therefore \quad L = \frac{NS^2}{440}$$

$$= \frac{(0.5 + 0.5) \times 175 \times 175}{440} = 69.60$$

Thus, S sight distance 175 metre is not less than L.

Let $S > L$,
$$L = 2S - \frac{440}{N}$$

$$= 2 \times 175 - \frac{440}{(0.5 + 0.5)} = -90$$

i.e. S is not greater than L.

Then the conclusion is grade change is too small and does not warrant designing a apex curve. Depending upon speed, length could be chosen. For example, if design speed is 65 km/hr, length of apex curve could be 40 meters as per IRC recommendations.

Problem 5.18: *Two grades + 2 % and – 2.5 % meet at apex. Overtaking sight distance to be provided for is 600 metres, calculate L.*

Solution:
$$L = \frac{NS^2}{9.6} \quad \text{when } L > S$$

$$L = 2S - \frac{9.6}{N} \quad \text{when } L < S$$

$$S = 600, L > S \text{ say}$$

$$N_1 = +2\% = 1 \text{ in } 50, N_2 = -2.5\% = -1 \text{ in } 40$$

$$N = N_1 + N_2 = \frac{1}{50} + \frac{1}{40} = 0.045$$

$$L = \frac{NS^2}{9.6}$$

$$= \frac{0.045 \times 600 \times 600}{9.6} = 1687.5 > 600.$$

Assumption correct, provide L = 1687 metres.

Problem 5.19: *Vertical grades +3 and –4 percent meet at sag point. Design speed is 80 km/hr. Perception brake time is 2.5 seconds. Friction coefficient between road surface and vehicle is 0.35. Find length of summit curve.*

Solution: Assume $S < L$ i.e. stopping sight distance $< L$

$$\text{S.S.D.} = 0.278\, V\, t + \frac{V^2}{254\, f} \quad \text{on flat grade}$$

$$= 0.278 \times 80 \times 2.5 + \frac{80^2}{254 \times 0.35}$$

$$= 128 \text{ m.}$$

Deviation angle = N = 3 + 4 = 7 %

$$L = \frac{NS^2}{5.4}$$

$$= \frac{0.07 \times (128)^2}{4.4} = 260.6 \text{ metre}$$

260.6 > 128. Assumption is correct.

$\therefore$ Length of summit curve = 260.6 metre.

Problem 5.20 : *Two grades 1 in 100 and 1 in 125 meet at summit. Speed is 80 km/hr. The summit curve is to be designed for overtaking sight distance of 470 metres. Determine length.*

Solution: $N = \dfrac{1}{100} + \dfrac{1}{125} = \dfrac{12.5 + 10}{1250} = \dfrac{22.5}{1250}$

Assume L > overtaking sight distance

Then $L = \dfrac{NS^2}{9.6} = \dfrac{22.5}{1250} \times \dfrac{(470)^2}{9.6} = 414.18 \text{ metre}$

That assumption proves incorrect. Therefore now assume L < S

$$L = 2S - \frac{9.6}{N} = 2 \times 470 - \frac{9.6 \times 1250}{22.5}$$

$$= 940 - 533.3 = 406.6 \text{ metre}$$

Assumption is correct. Therefore adopt this length.

Problem 5.21: *Two grades $\dfrac{1}{50}$ and $\dfrac{1}{100}$ meet at summit. The stopping sight distance and overtaking sight distances are 200 and 650 metres. Calculate length of summit curve to fulfil both these requirements. On the assumption that topography demands length of summit curve as maximum 500 metres.*

Solution: $N = \dfrac{1}{50} + \dfrac{1}{100} = \dfrac{3}{100}$

S. S. D. = 200 metre

Let L > SSD, $L = \dfrac{NS^2}{4.4} = \dfrac{3}{100} \times \dfrac{(200)^2}{4.4} = 272.72$

Assumption is correct in this case.

Now, let L > overtaking sight distance.

Then $L = \dfrac{NS^2}{9.6} = \dfrac{3}{100} \times \dfrac{(650)^2}{9.6} = 1320.3 \text{ metre.}$

This assumption is correct in this case. That is we cannot provide curve which will cater for both the criterias i.e. stopping sight distance and overtaking sight distance, since 1320 > 500 metres. Let us provide therefore intermediate sight distance.

I. S. D. = 2 S. S. D. = 2 × 200 = 400 metre

If L > S.D.　　　　　$L = \dfrac{NS^2}{9.6} = \dfrac{3}{100} \times \dfrac{(400)^2}{9.6} = 500$ metres.

Assumption is correct.

That is if we provide summit curve 500 metres, it will cater stopping sight distance and intermediate sight distance and will also be in limit of 500 m. So provide that.

Problem 5.22: *Descending grade of 1 in 20 and ascending grade of 1 in 30 meet to form valley curve. Design speed is 80 km/hr. Design valley curve to fulfil comfort condition and head light sight distance if f = 0.35 and braking time = 2.5 sec.*

Solution:　$N = \dfrac{1}{20} + \dfrac{1}{30} = \dfrac{5}{60}$

$$V = 80 \text{ km/hr} = \dfrac{80}{3.6} \text{ m/sec} = 22.2 \text{ m/sec.}$$

From the point of view of comfort,

$$L = 2\left[\dfrac{NV^3}{C}\right]^{1/2} \qquad C = \text{allowable rate of change of acceleration}$$

$$= 0.6 \text{ m/sec}^3$$

$$= 2\left[\dfrac{5}{60} \times \dfrac{(22.2)^3}{0.6}\right]^{1/2}$$

$$= 2 \times 38.98 = 77.96 \text{ m.}$$

From the point of view of head light sight distance, stopping sight distance.

$$= Vt + \dfrac{V^2}{2\,gf} = 22.2 \times 2.5 + \dfrac{(22.2)^2}{2 \times 9.8 \times 0.35} = 127.5 \text{ metres}$$

Let us assume L > S. S. D., then $L = \dfrac{NS^2}{(1.5 + 0.035s)}$

$$L = \dfrac{\dfrac{5}{60} \times (127.5)^2}{(1.5 + 0.035 \times 127.5)}$$

$$= \dfrac{1354.08}{5.962} = 227.21 \text{ metre}$$

L > S. S. D. ∴ Assumption is correct.

Therefore we have the length of sag curves to be 77.96 metres and 227.21 metres from two different considerations. Provide higher value of 227.21 metres.

Problem 5.23: *The traffic on a particular road as of today is 1000 p.cu/day. The traffic increase per year is 10 %. The present road width is 3 metres. Find when this road requires widening.*

Solution: Present traffic =1000 p.cu/day

It is single lane. Let it reach saturation after n years of service. When the traffic will be 2000 p.cu/day,

$$2000 = 1000 (1 + 0.1)^n$$

When n = 7,   R.H.S. $= 1000 \times 1.9487$

and when n = 8,   R.H.S. $= 1000 \times 2.143$

That is the road will require widening between 7th and 8th year.

Problem 5.24: *A single lane is to be widened to two lanes. Present traffic is 3000 p.cu/day. The cost of widening is Rs. 95 lakhs/km. Find internal rate of return.*

Solution: We have here

$$IRR = 5.42 - 0.167\,(95) + 0.0094\,(3000) + 0.208 \left(\frac{3000}{95}\right)$$

$$= 5.42 - 15.87 + 28.20 + 6.57$$

$$= 24.32\ \%$$

Problem 5.25: *Calculate stopping sight distance on a highway at a descending grade of 2 % for design speed of 80 km/hr. Total reaction time is 2.5 seconds and coefficient of friction between road and tyre is 0.35.*

Solution: Stopping sight distance

$$= 0.278\ Vt + \frac{V^2}{254\ (f \pm 0.01\ n)}$$

$$= 0.278 \times 80 \times 2.5 + \frac{(80)^2}{254\ (0.35 - 0.01 \times 2)}$$

$$= 130\ \text{metres.}$$

Problem 5.26: *For an upward gradient of 2 % and speed 80 km/hr., calculate safe stopping distance if perception and brake reaction time total is 2.5 seconds, and the coefficient of friction varies from 0.40 at 20 kmph to 0.35 at 100 kmph.*

Solution:

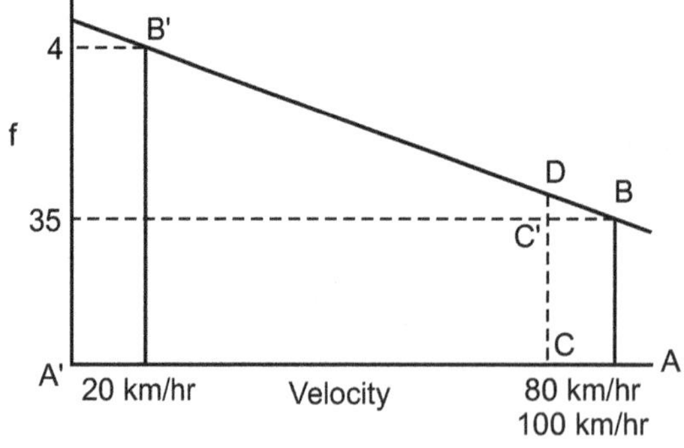

Slope of f versus velocity curve

$$= \frac{0.4 - 0.35}{100 - 20} = \frac{0.05}{80}$$

f at 80 km/hr.

$$= CD = AB + C'D$$

$$= 0.035 + \frac{0.05}{80}\ (100 - 80)$$

$$= 0.35 + 0.01 = 0.36$$

Fig. 5.26

Stopping sight distance (safe)

$$= 0.278\, V\, t + \frac{V^2}{254\,(f + 0.01\, n)}$$

$$= 0.278 \times 80 \times 2.5 + \frac{(80)^2}{254\,(0.36 + 0.01 \times 2)}$$

$$= 55.6 + 66.3 = 122 \text{ metres approximately}$$

Problem 5.27: *Calculate the camber for the following cases: (1) Major district Road, light rainfall, and thin bituminous surface, pavement is 4 metre wide. (2) Heavy rainfall, W.B.M. pavement, pavement 3.8 wide.*

Solution:

Case I : Camber of 1 in 50 is recommended

$$\text{Rise of crown with respect to edges} = \frac{4}{2} \times \frac{1}{50} = 0.04 \text{ m}$$

Case II: Camber of 1 in 33 is recommended

$$\text{Rise of crown with respect to edges} = \frac{3.8}{2} \times \frac{1}{33} = 0.057 \text{ m.}$$

Problem 5.28: *A 400 metre radius curve is laid to effect change of direction of road. The distance between the centre line of the road and the centre line of the inside lane is 1 metre. If the sight distance on this horizontal curve is 300 metres, determine the set back distance.*

Solution: Here, we have

$$\theta = \frac{S}{2\,(R - n)} \text{ radians} = \frac{300}{2\,(400 - 1)} = 0.375 \text{ radians}$$

$$= \frac{360 \times 0.375}{2\pi} \text{ in degrees} = 21.53^\circ$$

$$m = R - (R - n)\cos\theta = 400 - (400 - 1)\cos 21.53 = 29 \text{ meters.}$$

Problem 5.29: *For the uncontrolled intersection at the confluence of major and minor road, the respective design speeds are 40 and 30 km/hr. The intersection is located on level ground, and the coefficient friction between tyre and road surface is 0.35. Sketch the line of sight and building restrictions, if road widths respectively are 4 and 3.5 metre.*

Solution: Stopping sight distance for major road

$$= 0.278\, V + \frac{V^2}{254\left(f \pm \dfrac{n}{100}\right)}$$

$$= 0.278\, V + \frac{V^2}{254\, f} \quad ; n = 0 \text{ since level road}$$

$$= 0.278 \times 40 + \frac{V^2}{254 \times 0.35} = 0.278 \times 40 + \frac{(40)^2}{254 \times 0.35}$$

$$= 11.12 + 17.99 = 29.11 \text{ metre}$$

Stopping sight distance for minor road

$$= 0.278 \, V + \frac{V^2}{254 \times f} = 0.278 \times 30 + \frac{30^2}{254 \times 0.35} = 8.34 + 10.12$$

$$= 18.46 \text{ metre}$$

For intersection, the line of sight is shown in Fig. 5.27.

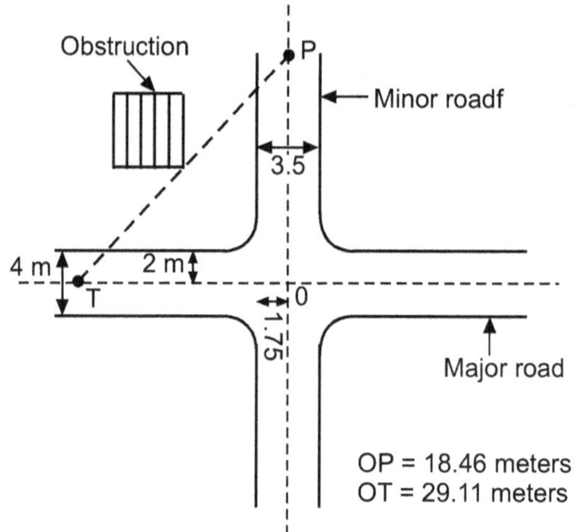

Fig. 5.27

Problem 5.30: *Determine the capacity of mini round about, which is located at a crossing of two highways each two lane widths, each lane being of 3.7 metres. The area within the intersection line is 100.0 m². The efficiency coefficient is 65. Find approximate capacity of mini round about.*

Solution: Here $\sum W$ = sum of basic road width = 8×3.7

$$= 29.6 \text{ say } 30 \text{ metres}$$

$$a = \text{area of junction widening} = 100 \text{ m}^2$$

$$k = 65$$

$$q = \text{pcu / hr capacity} = K \left(\sum W + a^{1/2} \right)$$

$$= 65 \left(30 + \sqrt{100} \right) = 40 \times 65 = 2600$$

i.e. 2600 pcu per hour.

Problem 5.31: *A particular highway is designed for 50 km/hr. as the speed. If the average spacing in metres of the moving vehicles is 0.5 metres, what would be capacity of the road?*

Solution: Here S = 0.5 metre, V = 50 km/hr.

Therefore, capacity in vehicles/hr/lane = $\dfrac{1000 \, V}{S}$

$$= \frac{1000 \times 50}{0.5} = 1 \text{ lakh vehicles/hr.}$$

Solution: Here L = 3.2, V = 50 km/hr., t = 1 second,

g = 10 metre/sec^2 as such

$$S = L + \frac{t\,V\,1000}{3600} + \left(\frac{V \times 1000}{3600}\right)^2 \times \frac{1}{2\,gf}$$

$$= L + 0.278\,Vt + \frac{V^2}{254\,f}$$

$$= 3.2 + 0.278 \times 50 \times 1 + \frac{50 \times 50}{254 \times 0.5}$$

$$= 3.2 + 14.0 + \frac{50 \times 50}{127}$$

$$= 3.2 + 14 + 20$$

$$= 37.2 \text{ metres about}$$

$$V = 50 \text{ km/hr.} \quad = \frac{50 \times 1000 \times 3.3}{60 \times 60}$$

$$= 46 \text{ ft/sec about}$$

$$\therefore \qquad S = 21 + 1.1\,V \text{ about}$$

$$= 21 + 1.1 \times 46 = 71 \text{ feet}$$

$$= 22 \text{ metres about.}$$

Solution: Here, we have w = 10 metres, e = 7 metres, l = 20 metres, p = 0.72, therefore

$$Q_p = \frac{280\,w\left(1 + \dfrac{e}{w}\right)\left(1 - \dfrac{p}{3}\right)}{1 + \dfrac{w}{l}}$$

$$= \frac{280 \times 10 \times \left(1 + \dfrac{7}{10}\right)\left(1 - \dfrac{0.72}{3}\right)}{1 + \dfrac{10}{20}} = \frac{2800 \times 1.7 \times 0.76}{1 + 0.5}$$

$$= 2380 \text{ vehicles at a time.}$$

Problem 5.34: *For a particular case, the rolling gradient is 1 in 20 and if a horizontal curve of 125 metre radius is to be introduced on this gradient, find out the compensated gradient on this curve.* **(Oct. 2002)**

Solution:

$$\text{Ruling gradient} = 5.0\%$$

$$\text{Grade compensation} = \frac{30 + R}{R} = \frac{30 + 125}{125}$$

$$= 1.24\%$$

$$\text{Maximum limit of grade compensation} = \frac{75}{R} = \frac{75}{125} = 0.6\%$$

$$\therefore \quad \text{Compensated gradient} = 5 - 0.6 = 4.4\%$$

Problem 5.35: *What is stopping Sight Distance? Find the non-passing sight distance on a highway at descending gradient of 2.5 percent for a design speed of 70 kmph. Assume other data suitably as per IRC recommendations only.*

Solution: Total reaction time t may be taken as 2.5 secs. and design coefficient of friction as $f = 0.35$, $V = 70$ kmph, $n = -0.025$ (descending gradient), $g = 9.8$ m/sec^2.

$$V = \frac{70}{3.6} = 19.44 \text{ m/sec.}$$

$$\begin{aligned}
SSD &= Vt + \frac{V^2}{2g\,(f \pm n\%)} \\[2mm]
&= 19.44 \times 2.5 + \frac{(19.44)^2}{2 \times 9.8\,(0.35 - 0.025)} \\[2mm]
&= 48.61 + \frac{377.91}{6.3765} \\[2mm]
&= 107.87 \text{ m} \approx 108 \text{ m} \\[2mm]
SSD &= 0.278\,Vt + \frac{V^2}{254\,(f \pm 0.01n)} \\[2mm]
&= 0.278 \times 70 \times 2.5 + \frac{70^2}{254\,(0.35 - 0.025)} \\[2mm]
&= 48.65 + \frac{4900}{82.55} = 108 \text{ m}
\end{aligned}$$

Problem 5.36: *For a 2 lane road with design speed of 75 kmph, has a horizontal curve of radius 450 metre. Design the rate of superelevation for mixed traffic flow conditions. Also find the amount by which the outer edge of the pavement to be raised when the width of pavement is 7.50 metre for this 2 lane road.* **(Oct. 2003)**

Solution: For mixed traffic conditions, the superelevation should fully conteract the centrifugal force for 75% of design speed.

$$e \;=\; \frac{V^2}{225\,R} \;=\; \frac{70^2}{225 \times 450} \;=\; 0.048$$

Since this value is less than 0.07, the superelevation of 0.048 may be adopted.

The total width of pavement, B = 7.5 m.

Raising of outer edge with respect to centre

$$E \;=\; \frac{B \cdot e}{2}$$

$$=\; \frac{7.5}{2} \times 0.048 = 0.18 \text{ m}$$

Problem 5.37: *Determine the safe O.S.D. for a design speed of 80 kmph for both one-way traffic and two-way traffic. You may assume the necessary data as per IRC recommendations only.* **(Oct. 2003)**

Solution:　　　　O.S.D. $= (d_1 + d_2)$ for one-way traffic

$$V \;=\; 80 \text{ kmph}$$

Assume　　　$V_b \;=\; V - 16 = 64 \text{ kmph and}$

$$A \;=\; 3.28 \text{ (maximum overtaking acceleration at 64 kmph for IRS std)}$$

$$t \;=\; 2 \text{ secs}$$

$$d_1 \;=\; 0.28\, V_b \cdot t$$

$$=\; 0.28 \times 64 \times 2 = 35.84 \text{ m}$$

$$d_2 \;=\; 0.28\, V_b \cdot T + 2.S$$

$$S \;=\; (0.2\, V_b + 6) = 0.2 \times 64 + 6 = 18.8 \text{ m}$$

$$T \;=\; \sqrt{\frac{14.4S}{A}} \;=\; \sqrt{\frac{14.4 \times 18.8}{2.5}} \;=\; 10.4 \text{ sec}$$

$$d_2 \;=\; 0.28 \times 64 \times 10.4 + 2 \times 18.8$$

$$=\; 186.368 + 37.6$$

$$=\; 223.96$$

∴　　　OSD $= 35.84 + 223.96$

$$=\; 259.80 \text{ m}$$

Problem 5.38: *What do you mean by Grade compensation on horizontal curves? For a particular case, the ruling gradient is 1 in 20 and if a horizontal curve of 125 metre radius is to be introduced on this gradient, find out the compensated gradient on this curve.*

(April 2004)

Solution:

$$\text{Ruling gradient} = 5\%.$$

$$\text{Grade compensation} = \frac{30 + R}{R} = \frac{30 + 125}{125}$$

$$= 1.25\%$$

$$\text{Maximum limit of grade compensation} = \frac{75}{R} = \frac{75}{125} = 0.6\%.$$

$$\therefore \quad \text{Compensated gradient} = 5 - 0.6 = 4.4\%$$

Problem 5.39: *Explain the terms (i) Stopping sight distance, (ii) Total reaction time of a driver in brief, only. State the factors on which S.S.D. depend. And hence determine S.S.D. for a given speed of 80 kmph for a single lane two-way traffic roads.*
Assume t = 2.5 secs and f = 0.35.

Solution:

$$\text{Stopping sight distance} = 0.278\ Vt + \frac{V^2}{254\ (f \pm 0.01\ n)}$$

$$= 0.278 \times 80 \times 2.5 + \frac{80^2}{254\ (0.35 - 0.01 \times 2)}$$

$$= 130 \text{ metres}$$

Problem 5.40: *Explain the terms in brief giving formulae for each:*
(i) Radius of relative stiffness, (ii) Equivalent radius of resisting section.
And hence, compute the radius of relative stiffness of 15 cm thick c.c. slab using the following data. E = 2,10,000 KSC, μ = 0.15 and K = 3 KSC per cm.

Solution:

$$K = 0.3$$

$$l = \left[\frac{Eh^3}{12\ K\ (2 - \mu^2)}\right]^{1/4}$$

$$= \left[\frac{210000 \times 15^3}{12 \times 3\ (2 - 0.15)^2}\right]^{1/4} = 67.0 \text{ cm}$$

Problem 5.41: *What considerations you will have to take while designing the length of vertical valley curves? State clearly giving reasons. And hence design the length of valley curve for a design speed of 80 kmph when a valley curve is formed by a descending grade of 1 in 25 meeting an ascending grade of 1 in 30. Assume allowable rate of change of centrifugal acceleration C = 0.60 m/sec²/sec.***(April 2005)**

Solution:

$$N = -\frac{1}{25} - \frac{1}{30} = \frac{11}{150}$$

$$V = 80 \text{ kmph}, \ V = \frac{80}{3.6}$$

$$= 22.2 \text{ m/sec}$$

(1) Comfort condition,

$$L = 2\left[\frac{NV^3}{C}\right]^{1/2} = 2\left[\frac{11}{150} \times \frac{(22.2)^3}{0.6}\right]^{1/2}$$

$$= 73.1 \text{ m}$$

(2) Head light S.D. conditions t = 2.5 secs, f = 0.35

$$\text{S.S.D.} = Vt + \frac{V^2}{2gf}$$

$$= 22.2 \times 2.5 + \left(\frac{22.2^2}{2 \times 9.8 \times 0.35}\right) = 127.3 \text{ m}$$

If L > SSD,
$$L = \frac{NS^2}{(1.5 + 0.035\,S)} = \frac{11 \times 127.3^2}{150\,(1.5 + 0.035 \times 127.3)}$$

$$= 199.5 \text{ m} \approx 200 \text{ m}$$

∴ Design value is 200 m.

Problem 5.42 : *The speed of overtaking and overtaken vehicles are 70 and 40 kmph respectively on two way traffic roads. If the acceleration of overtaking vehicle is 0.99 m/sec².*
(i) Calculate safe overtaking sight distance.
(ii) Mention the minimum length of overtaking zone assume t = 2 sec).   ***(May 2012)***

Solution: 1. Overtaking sight distance for two-way traffic :

$$= d_1 + d_2 + d_3$$

Assume the design speed as the speed of overtaking vehicle A.

$$v = 70 \text{ kmph}$$

$$v = \frac{70}{3.6} = 19.4 \text{ m/sec}$$

$$v_b = \frac{40}{3.6} = 11.1 \text{ m/sec}$$

Acceleration, a = 0.99 m/sec per sec.

$$d_1 = v_b \cdot t \text{ (Adopt t = 2 secs)}$$

$$= 11.1 \times 2 = 22.2 \text{ m}$$

$$d_2 = v_s \cdot T + 2 \cdot s$$

$$S = (0.7\,v_b + 6) = (0.7 \times 11.1 \times 6) = 13.6 \text{ m}$$

$$T = \sqrt{\frac{4 \cdot s}{a}} = \sqrt{\frac{4 \times 13.8}{0.99}} = 7.4 \text{ secs}$$

$$d_2 = 11.1 \times 7.47 + 2 \times 3.8 = 110.5 \text{ m}$$

$$d_3 = v \cdot T$$

$$= 19.4 \times 7.47 = 144.9 \text{ m}$$

$$\text{O.S.D.} = 22.2 + 110.5 + 144.9$$

$$= 277.6 \text{ m say } 278 \text{ m}$$

2. Mention the minimum length of overtaking zone = 3 (OSD)

$$= 3 (d_1 + d_2 + d_3) \text{ for two-way traffic} = 3 \times 278$$

$$= 834 \text{ meters}$$

Desirable length of overtaking zone $= 5 \times (\text{OSD})$

$$= 5 \times 278$$

$$= 1390 \text{ m}$$

Problem 5.43: *Calculate the extra widening required for a pavement within 7 m on a horizontal curve of radius 250 m if the longest wheel base of vehicle expected on be road is 7.0 m. Design speed is 60 kmph.* ***(Nov. 2012)***

Solution: Extra widening required

$$W_e = \frac{n l^2}{2R} + \frac{V}{9.5\sqrt{R}}$$

$$n = 2 \text{ (two lines for pavement width of 7.0 m)}$$

$$F = 250$$

$$V = 60 \text{ kmph}$$

$$W_e = \frac{2 \times 7^2}{2 \times 250} \times \frac{60}{9.5\sqrt{250}}$$

$$= 0.196 + 0.399$$

$$= 0.595 \text{ m say } 0.6 \text{ m}$$

Extra widening required = **0.6 m**

QUESTIONS

1. What constitutes "Geometric design" of highways?
2. What is critical length of grade? Are there any recommendations about it from IRC?
3. What are rotaries? How rotaries can function? What are the features of rotaries?
4. What are mini round abouts? Discuss their suitability.
5. Discuss the following types of intersections, their use and suitability: (a) Trumpet type interchange, (b) Four lagged interchange, (c) Clover-leaf, (d) Trumpet type interchange with toll plaza.
6. What are cycle tracks? Where these are provided? What purpose do they serve?

7. State IRC recommendations regarding summit and sag curves. What are the presuppositions in these recommendations?

8. Calculate stopping sight distance for a design speed of 100 km/hr on a level ground. Reaction time is 3 seconds and coefficient of friction is 0.4. Also calculate the stopping sight distance for an ascending grade of 1 in 50
   (**Ans.** Plain country 101.82 metres; Ascending grade 177.2 metres).

9. Write explanatory notes on (a) Shoulders, (b) Road Margins, (c) National highway in embankment, (d) Extra widening on curves, (e) Ideal transition curve.

10. Two lane pavement has a radius of 400 m. Design speed is 100 km/hr. Rate of change of centrifugal acceleration is max 0.8 and minimum 0.5. e = 0.07 maximum. Rate of attainment of super-elevation 1 in 150. Determine the length of transition curve.
    (**Ans.** 107.5 m)

11. Ascending grade of 1 in 50 and descending grade 1 in 30 form summit curve. Stopping sight distance is 180 metre. Determine length of summit curve.
    (**Ans.** 390 metre)

12. Valley curve is to be provided for descending grade of 1 in 30 and a level stretch from head light considerations. Stopping sight distance is 180 m. Determine the length.
    (**Ans.** 125 metre approximately)

13. What is meant by Single lane, Intermediate lane and Two lane pavement? What type of traffic plies on it?

14. Discuss the uses of (a) Kerbs, (b) Traffic separators with sketches.

15. What are road margins? Draw a sketch of road with road margins. Sketch a cross-section of a highway in urban area.

16. Outline the concept of "Capacity of road". On what factors does it depend? Derive expression for stopping sight distance.

17. What service road renders? Can it be measured and how?

18. Arrange the level of service in ascending or descending order with justification.

19. How road improvement decision can be based on the level of service?

20. Explain (a) Sight distance at intersection, (b) Safe overtaking sight distance, (c) PIEV concept.

21. Explain the concept of super-elevation. Why some curves may not require super-elevation? What part friction between tyre and road plays in determining super-elevation?

22. Why pavement is widened on curves?

23. State the general principles of horizontal and vertical alignment.

24. Present traffic on a particular road as of today is 5000 pcu/day. Traffic increase per year is 15 %. The present road width is 6 m. Find when this road would require widening. The maximum design service volume is 6000 pcu/day.   (**Ans.** 2 years)

25. A two lane traffic road carrying 22500 pcu/day is to be widened to four lanes at a cost of Rs. 174 lakh/km. Find Internal rate of return.   (**Ans.** 31.34 %)

26. What is meant by the term "Geometry of Highway"?

27. Describe the concept of passenger car unit. What are it's shortcomings?

    On a road 75 cycle rikshaw, 20 cars, and 1 bullock cart are plying per day. Determine the pcu per day of the road.   (**Ans.** 1345 pcu/day)

28. Describe the concept of Design vehicle and design speed. Comment on the shortcomings of this concept.

29. What parameters determine the terrain as plain rolling or steep?

30. Comment on the concept of "Ruling Gradient" and limiting gradient. How are these fixed?

31. Why camber is given to the pavement?

32. Discuss the concept of Right of the way "building lines, control lines."

Chapter 6
HIGHWAY DRAINAGE

6.1 INTRODUCTION

Appropriate drainage is important feature of good highway design in terms of ensuring required level of service and value for many are achieved. Highway drainage has two major objectives : Safety of the road user and longevity of the pavement. Speedy removal of surface water will help to ensure safe and comfortable conditions for the road user. Provision of effective sub-drainage will maximise longevity of the pavement and its associated earthworks. Highway drainage can therefore be broadly classified into two elements - surface run-off and sub-surface run-off : These two elements are not completely disparate in that some of the surface water may find its way into the road foundation through surfaces which are not completely impermeable, hence requiring removal by sub-drainage. Based on these fundamental principles, drainage methods in India are broadly divided into two categories :

- Combined systems, where the surface and sub-surface water are collected and transported in the same pipe, and

- Separate systems, where the two elements are collected and transported in separate pipes.

Within the broader definition of the two systems, there are a number of different drainage methods that are in use on Indian highways, some of them more common than others. Each method has its advantages and disadvantages and some may be more suitable in certain situations than the others. This paper describes some of the most common methods and provides an overview on their applications.

6.2 SIGNIFICANCE OF DRAINAGE

An increase in moisture content causes decrease in strength or stability of a soil mass; the variation in the soil strength with moisture content also depends on the soil type and mode of stress application. Highway drainage is important because of the following reasons :

- Excess moisture in soil sub-grade causes considerable lowering of its stability. The pavements are likely to fail due to sub-grade failure.

- Increase in moisture causes reduction in strength of many pavement materials like stabilized soil and water bound macadam.

- In some clayey soils, variation in moisture content causes considerable variation in volume of sugared. This sometimes contributes to pavement failure.

- One of the most important causes of pavement failure by the formation of waves and corrugations in flexible pavements is due to poor drainage.

- Sustained content of water with bituminous pavements causes failures due to stripping of bitumen from aggregates like loosening or detachments of some of the bituminous pavement layers and formation of pot holes.

- The prime cause of failures in rigid pavements by mud pumping is due to the presence of water in fine sub-grade soil.

- Excess water on shoulders and pavements edge causes considerable damages.

- Excess moisture causes increase in weight and thus increase in stress and simultaneous reduction in strength of the soil mass. This is one of the main reason of failure of earth slopes and embankment foundations.

- In places where freezing temperatures are prevalent in winter, the presence of water in the sub-grade and a continuous supply of water from the ground water can cause considerable damages to the pavement due in frost action.

- Erosion of soil from top of un-surfaced roads and slopes of embankments, cut and hill side is also due to surface water.

Requirements of Highway Drainage System

- The surface water from the carriageway and shoulder should effectively be drained off without allowing it to percolate to sub-grade.

- The surface water from the adjoining land should be prevented from entering the roadway.

- The side drain should have sufficient capacity and longitudinal slope to carry away all the surface water collected.

- Flow of surface water across the road and shoulders and along slopes should not cause formation of cross ruts or erosion.

- Seepage and other sources of underground water should be drained off by the sub-surface drainage system.

- Highest level of ground water table should be kept well below the level of sub-grade, preferably by at least 1.2 m.

- In waterlogged areas, special precautions should be taken, especially if detrimental salts are present or if flooding is likely to occur.

6.3 MECHANISM OF DAMAGE TO HIGHWAYS DUE TO FAULTY DRAINAGE

Lack of drainage affects the performance of highways in a number of ways. They are briefly discussed below :

- If the water falling on the pavement surface is not quickly drained away, it finds its way into the pavement layers through surface cracks, voids and joints (in cement concrete pavements). The water gets entrapped in the spaces between successive lifts of bituminous layers. The pavement is then in the "bathtub" condition, which may cause uplift pressures and result in reduced supporting power. Water may cause stripping of bitumen from aggregates and lower the binding strength of the pavement. In cement concrete slabs, "pumping" is caused, which causes loss of fines in the soil and void space.

- A classic example of this phenomenon of entrapped water frequently met within India is the raising of pavements attempted by earthwork or granular bases over a black-topped surface, which is left intact. This interface acts as an impervious layer to entrap water and causes "bathtub" condition. In the bitumenised road pavements, the development of 'potholes' is a common phenomenon mostly caused by the ingress of surface water, as illustrated in Fig. 6.1.

- The surface run-off or capillary water reaches the sub-grade soil, softens it and reduces its supporting power. Clayey soils are particularly affected by the ingress of moisture.

- Shoulders are rarely, if ever, surfaced. The bare earthen shoulders offer ready ingress of water. Lack of adequate outward slope presents longer opportunity for water to enter the sub-grade through the sides than if the shoulders were adequately sloped.

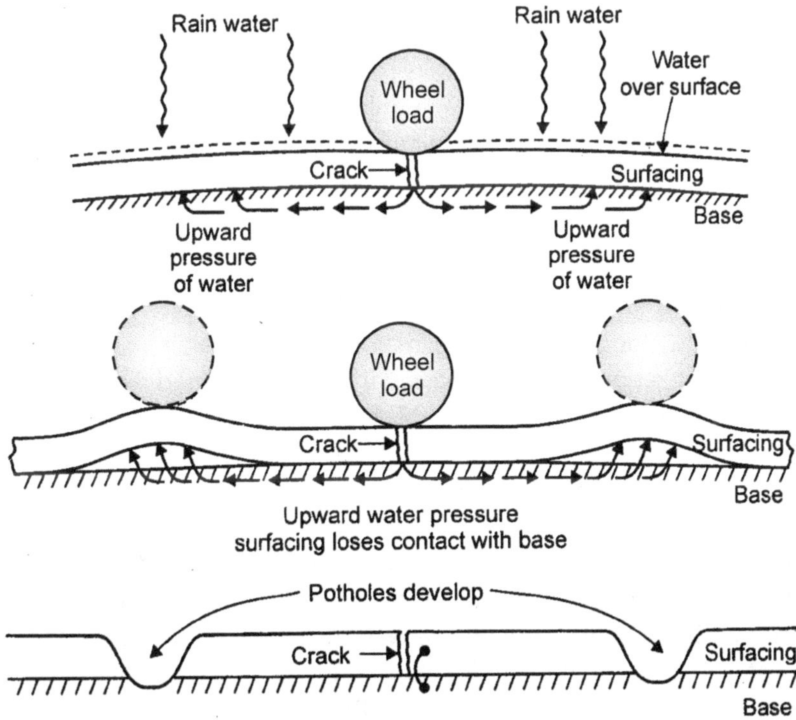

Fig. 6.1 : Development of potholes due to ingress of surface water

- In India, a commonly present road feature is the shoulders at a higher level than the road surface due to negligence of blading and dressing of the shoulders. During heavy downpour, water on the road surface does not get a free outlet and accumulates. Apart from finding its way through the cracks and voids in the pavement surface, the pavement edge at its junction with the earthen shoulder provides a possible entry point to the water. The water thus enters the sub-grade from the sides of the pavement.

- Clayey soils, which are susceptible to high volume change when changes in moisture content take place, swell and shrink alternating with wet and dry spells. Deep cracks are formed in the sub-grade. Heaving-up and deterioration of the pavement follow. Black-cotton soils, frequently found in India, suffer this distress condition.

- In high embankments, stability of slopes is jeopardised when water enters the soil mass, causing an increase in its weight and at the same time reducing its shear strength properties.

- In cut sections, seepage water can build up sufficient pressure to cause the failure of slopes.

- Landslides and subsidences are caused by a general lack of drainage. The Himalayan hill region abounds in locations where serious landslides and subsidences are caused, totally disrupting road traffic. The National Highways to Srinagar and Gangtok are typical examples.

- Frost action, which takes place entirely due to water finding its way into the pores of the soil mass and the pavement layers, is a serious cause of pavement failure at high altitudes in cold season.

- Heavy downpour on the slopes of embankments and cuts can cause excessive soil erosion and lead to rain-cuts and slop failures.

- Unless water from the streams is safely led across the highway through adequate vents, the water can accumulate against the embankment, causing afflux, slope erosion and softening of the sub-grade.

6.4 PRINCIPLES OF GOOD DRAINAGE

Since water is, beyond doubt, one of the main culprits causing failure of highways, the designer should aim at keeping the water away from the road-bed. This can be achieved by following some principles of drainage design. They are outlined below :

- The surface run-off over the pavement surface and the shoulders should be drained away as quickly as possible preventing the water from finding entry into the pavement layers from the top and into the sub-grade from the top and sides.

- Precipitation over the open land adjoining the highway should be led away from the highway through natural drainage channels or artificial drains. Suitable cross-drainage channels should be provided to lead the water across the highway embankment which may be cutting cross to the natural drainage courses.

- Consideration should be given to deal with the precipitation on the embankment and cut slopes such that erosion is not caused.

- Seepage and sub-surface water is detrimental to the stability of cut slopes and bearing power of sub-grades. Similarly, it can be of great importance in preventing frost action. An effective system of sub-surface drainage is a guarantee against such failures.

- Landslide-prone zones deserve special investigations for improving drainage.
- Poor embankment soils can perform satisfactorily if drainage is considered in the design.
- Water-logged and flood-prone zones demand detailed consideration for improving the overall drainage pattern of the area through which the highway is aligned.

6.5 METHODS OF DRAINAGE SYSTEM

There are two methods of drainage system as follows :

1. Surface drainage system and
2. Sub-surface drainage.

6.5.1 Surface Drainage System

- During the rainy season, water gets controlled at road surface and percolated into the road surface and the sub-grade and thereby weakness the sub-grade. To prevent this percolation of water into the sub-grade from the surface of the pavement, the following remedies have been suggested :
- Providing a water-tight or impervious type of road surfacing at the top most layer. i.e. wearing surface.

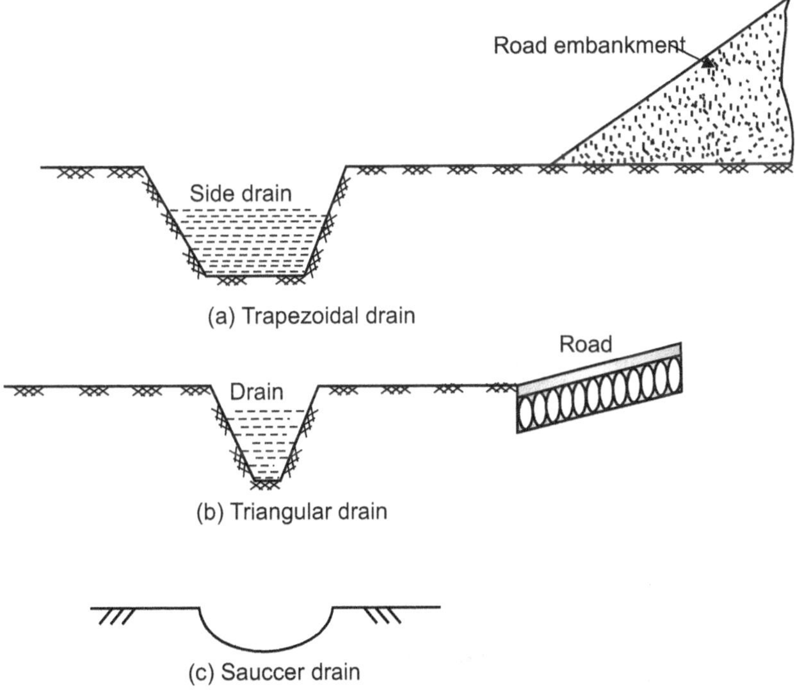

Fig. 6.2 : Surface drainage

- Providing sufficient cross and longitudinal slopes in the road surface.
- The top surface of the berms should be of an impervious material and should have proper slopes towards side drains.

- Providing side drains on both sides of the road. The drains should have a proper slope or gradient so that the water from the road surface should be drained off easily. The side drains should not be less than 1.85m or 6ft from the edge of the formation of the road. In case of cutting, the surface drains should be just after the edge of formation.
- In these places where the rainfall is heavily, the side drains should be trapezoidal in section and in those places where there is less rainfall the section of the drain is triangular or sauccer as shown in Fig. 6.2.
- The height of the embankment should be nearly 60 cm or 2 ft. above the highest flood level of the area.

It is Suitable for

- Slowly permeable clay and shallow soil.
- Regions of high intensity rainfall.
- To fields where adequate out lets are not available.
- The land with less than 1.5 % slope.

It can be Made by

- Land smoothing.
- Making field ditches.

Advantages and Disadvantages of Surface Drains

Advantages

- Low initial cost.
- Easy for inspection.
- Effective in low water table.
- Effective in low Permeability area.

Disadvantages

- Low efficiency.
- Loss of cultivable land.
- Interference to cultural operation.
- High Maintenance cost.

6.5.2 Sub-Soil or Sub-Surface Drainage

Water which penetrates into the ground will continue to flow underground until it meets with some impermeable materials, then the flow ceases and the water accumulates. The top surface of this underground water is called water table. The ground above this level will remain unsaturated and below this level, saturated. The water table generally tends to be parallel to the ground level, but the depth of water table below the ground level may vary and it depends upon the geological conditions.

If this water table is very near to the sub-surface of the road, the consistency of the soil will changes from dry to plastic state and the bearing capacity will consequently decrease. Another adverse effect which results from the increased moisture content is the volumetric increase which will ultimately cause crakes in the road surfacing. Hence it is essential to drain off this water to prevent the sub-grade, which is the foundation of the road from these adverse effects of sub-soil moisture. The method of removal of the sub-soil moisture is called sub-soil drainage.

Following are the conditions under which sub-soil drainage should be provided :

- If the road is through flat country and water stagnates on adjacent lands which makes the road bed soft and unstable.
- When the road is in cutting and there is considerable seepage in the slopes.
- When the surface of the road has the normal underground water table sufficiently below the road crust even then due to capillary action moisture may rise to the surface of the road or the sub-surface.
- When the soil is subjected to the action of springs.
- When the road is at the foot of a hill and water there from flow on the road and it damages the road.

Types of sub surface drainage :

- Pile drainage.
- Mole drainage.
- Vertical drainage.
- Well drainage or Drainage wells.

Method of Providing Sub-Soil or Sub-Surface Drainage

Pipe Drains : This method of sub-soil drainage is suitable when a road runs in a flat country with low embankments and where the sub-soil water accumulates below the sub-grade. In this method pipe drains are placed. Below the surface of the ground in the permeable saturated stratum.

The pipes are usually made of vitrified clay and are placed on a bed of sand, crushed stone, or clay 15 cm thick, with open joints butting against each other. To prevent the earth from above entering the pipes, through open joints, a tarred paper is sometimes provided to cover the joints. These pipes are placed in the trench with proper slopes both cross and longitudinal. The pipes are 15 to 20 cm in diameter. Cross or transverse pipes which are 6 to

10 cm in diameter are also laid at a distance of 6 m to 20 m apart. The trench is then filled with hard porous materials as shown in Fig. 6.3.

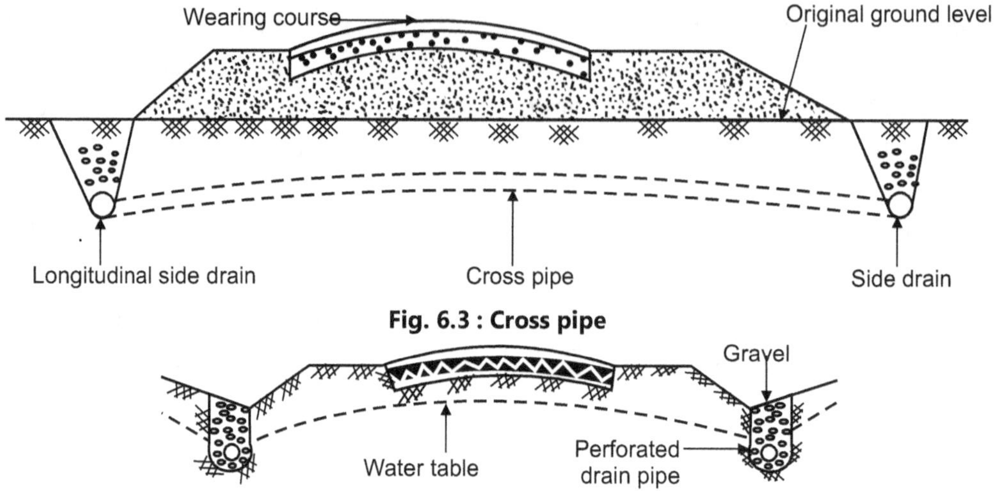

Fig. 6.3 : Cross pipe

Fig. 6.4 : Longitudinal pipe of sides of roads

The main longitudinal pipes may be laid in the centre or on both sides of the road depending upon the moisture conditions. The main pipe discharge their water into the surface drain.

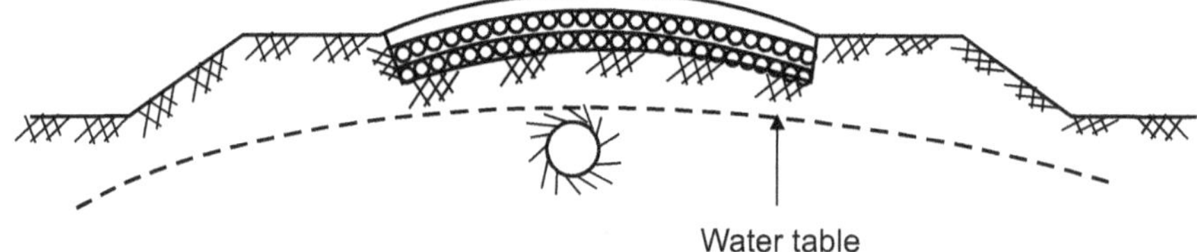

Fig. 6.5 : Longitudinal pipes in the centre of road

Kerb and Gullies

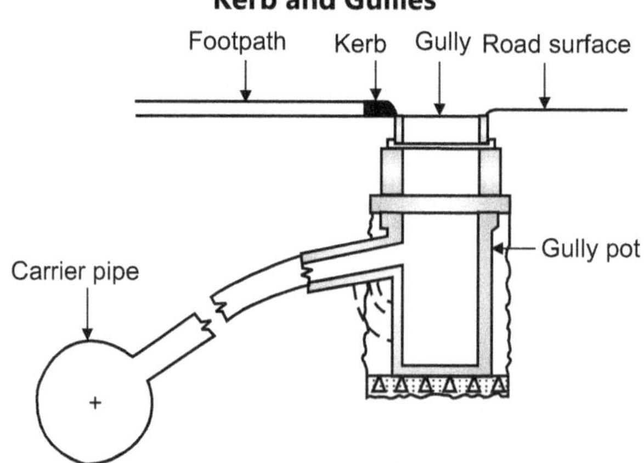

Fig. 6.6 : A typical scene of a kerb and gully drain and a layout of its construction

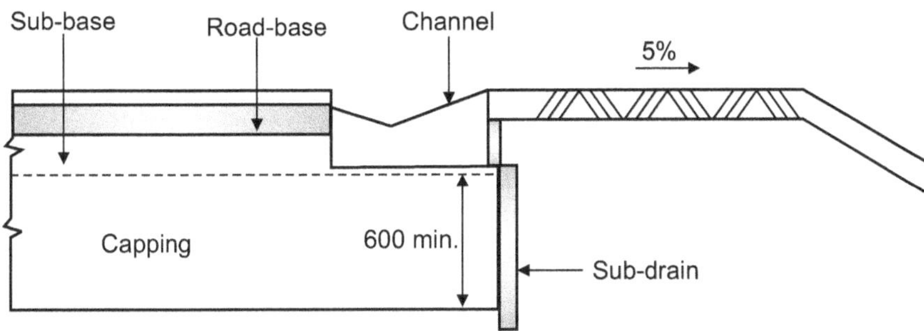

Fig. 6.7 : A typical scene of surface water channel drain and a layout of its construction

Surface water channels are normally of triangular/trapezoidal concrete section, usually slip-formed, set at the edge of hard strip or hard shoulder and flush with the road surface. They provide an economic alternative to edge channels and are the Agency's preferred edge-drain solution for rural locations (trunk roads and motorways). However, they may not be appropriate for roads with long stretches of zero longitudinal gradients. They provide a positive means of keeping the surface water on the surface for most of its journey thus avoiding the possibility of large quantities of water entering the road foundation and causing premature failures. Long length of channels, devoid of interruptions, can be constructed quickly and fairly inexpensively using slip-form techniques. They are capable of carrying large volumes of water over long distances and channel outlets can be located at appreciable spacing and to coincide with watercourses thus avoiding the need for a separate carrier pipe. They are easy to maintain and any long-term problems developing can be detected and monitored by simple visual inspection from the surface. Research suggests that properly designed channels pose no greater hazard than other common drainage features such as kerbs, embankments and ditches, and in most situations are potentially less hazardous.

6.6 TYPICAL DESIGNS OF SIDE DRAINS ON HILL ROADS

Some typical designs of side drains on hill roads are shown in Fig. 6.8.

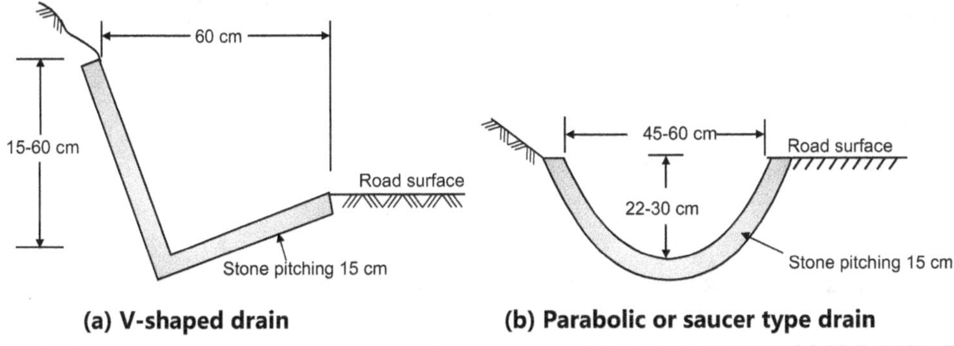

(a) V-shaped drain   **(b) Parabolic or saucer type drain**

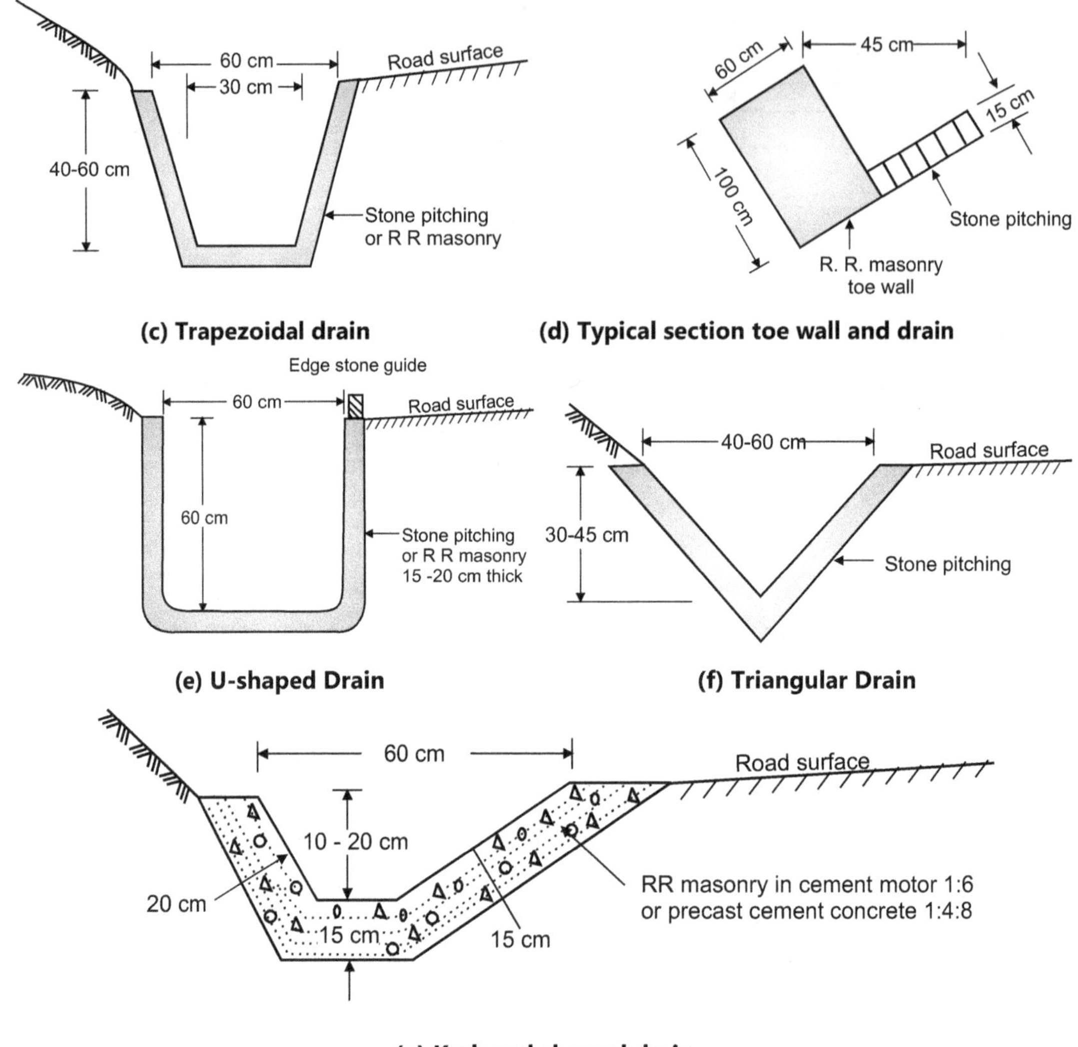

Fig. 6.8 : Typical designs of side chains on hill roads

6.7 ENVIRONMENT OF HIGHWAYS AND BYPASSES

6.7.1 Introduction

Environment of highways refers to the general appearance of the highway, its visual effect and the fringe benefits provided to the commuter. Road side amenity may be rest areas for long distance traveller laterally spaced at a sufficient distance apart preferably near a scenic spot and provided with toilets, water supply, food arrangements, overnight stay, etc. Another important offshoot of the environment of highways is landscaping and Road Side Arboriculture.

6.7.2 Land Scaping and Road Side Arboriculture

The highways should be so planned that they should appear part and parcel of the surroundings. Some of the principles of highway landscaping may be

- The alignment of the road should follow the natural terrain and harmoniously blend with it and it should preserve aesthetically valuable features, such as rock outcrops, waterfalls, architectural monuments etc. For example, for alignment between Satana and Khajuraho, the road while passing through the wooded area near Khajuraho passes near the Rajagarh Palace built by Chandelas. Road alignment in this part of the highway, is such that this palace is directly seen by the commuters plying on the road kindling in him the desire to see this off beat tourist attraction.

- Ugly scars due to cutting existing slope should be made good by vegetation, flatter slopes of embankments should be closely blended with the natural ground and vegetation should be grown on it to prevent erosion.

- All rotary islands and medians should be provided with flowering shrubs and borrow areas should be so treated that they do not leave ugly spot.

- The Architecture of bridges and culverts should be given careful thought.

6.8 ROAD SIDE ARBORICULTURE

The road side arboriculture refers to the road side trees and nursaries that are developed.
It has the following purposes.

- The trees afford shade, provide effective screen for unsightly views as slums, junks yard, storage depots etc.

- They yield fruits, wood, sometimes oil such as ucalyptus oil, making it a profitable proposition.

- Trees act as deterent to auto-exhaust and pollution due to it and to some extent prevent rain and wind erosion. Walking through boulevards is an experience. Many artists have drawn an inspiration from the trees that line the roads. For many writers. tree - line pathways have symbolized tranquility that is conducive to creative thinking. It should be noted that not only the highway department but also the railways are thinking of permanent way side plantations. In fact the Railway Board conducted a special study in December 1981 with the objective of evolving a plan of action of tree plantation along the track and the target has been set for 10 crores of trees in the next fifteen years. Time is not far off when not only our highways but even the rail-tracks will be tree lined.

6.8.1 The Principles to be Followed in Arboriculture

The principles that should be followed in road side development could now be discussed.

- In urban areas, road side plantation has aesthetic value. On wide urban roads, besides road plantation on road sides, medians or separator should be provided with shrubs, which reduce the head light glare during night driving. A typical arrangement is shown in Fig. 6.9. Wide crowned trees are not preferred. These obstruct the day light and are unsafe for night driving, therefore arrangement such as shown in Fig. 6.10 is not preferable but arrangement shown in Fig. 6.11 is preferable, in which carriageway is clear to the sky. Generally, trees are 12 metres away from the centre of the road. The general plan may be as shown in Fig. 6.9.

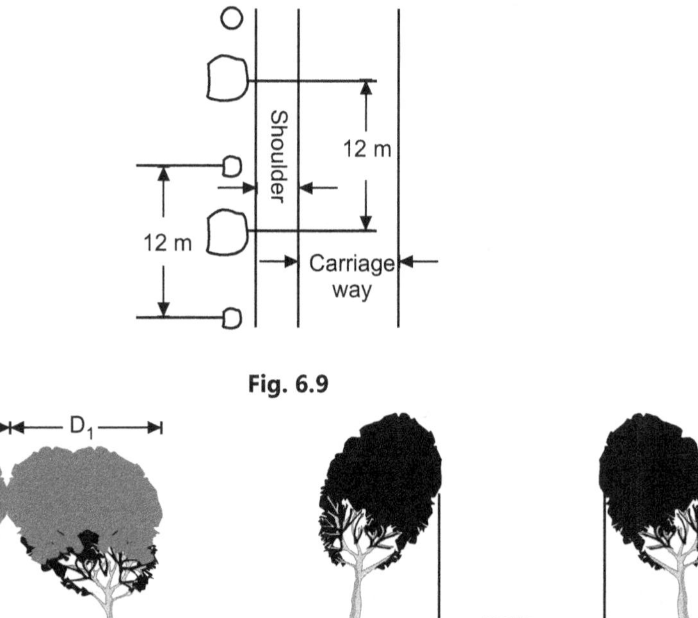

Fig. 6.9

Fig. 6.10

Fig. 6.11

- Plantation of the trees should be done on the advice of horticulturist. The species should be so selected that these are suitable for the existing soil type, and climate. The species should be fast developing, should be strong to resist heavy wind, if the road is passing through desert. In sub zero climate, proper trees should be chosen. The trees planted should be protected by either Iron guard, brick work or used bitumen drum, or a trench as shown in Fig. 6.12. The use of trench is of course recommended in rural areas.

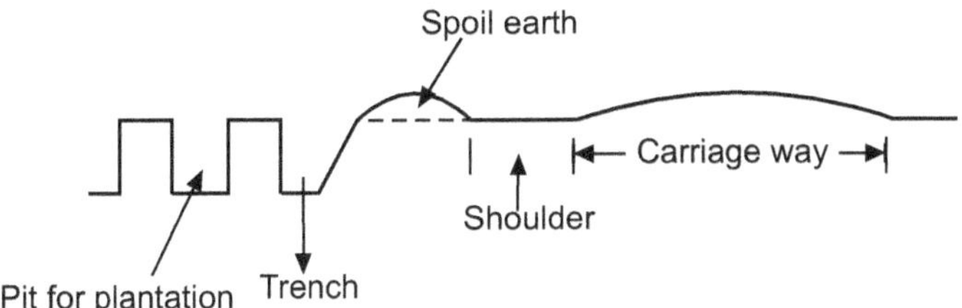

Fig. 6.12

• Nursary should be developed on the roadside so that there is a regular supply of plants. A typical layout of nursary is shown in Fig. 6.13. A nursary should be established 2 to 3 years in advance for transplantation. It is generally felt that new avenues would require about 180 and old avenues would require about 100 plants per km of road length for which nursary should be capable of supplying 270 plants for new avenues and 150 for old avenues, since seedling may die during the early growth.

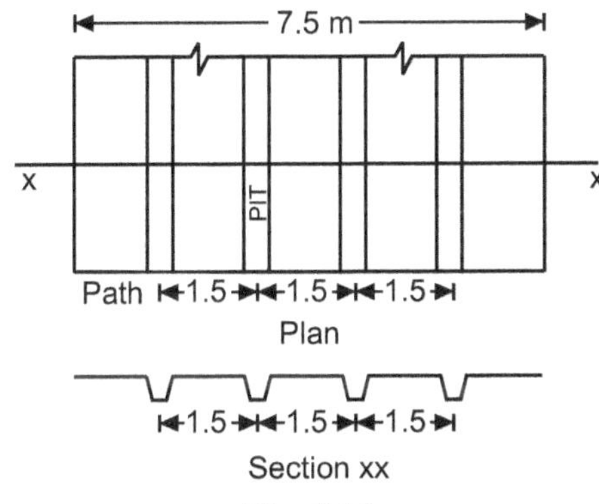

Fig. 6.13

• During the life time of the trees, these must be properly cared for with such operations such as deforking, lopping and felting. It must be stressed that growing healthy trees is a job of horticulturist and therefore he must be consulted at all stages. The civil engineer can make finances and skilled labour available to him and the job must be done under his supervision.

• If the road is located on embankment, providing turf on the side slopes, cuts and side drains give pleasing appearance. However, turf shoulders are generally not preferred as the grass grown on these shoulders can not resist traffic. The rain water that passes on road has in general more velocity due to smooth riding surface and it can cause erosion, hence in addition to road side plantation, woody plants or shrubs less than a metre high grown at sides can contain soil erosion effectively.

• As an example, how the trees can be provided to roadside, we give here the example of Amravati Bypass. The alignment of Amravati National Highway No. 6 Bye Pass of 17.8 km outside the Amravati Town is approved by ministry of transport. An amount of Rs. 25 lakhs was sanctioned in 1987 and the work was got done through specilised agency on regular contract of three years with the object of desired growth and survival of plants. The selection of tree species was declared on the basis of soil, rainfall, humidity, subsoil water, foliage, root depth fruition etc. with the help of experts. The entire proposed road was fenced on both sides. The tender documents for this work were such that the contractor has to grow specified trees upto specified height and growth with 90 % survival. The responsibility of giving proper watering agrochemicals, nutrients, pesticides etc. rested completely on the contractor.

Mr. Dhavad and Mr. A. K. Deo were the officers in charge and such a type of arboriculture was first taken-up on such a large scale in M. S. devising some what new tender documents.

6.8.2 Bypasses

The truck traffic passing through the main city is many a times responsible for ribbon development in India. It is good to provide bypass for such township for efficient movement of traffic and to control ribbon development. For example, truck going from Mumbai to Nagpur if it does not have cargo to be disembarked at Amravati, need not enter Amravati, if bypasses is provided for National Highway at Amravati. This will relieve truck traffic in the main city and the accompanied ribbon development with it. It should be remembered that adequate measures are taken to prevent recurrence of the phenomenon of ribbon development on the newly constructed bypasses. The bypasses are further discussed in this chapter elsewhere.

6.8.3 Service Roads

The concept of service roads or frontage roads in limiting the access on main highway, while simultaneously meeting the demand of abutting land owners for ingress and egress, has a lot of relevance. Such service roads prevent conjestion on the main way, reduce number of intersections, lessen the number of accidents and it is recommended that service roads should be insisted upon on highways where ribbon development has taken place, so also along new bypasses where it is feared in near future.

6.8.4 Removal of Road Side Encroachment and Control of Roadside Developments

The ribbon development always starts as an insignificant temporary structure along the highways and slowly develops into unsightly ribbon. Laws are existing in our country to evict these and what is required is a long term political will, non-corrupt organisation to nip such evil in the bud. Ribbon development and road side advertisements are twin evil that thrive on each other. In our country the roadside advertisement is generally controlled by municipal law, and they should be strictly enforced.

The state of Laws to Control Ribbon Development :

There have been some state laws such as the Bombay Highways act 1955, The Punjab Scheduled Road and controlled areas Restriction unregulated development Act 1963, The United Provinces Road side Land Control Act 1945, The Mysore Highway Act 1964. The

Mysore Public premises land (eviction rent recovery act 1972) which are in force in their respective territories. The deficiency of some of these acts are, they do not relate to National Highways. What is required is the unified approach throughout the nation, for which a model Highway Bill has been proposed by IRC, but it is not as yet accepted as legislation.

6.8.5 Road Traffic Noise

The road traffic noise can be controlled by variety of measures. Trucks, buses, and motor cycles are a major source of noise pollution. It is possible to control the noise level pollution by making the vehicles less noisy through legislation, but replacement of existing lorries and buses by new generation of quiet vehicles will take long time. Another misconceived notion in India for motorcycle riders is frequent use of horns and making noise by unnecessary acceleration, which must be curbed.

If we avoid existing residential area by diverting commercial through traffic away from the city streets, noticeable improvements in noise level can be obtained. Traffic management measures such as reducing the number of stopping, making one way streets, ban on lorries can also reduce noise levels

Good Engineering Designs :

Good engineering designs such as proper alignment, lesser grades, fewer stops at intersections, smoother road surface textures, and providing physical noise screens can reduce traffic noise considerably. Barriers are specially effective for elevated roads near low rise houses and if they are a part of the original design, they can be made visually acceptable. The usual tolerance level in residential area is around 70 dB (A). It has been found that a 11 feet concrete wall can provide good shield for noise. The eleven feet wall may not provide good appearance but a combination of five feet earth mond, topped by 6 feet wall can be pleasing and functional. The earth monds are better as they can both block and absorbs energy. Porous cinder block or expanded shale block, with the side away from the highway coated with stucco is advantageous. It has been proved beyond doubt that trees and plants do not serve any useful purpose they are porous to air flow vibrate easily and lack density and hence do not provide any sound benefit. There merit is to improve appearance and provide psychological shielding. The problem of noise on Indian roads, is not as yet well taken care of.

6.8.6 Air Pollution Due to Asphaltic Plant Operation

We have seen that the major pollution is due to particulate matter. To control particulate matters, it is required that much stress be given to control the particles of sizes beyond five microns. The control equipment available is of the following type.

(a) Dry mechanical collectors, (b) Wet scrubbers, and bag house (fabric filters). These equipments can be attached to the asphaltic plants and pollutants can be controlled to a very strict level. But the present cost of owning and operating such devices is coming in the way of their implementation. May be with growing awareness these equipments will be used more and more.

6.9 BYPASSES

Introduction :

A bypass is comparatively a post independence phenomenon. In the post independence time, the number of trucks and vehicles has increased drastically. The origin of destination study has indicated that some of the traffic need not enter the city at all. For example, a truck starting from Bombay, which has a cargo destined for Bangalore, need not enter Pune city if a bypass is available at Pune. This will relieve the conjestion in the city.

Advantages of Bypasses :

- The traffic which has no objects in a particular city does not enter the city. Thus traffic conjestion, pollution due to that traffic, noise due to that traffic, the possibilities of an accident due to that traffic are all lessened.

- The detention time of the transport vehicles is reduced and this results in reduction in operating cost of motor vehicle.

- The traffic need not get detained at octroi post; there is virtual absence of level crossing.

- The intangible benefits may include motor driver comfort, and improvement of social, economic, and regional structure.

- The land cost near the bypass may increase giving prosperity to the people, whose land is acquired for bypass construction.

- Sometimes the bypass is also required for strategic purposes in the case of border towns. For example, if it is border town, and a border road is passing through the main city, it is neither advisible nor proper to move military equipments through the interior of the city, and bypass if constructed will be ideal for military movements. The Road Hanumangarh, Suratgarh. Anupgarh could be quoted as an example.

This road initially belonged to Rajastan P.W.D. and was taken-up by Border Roads Organisation during May 1976 for strategic reasons. It was decided to extend the road to two lane specifications. As it was, this road passed through Surat garh town and the intensity of traffic on this highway has increased manifold due to strategic importance of this area, and during some periods. This necessitated an alternative route to bypass the township, and therefore Suratgarh bypass was conceived, construction work started in October 1985 and has got completed in March 1987. Another feature of this bypass which had strategic importance, is that this bypass was not only a desert road but also had to be constructed in an area where the alignment could not be changed. On one side, it had the Ghaggar river bed full of isolated ditches and on another side the built up area of Suratgarh township. As such there was hardly any scope for fixing the alignment of choice on the ground. This road partly runs through the river bed which necessitated the construction of a very high embankment ranging from 3 to 4 meters and partly it passes through a very high sand dune where cutting of the order of 4 meter was required.

6.9.1 Evaluation of Benefits from Bypass

Evaluation of tangible and intangible benefits from the bypass is somewhat difficult, but at the same, essential to justify the existence of bypass. Such attempts in India are not recorded. Kamdar, Desai el al had attempted to evaluate the benefits of national highway bypass around Vadodara city and as such it is described here.

(1) Vadodara a city of about 9,00,000 is located on Ahmedabad Bombay National Highway. NH 8. The highway passed through the city, but as the city grew fast with industrial development, the need for the bypass was felt. The construction of this bypass got completed in 1981. The total length of this bypass is about 26 kilometer, with seven meters carriage way.

(2) There were many tangible benefits such as reduction in operating cost of automobile, saving in time and less percentage of accidents. But there were many intangible benefits too. It was attempted to quantfy these intangible benefits.

There was a tremendous increase in the market value for the remaining land with the owner after acquisition of land. Because of the construction of bypass, there was reduction in monthly income of business establishments on old city routes and increase in monthly income on bypass route, the details of which are as under (as revealed by the answers to the questionaire)

Table 6.1

Activity	Percent Reduction in Monthly Income on Old City Route	Percent Increase in Monthly Income on Bypass Route
Hotels	51.36	48.16
Petrol Pumps	41.67	43.12
Motor Garages	48.86	51.00
Others	55.00	53.00

Approximately, there was as much reduction on old route, same was the increase on bypass, thus one may say that there was more equitable distribution of wealth in the community. To evaluate the effect of bypass on noise levels, the bypass was closed on 18th – 20th May 1982 and traffic diverted to old city route and noise observation, made at three relevant points. It was seen that there was 10 % decrease in noise level and because of the bypass night, noise level has decreased almost to a nill level.

All in all, one can say that bypass has proved it's worth.

Disadvantages:

This does not mean, that every thing is O.K. and there are no disadvantages with the bypass system, it it not so. These disadvantages are -

- Agricultural land is required to be acquired for the construction of bypass. The loss of this agricultural land is a national loss and there is proportionate loss of the individual whose lands have been acquired.

- There is a loss of business in the main city since some of the traffic simply does not enter the city.

- There is likely hood of some ribbon development along the bypass.

- The concept of bypass can not be a permanent solution. Sooner or later, the city sprawls towards the bypass and it gradually becomes a city thorough fare. This development is inevitable, however construction of bypass does smoothen and ease the flow of both through traffic and city traffic.

QUESTIONS

1. What is necessity of drainage?
2. Explain the drainages problem in hill roads.
3. Discuss the following with neat sketches with respect to sub-surface drainage.
   (a)   Lowering of water table.
   (b)   Control of seepage flow.
4. Write short note on:
   (a) Importance of drainages.
   (b) Surface drainages.
   (c) Sub-surface drainage.
   (d) Typical Designs of Side Drains on Hill Roads
5. What is Arboriculture? What role does it play in highway environment? Discuss any specific case.
6. What principles should be kept in view, while designing landscaping and road side arboriculture?
7. What are the benefits derived from road side arboriculture?
8. What is significance of drainage?

Chapter 7
HIGHWAY MATERIALS

7.1 CLASSIFICATION OF ROADS

The civil engineering materials that are used for highway construction are :

(1) Soils,

(2) Aggregate,

(3) Cement,

(4) Bitumen,

(5) Sand,

(6) Flyash,

(7) Certain stabilizing chemicals.

Whereas soil is essentially a part of subgrade, aggregate is used either as base course or as a part and parcel of cement concrete. Sand can be used in cement concrete or even bituminous surfacings. Flyash is used as replacement of cement, and stabilizing chemicals are used for stabilized bases. Materials that are used are no different from general civil engineering constituent materials, certain specific properties and performance are expected when they are used in highway construction. To assess these properties, certain tests have been developed. It is the object of this chapter to study these tests, understand their limitations and know, how the knowledge that is gathered from this testing can profitably be used. We shall first discuss the requirements of soil then aggregate and then bitumen the last. The test pertaining to other materials such as cement and sand are not specific. The tests regarding fly ash and stabilizing chemicals are discussed at the proper juncture.

Pavements are a conglomeration of materials. These materials, their associated properties, and their interactions determine the properties of the resultant pavement. Thus, a good understanding of these materials, how they are characterized, and how they perform is fundamental to understanding pavement. The materials which are used in the construction of highway are of intense interest to the highway engineer. This requires not only a thorough understanding of the soil and aggregate properties which affect pavement stability and durability, but also the binding materials which may be added to improve these pavement features.

Subgrade Soil : Soil is an accumulation or deposit of earth material, derived naturally from the disintegration of rocks or decay of vegetation that can be excavated readily with power equipment in the field or disintegrated by gentle mechanical means in the laboratory. The supporting soil beneath pavement and its special under courses is called subgrade. Undisturbed soil beneath the pavement is called natural subgrade. Compacted subgrade is the soil compacted by controlled movement of heavy compactors.

7.1.1 Desirable Properties

The desirable properties of subgrade soil as a highway material are :

- Stability.

- Incompressibility.

- Permanency of strength.

- Minimum changes in volume and stability under adverse conditions of weather and ground water.

- Good drainage.

- Ease of compaction.

7.1.2 Soil Types

The wide range of soil types available as highway construction materials have made it obligatory on the part of the highway engineer to identify and classify different soils. A survey of locally available materials and soil types conducted in India revealed wide variety of soil types, gravel, moorum and naturally occurring soft aggregates, which can be used in road construction. Broadly, the soil types can be categorized as Laterite soil, Moorum / red soil, Desert sands, Alluvial soil, Clay including Black cotton soil.

Gravel	Sand			Silt			Clay		
	Coarse	Medium	Fine	Coarse	Medium	Fine	Coarse	Medium	Fine
	0.6 mm		0.2 mm	0.02 mm		0.006 mm	0.0006 mm		0.0002 mm
2 mm				0.06 mm			0.002 mm		

Fig. 7.1 : Indian standard grain size soil classification system

Gravel : These are coarse materials with particle size under 2.36 mm with little or no fines contributing to cohesion of materials.

Moorum : These are products of decomposition and weathering of the pavement rock. Visually these are similar to gravel except presence of higher content of fines.

Silts : These are finer than sand, brighter in colour as compared to clay, and exhibit little cohesion. When a lump of silty soil mixed with water, alternately squeezed and tapped a shiny surface makes its appearance, thus dilatancy is a specific property of such soil.

Clays : These are finer than silts. Clayey soils exhibit stickiness, high strength when dry, and show no dilatancy. Black cotton soil and other expansive clays exhibit swelling and shrinkage properties. Paste of clay with water when rubbed in between fingers leaves stain, which is not observed for silts.

7.1.3 Tests on Soil

Subgrade soil is an integral part of the road pavement structure as it provides the support to the pavement from beneath. The subgrade soil and its properties are important in the design of pavement structure. The main function of the subgrade is to give adequate support to the pavement and for this the subgrade should possess sufficient stability under adverse climatic and loading conditions. Therefore, it is very essential to evaluate the subgrade by conducting tests. The tests used to evaluate the strength properties of soils may be broadly divided into three groups :

- Shear tests.
- Bearing tests.
- Penetration tests.
- **Shear Tests** are usually carried out on relatively small soil samples in the laboratory. In order to find out the strength properties of soil, a number of representative samples from different locations are tested. Some of the commonly known shear tests are direct shear test, triaxial compression test, and unconfined compression test.
- **Bearing Tests** are loading tests carried out on sub grade soils in-situ with a load bearing area. The results of the bearing tests are influenced by variations in the soil properties within the stressed soil mass underneath and hence the overall stability of the part of the soil mass stressed could be studied.
- **Penetration Tests** may be considered as small scale bearing tests in which the size of the loaded area is relatively much smaller and ratio of the penetration to the size of the loaded area is much greater than the ratios in bearing tests. The penetration tests are carried out in the field or in the laboratory.

7.1.3.1 Plate Bearing Test

This test is useful in determining the modulus of subgrade reaction, whose value is used in the design of rigid pavements. Fig. 7.2 shows the arrangement for plate test.

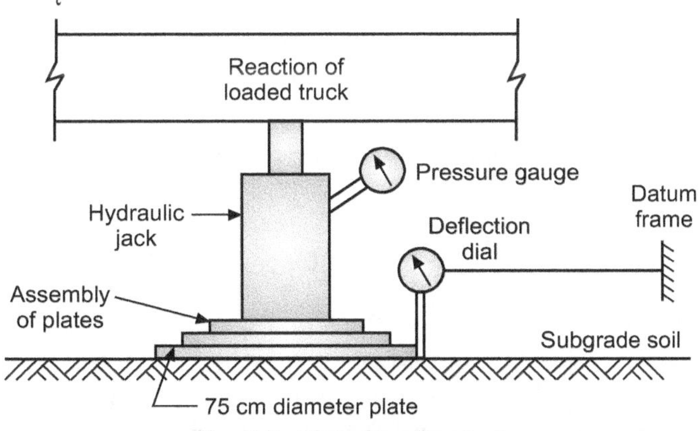

Fig. 7.2 : Plate bearing test

The plate used : Is generally 75 cm diameter of 25 mm thickness. Plate is located on the subgrade with sandwiched layer of sand in between for even distribution of load. In general, the load is applied through hydraulic jack. The deflection of the bearing plate is measured by dial gauges. Test naturally should be conducted on the subgrade when it is under worst moisture conditions, such as conditions of flooding. This may not always be possible. In such a case, artificial flooding should be resorted to, the initial seating load for the plate is 0.7 N/cm^2. For a 75 cm diameter plate, this load would work out to 310 kg. This seating load

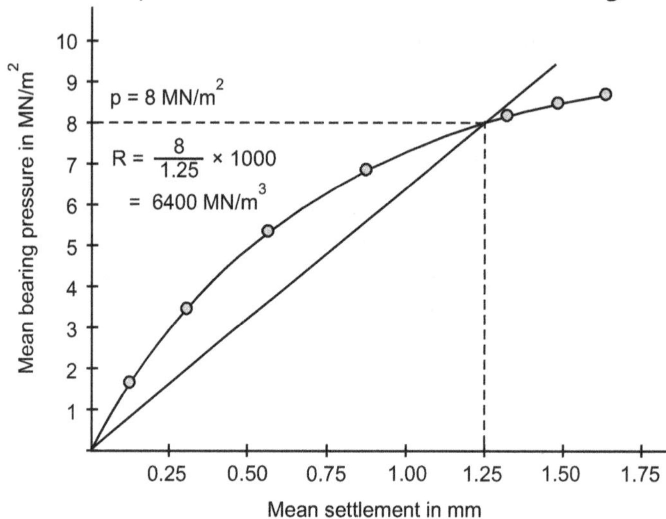

Fig. 7.3 : Load settlement curve for plate bearing test

should be applied, but then immediately released. The next increment of load should be such as to cause settlement of 0.25 mm approximately. When the load is acting on the plate, the rate of settlement decreases with time. Additional increment of load can be imposed when the rate of settlement is less than 0.025 mm/minute. This procedure should be repeated till a settlement of 1.75 mm results. A typical load settlement curve is shown in Fig. 7.3. If there is linear variation between stress and strain of the subgrade, the load settlement curve is straight line passing through the origin. Generally, this is not the case, and the load settlement line will be a curve. In such cases, the value of K, the modulus of subgrade reaction could be considered as the slope of the line passing through the origin and the point on the curve corresponding to settlement of 1.25 mm. For example, in the figure,

$$K = \frac{8}{1.25} \times 100 = 6400 \ MN/m^3.$$

When the plate load test is conducted in the worst conditions of the ground, there is no correction required in the K value. But when the test is conducted at a moisture content other than the saturated condition, a correction is required to the K value. To assess this correction, a soil sample is compacted at density and moisture content corresponding to the density and moisture content available when plate load test is conducted and its CBR value is determined, let this CBR be CBR_1. Now the sample at this density and moisture content is prepared and then saturated and its CBR is determined. Let this CBR be CBR_2. Then the ratio $\dfrac{CBR_2}{CBR_1}$ is a multiplier with which obtained K value must be multiplied to get the K value when ground would be saturated.

If a small diameter plate (30 cm diameter) is used, the K value could be converted to the standard 75 cm diameter plate value by the experimentally obtained correction. $K_{75} = 0.5\ K_{30}$, where K_{75} represents K value with 75 cm diameter plate and K_{30} represents K value with 30 cm diameter plate. This formula of course overestimates the foundation strength and should be used with care.

7.1.3.2 California Bearing Ratio Test

California bearing ratio test abbreviated as CBR test is a very popular test with highway engineers. It was first devised by O. J. Procter of California Division of Highways and is now a basis for the design of flexible pavements. The test can be conducted on remoulded specimen in the laboratory, or undistured specimen brought in the laboratory or in-situ on the subgrade soil itself. The diagrammatic sketch of the test is shown in Fig. 7.4. The mould has internal dimensions of 150 mm diameter and 175 mm height and generally is of phospher - bronze. The mould also has a detachable perforated base. This perforated base can be fitted either at the top or bottom. When filling the mould with soil, a disc 50 mm deep and 152 mm diameter is kept at the bottom and then the compaction is commenced. This procedure gives a soil specimen exactly of 127 mm height. CBR is essentially a penetration test and the penetration is caused by a plunger 50 mm diameter, penetrating at the centre of specimen at constant rate of strain of 1.25 mm/minute. When the machine to cause constant rate of strain is not available, ordinary hydraulic testing machine can be used, with rate of penetration controlled by the stop watch.

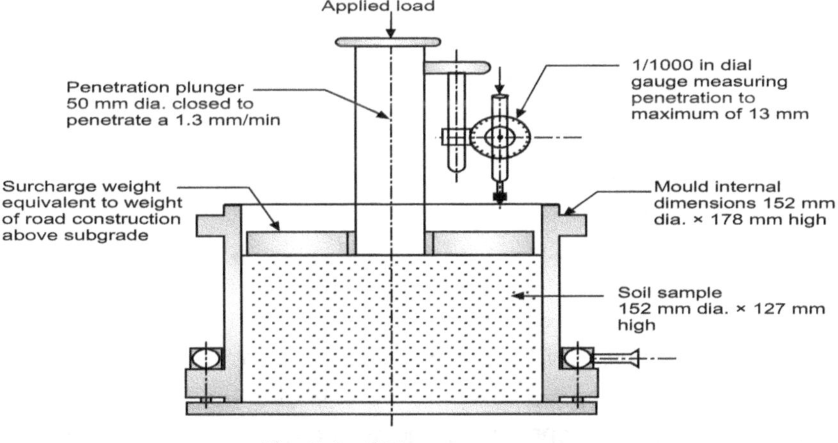

Fig. 7.4 : CBR test apparatus

For the in-situ test, loaded truck is used to provide the reaction and loading is through a screw jack. In actual field conditions, the subgrade is loaded by the weight of the pavement. To similiate these field conditions; surcharge weights are placed on the surface of the specimen. As a rough guide, 10 kg weight can be considered equal to 25 cm thick pavement. When conducting tests in the laboratory, the choice of the density and moisture content is very crucial. Naturally, the first choice is that the minimum state of compaction that might occur in the field. The design should be based on this CBR. Current standards in India suggest that subgrade should be compacted to at least 100 percent Proctor and hence this density could be used for test.

The recommended practice for new roads is to prepare the samples at optimum moisture content corresponding to Proctor compaction and get them soaked for four days and test them in this saturated condition. For existing roads, on which some modification is planned, the moisture content at which the testing should be done should be assessed just after the rains, in the field. In this particular case, the density of the specimen should be the field density, and not the maximum dry density. The water content and the field density should be determined at a distance of 0.6 to 1 meter from the pavement edge and directly below the pavement.

The procedure of soaking is dispensed within India, for :

- Roads in arid zones where the rainfall is less than 50 cms annually.

- Roads having a comparatively thick bituminous surfacing of impermeable nature and

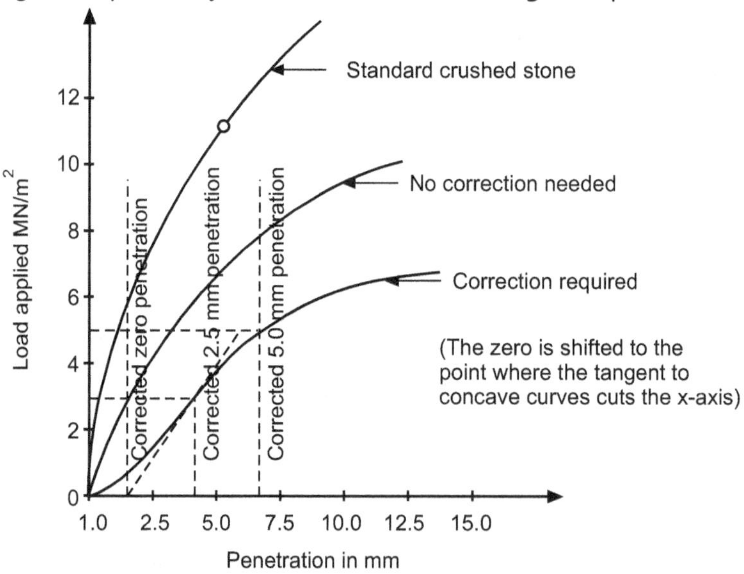

Fig. 7.5 : Load penetration curve

where the water table is too deep. To have an idea regarding the depth of water table, some sampling may be undertaken. Generally, if the water table is greater than one meter in sands, three meter in sandy clays, and six meter in heavy clays, the procedure of soaking may be dropped.

There is a school of thought that the CBR test should be conducted on samples, compacted at equilibrium moisture content. This school of thought has not received much backing in India.

After conducting the CBR test, the load penetration curve is drawn. A typical curve is shown in Fig. 7.5. Load penetration curve curving concave upwards, require correction. This correction is also shown in Fig. 7.5. The loads for penetration or 2.5 mm of 5 mm are noted. It has been seen that load of 6.895 MN/m^2 and 10.343 MN/m^2 cause the above penetrations in the case of standard crushed stones. The CBR value is expressed as a percentage of the actual load causing the penetrations of 2.5 mm or 5 mm to the standard loads just mentioned respectively. Thus,

$$\text{CBR} = \frac{\text{Load carried by specimen}}{\text{Load carried by standard crushed stone specimen}} \times 100$$

Two values of CBR can thus be obtained. The value at 2.5 mm is greater than that at 5 mm penetration, the former is adopted. If not, the test has to be repeated and if the new value of CBR at 5 mm penetration is still greater, this value of CBR will have to be used for design purposes. Some typical values of CBR of Indian soils are given in the table below.

Table 7.1

Type of Soil	Murum	Well Graded Sand	Sandy Clay	Silty Lay	Alluvial Silt	Black Cotton and Heavy Clays
CBR values	8 to 20	8 to 20	4 to 6	3 to 5	2 to 5	1 to 2

7.2 AGGREGATES

Introduction : Almost all the aggregates available in India and used for road construction are natural aggregates. The origin of all such aggregates could be igneous rocks, which are derived from the cooling of molten magma, or sedimentary rocks, which are formed due to action of water or ice, and metamorphic rocks which are end result of igneous or sedimentary rocks subjected to heat and pressure at deep depths of earth crust. Whereas the granite and basalt are both suitable for bituminous courses and cement concrete pavement, sedimentary rock such as quartzite which is reasonably hard and durable rock is good for bituminous courses and cement concrete pavement. It can also be used profitably for base courses. Limestone is good for base course but is not recommended for wearing course. Sandstone is good for road base. Laterites and Kankar are good for sub-base and base courses and their use as surface course is possible only in unimportant roads. In addition to the above terms designating the origin of the aggregate, some typical terms used in describing the aggregate are :

(1) Fine Aggregate : Aggregates mainly between 4.75 mm (5 mm) to 75 micron in size.

(2) Coarse Aggregate : Aggregate particles mainly larger than 5 mm in size.

(3) Crushed Rock : Aggregate obtained from the crushing of bedrock. All particles are angular.

(4) Screenings : The chips and dust or powder that are produced in the crushing of bedrock for aggregates.

7.2.1 Desirable Properties of Aggregates

Aggregate forms the major part of the pavement structure and it is the prime material used in pavement construction. Aggregates have to primarily bear load, stresses occurring on the roads and runways and have to resist wear due to abrasive action of traffic. Aggregate often serve as granular base-course underlying the superior pavements. Thus, properties of aggregates are of considerable significance.

Aggregates which are used in the surface course have to withstand the high magnitude of stresses, wear and tear due to abrasion. Such aggregates should have sufficiently high strength or resistance to crushing. These aggregates further need to be hard enough to resist the wear due to abrasive action of traffic. The specific gravity of stone is considered to be a measure for finding the suitability and strength characteristics of aggregates. Higher the specific gravity, better is the road aggregates. The presence of air voids or pores in stones is another property, which may indicate the suitability and strength characteristics of stones. More the voids, the strength is likely to be less, of course the specific gravity of such stones will also be lower.

The size of the aggregate is qualified by the size of square sieve opening through which the same may pass, and not the shape. Aggregates which happen to fall in a particular size range may have lesser strength and durability when compared with cubical, angular or rounded particles of the same stone. Hence too flaky and elongated aggregates should be avoided as far as possible. Rounded aggregates may be preferred in cement concrete mix due to better workability for the same proportion of cement paste and same water-cement ratio, whereas rounded particles are not preferred in granular base course and W.B.M. construction as the stability due to interlocking is lesser in these aggregates. In such construction, angular particles are preferred.

Heavy moving loads on the surface of flexible pavements may cause considerable deformation of the pavement layer resulting in possible relative movement and mutual rubbing of aggregate particles. This can cause wear on the points of contacts of the aggregates especially in the granular base course of flexible pavements. This action may not be of appreciable significance in bituminous concrete pavements. This Example is unlikely to exist in cement concrete roads as the pavement is rigid and no relative movement between the aggregate is possible before the pavement fails. The mutual rubbing action of the aggregates is termed as attrition and the resistance to wear due to attrition is considered as a desirable property for aggregates to be used in for W.B.M. construction, granular base, and surface course of flexible pavement.

Desirable properties of aggregates thus depend on type of pavement construction, traffic and climatic conditions. Above mentioned all properties need not necessarily be possessed by aggregates in a group for a particular construction. It is necessary, therefore, to carry out various tests on aggregates in order to ensure that not only are undesirable materials excluded from the pavements of highways, but also the best available aggregates are included.

7.3 TESTS ON AGGREGATES

The common tests on road aggregates in India are :
- Gradation and shape tests, consisting of, sieve analysis, flakiness index test and angularity number test.
- Specific gravity, porosity and water absorption.
- Estimation of deleterious materials such as clay lumps and soft particles.
- The strength test such as aggregate crushing.
- Hardness test such as Los-angeles abrasion.
- Aggregate impact.
- Aggregate polishing and stripping test. These are now discussed.

7.4 GRADATION TESTS

Introduction : This is the most common test performed on aggregates. Most specifications for concrete and asphalt mixes require a grain size distribution that will provide a dense, strong layer of aggregates.

A convenient system of expressing the gradation of aggregate is the one in which the consecutive sieve openings are doubled, such as 10 mm, 20 mm, 40 mm, etc. Under such a system, employing a logarithmic scale, lines can be spaced at equal intervals to represent the successive sizes. The aggregates used for making concrete are normally of the maximum size 80 mm, 40 mm, 20 mm, 10 mm, 4.75 mm, 2.36 mm, 600 micron, 300 micron and 150 micron. The aggregate fractions from 80 mm to 4.75 mm are termed as coarse aggregates and those from 4.75 mm to 150 micron are termed as fine aggregates.

From the sieve analysis, the particle size distribution in a sample of aggregate is found out. In this connection, a term known as "Fineness Modulus" is being used. Fineness modulus is a index of coarseness or fineness of the material. Fineness modulus is a factor obtained by adding the cumulative percentage of aggregate retained on each of the standard sieve ranging from 80 mm to 150 micron and dividing this sum by an arbitrary number 100. The larger the figure, the coarser is the material.

Experimental Procedure

(1) Apparatus

Table 7.2

Sr. No.	Type of Sieve	Sieve Designation
(1)	Square hole, perforated plates	80 mm, 63 mm, 50 mm, 40 mm, 31.5 mm, 25 mm, 20 mm,
(2)	Fine mesh, wire cloth	16 rag 12.5 mm, 10 mm, 6.3 mm, 4.75 mm, 3.35 mm, 2.36 mm, 1.18 mm, 600 micron, 300 micron, 150 micron, 75 micron

(2) Balance : The balance or scale shall be such that it is readable and accurate to 0.1 percent of the weight of the test sample.

Test Procedure : The sample shall be brought to an air-dry condition before weighing and sieving. This may be achieved either by drying at room temperature or by heating at a temperature of 100°C to 110°C. The air-dry sample shall be weighed and sieved successively on the appropriate sieves starting with the largest. Each sieve shall be shaken separately for not less than two minutes. Shaking shall be done with a varied motion, so that the material is kept moving over the sieve surface in frequently changing directions. Material shall not be forced through the sieve by hand pressure, but on sieves coarser than 20 mm, placing of particles is permitted.

On completion of sieving, the material retained on each sieve, together with any material cleaned from the mesh, shall be weighed. The results shall be calculated and reported as :

(a) The cumulative percentage by weight of the total sample passing each of the sieves, to the nearest whole number or

(b) The percentage by weight of the total sample passing one sieve, and retained on the next smaller sieve, to the nearest 0.1%.

7.5 SHAPE TESTS

Theory and Significance of Shape Tests : There are three mechanical measures of particle shape which may be included in the specification for road construction. These are the flakiness index, elongation index and angularity number. The flakiness index of an aggregate is the percentage by weight of particles whose least dimension (thickness) is less than three-fifth of their mean dimension; the mean dimension as used in each instance is the average of the two adjacent sieve aperture sizes between which the particles being measured is retained by sieving.

Elongation index of an aggregate is the percentage by weight of particles whose greatest length is greater than $1\frac{4}{5}$ ths times their mean dimension. The angularity number of an aggregate is the amount, to the nearest whole number, by which the percentage of voids exceeds 33 percent when aggregate is compacted in a specified manner in a standardized metal cylinder. Flat particles, thin particles, or long, needle shaped particles break more easily than cubical particles. Particles with rough, fractured faces allow a better bond with cements than the rounded, smooth gravel particles.

The standards for single-sized aggregates require that their flakiness indices should not be greater than 40 for 40 mm or larger size and 35 for aggregates which are 25 mm and smaller in sizes. Since other factors being equal, an aggregate composed of smooth rounded particles of a certain gradation will contain less voids than another aggregate of the same grading, but composed of angular particles, the angularity of an aggregate can be reflected in terms of the volume of contained voids when the aggregate is compacted. The angularity number may range from zero for a material composed of highly rounded beach-gravel particles to 10 or more for newly-crushed rock aggregates.

Apparatus : The apparatus shall consist of the following :

(a) Balance : The balance shall be of sufficient capacity and sensitivity and shall have an accuracy of 0.1% of the weight of the test sample.

(b) Metal Gauge or Thickness Gauge : The metal gauge shall be of pattern as shown in Fig. 7.6.

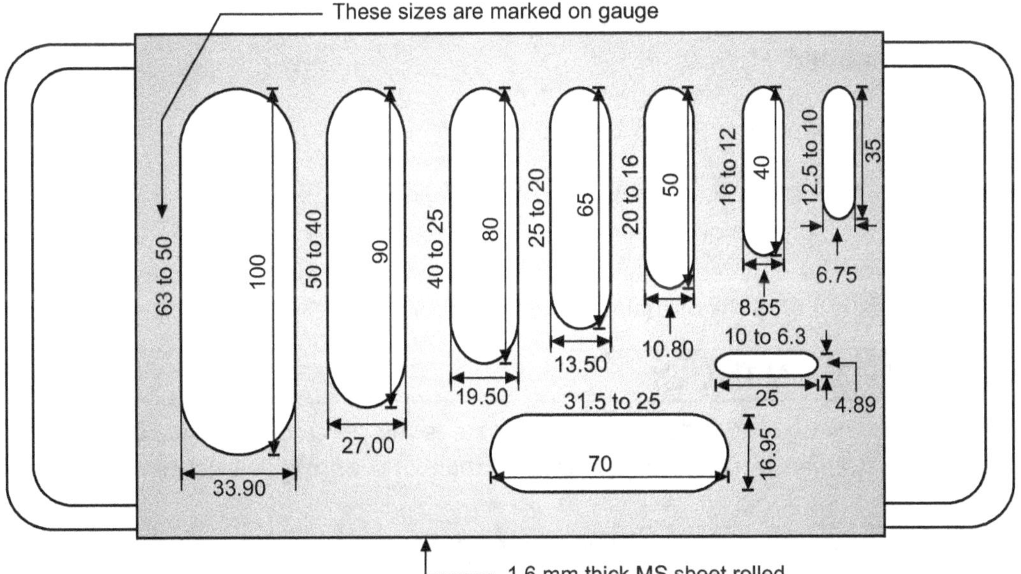

Note : *All dimensions are in millimetres*

Fig. 7.6 : Thickness gauge

(c) Sieves : Set of I.S. sieves.

Test Procedure : A sample of the aggregate to be tested is sieved through a set of sieves and separated into specified range as per the following table.

Table 7.3

Size of Aggregate		Thickness
Passing Through I.S. Sieve	**Retained on I.S. Sieve**	**Gauge**
63 mm	50 mm	33.90 mm
50 mm	40 mm	27.00 mm
40 mm	25 mm	19.50 mm
31.5 mm	25 mm	16.95 mm
25 mm	20 mm	13.50 mm
20 mm	16 mm	10.80 mm
16 mm	12.5 mm	8.55 mm
12.5 mm	10 mm	6.75 mm
10 mm	6.3 mm	4.89 mm

A quantity of aggregate shall be taken sufficient to provide a minimum two hundred number of pieces of any fraction to be tested.

Each fraction shall be gauged, in turn, for thickness on metal gauge as shown in Fig. 7.6. The width of slot used in the gauge shall be of dimension specified in the table for the appropriate size of material. Total amount passing the gauge shall be weighed to an accuracy of at least 0.1 percent of the weight of test sample.

Reporting of Result

$$\text{Flakiness index} \ = \ \frac{W_1}{W} \times 100$$

where, W_1 = Weight of flaky material from the whole sample.

         W = Total weight of sample.

(Flakiness index is the percentage by weight of particles in it whose least dimension (thickness) is less than 3/5 ths of their mean dimension.)

7.6 ELONGATION INDEX

Definition : The elongation index of an aggregate is the percentage by weight of particles whose greatest dimension (length) is greater than one and four-fifth times their mean dimension.

Apparatus for Test : The apparatus shall consist of the following :

(a) Balance

(b) Metal Gauge : The metal gauge shall be of the pattern shown in Fig. 7.7.

(c) Sieves : A set of I.S. sieves.

The sample of aggregate to be tested shall be sieved through a set of sieves and separated into specified range as per the following table :

Table 7.4

Size of Aggregate		Length
Passing through I.S. Sieve (mm)	**Retained on I.S. Sieve (mm)**	**Gauge**
63	50	–
50	40	81
40	25	58.5
31.5	25	–
25	20	40.5
20	16	32.4
16	12.5	25.6
12.5	10	20.2
10	6.3	14.7

The sample shall be sieved first with the use of I.S. sieves. Each fraction shall be gauged individually for the length on the metal gauge of pattern shown in Fig. 7.7. The total amount retained by the length gauge shall be weighed to an accuracy of at least 0.1% of the weight of the test sample. The elongation index is the total weight of material retained on the various length gauges, expressed as the percentage of the total weight of the sample gauged.

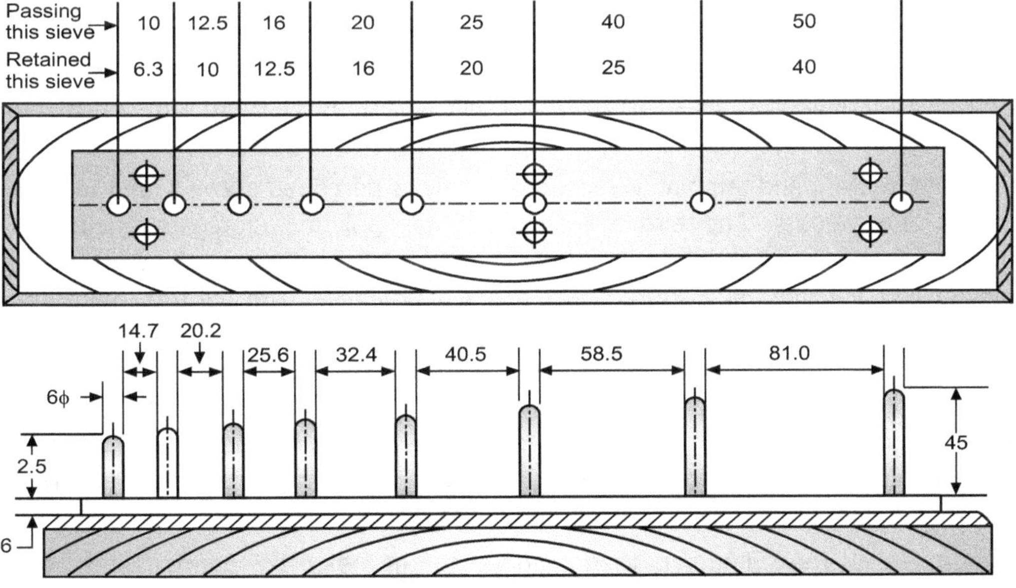

Fig. 7.7 : Length gauge

7.7 ANGULARITY NUMBER

The apparatus consists of :

- A metal cylinder closed at one end and of about 3 litre capacity, the diameter and height of it being approximately equal.

- Metal tamping rod of circular cross section 16 mm in diameter and 60 cm in length, rounded at one end.

- A metal scoop of about one litre heaped capacity of size $20 \times 12 \times 5$ cm.

- A balance of capacity 10 kg to weigh upto 1 gm.

The cylinder is calibrated by determining the weight of water at 27°C required to fill it. The amount of aggregate available should be sufficient to provide, after separation on the appropriate pair of sieves, at least 10 kg of the predominant size as determined by the sieve analysis on the 26, 16, 12.5, 10, 6.3 and 4.75 mm I.S. sieves. The test sample should consist of aggregate retained between the appropriate pair of I.S. sieves having square holes from the following sets :

20 and 16 mm, 16 and 12.5 mm, 12.5 and l0 mm, 10.0 and 6.3 mm, 6.3 and 4.75 mm. In testing aggregates larger than 20 mm, the volume of the cylinder shall be greater than three litre capacity. The sample of aggregate is dried in an oven at a temperature 100° to 110°C for 24 hours, and cooled in an air-tight container prior to testing. The scoop is filled and heaped to overflowing with the aggregate, which is placed in the cylinder by allowing it slide gently off the scoop from the lowest possible height. The aggregate in the cylinder is subjected to 100 blows of the tamping rod at the rate of about 2 blows per second. Each blow is applied by holding the rod vertical with its rounded end 5 cm above the surface of aggregate and releasing it. So that it falls vertically and no force is applied to the rod. The 100 blows should be distributed evenly over the surface of the aggregate.

The process of filling and tamping is repeated exactly as described above with a second and third layer of aggregates. The third layer should contain only the aggregate required to just fill up the cylinder level before tamping. After the third layer is tamped, the cylinder is filled to overflowing, and the extra aggregate is struck off the level with the top using tamping rod as a straight edge. Individual pieces of aggregate are then added and rolled into the surface by rolling the tamping rod across the upper edge of the cylinder, and this finishing process is continued as long as the aggregates do not lift the rod off the edge of the cylinder on either side, during rolling. The aggregate should not be pushed in or forced down and no downward pressure should be applied to the tamping rod, which is only rolled in contact with the top of the cylinder, on both sides.

The aggregate in the cylinder is then weighed to the nearest 5 grams. Three separate determinations are made and the mean weight of the aggregate in the cylinder is calculated. If the results of any one of the determination differ from the mean by more than 25 gm, three additional determinations are immediately made on the same material and the mean of all the size determination calculated.

Reporting of Results : The angularity number is calculated from the following formula :

$$\text{Angularity number} = 67 - \frac{100 \times W}{C \times G_A}$$

where,

W = Mean weight of aggregate in gram in the cylinder,

C = Weight of water in gram required to fill the cylinder,

and

G_A = Specific gravity of aggregate.

7.8 SPECIFIC GRAVITY AND WATER ABSORPTION TEST

Introduction : The specific gravity of an aggregate is considered to be a measure of strength or quality of material. Stones having low specific gravity are generally weaker than those with higher specific gravity values. The specific gravity test helps in the identification of stone. Water absorption gives an idea of strength of rock. Stones having more water absorption are generally considered unsuitable unless they are found to be acceptable based on strength and hardness test.

Specific gravity and water absorption of aggregates are important properties, especially in mix design for concrete and asphalt mixtures. With the aggregate for road works construction being proportioned by weight, as the usual practice, the specific gravity is of vital importance in determining the proper proportions of the resulting mixture.

Gradation specifications are valid only if the coarse and fine fractions have approximately the same specific gravities. If the value for the fine fraction is much greater than that for the coarse, the result is a mixture which, because of lack of fines, may be too harsh. On the other hand, if specific gravity of the coarse fraction is greater, a mixture which is too rich in fines may be obtained. When these conditions are encountered in practice, arbitrary gradation should not be used, but instead various gradation mixtures should be analysed carefully and evaluated on their own merits.

In reality, there are two specific gravities, depending on how measurement is made. As illustrated in Fig. 7.8 these are the bulk and apparent specific gravities. The bulk specific gravity is the ratio of the weight in air of a volume of aggregate (this includes voids which are permeable and impermeable) to the weight in air of an equal volume of distilled water. The apparent specific gravity is the ratio of the weight, in air of a volume of aggregate (including impermeable, but not permeable voids) to the weight in air of an equal volume of distilled water.

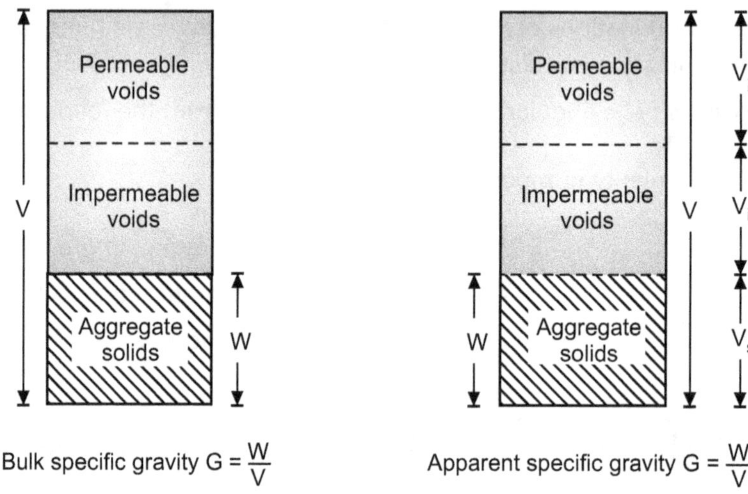

Fig. 7.8

Water absorption test is normally carried out in conjunction with the specific gravity test. Knowledge of the absorption properties of an aggregate is practically important in bituminous surfacing design, since the porosity of the aggregate affects the amount of binder required and additional binder material may have to be incorporated in the mixture to satisfy the absorption by the aggregate after the ingradients have been mixed. On the beneficial side, porous aggregates usually show better adhesion to the binder due to the mechanical interlock caused by the binder penetrating the particles.

The water absorption values allowed for road aggregates normally range from less than 0.1 percent to 2 percent for materials used in road surfacing, while values of upto 4 percent may be accepted in roadbases.

Apparatus for Test : The apparatus consists of following :

- A balance of capacity about 3 kg, to weigh accurate to 0.5 gm.
- A thermostatically controlled oven to maintain a temperature of 100°C to 110°C.
- A wire basket of not more than 6.3 mm mesh or a perforated container of convenient size with thin wire hangers for suspending it from the balance.
- A container for filling water and suspending the basket.
- An air-tight container of capacity similar to that of the basket.
- A shallow tray and two dry absorbent clothes, each not less than 75×45 cms.

Test Procedure : The weight of sample should not be less than 2000 gms. The sample shall be thoroughly washed first to remove finer particles and dust, drained and then placed in the wire basket and immersed in distilled water at a temperature between 22 to 32°C, with a cover of at least 5 cms of water above the top of basket. The entrapped air shall be removed from the basket by lifting it and then dropping. The basket and aggregate shall remain completely immersed during operation for the period of 24 ± 1/2 hours. Then take weight of basket plus aggregate in water, let it be A_1. Then remove the basket and the aggregate from water and allow them to drain for a few minutes, after which the aggregates shall be gently emptied from the basket on to one of the dry clothes and empty basket shall be returned to water and take its weight in water (A_2).

The aggregate placed on the dry cloth shall be gently, dried with the cloth, transferring it to second dry cloth when first will remove no further moisture. Then it is allowed to dry in absence of direct sunlight or heat, for not less than ten minutes. Take weight of dried aggregates (B). Then aggregates shall be placed in the oven in shallow tray, at a temperature of 100° to 110° C and maintained at this temperature for a period of 24 ± 1/2 hours. Remove it from oven and take its weight (weight C). This sample is oven dried and then crushed to smaller size (10 mm – 4.75 mm) and specific gravity test is carried out by use of pycnometer.

Procedure : A sample of about 1 kg for 10 mm to 4.75 mm or 500 gms of finer than 4.75 mm shall be placed in the bag and covered with distilled water at temperature of 22 to 32° C. Soon after immersion, air entrapped in or bubbles on the surface of the aggregates shall be removed by gentle agitation with the rod. The sample shall be immersed for 24 ± 1/2 hours. The water shall be carefully drained from the sample by decantation through filter papers, any material retained being returned to the sample. Then saturated and surface dried sample be weighed (weight A).

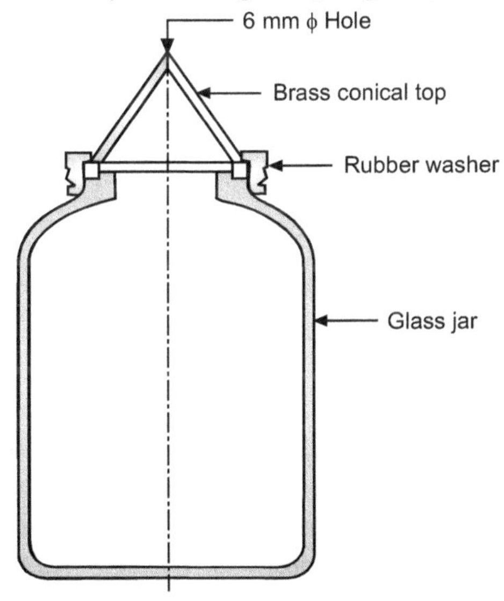

Fig. 7.9 : Pycnometer

Then aggregates shall be placed in the pycnometer which shall be filled with distilled water. Any trapped air shall be eliminated by rotating the pycnometer on its side, the hole in the apex of the cone being covered with finger. The pycnometer shall be trapped-up with distilled water to remove any froath from the surface. The pycnometer shall be dried on the outside and weighed (weight B).

Water shall be carefully drained from the sample by decantation through filter paper, and any material retained shall be returned to the sample. The sample shall be then ovendried to a temperature of 100° to 110°C for 24 ± 1/2 hrs., and then weighed (weight D).

Water shall be carefully drained from the sample by decantation through filter paper, and any material retained shall be returned to the sample. The sample shall be then ovendried to a temperature of 100° to 110°C for 24 ± 1/2 hrs., and then weighed (weight D).

Reporting of Results : Specific gravity, apparent specific gravity and water absorption shall be calculated as follows :

(1) For part I,

$$\text{Specific gravity} \; = \frac{C}{B-A}$$

$$\text{Apparent Specific gravity} \; = \frac{C}{C-A}$$

$$\text{Water absorption} \; = \frac{B-C}{C} \times 100$$

where, A = The weight in gm of saturated aggregate in water,

B = The weight in gm of the saturated surface - dry aggregate in air, and

C = The weight in gm of ovendried aggregate in air.

Use of Pycnometer

$$\text{Specific gravity} \; = \frac{D}{A-(B-C)}$$

$$\text{Apparent specific gravity} \; = \frac{D}{D-(B-C)}$$

$$\text{Water absorption} \; = \frac{(A-D)}{D} \times 100$$

where, A = Weight in gm of saturated surface dry sample

B = Weight in gm of pycnometer and sample and filled with distilled water

C = Weight in gm of pycnometer filled with distilled water only

D = Weight in gm of ovendried sample.

7.9 ESTIMATION OF DELETERIOUS MATERIALS

Deleterious substances are harmful or injurious materials. They include various types of weak or low-quality particles, and coatings that are found on the surface of the aggregate particles. Deleterious materials include organic coatings, dust, clay (lumps, shale, friable particles, easy to crumble), badly weathered particles, soft particles and particles which are dangerous to use because of their chemical composition. These substances may effect the bond between cement and aggregates or may break up during mixing or use. To find the deleterious materials, following tests are normally conducted :

- Dermination of clay lumps in the aggregate sample, and
- Determination of soft particles.

Determination of Clay Lumps

Object of Test : To determine clay lumps, present in the aggregate sample.

Apparatus for Test : The apparatus shall consist of the following :

(a) **Balance :** A balance or scale, sensitive to 0.1% of weight of the sample.

(b) **Containers.**

(c) **Sieves :** Sieves confirming to I.S. 460 -1962.

Test Procedure

Sample : Sample selected from material to be tested shall be first dried at a temperature not exceeding 110°C. Samples of fine aggregate shall consist of particles coarser than 1.18 mm I.S. sieves and shall weigh not less than 100 gms. Samples of coarse aggregate shall be separated into different sizes using 4.75 mm, 10 mm, 20 mm and 40 mm I.S. sieve. Total weight of different sizes shall not be less than the following table :

Table 7.5

Size of Particles Making-up the Sample	Weight of Sample (Minimum), gms
Over 4.75 mm to 10 mm	1000
Over 10 mm to 20 mm	2000
Over 20 mm to 40 mm	3000
Over 40 mm	5000

If the sample contains both fine and coarse aggregates, the material shall be separated into two sizes on 4.75 mm I.S. sieve, and sample of fine and coarse aggregate shall be prepared as per above table. Now, the sample shall be spread in a thin layer on the bottom of the container and examined for clay lumps. Any particles which can be broken into finely divided particles with fingers, shall be classified as clay lumps. After all discernible clay lumps have been broken, the residue from the clay lumps shall be removed by the use of sieves indicated below :

Table 7.6

Size of Particles Making-up the Sample	Size of Sieve for Sieving Residue of Clay
Fine aggregate (retained on 1.18 mm I.S. sieve)	850 micron
Over 4.75 mm to 10 mm	2.36 mm
Over 10 mm to 20 mm	4.75 mm
Over 20 mm to 40 mm	4.75 mm
Over 40 mm	4.75 mm

Reporting of Results : Particles of clay lumps shall be calculated to the nearest 0.1 percent in accordance with the following formula :

$$L = \frac{W - R}{W} \times 100$$

where

W = Weight of sample.

R = Weight of sample after removal of clay lumps.

L = Percentage age of clay lumps.

7.10 DETERMINATION OF SOFT PARTICLES

The apparatus consists of a brass rod, having a rockwell hardness of 65 to 75 RHB. A brass rod of about 1.6 mm diameter and of poor hardness inserted into the wood of an ordinary lead pencil is a convenient tool for field or laboratory use.

Sample : Aggregate for the test shall consist of materials from which the sizes finer than the 10 mm I.S. sieve have been removed. The sample shall contain at least 10% or more of following sizes :

10 to 12.5 mm,   12.5 to 20 mm

20 to 40 mm   and   40 to 50 mm

Each particle of aggregate under test shall be scratched with the brass rod using only a small amount of pressure (about 1 kg). Particles are considered to be soft if during the scratching process, a groove is made in them without deposition of metal from the brass rod or if separate particles are detached from the rock mass.

The report shall include the following information :

- Weight and number of particle of each size of each sample tested with the brass rod.

- Weight and number of each size of each sample classified as soft in the test.

- Percentage of test sample classified as soft by weight and by number of particles.

- Weighed average percentage of soft particles calculated from percentage in item (c) and based on the grading of sample of aggregate received for examination or, preferably on the average grading of material from that portion of the supply of which the sample is representative. In these calculations, sizes finer than the 10 mm I.S. sieve shall not be included.

7.11 AGGREGATE CRUSHING VALUE

Theory : Scope and Significance : Aggregate used in road construction, should be strong enough to resist crushing under traffic wheel loads. If the aggregates are weak, the stability of the pavements structure is likely to be adversely affected. Thus, the aggregate must have a durable resistance to crushing. The strength of aggregate is assessed by aggregate crushing test. The aggregate crushing value provides a relative measure of resistance to crushing under a gradually applied compressive load. To achieve a high quality of pavements, aggregate possessing high aggregate crushing value should be preferred.

The aggregate crushing value should not be more than 45 percent for aggregate used for concrete other than wearing surfaces, and 30 percent for concrete used for wearing surfaces such as runways, roads and field pavements.

Apparatus for Test : See Fig. 7.10. The apparatus for the standard test consists of the following :

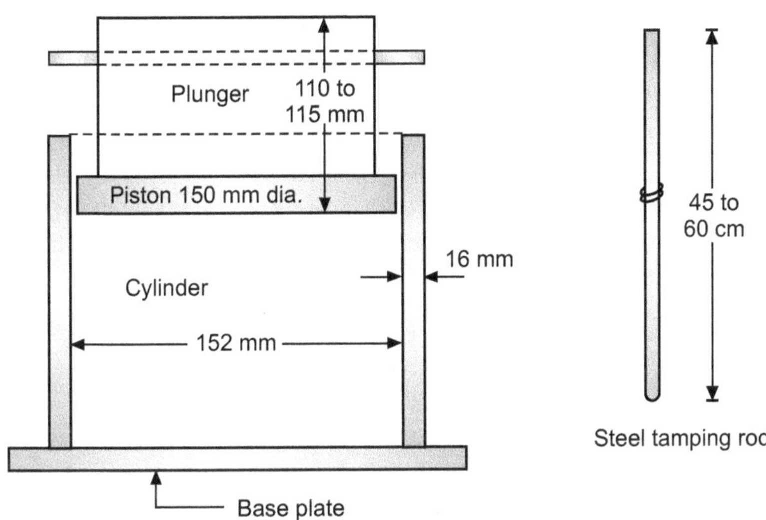

Fig. 7.10 : Crushing test apparatus

- Steel cylinder, with open ends and internal diameter 152 mm, square base plate, plunger having a piston diameter of 150 mm with a hole provided across the stem of the plunger so that rod could be inserted for lifting or placing the plunger in the cylinder.

- Cylindrical measure having internal diameter of 115 mm and height 180 mm.

- Steel tamping rod with one rounded end, having a diameter of 1.6 cm and length 45 to 60 cms.

- Balance of capacity 3 kg and accuracy upto 1 gm.

- Compression testing machine capable of applying load of 40 tonnes, at a uniform rate of loading of 4 tonnes per minute.

Test Procedure : The aggregate passing 12.5 mm I.S. sieve and retained on 10 mm I.S. sieve is selected for standard test. The aggregate should be in surface dry condition before testing. The aggregate may be dried by heating at a temperature 100° to 110°C for a period of 4 hours and tested after being cooled to room temperature. The cylindrical measure is filled by the test sample of aggregate in three layers of aproximately equal depth, each layer being tamped 25 times by the rounded end of tamping rod. After the third layer is tampad, the aggregate at the top of the cylindrical measure is leveled-off by using the tamping rod as a straight edge. About 6.5 kg of aggregate is required for preparing two test samples.

The test sample thus taken is then weighed. The same weight of the sample is taken in the repeat test. The cylinder of the test apparatus is placed in position on the base plate, one third of test sample is placed in this cylinder and tamped 25 times by the tamping rod. Similarly, two parts of the test specimen are added, each layer being subjected to 25 blows. The depth of material in the cylinder after tamping shall be 10 cm.

The surface of the aggregate is levelled and the plunger is inserted so that it rests on this surface in a level position. The cylinder with test sample and plunger in position is placed on compression testing machine. Load is then applied through the plunger at a uniform rate of 4 tonnes per minute until the total load is 40 tonnes. Aggregates including the crushed portion are removed from the cylinder and sieved on a 2.36 mm I.S. sieve. The material which possess this sieve is collected. The above crushing test is repeated on second sample of the same weight in accordance with above test procedure. Thus, two tests are made for the same specimen for taking average value.

Reporting of Results : Total weight of dry sample taken = W_1 gms – weight of the portion of crushed material, passing 2.36 I.S. sieve = W_2 gms.

$$\therefore \quad \text{Aggregate crushing value} = \frac{W_2}{W_1} \times 100$$

The value is usually recorded correct to first decimal place.

7.12 AGGREGATE ABRASION VALUE

Significance of Test : Apart from testing aggregates with respect to its crushing value, impact resistance, testing the aggregate with respect to its resistance to wear is an important test for aggregate to be used for road construction, ware house floors and pavement construction.

Aggregates must be sufficiently hard to resist the abrasive effects of traffic over a long period of time. The abrasive tests, which are generally carried out, are basically accelerated tests. Whether the aggregate abrasion value test is a simulation of abrasion under actual traffic condition is, of course, very debatable. Numerous testings have shown, that the aggregates with abrasion values greater than 15 are too soft for use in the wearing course of a bituminuous surfacing. The accelerated polishing test might be considered more representative of tyre surfacing interaction on the road way. In any case, an extensive investigations carried out by the 'Road Research Laboratory' has shown that the state of polish of the aggregate at the end of the 6-hour test approximates the state of polish reached after several months on a heavily-trafficked road or several years on a road carrying light traffic. Results reported indicate that an aggregate with a polished-stone coefficient of greater than 0.8 is likely to remain rough under any traffic conditions, while one with a value of 0.3 or lower will become so highly polished as to give rise to a dangerously slippery road surface when either wet or dry.

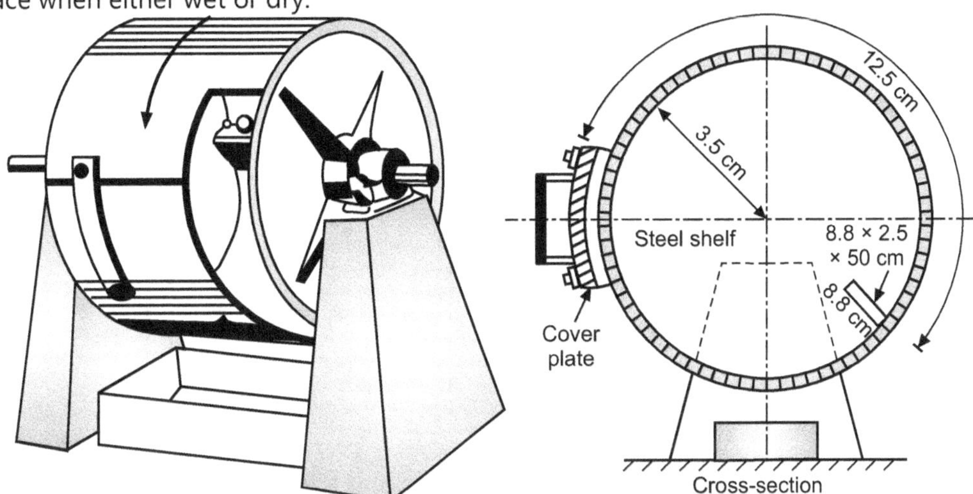

Fig. 7.11 : Los angeles abrasion testing machine

The Los Angeles abrasion test is actually an abrasion-cum-impact test due to the action of the steel balls in the drum as it is rotated. Normally, 'soft' limestones have Los Angeles values of over 50 percent, while very hard aggregates have values less than 20. Recommendations regarding the maximum percent wear given by the test vary, depending on the purpose for which the aggregate is to be used, the gradation, the testing procedures and the specifying authority. The abrasion value should not be more than 30 percent for wearing surfaces and not more than 50 percent for concrete other than wearing surface.

To determine abrasion value of aggregates by use of Los Angeles Abrasion testing machine, we require :

1. Los Angeles Abrasion testing machine. See Fig. 7.11.
2. Balance.
3. A set of I.S sieves
4. Abrasive charge, which consists of cast-iron spheres or steel spheres approximately 48 mm in diameter and each weighing between 390 to 445 gms.

Table 7.7 : Specified Abrasive Charge for Different Types of Gradings of Gggregates

Grading	Number of Spheres	Weight of Charge (gms)
A	12	5000 ± 25
B	11	4584 ± 25
C	8	3330 ± 20
D	6	2500 ± 15
E	12	5000 ± 25
F	12	5000 ± 25
G	12	5000 ± 25

Gradings of Test Samples

Table 7.8

Sieve Size		Weight in gm of Test Sample for Grade						
Passing, mm	Retained on mm	A	B	C	D	E	F	G
80	63	–	–	–	–	2500	–	–
63	50	–	–	–	–	2500	–	–
50	40	–	–	–	–	5000	5000	–
40	25	1250	-	–	–	–	5000	5000
25	20	1250	–	–	–	–	–	5000
20	12.5	1250	2500	-	-	–	–	–
12.5	10	1250	2500	-	–	–	–	–
10	6.3	–	–	2500	–	–	–	–
6.3	4.75	–	–	2500	-	–	–	–
4.75	2.36	–	–	–	5000	–	–	-

Test Procedure : The test sample consists of clean aggregate which has been dried in an oven at 105°C to 110°C and it should confirm to one of the gradings as shown in above table.

Test sample and abrasive charge is placed in the Los Angeles Abrasion testing machine and the machine is rotated at a speed of 20 to 33 revolutions per minute. For gradings A, B, C and D, the machine is rotated for 500 revolutions. For gradings E, F and G, it is rotated 1000 revolutions. At the completion of the above number of revolutions, the material is discharged from the machine and a preliminary separation of the sample made on a sieve coarser than 1.7 mm I.S. sieve. Finer portion is then sieved on a 1.7 mm I.S. sieve. The material coarser than 1.7 mm I.S. sieve is washed, dried in an oven at 105° to 110°C to a substantially constant weight and accurately weighed to the nearest gram.

Reporting of Results

$$\% \text{ Abrasion value} \ = \ \frac{\text{Material finer than 1.7 mm I.S. sieve}}{\text{Original weight of sample}} \times 100$$

7.13 METHOD OF TEST FOR DETERMINING AGGREGATES IMPACT VALUE COARSE AGGREGATES

This method covers the procedure for determining the aggregates impact value of soft and coarse aggregate used for bases and sub-bases of road pavements.

The apparatus shall consist of the following :

(1) The impact testing machine of the form shown in Fig. 7.12 and complying with the following :

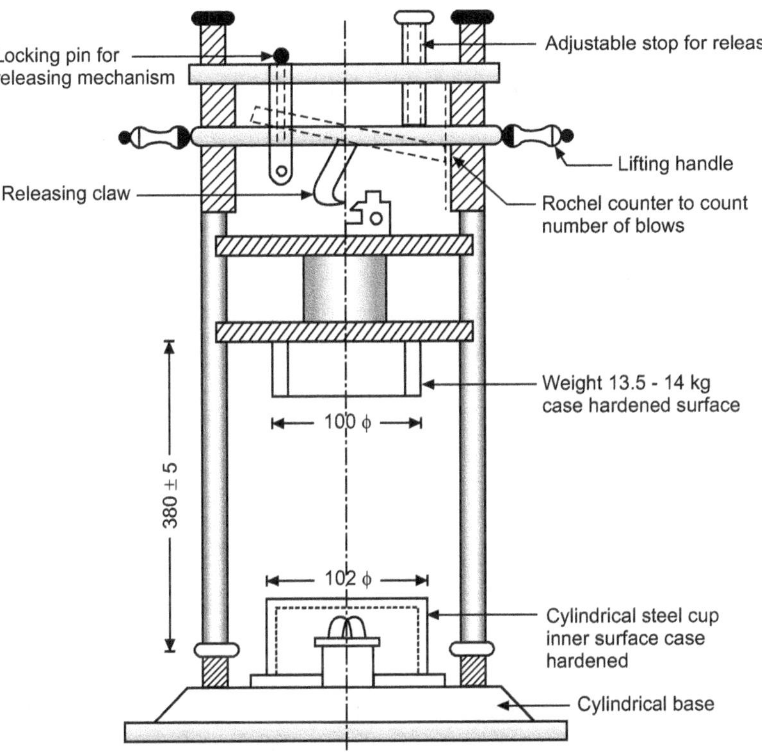

Fig. 7.12 : Aggregate impact testing machine

- Total weight neither more than 60 kg nor less than 45 kg.
- The machine shall have a metal base weighing between 22 and 30 kg with a plane lower surface of not less than 30 cm diameter, and shall be supported on a level concrete block or floor at least 45 cm thick. The machine shall be prevented from rocking either by fixing it to the block or floor or by supporting it on a level and plane metal plate cast into the surface of the block or floor.
- A cylindrical steel cup of the following internal dimensions and not less than 6.3 mm thick with its inner surface case-hardened, that can be rigidly fastened at the centre of the base and easily removed for emptying :

Diameter	102 mm
Depth	50 mm

- A metal hammer weighing 13.5 to 14.0 kg, the lower end of which shall be cylindrical in shape, 100 mm in diameter and 50 mm long, with a 2 mm chamfer at the lower edge, and case-hardened. The hammer shall slide freely between vertical guides so arranged that the lower (cylindrical) part of the hammer is above and concentric with the cup.

- Means for raising the hammer and allowing it to fall freely between the vertical guides from a height of 380 mm on to the test sample in the cup, and means for adjusting the height of fall within 5 mm.

- Means for supporting the hammer while fastening or removing the cup.

(2) Sieves : I.S. sieves of sizes 12.5 mm, 10 mm and 2.36 mm.

(3) Measure : A cylindrical metal measure, tared to the nearest gram, of sufficient rigidity to retain its form under rough usage, and of the following internal dimensions :

Diameter	75 mm.
Depth	50 mm.

(4) Tamping Rod : A straight metal tamping rod of circular cross-section 10 mm in diameter and 230 mm long, rounded at one end.

(5) Balance : Capacity not less than 500 g, readable and accurate to 0.1 g.

(6) Oven : A well-ventilated oven, thermostatically controlled to maintain a temperature of 100° to 110° C.

Preparation of Test Sample

- The test sample shall consist of aggregate the whole of which passes 12.5 mm I.S. sieve and is retained on a 10 mm I.S. sieve. The aggregate comprising the test sample shall be dried in an oven for a period of four hours till the time, the weight becomes constant at a temperature of 105° to 110°C and cooled.

- The measure shall be filled about one-third full with the aggregate and tamped with 25 strokes of the rounded end of the tamping rod. A further similar quantity of aggregate shall be added and a further tamping of 25 strokes given. The measure shall finally be filled to overflowing, tamped 25 times and the surplus aggregate struck-off, using the tamping rod as a straight-edge. The net weight of aggregate in the measure shall be determined to the nearest gram (weight of aggregate shall be used for the duplicate test on the same material).

- This oven-dried sample is immersed in water for three days.

- Wet sample after the immersion period is surface dried by suitable cloth.

Test Procedure

- The impact machine shall rest without wedging or packing upon the level plate, block or floor, so that it is rigid and the hammer guide columns are vertical.

- The cup shall be fixed firmly in position on the base of the machine and the whole of the test sample placed in it and compacted by a single tamping of 25 strokes of the tamping rod.

- The hammer shall be raised until its lower face is 380 mm above the upper surface of the aggregate in the cup, and allowed to fall freely on to the aggregate. The test sample shall be subjected to a total of 15 such blows each being delivered at an interval of not less than one second.

- The crushed aggregate shall then be removed from the cup and the whole of it sieved on the 2.36 mm I.S. sieve and washed with water till there is no further significant amount of loss. The fraction retained on the sieve shall be dried in an oven to the constant weight at 105 to 110 C and weighed to an accuracy of 0.1 g (weight B). The fraction retained on the sieve (weight B) shall be subtracted from the weight of the original oven-dried sample (weight A). The resultant weight (weight A – weight B) shall represent the fraction passing 2.36 mm I.S. sieve (weight C). Two tests shall be made.

Calculations

- The ratio of the weights of the fines formed to the total sample in each test shall be expressed as percentage of the oven dried, the result being recorded to the first decimal place :

$$\text{Aggregate impact value} = \frac{C}{A} \times 100$$

where, C = weight of the fines formed, and

A = weight of the ovendried sample.

Reporting of Results

- The mean of the two results shall be reported as aggregate impact value (wet) of the tested material. The detail result is as listed below.

  According to above procedure, the Aggregate Impact Test was conducted on following three Aggregates : (1) Basalt, (2) Granite, (3) Marble. Results are listed.

Table 7.9

Sr. No.	Aggregate	Ovendried Weight A in kg.	Weight of Fraction Passing through 2.36 mm Sieve in kg.	Impact Value	Height of Specimen	Settlement
1.	Basalt	0.5	0.045	9%	4.8 mm	0.8
2.	Marble	0.5	0.052	10.4%	4.7 mm	1.05
3.	Granite	0.5	0.053	10.6%	4.8 mm	0.8

The chief advantage of the aggregate impact test is that it determines the resistance to the impact of stones. The test can be performed in a short time even at construction site or at stone quarry as the apparatus is simple and portable. Well-shaped conical stones provide higher resistance to impact, when compared with the flaky and elongated stones.

7.14 AGGREGATE POLISHING TEST

The aggregates should not get polished under traffic. To test polishing characteristics of aggregates, the aggregates are embedded in a curved mould in cement sand mortar and then subjected to increased polishing caused by a rotating pneumatic wheel. The size of each specimen is 45 mm wide × 90.5 mm long. Rubber wheel is 20 cm diameter, 5 cm broad, loaded with 40 kg load at a tyre pressure of 3.15 ± 0.15 kg/cm^2 sand and water are fed to the machine when it is rotated at an r.p.m. of 320 – 325 for 3 hours 15 minutes. The specimen are thereafter tested for their polishing characters on British Portable tester. The British Portable tester is essentially a rubber sliding shoe which is mounted at the end of the pendulum. The slider when released, brushes past the specimen and comes to a halt. The instrument directly measures the polishing value on a graduated scale. Limestones have poor p.s.v's ranging from 35 to 40. Granites have values in the range of 40 – 48 and sand stone has a high value of about 55.

7.15 STRIPPING TEST

It is necessary that aggregate should adhere to the bitumen film for good performance. The stripping test measures the adhesion of bitumen to aggregates. The aggregates are mixed with 5 percent binder at the specified temperature with regard to the bitumen used. The coated aggregates are then immersed in water and kept undisturbed at controlled temperature for about 24 hours. The percentage of area uncoated due to action of water is now usually assessed, which itself is the stripping value. The maximum stripping value could be 25 percent. There is possibility that when aggregates come into close contact with water, bond between bitumen and aggregates may get loosened. This reduction in bond is called stripping, which possibility exists in the case of open-graded mixtures and surface dressings. Stripping should be avoided as it will lead to collapse of base structure.

7.16 BITUMEN

Bitumen is manufactured from crude oil. Bitumen is obtained as the last residue in fractional distillation of crude petroleum. Crude petroleum is a mixture of hydrocarbons of different molecular weights. In the petroleum refineries the individual components like LPG, naphtha, Kerosene, Diesel etc. are separated through the process of fractional distillation. The heaviest material obtained from the fractional distillation process is further treated and blended to make different grades of paving grade bitumen. The actual bitumen output can be controlled not only by selecting the appropriate crude but also by adopting varying processes in the refinery. The choice of process would depend on the availability of suitable crude, demand of the end products and total commercial viability of the complete refining process.

Definition : Bitumen is defined as "A viscous liquid, or a solid, consisting essentially of hydrocarbons and their derivatives, which is soluble in trichloroethylene and is substantially nonvolatile and softens gradually when heated. It is black or brown in colour and possesses waterproofing and adhesive properties. It is obtained by refinery processes from petroleum, and is also found as a natural deposit or as a component of naturally occurring asphalt, in which it is associated with mineral matte.

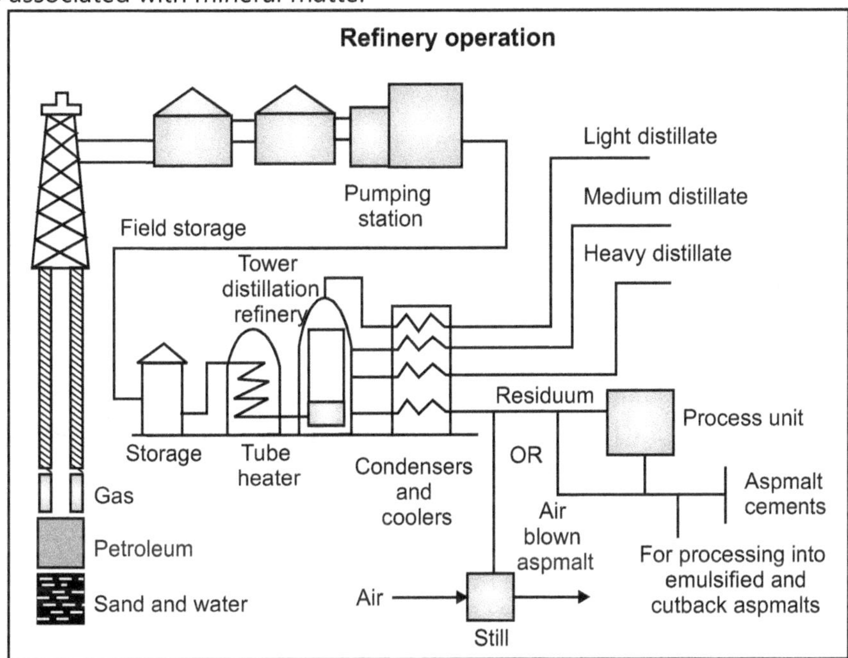

Fig. 7.13

7.16.1 Types of Bitumen

Bitumen or bituminous binder available in India is mainly of the following types :

• **Penetration Grade**

    Bitumen 80/100 : The characteristics of this grade confirm to that of S 90 grade of IS-73-1992. This is the softest of all grades available in India. This is suitable for low volume roads and is still widely used in the country.

    Bitumen 60/70 : This grade is harder than 80/100 and can withstand higher traffic loads. The characteristics of this grade confirm to that of S 65 grade of IS-73-1992. It is presently used mainly in construction of National Highways and State Highways.

    Bitumen 30/40 : This is the hardest of all the grades and can withstand very heavy traffic loads. The characteristics of this grade confirm to that of S 35 grade of IS-73-1992. Bitumen 30/40 is used in specialized applications like airport runways and also in very heavy traffic volume roads in coastal cities in the country.

•   **Industrial Grade Bitumen :** Industrial grade bitumen is also known as blown bitumen. This is obtained by blowing air into hot bitumen at high temperatures (normally beyond

180°C). Blowing hot air into bitumen at high temperatures results in structural changes in bitumen. Esters are formed in this process and these esters link up two different molecules and higher molecular weight material increases drastically. In the process the asphaltene content is increased which in turn results in higher softening points and very low penetration number. Industrial grade bitumen is used in industrial applications and in water proofing, tarfelting etc.

- **Cutback :** Cutback is a free flowing liquid at normal temperatures and is obtained by fluxing bitumen with suitable solvents. The viscosity of bitumen is reduced substantially by adding kerosene or any other solvent. Normal practice is to heat bitumen to reduce its viscosity. In some situations preference is given to use liquid binders such as cutback bitumen. In cutback bitumen suitable solvent is used to lower the viscosity of the bitumen. From the environmental point of view also cutback bitumen is preferred. The solvent from the bituminous material will evaporate and the bitumen will bind the aggregate. Cutback bitumen is used for cold weather bituminous road construction and maintenance. The distillates used for preparation of cutback bitumen are naphtha, kerosene, diesel oil, and furnace oil. There are different types of cutback bitumen like rapid curing (RC), medium curing (MC), and slow curing (SC). RC is recommended for surface dressing and patchwork. MC is recommended for premix with less quantity of fine aggregates. SC is used for premix with appreciable quantity of fine aggregates

- **Bitumen Emulsion :** Bitumen emulsion is a free flowing liquid at ambient temperatures. Bitumen emulsion is a stable dispersion of fine globules of bitumen in continuous water phase. Dispersion is obtained by processing bitumen and water under controlled conditions through a colloidal mill together with selected additives. The use of proper quality emulsifiers is essential to ensure that the emulsion has stability over time and also that it breaks and sets when applied on aggregates/road surface. It is chocolate brown free flowing liquid at room temperature. Bitumen Emulsions can be of two types cationic & anionic. Anionic bitumen emulsions are generally not used in road construction as generally siliceous aggregate is used in road construction. Anionic bitumen emulsions do not give good performance with siliceous whereas cationic bitumen emulsions give good performance with these aggregates. Therefore, cationic bitumen emulsions are far more popular than anionic bitumen emulsions.

- **Modified Bitumen :** Modified Bitumen are bitumen with additives. These additives help in further enhancing the properties of bituminous pavements. Pavements constructed with Modified Bitumen last longer which automatically translates into reduced overlays. Pavements constructed with Modified Bitumens can be economical if the overall lifecycle cost of the pavement is taken into consideration.

  - **Tar:** Tar is a viscous black liquid derived from the destructive distillation of organic matter. Most tar is produced from coal as a byproduct of coke production, but it can also be produced from petroleum, peat or wood.

7.16.2 Properties of Bitumen

- **Bitumen – A Visco-Elastic Material :** The properties of Bitumen can be defined in terms analogous to the Modulus of Elasticity of solid materials. In case of solids, Modulus of Elasticity E is defined by Hooke's law Bitumen is a Visco-elastic material. At high temperatures it behaves like a liquid and hence liquid flow properties like Viscosity are exhibited. However, at low temperatures bitumen behaves like a solid and hence solid properties like stress and strain become relevant. Similarly, for shorter loading time bitumen behaves like a solid whereas for longer loading times bitumen behaves like a liquid. The properties that bitumen exhibits in the intermediate temperature range and loading time are of great relevance as this range is very long and bitumen is handled in this temperature range most of the times.

  Due to the visco-elastic nature of bitumen, there is always a phase lag in stress & strain in case of repetitive loadings. For purely elastic material the phase lag is 00 and for purely viscous material the phase lag is 90^0. In case of bitumen since it is neither a liquid nor a solid at most temperatures hence the phase lag is always between 0^0 to 90^0. The above theory is extremely useful in studying fatigue characteristics, properties of creep & also tensile strength of bitumen.

- **Adhesion Properties of Bitumen :** Bitumen has excellent adhesive qualities provided the conditions are favourable. However in presence of water the adhesion does create some Examples. Most of the aggregates used in road construction possess a weak negative charge on the surface. The bitumen aggregate bond is because of a weak dispersion force. Water is highly polar and hence it gets strongly attached to the aggregate displacing the bituminous coating. The factors influencing aggregate bitumen adhesion are plenty and some of the factors influencing this property are as below:

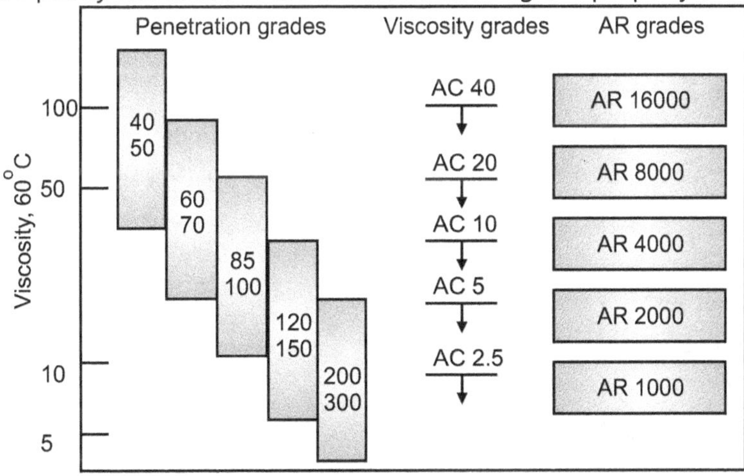

Fig. 7.14

- **External :** Rainfall, Humidity, Water pH, Presence of salts, Temperature, Temperature cycle, Traffic, Design, Workmanship, Drainage.

- **Aggregate :** Mineralogy, Surface texture, Porosity, Dirt, Durability, Surface area, Absorption, Moisture content, Shape, Weathering.
- **Bitumen :** Rheology, Constitution.
- **Mix :** Void content, Permeability, Bitumen content, Bitumen film thickness, Filler type, Aggregate grading, Mix type.

7.17 TESTS ON BITUMEN

Various tests are conducted to study the suitability of bitumen for various conditions. These tests are conducted as per present specification which contains some drawbacks. Although these specifications are supposed to bear relationship with those properties which directly govern the performance of mixes and bituminous pavements, these results are hardly used in the bituminous construction.

The present specifications which are used today to test the bitumen may have been specified to suit the conditions at the time, they were formulated but their usefulness is questionable today. As these tests are very simple and no elaborate equipment is required for conducting the tests, they continue to attract the attention of engineers. This does not mean that they should be completely abandoned but a more rational approach is needed to make them much more useful than what they are at present. Now days, methods of design of pavements and techniques of construction are improving, hence more sophisticated tests are needed to meet the present requirements.

The present tests either need modification as in case of ductility test or complete replacement by a more reliable test, as they provide little or no information to the Engineer who is directly responsible for the service performance of bituminous pavements or the manufacturers who play a pivotal role in the manufacture and supply of materials. This chapter deals with the Standard tests on Asphaltic Bitumen and their lacunas.

Tests on bitumen

There are a number of tests to assess the properties of bituminous materials. The following tests are usually conducted to evaluate different properties of bituminous materials.

- Penetration test
- Ductility test
- Softening point test
- Specific gravity test
- Viscosity test
- Flash and Fire point test
- Float test
- Water content test
- Loss on heating test

7.18 SOLUBILITY TEST

The pure bitumen is completely soluble in solvent like carbon disulphide and carbon tetrachloride. Hence any impurity in the form of inert materials, could be quantitatively analysed by dissolving the sample into those solvents. The standard procedure as per I.S. 1216 - 1978 is as follows :

Object : To determine the percentage of insoluble material in the bitumen.

Apparatus : Gooch crucible, conical glass flask of 20 ml capacity, carbon disulphide, carbon tetrachloride.

Procedure : Weight about 2 gm of the dry material correct to the nearest 0.001 gm into a 200 ml flask and add 10 ml of carbon disulphide or carbon tatrachloride. Stir the content of the flask and then allow it to stand loosely, cooled for a period of one hour, filter the content of the flask, through the flask, through the Gooch crucible prepared as per I.S. 1216 -1978. Moisten the asbestos pad with carbon disulphide before commencing the filtration and filter at a rate of not more than two drops per second at first. The filtrate shall be quite clear. Transfer the insoluble matter remaining in the flask to the crucible by washing out with steam of carbon disulphide from wash bottle. Wash the material retained in the crucible with successive small amounts of carbon disulphide until, the filtrate obtained is not discoloured. Allow the crucible to dry in air for 30 minutes, after which, place it in an oven at 110° C for one hour. Allow the crucible to cool in a desiccater and then weigh.

Matter soluble in carbon disulphide or carbon tetrachloride = A

We have,
$$A = \frac{(W_1 - W_2)}{W_1} \times 100$$

where W_1 = Weight in gm of dry sample,

W_2 = Weight in gm of insoluble material remained in the Gooch crucible.

Precision : The test result shall not differ from mean by more than following.

Table 7.10

Matter Soluble in Carbon Disulphide	Repeatability	Reproducibility
Below 98%	0.5	1.0
98 to 100%	0.1	0.2

Comments on the Test : The purpose of this test is to determine the insoluble material in bitumen such as salt etc. In addition, bitumen also contains carbon with fraction, soluble in carbon disulphide but insoluble in carbon tetrachloride. Actually it should not increase 2% in most of the road bitumen. But its percentage is high in that bitumen which are subjected to excessive heating. The insoluble material should be preferably less than 1%. In solubility test with carbon tetrachloride, if carbonaceous residue is over 0.5%, the bitumen is considered to be cracked. The minimum portion of the bitumen soluble in carbon disulphide is specified as 99%. This test is useful not only to ensure due care in refinery operations and to detect the contaminations caused due to shipments in dirty tanks, but also to determine the colloidal instability or stability of materials.

7.19 WATER CONTENT TEST

It is desirable that the bitumen contains maximum water content to prevent foaming of the bitumen when it is heated above the boiling point of water. The quantity of water present in the bituminous material is expressed as percentage by weight of the material.

- The standard procedure as per I.S. 1211 -1978 is as follows :

Object : To determine the water content of bituminous material.

Apparatus : Flask of capacity of 500 ml, condenser, receiver, a 100 ml graduated cylinder, heater, solvent (petroleum spirit with boiling range of 100° to 120°C).

Procedure : Place about 100 grams of sample, accurately weighed, in the flask and add 100 ml of solvent. Attach the flask to the condensing and collecting system and heat the flask at such rate that the condensate falls from the end of condenser at rate of two to five drops per second. Continue the distillation until the condensed water is no longer visible in any part of the apparatus except the bottom of the graduated tube and until the volume of water collected remains constant for period not less than five minutes.

Remove the ring of condensed water in the condensed tube, if any, by increasing the rate of distillation by few drops per second. Wash the droplet of water which adheres to the lower end of the condenser into the receiver with solvent using spray. Insert loose plug of cotton wool in the top of the condenser tube to prevent the condensation of atmospheric moisture in the condenser tube.

Allowable maximum water content = 0.2%.

Comments on the Test : Since percentage of water in the bitumen when heated above the boiling point of water is not to exceed 0.2% by weight. The specifications usually control the water content simply by stipulating that the material should not foam when heated to maximum road temperature. The weight of water condensed and collected is expressed by weight of original sample. The maximum water content of bitumen should not increase 0.2% by weight.

7.20 SPECIFIC GRAVITY

The density of bituminous binders is fundamental property frequently used as an aid in classifying the binder for use in paving jobs. The specific gravity value of bitumen is also useful in the bituminous mix design. The standard procedure as per I.S. 1209 -1978 is as follows. The ratio of the mass of an equal volume of substance and water, the temperature of both being specified. If the temperature of substance is t_1 °C and that of water is t_2 °C, the specific gravity is denoted by $S \times \dfrac{t_1}{t_2}$. The t_1 and t_2 shall be specified clearly.

Object : To find the specific gravity of the bituminous material (using specific gravity bottles.)

Apparatus : Specific gravity bottles of 50 ml capacity shall be used. One of the bottles shall be of 6 mm diameter neck and that of other having 25 mm diameter neck, constant temperature bath, thermometer.

Procedure : Clean, dry and weigh the specific gravity bottles together with the stopper (a).

Fill it with freshly boiled and cooled distilled water and insert the stopper firmly. Keep the bottle upto its neck for not less than half an hour in a beaker of distilled water maintaining at a temperature of 27°C or any other temperature at which specific gravity is to be determined. Wipe all surplus moisture from the surface with a clean dry cloth and weigh again (b). After weighing the bottle and water together (b), the bottle shall be dried again.

In case of solids and semisolids, bring small amount of the material to a fluid condition by gentle application of heat, care being taken to prevent loss by evaporation, when material is sufficiently fluid, pour a quantity into clean, dry specific gravity bottle mentioned above to fill atleast half. Slightly warm the bottle. Keep the material away from touching the sides above the final level of the bottle and avoid the inclusion of air bubbles. Weigh with the stopper (c).

Fill the specific gravity bottle containing the asphalt with freshly boiled distilled water placing the stopper loosely in the specific gravity bottle. Do not allow any air bubble to remain in the specific gravity bottle. Place the specific gravity bottle in the water bath and place the stopper in place. Allow the specific gravity bottle to remain in the water bath for period of not less than half an hour. Remove the bottle and wipe all the moisture and weigh it (d).

$$S \;=\; \text{Specific gravity of bitumen}$$

$$S \;=\; \frac{[c-a]}{(b-a)-(d-c)} \;=\; \frac{(c-a)}{(b-a)-(d-c)}$$

where,

a　=　Mass of specific gravity bottle.
b　=　Mass of specific gravity bottle filled with distilled water.
c　=　Mass of specific gravity bottle about half filled with the material.
d　=　Mass of specific gravity bottles about half filled with the material and rest with distilled water.

Comments on the Test : The density of bitumen binder is a fundamental property frequently used as an aid in classifying the binders for use in paving jobs. In most applications, the bitumen is weighed out finally when used with aggregate system. Specific gravity is not required except when weight-volume relationship is needed for filling and shipping purpose and for design of bituminous mixes. Increased amount of aromatic type compounds or mineral impurities cause an increase in the specific gravity.

Generally, specific gravity of pure bitumen is in the range of 1.01 to 1.03. The specific gravity of cut back bitumen may be lower depending on the type and proportion of dilution used. The tars have specific gravity ranging from 1.10 to 1.25.

7.21 FLASH AND FIRE POINT TEST

Bituminous material leaved out volatiles at high temperatures, depending upon their grade. These volatiles catch fire causing flash. This condition is very hazardous and it is therefore essential to qualify this temperature for each bitumen grade, so that paving engineer may restrict mixing and application temperature. This test is necessary to know the flash point and fire point of the bitumen. The flash point of the bitumen is the lowest temperature at which the application of test flame causes the vapours from the material momentarily given in the form of flash under specified condition. The flash point is the lowest temperature at which the application of test flame causes the material to ignite and burn at least for 5 seconds under specified condition of test. The standard procedure as per I.S. 1209 -1978 is as follows :

Apparatus : Pensky-Markens closed tester consisting of cup, lid, stirring device, cover proper, shutter, flame exposure device, stove, top plate, air bath, thermometer etc. See Fig. 7.15.

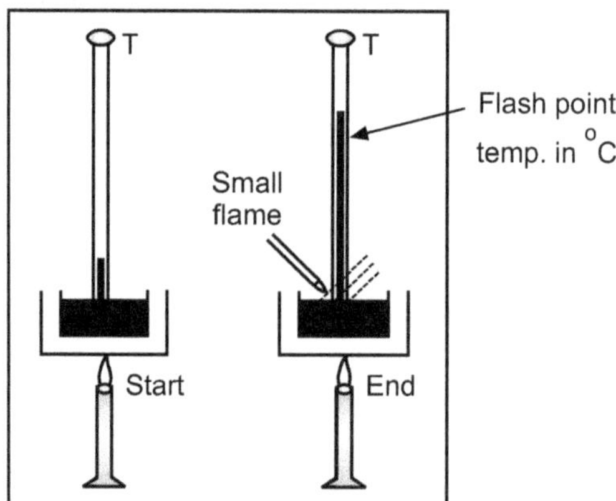

Fig. 7.15 : Flash point test

Procedure : Clean and dry all parts of the apparatus and its accessories thoroughly before the test is started. Take particular care to avoid the presence of any solvent used to clean the apparatus after previous test. Fill the cup with material to be tested upto the level indicated by the filling mark. Place the lid on the cup and set the latter on the stove. Take care that the locating devices are properly engaged. Insert the thermometer high on low range as required. Light and adjust the test flame such that it is of the size of a bed of 4 mm in diameter. Apply heat at such rate that the temperature recorded by the thermometer increases between 5° to 6°C.

Turn the stirrer at a rate of approximately 60 revolutions per minute. Apply the test flame at each temperature reading which is multiple of 1°C, upto 104°C. For temperature above 104°C, apply the test flame at each temperature reading which is multiple of 2°C. The first application of test flame being made at a temperature at least 17°C below the actual flash point. Apply the test flame by operating the device controlling the shutter and test flame burner so that the flame is lowered in 0.5 seconds, left in its lower position for one second and quickly raised to its high position. Discontinue the stirring during application of test flame.

Table 7.11

Sr. No.	Flash Point	Fire Point
1.	178°C	210°C
2.	182°C	208°C
3.	180°C	203°C

Comments on the Test : This test is essential for safety measures. This test is conducted to determine the temperature upto which the bitumen can be safely heated. The minimum specified flash point of bitumen used for pavement construction in Pensky- Markens closed type test is 175°C. The first application at test flame to be made below the actual flash point by an amount of 17°C.

7.22 SPOT TEST

This test is used for detecting overheated or cracked bitumen. This test is considered to be more sensitive than the solubility test for detection of cracking. About 2 gm of bitumen is dissolved in 10 ml of naphtha. A drop of this solution is taken out and placed on filter paper, one after one hour and second after 24 hours after the solution is prepared. If the stain of the spot on the paper is uniform in colour, the bitumen is accepted as uncracked. But if the spot forms dark brown or black circle in the centre with an angular ring of light colour surrounding it, the bitumen is considered to be overheated or cracked.

Comments on the Test : Although this test is not specified by Indian standard code, it is used in foreign countries like U.S.A., as this test is considered to measure homogeneous (colloidal stability) characteristic of asphalt. This test is again considered to be a controversal one due to the fact that it does not always detect the cracked materials in blend of cracked and normal materials.

7.23 VISCOSITY TEST

It is a standard test as specified by I.S. 1206. **Viscosity** is the property of bitumen by which it resists flow due to internal friction. Viscosity is measured by Redwood viscometer. According to this method, viscosity is measured by determining the time taken by 50 ml of material to flow through specified orifice under standard temperature. The test is conducted at required temperature.

Apparatus : Tar viscometer, cup, valve, water bath, stirrer, thermometer, stop watch. See Fig. 7.16.

Procedure : Adjust the tar viscometer so that the top of tar cup is levelled. Heat the water in the water bath to the temperature specified for the test.

Clean the tar cup orifice of viscometer with suitable solvent and dry them roughly. Warm and stir the water under the temperature which is 20°C above the temperature specified for the test, pour the material into the cup. Place the thermometer in the material and stir it until temperature is exactly equal to specified temperature. The material is to be filled in the cup upto the index mark. The viscometer should be levelled before filling the material.

Lift the valve and suspend it on the valve support. Start the stop watch and determine the time required for collection of 50 ml of the material. Note the time in seconds.

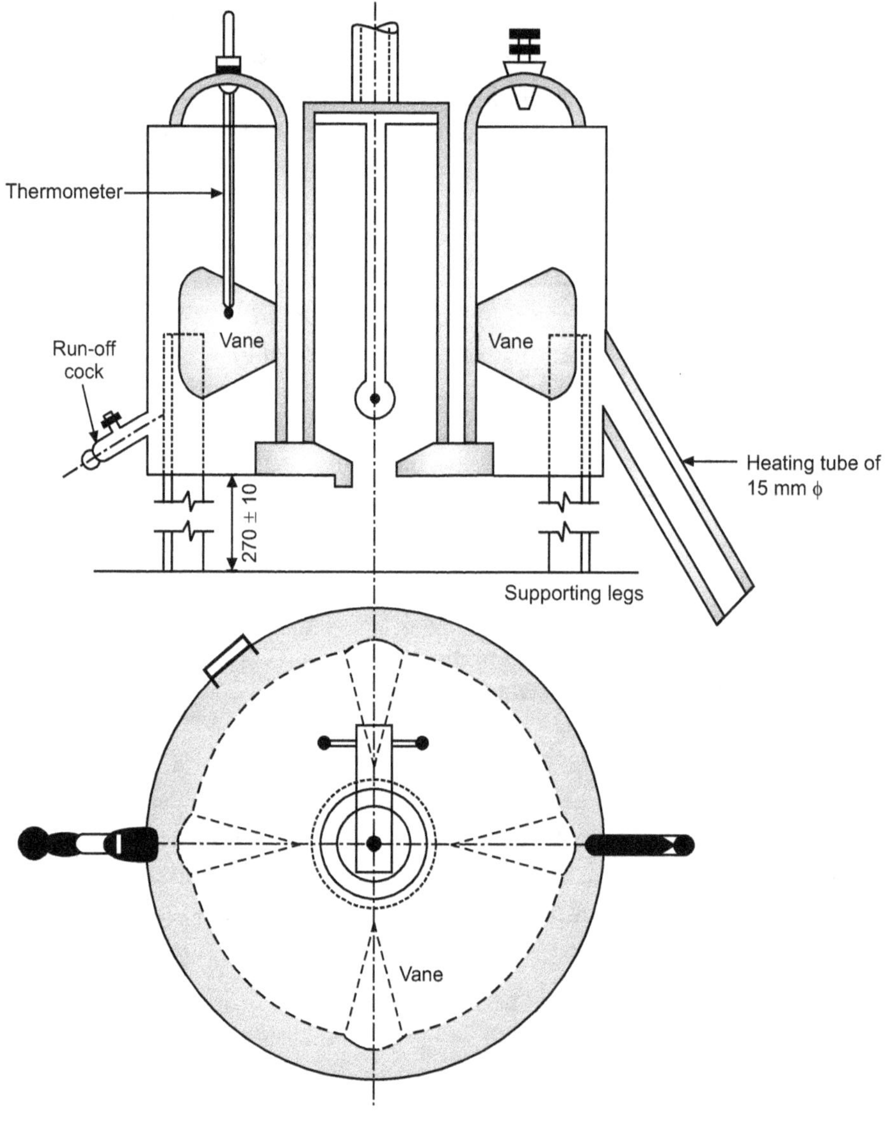

7.16 : Tar viscometer

Precision : The result of repeat determinations on portions of same sample shall fall within ± 4% of the average of several readings.

Test Result : Test conducted with Redwood viscometer with 10 mm orifice.

Road Tar of grade = R. T. 1

Test temperature = 45°C

Table 7.12

Sr. No.	Viscosity	Mean	Precision
1.	24 sec.		– 21.3%
2.	28 sec.		– 8.2%
3.	33 sec.	30.5 sec.	+ 8.2%
4.	27 sec.		– 11.4%
5.	31 sec.		+ 1.64%
6.	34 sec.		+ 11.5%
7.	35 sec.		14.8%
8.	31 sec.		+ 1.64%
9.	21 sec.		– 4.92%
10.	33 sec.		+ 8.2%

As per I.S. 1206 -1978, precision allowed is ± 4% from the mean of several readings.

7.24 LOSS ON HEATING TEST

It is standard test as per I.S.1212 -1978. It is loss in weight (exclusive of water) of oil of a bituminous material when heated to a standard temperature and under specified conditions. The standard procedure as per I.S. code is as follows :

Apparatus : Oven, perforated metal shelf, container, thermometer etc.

Procedure : Stir and agitate thoroughly the material as received, warm it if necessary, to ensure a complete mixture before a portion is removed for the test. Heat the container in an oven at 100° to 110°C for 30 minutes, cool and weigh. Weigh into the container 50 gms at the material correct to the nearest 0.01 gm. Bring over to the temperature of 163°C and place the sample container in the oven. Close the oven and rotate the shelf during entire test at a rate of 5 to 6 revolutions per minute. The temperature being maintained at 163°C for 5 hours. The 5 hours period shall start when the temperature reaches 162°C and in no case shall the total time during which sample is in the oven, be more than 5 hours and 15 minutes. At the end of specified period, remove the container, cool to the room temperature and weigh it. When extreme accuracy is required, only one material, that is two containers shall be placed in the oven - at one time.

Precision : Result of duplicate shall not differ by following :

Table 7.13

Loss on Heating	Repeatability	Reproducibility
0 to 0.5%	0.1	0.2
0.5 to 1.0	0.2	0.4
1.0 to 2.0	0.3	0.6
Above 2.0	10% of mean	20% of mean

Test Result

$$\text{Duration of heating} = 5 \text{ hours}$$
$$\text{Grade of Bitumen} = 80/100$$
$$\text{Test temperature} = 163° \text{ C}$$

Table 7.14

Sr. No.	Wt. of Sample before Heating	Wt. of Sample After Heating	Percentage Loss
1.	50 gm	49.0 gm	2%
2.	50 gm	49.5 gm	1%
3.	50 gm	45.5 gm	3%
4.	50 gm	48.0 gm	4%
5.	50 gm	48.5 gm	3%
6.	50 gm	49.0 gm	2%
7.	50 gm	49.0 gm	2%
8.	50 gm	48.5 gm	3%
9.	50 gm	49.0 gm	2%
10.	50 gm	48.5 gm	3%

7.25 DUCTILITY TEST

Ductility test is standard test described in I.S. 1208 -1978. See Figs. 7.17 and 7.18. The **ductility** of bitumen is measured as the distance in centimeter to which a briquette specimen of bitumen will elongate before breaking, when the briquette is pulled apart at specified speed and temperature. The usual speed is 5 cm per minute and test temperature of water bath is 27°C. The ductility value signifies the property by which a bitumen can exist without breakings.

The standard procedure is as follows :

Object : To determine ductility of Bitumen.

Apparatus : Mould, Water bath, Testing machine, Thermometer etc.

Procedure : Unless otherwise specified, the test shall be conducted at 27°C and at rate of pull 50 mm/minute.

Completely melt the bituminous material to be tested to a temperature of 75° to 100°C above the approximately softening point until it becomes thoroughly fluid. Assemble the mould on the brass plate and in order to present the material under test from sticking, coat the surface of the sides of the mould with mixture of equal parts of glycerine and dextrine.

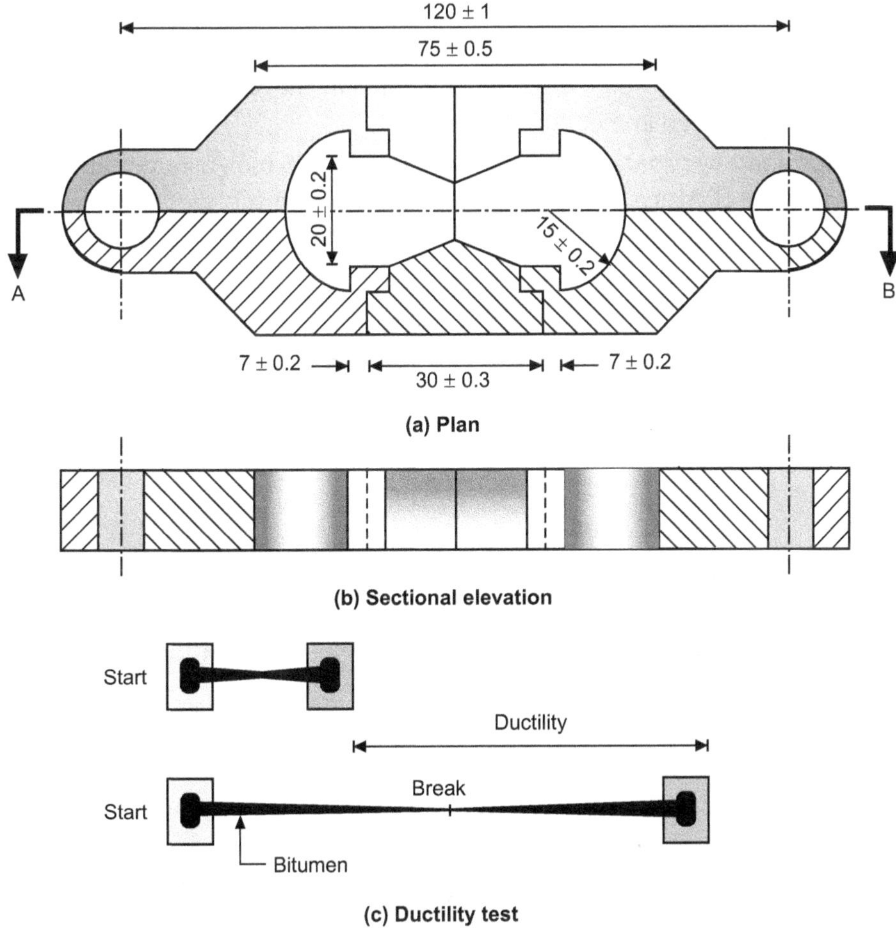

Fig. 7.17 : Ductility test

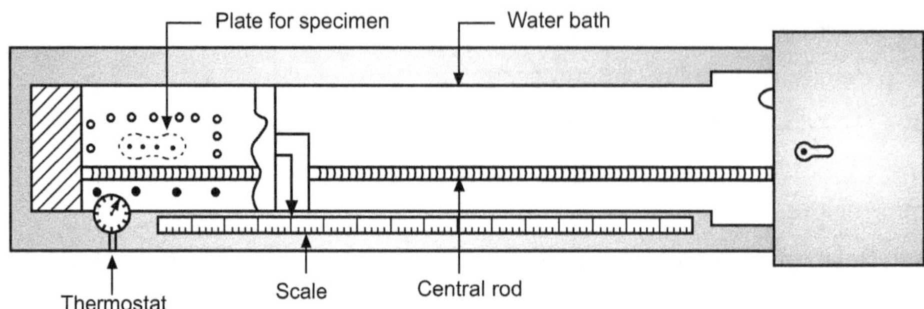

Fig. 7.18 : Ductility machine

Fill the material in the mould until it is more than level full. Leave it to cool at the room temperature for 30 to 40 minutes and then place in water bath maintained at 27°C for 30 minutes after which, cut off the excess bitumen by means of hot straight edged knife so that the mould shall be just level full. Place the briquette in the water bath. Remove the side pieces and test the specimen immediately.

Pull the two clips apart horizontally at a uniform speed of 50 mm/minute until the briquette ruptures. Measure the distance in centimeters through which the clips have been pulled, to produce rupture.

Precision : The test result shall not differ by the following :

Table 7.15

Repeatability	Reproducibility
10%	20%

Test Result

(1)   Grade of bitumen = 80/100

Rate of Pull = 50 mm/minute

Test temperature = 27°C

Table 7.16

Sr. No.	Ductility (cm)	Mean Ductility (cm)
1.	45	
2.	41	43.4 cm
3.	42	
4.	46	
5.	43	

(2)   Grade of bitumen = 60/70

Rate of pull = 50 mm/minute

Temperature = 27°C

Table 7.17

Sr. No.	Ductility (cm)	Mean Ductility (cm)
1.	41	
2.	38	39 cm
3.	40	
4.	39	
5.	37	

Lacunas in the Test : Test is conducted at 27°C but the maximum temperature on the road is normally more than 27°C and hence laboratory condition and practical condition are different. On roads, bituminous pavements are subjected to traffic loads but this test is conducted in the laboratory at uniform speed which is 50 mm/minute. Bituminous pavement contains aggregates along with bitumen, known as asphalt concrete which is subjected to traffic loads. But the laboratory sample is tested without aggregates.

The test is believed to measure the adhesiveness and plasticity of the bitumen. The bitumen may satisfy the ductility requirements. The materials with very high ductility are generally adhesive and have good cementing properties. High ductility is associated with high temperature susceptibility. The ductility value gets seriously affected by pouring temperature, dimensions of Briquette, level of Briquette in water bath, test temperature and rate of pulling.

Effect of temperature of water bath on ductility

(1)   Grade of bitumen = 80/100

            Rate of pull = 50 mm/min.

Table 7.18

Sr. No.	Temperature of Bath ($^{\circ}$C)	Ductility (cm)
1.	27°C	43 cm
2.	32°C	39 cm
3.	46°C	33 cm
4.	51°C	29 cm
5.	55°C	25 cm

(2)   Grade of bitumen = 60/70

            Rate of pull = 50 mm/min.

Table 7.19

Sr. No.	Temperature of Water Bath (°C)	Ductility (cm)
1.	27°C	39 cm
2.	31°C	36 cm
3.	45°C	31 cm
4.	50°C	28 cm
5.	54°C	23 cm

The ductility gets affected by change in temperature of water bath. Ductility value gets reduced with increase in water bath temperature. The ductility value also gets reduced with increase in rate of pull. The ductility value when rate of pull was 50 mm/minute was less when the rate of pull was 10 mm/minute even though grade of bitumen was same. When ductility is calculated at strain controlled condition, it is found that the ductility value gets affected by size of aggregates. The ductility value gets reduced with increase in size of aggregates. Ductility value is also affected by load applied vertically downward. It gets reduced with increase in load. If ductility value by standard test is compared with ductility value by stress controlled test, it is found that later value is 0.65 times the standard value. The ductility values get affected by pouring temperature, dimensions of briquette, level of briquette in water bath, test temperature and rate of pulling. If the temperature of the bath is increased, the ductility gets reduced, to a significant extent but the rate of pull does not have significant effect on ductility. Even if the rate of pull is decreased to 10 mm/minute, ductility gets increased by hardly 5%.

In actual field conditions, the ductile property of the bitumen is in conjunction with aggregate. To test the ductility property of bitumen in conjunction with the aggregate, author devised a modified test. This method consisted of taking equal sized aggregates which are kept touching each other. The bitumen of specified grade is poured just enough to coat the aggregates and the two aggregates are then pulled apart in vertical direction with a fixed load and length of bitumen thread is measured at the point of breaking. The fixed load employed was 30 gm. The following table shows typical results obtained by us.

Table 7.20 : Grade of Bitumen - 80/100

Aggregate Size in mm	10	12	20	25	40
Ductility in cm	33	32	30	25	24

In general, the larger-sized particles reduce the ductility. The magnitude of the stretching load employed has also a pronounced effect on the ductility values. If the stretching load increases, the ductility gets reduced, the following table examplifies this point.

Table 7.21 : Grade 80/100 Temperature 28°C 40 mm Aggregate

Stretched Load (gm)	10	20	30	40	50
Ductility in cm	35	33	29	29	23

7.26 PENETRATION TEST

This is standard test as per I.S. 1203 -1978. The penetration test determines the hardness or softness of the bitumen by measuring the depth in tenth's of a millimetre to which standard loaded needle will penetrate vertically in five minutes. The penetration of bituminous material is the distance in tenths of a millimeter that a standard needle will penetrate vertically into a sample of the material under standard conditions of temperature, load and time. The standard procedure is as follows :

Object : To determine the penetration value of the bitumen.

Apparatus : Container, needle, water bath, transfer dish, Penetration apparatus (See Fig. 7.19), thermometer, time device etc.

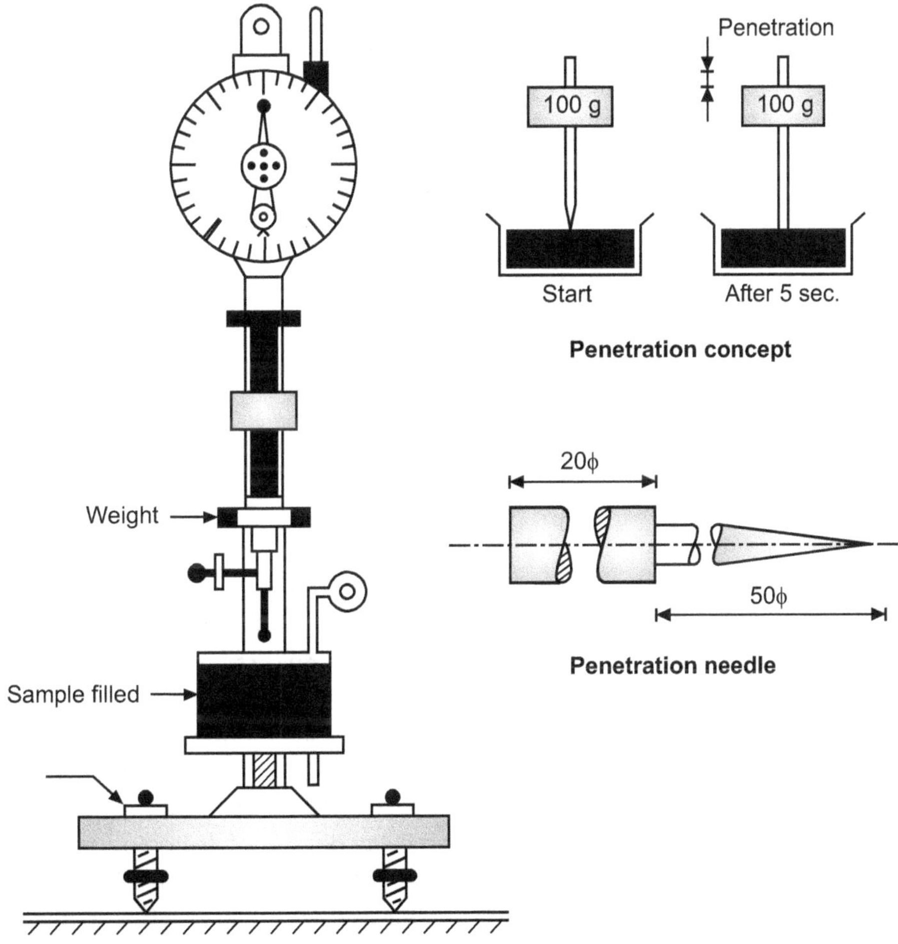

Fig. 7.19 : Penetrometer

Procedure : Soften the material to pouring temperature not more than 60°C for tars and not more than 90°C for bituminous materials above the approximate softening point and see that it is homogeneous and is free from air bubbles and water by stirring. Pour the material into the container to a depth at least 10 mm in excess of the expected penetration.

Protect the sample and allow it to cool. Place it in the bath which is to be kept at 25° C. Unless otherwise specified, the test is carried out at 25°C.

Adjust the needle to make contact with the surface of the sample. Bring the pointer to zero. Release the needle and measure the distance penetrated. Make three determinations and express in one tenth of a millimeter.

Precision : The duplicate result shall not differ by following :

Table 7.22

Penetration	Repeatability	Reproducibility
Below 50	1 unit	4 units
Above 50	3% of their mean	8% of their mean

Test Result

Grade of bitumen   = 80/100

Test temperature   = 25°C

Table 7.23

Sr. No.	Penetration	Mean
1.	86	
2.	92	
3.	81	
4.	87	87
5.	82	
6.	89	
7.	88	
8.	93	
9.	85	
10.	87	

7.27 DETERMINATION OF SOFTENING POINT OF BITUMEN

Bitumen does not suddenly change from solid state to liquid state but as the temperature increases, it gradually becomes softer until it flows readily. All semi-solid state bitumen needs sufficient fluidity before they are used for application with the aggregate mix. For this purpose, bitumen is sometimes cut back with a solvent like kerosene. The common procedure however is to liquify the bitumen by heating. The **'softening point'** is the temperature at which the substance attains particular degree of softening under specified condition of test. For bitumen it is usually determined by 'Ring and Ball test'. A brass ring containing the test sample of bitumen is suspended in liquid like water or glycerine at a given temperature. A steel ball is placed upon the bitumen and the liquid medium is then heated at a specified rate. The temperature at which the softened bitumen touches the metal plate placed at a specified distance below the ring is recorded as the softening point of a particular bitumen. The apparatus and test procedure are standardized by ISI. It is obvious that harder grade bitumen possess higher softening point.

Apparatus required for performing the test is shown.

Apparatus : It consists of ring and ball apparatus.

- **(a) Steel Balls :** They are two in number. Each has a diameter of 9.5 mm and weight 2.5 ± 0.05 g.
- **(b) Brass Rings :** There are two rings of following dimensions.

Table 7.24

Sr. No.	Particular	Dimension
1.	Depth	6.4 mm
2.	Inside ϕ @ bottom	15.9 mm
3.	Inside ϕ @ top	17.5 mm
4.	Outside diameter	20.6 mm

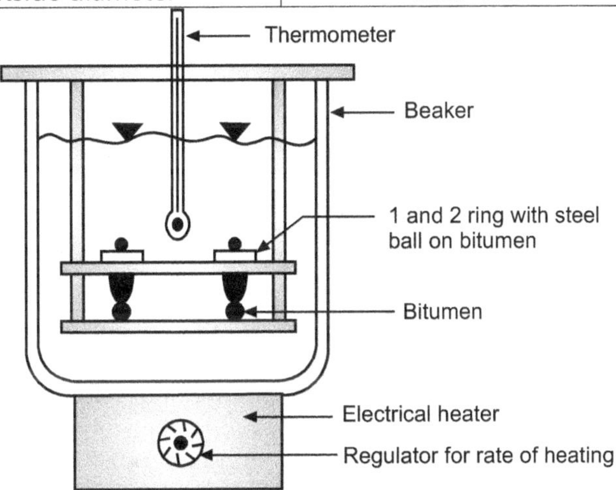

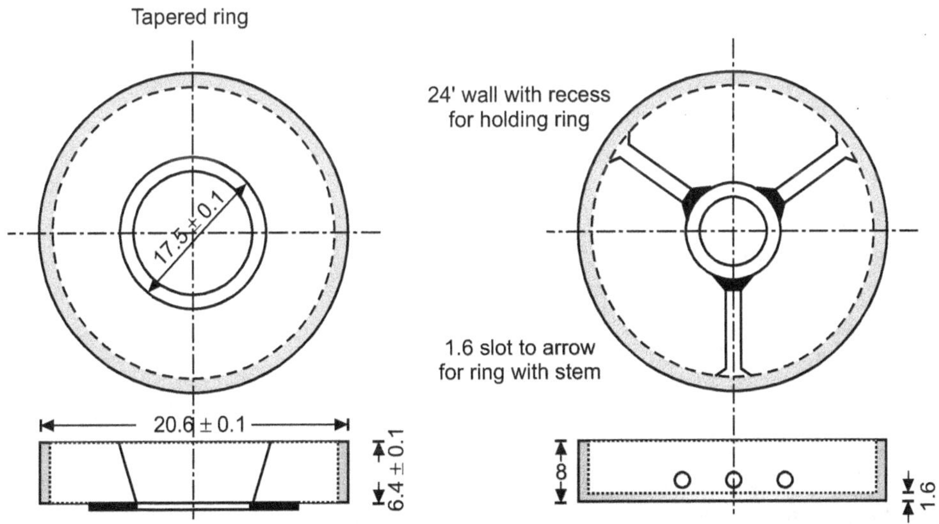

Fig. 7.20 : Softening point apparatus

(c) **Support :** The metallic support is used for placing a pair of rings. The upper surface of rings is adjusted to be 50 mm below the surface of water or liquid contained in bath. A distance of 25 mm between the bottom of rings and top surface of the bottom plate of support is provided. It has a housing for a suitable thermometer.

(d) **Bath and stirrer :** A heat resistant glass container of 85 mm diameter and 120 mm depth is used. Bath liquid is water for materials having softening point below 80°C and glycerine for materials having softening point more than 80°C, mechanical stirrer is used for insuring uniform heat distribution at all times throughout the bath itself.

Procedure : Sample material is heated to a temperature between 75°C and 100°C above the approximate softening point until it is completely fluid and is poured and heated in rings. To avoid sticking of metal plates to bitumen, coating is done to this with a solution of glycerine and dextrine. After cooling the rings in air for about 30 minutes, the excess bitumen is trimmed and rings are placed in the supports as discussed in item (c) above. At this time, the distilled water is kept at 50°C. This temperature is maintained for 15 min. after which balls are placed in position. The temperature of water is raised at uniform rate of 5°C per minute with a controlled heating unit, until the bitumen softens and touches bottom plate by sinking the balls. At least two observations are made. For material whose softening point is above 80°C, glycerine is used as a heating medium and the starting temperature is 35°C.

Results : The temperature at instant when each of the ball and sample touches the bottom plate of support is recorded as softening point value. The mean determinations are noted. It is essential that the mean value of the softening point temperature does not differ from individual observations by more than following limits :

Table 7.25

Softening Points	Repeatability	Reproducibility
Below 30°C	2°C	4°C
30°C – 80°C	1°C	2°C
Above 80°C	2°C	4°C

Discussion : As in the other physical tests on bitumen, it is essential that the specifications discussed above are strictly observed. Particularly, any variation in the following points would affect the result considerably :

(1) Quality and type of liquid.
(2) Weight of balls.
(3) Distance between bottom ring and bottom plate.
(4) Rate of the heating.

Impurity in water or glycerine has been observed to affect the results considerably. It is logical to observe the lower softening point if the weight of the ball is excessive. On the other hand, the increased distance between the bottom of the ring and bottom base plate increases the softening point.

Applications of Softening Point Test : Softening point is essentially a temperature at which the bituminous binders have an equal viscosities. Softening point of tar therefore, is related to the equiviscous temperatures i.e. (e.v.t.). The softening point found by the ring and ball apparatus is approximate.

Observations

(1) Bitumen grade   = 80/100

(2) Approximate softening point   = 48.5° C

(3) Liquid used in bath water/glycerine = water

Table 7.26

Time in Minutes	Temperature		Time in Minutes	Temperature	
	Ball 1	**Ball 2**		**Ball 1**	**Ball 2**
0	5.0	5.0	11	24.0	24.0
1	7.0	7.0	12	26.5	26.5
2	7.5	8.0	13	30.0	30.0
3	9.0	9.5	14	32.5	32.5
4	10.0	11.0	15	36.5	36.5
5	13.0	12.0	16	39.0	39.0
6	14.0	13.0	17	42.0	42.0
7	15.0	14.0	18	46.0	46.0
8	17.0	16.0	18' 54"	48.0	–
9	18.5	18.0	19	–	48.0
10	20.5	21.5	19' 25"	–	49.0

Table 7.27

Test Property	Sample no. 1		Sample no. 2		Mean Value of Softening point
	Ball 1	**Ball 2**	**Ball 1**	**Ball 2**	
Temp. °C at which sample touches bottom	48°C	49°C	–	–	48.5°C
Repeatability	1°C	1°C	–	–	1°C
Reproducibility	2°C	2°C	–	–	2°C

Test Result : Grade of Bitumen 80/100

Table 7.28

Sr. No.	Ball No. 1 in °C	Ball No. 2 in °C	Softening point, °C
1.	39	40	39.5
2.	49	38	39
3.	42	40	41
4.	43	42	42.5
5.	40	41	40.5
6.	40	40	40
7.	42	43	42.5
8.	40	42	41

7.28 BITUMINOUS MATERIALS

While discussing the test, we have used the word "bitumen". Bitumen is a petroleum product obtained by the specific distillation of petroleum crude. Bitumen can also be found in natural form but bulk of the supply of bitumen is through distillation of petroleum crude. Bitumen is completely soluble in carbon disulphide or carbon tetrachloride. The grades of bitumen used for the construction work of roads and air field pavements are called paving grades and those used for water proofing of structures and industrial floors are industrial grades. When the viscosity of bitumen is reduced by specific amount by a volatile dilutant, it is called cut back, on the other hand when the bitumen is suspended in a finely divided condition in aqueous medium and stabilized with an emulsifier, the material is known as emulsion. Similarly when bitumen contains some inert mineral, it is called as asphalt. Asphalt could be found naturally or artificially prepared. Compared to bitumen 'tar' is not derived from crude petroleum. It is obtained by the destructive distillation of coal or wood. Tar is soluble only in toluene. Tar in general has inferior weather resisting properties, change in viscosity of tar with temperature is considerable - not an asset from the point of road construction. Therefore, bitumen is generally preferred. As civil engineers, we are not interested in the production process of tar or bitumen.

7.29 BITUMEN MIXES

Bitumen along with aggregate can form tough paving surface. Aggregate should be sharp (not rounded). The maximum size of aggregate depends upon the thickness of the layer. For base course, maximum size of aggregate would be 2.5 to 5 cm. For surface course 1.25 to 1.87 cm size maximum aggregate may be O.K. The mix should be such that voids formed in the coarse aggregate should be filled by smaller-sized particles and bitumen should act as binder to all. As an example, the two recommended gradations for 40 mm thick bituminous surface are given in the table below.

Table 7.29

Sieve Size	Percent Passing by Weight	
mm	Grade 1	Grade 2
20	–	100
12.5	100	80 – 100
10.0	80 – 100	70 – 90
4.75	55 – 75	50 – 70
2.36	35 – 50	35 – 50
0.600	18 – 29	18 – 29
0.300	13 – 23	13 – 23
0.150	8 – 16	8 – 16
0.0075	4 – 10	4 – 10
Binder content, percent by weight of mix.		
	5 – 7.5	5 – 7.5

Since the bitumen aggregate mix consists of aggregate and bitumen, the usual Example is to find the properties of the mix knowing the properties of the individual i.e. the aggregate and the binder. This is easily done. For example, if W_1, W_2, W_3, W_4 are percent by weight of aggregates 1, 2, 3, 4 in a bituminous mix and G_1, G_2, G_3, G_4 are the specific gravities of the respective aggregates, then G_s, the specific gravity of blended aggregate mix will be,

$$G_s = \frac{100}{\dfrac{W_1}{G_1} + \dfrac{W_2}{G_2} + \dfrac{W_3}{G_3} + \dfrac{W_4}{G_4}}$$

The proportion G_1, G_2, G_3 etc. are to be so fixed that minimum voids should be left in the aggregate mix and dense matrix should result. This can be done by triangular chart method or Rothfuch's method. To this aggregate mix, let us assume W_b is percent by weight of bitumen is added, V_b percentage of bitumen by volume

$$G_T = \text{Maximum specific gravity of mix} = \frac{100}{\dfrac{100 - W_b}{G_a} + \dfrac{W_b}{G_b}}$$

This is the maximum specific gravity, provided bitumen occupies all the void volume. If this does not occur, and G is actual specific gravity of mix then percent air voids in the specimen would be given by,

$$V_v = \text{Percent air voids} = \frac{100\,(G_T - G)}{G_T}$$

and the percent voids filled with bitumen will be given by (VFB) V.F.B. $= \dfrac{100\, V_b}{100 - \dfrac{G}{W_a}}$, where

W_a is aggregate content percent by weight. Actually the attempt should be such that all the void volume in the aggregate mix should be occupied by bitumen leaving no air voids. This is impracticable. Another criteria is that bitumen percentage in the bitumen-aggregate mix should be such that the mix should have requisite strength and flexibility. To assess this and thus aid in finding out the bitumen content, tests have been devised. There are Marshall stability, Hubbard field method and Hueom method. We shall discuss these.

Marshall Method : This method and test is applicable to the hot-mix design of bitumen and aggregate with aggregate maximum size of 2.5 cm. For paving jobs the test is suitable. Essentially it consists of testing a 10.16 cm diameter 6.35 height cylindrical bitumen aggregate specimens. The load is peripheral. The load is applied at the rate of 5 cm/minute i.e. strain controlled and the Marshall stability value is the maximum load in kg before failure and the flow value is the deformation of specimen in 0.25 mm. units upto maximum load. To the first trial aggregate mix. which is heated to 175°C to 195°C, bitumen which is heated to 120° to 145° C should be added (say 5.5 to 4% by weight of material aggregate) thoroughly mixed at the desired temperature and moulded. The moulds should be cooled and then weighed in air and under submergence. Prior to testing these moulds should be heated to 60° + 1° for about 30 to 40 minutes and then tested peripherally. The suitable equipments such as heaters, tamper should be available. Sometimes one cannot get the exact height of 63.5 mm. In such a case, the Marshall stability value, obtained from such a not upto the mark specimen, is to be corrected with the help of the following table :

Table 7.30 : Correction Factors for Marshall Stability Value

Volume of Specimen in CCs	Thickness of Specimen	Correction Factor
457 – 470	57.1	1.19
471 – 482	58.7	1.14
483 – 495	60.3	1.09
496 – 508	61.9	1.04
509 – 522	63.5	1.00
523 – 535	65.1	0.96
535 – 546	66.7	0.93
547 – 559	68.3	0.89
560 – 573	69.9	0.86

Maintaining the aggregate percentage, we have to go on increasing the bitumen content in increments of 0.5 percent upto about 7.5 or 8.0 percent bitumen by weight of total mix. The percent air voids in the specimen (V_v) could be computed by $V_v = \dfrac{G_T - G_m}{G_m} \times 100$, where , G_T is specific gravity of mixture and G_m bulk density of specimen. Bulk density of specimen could be obtained since we have weighed the specimen in air and under submergence. Now, the graphs are plotted. These graphs generally are

- Percent bitumen against Marshall stability value,

- Bitumen percent against flow value,

- Bitumen percentage against unit weight,

- Bitumen percent against percent voids in total mix (V_v) and

- Bitumen percentage against percent voids filled with bitumen VFB.

The purpose of Marshall test is to find out optimum bitumen content so that the mix has the requisite strength (Marshall stability No.) and flexibility (i.e. the flow value). The optimum bitumen content for the mix design is the average value of the following three bitumen contents found from the graphs of the test results :

(1) Bitumen content corresponding to maximum stability,

(2) Bitumen content corresponding to maximum unit weight,

(3) Bitumen content corresponding to the median of designed limits of percent air voids in total mix (4%). For type of pavement, certain Marshall stability value and flow value are recommended. One can check-up whether the optimum binder content found out from testing is more or less as per these recommendations or not. If so, the aggregate percentage mix and optimum binder mix so found out is O.K. As an example the following table is provided. However, many such tables are available.

Table 7.31 : Marshall Mix Design for Bituminous Concrete

Test Property	Recommended Value
Marshall stability (kg)	340 (minimum)
Flow value, 0.25 mm units	8 to 16
Air voids in total mix. V_v%	3 to 5
Voids filled with bitumen VFB%	75 to 85

Modified Hubbard : Field method of bituminous mix design. Though developed initially to design sheet asphalt mix, now it can be used with modifications to design bituminous mixes having coarse aggregate upto 19 mm size. The principle of the test is to prepare aggregate bitumen mould 15.24 cm diameter 6 to 87 cm height.

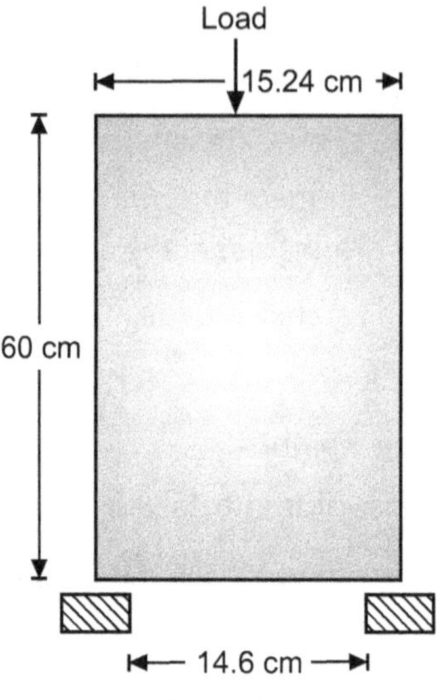

Fig. 7.21

This specimen is extruded through a ring of 14.6 cm diameter under load. The load that is required to do this is known as Hubbard - Field stability. The other graphs are same as in Marshall stability test. Test therefore would consist of :

- **Preparation of Specimen :** Aggregate in the desired proportions and the bituminous material are heated to the prescribed temperature and placed in preheated mould and tamped by 30 blows on each side. Static load of 4536 kg is applied for two minutes and specimen cooled to 37.8°C under same compressive load. Specimen is now removed, weighed and measured.

- Now the specimen is tested at 60° C under the rate of deformation of 6.1 cm/minute. It should be remembered that whereas one end of the specimen is loaded, the other end rests on ring of 14.6 cm. and the sample is getting extruded through this ring. The maximum load recorded is the stability value. The experiment is repeated with different bitumen content and the graphs that are plotted are : (i) Stability versus bitumen content, (ii) Unit weight versus bitumen content, (iii) Percent void in total mix versus the bitumen content, (iv) Percent aggregate voids versus bitumen content.

To determine optimum binder content the first step is to find bitumen content corresponding to 3 to 3.5 percent air voids in the total mix. For this bitumen content read the stability number from the graph. Certain values of stability number have been prescribed as shown in the table below :

Table 7.32 : Recommended Stability Number

Property	Medium and Light Traffic	Heavy and Very Heavy Traffic
Stability kg	545 – 910	7510
Voids, total mix.%	2 – 5	2 – 6

If the stability value is within specified limit, the mix is satisfactory. Otherwise change aggregate percentage and repeat the tests i.e. redesign. The final selection should depend upon economics and strength.

Comparison between Hubbard and Marshall Test : The most important aspect in Marshall test is peripheral load which is applied and flow value is recorded. Whereas in the Hubbard test cylinder is subjected to compressive load on flat end, the other end being resting on extrusion ring. Therefore, the sample is being extruded under compressive load. No flow value is observed. But there is large similarity in design methods since it is done through graphs.

Hueom Method of Bituminous Mix Design : This method consists of conducting two tests on bituminous mix : (1) stabilometer test and (2) cohesometer test. Stabilometer test is akin to triaxial test, whereas cohesometer test is akin to direct shear test. For stabilometer test, we have test specimen of 10 cm diameter and 6.25 cm height of specified mix. We generally prepare three specimen having same aggregate mix but binder content 0.5 to 1.0 percent above and 0.5 to 1.0 percent below the estimated binder content. The specimen are prepared at 110°C using kneading compactor. These specimens are now cooled at room temperature for one hour and placed in water pan for 24 hour for possible swell measurements. After the swell measurement the specimen is to be tested at 60°C in the stabilometer. The confining pressure applied is 0.35 kg/cm^2, vertical loads are then applied in the sequence of 227, 454 and in increments of 454 kg upto a maximum of 2722 kg. Due to application of vertical load, confining pressure may change, which is now reset to 0.35 kg/cm^2. The confining pressure is now increased to 7 kg/cm^2. The confining pressure is set by rotation of handle and number of turns of handle directly gives displacement of specimen. The specimen from the stabilometer test is now recovered and subjected to cohesiometer test. Of course before subjecting the sample to cohesometer test, it should be maintained at 60°C for two hours. Cohesometer test is direct shear test. The actuating load is being provided by lead shots. The stabilometer resistance value R and cohesometer value C can be computed by

$$C = \frac{L}{W\,(0.2\,H + 0.0176\,H^2)} \quad \text{and } R = 100 - \frac{100}{\dfrac{2.5}{D_2}\left(\dfrac{P_v}{P_h} - 1\right) + 1}$$

where,

C　=　Cohesometer value.

L　=　Weight of shots (lead) in gms.

W　=　Diameter or width of specimen in cm.

H　=　Height of specimen in cm.

For stabilometer value R,

P_V = Vertical pressure applied.

P_h = Horizontal pressure transmitted at this P_h.

D_2 = Displacement of stabilometer fluid necessary to increase the fluid pressure from 0.7 to 7.0 kg/cm^2 measured in number of revolutions of calibrated pump handle.

For different types of traffic, the recommeded values of these parameters are given below :

Table 7.33

Test	Criteria		
Value	High Traffic	Medium Traffic	Heavy Traffic
Stabilometer value R	> 30	> 35	> 37
Cohesometer value C	> 50	> 50	> 50
Swell mm	< 0.76	< 0.76	< 0.76
Air void present	> 4	> 4	> 4

SOLVED PROBLEMS

Peoblem 7.1 : *The following data refer to observation taken for angularity number*

(1) Size of aggregate = 20 mm – 16 mm.

(Passing through 20 mm and retained on 16 mm)

(2) Specific gravity of aggregate = 2.856 = G_A.

(3) Weight of water required to fill the metal cylider = 3000 gms = C.

(4) Weight of aggregate required to fill the cylinder = W = 3880 gms.

Find angularity number.

Solution :

$$\text{Angularity number} = 67 - \frac{100 \times W}{C \times G_A}$$

$$= 67 - \frac{100 \times 3880}{2.856 \times 3000}$$

$$= 67 - \frac{100 \times 3880}{2.856 \times 3000}$$

$$= \textbf{21.71} \qquad \qquad \textbf{... Ans.}$$

Peoblem 7.2 : *For aggregate passing 40 mm and retained on 10 mm, following observations were taken*

 (i) *Weight of basket = 110 gm.*

 (ii) *Weight of basket + sample = 960 gm.*

 (iii) *Weight of saturated surface dry sample = 1310 gm.*

 (iv) *Weight of oven-dried sample = C = 1280 gm.*

 Find specific gravity, apparent specific gravity and water absorption.

Solution : Weight of sample in water = 960 – 110 = 850 gm

(1) Specific gravity

$$= \frac{1280}{1310 - 850}$$

$$= \textbf{2.78} \qquad \textbf{... Ans.}$$

(2) Apparent specific gravity $= \dfrac{1280}{1280 - 850} = \textbf{2.976}$ **... Ans.**

(3) Water absorption

$$= \frac{1310 - 1280}{1280} \times 100$$

$$= \textbf{2.34\%} \qquad \textbf{... Ans.}$$

Peoblem 7.3 : *From the following observations, determine water absorption, specific gravity and apparent specific gravity.*

 Size of aggregates 10 mm to 4.57 mm

 (1) *Weight of pycnometer + water = 1380 gm = C.*

 (2) *Weight of pycnometer + water + sample = B = 1705 gm.*

 (3) *Weight of pycnometer = 540 gm.*

 (4) *Weight of ovendried sample = 495 gm = D.*

 (5) *Weight of saturated surface-dried sample = 506 gm = A.*

Solution :

(1) Applied specific gravity

$$= \frac{495}{495 - (1705 - 1380)}$$

$$= \textbf{2.911} \qquad \textbf{... Ans.}$$

 Weight of saturated surface-dried sample = 506 gm

(2) Water absorption

$$= \frac{506 - 495}{495} \times 100$$

$$= \textbf{2.22\%} \qquad \textbf{... Ans.}$$

(3) Specific gravity $= \dfrac{495}{506 - (1705 - 1380)} = \textbf{2.734}$ **... Ans.**

QUESTIONS

1. Explain the procedure involved in aggregate crushing valve.

2. What are various test carried out on bitumen? Explain any one briefly?

3. What are various test carried out on soil? Explain any one briefly?

4. What are various test carried out on aggregates? Explain any one briefly?

5. Discuss various tests on aggregates for their stability.

6. Define terms (i) Flakiness Index (ii) Elongation Index, and also state the importance of that.

7. Write short notes on :

   (a) Bitumen and tar.

   (b) Impact test on aggregates.

   (c) CBR.

   (d) Plate load test.

   (e) Flakiness index test.

   (f) Angularity number test.

   (g) Specific gravity, porosity and water absorption.

   (h) Aggregate crushing value test.

   (i) Los-angeles abrasion.

   (j) Aggregate impact.

   (k) Aggregate polishing and stripping test.

   (l) Viscosity Test.

   (m) Fire and flash point test.

8.1 OVERVIEW

A highway pavement is a structure consisting of superimposed layers of processed materials above the natural soil sub-grade, whose primary function is to distribute the applied vehicle loads to the sub-grade. The pavement structure should be able to provide a surface of acceptable riding quality, adequate skid resistance, favourable light reflecting characteristics and low noise pollution. The ultimate aim is to ensure that the transmitted stresses due to wheel load are sufficiently reduced, so that they will not exceed bearing capacity of the subgrade. Two types of pavements are generally recognized as serving this purpose, namely **flexible pavements** and **rigid pavements**. This chapter gives an overview of pavement types, layers and their functions and pavement failures. Improper design of pavements leads to early failure of pavements affecting the riding quality also.

8.2 REQUIREMENTS OF A PAVEMENT

The pavement should meet the following requirements :

- Sufficient thickness to distribute the wheel load stresses to a safe value on the sub-grade soil.
- Structurally strong to withstand all types of stresses imposed upon it.
- Adequate coefficient of friction to prevent skidding of vehicles.
- Smooth surface to provide comfort to road users even at high speed.
- Produce least noise from moving vehicles.
- Dust-proof surface so that traffic safety is not impaired by reducing visibility.
- Impervious surface, so that sub-grade soil is well protected.
- Long design life with low maintenance cost.

8.3 TYPES OF PAVEMENTS

The pavements can be classified based on the structural performance into two, flexible pavements and rigid pavements. In flexible pavements, wheel loads are transferred by grain-to-grain contact of the aggregate through the granular structure. The flexible pavement, having less flexural strength acts like a flexible sheet (For example, bituminous road). On the contrary, in rigid pavements, wheel loads are transferred to sub-grade soil by flexural strength of the pavement and the pavement acts like a rigid plate (For example cement concrete roads). In addition to these composite pavements are also available. A thin layer of flexible pavement over rigid pavement is an ideal pavement with most desirable characteristics. However, such pavements are rarely used in new construction because of high cost and complex analysis required.

8.3.1 Flexible Pavements

Flexible pavements will transmit wheel load stresses to the lower layers by grain-to-grain transfer through the points of contact in the granular structure (See Fig. 8.1).

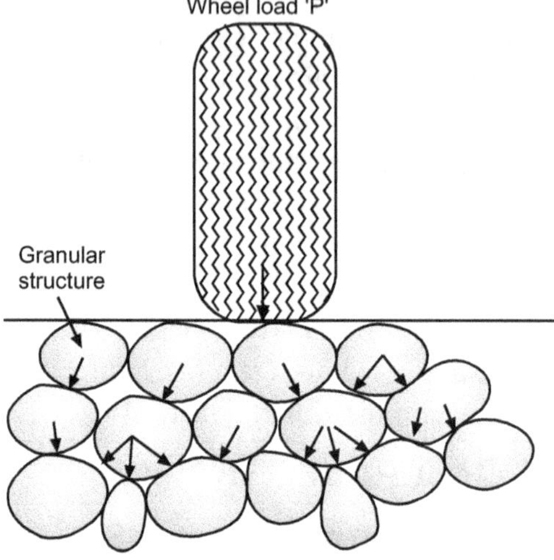

Fig. 8.1 : Load transfer in granular structure

8.3.1.1 Deflection on Flexible Pavement

The wheel load acting on the pavement will be distributed to a wider area and the stress decreases with the depth. Taking advantage of this stress distribution characteristic, flexible pavements normally has many layers. Hence, the design of flexible pavement uses the concept of layered system. Based on this, flexible pavement may be constructed in a number of layers and the top layer has to be of best quality to sustain maximum compressive stress, in addition to wear and tear. The lower layers will experience lesser magnitude of stress and less quality material can be used. Flexible pavements are constructed using bituminous materials. These can be either in the form of surface treatments (such as bituminous surface treatments generally found on low volume roads) or asphalt concrete surface courses (generally used on high volume roads such as national highways).

8.3.1.2 Types of Flexible Pavements

The following types of construction have been used in flexible pavement :

- Conventional layered flexible pavement,
- Full-depth asphalt pavement and
- Contained Rock Asphalt Mat (CRAM).

Conventional Flexible Pavements : are layered systems with high quality expensive materials placed at the top where stresses are high and low quality cheap materials are placed in lower layers. Full-depth asphalt pavements are constructed by placing bituminous layers directly on the soil sub-grade. This is more suitable when there is high traffic and local materials are not available.

Contained rock asphalt mats are constructed by placing dense/open-graded aggregate layers in between two asphalt layers. Modified dense graded asphalt concrete placed above the sub-grade will significantly reduce the vertical compressive strain on soil sub-grade and protect from surface water.

8.3.2 Typical Layers of a Flexible Pavement

Typical layers of a conventional flexible pavement include seal coat, surface course, tack coat, binder course, prime coat, base course, sub-base course, compacted subgrade and natural subgrade (See Fig. 8.2).

Seal Coat : Seal coat is a thin surface treatment used to water-proof the surface and to provide skid resistance.

Tack Coat : Tack coat is a very light application of asphalt, usually asphalt emulsion diluted with water. It provides proper bonding between two layer of binders course and must be thin, uniformly cover the entire surface and set very fast.

Prime Coat : Prime coat is an application of low viscous cutback bitumen to an absorbent surface like granular bases on which binder layer is placed. It provides bonding between two layers. Unlike tack coat, prime coat penetrates into the layer below, plugs the voids and forms a water- tight surface.

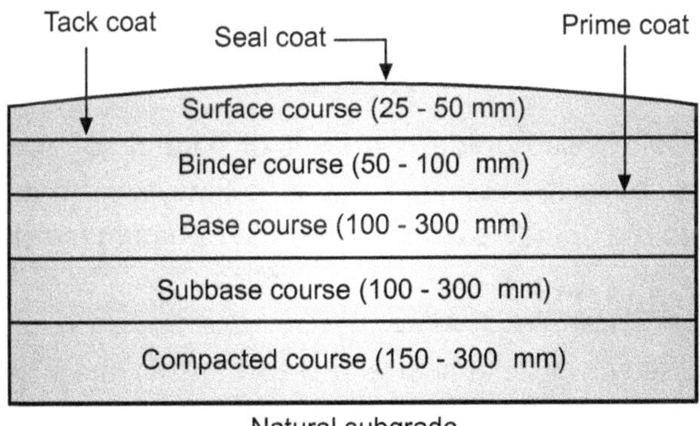

Fig. 8.2 : Typical cross-section of a flexible pavement

Surface Course : Surface course is the layer directly in contact with traffic loads and generally contains superior quality materials. They are usually constructed with dense graded asphalt concrete (AC). The functions and requirements of this layer are :

- It provides characteristics such as friction, smoothness, drainage etc. Also it will prevent the entrance of excessive quantities of surface water into the underlying base, sub-base and sub-grade.

- It must be tough to resist the distortion under traffic and provide a smooth and skid-resistant riding surface.

- It must be water proof to protect the entire base and sub-grade from the weakening effect of water.

Binder Course : This layer provides the bulk of the asphalt concrete structure. It's chief purpose is to distribute load to the base course. The binder course generally consists of aggregates having less asphalt and doesn't require quality as high as the surface course, so replacing a part of the surface course by the binder course results in more economical design.

Base Course : The base course is the layer of material immediately beneath the surface of binder course and it provides additional load distribution and contributes to the sub-surface drainage. It may be composed of crushed stone, crushed slag and other untreated or stabilized materials.

Sub-Base Course : The sub-base course is the layer of material beneath the base course and the primary functions are to provide structural support, improve drainage and reduce the intrusion of fines from the sub-grade in the pavement structure. If the base course is open graded, then the sub-base course with more fines can serve as a filler between sub-grade and the base course. A sub-base course is not always needed or used. For example, a pavement constructed over a high quality, stiff sub-grade may not need the additional features offered by a sub-base course. In such situations, sub-base course may not be provided.

Sub-grade : The top soil or sub-grade is a layer of natural soil prepared to receive the stresses from the layers above. It is essential that at no time, soil sub-grade is overstressed. It should be compacted to the desirable density, near the optimum moisture content.

8.4 RIGID PAVEMENTS

Rigid pavements have sufficient flexural strength to transmit the wheel load stresses to a wider area below. A typical cross-section of the rigid pavement is shown in Fig. 8.3. Compared to flexible pavement, rigid pavements are placed either directly on the prepared sub-grade or on a single layer of granular or stabilized material. Since there is only one layer of material between the concrete and the sub-grade, this layer can be called as base or sub-base course.

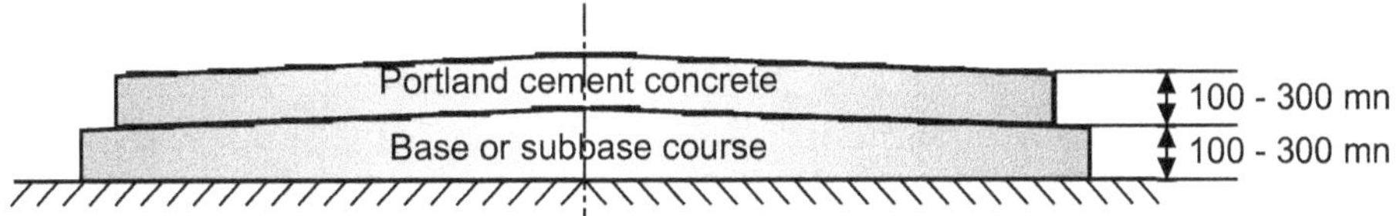

Fig. 8.3 : Typical cross-section of rigid pavement

In rigid pavement, load is distributed by the slab action and the pavement behaves like an elastic plate resting on a viscous medium (See Fig. 8.3). Rigid pavements are constructed by Portland Cement Concrete (PCC) and should be analyzed by plate theory instead of layer theory, assuming an elastic plate resting on viscous foundation. Plate theory is a simplified version of layer theory that assumes the concrete slab as a medium thick plate which is plane before loading and to remain plane after loading. Bending of the slab is due to wheel load and temperature variation and the resulting tensile and flexural stress.

8.4.1 Types of Rigid Pavements

Rigid pavements can be classified into four types :

- Jointed plain concrete pavement (JPCP),
- Jointed reinforced concrete pavement (JRCP),
- Continuous reinforced concrete pavement (CRCP) and
- Pre-stressed concrete pavement (PCP).

Jointed Plain Concrete Pavement : They are plain cement concrete pavements constructed with closely spaced contraction joints. Dowel bars or aggregate interlocks are normally used for load transfer across joints. They normally has a joint spacing of 5 to 10 m.

Jointed Reinforcement Concrete Pavement : Although reinforcements do not improve the structural capacity significantly, they can drastically increase the joint spacing to 10 to 30 m. Dowel bars are required for load transfer. Reinforcements help to keep the slab together even after cracks.

Continuous Reinforced Concrete Pavement : Complete elimination of joints are achieved by reinforcement.

8.4.2 Advantages of Rigid Pavement

- Rigid lasts much longer i.e 30+ years compared to 5-10 years of flexible pavements.
- In the long run it is about half the cost to install and maintain. But the initial costs are somewhat high.
- Rigid pavement has the ability to bridge small imperfections in the subgrade.
- Less Maintenance cost and Continuous Traffic and Flow.
- High efficiency in terms of functionality.

8.5 COMPARISON OF FLEXIBLE AND RIGID PAVEMENT

Sr. No.	Flexible Pavements	Rigid Pavements
1	Deformation in the sub grade is transferred to the upper layers.	Deformation in the subgrade is not transferred to subsequent layers.
2.	Design is based on load distributing characteristics of the component layers.	Design is based on flexural strength or slab action.
3.	Have low flexural strength.	Have high flexural strength.
4.	Load is transferred by grain to grain contact.	No such phenomenon of grain to grain load transfer exists.
5.	Have low completion cost but repairing cost is high.	Have low repairing cost but completion cost is high.
6.	Have low life span (High Maintenance Cost).	Life span is more as compare to flexible (Low Maintenance Cost).
7.	Surfacing cannot be laid directly on the sub grade but a sub base is needed.	Surfacing can be directly laid on the sub grade.
8.	No thermal stresses are induced as the pavement have the ability to contract and expand freely.	Thermal stresses are more vulnerable to be induced as the ability to contract and expand is very less in concrete.
9.	Thats why expansion joints are not needed	Thats why expansion joints are needed
10.	Strength of the road is highly dependent on the strength of the sub grade.	Strength of the road is less dependent on the strength of the sub grade.
11.	Rolling of the surfacing is needed.	Rolling of the surfacing in not needed.
12.	Road can be used for traffic within 24 hours.	Road cannot be used until 14 days of curing.
13.	Force of friction is less Deformation in the sub grade is not transferred to the upper layers.	Force of friction is high.
14.	Damaged by Oils and Certain Chemicals.	No Damage by Oils and Greases.

8.6 FACTOR AFFECTING PAVEMENT DESIGN

There are many factors that affect pavement design which can be classified into four categories as traffic and loading, structural models, material characterization, environment. They will be discussed in detail in this chapter.

8.6.1 Traffic and Loading

Traffic is the most important factor in the pavement design. The key factors include contact pressure, wheel load, axle configuration, moving loads, load, and load repetitions.

Contact Pressure: The tyre pressure is an important factor, as it determines the contact area and the contact pressure between the wheel and the pavement surface. Even though the shape of the contact area is elliptical, for sake of simplicity in analysis, a circular area is often considered.

Wheel Load: The next important factor is the wheel load which determines the depth of the pavement required to ensure that the sub grade soil is not failed. Wheel configuration affects the stress distribution and defection within a pavement. Many commercial vehicles have dual rear wheels which ensure that the contact pressure is within the limits. The normal practice is to convert dual wheel into an equivalent single wheel load so that the analysis is made simpler.

Axle Configuration: The load carrying capacity of the commercial vehicle is further enhanced by the introduction of multiple axles.

Moving Loads: The damage to the pavement is much higher if the vehicle is moving at creep speed. Many studies show that when the speed is increased from 2 km/hr to 24 km/hr, the stresses and defection reduced by 40 per cent.

Repetition of Loads: The influence of traffic on pavement not only depends on the magnitude of the wheel load, but also on the frequency of the load applications. Each load application causes some deformation and the total deformation is the summation of all these. Although the pavement deformation due to single axle load is very small, the cumulative effect of number of load repetition is significant. Therefore, modern design is based on total number of standard axle load (usually 80 KN single axle).

8.6.2 Structural Models

The structural models are various analysis approaches to determine the pavement responses (stresses, strains, and defections) at various locations in a pavement due to the application of wheel load. The most common structural models are layered elastic model and visco-elastic models.

Layered Elastic Model: A layered elastic model can compute stresses, strains, and defections at any point in a pavement structure resulting from the application of a surface load. Layered elastic models assume that each pavement structural layer is homogeneous, isotropic, and linearly elastic. In other words, the material properties are same at every point in a given layer and the layer will rebound to its original form once the load is removed. The layered elastic approach works with relatively simple a mathematical model that relates stress, strain, and deformation with wheel loading and material properties like modulus of elasticity and poissons ratio.

8.6.3 Material Characterization

The following material properties are important for both flexible and rigid pavements.

- When pavements are considered as linear elastic, the elastic moduli and poisson ratio of sub-grade and each component layer must be specified.
- If the elastic modulus of a material varies with the time of loading, then the resilient modulus, which is elastic modulus under repeated loads, must be selected in accordance with a load duration corresponding to the vehicle speed.
- When a material is considered non-linear elastic, the constitutive equation relating the resilient modulus to the state of the stress must be provided.

  However, many of these material properties are used in visco-elastic models which are very complex and in the development stage.

8.6.4 Environmental Factors

Environmental factors affect the performance of the pavement materials and cause various damages. Environmental factors that affect pavement are of two types, temperature and precipitation and they are discussed below:

Temperature

The effect of temperature on asphalt pavements is different from that of concrete pavements. Temperature affects the resilient modulus of asphalt layers, while it induces curling of concrete slab. In rigid pavements, due to difference in temperatures of top and bottom of slab, temperature stresses or frictional stresses are developed. While in flexible pavement, dynamic modulus of asphaltic concrete varies with temperature. Frost heave causes differential settlements and pavement roughness. Most detrimental effect of frost penetration occurs during the spring break up period when the ice melts and sub-grade is a saturated condition.

Precipitation

The precipitation from rain and snow affects the quantity of surface water infiltrating into the sub-grade and the depth of ground water table. Poor drainage may bring lack of shear strength, pumping, loss of support, etc.

8.7 The CONCEPT OF "EQUIVALENT WHEEL LOAD", "REIGIDITY FACTOR," REPEITION" AND "IMPACT"

Before we take up the actual design of pavements, we have to know certain concepts, these concepts are :

8.7.1 Equivalent Wheel Load

Most of the loads that pass on highways are not single wheels. For example, in the case of trucks we have axle loads. In such cases, two wheels are placed closely together. In such cases, pressure bulb created by these two wheels are likely to overlap. Most of the design methods are based on single wheel loading. Therefore, these dual wheels have to be replaced by single wheel called **equivalent wheel**. We have two criteria here. An equivalent single wheel load of wheel assembly based on equivalent deflection criterion will be defined as that, single wheel load having the same contact pressure which produces the value of maximum deflection at a given depth. On the other hand, equivalent single wheel load of tyre assembly based on equivalent stress criterion may be defined as that, single wheel load which produces the same value of maximum stress at the desired depth.

Equivalent deflection criterion is generally considered more suitable. According to the observations made by U.S. corps of Engineers, if we consider two wheel spaced 'd' from their inner faces, then at depths greater than $\frac{d}{2}$, stresses induced due to each load, start overlapping and at a depth '2s', where 's' is the distance between the centre lines of tyre, the dual wheel assembly acts as if it is a single unit carrying a load equal to double the each wheel load (i.e. $2 \times P$). In order to determine single wheel load at any depth, it is assumed that the value of equivalent single wheel load varies as the logarithm of the thickness of pavement between '$\frac{d}{2}$' and 2s. The equivalent single wheel load is first determined for an estimated design thickness of the pavement with the help of this assumption. This wheel load is then used in the design procedure and the thickness of the pavement is calculated. In case thickness so obtained is equal to the estimated thickness, then the equivalent single wheel load so considered is correct, otherwise more trials are to be made till the calculated thickness more or less equals the estimated thickness.

8.7.2 Rigidity Factor

Theoretically, if the tyre inflation pressure is p and the contact area is A, then the load that is actuating on the pavement is pA. This is on the assumption that the applied surface pressure is equal to tyre inflation pressure. Actually surface pressure is generally greater than tyre inflation pressure, when the tyre inflation pressure is less than 7 kg/cm^2. The contact surface pressure becomes less than tyre pressure for values of tyre pressure greater than 7 kg/cm^2. The ratio between the contact surface pressure to tyre inflation pressure is known as rigidity factor. The knowledge of stress-distribution from the principles of soil mechanics tells us that, effects of high tyre inflation pressure are more pronounced in the upper layers only and less effects at greater depths. Thus, the tyre inflation pressure will control the quality of material in the upper layer but not the total pavement thickness requirements. This is the reason, why in the case of iron tyred traffic, that is bullock carts, the stresses in the pavement surface are very high requiring strong material for surfacing courses.

8.7.3 Effect of Repetition of Loads

It is not the application of wheel load but the repetitive application of wheel load that causes deleterious effects on the highway. Elastic and plastic deformations are caused in the highway pavement due to repetition of wheel load. The repeated load application causes breaking down of base course aggregate material. The sucking and kneading action of the wheel load may cause working upwards of soil in the sub-grade. As per the findings of the A.A.S.H.O. road test, for a given axle load, the pavement thickness required to provide a given service is proportional to the logarithm of the number of repetition of the axle load.

As per Mcleod, a flexible highway pavement designed for one million coverages of the design load in 25 years requires 25 % of the design thickness only for one coverage. In the case of mixed traffic on highways, we can replace different wheel loads to an equivalent wheel load by using this concept. Suppose that P_1 is the wheel load which causes failure of the pavement in 'n_1' applications and P_2 is the wheel load which causes the same degree of failure in the same pavement, then Mcleod theorised that $P_1 n_1 = P_2 n_2$.

In order to determine equivalent load factors curves with 25%, designed thickness are plotted for various wheel loads on vertical axis against one application and total 100 % thickness on a vertical axis, drawn at one million repetitions. On the assumption that 25 cm thickness is required for highway pavement (generally flexible) on an ordinary sub-grade soil then for this 25 cm thickness of pavement respective repetitions could be read from this figure for different load applications and are shown in Table 8.1 below.

Table 8.1 : Load Repetitions for Failure

Wheel Load, kg	Load Repetitions for Failure
2268	1,05,000
2725	50,000
3170	22,500
3630	13,000
4080	6,500
4530	3,300
4990	1,700
5440	1,000

The table helps us in determining what is known as equivalent load factor. For example, a wheel load of 2268 kg when applied 1, 05,000 fails the pavements, whereas 2720 kg wheel load requires 50,000 repetitions for failing the pavement. Therefore, 2720 kg wheel load may be considered equivalent to 1,05,000/50,000 i.e. 2.1 times the wheel load 2268 kg. That is equivalent wheel load factor for 2720 kg wheel is 2.1. These equivalent load factors were suggested by Liddle, on the basis of A.A.S.H.O. test to convert the vehicle to standard 8200 kg and are tabulated below. Equivalent load factor for any other standard weight axle could be had by assuming linear law.

Table 8.2 : Equivalent Factor

Axle	Equivalent Factors	
Loads	Single Axle	Tandom Axle Sets
910	0.0002	
1810	0.0025	
2720	0.01	0.0009
3630	0.04	0.0027
4540	0.08	0.01
5440	0.18	0.02
6350	0.34	0.03
7260	0.60	0.05
8160	1.00	0.08
9070	1.59	0.09
9980	2.43	0.11
10890	3.59	0.17
11790	5.15	0.24
12700	7.21	0.34
13610	9.88	0.47
14520	13.29	0.63
15430	17.57	0.82
16320	22.89	1.07
17320	29.40	1.38
18140	37.31	1.75
19070	46.82	2.19

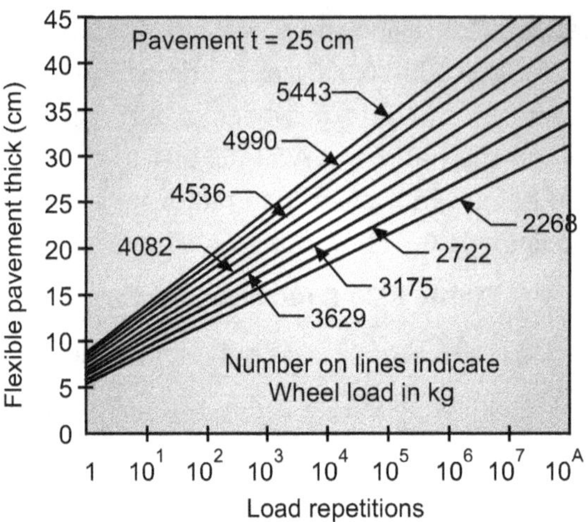

Fig. 8.4

The above table is based on the tests conducted by American Association of State Highways officials at Illinois and may vary from country to country. A general equation for equivalent factor can be stated as,

$$\text{Equivalent factor} = \left(\frac{W_i}{8200}\right)^A$$

The exponent A may vary from 2.5 to 4.6 depending upon the thickness of asphaltic pavement and its temperature. It should be noted, we in India have not been in a position to conduct such exhaustive tests such as A.A.S.H.O. due to monetary constraint. In the above equation, 8200 kg is considered standard wheel load.

Impact : As far as flexible pavements are considered, no impact allowance need be made. This is because of the fact that the traffic load comes rapidly and the strength of material tested rapidly is higher than when it is tested in a static condition. As the speed of the vehicle increases, stresses and deflections in the road surface decrease. For rigid pavements, joints do suffer due to impact. Generally, the impact allowance of 20 % is commonly used for the design of rigid pavements. But that is not a hard and fast rule.

8.8 METHODS OF DESIGNING FLEXIBLE PAVEMENTS

8.8.1 North Dakota Cone Test Method

This method was devised by North Dakota State Highway Department. The method essentially consists of pushing a cone in the sub-grade. The half angle of the cone is 7° 45'. The cone is pushed into the ground for successive weights of 5, 10, 20, 30, 40 kg and deflection under each load is obtained. Since, theoretically the penetration for 10 kg load should be half that of 40 kg load, the value of correction is $C = \Delta\,40 - 2\,\Delta\,10$, where $\Delta\,40$ and $\Delta\,10$ are penetrations at 40 and 10 kg load. This correction is added to each of the observed deflection to get true penetration. Suppose for the load W, the true penetration is h, then the radius of the bearing area is $h \tan \dfrac{\theta}{2}$ and the bearing area is $\dfrac{\pi}{4}\left(2\,h \tan \dfrac{\theta}{2}\right)^2$ or π $h^2 \tan^2 \dfrac{\theta}{2}$ and therefore, the bearing pressure for the load W is $\dfrac{W}{\pi\,h^2 \tan^2 \dfrac{\theta}{2}}$. See Fig. 8.5 for

each value of W i.e. 5 kg, 10 kg, 20 kg etc., we shall have different penetration and as such, we can get bearing pressures corresponding to different load. Averaging these bearing pressures, we can get bearing pressure for the ground. Boyd, has obtained the total thickness of the flexible pavement from this data as

$$h = \frac{72.45}{(\text{Bearing pressure})^{0.388}}$$

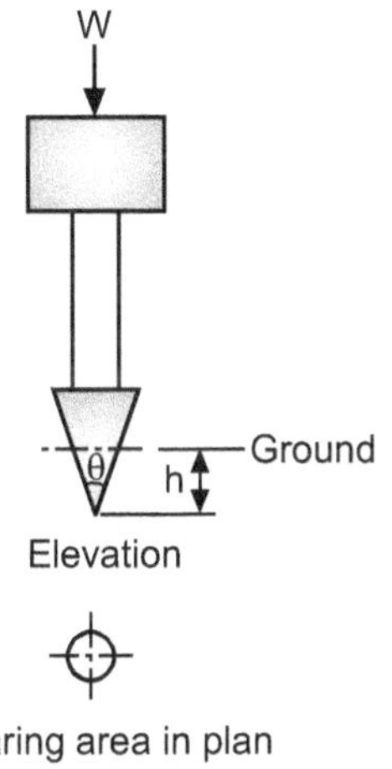

Fig. 8.5

The discussed equation was obtained on the basis of cone bearing value data for many highways in Dakota U.S.A. It is also stated by Dakota Highway officials that, for cone bearing pressure of 28 kg/cm² or more, the minimum total thickness of 24 cm should be provided. This section may consist of 12.50 cm sub-base, 5 cm of stabilised aggregate base and 6.5 cm of asphaltic concrete wearing course. When the cone bearing pressure is less than 28 kg/cm², additional sub-base is to be provided.

It is very clear that the method is useful for fine grained sub-grades, but when there are somewhat coarser particles in the sub-grade, one is likely to get eratic readings, and the method will fail in that case. The method is possibly very good for cement stabilized base coarse.

8.8.2 Methods Based on Plate Bearing Tests

The basis of these methods is to determine modulus of elasticity of sub-grade and from that, determine the pavement thickness. Originally this method was devised by U.S. Navy for air field pavements, but now is extensively used for highway pavements also. The method involves the following steps :

Step 1 :

A plate bearing test is conducted on the sub-grade. Preferably test should be conducted during the severest season. The circular plate is loaded in increments of 20 % of safe load for the final deflection of 6.25 mm. For a two layer system, modulus of elasticity of the sub-grade is given by

$$E_{sub} = \frac{1.18 \, p_1 \, a}{\Delta_1}$$

where, E_{sub} = Modulus of elasticity of sub-grade in kg/cm^2.

p_1 = Pressure on plate for Δ_1 deflection in cm in test on sub-grade.

a = Radius of plate.

Δ_1 = Deflection in cm.

Naturally, for each value of Δ and p, we can get E_{sub}, average value of observations may be taken for computation purposes. Now, base course of 15 to 30 cm thick is now constructed over the same area. The compacted density and moisture content of this constructed course should be the same as the base course to be constructed in the field. The base course constructed could be 4.5 m × 4.5 m or even upto 6 m × 6 m. At the centre of this course, the plate bearing test is now conducted as previously. Let p_2, Δ_2 be the pressure and deflection values in test 2. At this stage, we make use of Burmister analysis for two layer system.

8.8.3 Burmister Analysis for two Layer System

In the flexible pavement system, the system consists of layers of decreasing modulus of elasticity. Burmister considered an elastic slab of finite depth but of infinite horizontal extent placed on semi-infinite material of lower modulus of elasticity and the upper slab being loaded by a circular area. This more or less reflects the state of affairs in the flexible pavement. For a value of Poisson's ratio equal to 0.5 and for different ratios of modulus of elasticities of base and sub-grade, vertical stresses were computed by Burmister and shown in Fig. 8.6. The use of this figure is comparatively easy. Let us suppose that, plate that is loaded on the base is 0.5 meter radius and the intensity of loading is say 15 kg/cm^2. We require the state of stress at z = 1 meter. Then $\frac{z}{a} = \frac{1}{0.5} = 2$. Further, it is given that

$\dfrac{E_{\text{base course}}}{E_{\text{sub-grade}}}$ = 5, then vertical stress influence coefficient is 0.2 about and stress at this point is 15 × 0.2 = 3.0 kg/cm² about. Now suppose we want to know state of stress at z = 0.25 meter. Now $\dfrac{z}{a}$ = $\dfrac{0.25}{0.5}$ = 0.5.

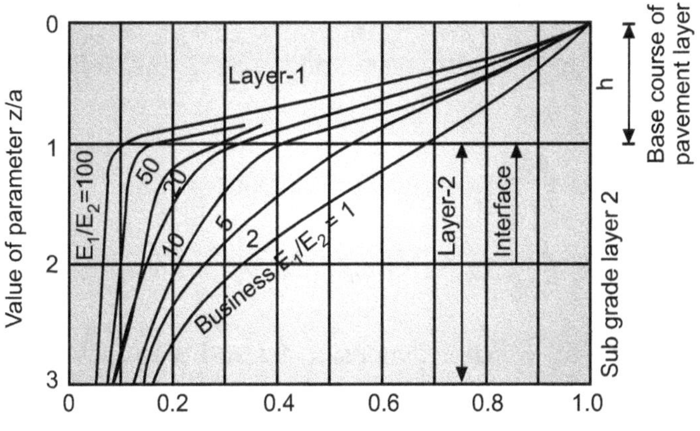

Fig. 8.6

For this value of $\dfrac{z}{a}$ = 0.5 $\dfrac{E_{\text{base}}}{E_{\text{sub}}}$ = 5, we have $\dfrac{6z}{p}$ = 0.9 and the stress at this point is

0.9 × 15 = 13.5 kg/cm² . When $\dfrac{E_{\text{base}}}{E_{\text{sub}}}$ = 1, it is Boussinesque stress distribution. Since, all the

curves for $\dfrac{E_{\text{base}}}{E_{\text{sub}}}$ lie to the left of the curve for $\dfrac{E_{\text{base}}}{E_{\text{sub}}}$ = 1, it shows that, when we provide

two layers, the stresses are reduced as compared to the case when we provide only one

layer i.e. $\dfrac{E_1}{E_2}$ = ± 1. When $\dfrac{z}{a}$ > 3, all the curves cluster towards each other showing that for

$\dfrac{z}{a}$ > 3, stresses in two layered medium and single layer medium are somewhat same. The

same graph also shows that the clustering of the curves is occurring after $\dfrac{z}{a}$ = 2.5. That is

there is no point in increasing the thickness of the layer 2 beyond $\dfrac{z}{a}$ = 2.5. Experiments in

the field have also indicated that the capacity of granular materials to carry load per cm of
its thickness decrease rapidly after reaching a maximum at a thickness approximately equal
to the diameter of loaded area. The source of error in the graph and in general in using the
Burmister theory for pavement thickness are :

- Elastic properties of the soil below a certain depth have very small effect on the stresses and displacements in the pavement and sub-grade. As far as stresses are concerned, the statement is O.K. but may not be alright as regards displacement.
- Burmister had assumed that Poisson's ratio will be 0.5 for all the layers while constructing the graph. This can cause error in the construction of the graph. On the assumption of rough interface between layer 1 and layer 2, irrespective of the ratio of $\dfrac{E_{base}}{E_{sub}}$ and the relative thickness of layer 1 and layer 2, the deflection of the two layer system was obtained as,

$$\Delta \;=\; 1.15\,\frac{pa}{E_{sub}}\;F_w \;-\; \text{for flexible plate}$$

$$\text{and}\qquad \Delta \;=\; 1.18\,\frac{pa}{E_{sub}}\;F_w \;-\; \text{for rigid plate}$$

F_w = displacement factor which is dimensionless and is a function of $\dfrac{E_1}{E_2}$ as well as the depth to radius ratio.

The curves of F_w against the thickness h in multiples of radius are shown in Fig. 8.7. Making use of this in Burmister analysis, we can now write

$$F_w \;=\; \frac{E_{sub}\,\Delta_2}{1.18\,p_2\,a}$$

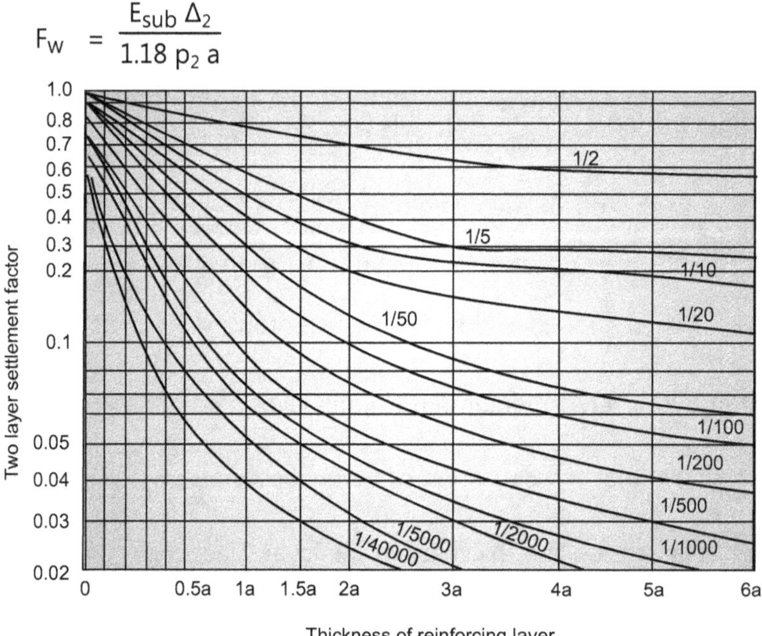

Fig. 8.7

In the case of flexible pavement design, we know h, the thickness of top bituminous layer a, the radius of bearing plate used for test, p_2 the bearing pressure for deflection Δ_2 and E_{sub} modulus of elasticity of sub-grade. The substitution of these factors in the above equation would yield F_w, the settlement factor. Now knowing the settlement factor F_w, h, a and using Fig. 8.7, we get the value $\dfrac{E_{base}}{E_{sub}}$, where E_{base} is modulus for the layer 1 that is the top layer or base course. We know the value E_{sub}, therefore we can get the value of modulus of elasticity for base course.

Let the wheel load be W and the tyre inflation pressure be pif, then approximate contact area will be $\dfrac{W}{pif}$. This is more or less on the assumption that supports furnished by side-walls of tyres is ignored. We may assume as U.S. Navy has done, that side wall support is ten percent and thus contact pressure may be assumed to be greater than tyre pressure by a factor equal to 1.1 and contact area is equal to wheel load divided by 1.1 × tyre pressure or $0.9 \times \dfrac{\text{wheel load}}{\text{tyre pressure}}$. We must remember here that, as far as plate bearing test is concerned, the plate can be considered as rigid but the wheel tyre can not be considered as rigid. In fact it is quite akin to a flexible plate. Therefore, we must make use of flexible plate equation to get settlement factor F_w. That is

$$\Delta_2 = \frac{1.5\, p_2\, a}{E_{base}}\, F_w$$

Here we assume Δ_2 = 0.5 cm and get the corresponding value of p_2 from the actual test conducted and $F_w = \dfrac{0.5 \times E_{base}}{1.5\, p_2\, a} = \dfrac{E_{base}}{3\, p_2\, a}$. Thus we now know the settlement factor for flexible plate and $\dfrac{E_{base}}{E_{sub}}$. For this couplet, we can get the thickness h as a multiple of 'a' from Fig. 8.7. Thus, we have obtained the initial tentative thickness of base course.

Steps 2 and 3:

This theoretical thickness is now to be verified. Let us suppose that the road is passing through fill section. Then on the actual alignment, we construct bases of varying thickness i.e. 0.5, 0.75, 1, 1.25, 1.5 times the theoretical thickness. Plate bearing test is conducted on each of this base. The plate has a radius corresponding to the effective contact area of radius 'a' and the load to be employed is a wheel load. Of course prior to the construction of the base course, the sub-grade should be in its weakest condition. All these tests should preferably be conducted in the severest season i.e. rainy season. If this is simply impossible, the sub-grade should be thoroughly saturated before constructing the base. Now in this plate load test, for a particular thickness of the base, we have the plate which has a radius corresponding to the effective contact radius and the load equal to wheel load. We thus, know the settlement for this combination. We plot this settlement against the thickness of the base. The thickness which produces the settlement of 5 mm is the required thickness.

In addition to base course, we have on it's top the bituminous surfacings. The added bituminous concrete surfacing is considered as additional and is not considered in arriving the thickness of the base. As a guide, the following table may be consulted for finding the thickness of bituminous concrete pavement. The table gives thickness depending upon wheel load.

Table 8.3 : Pavement Surface Thickness

Wheel Load (kg)	Thickness (cm)
6800 kg and soil cement or macadam base.	3.75
6800 kg or less other bases.	5.0
6800 to 11375 kg.	6.25
11375 to 22750 kg.	7.50
22750 kg and greater.	10.0

In general, the base course should have strength of 60 to 80 CBR for tyre pressure upto 10.5 kg/cm^2 or greater than 10.5 kg/cm^2.

8.8.4 Mcleod Method

Mcleod method is actually for the design of flexible pavement used in runways. This method was the result of extensive series of tests conducted on existing air fields in Canada. Surface, base and sub-grade of the runways were tested for plate load, CBR, triaxial compression etc. and the method evolved. This test data had indicated that, if the repetitive plate load test is carried on base/sub-grade the load at the surface is a direct function of sub-grade support for a fixed thickness of pavement. This relationship is shown in Fig. 8.8 and for a fixed deflection. This proposed deflection was 12.5 mm for runways and 9 mm for taxiways apron and turn around design. The analysis of the extensive data resulted in the following equation :

$$T_{base} = K \log_{10} \frac{P}{S}$$

where, T_{base} = Thickness of base.

P   = Applied wheel load in kg at 12.5 mm deflection for runways and wheel load corresponding to 9 mm deflection for taxiways aprons and turn around designs for same contact area pertaining to P.

s = Support of sub-grade in kg for respective deflection and same contact area.

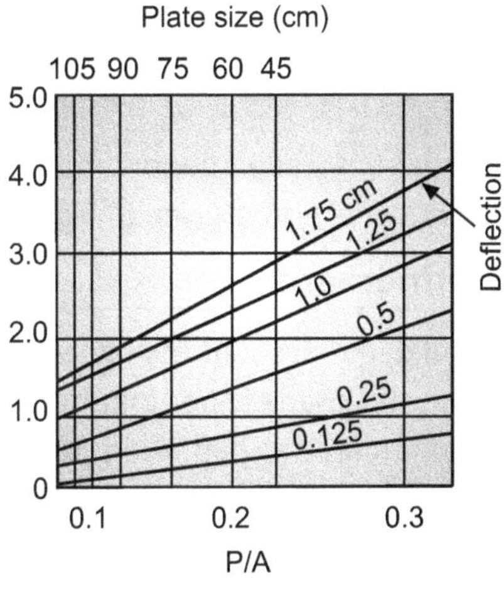

Fig. 8.8

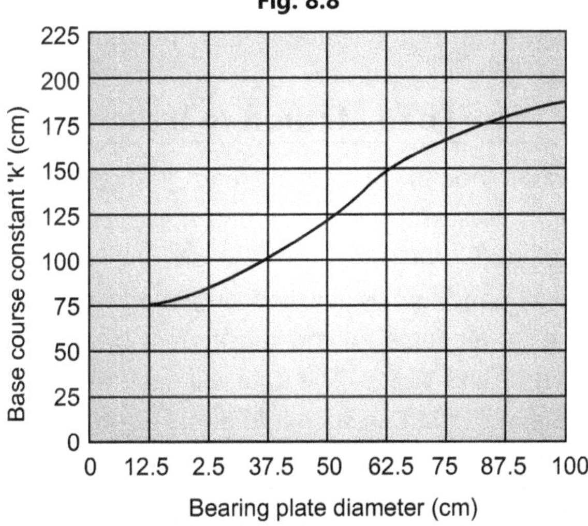

Fig. 8.9

The base course constant K varies with the diameter of the plate employed and this variation is shown in Fig. 8.9. Though first evolved for air port runways, the method can be profitably used for highways also. It should be remembered that the thickness obtained is for crushed stone base. If stronger base is to be used, the thickness of crushed stone base should be divided by suitable conversion factor. The suitable conversion factors are given in Table 8.4.

Table 8.4

Base Material	Conversion Factor
High quality asphalt concrete.	2.0
Asphaltic pavement.	1.5
Water Bound Macadam Base.	1.5
Crushed stone.	1.0

The empirical relationship between sub-grade support for 75 cm diameter plate at 5 mm deflection and support at any other deflection is given in Fig. 8.9.

8.8.5 Effect of Lateral Confinement

The method discussed does not take into account the lateral confinement of the sub-grade. In actual practice, the base and the sub-grade is not that free for lateral expansion, that is, it is somewhat laterally confined. Mehdiratta, had tried to evaluate the effect of lateral confinement on pavement analysis. His studies has indicated that, by introducing vertical diaphragms of rigid material like stone slabs along the pavement edge, it is possible that reduced thickness of pavement could be used, thus lowering down the construction cost. Though the method holds promise, the author is of the opinion that, large scale field trials are required to justify this conclusion.

8.8.6 Application of Plate Load Method to Indian Conditions

In Indian conditions, water bound macadam road is first constructed between two destinations. When traffic increases, this water bound macadam road is to be black topped to cater for the increased traffic. In such case, the existent water bound macadam road which may be in denuded condition is levelled and made up. Since, this water bound macadam road is now the base course for the subsequent bituminous layer, the plate load tests have to be conducted on this W.B.M. The data will generally indicate that, the thickness of W.B.M. is not upto the expectation. In such additional aggregate is added to this W.B.M. course, so as to make-up its thickness to the desired and computed level.

8.9 C.B.R METHOD OF DESIGN OF FLEXIBLE PAVEMENTS

Where information regarding vehicle damage factor and cumulative number of standard axles on annual basis is available, modified CBR method is to be used. Where such information is not available, simple CBR design curves given in Fig. 9.7 could be used. For this purpose, the traffic is first classified in the category of A, B, C, D, E as follows. However, where such information is available, Fig. 9.8 should be used for modified CBR method.

Table 8.5 : Classification of Traffic for Design

Traffic Commercial Vehicles per Day	CBR Design Curve Applicable
0 – 15	A
15 – 45	B
45 – 150	C
150 – 450	D
450 – 1500	E

The next step is to estimate the future traffic. For this purpose, the formula used is as follows,

$$F_t \;=\; P\,(1 + r)^{n + x}$$

where,

F_t = Number of commercial vehicles per day for design.

P = Number of commercial vehicles per day at last count.

r = Annual growth rate of commercial traffic.

n = Number of years between the last count and the year of completion of construction.

x = Design life in years.

As far as CBR method is concerned, for two lane traffic, the design will be based on the number of commercial vehicles per day in both directions, whereas single lane roads should be designed for twice the traffic in both the directions.

Where the traffic is increasing rapidly, it is possible that single lane may require upgrading to two lane standards within a short period and this should be borne in mind when determining pavement thickness.

Again just as in the case of modified CBR method, CBR method also gives total thickness of the pavement and some guide regarding minimum thickness of individual courses, such as sub-base, base etc. is required, so that the total thickness can be made-up. The guide that is recommended by I.R.C. is given below.

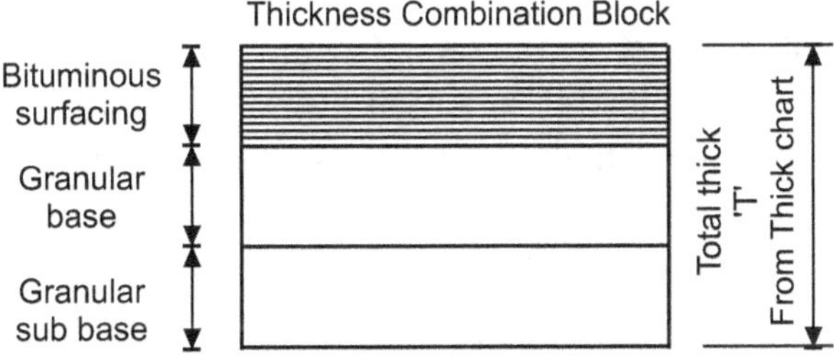

Fig. 8.10 : Structural section

Cumulated standard axles million (M)	Minimum thickness of component layers compacted thickness (mm)		
	Surfacing (X)	Base (Y)	Sub-base (Z)
0.5 M	20 mm PC/2-Coat SD	150	(T – 150) Minimum thickness 100 mm on sub-grades of CBR less than 20 %
0.5 – 2 M	20 mm PC/MS	225	(T – 225) Minimum thickness 150 mm on sub-grades of CBR less than 20 %
2 – 5 M	20 mm PC/MS/SDC + 50 mm/75 mm BM	250	(T – 300/325) Minimum thickness 150 mm on sub-grades of CBR less than 30 %
5 – 10 M	25 mm SDC/AC + 60 to 80 mm DBM	250	(T – 335 to 355) Minimum thickness 150 mm on sub-grades of CBR less than 30 %
10 – 15 M	40 mm AC + 65 to 80 mm DBM	250	(T – 355 to 370) Minimum thickness 150 mm on sub-grades of CBR less than 30 %
15 – 20 M	40 mm AC + 80 to 100 mm DBM	250	(T – 370 to 390) Minimum thickness 150 mm on sub-grades of CBR less than 30 %
20 – 30 M	40 mm AC + 100 to 115 mm DBM	250	(T – 390 to 405) Minimum thickness 150 mm on sub-grades of CBR less than 30 %

SD   – Surface dressing to the MOST specification/IRC standards.

PC   – Premix Carpet to the MOST specification/IRC standards.

MS   – Mix Seal Surfacing to the MOST specification.

SDC – Semi-dens Carpet to the MOST specification.

AC   – Asphaltic Concrete to the MOST specification.

BM   – Bituminous Macadam Binder Course to the MOST specification.

DBM – Dense Bituminous Macadam Binder Course.

Note : (i)   If the CBR of the sub-grade is more than the minimum requirement for the sub-base, no sub-base is required.

(ii)   Binder course of thickness more than 80 mm should be laid in two layers.

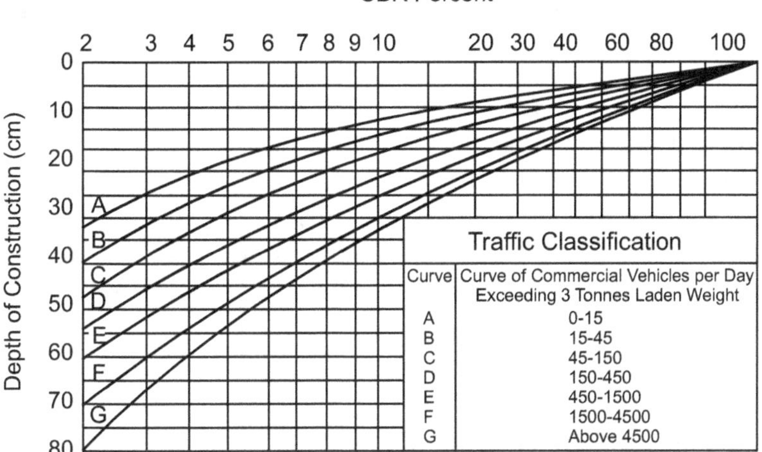

Fig. 8.11

8.10 PROPERTIES OF THE BASE, SUB-BASE AND SURFACINGS

The inherent drawback in CBR or modified CBR method is that, once the CBR of the sub-grade that is the vergin soil and traffic data that is number of commercial vehicles/day are known, the total thickness of the pavement is fixed. Some guidance is available regarding the individual thickness of base, sub-base etc., but essentially the total thickness of the pavement is unchanged. Having decided the total thickness and the individual thickness of base, sub-base etc., we shall now discuss the desirable properties, which these courses should possess. Some guidance is available regarding this from I.R.C.

8.11 THE IMPORTANCE OF MEASUREMENT OF CBR IN I.R.C. METHOD AND SELECTION OF DRY DENSITY AND MOISTURE CONTENT

It will be seen that in the modified California bearing ratio method, the CBR of the sub-grade is the main criterion on which total thickness of the pavement would depend. Therefore, the dry density and the moisture content of the sub-grade at which CBR is determined is very important.

Indian Roads Congress has recommended that the tests should be performed on the remoulded samples of soil in the laboratory preferably by static compaction and alternative by dynamic compaction. In-situ tests are not recommended for design purposes as it is felt that it is difficult to simulate critical conditions of dry density and moisture content in the field. The test conditions in the laboratory should reproduce as closely as possible the weakest conditions likely to occur under the road after construction.

8.12 COMPARISON BETWEEN C.B.R. AND MODIFIED C.B.R. METHOD

I.R.C. - 37 - 1984 has suggested the use of C.B.R. as well as Modified CBR method. The comparison between these methods is as follows :

- In the old standards of I.R.C., C.B.R. method that was suggested was closely on the lines of the method suggested by Road Research Laboratory U.K. and was applicable even upto 4500 commercial vehicles (less than 3 tons) per day. I.R.C. - 37 - 1984 has modified this, so that traffic intensity of 1500 vehicles can only be taken. This is it's drawback.
- C.B.R. method does not take into account the damaging effects of heavier wheel loads and their frequency, specially loads above 8160 kg single axle loads.
- As per the old standards of I.R.C., C.B.R. method was not considering multilanes or single and duel carriage-way. By introducing clause 3.2.4.2, C.B.R. method now introduced is capable of taking two lane traffic.
- In the old standards of I.R.C., an equivalency factor of upto 2 for bituminous constructions was permitted to equate the thickness of the bound base to that of water bound macadam. I.R.C. 78 - 1984 has recommended equivalent factor of 1.5 for bituminous macadam or lean cement concrete base and an equivalent factor 2 for dense bitumen macadam. I.R.C. 78 - 1984 further states that the equivalence factors are but a suggestion.
- In the old standards of I.R.C., the design curves gave the total thickness of pavement for different traffic intensities and C.B.R. value of sub-grade. The curves were not giving individual thickness base, sub-base etc.

IRC - 37 - 1984, by recommending minimum thickness of base, sub-base etc. has removed this lacuna to a certain extent.

8.13 MODIFIED C.B.R. METHOD

Modified C.B.R. method is certainly better than the C.B.R. method. It's upgradation over C.B.R. method is as follows :

- By considering the vehicle damage factor, and cumulative standard axles, the method is now capable of taking higher traffic intensities and higher loads.
- By suitably incorporating the factors, it is now possible to consider, two-lane, four lane carriage-ways.
- The equivalency factors are incorporated in modified C.B.R. method but slight flexibility is given in their use.
- The C.B.R. and the modified C.B.R. method both give essentially total thickness of pavement based on C.B.R. of the sub-grade and traffic. This lacuna stays.

Anomoly in IRC 37 - 1984 :

IRC 37 - 1984 "Guidelines for the design of flexible pavement" clause 3.2.3 Table 8.1 indicate values of vehicle damage factor. In this table, thick bituminous surfacing has higher vehicle damage factor than the thin bituminous surfacing. Thus, for the same initial traffic, annual growth rate and design life, application of equation in clause 3.2.3.1 in IRC 78 - 1984 will yield higher cumulative standard axles for thick bituminous surfacings and comparatively lower cumulative standard axles for thin bituminous surfacings. This therefore will yield more total pavement thickness for thick bituminous surfacings than that for thin bituminous surfacings for the same intensity of traffic (vehicles/day), which is certainly not correct. It therefore appears that vehicle damage factors for thin bituminous surfacings should be interchanged for the thick bituminous surfacings for the same intensity of traffic. Fortunately, since the number of cumulative axles plotted in Fig. 8.12 is in log scale and as such the change in total pavement thickness due to change in cumulative axles is somewhat less. Otherwise, this anomoly would have led to serious shortcomings.

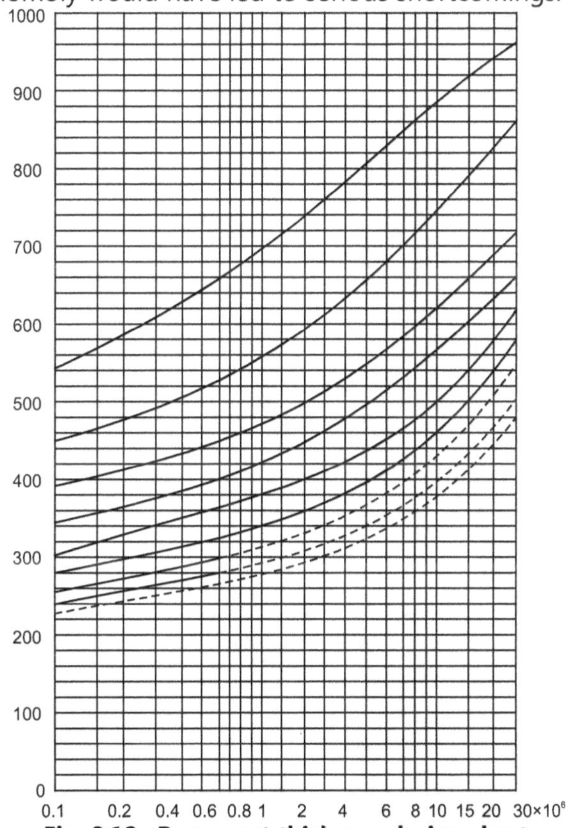

Fig. 8.12 : Pavement thickness design chart

Note : 1.   Read total pavement thickness from continuous curves

2.   Use dotted curves for proportioning sub-base thickness

8.14 IRC METHOD OF DESIGN OF FLEXIBLE PAVEMENTS

8.14.1 Overview

Indian roads congress has specified the design procedures for flexible pavements based on CBR values. The Pavement designs given in the previous edition IRC : 37-1984 were applicable to design traffic up to only 30 million standard axles (msa). The earlier code is empirical in nature which has limitations regarding applicability and extrapolation. This guideline follows analytical designs and developed new set of designs up to 150 msa.

Scope : These guidelines will apply to design of flexible pavements for Expressway, National Highways, State Highways, Major District Roads and other categories of roads. Flexible pavements are considered to include the pavements which have bituminous surfacing and granular base and sub-base courses conforming to IRC/ MOST standards. These guidelines apply to new pavements.

Design Criteria : The flexible pavements has been modeled as a three layer structure and stresses and strains at critical locations have been computed using the linear elastic model. To give proper consideration to the aspects of performance, the following three types of pavement distress resulting from repeated (cyclic) application of traffic loads are considered :

- Vertical compressive strain at the top of the sub-grade which can cause sub-grade deformation resulting in permanent deformation at the pavement surface.

- Horizontal tensile strain or stress at the bottom of the bituminous layer which can cause fracture of the bituminous layer.

- Pavement deformation within the bituminous layer. While the permanent deformation within the bituminous layer can be controlled by meeting the mix design requirements, thickness of granular and bituminous layers are selected using the analytical design approach so that strains at the critical points are within the allowable limits. For calculating tensile strains at the bottom of the bituminous layer, the stiffness of Dense Bituminous Macadam (DBM) layer with 60/70 bitumen has been used in the analysis.

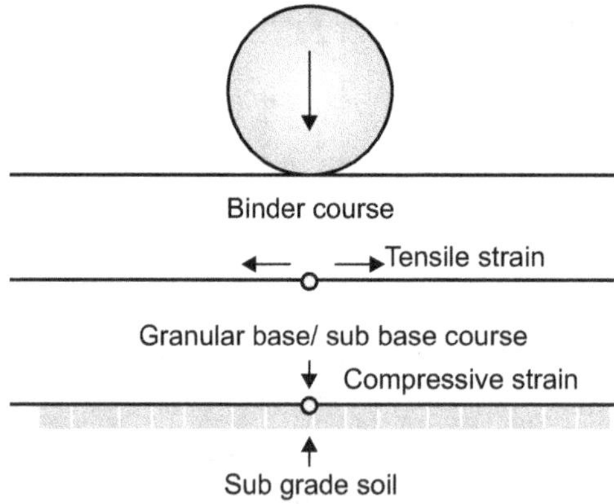

Fig. 8.13 : Critical locations in pavement

A and B are the critical locations for tensile strains (ε_t). Maximum value of the strain is adopted for design. C is the critical location for the vertical subgrade strain (ε_z) since the maximum value of the (ε_z) occurs mostly at C.

Fatigue Criteria : Bituminous surfacing of pavements display flexural fatigue cracking if the tensile strain at the bottom of the bituminous layer is beyond certain limit. The relation between the fatigue life of the pavement and the tensile strain in the bottom of the bituminous layer was obtained as :

$$N_1 \;=\; 2.21 \times 10^{-4} \times \left(\frac{1}{\varepsilon_t}\right)^{3.89} \times \left(\frac{1}{E}\right)^{0.854} \qquad \text{...(8.1)}$$

In which N_1 is the allowable number of load repetitions to control fatigue cracking and E is the Elastic Modulus of bituminous layer. The use of equation 28.1 would resulting fatigue cracking of 20% of the total area.

Rutting Criteria : The allowable number of load repetitions to control permanent deformation can be expressed as :

$$N_1 \;=\; 4.1656 \times 10^{-8} \times \left(\frac{1}{\varepsilon_z}\right)^{4.5337} \qquad \text{...(8.2)}$$

N_r is the number of cumulative standard axles to produce rutting of 20 mm.

Design Procedure : Based on the performance of existing designs and using analytical approach, simple design charts and a catalogue of pavement designs are added in the code. The pavement designs are given for subgrade CBR values ranging from 2 % to 10 % and design traffic ranging from 1 msa to 150 msa for an average annual pavement temperature of 35 C. The later thicknesses obtained from the analysis have been slightly modified to adapt the designs to stage construction. Using the following simple input arameters, appropriate designs could be chosen for the given traffic and soil strength :

- Design traffic in terms of cumulative number of standard axles; and
- CBR value of sub grade.

Design Traffic : The method considers traffic in terms of the cumulative number of standard axles (8160 kg) to be carried by the pavement during the design life. This requires the following information :

- Initial traffic in terms of CVPD.

- Traffic growth rate during the design life.

- Design life in number of years.

- Vehicle damage factor (VDF).

- Distribution of commercial traffic over the carriage way.

Initial Traffic : Initial traffic is determined in terms of commercial vehicles per day (CVPD). For the structural design of the pavement only commercial vehicles are considered assuming laden weight of three tonnes or more and their axle loading will be considered. Estimate of the initial daily average traffic flow for any road should normally be based on 7-day 24-hour classified traffic counts (ADT). In case of new roads, traffic estimates can be made on the basis of potential land use and traffic on existing routes in the area.

Traffic growth rate Traffic growth rates can be estimated (i) by studying the past trends of traffic growth and (ii) by establishing econometric models. If adequate data is not available, it is recommended that an average annual growth rate of 7.5 percent may be adopted.

Design Life : For the purpose of the pavement design, the design life is defined in terms of the cumulative number of standard axles that can be carried before strengthening of the pavement is necessary. It is recommended that pavements for arterial roads like NH, SH should be designed for a life of 15 years, EH and urban roads for 20 years and other categories of roads for 10 to 15 years.

Vehicle Damage Factor : The vehicle damage factor (VDF) is a multiplier for converting the number of commercial vehicles of different axle loads and axle configurations to the number of standard axle-load repetitions. It is defined as equivalent number of standard axles per commercial vehicle. The VDF varies with the axle configuration, axle loading, terrain, type of road, and from region to region. The axle load equivalency factors are used to convert different axle load repetitions into equivalent standard axle load repetitions. For these equivalency factors refer IRC : 37 2001. The exact VDF values are arrived after extensive field surveys.

Vehicle Distribution : A realistic assessment of distribution of commercial traffic by direction and by lane is necessary as it directly affects the total equivalent standard axle load application used in the design. Until reliable data is available, the following distribution may be assumed. Single lane roads : Traffic tends to be more channelized on single roads than two lane roads and to allow for this concentration of wheel load repetitions, the design should be based on total number of commercial vehicles in both directions.

Two-lane single carriageway roads : The design should be based on 75 % of the commercial vehicles in both directions.
Four-lane single carriageway roads : The design should be based on 40 % of the total number of commercial vehicles in both directions.
Dual carriageway roads : For the design of dual two-lane carriageway roads should be based on 75 % of the number of commercial vehicles in each direction. For dual three-lane carriageway and dual four-lane carriageway the distribution factor will be 60 % and 45 % respectively.

Pavement Thickness Design Charts : For the design of pavements to carry traffic in the range of 1 to 10 msa, use chart 1 and for traffic in the range 10 to 150 msa, use chart 2 of IRC : 37 2001. The design curves relate pavement thickness to the cumulative number of standard axles to be carried over the design life for different sub-grade CBR values ranging from 2 % to 10 %. The design charts will give the total thickness of the pavement for the above inputs. The total thickness consists of granular sub-base, granular base and bituminous surfacing. The individual layers are designed based on the recommendations given below and the subsequent tables.

8.14.2 Pavement Composition

Sub-Base : Sub-base materials comprise natural sand, gravel, laterite, brick metal, crushed stone or combinations thereof meeting the prescribed grading and physical requirements. The sub-base material should have a minimum CBR of 20 % and 30 % for traffic upto 2 msa and traffic exceeding 2 msa respectively. Sub-base usually consist of granular or WBM and the thickness should not be less than 150 mm for design traffic less than 10 msa and 200 mm for design traffic of 1:0 msa and above.

Base : The recommended designs are for unbounded granular bases which comprise conventional Water Bound Macadam (WBM) or Wet Mix Macadam (WMM) or equivalent confirming to MOST specifications. The materials should be of good quality with minimum thickness of 225 mm for traffic up to 2 msa an 150 mm for traffic exceeding 2 msa.

Bituminous Surfacing : The surfacing consists of a wearing course or a binder course plus wearing course. The most commonly used wearing courses are surface dressing, open graded premix carpet, mix seal surfacing, semi-dense bituminous concrete and bituminous concrete. For binder course, MOST specifies, it is desirable to use Bituminous Macadam (BM) for traffic upto o 5 msa and Dense Bituminous Macadam (DBM) for traffic more than 5 msa.

SOLVED PROBLEMS

Problem 8.1 : *Design the pavement for construction of a new bypass with the following data :*
1. *Two lane carriage way.*
2. *Initial traffic in the year of completion of construction = 400 CVPD (sum of both directions).*
3. *Traffic growth rate = 7.5%.*
4. *Design life = 15 years.*
5. *Vehicle damage factor based on axle load survey = 2.5 standard axle per commercial vehicle.*
6. *Design CBR of subgrade soil = 4%.*

Solution : (1) Distribution factor = 0.75.

$$(2)\ N = \frac{365 \times [(1 + (0.075)^{15} - 1)]}{0.075} \times 400 \times 0.75 \times 2.5$$

(3) Total pavement thickness for CBR 4% and traffic 7.2 msa from IRC : 37 2001 chart 1 = 660 mm.

(4) Pavement composition can be obtained by interpolation from Pavement Design Catalogue (IRC : 37 2001).

(a) Bituminous surfacing = 25 mm SDBC + 70 mm DBM.

(b) Road-base = 250 mm WBM.

(c) Sub-base = 315 mm granular material of CBR not less than 30%.

Problem 8.2 : *Design the pavement for construction of a new two lane carriageway for design life 15 years using IRC method. The initial traffic in the year of completion in each direction is 150 CVPD and growth rate is 5%. Vehicle damage factor based on axle load survey = 2.5 std axle per commercial vehicle. Design CBR of subgrade soil = 4%.*

Solution :

(1) Distribution factor = 0.75

(2) $N = \dfrac{365 \times [(1 + (0.05)^{15} - 1)]}{0.05} \times 300 \times 0.75 \times 2.5$

$= 4430348.837$

$= 4.4.$ msa

(3) Total pavement thickness for CBr 4 % and traffic 4.4. msa from IRC : 372001 chart 1 = 580mm

(4) Pavement composition can be obtained by interpolation from pavement Design Catalogue (IRC : 37 2001).

(a) Bituminous surfacing = 20mm PC + 50mm BM

(b) road-base = 250mm Granular base

(c) sub-base = 280mm granular material.

8.15 INTRODUCTION TO RIGID PAVEMENTS

Pavements could be classified as rigid or flexible. Bituminous pavements, Water Bound Macadam roads, stabilized bases etc. could be classed as flexible pavement whereas concrete pavements are rigid pavements.

8.15.1 Action of Rigid and Flexible Pavement

The flexible pavement layer transmits the stresses to the lower layer by grain to grain transfer. The vertical stress is maximum on the pavement surface and is equal to contact pressure. The stresses get decreased at lower layers in the shape of truncated cone. Therefore, the lower layer in the pavement structure could be of less strength and the topmost layer will have the highest strength. The top layer has also to cater for wearing action of wheel load. In general the strength and rigidity of flexible pavement is much less than that of the rigid pavement. Due to this the flexible pavement layers mirror the deformation of the lower layers on the surface of top layer, hence the name flexible. Since the layers are arranged one over the other in increasing strength order, stress distribution pattern is constrained. On the other hand rigid pavement possesses considerable flexural strength and rigidity. Most of the times, it is a concrete slab laid on sub-grade. Therefore stresses are not transferred from grain to grain to the lower layer. In fact due to slab action large amount sub-grade area takes-up stresses, therefore, it is the stresses generated in the concrete slab due to placement of wheel - load and temperature stresses generated that are the guiding factor. Due to it's rigidity, the rigid pavement does not get deformed to the shape of the lower surface as it can very easily bridge the minor variations of the lower layer. Cement concrete pavement surface is a good wearing surface, many a times it can be laid directly on the compacted sub-grade.

8.15.2 Methods of Pavement Design

Following methods of pavement design will be considered :
(a) Westergaard method,
(b) Goldbeck or Older's method,
(c) Spangler's Equation,
(d) Pickett's Equation,
(e) I.R.C. method.

(a) Westergaard Method : Westergaard in 1920 developed an equation for an elastic plate resting on subgrade. He assumed that :
- Cement concrete slab is homogeneous, isotropic elastic thin plane resting on the sub-grade below.
- Pavement slab is infinite in extent and the subgrade can be considered as if it is a dense liquid.
- The reaction of the subgrade is in vertical direction only and is proportional to the settlement of the slab, the coefficient of proportionality between them being the modulus of subgrade reaction.
- The slab has uniform thickness.
- In order to express deformation characteristics of the pavement, he coined the term, the radius of relative stiffness (l) which is,

$$l = \sqrt[4]{\frac{Eh^3}{12\,(1-\mu^2)\,k}}$$

where E, μ and h are respectively modulus of elasticity, Poisson's ratio and thickness of slab and k is modulus of subgrade reaction. He further defined equivalent radius of resisting section as b = a for $\frac{a}{h} \geq 1.724$ and b $= \sqrt{1.6\,a^2 + h^2} - 0.675$ for $\frac{a}{h} \leq 1.724$.

With these assumptions, he used theory of thin plates resting on elastic foundation along with Ritz method of successive approximation and the principle of maximum energy to determine tensile stresses at the edge corner and interior loading.

$$\text{Edge loading, tensile stress} = \frac{0.52\,P}{h^2}\left[4\log_{10}\left(\frac{l}{b}+0.359\right)\right]$$

$$\text{Corner loading, tensile stress} = \frac{3P}{h^2}\left[1-\left(\frac{a\sqrt{2}}{l}\right)^{0.6}\right]$$

$$\text{Interior loading, tensile stress} = \frac{0.3162\,P}{h^2}\left[4\log_{10}\frac{l}{b}+1.069\right]$$

where, P is the wheel load and a radius of wheel load distribution. Corner loading is generally very severe. It develops negative bonding moment at the top of slab causing maximum tensile stress at the top surface parallel to the bisector of the corner angle. The maximum stress does not occur at the load point, but at a distance d along the corner bisector given by the relation d $= 2.38\sqrt{al}$ where the terms a, and l are already described.

After computing stresses as per Westergaard, the thickness of pavement should be such that the stresses are within limit. The ideas propunded by Westergaard have been extensively used in I.R.C. method.

(b) Kelly Method : Teller and Southerland had carried out, what is now known as Arlington tests (1939). Kelly developed following equation based on these tests. The equation is valid for corner loading. Corner loading, tensile stress ,

$$= \frac{3P}{h^2}\left[1-\left(\frac{a\sqrt{2}}{l}\right)^{1.2}\right]$$

Kelly equation is incorporated in I.R.C. method. Kelly's equation for corner loading was simplified by Spangler (1942) and which is given below. Corner loading tensile stress

$$= \frac{3.2P}{h^2}\left(1-\frac{a\sqrt{2}}{l}\right)$$

(c) Pickett Equation : Pickett (1951) proposed semi-empirical formulae both for protected and unprotected corners. These equations are

Unprotected corner, tensile stress

$$= \frac{4.2P}{h^2}\left[1-\frac{\sqrt{a/l}}{0.925+0.22\,\frac{a}{l}}\right]$$

For the protected corner,

$$\text{tensile stress} = \frac{3.36P}{h^2}\left(1-\frac{\sqrt{a/l}}{0.925+0.22\frac{a}{l}}\right)$$

(d) Goldbeck or Older's Method : When the circular loaded area occupies the corner of the pavement, pavement acts as a cantilever. By assuming that the bending moment acts on a plane diagonally across the corner and that it is distributed uniformly over the cross-section, Goldbeck obtained stress due to corner load as

$$\text{Corner load, tensile stress} \;=\; \frac{3P}{h^2}$$

8.15.3 Design of Rigid Pavements as per IRC

Design of rigid pavement based on the guidelines provided by IRC : 58 – 1988 proceeds on the basis of following lines.

Design Wheel Load : Axle loads of commercial vehicles have increased considerably. There is revision of legal limit on the maximum laden axle loads of commercial vehicles from 8160 kg to 10200 kg so that the maximum wheel load now is 5100 kg. For most of the commercial highway vehicles, the tyre inflation pressure could be taken from 5.3 to 7.3 kg/cm^2. Generally, the later value is taken so that maximum pressure is transmitted to the pavement.

Traffic Intensity : Repetitive loading caused due to traffic is a major devastating force for the highways. These effects may not be of much consequence in case of low traffic intensities because of considerable time lag between successive passes but has significant importance in the case of heavily trafficked pavements as the fatigue strength of concrete reduces with increase in the number of load repetitions. It is very clear that the maximum intensity of traffic will occur at the end of the design life of the road. It is considered adequate by I.R.C. to consider 20 years traffic for the rigid pavement. This traffic projection for main highways may be based on the following equation suggested by I.R.C.

$$T \;=\; P\,(1 + r)^{n\,+\,20}$$

where, T =   Design traffic intensity in terms of number of commercial vehicles

        (laden weight $\geq$ 3 tonnes) per day,

   P   = Traffic intensity at last traffic count,

   r   = Annual rate of increase of traffic intensity, and

   n   = Number of years since the last traffic count and commissioning the new concrete pavement.

The traffic intensity P should be based on seven days average based on 24 hours count, in exceptional cases three days count may be used. When data is not available, the value of r may be taken as 7.5 for rural roads and 10 for urban roads. Based on traffic intensity, the rigid pavement may be classed in the following categories for the purpose of design.

Table 8.6 : Traffic Classification for Rigid Pavement Design

Traffic Classification	Design Traffic Intensity Cehicles (Laden Weight > 3 Tonnes) Per Day at the End of Design Life
A	0 – 15
b	15 – 45
c	45 – 150
d	150 – 450
e	450 – 1500
f	1500 – 4500
g	> 4500 and all express ways

Environmental Parameters : The difference in temperature between the top and bottom surfaces of the concrete slab largely determines the thickness of the slab. Similarly, mean temperature cycles daily and annually of concrete pavement affect the maximum spacing of contraction and expansion joint in the pavement and for maximum safe spacing of expansion joint, this data is required. As far as the temperature differential between the top and bottom of slab is concerned, the following table prepared by Central Road Research Institute and incorporated in IRC 5.8 – 1988 may be used.

Table 8.7 : Temperature Differentials in Concrete Roads

Zone	States	10	15	20	25	30
I	Punjab, U.P., Rajastan, Gujrat, Haryana, North M.P., excluding Hilly regions and coastal area	10.2	12.5	20	25	30
II	Bihar, West Bengal, Assam, Eastern Orissa	14.4	15.6	16.4	16.6	16.8
III	Maharashtra, Karnataka, South M.P., Andhra Pradesh, Western Orissa, North Madras	14.75	17.3	19.0	20.3	21.0
IV	Kerala and South Madras	13.2	15.0	16.4	17.6	18.1
V	Coastal regions bounded by hills	12.8	14.6	15.8	16.2	17.0
VI	Coastal areas unbounded by hills	13.6	15.5	17.0	19.0	19.2
	For hilly regions, actual observations should be conducted					

As far as the second point regarding mean temperature cycle is concerned, extensive data is not available, and as such somewhat conservative recommendations have been made by I.R.C.

8.15.4 Foundation Strength and Surface Characters

Modulus of subgrade reaction is the best way of expressing foundation strength. Limiting design deflection for concrete pavement is 1.25 mm and as such modulus of subgrade reaction value (K value) should be at this deflection. Test should be run on 75 cm diameter plate and one test per km per lane as a minimum is recommended. Sometimes 30 cm plate is used for plate test and in this case the following equation could be used

$$K_{75} = 0.5\, K_{30}$$

where, K_{75} and K_{30} are the K values obtained on 75 cm and 30 cm diameter plate. When the subgrade is uniform, the equation is all right. For layered construction, the above equation over-estimates the subgrade strength and should be used with caution. The plate test should be conducted on the subgrade, when it is placed in the most unfavourable climatic condition. A test just after the monsoon is the best. When plate test is not carried, approximate K value can be calculated based on CBR value by making use of the following table.

Table 8.8 : Approximate K Value Corresponding to CBR Value for Homogeneous Sub-grades

CBR Value % Soaked 4 Days	2	3	4	5	7	10	20	50	100
K value, kg/cm^3	2.08	2.77	3.46	4.16	4.84	5.54	6.92	13.85	22.16

If the K value of the subgrade is less than 5.5 kg/cm^3, the subgrade should preferably be stabilized to attain higher value. For rocky sub-grades with K value more than 5.5 kg/cm^3, the pavement can directly be laid on the subgrade after providing levelling course. These provisions do not apply to the clayey and expansive sub-grades which are dealt with separately.

Foundation Surface Characters : Smoothness or roughness of the foundation affects concrete slab movement and therefore joint spacing. The maximum safe spacing of joints increases with increase in surface roughness of the foundation in the case of expansion joints and decreases in the case of contraction joint. The following table classifies the foundation.

Table 8.9 : Types of Rigid Pavement Foundations According to their Surface Characters

Type of Foundation	Surface Characters
Compacted sand and gravel. Smooth foundation covered with water-proof paper	Very smooth
Compacted sand, gravel and clinker, stabilized soil, Rough foundation covered with water-proof paper	Smooth
Water bound macadam, soil gravel mix, Rolled lean concrete, lime pozzolona concrete etc.	Rough

The foundations adopted in our country are generally rough or smooth and these are considered by I.R.C.

Concrete Characteristics : Stresses induced in the concrete pavement i.e. rigid pavement are either due to bending or it's prevention and flexural strength of concrete is the governing criterion. This strength should not be less than 40 kg/cm² (40000 kN/m). This strength can be obtained from the concrete mix design strength by the following equation. Thus, if

$\bar{S}$ = Structural design value for concrete strength to be considered for the design of concrete pavement.

S = Mix design value of concrete strength.

t = Tolerence factor for the desired confidence level.

σ = Expected standard deviation of field test samples based on the knowledge of the type of the control. viz very good, good or fair then

$$\therefore \qquad S = \bar{S} + t \cdot \sigma$$

That is the mix design strength should be slightly higher than the minimum flexural strength available in the field. To use the above equation, the values of t and σ for concrete compressive strength value of 280 kg/cm² (Table 8.10) are given in table below.

Table 8.10 : Quality Control and Values of t, σ to be Achieved

Quality Control	t	σ 1 kg/cm² = 100 kN/m²	Mix Design Strength, kg/cm² 1 kg cm² = 100 kN/m²
Very good	1.50	22 kg/cm²	315 kg/cm²
Good	1.50	33 kg/cm²	330 kg/cm²
Fair	1.50	52 kg/cm²	350 kg/cm²

8.15.5 The Quality Control

Very good, good, fair is described as follows :

Very good : Rigid and constant supervision of quality control team. Weigh batching use of graded aggregate with moisture determination of aggregates.

Good : Constant supervision of quality control team. Weigh batching. Use of graded aggregates with its moisture determination.

Fair : Control with volume batching for aggregates with occasional checking of quality control team for aggregate moisture and other things. The values given in the above table may vary plus or minus 7 %, 10 % and 15 % depending upon the quality control viz. very good, good or fair.

8.15.6 Modulus of Elasticity and Poisson's Ratio

The elastic modulus E of the concrete increases with increase in it's strength whereas the Poisson's ratio decreases with increase in value of E_o. Though experiments are best to ascertain these values for a concrete of flexural strength between 38 to 42 kg/cm^2, the value of E may be assumed to be 3×10^5 kg/cm^2 and the value µ to be 0.15.

8.15.7 Coefficient of Thermal Expansion

The coefficient of thermal expansion α of the concrete of the same mix proportion varies with the type of aggregate being high for siliceous aggregates, medium for igneous rocks and low for calcareous ones. For design purposes, a value of $\alpha = 10 \times 10^{-6}/{}^\circ C$ may be adopted.

8.16 DESIGN OF RIGID PAVEMENTS

Design of rigid pavement i.e. concrete pavement as per I.R.C. is split up in certain stages. These stages may be :

- Determination of slab thickness and spacing and layout of joints,
- Design of reinforcement at joints,
- Design of longitudinal reinforcement. These steps are now discussed.

Design of Rigid Pavement : The factors commonly considered for the design of pavement thickness are traffic loads and temperature variations as the two additives. The effects of moisture changes and shrinkage being generally opposed to temperature. These are of small magnitudes and would ordinarily relieve the temperature effects to some extent and as such are not normally considered relevant for the thickness design of pavement. We shall therefore consider the temperature and load effects only.

8.16.1 Temperature Effects

The top of the concrete slab is hotter than the bottom during the day and cooler during the night. The slab therefore warps upwards (top convex) during the day and downwards (top concave) during the night. The self weight of the slab tries to restraint this warping tendency, thus inducing stresses called temperature stress. These stresses are therefore flexural in nature being tensile at the bottom during the day at top and tensile at top during the night. Since resistance offered to warping at any section of the slab is a function of the weight of the slab upto that section, corners have very little resistance. The resistance or restraint is maximum in the slab interior and somewhat less at the edge. Therefore the temperature stresses induced in the pavement are negligible in the corner range and maximum at the interior.

8.16.2 Traffic Load Effects

Corner of the pavement slab is discontinuous in two directions, and maximum stress is caused here. The edge is discontinuous in one direction and as such has lower stress whereas traffic load causes least stress in the interior where the slab is continuous in all the directions. Furthermore, the corner of the slab tends to bend like a cantilever, thus inducing tension at top, interior, like a beam inducing tension at bottom. As far as edge is considered, main bending is along the edge, like a beam giving maximum tension at bottom.

8.16.3 The Combined Effect of Temperature and Load

The maximum combined tensile stresses in the three regions of the slab will thus be caused when the effects of temperature and loads are additive. This would occur during the day in the case of interior and edge region at the time of maximum temperature difference in the slab. In the corner region, the temperature stresses are negligible but the load stress is maximum at night when the corners of the slab exhibit tendency to lift updue to warping and loose partly the foundation support. Considering the total combined stress for the three regions viz corner edge and interior, it is therefore felt by IRC that both the corner and edge regions should be checked for total stresses and design of slab thickness based on the more critical conditions of the two. We therefore now set to calculate stresses in the regions as a prelude to design of pavement.

8.16.4 Calculation of Stresses

Edge Stresses : The edge stresses will be caused due to load and due to temperature. We shall consider these one by one.

Edge Stresses Due to Load : The load stress in the critical edge region may be obtained per Westergaard analysis and further modified by Teller and Sutherland. The following formula is suggested by I.R.C.

$$\sigma l e = 0.529 \frac{P}{h^2} (1 + 0.54\,\mu) \left(4 \log_{10} \frac{l}{b} + \log_{10} b - 0.4048 \right)$$

where, $\sigma l e$ = load stress in the edge regions in kg/cm^2
P = design wheel load in kg
h = pavement slab thickness in cm
μ = Poisson's ratio for the concrete
E = modulus of elasticity for concrete, kg/cm^2
K = reaction modulus of the pavement foundation, kg/cm^3

l = radius of relative stiffness = $\sqrt[4]{\dfrac{Eh^3}{12\,(1 - \mu^2)\,K}}$

b = radius of equivalent distribution of pressure area

= a for $\dfrac{a}{h} \geq 1.724$

= $\sqrt{1.6\,a^2 + h^2} - 0.675\,h$ for $\dfrac{a}{h} \leq 1.724$

a = radius of contact area, contact area to be assumed circular

For ready reference, following tables may be consulted to ascertain the values of l and b directly. It should be noted that the formula suggested by IRC is in metric units and not in S.I. units.

Table 8.11 : The Values of Radius of Relative Stiffness for Different Values of Pavement Thickness and Foundation Reaction Modulus K, E for Concrete $= 30 \times 10^5$ kg/cm²

h in	Radius of relative stiffness (cm) for different values of (kg/cm³)				
cm	K = 6	K = 8	K = 10	K = 15	K = 30
15	61.44	57.18	54.08	48.86	41.09
16	64.49	60.02	56.76	51.29	43.31
17	67.49	62.81	59.40	53.67	45.14
18	70.44	65.56	62.01	56.03	47.07
19	73.36	68.28	64.57	58.35	49.06
20	76.24	70.95	67.10	60.63	50.99
21	79.08	73.59	69.60	63.89	52.89
22	81.89	76.20	72.08	65.13	54.77
23	84.66	78.80	74.52	67.33	56.62
24	87.41	81.35	76.94	69.31	58.45
25	90.13	83.88	79.32	71.68	60.28

Table 8.12 : Radius of Equivalent Distribution of Pressure Section b, in Terms of Radius of Contact a and Slab Thickness 'h' i.e. Table of $\dfrac{a}{h}$ Against $\dfrac{b}{h}$

a/h	b/h	a/h	b/h
0.0	0.325	1.0	0.937
0.1	0.333	1.1	1.039
0.2	0.357	1.2	1.143
0.3	0.387	1.3	1.250
0.4	0.446	1.4	1.358
0.5	0.508	1.5	1.470
0.6	0.580	1.6	1.582
0.7	0.661	1.7	1.695
0.8	0.747	1.724	1.724
0.9	0.840	> 1.1724	a/h

Edge Stresses Due to Temperature : Bradbury's coefficient along with Westergaard analysis may be employed in this case. The formula recommended by I.R.C. is

$$\sigma te = \frac{E\,\alpha\,\Delta t}{2} \cdot C,$$

where,

    σte = Temperature stress in the edge region.

    Δt = Maximum temperature differential during day between top and bottom of the slab.

    C = Bradbury's coefficient. This can be had from the charts, knowing the values of L/l and W/l.

    L = Slab length, or spacing between consecutive contraction joints.

    W = Slab width and

    l = Radius of relative stiffness,

The Bradbury's coefficient may be obtained from table.

Table 8.13 : Values of Coefficient C based on Bradbury's Chart

L/l or W/l	C
1.	0.000
2.	0.040
3.	0.175
4.	0.440
5.	0.720
6.	0.920
7.	1.030
8.	1.075
9.	1.080
10.	1.075
11.	1.050
12 and above	1.000

The intermediate values of C for the values of $\frac{L}{l}$ or $\frac{W}{l}$ may be incorporated and α is coefficient of thermal expansion for the concrete.

Design Charts : Figs. 8.14 and 8.15 give ready to use design charts for calculation of load stresses in the edge corner regions of rigid pavement slabs for the design wheel load of 5100 kg.

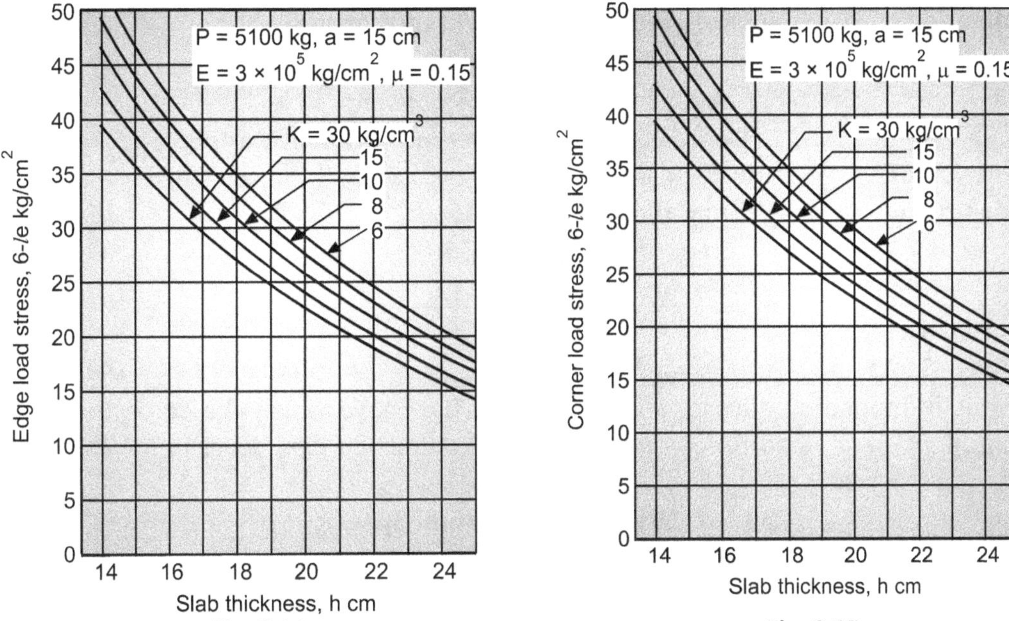

Fig. 8.14   **Fig. 8.15**

Fig. 8.16 gives a design chart for calculation of temperature stresses in the edge region. Having known the stresses at the different regions of the slab, we now set to design rigid pavement.

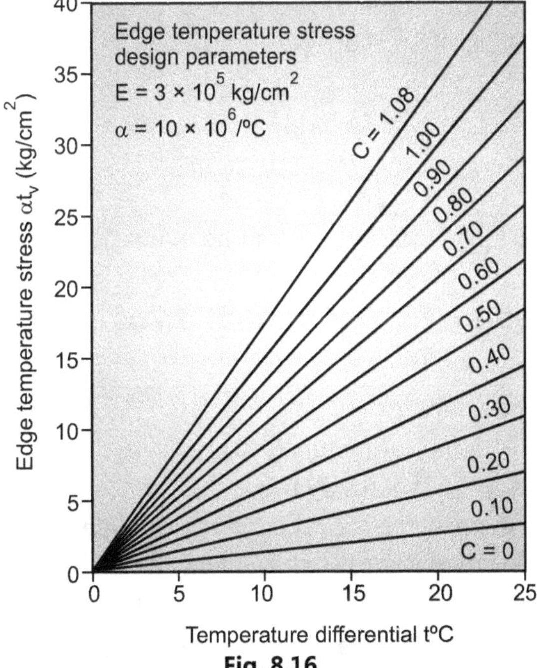

Fig. 8.16

Determination of Slab Thickness and Spacing and Layout of Joints :

The table below recommended may be followed for spacing of joints.

Table 8.14 : Expansion Joint Spacing

Period of Construction	Degree of Roughness of Foundation	Maximum Expansion Joint Spacing Slab Thickness (cm)		
		15	20	25
Winter	Smooth	50	50	60
(oct. – march)	Rough	140	140	140
Summer	Smooth	90	90	120
(April – Sept.)	Rough	140	140	140

The degree of roughness is as specified previously. The above table is based on the study conducted by Central Road Research Institute. For contraction joint spacing, the following table may be followed.

Table 8.15 : Contraction Joint Spacing

Slab Thickness, cm	Maximum Contraction Joint Spacing, cm	Suggested Reinforcement in Welded Fabric in kg/m^2 for Reinforced Pavements
Unreinforced slabs		
10	4.5	
15	4.5	
20	4.5	
Reinforced slabs		
10	7.5	2.2
15	13.0	2.7
20	14.0	3.8

Having tentatively decided joint spacing, we can now design slab thickness in the following steps.

8.16.5 Design Procedure for Determination of Rigid Pavement Thickness

The following steps may be taken :

- Design values for the various parameters E, M are fixed.
- Joint spacing and lane width tentatively fixed.
- Maximum temperature stress for critical edge region determined by equation or figure. To do this tentative design, thickness of pavement slab will have to be assumed.
- Calculate residual available strength of concrete for supporting load.
- Calculate edge load stress from equation or figure and calculate factor of safety thereon.

- If factor of safety is slightly more than one, the design is OK. If it is less than one or much more than 1, steps 3 to 5 to be repeated till the factor of safety is one or slightly more than one. Let this thickness be h_s.

- Depending upon the traffic intensity, the provided thickness may be obtained from the following equation :

$$h_p = h_s + h_t$$

The values of h_t may be obtained from the following table :

Table 8.16 : Values of h_t

Traffic Classification	A	B	C	D	E	F	G
h_t (cm)	− 5	− 5	− 2	− 2	+ 0	+ 0	+ 2

8.17 PROVISION OF REINFORCEMENT

The rigid pavement will have to be reinforced at the joints. In addition, suitable reinforcement will have to be given in the body of the pavement.

8.17.1 Reinforcement at Transverse Joint

Mild steel dowel bars are provided at transverse joint to relieve load stresses at the edge and corner regions. The load transfer capacity of a single dowel bar in shear, in bending and in bearing on concrete is given by the following equations as per Bradbury's analysis.

$$\bar{P}_s = 0.785\ d^2\ f_s'$$

$$\bar{P}_{bn} = \frac{2\ d^3\ f_c}{r + 8.8\ z} \quad \text{and}$$

$$\bar{P}_{be} = \frac{f_c\ r^2\ d}{12.5\ (r + 1.5\ z)} \quad \text{where,}$$

$\bar{P}_s, \bar{P}_{bn}, \bar{P}_{be}$ are the load transfer capacity of single dowel bar in shear, bending and bearing on the concrete, d, and r are the diameter and length of dowel bar, f_s', f_s are respectively permissible shear and flexural stress in dowel bar and f_c is the permissible bearing stress in the concrete and z is the joint width. It is generally assumed that for balanced design, capacity of bar in bending and bearing should be equal which means we should equate these equations. When we do this, we get the following equations for known or assumed values of z and d.

$$r = 5d\left[\frac{f_s}{f_c} \times \frac{r + 1.5\ z}{r + 8.8\ z}\right]^{\frac{1}{2}}$$

For known values of z and d, r can be obtained by trial and then the equation for $\bar{P}_s$ or $\bar{P}_{bn}$ would give us load transfer capacity of single dowel bar. To calculate spacing of dowel bars, we first determine the required capacity factor from the following equation.

$$\text{Required capacity factor} \;=\; \frac{\text{Required load transfer capacity of system}}{\text{Load transfer capacity of single bar}}$$

The dowel bars are effective in load transfer on either side of load position upto 1.8 times the radius of relative stiffness. We may assume linear variation of capacity factor for a single dowel bar from L under the load to zero at a distance 1.8 l therefrom. For different spacings, the capacity factors could be calculated and the spacing which confirms to the required capacity factor may be selected for adoption. Dowel bars are not satisfactory for the thickness of slab less than 15 cm. There is an illustrated example at the end to high-light the points. It is to be noted that for dummy contraction joint, no dowel bars need be provided since aggregate interlock is sufficient in this case for load transfer. But the dowel bars are a must in the case of full depth construction joint. Typical tentative dowel bar arrangement for 20 mm wide expansion joint with 40 % load transfer are given in the table below.

Table 8.17 : Typical Dowel Bar Arrangement

Design Loading	Slab Thickness, cm	Dowel Bars		
		Diameter, mm	Length, mm	Spacing, mm
5100 kg	15	25	500	200
	20	25	500	250
	25	25	500	300

For working the above table, the values of design parameters assumed are f_s = 1400 kg/cm^2, f_c = 100 kg/cm^2, E_c = 3 × 10^5 kg/cm^2, K_s = 8.3 kg/cm^2 joint width 20 mm and load transfer 40 per cent.

8.17.2 Reinforcement for Longitudinal Joints

Theoretically, no reinforcement is required for longitudinal joints. Practically these joints are required in service, for example in the case of heavy traffic, expansive sub-grades etc. The area of steel required per meter length of the joint may be computed by considering

    b = Distance between the joint in question and the nearest free joint or edge in metres.

    f = Coefficient of friction between pavement and the subgrade.

    W = Weight of slab in kg/m^2, and

    S = Allowable working stress in kg/m^2.

Therefore bW would represent the total weight of the slab and fbW would represent total frictional force between the pavement and the subgrade per metre length of slab. Assuming that this force is taken by steel, we have

    A_s = Area of steel in cm^2 required per metre length of joint.

$$= \frac{fbW}{S}$$

To find length of this bar, it is assumed that the bond strength of the bar developed equals the working stress of the steel. If P is the perimeter of bar in cm and B is the bond stress in kg/cm^2, then the bond strength of the bar is LBP. The strength of steel bar is SA. Therefore,

$$LBP = SA \quad \text{and} \quad L = \frac{SA}{BP}$$

It is generally assumed that the length of any tie bar should be such it develops a bond strength twice that required that is the factor of safety should be two. Using this concept, we have

$$L = \frac{2SA}{BP}$$

The bond strength of plain and deformed tie bars may respectively be assumed as 17.5 kg/cm^2 and 24.6 kg/cm^2. To prevent warping at the joints and concentration of tensile stresses, the maximum diameter of the bar is limited to 20 mm and these should not be spaced more than 75 cm apart. The calculated length may be increased by 5 – 8 cm to account for inaccuracy of placement. As a guidance, for central longitudinal joint in double lane rigid pavements with lane width of 3.5 m, typical bar details are given below on the basis of f = 1.5, W = 24 kg/m^2/cm of slab thickness and s = 1400 kg/cm^2.

Table 8.18 : Central Longitudinal Joint Two Lane Pavement

Slab Thickness	Tie Bar Details			
	Diameter mm	Maximum Spacing	Minimum Length (cm)	
			Plain Bars	Deformed Bars
15	8	38	40	30
	10	60	45	35
20	10	45	45	35
	12	64	55	40
25	10	30	45	35
	12	45	55	40
	14	62	65	46

8.18 JOINTS IN CEMENT CONCRETE PAVEMENTS

Introduction : Joints are the weakest link in the concrete pavement but it is also the necessary evil. Generally, all the deterioration of concrete pavement is in the vicinity of the joints and hence these are to be planned and constructed with due care. Joints are necessary in the concrete pavement due to following reasons :

- These allow concrete slab to expand and contract under the action of temperature and moisture changes, thus relieving the warping stresses due to temperature.

- These allow pavement to be laid in bays in lanes of convenient widths.
- These allow suitable measure for breaking at the end of days work. As far as possible, the number of joints should be kept minimum since laying of joints interferes with the progress of concreting and riding quality of a road is reduced if the joints are more in numbers. A good joint should have the following properties : (1) It must be waterproof and should not allow dirt or stone grit to enter it. (2) Free movement should be available at the joint. (3) It should not cause unnecessary hindrance in the concreting operations and should not be very weak so as to pose structural weakness and (4) It should not hamper the riding quality of the road to a significant extent.

Types of Joints : There are three general types of joints viz. (1) Expansion joint, (2) Contraction joint and (3) Warping joint. These are now discussed.

Expansion Joint : These joints provide the room for the expansion of the pavement. The compressive stresses that might be generated because of prevention of expansion are thus reduced and bulking of concrete slab is avoided.

Contraction Joint : These provide room for the contraction of the concrete slab, that might occur due to change in temperature, the tensile stresses are thus relieved, and warping is reduced.

Warping Joint : These joints relieve the stresses due to warping and are commonly used for longitudinal joints dividing the pavements into traffic lanes.

Construction Joints : These are provided whenever construction operations require them. These are generally full depth joints and may belong to any of the above types. All these joints can be located in the transverse way that is perpendicular to the direction of traffic on the road or in longitudinal way that is in the direction parallel to the direction of traffic on the road. The details of different joints are shown in Fig. 8.17.

Transverse Joints : These joints can be expansion, contraction or construction and should make a right angle with the centre line of the pavement. Contraction and expansion joints should be continuous from edge to edge of the pavement through all lanes, constructed at the same or different times.

8.18.1 Details of Joints

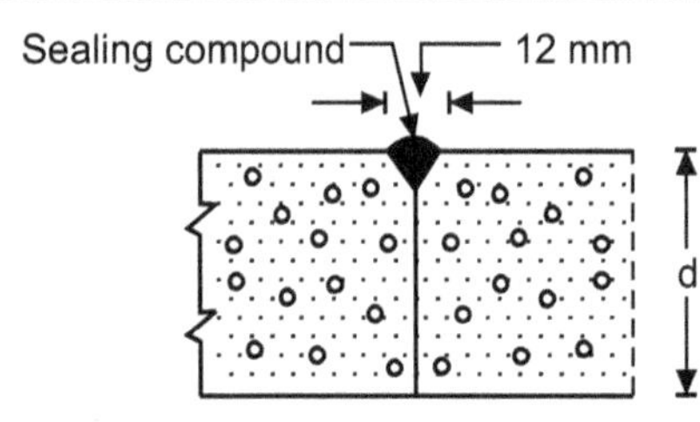

Plain butt joint (for longitudinal warping and construction joints)

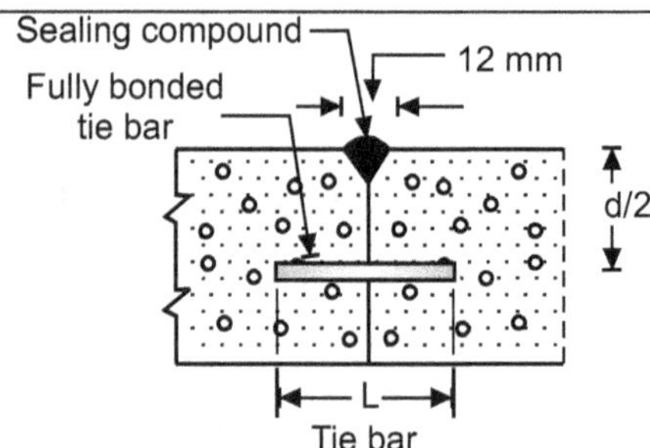

Butt joint with tie bar (for longitudinal warping joint)

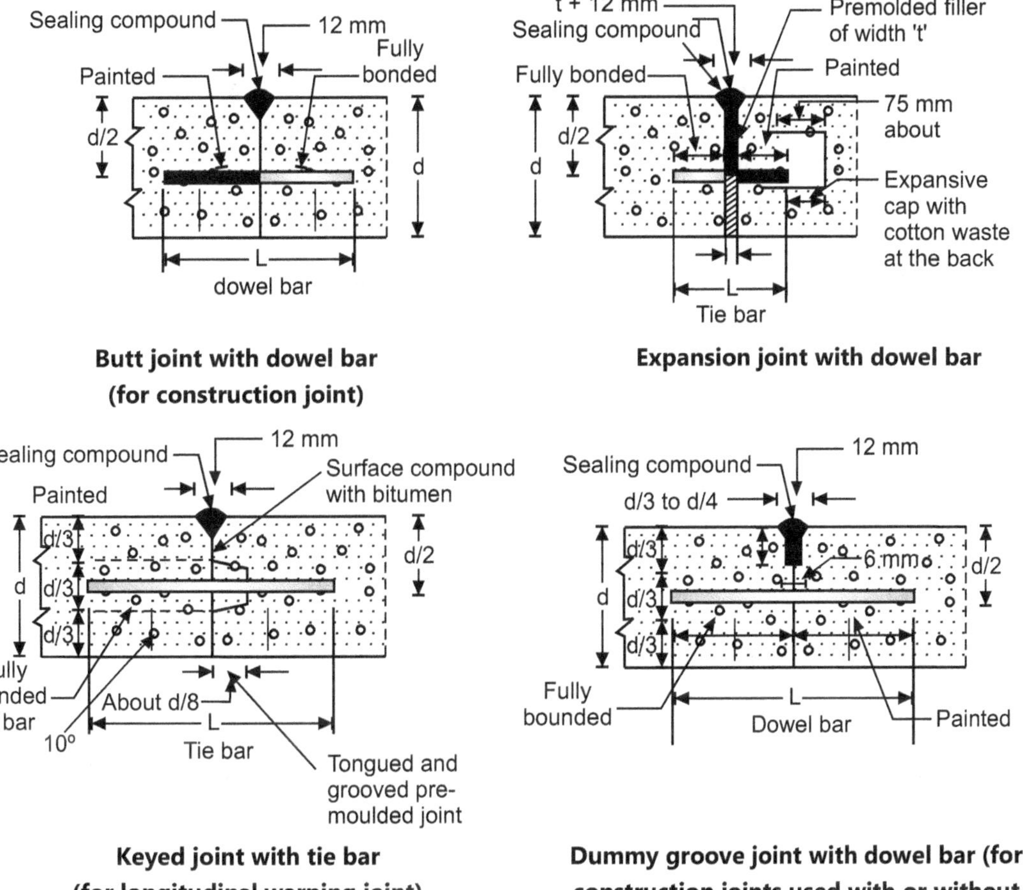

Butt joint with dowel bar

(for construction joint)

Expansion joint with dowel bar

Keyed joint with tie bar

(for longitudinal warping joint)

Dummy groove joint with dowel bar (for construction joints used with or without dowel)

Fig. 8.17

Note

(a)   Maximum radius for rounding of corners of slab-6 mm.

(b)   L = Length of dowel or tie bar.

(c)   d = Slab thickness.

(d)   t = Expansion joint width / premoulded filter board width.

Transverse Expansion Joint : These extend over the entire width of the pavement. Dowel bars are generally required at these joints to transfer the wheel load to the adjacent slab, however no dowel bars need be given for slabs less than 150 mm thickness. The gap between the adjacent slab is filled by premoulded expansion joint filler broad, confirming to

I.S. 1838 - 1961. The top of the filler board should be 25 mm below the surface of the pavement. The dowel bar that is provided at the expansion joint is simply a load transfer device in the form of simple round steel bar, one half of which is anchored in either slab while the other half is free to move longitudinally within the adjacent slab. The free longitudinal movement of the dowel bar is ensured by coating the free half end of the dowel bar with a thin coating bitumen over it. An expansion cap is provided at the end to offer a space of about 2.5 cm for movements during expansion. These dowel bars should be placed parallel to each other and to the centre of line of the pavement.

Transverse expansion joints are essentially dummy groove type. These should be constructed by forming in the surface of the slab a slot not less than 6 mm wide and having a depth equal to one third to one fourth the depth of the pavement at the thinnest part of its section. The slot may be formed by pushing, into the concrete a flat bar or the wedge of a 'T' bar using a suitable vibratory device, removing the bar and keeping the slot open. T bar is generally preferred. No spalling of the concrete should occur when the bar is being removed and the edge of the joint should be rounded with an edging tool before the concrete hardens.

Transverse Construction Joint : Transverse construction joint should be provided whenever placing of concrete is suspended for more than 30 minutes. It must be remembered that constructing activity should always be suspended (except in the case of emergency) at the regular site of expansion or contraction joint. If the concreting activity is stopped at the site of an expansion joint a regular expansion joint with dowel bars should be provided. If the concreting operation are stopped at the site of contraction joint or any such other place, the construction joint should be of butt type with dowels.

Longitudinal Joints : These should be of the plain butt type and formed by placing the concrete against the face of the slab concreted earlier. The face of the slab concreted earlier should be painted with bitumen with bitumen before placing of fresh concrete. Tie bars should be used at longitudinal joints and these should be supported so as not to be displaced during concreting operations. Tie bars should be bonded in the slabs across the longitudinal joints and while casting the first slab, these should be bent so that one end of them lies along the forms. After removal of the forms bars should be straightened so that they extend into the concrete placed on the other side of the joint.

Direction of Transverse Joints : All the transverse joints should be constructed in line across the full width of the pavement. It has been seen that where transverse joint has been staggered on either side to the longitudinal joint, cracking has often occurred in line with the joint in the adjacent slab, therefore staggered joints are not preferred. Similarly transverse joints should always be at right angles to the direction of traffic, any other angle that is the skew joint increases the risk of cracking at the acute angles and may also tend to make the slab move sideways. It follows from the above discussion that acute angled corners should also be avoided. Where these corners are unavoidable, as in the case of intersections, the corners should be strengthened by using adequate amount of reinforcement.

Spacing of joints, Reinforcement, Tie bars Dowels have been already discussed. Reinforcement in the concrete slab is not intended to contribute towards its flexural strength, therefore its position is not important. But general guidance is that the position of reinforcement should be such that it should be protected from corrosion. Since cracks starting with higher tensile stresses at the top surface are more critical to the riding characteristics of the pavement where they tend to open, the general preference is for the placing of the reinforcement about 50 mm below the surface. This is accomplished by striking-off the concrete such that the compacted layer is 50 mm below the final surface, placing the reinforcement and then placing the remainder of the concrete. Reinforcement is often continued across dummy groove joints to serve the same purpose as tie bars but at all full depth joints, the reinforcement is kept at least 50 mm away from the face of the joint or edge.

Sealing of Joints : After the curing period is over but before the pavement is opened to traffic, the transverse expansion, contraction, as well as longitudinal joint should be thoroughly cleaned and cleared of all the foreign material, if necessary by blowing the compressed air in it. All the contact faces of the joint should be cleaned by wire brush. The edges of the joint should be primed with thin bituminous paint, which should be allowed to dry out before the sealing compound is applied. The typical composition of the primer may be as follows.

Sr. No.	Primer	Percentage by Weight
1.	Bitumen (200 penetration grade)	66 (blended hot)
2.	Light Creosote Oil	14 (Blended hot or cold)
3.	Solvent Naphtha	20 (Blended cold)

The bitumen 200 penetration grade should be melted and fluxed with light creosote oil and when the mixture becomes cold, solvent naphtha should be added to form the ideal primer. In no case, bituminous emulsions be used as primers. There are many sealing compound, manufactured by many agencies. Generally, the sealing compound should not be heated above 200° C. Even a temperature of 180° C should not be continued for long periods. Sealing compound should be powered into the joint opening only and as far as possible, it should not be allowed to spill on the concrete surface. Sometimes the exposed surface of the sealing compound is dusted with dry hydraulic lime to prevent tackiness. The line of separation between adjacent slabs of concrete should be cleaned and painted with 200 penetration grade bitumen.

Opening the Road to Traffic : The traffic should not be allowed to ply on concrete roads for 28 days after the formation of concrete, when ordinary portland cement, portland blast furnace slag cement, or portland pozzolona cement are used. Before the road is opened to traffic the joints must be properly sealed.

QUESTIONS

1. Bring out the difference between rigid and flexible pavement.

2. Which loading is severe in Westergaard theory?

3. How do we calculate traffic intensity as per I.R.C. method of design of rigid pavements and how traffic is classified in it?

4. Discuss in brief methods for design of flexible pavements

5. Discuss the different type of consideration made in the design of rigid pavement as per IRC.

6. Outline the steps in the design of rigid pavement as per I.R.C.

7. Explain in detail about Marshal Stability teat, with neat diagram.

9. Draw the neat sketches for the cross-section of Flexible and Rigid pavements. Mention in detail about the materials used, their properties, merits and demerits and failure of the pavements in Rainy Season.

Chapter 9
CONSTRUCTION

9.1 MODERN EQUIPMENT FOR ROAD CONSTRUCTION

Road making plants and machinery is used in various jobs. The various works includes in the road construction are:

- Clearing trees, shrubs, jungles etc.
- Forming the soil, to level by cutting ridges or filling hollows.
- Spreading the metal and rolling
- Surfacing or applying wearing course.

(a) The following equipment and plants are generally used for clearing the jungles, shrubs etc :

- Bull dozer
- Rooter
- Tractor
- Towed scraper
- Shovel unit with trucks

(b) For cutting, filling and preparing the formation or sub grade for a road, the following machinery is generally used :

- Tractor dozer
- Grader
- Shovel
- Clamshell
- Trucks
- Trench cutter
- Plough rollers

(c) For spreading the road metal or aggregates on the prepared sub-grade and rolling the same, the following plants and equipments are used :

- Crusher
- Trucks
- Aggregates Distributor and
- Rollers

(d) The surfacing generally consists of Bituminous surfacing and concrete surfacing

For Bituminous pavements following plants and equipments are used :

- Bituminous Boiler
- Sprayer

- Aggregate Spreader
- Bitumen Mix Spreading Machine Paver
- Grouting Machine
- Rollers

For cement concrete pavements the following plants and equipments are used;

- Central Batching And Mixing Plants
- Concrete Mixers
- Concrete Pavers
- Concrete Spreader And Finisher
- Concrete Vibrators

9.2 WATER BOUND MACADAM WEARING COURSE

The water bound macadam road is one of the oldest method of road construction known to mankind. The road metals used for the construction of this road are known as macadam. The W. B. M. Road is used as village road, or as a base for the important modern roads such as surface painted roads, premixed carpet, bituminous macadam and cement concrete roads. This type of road consists of road metals bound together with water only. The smaller pieces of the metals are used to filled up the voids

Normally the wearing surface itself takes the load of the wheels and then the load is transferred on the lower surfaces. Therefore this should be sufficiently strong so that it can bear the traffic load without getting damaged. After rolling the thickness of wearing coat should be 11.5 cm. For the first time this thickness should be from 7.5 cm to 11.5 cm or according to the drawing details.

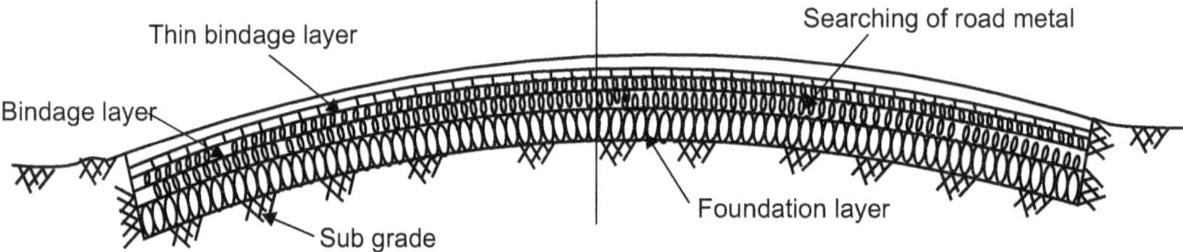

Fig. 9.1 : Waterbound macadam road

Table 9.1 : Physical Requirements of Coarse Aggregates for Water Bound Macadam for Sub-Base Course

Test	Test Method	Requirement
1. * Los Angeles Abrasion Value	IS : 2386 (Part IV)	40 per cent (Max)
Or	IS : 2386 (Part IV)	30 per cent (Max)
*Aggregate Impact Value	Or IS : 5640**	
2. Combined Flakiness and Elongation Indices (Total)***	IS : 2386 (Part I)	30 per cent (Max)

Table 9.2 : Grading Requirements of Coarse Aggregates

Grading No.	Size Range	IS Sleve Designation	Percent by Weight Passing
1.	90 mm to 45 mm	125 mm	100
		90 mm	90-100
		63 mm	25-60
		45 mm	0-15
		22.4 mm	0-5
2.	63 mm to 45 mm	90 mm	100
		63 mm	90-100
		53 mm	25-75
		45 mm	0-15
		22.4 mm	0-5
3.	53 mm to 22.4 mm	63 mm	100
		53 mm	95-100
		45 mm	65-90
		22.4 mm	0-10
		11.2 mm	0-5

Table 9.3 : Grading for Screenings

Grading Classification	Size of Screenings	IS Sleve Designation	Percent by Weight Passing the IS Sleve
1.	13.2 mm	13.2 mm	100
		11.2 mm	95-100
		5.6 mm	15-35
		180 micron	0-10
2.	11.2 mm	11.2 mm	100
		5.6 mm	90-100
		180 micron	15-35

Table 9.4 : Approximate Quantities of Coarse Aggregates and Screenings Required for 100/75 mm Compacted Thickness of Water Bound Macadam (WBM) Sub Base/Base Course for 10m² Areas

Classification	Size Range	Compacted Thickness	Loose Qty.	Screenings			
				Stone Screening		Crushable Type such as Moorum or Gravel	
				Grading Classification and Size	For WBM sub-base/base course (Loose Quantity)	Grading Classification and Size	Loose Quantity
Grading 1	90 mm to 45 mm	100 mm	1.21 to 1.43 m³	Type A 13.2 mm	0.27 to 0.30 m³	Not uniform	0.30 to 0.32 m³
Grading 2	63 mm to 45 mm	75 mm	0.91 to 1.07 m³	Type A 13.2 mm	0.12 to 0.15 m³	--do--	0,.22 to 0.24 m³
-do--	-do--	--do--	-do--	Type B 11.2 mm	0.20 to 0.22 m³	--do--	--do--
Grading 3	53 mm to 22.4 mm	75 mm	-do--	-di--	0.18 to 0.21 m³	--do--	--do--

9.2.1 General Guideline and Procedure for Water Bound Macadam

- Thickness of a compacted layer should be 100 mm for 90-45 mm, size aggregates and 75 mm for 63-45 mm or 53-22.4 mm size aggregates.

- Screenings should generally be of the same material as coarse aggregate. However, if the use of screenings is not feasible, some other non-plastic material, such as, moorum or gravel (other than rounded river borne material) having liquid limit and plasticity index below 20 and 6 respectively may be used provided fraction passing 75 micron sieve does not exceed 10 per cent.

- Binding maternal need not be used if the layer is to serve as base (or is to receive black topping), or where crushable type of screenings, like, moorum is used.

- It is a good practice to lay a sub-base of granular/stabilised material before laying WBM. This is particularly important where the sub grade is of clayey type.

- Where the WBM is to be laid directly over sub grade, a 25mm thick layer of stone screenings (Grading B) "inverted choke" should be spread on the prepared sub grade before the application of aggregate is taken up. In case of fine sand or silty or clayey sub grade it is advisable to lay 100 mm thick insulating layer of screening or coarse sand on the top of fine grained soil. A preferred alternative to inverted choke is the use of appropriate geosynthetics mesh.

- Arrangements for water, rollers in working order and templates/ other tools and equipment for checking the quality of the materials and work must be available at site before the work of laying is started.

- The quantities of coarse aggregates and screenings will vary, depending on the actual grading.

- Arrangements for lateral confinement of aggregates must be provided. This can conveniently be done by raising the shoulders in stages equal in thickness to each layer of WBM.

- The coarse aggregate should be spread uniformly and evenly on the prepared subgrade /sub-base by using templates placed across the road about 6 m apart. The thickness of each compacted layer should not be more than 100 mm in grading 1 and 75 mm for grading 2 and 3. Wherever possible, mechanical devices should be used to spread the aggregates uniformly so as to minimise the need for manual rectification afterwards.

- The spreading should be done from stockpiles or directly from vehicles. No segregation of large or fine aggregates should be allowed.

- The surface should be checked frequently while spreading and rolling so as to ensure the specified regularity of slopes and camber.

- The coarse aggregate should not normally be spread more than three days in advance of the subsequent construction operations. Three wheeled power rollers at 80 to 100 kN or tandem or vibratory rollers at 80 to 100 kN static weight should be used for rolling. Except on supper elevated portions, where the rolling should proceed from inner edge to outer edge, rolling should begin from the edge gradually progressing towards centre. Successive passes should uniformly overlap the proceeding by at least one half widths.

- In case screening are to be applied, rolling should be discontinued when the aggregate are partially compacted with sufficient void space to permit application of screening. During rolling slight sprinkling of water may be allowed. Complete rolling is indicated by a loose stone piece getting crushed under the roller without sinking.

- After the coarse aggregate has been rolled, screening to completely fill the interstices should be applied gradually over the surface. Screening should not be damp or wet at the time of application. These should not be dumped in piles but applied at a uniform rate, in three or more applications, so as ensure filling of all voids. Dry rolling should be done while the screenings are being spread so that vibrations of the roller cause screenings to settle into the voids of coarse aggregate. Dry rolling should accompanied by brooming. These operations should continue until no more screenings can be forced into the voids of coarse aggregate.

- Spreading, rolling and brooming of screens shall be carried out in only such lengths which are likely to be completed within one day's operation.

- After screenings have been applied, the surface should be copiously sprinkled with water, swept with hand brooms and rolled. This operation should be continued with additional screenings, applied as necessary, until the coarse aggregates has been thoroughly keyed, well broomed, firmly set in its full depth and a grout has been formed of screenings.

- The base or sub grade should not get damaged due to use of excessive quantities of water. In case lime treated soil sub-base, construction of water bound macadam should be taken up only after sub-base has picked up enough strength.

- Apply binding material, wherever required, in a similar fashion as screening. Continue rolling till full compaction is achieved.

- After the final compaction of WBM course, the pavement should be allowed to dry overnight. Next morning hungry spots should be filled with screenings or binding material, lightly sprinkled with water, if necessary and rolled.

- No traffic should be allowed on the road until the macadam has set. The compacted WBM Course should be allowed completely dry and set before the next pavement course is laid over.

- WBM work should not be carried out when the atmospheric temperature is less than 0° C in the shade.

9.3 WET MIX MACADAM

9.3.1 Description

Wet Mix Macadam is a pavement layer where crushed graded aggregates and granular material, like, graded course sand are mixed with water in mixing plant and rolled to a dense mass on a prepared surface. It has many advantages over the WBM construction. These include superior gradation of aggregate, faster rate of construction, higher standard of densification that can be achieved, less consumption of water and stricter standards of quality achievable. The specification can be adopted for sub-base and base courses. The work may be done in many layers. The thickness of an individual layer shall not be less than 75 mm and can be up to 200 mm provided suitable type of compacting equipment is used.

9.3.2 Aggregate

Physical Requirement: Coarse aggregates shall be crushed stone/crushed gravel/shingle, not less than 90 per cent by weight of gravel / shingle pieces retained on 4.75 mm sieve and shall have at least two fractured faces. The aggregates shall conform to the physical requirements set forth in Table 1. If the water absorption valve of the coarse aggregate is greater than 2 %, soundness test be carried out on the material as per IS: 2386 (Part V)

Table 9.5 : Physical Requirement of Coarse Aggregates for Wet-Mix

	Test	Test Method	Requirement
1	Los Angles Abrasion Valve	IS: 2386 (Part IV)	40 % (Maximum)
2	Aggregate Impact Valve	IS: 2386 (Part IV)	30 % (Maximum)
3	Combined Flakiness And Elongation Indices	IS: 2386 (Part I)	30 % (Maximum)

Grading Requirement: The aggregates bay confirm to the grading given in table. Material finer than 425 micron shall be Plasticity Index (PI) not exceeding 6. The nominal size of aggregate to be used case would depend on availability. While both the grading can be used for base / sub base courses. Course using Grading No 1 shall not be laid over the course using Grading No 2.

I S Sieve Designation	% By Weight Passing Sieve	
53 mm	100	
45 mm	95.10	
26.5 mm		100
22.4 mm	60.80	50.10
11.2 mm	40.60	
4.75 mm	25.40	35.55
2.36 mm	15.30	
600 u	8.22	10.30
75 u	0.8	2.9

The final grading within the limits set forth in table shall be well graded from coarse to fine and shall not vary from the lower limit on one sieve to the higher limit on the adjacent sieve or vice versa.

9.3.3 Construction Operation of WMM

9.3.3.1 Weather and Seasonal Limitations

The work of laying of wet mix macadam shall not be done during rain.

9.3.3.2 Preparation of Base

The surface of the sub-grade/sub-base/base to receive the WMM course shall be prepared to the specified lines and cross-fall (camber) and made free of dust and other extraneous matter. Any ruts or soft yielding places shall be corrected in an approved manner and rolled until firm surface is obtained, if necessary by sprinkling water. As far as possible, laying of

WMM course over an existing thick bituminous layer may be avoided since it will cause problems of internal drainage of the pavement at the interface of two courses. It is desirable to completely excavate the existing thin bituminous wearing course where WMM is proposed to be laid over it. However, where the intensity of rain is low (less than 1300 mm), and the interface drainage is efficient, WMM can be laid over the existing thin bituminous surfacing by cutting 50 mm x 50 mm furrows at an angle of 45 degrees to the center line of the pavement at one meter intervals on the existing road. The directions and depth of furrows shall be such that they provide adequate bondage and also serve to .drain water to the existing granular base course beneath the existing thin bituminous surface.

9.3.3.3 Provision of Lateral Confinement of Wet Mix

While constructing WMM, arrangement shall be made for the lateral confinement of wet mix. This shall be done by laying materials adjoining shoulders along with that of wet mix layer. The sequence of operations shall be such mat the construction of the shoulder is done in layers each matching the thickness of the adjoining pavement layer. Only after a layer of pavement and corresponding layers in shoulder have been laid and compacted, the construction of the next layer of pavement and shoulder shall be taken up.

9.3.3.4 Preparation of Mix

WMM shall be prepared in an approved mixing plant of suitable capacity having provision for controlled addition of water and forced/positive mixing arrangement, like, pugmill or pan type mixer. For small quantity of wet mix work, mixing may be done in ordinary concrete mixers. The Specifications and requirements for equipment for WMM are discussed in Part II. The equipment should conform to requirements detailed in Part II. Optimum moisture for mixing shall be determined in accordance with IS:2720 (Part VIII), after replacing the aggregate fraction retained on 19 mm sieve with material of 4.75 to 19 mm size. However, the OMC and required number of passes to achieve the desired density may be determined at site during proof rolling, using the roller selected for compaction. While adding water, due allowance should be made for evaporation losses. However, at the time of compaction, water in the wet mix should not vary by more than ± 1 per cent

9.3.3.5 Spreading of Mix

Immediately after mixing, the mixed material shall be transported to site and spread uniformly and evenly upon the prepared subgrade /sub-base / base in required quantities. Hauling of the mix over a freshly completed stretch is not permitted.

The mix may be spread either by a paver finisher or motor grader or a combination of both. However, the use of paver finisher should be preferred to motor grader for spreading. For portions where mechanical) means cannot be used, manual method of spreading can be adopted. The equipment used for spreading shall be capable of spreading the material uniformly all over the surface. Its blade shall have hydraulic controls suitable for initial adjustments and maintaining the same so as to achieve the specified slope and grade.

The paver finisher shall be self-propelled, having the following features:-

(i)   Leading hoppers and suitable distributing mechanism

(ii) The screed shall have tamping and vibrating arrangement for imparting initial compaction to the layer as it is spread without knitting or otherwise disturbing the surface profile.

(iii) The paver shall be equipped with necessary control mechanism so as to ensure that the unfinished surface tree from surface blemishes.

The surface of the layer as spread shall be carefully checked with templates and all high or low spots remedied by removing or adding wet mix material as may be required. The layer thickness may be checked by depth blocks during construction. No segregation of coarse or fine particles shall be allowed. The layer as spread shall be of uniform gradation and shall not have pockets of fine materials.

9.3.3.6 Compaction

After the mix has been laid to the required thickness, grade and cross-fall/camber, the same shall be uniformly compacted to the full depth with a suitable roller. If the thickness of the single compacted layer does not exceed 100 mm, a smooth wheel roller of 80 to 100 kN weight may be used. For compacting single layer of higher thickness upto 200 mm, the compaction shall be done with the help of vibratory roller of minimum 80-100 kN static weight or equivalent capacity to achieve the desired density. The speed of roller shall not exceed 5km/hr.

In portions having uni -directional cross-fall/super elevation, rolling shall commence from the lower edge and progress gradually towards the upper edge. Thereafter roller should progress parallel to the center line of die road, uniformly over-lapping each preceding track by at least one-third width until the entire surface has been rolled upto the centre line. The process of compaction is then to be repeated from the other edge of the pavement upto die centre line, until the entire pavement is compacted. Any displacement occurring as a result of reversing of the direction of a roller or from any other cause shall be corrected. Along forms, kerbs, walls or other places not accessible to the roller, die mix shall be thoroughly compacted with mechanical tampers or a plate compactor. Skin patching of an area without scarifying the surface to permit proper bonding of the added material shall not be permitted.

Rolling should not be done when the subgrade is soft or yielding or when it causes a wave-like motion in the sub-base/base course or sub-grade. If irregularities develop during rolling which exceed 12 mm when tested with a 3 meter straight edge, the surface should be loosened and premixed material added or removed as required before rolling again so as to achieve a uniform surface conforming to the desired grade and cross-fall. In no case should the use of unmixed material be permitted to make up the depressions.

Rolling shall be continued till the density achieved is at least 98 per cent of the maximum dry density for the material as determined by the method outlined in IS: 2720 (Part VIII).

After completing, the finished surface shall present a well-closed appearance, free from movement under compaction equipment or any compaction marks, ridges, cracks and loose material. All loose, segregated or otherwise defective areas shall be made good to the full thickness of the layers and re-compacted.

Longitudinal joints and edges shall be constructed true to the delineating line parallel to the centre line of the road. All longitudinal and transverse joints shall be cut vertical to the full thickness of the previously laid mix before laying the fresh mix.

9.3.4 Important Considerations in Construction Process

While due care and attention is required on the whole process of WMM construction, the following are important points needing more attention:-

(i) Sometimes because of moisture in the fines, these will not flow out from the bin of the three-bin feeder to the belt. In such situation, it would be necessary to have a small vibrator fitted on one of the side walls of the bin to intermittently shake it.

(ii) Control on water in the mix is of utmost importance; hence there should not be any variation in the grading, particularly of fines as it will affect the moisture content and uniform mixing. Similarly, excessive fluctuations in the moisture content of the fines should be avoided. If necessary, slight increase may be made in the moisture contents to account for the moisture loss in transit to the laying site.

(iii) Excessive sill or clay in fines should not be permitted, as besides spoiling the quality of mix, it will cause clogging in pugmil and storage silo.

(iv) The mixed material should be transported directly to site. Stockpiling of mixed material should be discouraged as excessive handling is the cause of segregation and moisture loss, both of which arc detrimental to the quality of the wet mix macadam.

(v) There should be minimum joints in laying wet mix macadam. To ensure this, the daily output should at least be 500 linear meters. The width of laving also should be so adjusted to avoid the necessity of laying narrow strips e.g. against kerbs.

(vi) Single paver of 7m width or two pavers each of 3.5m width working in tandem within the short distances should be used for obtaining good results.

9.3.5 Setting and Drying

After final compaction of the wet mix macadam course, the road shall be allowed to dry for 24 hours before overlaying with any bituminous layer.

9.3.6 Opening to Traffic

No vehicular traffic except construction vehicles shall be allowed on the finished WMM surface till the subsequent bituminous course is laid.

Layout of WMM Plant

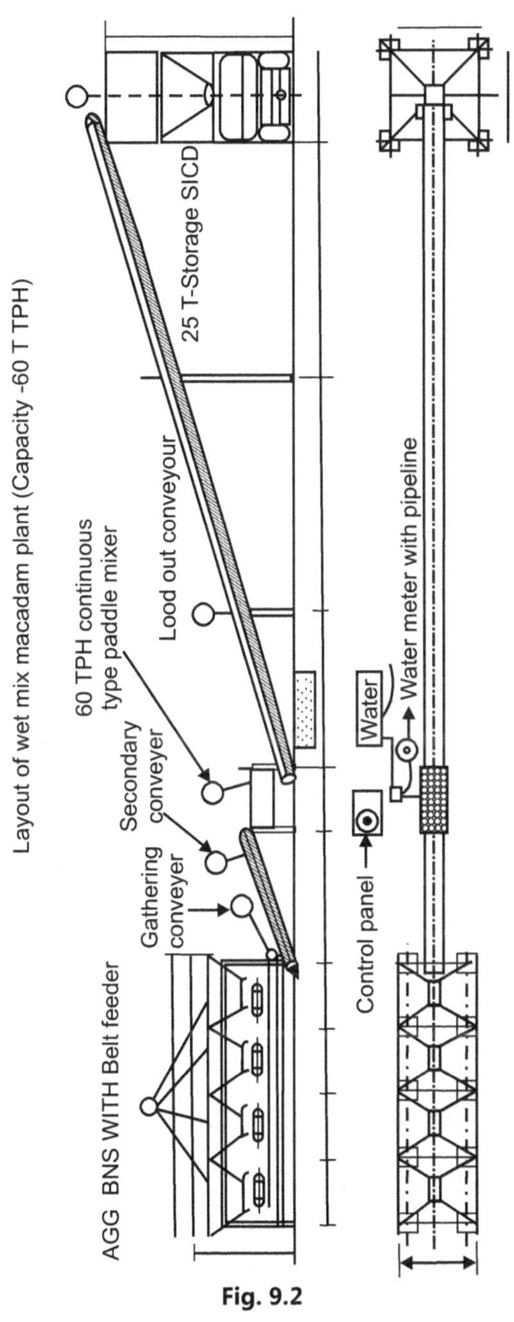

Fig. 9.2

source IRC:109-1997 **publication**

9.4 GSB

A granular subbase course is that part of the pavement structure constructed to provide a foundation for the base course, to distribute the superimposed loading to the subgrade and to provide drainage beneath the base and surface courses. It usually consists of natural sand or a mixture of sand with gravel, excavated and constructed with grading equipment as an item under a grading contract. Before placing the subbase material, the subgrade or foundation must be properly prepared. It should be smooth, shaped to conform to required crown and grade, and be compacted to the required density. Where travel of the placing equipment ruts or disturbs the foundation, means must be employed to correct these conditions ahead of placing the subbase material. If the subbase is constructed on a rutted foundation, the roadbed will not drain properly and areas of weakness may develop in the pavement structure. Placing, shaping, and compacting the subbase material to conform its full width to the required grade, section, and density are necessary for satisfactory construction of the proposed base course. The inspector should frequently check the subbase course for correct depth and spread.

Aggregates are used in granular base and subbase layers below the driving surface layer(s) in both asphalt concrete and Portland cement concrete pavement structures. The aggregate base layers serve a variety of purposes, including reducing the stress applied to the subgrade layer and providing drainage for the pavement structure. The granular base layer is directly below the pavement surface and acts as the load bearing and strengthening component of the pavement structure. The granular subbase forms the lowest (bottom) layer of the pavement structure, and acts as the principal foundation for the subsequent road profile, provides drainage for the pavement structure, and protects the structure from frost. Granular bases are typically constructed by spreading the materials in thin layers of 150 mm (6 in) to 200 mm (8 in) and compacting each layer by rolling over it with heavy compaction equipment.

9.4.1 Granular Sub-Base

The material for granular sub-base should generally conform to the grading indicated in Tables 9.6 and 9.7 or combination thereof.

Table 9.6 : Grading for coarse-graded granular sub-base materials

IS sieve designation	Percent by Weight Passing the IS sieve		
	Grading I	Grading II	Grading III
75.0 mm	100	-	-
53.0 mm	80-100	100	-
26.5 mm	55-90	70-100	100
9.50 mm	35-65	50-80	65-95
4.75 mm	25-55	40-65	50-80

IS sieve designation	Percent by Weight Passing the IS sieve		
	Grading I	Grading II	Grading III
2.36 mm	20-40	30-50	40-65
0.425 mm	10-25	15-25	20-35
0.075 mm	3-10	3-10	3-10
CBR value (minimum)	30	25	20

Table 9.7 : Grading for Coarse-graded Granular sub-base materials

IS sieve designation	Percent by Weight Passing the IS sieve		
	Grading I	Grading II	Grading III
75.0 mm	100	-	-
53.0 mm	-	100	-
26.5 mm	55-75	50-80	100
9.50 mm	-	-	-
4.75 mm	10-30	15-35	25-45
0.075	<10	<10	<10
CBR Value (Minimum)	30	25	20

Note : The material passing 425 micron (0.425 mm) sieve for all the three gradings when tested according to IS : 2720 (Part V) shall have liquid limit plasticity index not more than 25 and 6 per cent respectively.

Placing

- Place granular sub-base after subgrade is inspected and approved by concern.
- Construct granular sub-base to depth and grade in areas indicated.
- Ensure no frozen material is placed.
- Place material only on clean unfrozen surface, free from snow or ice.
- Place granular sub-base materials using methods which do not lead to segregation or degradation.
- Place material to full width in uniform layers not exceeding 150 mm compacted thickness. Owner's Representative may authorize thicker lifts (layers) if specified compaction can be achieved.
- Shape each layer to smooth contour and compact to specified density before succeeding layer is placed.
- **Remove and replace portion of layer in which material has become segregated during spreading.**

Compaction

- Compaction equipment to be capable of obtaining required material densities.
- Compact to density of not less than 98% corrected maximum dry density.
- Shape and roll alternately to obtain smooth, even and uniformly compacted sub-base.
- Apply water as necessary during compaction to obtain specified density.
- In areas not accessible to rolling equipment, compact to specified density with mechanical tampers approved by Owner's Representative.
- Correct surface irregularities by loosening and adding or removing material until surface is within specified tolerance.

9.5 CONSTRUCTIONS OF BITUMINOUS PAVEMENTS

Bituminous pavements are composed of a mixture of bitumen and/or tar and mineral aggregates. Due to greater demand of cement in large number of projects in recent years, in India greater percentage of roads that exist today is Black Top. All the state P.W.D.'s, central P.W.D.'s and other agencies at present use mostly the bituminous materials for the surfacing of roads. Unfortunately, the world oil crisis has shot up the price of bitumen With Indian roads consuming approximately 11 lac tonnes of bitumen annually; this involves precious and scarce foreign exchange. Various types of bituminous pavements having thickness ranging between 0.75 cm to as high as 15 to 22 cm have been developed. When properly used and constructed, these pavements have long and economic lives. They serve the following main functions:

(a) Provide smooth and good riding surface;

(b) Provide high resistance to surface wear;

(c) Provide skid resistant surface;

(d) Protect the underlying layer and sub-grade from detrimental actions of water and other natural agencies i.e., it seals the ingress of rain water.

9.6 TYPES OF BITUMINOUS PAVEMENTS

Based on methods of construction, bituminous pavements can be classified under the following categories :

(1) Surface Treatments : They include :

- Prime coat,
- Tack coat,
- Surface dressing, and
- Seal coat.

(2) Grouted or Penetration Macadam : They include :

- Semi-grouted macadam, and
- Fully-grouted macadam.

(3) Road Mix Surfaces : They include :

- Open graded mixes,
- Dense graded mixes, and
- Sand asphalt.

(4) High Type Bituminous Pavements : They include hot premixed surfaces. For example,

- Bituminous macadam,
- Bituminous concrete or asphaltic concrete,
- Sheet asphalt or rolled asphalt,
- Sand asphalt,
- Mastic asphalt, and
- Tar concrete.

Bituminous pavements can also be classified on the basis of mixing and construction techniques. They are : (1) Road mix, and (2) Central plant mix.

Choice of binder type e.g. straight run bitumen, tar, cut back or emulsion depends upon the type of the pavement, availability of materials and equipments, climatic condition etc. The specifications for Road and Bridge works issued by the M.O.T. (Roads Wing) Government of India and published by Indian Roads Congress gives detailed specifications for the Single Coat Surface Dressing, Double Coat Surface Dressing, 20 mm open Graded Premixed Carpet, Mixed Seal Surfacing, Built up Spray Grout Base Courses, Bituminous Bound Macadam base/binder Courses Semi-dense Carpet and Bituminous Concrete. These bituminous courses are roughly in ascending order of superiority for their use in road construction.

Fig. 9.3

Fig. 9.4

9.6.1 Surface Treatments

These are the works carried out to alter the qualities of a wearing surface. The different types of surface treatments are briefly described below :

Prime Coat : This consists of application of a low viscosity cut back e.g. RC-0, MC-1 or SC-1 as primers on an existing base of previous texture like WBM base. The various functions of a prime coat are :

- It plugs capillary voids and water proofs the existing base.
- It coats and blends dust and loose particles thereby hardening and toughening the surface.
- It provides adhesion between new and old surface.
- It serves as a table for road mix paving jobs.

Tack Coat : It is a treatment which is given to the under side of a surface or some other course to bind the previously prepared layer to the superimposed layer. It involves a simple single application of a bituminous binder for example, a bitumen emulsion, a cut back or a low viscosity tar to a previously prepared surface. They are commonly used when a new wearing surface is to be placed on an old bituminous surfacing, or on new or old concrete pavement, or on a brick, stone or black pavement, or on a primed granular base course. The surface on which the tack coat is to be applied should be thoroughly swept and cleaned of dust and other foreign matters. The rate of spread of straight run bitumen may be 5 kg/10 m^2 area for an existing bitumen treated surface and 10 kg/10 m^2 area for an untreated WBM surface.

Surface Dressing : They normally consist of a layer of small aggregates such as chippings of stone, slag or gravel on a thin layer of binder which is freshly applied to an existing road surface. A surface dressing when provided on earth or gravel or WBM road, provides non-skid surface, improves night visibility, arrests disintegration and provides a clear demarcation between the carriage-way and the shoulders. It does not help in increasing the load carrying capacity but provides dust free and water proof surface Normally, specifications suggested for use in surface dressing are single coat surface dressing, double coat surface dressing, open graded premix carpet and mix-seal surfacing. Whereas, it is accepted that two coat surface dressing and 20 mm premixed carpet with seal coat are most commonly used specifications for light surfacing, the former consumes about 11 tonnes of bitumen for 1 km length of single lane road, the latter consumes about 13 tonnes of bitumen. Thus, a saving of nearly 15 % bitumen can be achieved if we go in for surface dressing rather than premixed carpet. For lighter traffic even one coat surface dressing may be sufficient, where suitably graded stone aggregates are available, mix-seal type of surfacing which requires some quantity of bitumen as two coat surface dressing should be preferred to 20 mm premixed carpet.

Construction Procedure : The surface dressing should consist of one or two coats, each consisting of a layer of bituminous binder sprayed on a prepared base followed by a cover of stone chippings. The surface dressing should be carried out only when the atmospheric temperature is above 16°C and the weather is dry and clear.

Materials

(1) Bitumen : The grade of the straight run bitumen is chosen depending upon the climatic conditions of the region in which surface dressing is to be constructed. In most parts of India 80/100 and 180/200 grade bitumen is used. Heavier grade cut backs, rapid setting emulsions or heavier grade tars may also be used. For single surface dressings on WBM base course, quantity of bitumen needed ranges from 17 to 195 kg per 10 m^2 area and 10 to 12 kg per 10 m^2 area in case of renewal of black top surfacing. For second coat of surface dressing, the quantity of bitumen needed ranges from 10 to 12 kg per 10 m^2 area. Bulk bitumen lorries with tanks of capacity ranging from 5,000 to 15,000 litres are used to transport bulk bitumen.

(2) Aggregates : The stone chippings should consist of clean durable and uniform quality aggregates of following properties :

Table 9.8

Shape	Cubical
Los Angeles value	less than 35 %
Aggregate impact value	less than 30 %
Flakiness index value	less than 25 %
Water absorption	less than 1 %
Stripping	less than 25 %

The aggregates should also be free of elongated, flaky, soft pieces, salt, alkali vegetable matters and dust coatings. The quantity of aggregates used in first coat of surface dressing should be 0.15 m^3 per 10 m^2 area of 12 mm nominal size. On the other hand, the quantity of aggregate used in second coat of surface dressing should be 0.10 m³ per 10 m² area and of 10 mm nominal size.

Equipment : The equipments used for construction of surface dressing are :

List of Equipments and Tools for Surface Dressing Works

- Bitumen boiler (Preferable oil fired with pressure burner).
- Spraying unit such as, a self propelled bitumen sprayer.
- Spraying cans.
- Road roller (8-10 tonnes).
- Buckets (G.I. Sheet) 6 to 10 litres capacity.
- Wire brushes.
- Coir brushes.
- Gunny bags.
- Baskets lined with gunny cloth.
- Empty drums or G.I. sheet tanks for storage of water (200 litres capacity).
- Road barriers.
- Diversion boards.
- Thermometers (dial type, distant reading 0° - 250°C).
- Tractor or bullock cart to drag bitumen boiler.
- Hammer and cutter to open bitumen drums.
- Chain pulley arrangements for loading of drums into boiler.
- Spades or Punjas.
- Measuring Tape.
- Camber Board.
- Straight Edge (3 metres).
- Gritters.
- 30 and 15 litre capacity containers for checking quantity of aggregates.

Preparation of Base : Before laying the surface dressing, it is essential to prepare the base in accordance with specified grade and cross-section. The prepared surface should also be thoroughly cleaned first with hard brushes, then with softer brushes and finally by blowing with gunny bags.

Application of Binder : Bitumen heated at 163 to 177°C is uniformly sprayed with the help of a mechanical sprayer or pouring can.

Application of Stone Chippings : Soon after the application of binder, the stone chippings are uniformly spread either by means of a mechanical gritter or manually with a twist of the basket containing the aggregates.

Rolling : Soon after the spreading of stone chippings, the entire surface should be rolled with a 8-10 tonne smooth wheeled roller. Rolling should start from the edges and progress towards the centre in such a way, so that each pass of the roller should uniformly overlap not less than one-third of the track made in the preceding pass. The rolling should continue till surface is firmly bedded.

Application of Second Coat : The second coat should be applied immediately after laying the first coat by method similar to the one as described above for single coat dressing. The surface should be checked with a 3m straight edge for longitudinal profile and with a camber template for cross profile. The permitted tolerances of surface irregularities are 10 mm for longitudinal profile and 6 mm for cross profile. The road should not be open to traffic before 24 hrs.

Surface Dressing under Abnormal Conditions : Surface dressing can be laid even under abnormal conditions for example, cold and wet weather, steep grades and super elevations, etc. This involves additional expenditure and careful control. In hill roads, due to steep gradients abnormal shear stresses are created by gear changing while going upgrade and braking during down going. Binders of normal viscosity as used in plain regions will not be able to take these higher stresses. This necessitates using higher viscosity binders to hold the chippings on the hill roads.

The higher viscosity binder becomes viscous and will not allow proper penetration and wetting of aggregates. If lower viscosity binders like cut back with harder grade asphaltic cement is used, the binder flows down the grade when applied and will be in the form of a non-uniform film.

The various methods to overcome the above difficulties are :

(1) Using Heated Aggregates : In this method, the heated higher viscosity binder is spread, so that it can be applied in a thin film. As soon as it reaches the surface, it gets sufficiently hard to resist flow down the grade. To facilitate easy penetration and wetting of aggregates, pre-heated aggregates are spread on the binder film and lightly rolled. The heated aggregates will be able to soften the binder, penetrate and get coated easily.

(2) Use of Equipment : Equipment can be used for surface dressing on steep gradients, superelevation and cold weather conditions in most parts of the country under the prevailing cold weather conditions without deviating from the conventional method of construction.

(3) Use of Pre-coated Chippings : In this method, the pre-coated chippings with higher viscosity binder are spread on the surface and rolled when still warm. At high altitudes, when the air temperatures are very low, cut back bitumen may be used as the binding material.

(4) Use of Adhesive Agents : During wet weather, binder treated with adhesive agents for example, long chain amines or long chain aliphatic diamines or long chain amides should be used as a binding material for surface dressing.

SEAL COAT : It is a final thin coat either over a previous bituminous pavement or over an existing worn out bituminous pavement. The main purposes of a seal coat are :

* To waterproof the surface.
* To provide a more desirable surface texture.
* To reduce slipperiness.
* To improve visibility.
* To build up pavement structure.

The seal coat can be of following two types :

Type I Seal Coat : It consists of an application of a layer of bituminous binder followed by a cover of stone chippings.

Type II Seal Coat : It consists of a premixed seal coat comprising of a thin application of aggregates premixed with bituminous binder.

Construction Procedure : In case of type I seal coat, the heated bitumen 9.8 kg per   10 m^2 area and 6 mm stone chippings 0.09 m^3 per 10 m^2 area are used in a manner similar to the one described for surface dressing. For the construction of type II seal coat, the preheated bitumen and aggregates mixed in a specified proportion are spread uniformly on the surface to be sealed. The quantity of aggregates (passing 1.7 mm sieve and retained on 180 micron sieve) to be utilized should be 0.06 m^3 per 10 m^2 area and bitumen 6.8 kg. per 10 m^3 area.

The mix after it has been spread uniformly on the bituminous surface to be sealed should be rolled with 6-9 tonne smooth-wheeled power rollers till a smooth uniform surface is obtained. The traffic may be allowed soon after final rolling, when the premixed material has cooled down to the surrounding temperature. The quality control of work should be similar to the one described earlier for surface dressing.

9.6.2 Grouted or Penetration Macadam

This is a type of construction in which a bituminous binder is applied in a fluid state to partially compacted aggregate layer. When binder is allowed to penetrate to full depth, it is known as full grouted macadam and when it is allowed to penetrate half the depth, it is known as semi-grout macadam. Full-grout macadam construction generally 5 to 8 cm thick is used in regions of very heavy rainfall. Semi-grout macadam construction generally 5 cm thick is used in regions of average rainfall and medium traffic.

Construction Procedure : Generally, grouted macadam consists of two layer composite construction of compacted crushed coarse aggregates with application of bituminous binder after each layer and key aggregates on the top of the second layer. This is also known built-up spray grout base course. This should be constructed only in dry weather when the atmospheric temperature is above 16ºC.

Materials : The binder should be straight run bitumen of grade 80/100 or 60/70 or 30/40 of quantity 50 and 68 kg per 10 m^2 area for 5 cm and 7.5 cm compacted thickness respectively.

Road tars i.e. RT-4 and cut backs can also be used. Normally, the aggregates used are crushed stone or crushed gravel. They should be clean, cubical in shape, free of organic matters, hydrophobic and of low porosity. The various physical requirements of stone aggregates should be as follows :

Table 9.9

Shape	Capital
Los Angeles value	Less than 50 %
Aggregate Impact value	Less than 40 %
Flakiness index value	Less than 25 %
Stripping value	Less than 25 %
Water absorption	Less than 1 %

The coarse aggregates and key aggregates required for 5 cm compacted thickness should be 0.60 m^3 and 0.15 m^3 per 10 m^2 area respectively. Their gradings should be as indicated in the table below :

Table 9.10

Sieve Size	Percent by Weight Passing the Sieve	
	Coarse Aggregate	Key Aggregate
50 mm	100	–
25 mm	35.70	–
20 mm	–	100
12.5 mm	0.15	35.70
4.75 mm	–	0.15
2.36 mm	0.5	0.5

The various construction operations for example, preparation of base, application of tack coat, spreading and rolling of aggregates for the first layer should be similar to the one as described earlier. Heated binder should be sprayed on aggregate layer at the rate of 12.5 kg/10 m^2 in a uniform manner with the help of mechanical sprayers. Soon after the first application of binder, the second layer of coarse aggregates should be spread and rolled. Again, the second aggregates layer should be given a binder spray at the rate of 12.5 kg/10 m^2 area. Immediately, after the application of binder, key aggregates should be spread uniformly at the rate of 0.13 m^3/10 m^2. The surface should then be rolled with a 8 - 10 tonne smooth wheeled roller till the key aggregates are firmly in position. The road surface should be open to traffic after 24 hours.

9.6.3 Road Mix Surface

In this type of construction, the binder and aggregates are mixed on the top of an existing surface or a base. If the aggregates used are of uniform size, then the road mix is known as open graded mix. In dense graded mix, the aggregates used are well graded. In case of mix in place sand asphalt construction, the naturally occurring sand is mixed with liquid asphalt to form the wearing surface. The road mix surfaces are suitable for light to moderate traffic conditions, on old or new bases. These mixes have got following advantages over penetration macadam :

- Saving in quantity of bitumen,

- Better coating of aggregates, and

- Increased stability.

9.6.4 High Type Bituminous Pavements

These types of pavements use central plant mix for its construction. The various high type of bituminous pavements using premixed aggregates described in this chapter are bituminous macadam, bituminous concrete and mastic asphalt.

Bituminous Macadam or Bitumen Bound Macadam : This consists of a single construction 5 cm or 7.5 cm thick of compacted crushed aggregates premixed with a bituminous binder. This type of construction utilizes quite flexible gradation control and provides an economical and strong base course. It has been established that a thinner section of bitumen bound macadam is equivalent to a thicker section of WBM or gravel base course section. This is because of the fact that the load distribution through the bitumen bound macadam is comparatively on a wider area and the surface is more resistant to deformation. Bitumen bound macadam can be advantageously used in snow bound hilly terrain, regions of high ground water table and in areas where medium type of aggregates are available.

Construction Procedure : Bitumen bound macadam should be laid during dry weather only. Before actual construction, the base should be prepared, shaped and conditioned to a specified grade and cross-section. The prepared surface should be thoroughly cleaned and made free from dust.

Materials : The various binders used are : straight run bitumen, road tar, cut back or emulsion. The straight run bitumen grade 30/40 or 60/70 or 80/100 is chosen depending upon the climatic conditions. The quantity of the bitumen needed depends upon the grading adopted in the design. The crushed stone aggregates to be used should be clean strong, durable, cubical in shape, hydrophobic, low porosity and free from organic and other deleterious matters. The various physical requirements of aggregates should be as shown below :

Table 9.11

Shape	Capital
Los Angeles Value	less than 35 %
Aggregate impact value	less than 30 %
Flakiness index value	less than 25 %
Stripping	less than 25 %
Water absorption	less than 1 %

The aggregate gradings both for 7.5 cm and 5 cm thick bitu-minous macadam should confirm to the followings. The binder content for premixing generally varies from 3 to 4.5 % for grading I, grading II and 3.5 to 6% for grading III. As per Asphalt Institute classification, 5 cm and 7.5 cm bitumen bound macadam falls under open mix type category. Marshall and Hubbard field methods of mix design are considered unsuitable for such type of mixes. Even though the Hveem's method is listed as doubtful by the Asphlt Institute for this type of mixture, this method of mix design is adopted for determination of optimum bitumen content to obtain the laboratory mix design.

Table 9.12 : Aggregate Grading for 50 cm Compacted Thickness of Bitumen Bound Macadam

Sieve	Percent by Weight Passing the Sieve		
Size	Grading I	Grading II	Grading III
63 mm	–	–	–
50 mm	100	100	–
40 mm	–	90 - 100	–
25 mm	37 - 70	50 - 80	100
20 mm	–	–	70 - 100
12.5 mm	0 - 15	10 - 30	–
10 mm	–	–	35 - 60
4.75 mm	–	–	15 - 35
2.36 mm	0 - 5	–	5 - 20
0.075 mm	0 - 3	0 – 5	0 - 4

Table 9.13 : Aggregate Grading for 7.5 cm Compacted Thickness of Bitumen Bound Macadam

Sieve Size	Percent by Weight Passing the Sieve		
	Grading I	Grading II	Grading III
63 mm	100	–	100
50 mm	90 - 100	–	100
40 mm	35 - 65	100	100
25 mm	20 - 40	70 - 100	70 - 100
20 mm	–	50 - 80	50 - 80
12.5 mm	5 - 20	–	–
10 mm	–	–	25 - 50
4.75 mm	–	10 - 30	10 - 30
2.36 mm	–	5 - 20	5 - 20
75 micron	0 - 5	0 - 5	–

It is essential to lay a tack coat over the base before laying bitumen bound macadam construction. The quantity of binder for tack coat should be 5.0 to 7.5 kg per 10 m^2 for bituminous base and 7.5 to 10 kg per 10 m^2 for untreated WBM layer.

Preparation of Mix : In a hot mix plant, the bitumen and aggregates are separately heated to a temperature in the range of 155 –163° C and 150 –177°C respectively. At no time the difference in temperature between the aggregates and bitumen should exceed 14 C. The mixing is so through, so that a homogeneous mixture is obtained in which all particles of the aggregates are coated uniformly. The mixture is carried to the site through vehicle or a wheel barrow. For small premix work and in places where mixing plant is not available hand operated drum mixer should be used.

List of Equipments for thin Premix Carpet and Bituminous Macadam

- Drying and mixing unit.
- Bitumen boiler (preferably oil fired with pressure burner).
- Chain pulley arrangement for lifting of drums.
- Road roller (8-10 tonnes).
- Bitumen sprayer with spray-bar or spraying cans with 18 litres capacity.
- Buckets (G.I. sheets) 6 to 12 litres capacity.
- Spring balance (10 kg).
- Baskets (lined with gunny cloth).
- Wire brushes.
- Coir brushes.
- Gunny bags (old).
- Empty drums or G I. sheet tanks for storage of water (200 litres capacity).
- Spades.
- Rakes (big).

- Rakes (small) with long handles for levelling of mix.
- Templates.
- Camber board.
- Straight-edge (3 metres).
- Measuring Tape.
- Thermometers (dial type, mercury in steel, distant reading 0°C to 250°C).
- Wheel barrow.
- Shovels.
- Gum boots.
- Hammer cutter for opening of bitumen drums.
- Angle iron or wooden strips of required dimensions for edges.
- Road barriers.
- Diversions boards.
- Red lamps.
- 30 and 15 litre capacity containers for checking quantity of aggregates.

Spreading : The mix should be spread immediately after mixing by means of a self-propelled mechanical paver with suitable screeds capable of spreading, tamping and finishing the mix. The temperature of the mix at the time of laying should be maintained in the range of 121-163°C.

Rolling : Soon after the spreading of the mix the rolling is done with 8 to 10 tonnes tandem roller. The rolling is commenced from the edges of the pavement and progressed towards the centre and uniform overlapping is provided. The roller wheels should be kept damp to avoid the bituminous material from sticking to the wheels The pavement surface should be checked and may be permitted 10 mm and 6 mm tolerances of surface regulating in longitudinal and cross profile respectively. Built-up spray grout can be structurally equated to Bituminous Macadam (with an equivalency factor of 1 : 1.5. This implies that, whereas the quantity of bitumen required for a 50 mm thick. Bituminous Macadam Course is about 19 tonnes per 1 km length of a single lane road, the quantity of bitumen required for a structurally Equivalent layer of 75 mm built-up spray grout is only 13 tonnes involving a saving of bitumen of nearly 50 %.

Bituminous Concrete or Asphaltic Concrete

This is an intimate mixture of coarse aggregate, fine aggregates, mineral filler and bitumen. This hot mix, hot laid construction is probably the most stable and durable bituminous road mixture in India. This is also a dense, impervious, waterproof construction suitable for the most heavily travelled roads. It possesses considerable mechanical strength and this makes it to withstand high stresses without causing undue strain in the upper layer of the pavement structure. It has been found that unit thickness of bituminous concrete layer is Equivalent to three times thick crushed stone layer and four times thick sand-gravel layer. Bituminous concrete is normally used as the wearing course on the major roads and very often also as base course. As per Asphalt Institute, Maryland, USA. the bituminous concrete construction should be done in two layers i.e. binder course and wearing course. The different thickness requirement for various traffic conditions are given below :

Table 9.14

Traffic	Thickness Requirement		Total
	Binder Course	Wearing Course	
Light	–	5 cm	5 cm
Medium to heavy	4 to 5 cm	4 to 2.5 cm	8 cm
Very heavy	6 to 8 cm	4 to 2.5 cm	10 cm

Asphaltic concrete mix is designed on the basis of stability and durability considerations. The mix should meet the following requirements :

Table 9.15

Description	Requirements
1. Marshall stability, determined on Marshall specimens compacted by 50 compaction blows on each end.	227 kg
2. Marshall flow value (0.1 mm units).	20 - 45
3. Per cent voids in mix.	3 - 5
4. Per cent voids in mineral aggregate filled with bitumen.	75 - 85
5. Binder content per cent by weight of mix.	5 - 7.5

Construction Procedure : Bituminous concrete should be laid during dry weather conditions only.

Materials

(1) Binder : The straight-run bitumen grade 30/40 or 60/70 or 80/100 is chosen depending upon the climatic conditions. The quantity of bitumen needed varies from 5.0 to 7.5 % by weight of mix.

(2) Coarse Aggregates : The crushed coarse aggregates to be used should be clean, strong, durable, cubical in shape, hydrophobic, of low porosity and free of organic or other deleterious matters. The physical requirements of the aggregates should conform to the one described for bitumen bound macadam.

(3) Fine Aggregates : The aggregates (passing 2.36 mm sieve and retained on 0.75 mm sieve) should be clean, hard, durable, uncoated, dry, and free from soft, or flaky pieces and organic or deleterious matters.

(4) Filler : The filler (passings 600 micron sieve) should be inert material for example, stone dust, cement, hydrated lime, fly-ash or other non-plastic matter.

(5) Gradation of Aggregates : The combined grading of mineral aggregates and filler should conform to any of the two gradings given below :

Table 9.16

Sieve Size	Per Cent by Weight Passing the Sieve	
	Grading I	Grading II
20 mm	–	100
12.5 mm	100	80 - 100
10 mm	80 - 100	70 - 90
4.75 mm	55 - 75	50 - 70
2.36 mm	32 - 50	35 - 50
600 micron	18 - 29	18 - 29
300 micron	13 - 23	13 - 23
150 micron	8 - 16	8 - 16
75 micron	4 - 10	4 – 10

Generally, for compacted layer thickness of 25-40 mm any of the two gradings could be used but for layer thickness of 40-50 mm only grading No. 2 should be used. The permissible variations from the job mix formula should conform to the following limits :

Description of Ingredient	Permissible Variation by Weight of Total Mix
Aggregate passing 4.75 mm sieve	± 5.0 per cent
Aggregate passing 2.36 mm sieve	± 4.0 per cent
Aggregate passing 600 micron sieve	± 3.0 per cent
Aggregate passing 75 micron sieve	± 1.0 per cent
Binder	± 3.0 per cent

Construction Operations : The various construction operations include preparation of base, application of tack coat, preparation of mix, spreading and rolling. During the preparation of base course all the irregularities including pot-holes or ruts are removed. It is desirable to lay a bituminous leveling course on an existing extremely wavy pavement. The construction operations like : application to tack coat, preparation of mix and spreading are similar to the one described for bitumen bound macadam construction.

Soon after the spreading of mix by paver the surface should be thoroughly compacted by rolling with all set of rollers moving at less than 5 kmph speed. It is always desirable that the initial rolling should be done with 8-12 tonne three wheel rollers. The surface finishing should be carried out by with 8-10 tonne tandem roller or pneumatic rollers. The rolling process is similar to the one described earlier. The rolling should be continued till the density achieved is at least 95 % of that of the laboratory Marshall specimen.

Field Controls : The various field controls include : (1) Aggregates grading control, (2) Binder grade control, (3) Temperature control for aggregates, and (4) Temperature control for mix during mixing and compaction. It is recommended that at least one test for above field controls must be carried cut for every 100 tonnes of mix discharged by plant. The field density should also be checked once for every 1000 m^2 of compacted surface. The permitted tolerances of surface regularity are 8 mm and 4 mm for longitudinal and cross-profile respectively.

Mastic Asphalt : Mastic asphalt is superior to other types of surfacings because of its ability to take very heavy shear stresses without deformation. That is why mastic asphalt is recommended for very heavy traffic and in places where the braking and accelerating stresses are very heavy for example, bus-stops and round abouts. Mastic asphalt has not found any importance in our country due to :

(a) Non-availability of machinery required-to heat and mix at very high temperature.
(b) Non-availability of highly skilled labour to handle the mix in spreading at high temperature of 200°C.
(c) Non-availability of the grading of asphalt required.
(d) Very high cost due to large quantity of binder used.

9.7 CEMENT CONCRETE PAVEMENTS

Cast in place concrete is used in very diverse applications for the construction of road pavement because of numerous advantages i.e. :

- Great rigidity and consequently a good distribution of the loads on the foundation and excellent fatigue behaviour,
- Great resistance to wear and rutting and edges that do not erode ;
- Not affected by oil, organic substances, chemicals;
- Bright colour, skid resistance and safety in winter;
- Environmentally friendly.

Concrete pavements lasts long too and require little maintenance, at least if they have been designed properly and executed professionally. If this is not the case, significant premature damage is liable to occur, resulting in high maintenance costs.

Following, all aspects of the execution of monolithic pavements are discussed. This bulletin is intended to be a reference publication for people who are responsible for the execution of the works and for the supervision of construction. The evaluation of both older and recent concrete pavements demonstrates time and again how important the quality of the execution is. It requires special attention, both from the contractor executing the works and from the people ensuring that the specifications are complied with.

There are different types of monolithic pavements.

(1) Plain Concrete - Short Pavement Slabs : This type of pavement consists of successive slabs whose length is limited to about 25 times the slab thickness. At present it is recommended that the paving slabs not be made longer than 5 m, even if the joints have dowels to transfer the loads. The movements as a result of fluctuations in temperature and humidity are concentrated in the joints. Normally, these joints are sealed to prevent water from penetrating the road structure. The width of the pavement slabs is limited to a maximum of 4.5 m.

(2) Reinforced Concrete

(a) Continuously Reinforced Concrete : Continuously reinforced concrete pavements are characterised by the absence of transverse joints and are equipped with longitudinal steel reinforcement. The diameter of the reinforcing bars is calculated in such a way that cracking can be controlled and that the cracks are uniformly distributed (spacing at 1 to 3 m). The crackwidth has to remain very small, i.e. less than 0.3 mm.

(b) Reinforced Pavement Slabs : Reinforced concrete pavement slabs are almost never used, except for inside or outside industrial floors that are subjected to large loads or if the number of contraction joints has to be limited.

(c) Steel Fibre Concrete : The use of steel fibre concrete pavements is mainly limited to industrial floors. However, in that sector they are used intensively. For road pavements steel fibre concrete can be used for thin or very thin paving slabs or for very specific applications.

9.7.1 Preparation of the Subgrade or the Base

The road subgrade has to be prepared carefully, in order to realize everywhere a pavement structure of an adequate and uniform thickness. This allows to provide a homogeneous bond between the concrete slab and its foundation which is important for the later behaviour of the pavement structure For roads with a base, drainage of the water must be provided. Mud, leaves, etc. have to be removed When the base is permeable, it should be sprayed with water in order to prevent the mixing water from being sucked out of the concrete.

However, if the base is impermeable (e.g. if the concrete is placed on a watertight asphalt concrete interlayer) it can be necessary under warm weather conditions to cool down this layer by spraying water on the surface.

The following points are important for roads without a foundation :

- Drainage of all surface water;
- Good compaction of the subgrade;
- Filling and compaction of any ruts caused by construction traffic;
- It is forbidden to level the subgrade by means of a course of sand. If the subgrade has to be levelled, it is advisable to do this by using a granular material: either slag or coarse aggregate e.g. with a grain size 0/20;
- Provide an additional width of the subgrade for more lateral support.

It must always be avoided that water is sucked from the cement paste into the substructure or the base. This can be accomplished by either moderately moistening the subgrade, or by applying a plastic sheet on the substructure of the pavement. The latter work must be done with care, to prevent the sheet from tearing or being pulled loose by the wind.

9.7.2 Mixing and Transport of Concrete

Concrete Mixing Plant : The concrete mixing plant must have a sufficient capacity in order to be able to continuously supply concrete to the paving machines. The mix constituents and admixtures have to be dosed very accurately. The number of aggregate feed bins has to equal at least the number of different aggregate fractions. The bins shall have raised edges to prevent contamination of the aggregate fractions. The equipment for loading the materials shall be in good condition and shall have sufficient capacity to be able to continuously feed the bins. The bucket of the loaders shall not be wider than the bins. The content of the cement silos and the water tank are in proportion to the production rates. For small works, permanent concrete mixing plants are often called on. In that case, mixing plants that are inspected and that can deliver BENOR (Belgian quality certification) concrete should be used. Furthermore it is useful and even essential to have a communication system between the concrete mixing plant and the construction site in order to coordinate the batching and paving operations.

Transport of the Concrete : Sufficient trucks must be available to continuously supply the paving machines. The number depends on the yield at the construction site, the loading capacity of the trucks and the cycle time (i.e. the transport time plus the time required to load and unload a truck). The loading capacity and the type of truck to be used depend on the nature of the work, the haul roads and the concrete paving machines.

Fig. 9.5 : Preparation of the subgrade or the base

Usually, the specifications prescribe that the concrete has to be transported in dump trucks as paving concrete consists of a relatively dry mix having a consistency that makes transport and unloading in truck mixers difficult. Furthermore, dump trucks can discharge the concrete faster. For small works and in urban areas, the use of truck mixers is increasingly accepted. Under these circumstances an admixture (e.g. a superplastifier) can be mixed in just before discharging the concrete. The necessary measures have to be taken to prevent changes of the water content and temperature of the concrete during transport. To this end, the specifications prescribe to cover the dump trucks by means of a tarpaulin.

Fig. 9.6 : Placing of concrete

9.7.3 Fixed-Form Concrete Paving

Setting up the Side Forms : In order to place the side forms properly the alignment of the road has to be staked out carefully. This is usually accomplished by driving iron rods firmly into the subgrade soil or the base at a spacing of maximum 5m. After the elevations corresponding to the top of the forms have been marked on the rods, they are connected with a string line that represents the top of the forms. The form sections have to be properly supported on the base at all points. The inner surfaces of the forms shall be installed vertically and on line. In curved areas shorter or bent form sections are used, so as to better match the alignment of the curve. After the form sections have been properly aligned over a certain distance, they are secured by means of stakes. As the side forms serve as the reference for guiding the vibratory screed, the tolerances for the evenness shall not be exceeded. To accurately place the forms, a rigid template having the same width as the concrete pavement must be available on site, so that it can be checked at any time whether or not the form sections are set up parallel. The inside surface of the forms should be cleaned and oiled or coated with a form release product, to prevent spalling when the forms are stripped and to facilitate cleaning of the formwork elements before they are used again.

In urban areas, the formwork is often substituted by rows of paving bricks. These are placed on a bed of mortar or concrete with a cement content of at least 350 kg/m3. The rows of paving bricks divide the pavement surface into rectangular sections. They have to be placed a few days before the concrete is cast. If the surface of the stones is uneven, a thin plate is laid on top of them to make the sliding surface for the vibratory screed as smooth as possible.

Equipment : All equipment necessary for executing the paving must be present on site and has to function properly. This concerns primarily : manual needle vibrators and vibrating screed, equipment for floating the concrete surface, for applying the curing compound, for sawing the joints, etc. The profile of the finishing equipment has to be even, in order to obtain good final pavement smoothness. To check this, a gauge is placed at each end of the screed to be controlled. Subsequently, a string is tensioned between the two gauges and the distance between the string and the finishing surface of the screed is measured at various points. Another method consists of checking the evenness with a level and leveling rod. The consolidation equipment has to generate uniform vibrations with the right frequency and amplitude.

Fig. 9.7

Fig. 9.8

9.7.4 Slipform Concrete Paving

Preparation of the Track Runway : The quality of the runway for the tracks of the paving equipment is undoubtedly one of the most important factors that contribute to the realisation of a smooth pavement surface. In connection therewith, the following criteria have to be met :

- Sufficient bearing capacity, so that the slipform paver can proceed without causing deformations;
- Good skid resistance to prevent the tracks from slipping, especially when paving on a slope;

- Good evenness to avoid that the self-levelling systems have to compensate for excessive differences in height. The track runway is a determining factor for the steering and consequently its surface has to at least as smooth as the concrete paving surface itself. The runway surface has to be permanently cleaned prior to the passage of the tracks. The track runway has to be wide enough taking into account:
- The greatest width of the paving machine plus an extra width (especially on embankments);
- The necessary space for placing the sensor lines.

Furthermore, if the longitudinal slope is 4 % or more, the track runway has to be stabilised to prevent slipping. In addition to this the tracks can be equipped with plates or hooks or the paving can preferably progress own hill.

9.8 JOINTS

Provisions of joints are necessitated due to :
- Expansion, contraction and warping of concrete slabs resulting from temperature and moisture changes;
- Facilitate a break in the construction at the end of day's work or for any unexpected interruption to work progress; and
- Construction of pavements in lanes of convenient width.

9.8.1 Types of Joints

Transverse joints are of the following types :

(a) Expansion Joints : These provide for space in concrete to allow for expansion of slab. The practice with regard to spacing of expansion joints vary from 20 metres to a few hundred metres. Recent practice is to omit expansion joints and provide the same at junctions of roads with structure, like, bridges, etc.

(b) Contraction Joints : These joints are provided in concrete pavements to prevent stresses induced as a result of ambient temperature falling below the laying temperature. These are normally 3 to 5 mm, width and provided upto $1/3^{rd}$ to $1/4^{th}$ the slab thickness. Spacing of contraction joints is generally 5 metres. For reinforced concrete pavements the maximum spacing varies from 7.5 m to 17.0 m depending upon thickness of slabs.

Fig. 9.9 : Expansion joints

Fig. 9.10 : Construction joints

(c) Construction Joints : These joints are provided at the end of a day's work or when the work is stopped unexpectedly due to interruption for more than 30 minutes. These are either contraction joints or expansion joints.

(d) Longitudinal Joints : These are required when the width of concrete pavement is more than 4 metres wide. These are intended to Provide for warping and even uneven settlement of subgrade. Generally, the joints are butt type dummy type joints are also used. These are saw cut joints for at least 1/3rd of the depth of slab.

QUESTIONS

1. Explain the details the construction procedures for cement concrete roads.
2. Explain the details the construction procedures for bituminous road construction.
3. Explain different types of joints in cement concrete pavements.
4. Explain the details the construction procedures for Water Bound Macadam Road construction.
5. Differentiate between Highway pavement and Airport pavement.
6. Write short notes on the following:
    (a) WMM
    (b) WBM
    (c) GSB
    (d) BC
    (e) BM
    (f) Cement concrete road
    (g) Bituminous pavement

Chapter 10
INTRODUCTION TO AIRPORT ENGINEERING

10.1 MEANING OF TRANSPORT

Transport refers to the activity that facilitates physical movement of goods as well as individuals from one place to another. In business, it is considered as an auxiliary to trade, that means, it supports trade and industry in carrying raw materials to the place of production and distributing finished products for consumption. Individuals or business firms that engage themselves in such activities are called transporters. Generally, transporters carry raw material, finished products, passengers etc. from one place to another. So it removes the distance barrier. Now-a-days goods produced at one place are readily available at distant places. People move freely throughout the world because of transport. It is associated with every step of our life. Without transport, we, as well as business units cannot move a single step. Let us discuss its importance.

Fig. 10.1

10.2 IMPORTANCE OF TRANSPORT

Followings are the points of importance of transport.

- **Makes available raw materials to manufacturers or producers :**

Transport makes it possible to carry raw materials from places where they are available, to places where they can be processed and assembled into finished goods.

- **Makes available goods to customers :**

Transport makes possible movement of goods from one place to another with great ease and speed. Thus, consumers spread in different parts of the country have the benefit of consuming goods produced at distant places.

- **Enhances standard of living :**

Easy means of transport facilitates large-scale production at low costs. It gives consumers the choice to make use of different quantitites of goods at different prices. So it raises the standard of living of the people.

- **Helps during emergencies and natural calamities :**

In times of national crisis, due to war or internal disturbance, transport helps in quick movement of troops and the supplies needed in the operation.

- **Helps in creation of employment :**

Transport provides employment opportunity to individuals as drivers, conductors, pilots, cabin crew, captain of the ship etc. who are directly engaged in transport business. It also provides employment to people indirectly in the industries producing various means of transport and other transport equipments. People can also provide repairing and maintenance services by opening service centers at convenient locations.

- **Helps in labour mobility :**

Transport helps a lot in providing mobility to workers. You may be aware that people from our country go to foreign countries to work in different industries and factories. Foreingers also come India to work. In India, people also move from one part to another in search of work. Similarly, it is not always possible to have workers near the factory. Most industries have their own transport system to bring the workers from where they reside to the place of work.

- **Helps in bringing nations together :**

Transport facilities movement of people from one country to another. It helps in exchange of cultures, views and practices between the people of different countries. This brings about greater understanding among people and awareness about different countries. Thus, it helps to promote a feeling of international brotherhood.

10.3 MODES OF TRANSPORT

We fine the basically transport is possible through land, air or water, which are called the different modes of transport. On land we use trucks, tractors etc., to carry goods; train, bus, cars etc. to carry passengers. In air, we find aeroplanes, helicopters to carry passengers as well as goods. Similarly in water we find ships, steamers etc., to carry goods and passengers. All these are known as various means of transport. Let us discuss about various modes of transport. The modes of transport can be broadly divided into three categories.

- Land transport (Road, Railway Pipelines transport, Ropeway transport).
- Water transport (Inland water transport, Ocean transport).
- Air transport.

10.4 AIR TRANSPORTATION

This is the fastest mode of transport. It carries goods and passengers through airways by using different aircrafts like passenger aircraft, cargo aircraft, helicopters etc. Besides passengers it generally carries goods that are less bulky or of high value. In hilly and mountainous areas where other mode of transport is not accessible, air transport is an important as well as convenient mode. It is mostly used for transporting goods and passengers during natural calamities like earthquake and floods etc. During war, air transport plays an important role in carrying soldiers as well as supplies to the required areas.

Air transport may be classified as domestic and international air transport. While domestic air transport mainly facilitates movement within the country, international air transport is used for carrying goods and passengers between different countries. Air transport is carried out in fixed air routes, which connect almost all the countries.

10.4.1 Advantages of Air Transport

The following are some of the advantages of air transport :

- **High Speed :**

Air transport is the fastest mode of transport and therefore suitable carriage of goods over a long distance requiring less time. There is no substitute for air transport when the transport of goods is required urgently.

- **Quick Service :**

Air transport provides comfortable, efficient and quick transport service. It is regarded as best mode of transport for transporting perishable goods.

- **No Infrastructure Investment :**

Air transport does not give emphasis on construction of tracks like railways. As no capital investment in surface track is needed, it is a less costly mode of transport.

- **Easy Access :**

Air transport is regarded as the only means of transport in those areas which are not easily accessible to other modes of transport. It is therefore accessible to all areas regardless the obstruction of land.

- **No Physical Barrier :**

Air transport is free from physical barriers because it follows the shortest and direct routes where seas, mountains and forests do not obstruct.

- **Natural Route :**

Aircrafts travels to any place without any natural obstacles or barriers. Because the custom formalities are complied very quickly. It avoids delay in obtaining clearance.

- **National Defence :**

It plays a significant role in the national defense of the country because modern wars are conducted with the help of aero planes. Airways has a upper hand a destroying the enemy in a short period.

10.4.2 Disadvantages of Air Transport

In spite of many advantages air transport has a number of disadvantages. These disadvantages are :

- **Risky :**

Air transport is the most risky from transport because a minor accident may put a substantial loss to the goods, passengers and the crew. The chances of accidents are greater in comparison to other modes of transport.

- **Very Costly :**

Air transport is regarded as the costliest mode of transport. The operating cost of aero-planes are higher and it involves a great deal of expenditure on the construction of aerodromes and aircraft. Because of this reason the fare of air transport are so high that it becomes beyond the reach of the common people.

- **Small Carrying Capacity :**

The aircrafts have small carrying capacity and therefore these are not suitable for carrying bulky and cheaper goods. The load capacity cannot be increased as it is found in case of rails.

- **Unreliable :**

Most of the air transports are uncertain and thus, unreliable because these are controlled by weather conditions. It is seriously affected by adverse weather conditions. Fog, snow and heavy rain weather may cause cancellation of some flights.

- **Huge Investment :**

Air transport requires huge investment for construction and maintenance of aerodromes. It also requires trained, experienced and skilled personnel which involves a substantial investment.

10.4.3 Limitations of Air Transport

It has the following limitations :

- It is relatively more expensive mode expensive mode of transport.
- It is not suitable for transporting heavy and bulky goods.
- It is affected by adverse weather conditions.
- It is not suitable for short distance travel.
- In case of accidents, it results in heavy losses of goods, property and life.

10.4.4 Different Means Air Transport

Mean	Domestic air transport	International air transport
	Aeroplanes, Helicopter	Aeroplane

10.5 IMPORTANT TECHNICAL TERMS

- **Aerodrome :**

A defined area on the land or water intended to be used either wholly or in part for the arrival, departure and movement of airport.

- **Aerodrome elevation :**

The elevation of highest points of the landing area.

- **Aerodrome identification sign :**

A sign placed on or adjacent to an aerodrome to aid in identifying the aerodrome from the air.

- **Aerodrome reference point :**

The designated geographical location of an aerodrome.

- **Apron :**

A defined area, on a land aerodrome, intended to accommodate aircraft for purposes of loading or unloading passengers or cargo, refueling, parking or maintenance.

- **Clearway :**

A defined rectangular area on the ground or water at the end of a runway in the direction of take-off and under control of the competent Authority selected or prepared as a suitable area over which an aircraft may make a portion of its initial climbs to a specified height.

- **Holding bay :**

An area where aircraft can be held, or bye-passed, to facilitate efficient ground traffic movement.

- **Instrument runway :**

A runway intended for the operation of aircraft using non-visual aids.

- **Landing direction indicator :**

A device used to indicate visually the direction currently designated for landing and for take-off.

- **Landing area :**

That part of the movement area intended for the landing or take-off run of aircraft.

- **Manoeuvring area :**

That part of an aerodrome to used for the take-off and landing of aircraft associated with take-off and landing, excluding aprons.

- **Markers :**

Objects, other than landing direction indicators, wind direction indicators and flags, used to indicate obstruction or to convey aeronautical information by a day.

- **Marking :**

Signs displayed on surfaces in order to convey aeronautical information.

- **Movement area :**

That part of an aerodrome intended for the surface movement of aircraft, including manoeuvring area and aprons.

- **Non-instrument runway :**

A runway intended for the operation of aircraft using visual approach procedures.

- **Runway :**

A defined rectangular area on a land aerodrome prepared for landing and take-off run of aircraft along its length.

- **Runway selected basic length :**

The length selected by the competent authority as a basis for the design of runway and associated physical characteristics of the land aerodrome.

- **Runway visual range :**

The maximum distance in the direction of take-off or landing at which the runway or the specified lights or markers delineating it can be seen from a position above a specified point on its centre line at a height corresponding to the average eye-level of pilots at touchdown.

- **Shoulders :**

An area, adjacent to the edge on a paved surface so prepared as to provide a transition between the pavements and the adjacent surface for aircraft running off the pavement.

- **Signal area :**

An area on an aerodrome used for the display of ground signals.

- **Stoppage :**

A defined rectangular area on the ground at the end of a runway in the direction of take-off designated and prepared by the competent authority as a suitable area in which an aircraft can be stopped in the case of an interrupted take-off.

- **Taxiway :**

A defined path on a land aerodrome selected or prepared for the use of taxiing aircraft.

- **Threshold :**

The beginning of that portion of the runway usable for landing.

- **Reference point :**

That position of the aerodrome whose reference point shall be permanently established and shall be given in terms of the nearest second of latitude and longitude. The position of the same shall be near to the geometric centre of the landing area as in practicable.

- **Aerodrome elevation :**

The aerodrome elevation shall be given in terms of the nearest meter or feet.

10.6 AIRPORT COMPONENT

An airport has to major components
- Airside
- Landside Distinction

Airside :

The following airside features are depicted on the (airport layout plan) ALP :
- Runways, runway shoulders, blast pads, runway marking.
- Taxiways, taxiway shoulders, aprons.
- Navigational Aids (ILS, PAPI, MALS, MALSR, rotating beacon, segmented circle).

- Boundaries and dimensions associated with Object Free Areas (OFA's), Runway Safety Areas (RSA's), Runway Protection Zones (RPZ's), Building Restriction Lines (BRL's), Glide Slope Critical Areas.

Landside :

The following landside features are depicted on the ALP :

- Major buildings with building indentification numbers.
- Parking areas, fencing.
- On-airport access roads, adjacent off-airport roadways, railroads.
- Other physical features including ten-foot topographic contours, stream, lines, the earthen dam and Cement Creek Reservoir.

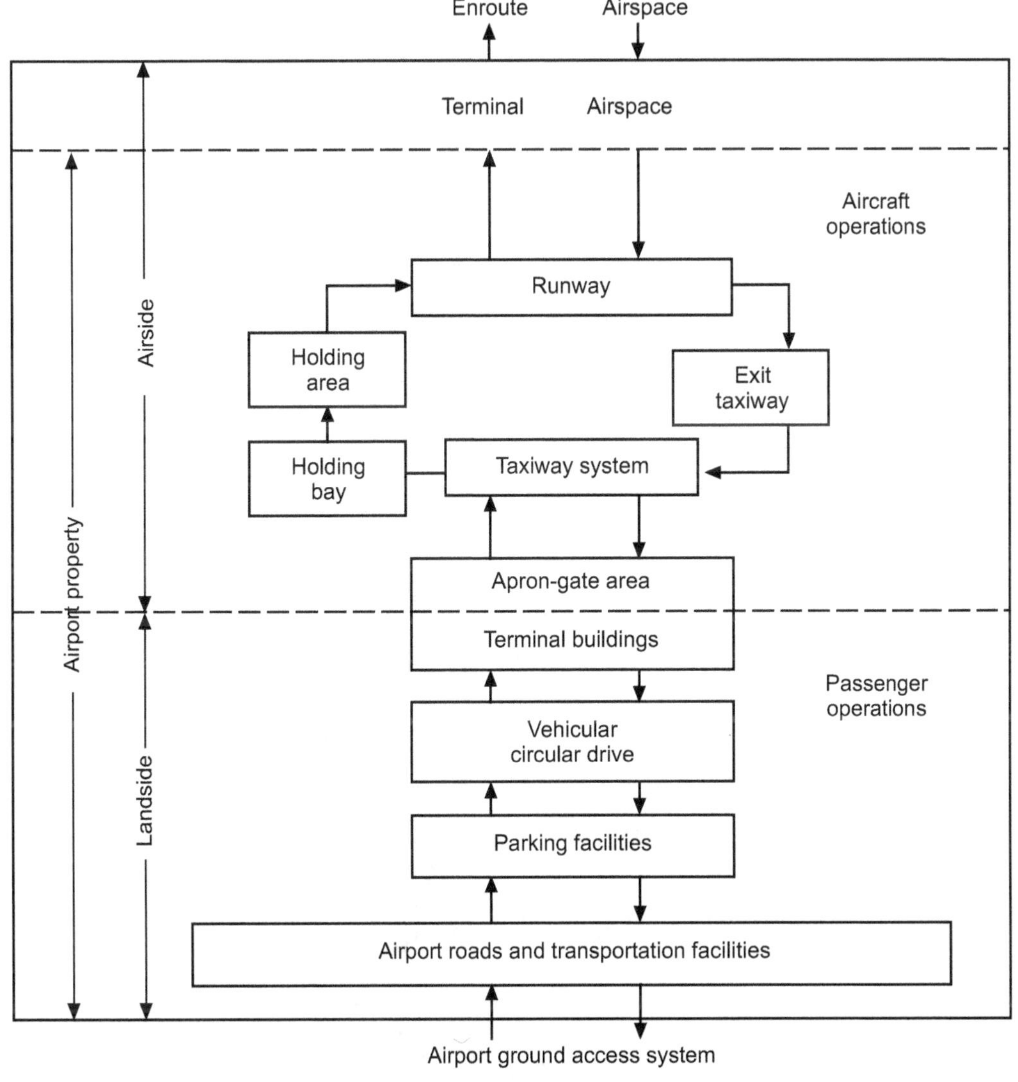

Fig. 10.2

Proposed landside development areas are depicted as shaded/hatched. These areas show locations suitable for hangars and other aviation related structures.

A runway, the most essential component of an air-port, enables landing and take-off of airplanes. For all but the crudest airports, it is a paved strip. Many air-ports have more than one runway. Parallel runways are two runways laid out in the same direction to accommodate operations when the capacity of a single runway is exceeded.

Taxiways provide a convenient means for air-craft to enter and exit a runway. They are usually paved strips connecting runways with each other and with aircraft parking area.

Parking aprons are typically paved areas adjacent to a terminal building that aircraft uses as an approach to the building and to stop to permit passengers and crew to enter or exit the aircraft. Aprons usually incorporate fuel systems, electrical power supply, and facilities for servicing aircraft.

A terminal building usually is incorporated in an airport to provide a transition for passengers and crew from ground to air and vice versa. It houses waiting rooms for passengers and facilities for baggage and cargo handling. Also, it general contains airline ticketing counters and offices. It is served by automobile access roads, and typically parking spaces for autos are provided nearby.

Control towers are built at many busy air ports for air-traffic control. They provide a raised area from which traffic controllers can observe run-ways, taxiway and aprons.

10.7 AIRPLANE PARTS AND FUNCTION

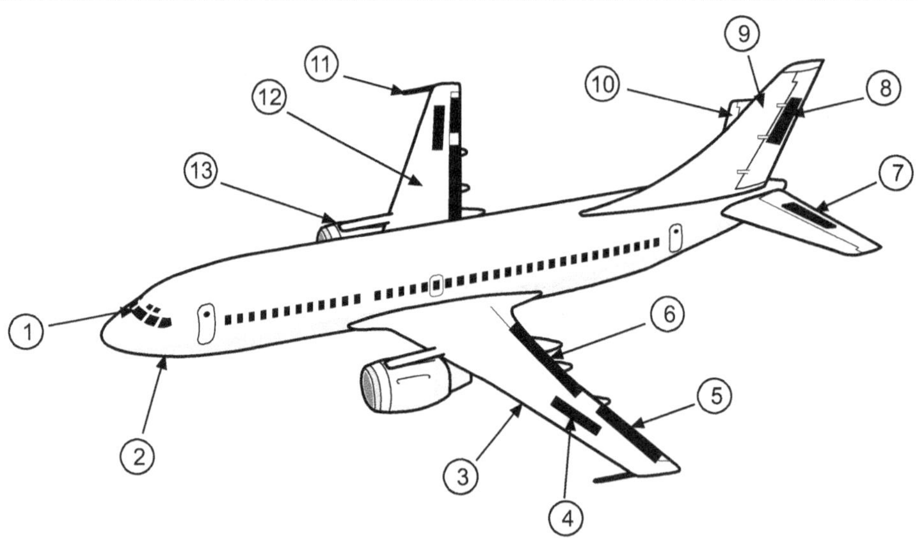

Fig. 10.3

Sr. No.	Airplane Part Name	Function
1.	Cockpit	Command and control
2.	Fuselage	Hold things together-carry payload
3.	Slats	Increase lift, drag and roll
4.	Spolier	Change lift, drag and roll
5.	Aileron	Change roll
6.	Flaps	Increase lift and drag
7.	Elevator	Change pitch
8.	Rubber	Change yaw
9.	Vertical Stabilizer	Control Stabilizer
10.	Horizontal Stabilizer	Control pitch
11.	Winglet	Decrease drag
12.	Wing	Generate lift
13.	Turbine Engine	Generate thrust

10.8 AIRPORT PLANNING

10.8.1 Planning for Airport Development

Airport planning can be divided into two categories, airport system planning and individual airport planning. Airport system planning deals with the interaction between airports, as well as the planning of airports at a regional or national level. Such planning is required for national or statewide funding schedules that support airport development and for ensuring a systematic approach to the allocation of funding among the many eligible airport. It covers the management of multiple airports in the large metropolitan region.

As for the second category, comprehensive planning for the development of a specific airport is usually in an airport master plan. Such a master plan is list of comprehensive concepts for long term development of an existing airport or construction of a new airport and presents the complete development concepts, utilizing graphical representation where appropriate and the data and rationale upon which the plan is based. The basic common objectives are :

- Developing and presenting the facilities of the airport, airspace infrastructure and vicinity land uses, at present and in the future.
- Estimating the environmental effects of facility construction and operation.
- Forecasting future air transportation demands to determine the requirement capacity for each facility at each time phase.
- Scheduling of development phases in the plan, and planning financial support for the implementation plan.

- Evaluating costs and benefits and economic gain of various alternatives airport development concepts.

10.8.2 Economic Impacts and Economic of Airport Development

Since transport demand is a derived demand, user benefits are demonstrated self evidently by the revealed demand. However, the costs to provide all the required services should be carefully considered and compared with their economic benefits. The most salient benefits of airport development are those derived from local employment and the stimulation of the regional economy. A major commercial airport contributes lot of jobs to the local economy and the presence of a convenient airport is instrumental in companies' decisions to locate in the region. The most notorious disadvantages of airport development and operation are noise and other environmental impacts. The mitigate the problems associated with environmental impacts, substantial capital resources are frequently required.

A large one-time investment is required to develop a commercial airport and its ongoing operation can be generating quite considerable continuous annual revenue. So part of airport planning is to be determine if the development of the airport will be profitable, which entails detailed analysis of the costs and revenues resulting from airport operation. It is generally recognized that large commercial airports with high utilization rates can be operated as successful business. Their revenues can cover their full costs, including capitals charades. However, some small and medium sizes airport cannot generate enough profit to cover full costs including capital costs.

10.9 AIRCRAFT CHARACTERISTICS

Following are the characteristics of a conventional type air craft

Aircraft capacity

- Aircraft speed
- Aircraft weight and wheel arrangement
- Fuel spilling
- Jet blast
- Minimum circling radius
- Minimum turning radius
- Noise
- Range
- Size of aircraft
- Take off and landing distance
- Type of propulsion
- Tyre pressure and contact area

10.9.1 Impacts of Aircraft Characteristics on Airport Design

Advances in aircraft technology have led to improvements in the system performance of air transportation. Technological advances in speed, range and operating systems have greatly contributed to the high growth rate of the industry. As a major component in an air transportation system, an airport should accommodate future changes in aircraft design and performance associated with overall improvements of system performance. Airlines expect to operate any type of aircraft with low direct operating costs to serve market need properly. Consequently, while airlines choose which types of aircraft to operate with view to maximizing their economic efficiency, the airport need to provide landing fields for airlines while maximizing operational safety and efficiency. Furthermore, gradually increasing concerns for the environmental factors are influencing airport design, partly through influence on aircraft technology.

First, runway length continually increased until the 1960s to accommodate faster and larger aircraft. Then, improvement in engine techniques led to stabilization and even decrease in runway length in the 1980s and 1990s until the 1960s; airlines had selected aircraft with the sole consideration of economic efficiency through low operating costs. Since then, however, noise problems surrounding airports have forced airlines to compromise between costs and aircraft noise levels. Generally, long-range aircraft require longer runways for take-off and landing than medium and short-term aircraft. The required length for each aircraft type is determined by the aircrafts' design capability and the safety regulations.

The required strength of the landing field is determined by the weights of operated aircrafts such as absolute weights, weight per wheel, pressure per wheel, and frequency of operation. The distribution of the weight between the main gears and the nose gear varies according to aircraft type and its centre of gravity. Aircraft manufactures publish a variety of data on the weight of each aircraft type, such as maximum landing weight, operating empty weight, zero fuel weight, etc.

Aircraft dimensions, defined by the wingspan and fuselage length, influence the size of the aircraft movement area and the configuration of the terminal building. The length of the fuselage are the factors that determine queuing distances and the spacing of pre takeoff waiting areas. The minimum radius swept by the extremity of the aircraft determines the size of apron and parking space. It is important to understand the aircrafts geometry of movements. The largest radius is the critical factors with respect to clearance to buildings or adjacent aircraft. The width of taxiway is the influenced by the track width between the wheels, and the spacing of taxiways is determined mainly by the wingspan.

10.9.2 Main Aircraft Characteristic

Types of aircraft, wingspan, length, wheel base, wheel track, runway length, passenger capacity, maximum weight etc. are the main characteristics of airport.

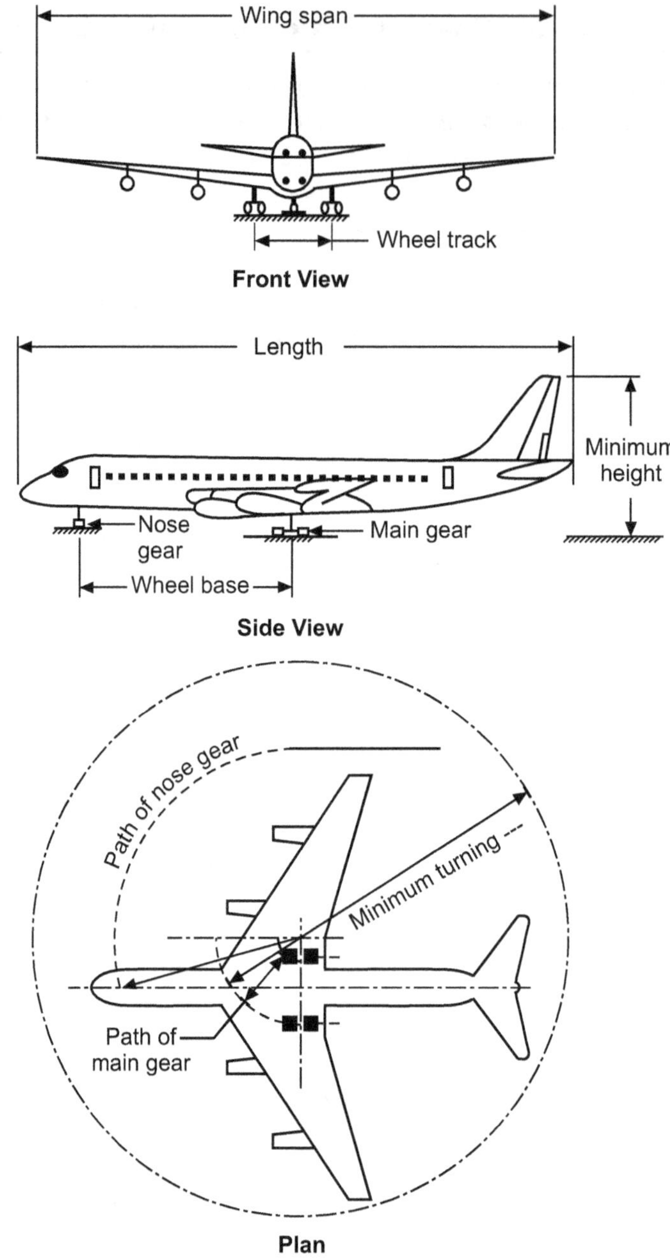

Fig. 10.4 : Aircraft dimensions

10.9.2.1 Aircraft Characteristic for Airport Planning

- Airplane Description
- Airplane Performance
- Ground maneuvering

- Terminal servicing
- Operating conditions, and
- Pavement Data

These airplane characteristics data is required for general airport palnning.

The airport palnner may also want to consider the information presented from following organizations which is also useful for planning of airport and regarding future aircraft growth trends :

- Aerospace Industries Association
- Airports Council International
- Air Transport Association of America
- International Air Transport Association
- International Coordinating Council of Aerospace Industries Association
- International civil aviation organization.

10.9.2.2 Airplane Description

General Airplane Characteristics

- **Maximum Design Taxi Weight (MTW)** : Maximum weight for ground maneuvering as limited by aircraft strength (MTOW plus taxi fuel).
- **Maximum Design Landing Weight (MLW)** : Maximum weight for landing as limited by aircraft strength and airworthiness requirements. (This is the maximum weight at the start of the take-off run.)
- **Operating Empty Weight (OEW)** : Weight of structure, power plant, furnishing, systems, unusable fuel and other unusable propulsion agents and other items of equipment that are considered part of a particular airplane configuration. OEW also includes certain standard items, personnel, equipment and supplies necessary for full operations, excluding usable fuel and payload.
- **Maximum Design Zero Fuel Weight (MZFEW)** : Maximum weight allowed before usable fuel and other specified usable agents must be loaded in defined sections of the aircraft as limited by strength and airworthiness requirements.
- **Maximum Payload** : Maximum design zero fuel weight minus operational empty weight.
- **Maximum Cargo Volume** : The maximum space available for cargo.
- **Usable Fuel** : Fuel available for aircraft propulsion.

General Airplane Dimensions

- Ground Clearances
- Interior Arrangements
- Cabin Cross Section
- Lower Compartment
- Door Clearances

10.9.2.3 Airplane Performance

- General Information
- Payload-Range
- FAR Takeoff Runwa Length Requirements.
- FAR Landing Runway Length Requirements.

10.9.2.4 Ground Maneuvering

General Information

For ease of presentation, these data have been determined from the theoretical limits imposed by the geometry of the aircraft and where noted, provide for a normal allowance for the slippage. As such, they reflect the turning capability of the aircraft in favourable operating circumstances. The data should only be used as guidelines for determining such parameters and to obtain the maneuvering characteristics of this aircraft type. In the ground operating mode, varying airline practices may demand that more conservative turning procedures be adopted. Airline operating techniques will vary in level of performance over a wide range of circumstances throughout the world. Variations from standard aircraft operating patterns may be necessary to satisfy physical constraints within the maneuvering area, such as adverse grades, limited space, or high risk of jet blast damage. For these reasons, ground maneuvering requirements should be co-ordained with the using airlines prior to layout planning.

- Turning Radii, No Slip Angle
- Minimum Turning Radii
- Visibility from Cockpit
- Runway and Taxiway Turn Paths
- Runway Holding Bay (Apron)

10.9.2.5 Terminal Servicing

Fig. 10.5 shows the typical airplane servicing arrangement.

- Airplane Servicing Arrangement (Typical)
- Terminal Operations, Turnaround Station
- Terminal Operations, En Route Station.
- Ground Service Connections.
- Engine Starting Pneumatic Requirements.
- Ground Pneumatic Power Requirements.
- Preconditioned Airflow Requirements.
- Ground Towing Requirements.

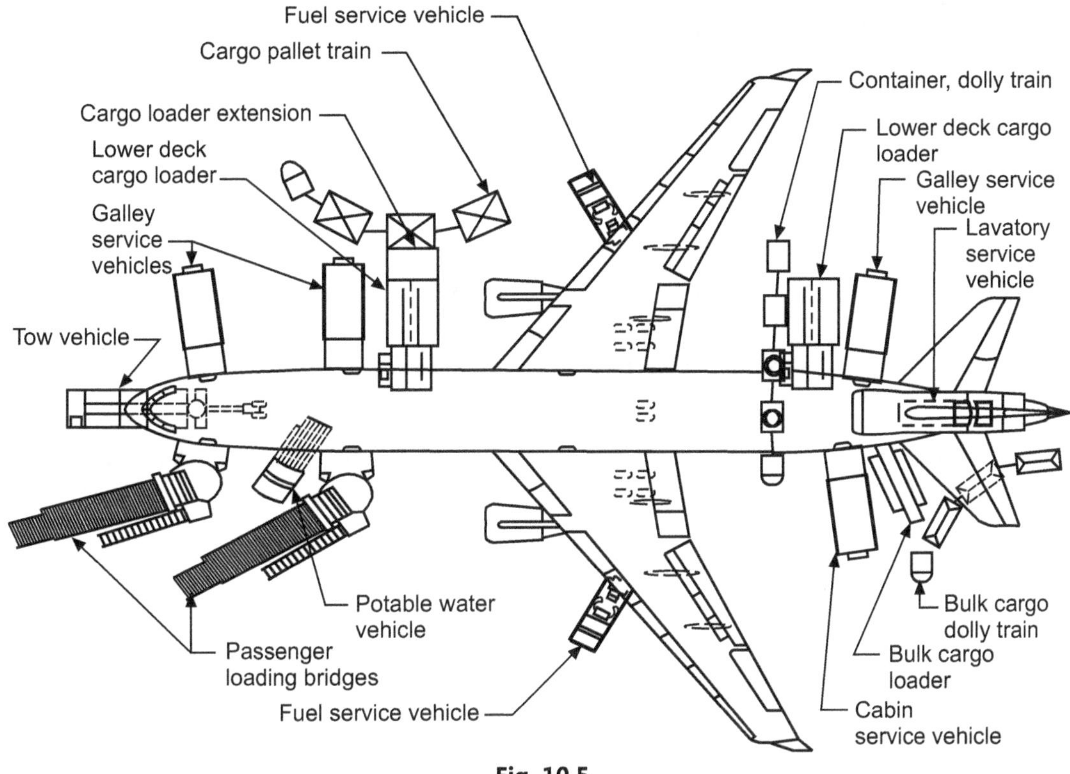

Fig. 10.5

10.9.2.6 Operating Conditions

- Jet Engine Exhaust Velocities and Temperatures
- Airport and Community Noise

10.9.2.7 Pavement Data

- **General Information :** A brief description of the pavement charts that follow will help in the their use for airport planning. Each airplane configuration is shown with a minimum range of four loads imposed on the main lading gear to aid in interpolation between the discrete values shown. Pavement requirements for commercial airplanes are customarily derived from the static analysis of loads imposed on the main landing gear struts.

- Footprint.
- Maximum Pavement Loads.
- Landing Gear Loading on Pavement.
- Flexible Pavement Requirements.
- Flexible Pavement Requirements, LCN Conversion.
- Rigid Pavement Requirements.
- Rigid Pavement Requirements, LCN Conversion.

10.10 AIRPORT PLANNING

Airport planning requires more intensive study and forethought as compared to planning of other modes of transport. This is because aviation is the most dynamic industry and its forecast is quite complex. Unlike rail, road and water transportation, air transportation has yet not reached a steady state in design.

It is very difficult to predict for the airport, satisfying the present needs, whether this airport shall prove adequate for the new type of aircrafts which may emerge every years hence, therefore it is required to keep in touch with recent trends and also with likely future projections in the aviation activities.

10.11 SELECTION OF SITES FOR AIRPORT

The selection of a suitable site for an airport depends upon the class of airport under consideration. However, if such factors are required for the selection of the largest facility are considered, the development of the airport by the stages will be made easier and economical.

The factors listed below are for the selection of a suitable site for a major airport installation.

- Regional Plan
- Airport Use
- Proximity to other airport
- Ground accessibility
- Topography
- Obstructions
- Visibility
- Wind
- Noise nuisance
- Grading, drainage and soil characteristics
- Further development
- Availability of utilities from town
- Economic Consideration

10.12 SURVEY FOR SITE SELECTION

Keeping in view the various factors which influence the site selection, the types of surveys to be carried out at each site are as follows.

- Traffic survey
- Metrological Survey
- Topographical Survey
- Soil Survey
- Drainage Survey
- Material Survey

(a) Traffic Survey :

To determine the amount of air traffic including the anticipated traffic for future.

(b) Metrological Survey :

To determine direction, duration and intensity of wind, rainfall, fog, temperature and barometric pressure etc.

(c) Topographical Survey :

Topographical Survey is very important :

- To prepare contour map showing three meter contours and other features such as tress, streams, hillocks etc.
- To prepare a map showing such consideration objects as pole lines, building roads etc. as per obstruction, removal and marking. These maps will be helpful in the jobs of clearing, grading and drainage.

(d) Soil Survey :

To determine soil types from the trial pits and ground water table. This assists in the design of runway, taxiway, terminal buildings and the drainage system.

(e) Drainage Survey :

Drainage survey is very important for following reasons :

- To determine the quantity of storm water for drainage, this can be obtained from the rainfall intensity and contour maps.
- To locate possible outlets for drain water in the vicinity of the site.
- To study the possibility of intercepting or diverting fully the natural streams or nallas flowing towards the site under consideration.

(f) Material Survey :

To ascertain the availability of suitable constructional materials at a reasonable cost and the mode of transportation of these materials to the site.

10.13 DRAWING TO BE PREPARED FOR AIRPORT PLANNING

The survey to be conducted at the various possible sites will guide in the site selection of the most suitable site. The following plans are to be prepared for the finally selected site.

- Topographical plan showing original and finally proposed contours, locations of trees, streams, buildings, roads, property lines etc.
- Obstruction map showing safe approach and take-off zone as well as turning zone for aircraft.
- Drainage plan, showing the layout of proposed buildings, runway, taxiways and drainage network. The proposed ground contours and the cross-sections and longitudinal profiles of runways and taxiways should also be plotted. The size of pipe, percentage gradients and such other details of the drainage network should be clearly indicated.
- Airport master plan, showing the ground contours layout of runways, taxiways, terminal buildings control towers, hangers, aprons, roads, and parking areas etc. It

provides means by which an airports may be efficiently constructed in stages to meets both the immediate and the further requirements. Preparation of a master plan guide in the development of airport in a logical sequence there by resulting in a better airport at a minimum cost.

POINTS TO REMEMBER

- Importance of transport and of importance of air transport.
- Advantages and disadvantages of air transport.
- Important technical terms related to air transport.
- Airplane different parts and its function.
- Aircraft characteristic for airport planning i.e.

  (a) Airplane description, (b) Airplane performance, (c) Ground maneuvering, (d) Terminal servicing, (e) Operating conditions and Pavement data.
- Factors required for site selection for major airport.
- Different types of surveys and drawings for airport planning.

QUESTIONS

1. What are advantages and limitation of air transportation ?
2. What is an aircraft ? State its characteristics and explain any 2 in brief.
3. Explain the planning concept of airport buildings.
4. What are the characteristics of a good airport planning ?
5. Discuss in detail the factors affecting the choice of selection of site for an airport.
6. Enlist various component parts of airplane and its function.
7. What are the facilities to be provided in the terminal building of an international airport ?
8. Define the following terms :

(1) Airport reference temperature	(7) Apron
(2) Airside	(8) Clearway
(3) Clam period	(9) Holding bay
(4) Airport capacity	(10) Runway
(5) Aerodrome	(11) Raxiway
(6) Aerodrome elevation	(12) Threshold

11.1 TERMINAL DESIGN AND AIRPORT LAYOUT

1. Terminal Area :

It is the portion of an airport other than the landing area. It is serves as a focal point for activities on the airport. It includes terminal and operational buildings; vehicle parking area, aircraft service hanger etc.

2. Building and Building Area :

The purpose of airport building is to provide shelter and space for various surface activates related to the air transportation. As such they are panned for the maximum efficiency, convenience and economy. Location of building area with respect to runway and taxiway should provide adequate space for further expansion of all structures.

3. Terminal Building :

Terminal building usually refers to a building mainly used for passengers, airline and administration facilities. Its layout is such as to offer the emplaning passengers, the convenient and direct access from the vehicle platform or street side of the building. A type plan terminal building as evolved and supplied by the government Architect should be followed.

4. Typical Airport Building :

The pattern of runway to be finally adopted at the site depends upon the volume of air traffic to be handed, direction. Duration and intensity of wind, availability of suitable approaches etc. the following are the basic pattern.

- Single runway
- Parallel runway
- Intersecting runway
- Non-intersecting runways

The actual runway pattern may consist of a combination of two or more number of basic patterns. A typical airport for the runway configuration is illustrated in Fig. 11.5 and 11.6.

Characteristics of airport layout :

- It grants maximum functional efficiency with the minimum utilization of the space.
- It has adequate space for the loading aprons.

- It has sufficient terminal building facilities.
- It provides excellent control tower visibility.
- Minimum cost of construction.
- The operation of landing, taxiing and take-off the aircraft are carried out smoothly without interfering with each other.
- The overall arrangement of the components is such that the further expansion is easily permitted.
- Minimum the taxiway distance between the loading apron and the runway ends.
- Safe approach of runway lengths and approaches.

11.2 TYPICAL AIRPORT LAYOUT

The layout of an airport mainly depends on the basic patterns or configurations of the runways. The other airport elements are then correlated in such a fashion that an integrated layout is developed giving smooth flow of traffic, keeping the taxi distances to a minimum, providing shortest route for the passengers etc. Fig. 11.1 to Fig. 11.4 shows typical airport layouts.

Fig. 11.1 shows an airport layout for a single runway. Fig. 11.2 shows an airport layout with two parallel runways.

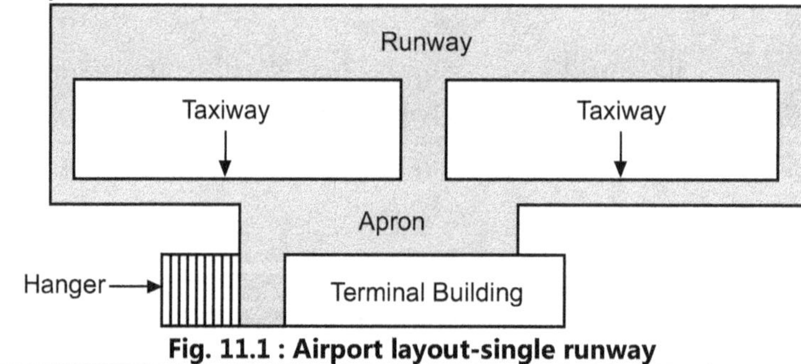

Fig. 11.1 : Airport layout-single runway

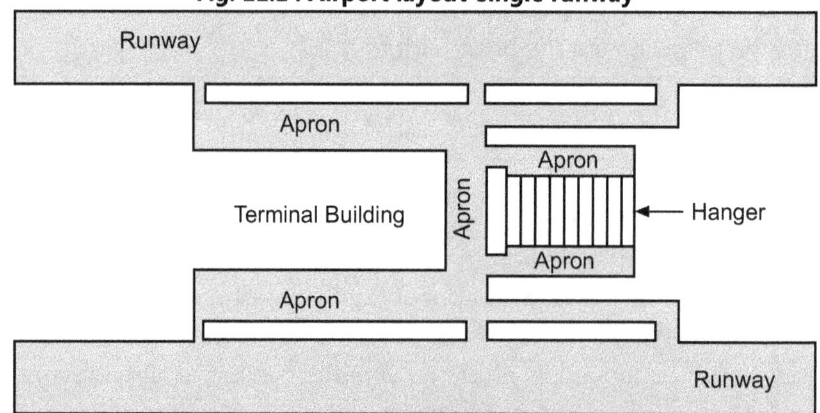

Fig. 11.2 : Airport layout-two parallel runway

Fig. 11.3 shows an airport layout with three non-intersecting runways. Fig. 11.4 tangential runways airport layout squiring small length of taxiways.

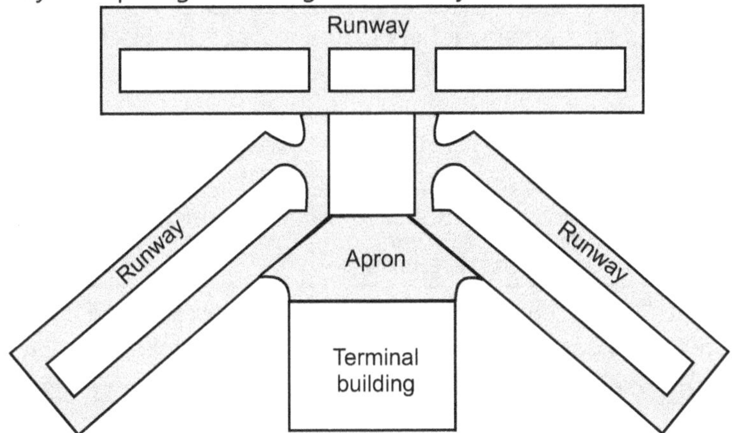

Fig. 11.3 : Airport layout – three non-intersecting runways

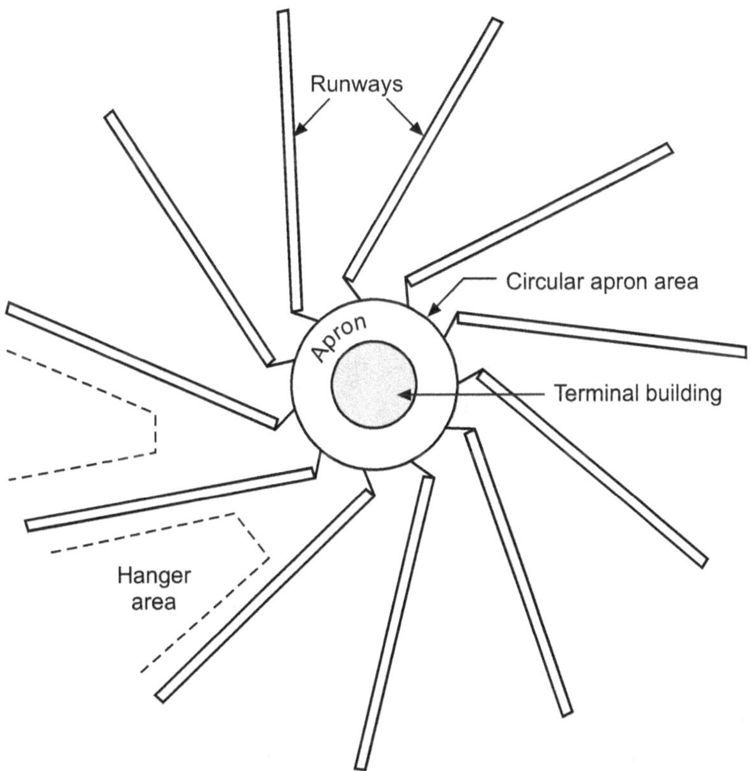

Fig. 11.4 : Airport layout – tangential runways

11.3 AIRPORT OBSTRUCTIONS

11.3.1 General

The site for airport should be selected that, it does not obstruct the safe landing and take-off of aircrafts. Steps should also be taken to curb possibility of developing any future obstruction. The purchase of the entire flight approach areas, and the turning areas, to prevent the undesirable growth of structure is not always feasible economically. As such zoning ordinances regarding the permissible height of structures and the land used within the airport boundary, need implementation, as soon as the site is selected for the airport.

11.3.2 Classification of Obstructions

The term objects as used below includes both temporary and permanent objects. Obstruction to safe air navigation are broadly divided into the following two categories :

- Objects protruding above, certain imaginary surfaces, as prescribed in Fig. 11.5 and Fig. 11.6.
- Objects exceeding their limiting heights above the ground surface in approach zones and turning zones.

11.3.3 Definitions of imaginary Surfaces and Areas

1. Take-off climb area :

A specified portion of the surface of the ground beyond the end of a runway or clear-way in the direction of take-off. It is an area within which it may be necessary to take one or more of the following actions :

- restrict the creation of new obstruction.
- remove objects or mark objects in order to ensure a satisfactory level of safety and efficiency for aero plane operations during the take-off climb phase.

2. Take-off climb surface :

A specified portion of an inclined plane or other specified surface limited in plan by the vertical projection of the take-off climbs area and chosen so as to establish the heights above which the action described in (i) above may need to be taken.

3. Approach area :

The specified portion of the surface of the ground preceding the threshold. It is an area within which it may be necessary to take one or more of the following actions : Restrict the creation of the new obstructions; remove objects or mark objects in order to ensure a satisfactory level of safety and regularity for aero plane operations during the approach phase.

4. Approach surface :

A specified portion of an inclined plane or a combination of planes limited in plan by the vertical projection of the approach area and chosen so as to establish the heights above which the action described in (ii) above may need to be taken.

5. Inner horizontal surface :

A specified portion of a horizontal plane located above an aerodrome and its immediate environment. This surface establishes the height above which it may be necessary to take one or more of the following actions :

- restrict the creation of new obstructions;

- remove objects or mark objects to ensure a satisfactory level of safety and regularity for aero planes maneuvering visually in the aerodrome circuit before commencing the approach phase.

6. Conical Surface :

A specified surface sloping upwards and outwards from the periphery of the inner horizontal surface and establishing the vertical limits above which it way be necessary to take one or more of the following actions :

- restrict the creation of new obstructions;
- remove the object or mark objects in order to ensure a satisfactory level of safety and regularity for aeroplanes maneuvering visually in the vicinity of an aerodrome.

7. Transitional surface :

A specified surface sloping upwards and outwards from the edge of the approach surface and from a line originating at the end of the inner edge of each approach area, drawn parallel to the runway centerline in the direction of landing. The transitional surface establishes the heights above which it may be necessary to take one or more of the following actions :

- restrict the creation of the new obstructions;
- remove objects or mark objects in order to ensure a satisfactory level of safety and regularity for aeroplanes flying at low altitude and displaced from the run way centre line in the approach or missed approach phases.

8. Outer horizontal surface :

A specified portion of a horizontal plane located above the environment of an aerodrome beyond the horizontal limits of the conical surface, where applicable. The surface establishes a level above which consideration may need be given to the control of new construction to facilitate practicable or efficient instrument approach procedures.

11.3.4 Take-Off Climb Area and Surface

A take-off climb area shall be established for each runway direction intended to be used for the take-off of aeroplanes.

The limits of the take-off climb area shall comprise :

- An inner edge of specified length perpendicular to the centre line of the runway at the end of the clear way, where such is provided, or at a distance of 60 m. (200 ft.) where the runway code latter A, B or C. 30 m. where the runway code letter is D or E; measured horizontally (in the direction of take-off), from the end of the runway, when no clear way is provided.

- Two sides originating at the ends of the inner edge, diverging uniformally at a specified rate from the vertical projection of the take-off flight path to a specified maximum lateral distance and continuing thereafter at that distance from the vertical projection of the flight path to produce a specified overall width referred to as the 'Final Width'.

- An outer edge normal to the vertical projection of the take-off flight path.

The dimensions of the take-off climb area measured horizontally shall be not less than the appropriate dimensions specified in Table 11.1 except that a lesser length may be adopted where such lesser length would be consistent with procedural measures adopted to govern the outward flight of aeroplanes.

Table 11.1 : Dimensions of the take-off climb area

Runway code letter	A, B, C		D	E
	Main take-off runways	other runways		
1	2	3	4	5
Length of inner edge	180 m	180 m	80 m	60 m
Divergence (each side)	12.5 %	12.5 %	10 %	10 %
Final Width	1200 m	1200 m	580 m	380 m
Length	1500 m	12000 m	2500 m	1600 m
Slope	2 %	2.5 %	4 %	5 %
	(1 : 50)	(1 : 40)	(1 : 25)	(1 : 20)

11.3.5 Approach Area and Surface

An approach area shall be established for each runway direction intended to be used for the landing of aeroplanes. The limit of the approach area shall comprise :

- An inner edge of specified length perpendicular to the centre line of the runway at a distance of 60 m. where the runway code letter is A, B, or C; 30 m. where the runway code letter is D or E; measured horizontally from the threshold away from the direction of landing;

- Two sides criginating at the ends of the inner edge diverging uniformly at a specified rate from the extended centre line of the runway;
- An outer edge parallel to the inner edge.

The dimensions of the approach area measured horizontally shall not be less than the appropriate dimensions specified in Table 11.2 below :

Table 11.2 : Dimensions of the approach area

Runway Code Letter	Instrument approach	Other approach areas			
	A, B, C	A, B	C	D	E
1	2	3	4	5	6
Length of inner edge	300 m	150 m	150 m	80 m	60 m
Divergence (each side)	15 %	10 %	10 %	10 %	10 %
Length	15000 m	3000 m	3000 m	2500 m	1600 m
Slope for inner 300 m (10,000 ft) of length	2 % (1 : 50)	2.5 % (1 : 40)	3.33 % (1 : 30)	4 % (1 : 25)	5 % (1 : 20)
Slope beyond 300 m	2.5 % (1 : 40)	-	-	-	-

The lower limit of approach surface shall be a horizontal line in the vertical plane containing the inner edge of the approach area and at the elevation of the mid-point of the threshold.

The slope of the approach surface measured above the horizontal line in the vertical plane containing the centre line of the runway shall be as specified in Table 11.2 above.

11.3.6 Inner Horizontal Surface

The inner horizontal surface shall be contained in a horizontal plane located 45 m above the elevation datum determined by the Component Authority. The inner horizontal surface shall extend to a horizontal distance of at least

400 m.	..	Where the runway code letter of longest runway is A, B or C;
2500 m.	..	Where the runway code letter of longest runway is 'D';
2000 m.	..	Where the runway code letter of longest runway is 'E';

measured from a point or points on the aerodrome as determined by the Component Authority.

Fig. 11.5 and 11.6 show all the imaginary surfaces.

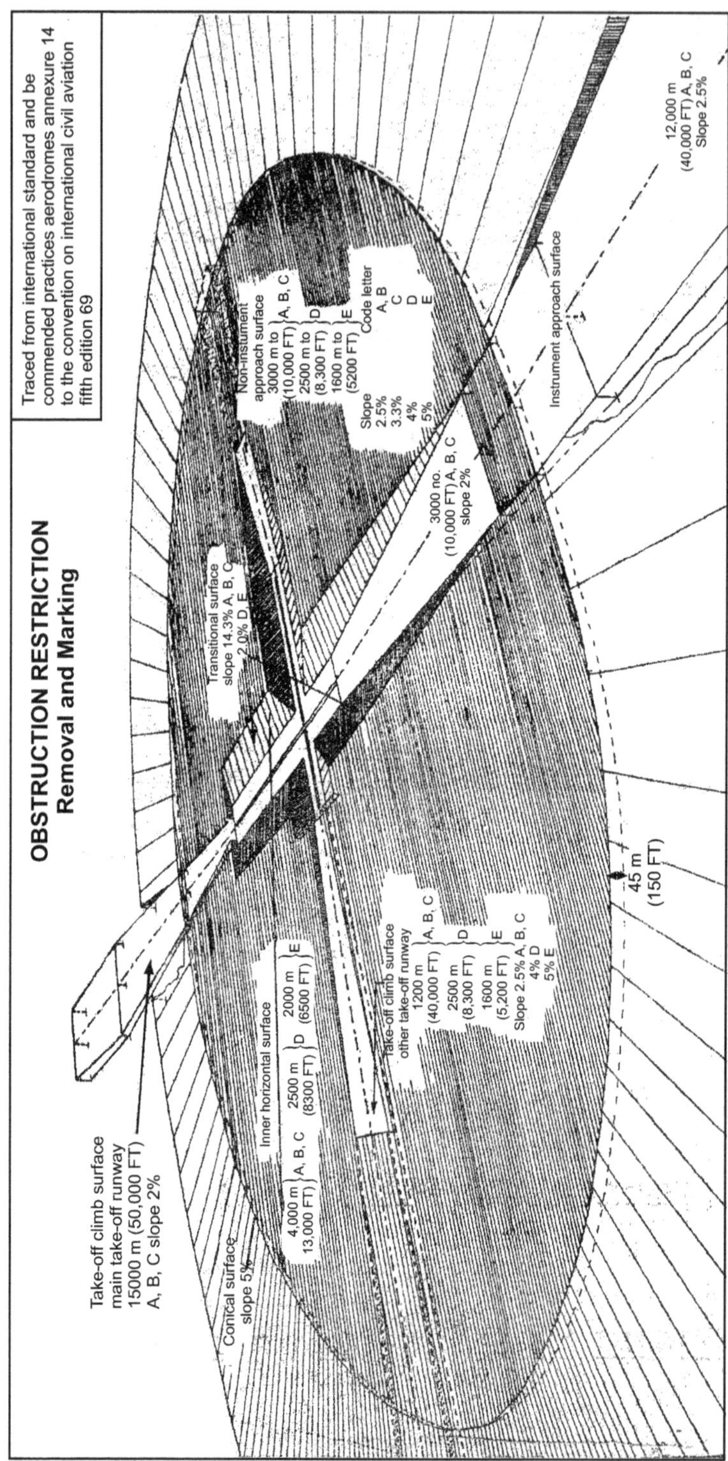

Fig. 11.5 : Perspective View (Plan) of a Typical Land Aerodrome

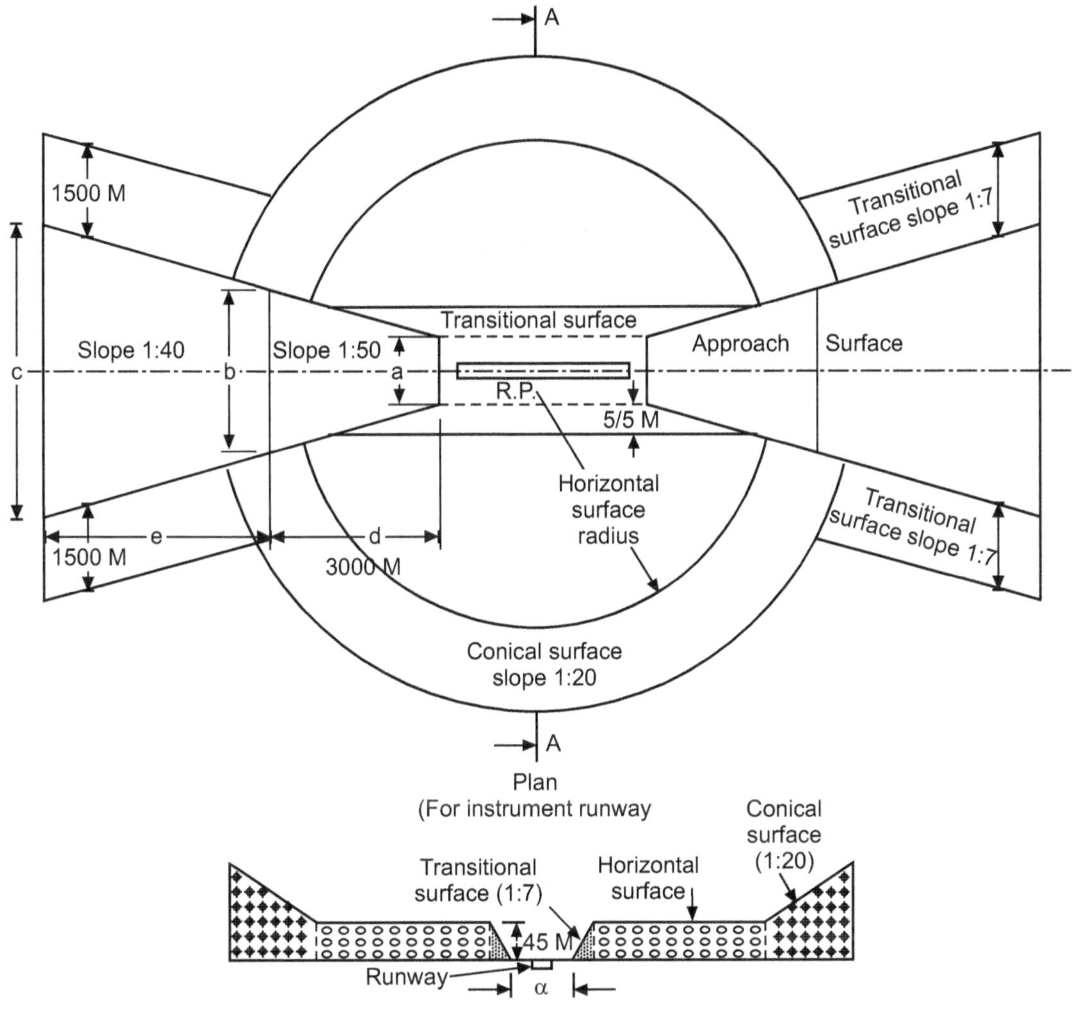

Section on AA

Diamensions of Approach Surface

i) For Instrumental Runway
    a = 300 m, b = 1200 m.
    c = 4800 m, d = 3000 m.
    and E = 1200 m.

ii) For Non-Instrumental Runway
    a = 75 m (For Small Airport)
       = 150 m (For Large Airport)
    b = 675 m (For Small Airport)
       750 m (For Large Airport)
    c = b (for All Size Airport)
    d = 3000 m (For All Size Airport)

Slope is 1 : 20 for small airports and 1 : 40 for Large Airports

Fig. 11.6 : Imaginary surfaces showing obstruction zones

11.3.7 Approach Zone

During landing, the glide path of an aircraft varies from a steep to a flat slope. But during take-off the rate of climb of aircraft is limited by its wing loading and engine power. As such wide clearance areas, known as approach zones are required on either side of runway along the direction of landing and take-off of aircrafts. Over this area the aircraft can safely gain or loose altitude. The whole of this area has to be kept free of obstructions and as such zoning laws are implemented in this area. The plan of approach zone is the same as that of the approach surface vide Fig. 11.6. The only difference between the two is that while approach surface is an imaginary surface, the approach area indicates the actual ground area.

11.3.8 Turning Zone

If during the take-off, the engine fails or the pilot elects to land for any reason, the aircraft will have to take a turn and come in line with runway before landing. The area of airport, other than the approach area, which is used for turning operation of aircraft is called turning zone. This area may be up to 10 Km. (6 miles) in diameter.

11.4 HOLDING APRON

Holding aprons is the designated portion placed adjacent to the ends of runways for allowing to check aircraft instruments and engine operation prior to take-off and also to wait till clearance for takeoff is given. Holding aprons are usually provided near the runway ends and are made sufficiently large so that if one aircraft is unable to take-off because of some defect of machinery, another aircraft can bye pass it for the take-off.

11.5 LOADING APRONS

The paved area adjacent and in front of the thermal building is known as the apron and it is used for loading and unloading of the aeroplanes as well as for fuelling and minor servicing and check-up of the aeroplanes.

The aeroplanes are berthed on the aprons before they are loaded and unloaded. Hence, the loading apron is also known as the *parking apron*. It is desirable to provide cement concrete pavement for the aprons to resist the effects of jet blast and fuel spillage.

The dimensions of the loading apron depends upon the number of loading positions or gate positions required, the size of aircraft and the parking system to be adopted. The aircraft loading positions or stands are designed by the circles of varying diameters. The span of diameter depends on the wing span, length and turning radius of the aircraft which will use the airport. the number of aircraft stands to be provided is determined from peak aircraft movements per hour. Generally a clearance of 7.5 m is provided between the aircrafts parked on the adjacent aircraft stands.

11.6 HOLDING APRONS

The portion of paved area which is provided adjacent to the ends of runway in case of busy airports is known as the holding apron. They are also sometimes referred to as the run-up or warm-up pads. The taking-off aircraft coming from the loading apron is held on the holding apron for some time so that the aircraft instrument and engine operation may be checked prior to the take-off of the aircraft.

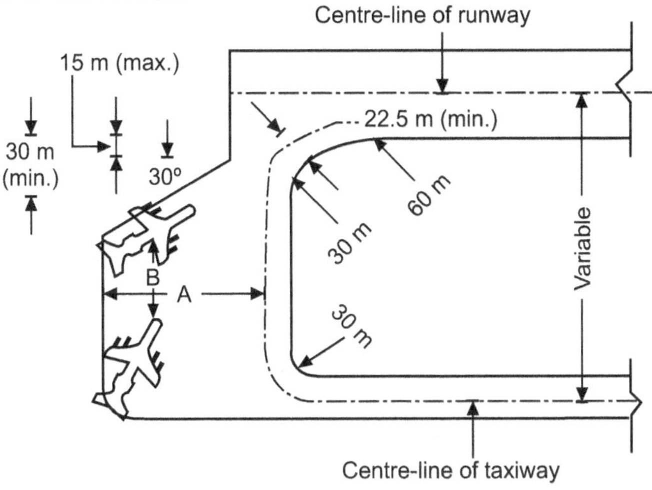

Fig. 11.7

Following points should be noted in concentration with the holding aprons :

1.   Configuration : The holding apron should be of sufficient area to accommodate three or four aircrafts of the largest size expected to be handled by the airport. There are many configurations of the holding aprons. A satisfactory method for establishing the size of the holding apron is to make use of the plastic models of the aircraft. Fig. 11.7 shows the configuration of the holding apron for two aircrafts as suggested by the FAA. The dimensions A and B vary with the type of the aircraft.

2.   Entry to the runway : As far as possible, the holding apron should be located so as to permit aircraft departing therefrom to enter the runway at an angle less than 90°. It will permit the pilot to turn the aircraft rapidly from the taxiway.

3.   Facility of bypass : The holding aprons are made large enough so that if an aircraft is unable to take-off due to any reason, another aircraft ready to take-off can bypass it. If this facility is not provided, the damaged aircraft will have to proceed down the runway at exit at the nearest exit taxiway to reach the terminal area. This would consume more time and reduce the airport capacity.

4.   Holding bays : These are relatively small aprons placed at a convenient location in the airport for the temporary storage of the aircraft. The number of gates at some airports may be insufficient to handle the demand during a busy period of the day. Under such circumstances, the aircrafts are routed by the air traffic control to a holding bay and they are held there until a gate becomes available.

5.   Location : The airport should be permitted to enter the runway as close to the end of the runway as possible. The holding aircraft should be placed outside the bypass route so that the blast from the holding aircraft will not be directed towards the bypass route.

6.   Peak demands : The peak traffic volume at many airports exceeds the capacity of a holding apron. It results in aircraft queues on the taxiway leading to the end of the runway. Despite this situation, the provision of a holding apron is useful for allowing one aircraft to bypass another.

11.7 APRONS (KNOWN AS PARKING LOT)

It indicates a defined area of the airport to accommodate aircrafts for loading and unloading of cargo and passengers, parking, refueling etc. it is usually paved and is located in fornt of the building or adjacent to hangars.

Aprons should be provided as end when necessary to permit the on and off loading of passengers, cargo or mail as well as the servicing of aero planes without interfering with the aerodrome traffic.

11.8 AIRPORT GRADING AND DRAINAGE

11.8.1 Airport Grading

The site selected for airport may have undulating ground profile. The entire area is properly graded to enable the quick drainage of storm water and also to facilitate the construction of various airport elements.

The grading is done with minimum cost of earthwork. Special considerations are given to the grading operations for the airports which are under stage construction. The grading for each construction is planed in such a way that the resulting grades conform well to the final grades. The following points are observed in the grading :

- Generally the formation level of murum bank should be 0.3 m above the ground level.
- The amount of cut and fill should, as far as possible, balance each other. The haulage distance and the amount of earthwork to be moved should also be kept to a minimum.
- Sub-grade soil should, as far as practicable, be of a uniform character to ensure a uniform sub-grade support. If very poor soils such as B. C. soil are met, it should be completely removed till murum or better soil is met with.
- Proper surface and sub-surface to be prepared, drainage should be done to ensure the stability of the pavements and the embankments.
- Grading plans should be prepared to carry the surface water away from the runways, taxiway, apron areas and building area.
- The areas at the end of landing strips should also be graded as a precautionary measure.

- The choice of the equipment for clearing, grading and compaction should be detriment considering the nature of the material involved, the job size, local practice and construction time assigned etc.

11.8.2 Airport Drainage

For design of drainage system certain basis information are collected. This data consists of the following :

- A contour map of the airport site and land adjacent to the site showing all natural water-courses, the area contributing run-off on the site and possible outfalls and ditches is prepared. The contour interval should not be more than 0.6 m.
- An additional map is prepared showing the existing layout of the runways. The contour interval should be 0.3 m. The map should be used as the drainage working drawing.
- The rainfall data that is frequency, intensity and duration of storms for a period of 5 to 10 years from the metrological department. The rainfall intensity duration curve is then developed for the site.
- Centre line profiles of the runway, taxiway and apron area with necessary cross-section are prepared.

11.8.3 Surface Drainage

The design capacity of the storm water system should be adequate.

11.9 RESCUE AND FIRE FIGHTING SERVICES AND EQUIPMENTS AT AERODROME

- Provision of highly mobile rescue vehicles.
- Major vehicles carrying extinguishing media.
- Telephone connection.
- General alarm system for rescue and fire-fighting services at aerodromes.
- Ambulance and medical facilities.
- **Personnel :** Fully trained personnel to operate the rescue and fire-fighting equipment at maximum capacity

11.10 VISUAL AIDS

The pilot needs aids while landing or taking off during all weathers and at every time. The pilot usually takes help of the perspective view of the runway and other ground reference marks during the landing operations. Runway threshold, runway edges and runway centre line are amongst the most essential item which should be clearly visible to the pilot in order to enhance the day-time visibility, runways, taxiways and other allied structures are marked with lines and numbers.

All markings should be clear and should provide the maximum practicable contrast under all conditions. In the day-time during poor weather conditions, or at night, the visibility reduces considerably. It is essential to provide adequate lighting in the airport which should convey the similar information to the pilot during visibility conditions as the markings do in daytime.

11.11 RUNWAY CENTRE LINE MARKING

It shall consist of a broken line of longitudinal strips of uniform length, uniform spaced and extending along the whole length of the runway. The lengths of the stripes shall be at least equal to the lengths of the gaps. The spacing between the beginnings of two successive stripes shall not be less than 50 m and not more than 75 m. The width of the stripes shall be not less than 0.45 m for instrument runways and not less than 0.3 m for other runways.

11.12 THRESHOLD MARKING

The threshold should normally be located at the extremity of the runway unless operational considerations justify the choice of another location. When the threshold is located at the runway extremity, the threshold marking shall normally commence 6m from the runway extremity, but where are runway or taxiway intersections near the threshold the competent authority may exercise direction in adjusting the location of the threshold marking.

Runway threshold marking shall consist of a series of longitudinal stripes of uniform dimensions disposed symmetrically about the centre lines of the runway refer Fig. 11.8.

The stripes shall be extended laterally to within 3 m of the edge of the runway or to a distance of 27 m on either side of the runway centre lines whichever results in the smaller lateral distance. Where the runway designations marking are placed within the threshold marking there shall be a minimum of three stripes on each side of the centre line of the runway. Where the runway designation marking is placed above the threshold marking, the stripes shall be continued across the threshold. The stripes shall be at least 30 m long and approximately 1.80 m wide spacing of approximately 1.80 m between them except where the stripes are continued across the threshold, a double spacing shall be used to separate the two stripes nearest the centre line of the runway and the case where the designation marking is included within the threshold this spacing shall be 22.5 m.

11.12.1 Surface Drainage

The side strips markings should consist of two lines extending between the runway threshold markings parallel to and equidistant from the centre line of the runway. These lines should have an overall width of at least 0.9 m with their outer approximately on the runway, except where the runway is wider than 45 m. when they should have a spacing of 42 m between their inner edges. The stripes markings may consist of a solid line of a series of stripes providing an effect equivalent to a solid line.

11.12.2 Taxi-way Marking

It should be white or yellow colour. The centre line markings of taxiway should be 0.5 m in width and continuous in length. Taxi-holding position markings should be displayed at all intersections of paved taxi-way with runways.

Holding position shall not be closer to the runway centre line than 75 m where the runway code letter is A or B or C Fig. 11.9

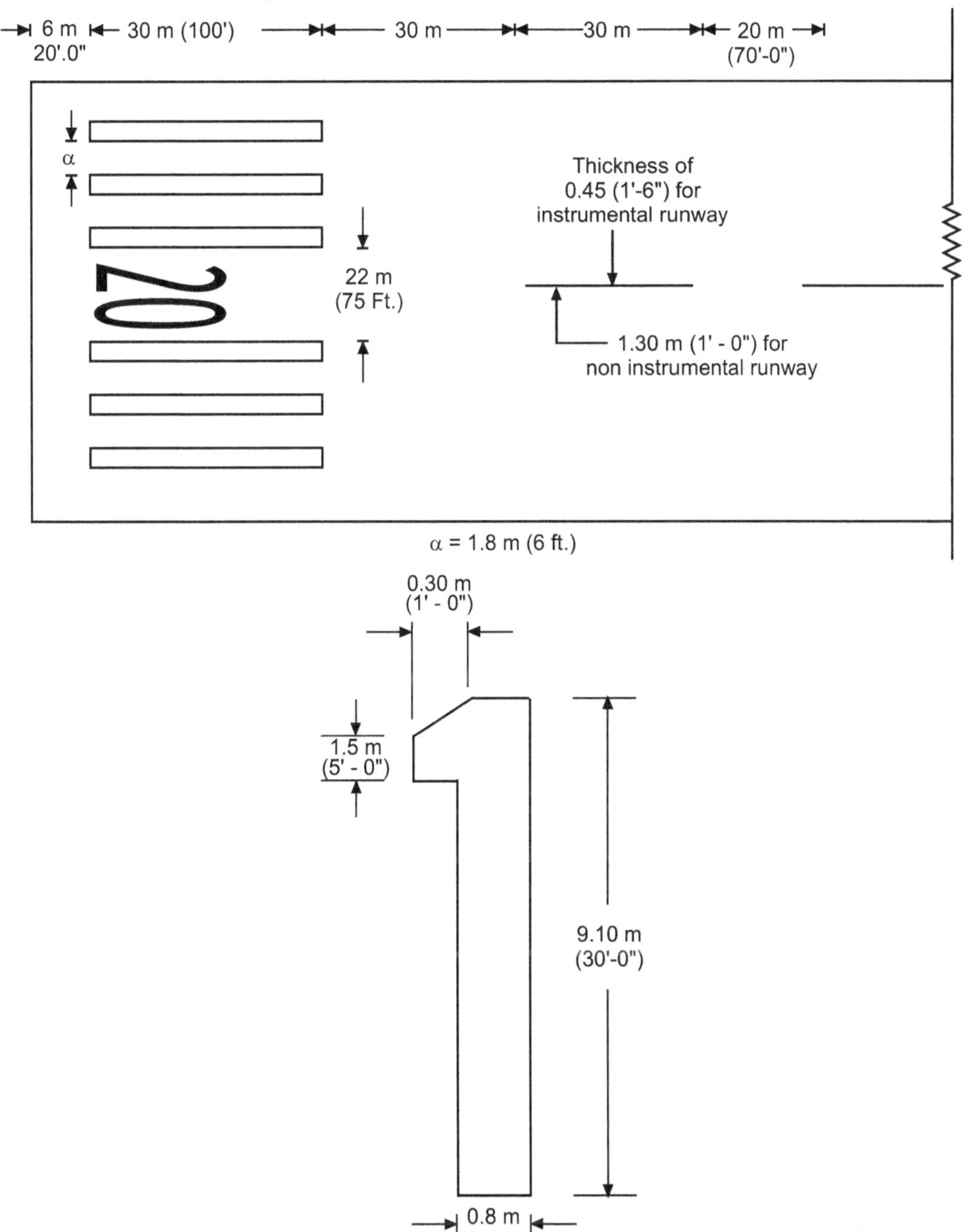

Fig. 11.8 : Lettering for Runway Markings

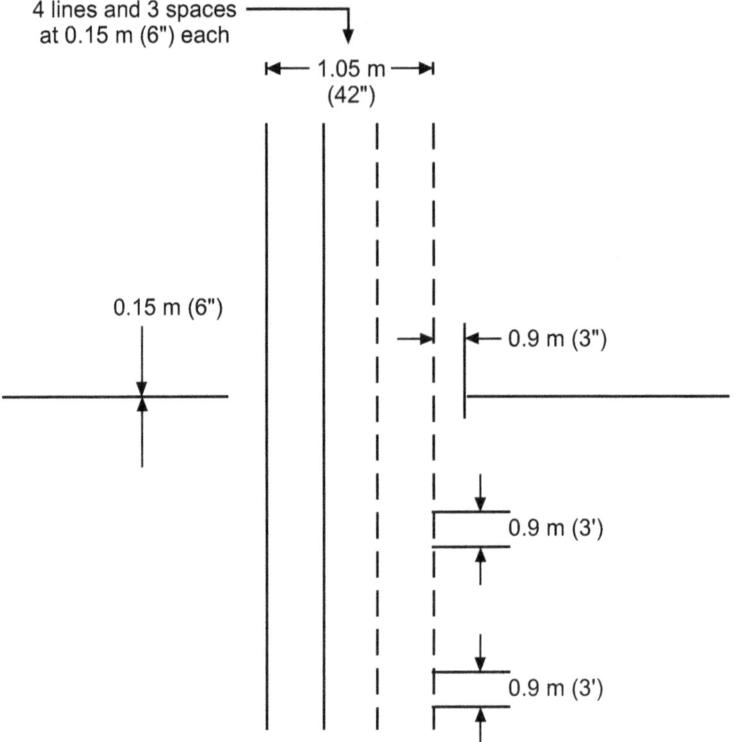

Fig. 11.9 : Taxi Holding Position Marking

QUESTIONS

1. What are the characteristics of a good airport layout ?
2. What are the different control surfaces at an airport ? Explain the concepts of airport zoning with the help of sketches.
3. Describe the various facilities required in a typical airport terminal building.
4. Explain in detail about airport zoning.
5. Write notes on
   (a) Aprons
   (b) Hangers
   (c) Wind Rose Diagram
   (d) Runway Configuration
   (e) Airport Obstruction
6. Draw neat sketch of typical airport layout of single runway.

Chapter 12
RUNWAYS AND TAXIWAYS

12.1 RUNWAY ORIENTATION

Runway is usually oriented in the direction of prevailing winds. The head wind i.e., the direction of wind opposite to the direction of landing and take-off, provides greater lift on the wings of the aircraft when it is taking-off. As such the aircraft rises above the ground much earlier and in a shorter length of runway. During landing the head wind provides a braking effect and the aircraft comes to a stop in a smaller length of runway. Landing and take-off operations, if done along the wind direction, would require longer runway.

12.2 CHOICE OF MAXIMUM PERMISSIBLE CROSS WIND COMPONENT AND COVERAGE

It is not possible to obtain the direction of wind along the direction of the centre line dof runway throughout the year. On some day of the year or hour of the day, the wind may blow making certain angle θ with the centre line of the runway. If the direction of the wind is at an angle to the runway centre line, its component along the direction of runway will be V Cos θ and that normal to the runway centre line will be V Sin θ, where V is wind velocity. The normal component of the wind is called cross wind component and may interrupt the safe landing and take-off the aircrafts.

In the application of the above it should be assumed that landing or taking-off of acroplanes is in normal circumstances precluded when the cross wind component exceeds :

- 37 kph in the case of aeroplanes requiring a runway selected basic length of A or B.
- 24 kph in the case of aeroplanes requiring a runway selected basic length of C.
- 18.5 kph in the case of aeroplanes requiring a runway selected basic length of D and E.

Note : When low runway frictional characteristics are encountered with some frequency, it may be desirable to assume a cross wind component not exceeding 24 Kph in the case of aeroplanes requiring a runway selected basic length A, B or C.

The percentage of time in a year during which the cross wind component remains within the limits as specified above is called wind coverage.

The number of runways at an aerodrome and their orientation should be such that as far as large a percentage of time as practicable, but for less than 95 percent, there is at least one runway for which the surface wind velocity component at right angles to its longitudinal axis will not preclude the landing or taking off of aeroplanes that the aerodrome is intended to serve.

12.3 WIND ROSE

The wind data i.e. direction, duration and intensity are graphically represented by a diagram called wind rose. The wind statistic used should extended over as long a period as possible, preferably not less than five years. Such wind data can be obtained from Office of the Deputy Director General of Observatories, Pune 411 005, known as Simla House.

The wind considered should be that measured in accordance with the procedure prescribed by the World Meteorological Organisation for the measurement of surface wind for synoptic observation.

The observations used should be made at least eight times daily and spaced at equal intervals of time.

A typical wind data and the method of analysis for obtaining the most suitable direction of the runway is given in Table 12.1.

In this table the duration of wind for any one direction covers an angle of 22.5 degrees as shown in Fig. 12.3.

It is assumed that the wind may come from any point within the 22.5 degree sector.

The wind rose diagram can be plotted in two types as shown in Fig. 12.3 and 12.4.

Table 12.1 : Wind Data*

Wind Direction	Duration of wind, percent**			Total in each direction per cent
	6.4 to 25 Kph	25 to 40 Kph	40 to 60 Kph	
1	2	3	4	5
N	7.4	2.7	0.2	10.3
NNE	5.7	2.1	0.3	8.1
NE	2.4	0.9	0.6	3.9
ENE	1.2	0.4	0.2	1.8
E	0.8	0.2	0.0	1.0
ESE	0.3	0.1	0.0	0.4
SE	4.3	2.8	0.0	7.1
SSE	5.5	3.2	0.0	8.7
S	9.7	4.6	0.0	14.3
SSW	6.3	3.2	0.5	10.0
SW	3.6	1.8	0.3	5.7
WSW	1.0	0.5	0.1	1.6
W	0.4	0.1	0.0	0.5
WNW	0.2	0.1	0.0	0.3

Wind Direction	Duration of wind, percent**			Total in each direction per cent
	6.4 to 25 Kph	25 to 40 Kph	40 to 60 Kph	
1	2	3	4	5
NW	5.3	1.9	0.0	7.2
NNW	4.0	1.3	0.3	5.6
Total Percentage				86.5

*   Average of 8 Years period

**   Percentage of time during which wind intensity is less than 6.4 Kph is 100-86.5 = 13.5 percent

This period is called as calm period and this period does not influence the operation of landing and take-off because of low-wind intensity.

12.3.1 Type I Wind Rose

This type of wind rose is illustrated in Fig. 12.3. The radial lines indicate the wind direction and each circle represents the duration of wind. From the Table 12.3 it is observed that the total percentage of time in a year during which the wind blows from North direction is 10.3 percent. This value is plotted along the North direction in Fig. 12.3.

Similarly, other values are also plotted along the respective directions. All plotted points are then joined by straight lines as shown in Fig. 12.3. The best direction of runway is usually along the direction of the longest line on wind rose diagram. In Fig. 12.3 the best orientation of runway is thus along NS direction. If deviation of wind direction up to (22.5° + 11.25°) from the direction of landing and take-off is permissible, the percentage of time in a year during which the runway can safely be used for landing and take-off, will be obtained by summing the percentages of time along NNW, N, NNE, SSE, S and SSW directions. This comes to 57.0 percent. Calm period, i.e. the percentage of time during which wind intensity is less than 6.4 Kph is also added to the above period. The total percentage of the time, therefore, comes to 57.0 + 113.5 = 70.5. This type of wind rose does not account for the effect of cross wind component.

12.3.2 Type II Wind Rose

This type of wind rose is illustrated in Fig. 12.4. The wind data as in the previous type, i.e. of Table 12.3 also used for this case. Each Circle represents the wind intensity of scale 1 cm = 14 Kph. The value centered in each segment represents the percentage of time in a year during which the wind, having a particular intensity, blows from the respective direction. The procedure for determining the orientation of runway from this type of Wind rose in described below :

- Draw three equi spaced parallel lines on a transparent paper strip in such a way that the distance between the two nearby parallel lines (i.e. from centre line of runway to end line of runway) is equal to the permissible cross wind component. This distance is measured with the same scale with which the wind rose diagram is drawn. In Fig. 12.4 the cross wind component is assumed as 25 Kph in this example.

- Place the transparent paper strip over the wind rose diagram is such a way that the centre line passes through the centre of the diagram.

- With the centre of wind rose, rotate the tracing paper and place it in such a position that the sume of all the values indicating the duration of wind, within the two outer parallel lines, is the maximum. The runway should be thus oriented along the direction indicated by the central line. The wind coverage can be calculated by summing-up all the percentages shown in each segment. The percentage value is assumed to be equally distributed over the entire area of the segment. When one of the outer parallel lines of the transparent strip crosses a segment, a fractional part of the percentage appearing in that segment within the outside lines is also counted in the summation. Fractional areas are determined by judgement to the nearest decimal place or by using graph paper.

  In Fig. 12.4 the maximum wind coverage in percent is obtained as : 13.5 (Calm period) + 7.40 + 5.70 + 2.40 + 1.20 + 0.80 + 0.30 + 4.30 + 5.50 + 9.70 + 6.30 + 3.60 + 1.00 + 0.40 + 0.20 + 5.30 + 4.00 + 2.70 + 2.10 + 0.50 + 0.10 + 0.03 + 2.10 + 3.20 + 4.60 + 3.20 + 1.10 + 0.30 + 0.02 + 1.50 + 1.30 + 0.20 + 0.20 + 0.00 + 0.00 + 0.30 + 0.25 = 96.50

- Read the bearing of the runway on the outer scale of the wind rose where the central line on the transperent paper crosses the angular scale. In Fig. 12.4 the best orientation of runway is along the direction where whold circle bearing is zero degree i.e. along 'NS' direction.

- If the coverage provided by a single runway is not sufficient, two or more number of runways are planned in such a manner that the total coverage provided by them is as required i.e. suppose in this case if the coverage comes to 90 percent, the another direction shall be tried by trial and error method so as to get remaining 5 per cent wind coverage, so as to got total coverage of 95 per cent vide para 3.2.

12.4 SELECTED BASIC LENGTH OF RUNWAY

The selected basic length of each runway should be the length that would be required at a level site at sea level in standard atmospheric conditions and in still air to meet the needs of the aeroplanes for which the runway is provided.

Runway selected basic lengths for various types of aeroplanes and as recommended by ICAO Annexe - 14 are given in Table 12.2.

Table 12.2 : Runway-Selected Basic Lengths for Various Types of Aeroplanes

Code Letter	Runway selected basic length
A	2100 m (7000 ft.) and over
B	1500 m. (5000 ft.) upto but not including 2100 m. (7000 ft.)
C	900 m. (3000 ft.) upto but not including 1500 m. (5000 ft.)
D	750 m. (2500 ft.) upto but not including 900 m. (3000 ft.)
E	600 m. (2000 ft.) upto but not including 750 m. (2500 ft.)

Note : All air fields in Maharashtra will have total dimensions of 1830 × 305 m (6000' × 1000'). The basic runway length shall be 1370 m × 45 m (4500' × 150') with 23 m (75') hard side shoulders on each side of runway. The threshold lengths should be 76 m (250') on either side made-up of hard surface.

12.5 ACTUAL LENGTH OF RUNWAY

The selected basic runway length as given in Table 12.2 is for mean sea level elevation, having standard atmospheric conditions. The actual length of the runway at an aerodrome should be not less than its selected basic length corrected to take into account the different local factors that influence the performance of aeroplanes.

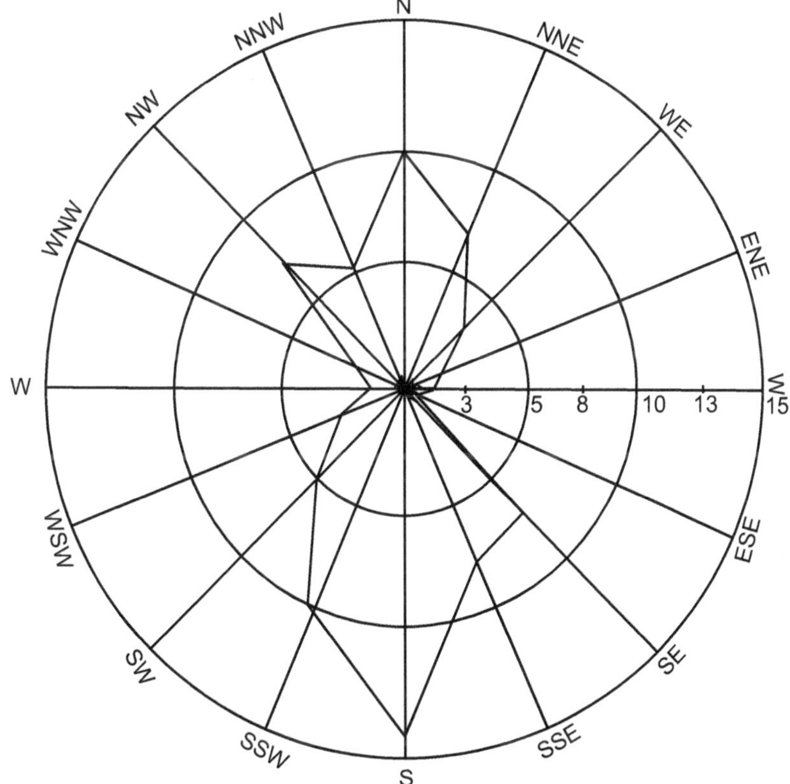

Fig. 12.1 : Wind Rose Diagram (without Consideration of Cross Component)

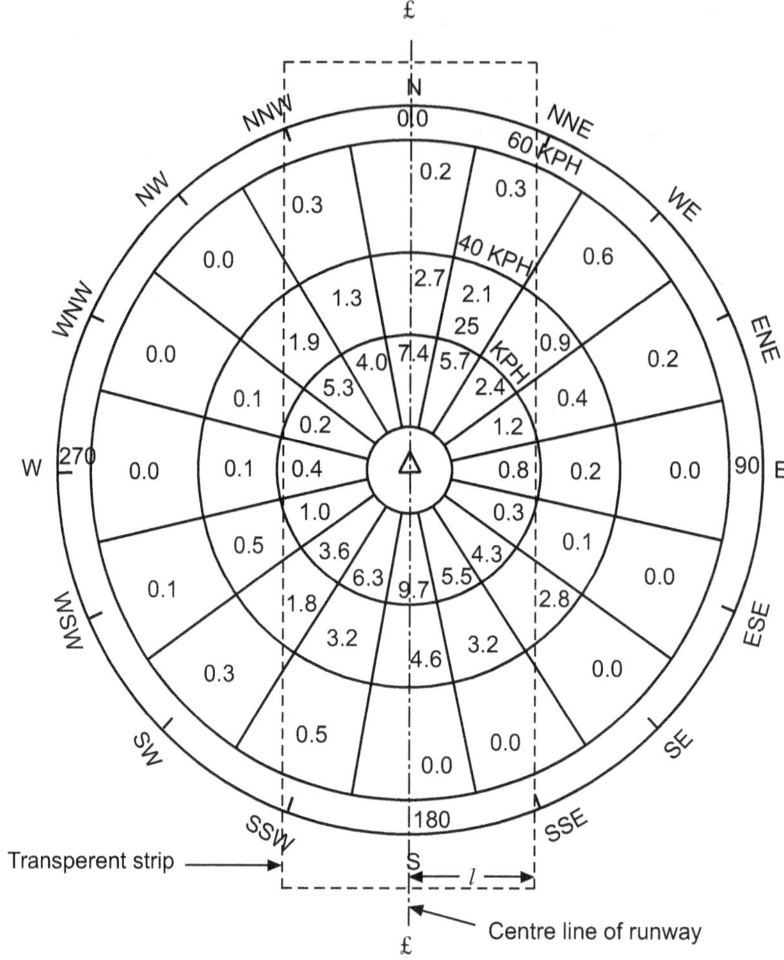

Reference : £ = Permissible cross wind component

Fig. 12.2 : Wind Rose Diagram

(With consideration of Cross Wind Component)

Necessary corrections are therefore applied for change in elevation temperature and gradient for the actual site of construction.

Standard atmosphere is defined as follows :

(a) The air is a perfect dry gas.

(b) The physical constant are :

    (1) Sea Level Mean Molecular Weights :

$$M_o = 28.9644 \times 10^{-3} \text{ K./Mole.}$$

    (2) Seal Level Atmospheric Pressure :

$$P_o = 1013.250 \text{ Millibars}$$
$$= 1.013250 \times 10^5 \text{ newtons m}^{-4}.$$

(3)   Sea Level Temperature :
$$T_o \ = \ 15°\ C\ (59°F)$$
$$T_o \ = \ 288.15°\ K\ C\ (518.67^3 R)$$

(4)   Sea Level Atmospheric Density :
$$P_o \ = \ 1.2250\ Kg.\ m^{-3}$$

(5)   Temperature of the ice point :
$$T_1 \ = \ 273.15°\ K\ (491.67°\ R)$$

(6)   Universal Gas Constant :
$$R \ = \ 8.31432\ Joules\ (°K)^{-1}$$

1. Correction For Elevation :

As the elevation increase, the air density reduces. This in turn reduces the lift on the wings of the aircraft and the aircraft requires greater ground speed before it can rise into the air. The achieve greater speed, longer length of runway in required. ICAO recommends that the basic length of runway should be increased at the rate of 7 percent per 300 m (1000 feet) rise in elevation above the mean sea level.

2. Correction For Temperature :

The rise in airport reference temperature has the same effect as that of the increase in elevation.

The length of runway determined under (A) should be further increased at the rate of one percent for every 1° Centigrade rise of aerodrome reference temperature above the standard atmospheric temperature at that elevation.

The temperature gradient of the standard atmosphere from the mean sea level to the altitude at which the temperature becomes -15.5°C is -0.0065°C per meter. The temperature gradient becomes zero at the elevation above the altitude at which the temperature is -15.5°C.

ICAO further recommends that, if the total correction for elevation plus temperature exceeds 35 percent of the basic runway length, these corrections should then be further checked-up by conducting specific studies at the site by model tests.

The aerodroms reference temperature should be the monthly mean of the mean daily temperature for the hottest month of the year (T_1) (The hottest month being that which has the highest mean daily temperature), plus one-third of the difference between the monthly mean of the maximum daily temperature for the same month (T_2) and the above mentioned monthly mean temperature (T_3), i.e.

$$T_1 \ + \ \frac{T_2 - T_1}{3}$$

Both T_1 and T_2 should be averaged over a period of one year vide Example given below,

3. Correction for Gardent :

Steeper gradient results in greater consumption of energy and as such longer length of runway is required to attain the desired ground speed.

FAA recommends that the runway length after having been corrected for elevation and temperature should be further increased at the rate of 20 percent for every 1 percent of effective gradient. **EFFECTIVE GRADIENT** is defined as the maximum difference in elevation between the highest and the lowest points of runway divided by the total length of runway vide Example given below.

SOLVED PROBLEMS

Problem 12.1 :

The following Problems illustrates the application for the various corrections mentioned above :

(a) Runway selected basic length under standard conditions is 1620 m.

(b) The airport site has an elevation of 270 m.

(c) Reference temperature = 32.90 °C.

(d) Effective gradient of 0.20 per cent.

   (1) Runway length required after correction for elevation

$$= \left(\frac{1620}{1} + \frac{7}{100} \times \frac{1620}{1} \times \frac{270}{300} \right) = 1722 \text{ m}$$

   (2) Determination of standard atmospheric temperature at the given elevation

$$= \quad 15° - 0.0065 \times 270$$

$$= \quad 13.24°C$$

   (3) The airport reference temperature is 32.90°C

      Rise of temperature = 32.90° − 13.24°C = 19.66°C

   (4) Runway length required after correction for temperature

$$= \quad 1722 + \frac{1722}{100} \times 19.66 = 2060.54 \text{ m Say } 2061 \text{ m.}$$

   (5) The total correction in percentage due to Elevation and Temperature

$$= \quad \frac{2061 - 1620}{1620} \times 100 = 27.2 \text{ percent.}$$

      this should be less than 35 percent.

   (6) Runway length after correction for gradient

$$= \quad 2061 + \frac{20}{100} \times 2061 \times 0.20 = 2143.44 \text{ m.}$$

      Rounding the above value to the nearest 10 m.

      Runway length required is 2150 m.

Problem 12.2:

The length of Runway under standard conditions is 2100 m. The Airport site has an elevation of 270 m above mean sea level. Its reference temperature is 30 ℃. If the runway is to be constructed with an effective gradient of 0.20%. Determine the converted runway length. Also, carryout the usual checks as per ICAO.　　　　　**(May 2012)**

Solution:

  (1) Runway length under standard conditions is = 2100 m.

  (2) The air-port site deviation = 270 m.

  (3) Reference temperature = 30°C.

  (4) Effect gradient 0.20%.

  (1) Runway length required after correction for elevation

$$= \left(\frac{2100}{1} + \frac{7}{100} \times \frac{2100}{1} \times \frac{270}{300} \right) = 2232.3 \text{ m say } 2233 \text{ m}$$

  (2) Determination of standard atmospheric temperature at the given elevation

$$= 15° - 0.0065 \times 270$$
$$= 13.24°C$$

  (3) The airport reference temperature is 30°C.

      Rise of temperature = 30 − 13.24 = 16.76°C

  (4) Runway length required after correction for temperature

$$= 2233 + \frac{2233}{100} \times 16.76 = 26.07.25 \text{ m say } 2607 \text{ m}$$

  (5) The total correction in percentage due to elevation and temperature

$$= \frac{2607 - 2100}{2100} \times 100 = 24.14\%$$

  (6) Runway length after correction for gradient

$$= 2607 + \frac{20}{100} \times 2607 \times 0.20$$

$$= 2711.28$$

Rounding the above value to the nearest 10 m.

$$\boxed{\text{Runway length required is 2720 m}}$$

Problem 12.3: *The length of runway under standard conditions is 600 m. The airport site has an elevation of 100 m above mean sea level. Its reference temperature is 28 ℃. If the runway is to be constructed with an effective gradient of 0.5%, determine the corrected runway length. Also carryout the usual checks as per ICAO.*　　　　　**(Nov. 2012)**

Solution:

(1) Runway under standard condition is 600 m.

(b) Airport site elevation = 100 m.

(c) Reference temperature = 28°C.

(d) Effective gradient = 0.5%.

(1) Runway length required after correction for elevation

$$= \left(\frac{600}{1} + \frac{7}{100} \times \frac{600}{1} \times \frac{100}{300}\right) = 614 \text{ m}$$

(2) Determination of standard atmospheric temperature at the given elevation

$$= 15° - 0.0065 \times 100$$

$$= 14.35°C$$

(3) The airport reference temperature is 28°C.

$$\text{Rise of temperature} = 28 - 14.35 = 13.65°C$$

(4) Runway length required after correction for temperature

$$= 614 + \frac{614}{100} \times 13.65$$

$$= 697.82 \text{ m say } \textbf{698 m}$$

(5) The total correction in percentage due to elevations and temperature.

$$= \frac{698 - 600}{600} \times 100 = 16.33\%$$

According ICAO this should be less than 35%.

(6) Runway length after correction for gradient.

$$= 698 + \frac{20}{10} \times 698 \times 0.5$$

$$= 698 + 69.9 = 767.8 \text{ m say } \textbf{768 m}$$

Runway length required = 768 m

12.6 RUNWAY GEOMETRIC DESIGN

The following items need consideration in the geometric design of runways :

- Runway length and Width.
- Width and length of landing strip.
- Transverse gradient.
- Longitudinal and effective gardient.
- Rate of change of longitudinal gradient.
- Sight Distance.

(a) Runway Length and Width :

The basic runway length as recommended by ICAO are shown in Table 12.2. The ICAO recommends that the width of each runway should not be less than :

- 45 m where the runway code letter "A or B".
- 30 m where the runway code letter is "C".
- 23 m where the runway code letter is "D".
- 18 m where the runway code letter is "E".

(b) Width and Length of Landing Strip :

Landing strip consists of the runway, which is a paved area plus the shoulder on either side of the runway. The shoulders are usually upward as they are used during emergency i.e. when there is some abnormality in the aircraft operation. They may at the most be prepared of stabilised soil or be turfed.

The length of strip should extend beyond the end of the runway or stop way if provided for a distance of at least :

- 60 m where the runway code letter is A, B or C.
- 30 m where the runway code letter is D or E.

Width of strip including a runway other than an instrument runway should extend on each side of the centre line of the runway or stop way throughout the length of the strip for a distance of at least :

- 75 m where the runway code letter is A, B or C.
- 40 m where the runway code letter is D.
- 30 m where the runway code letter is E.

Note : The overall dimensions as well as the dimension of runway adopted for Maharashtra are given below Table 12.2.

(c) Transverse Gradient :

Transverse gradient is essential for quick drainage of surface water. If surface water is allowed to paod on the runway, the aircraft can meet servere hazards. To promote the most rapid drainage of water, the transverse slopes of a runway should be as sleep as is compatible with the handing characteristics of the aeroplanes the runway is intended to serve but should not exceed :

- 1.5 per cent where the runway code letter is A, B or C;
- 2 per cent where the runway code letter is D or E.

Transverse slopes on that portion of a strip to be graded should be adequate to prevent the accumulation of water on the survace but should not exceed :

- 2.5 percent for strips where the runway code letter is A, B or C, and
- 3 percent for strips where the runway code letter is D or E.

except that for the first 3 m outward from the runway or stopway edge the slope may be as great as 5 percent to facilitate drainage.

The transverse slope on any portion of a strip beyond that to be graded for acroplanes accidently running off the runway should not exceed an upward slope of 5 percent as measured in the direction away from the runway.

(d) Longitudinal and Effective Gradient :

The longitudinal gradient of runway increases the required runway length.

ICAO gives the following recommendations for the longitudinal slope :

"The slope computed by dividing the difference between the maximum and minimum elevation along the runway centre line by the runway lengths should not exceed :

- 1 per cent where the runway code letter is A, B or C;
- 2 per cent where the runway code letter is D or E;

Along no portion of a runway the logitudinal slope exceed :

- 1.25 per cent where the runway code letter is A or B;
- 1.5 per cent where the runway code letter is C;
- 2 per cent where the runway code letter is D or E.

Additionally for runways of code letter A or B for the first and last quarter of the length of the runway the slope should not exceed 0.8 per cent.

The longitudinal slopes along that portion of the strip to be graded should not exceed -

- 1.5 per cent where the runway code letter is A;
- 1.75 per cent where the runway code letter is B;
- 2 per cent where the runway code letter is C, D or E.

(e) Rate of Change of Longitudinal Gradient :

The abrupt change of longitudinal gradient restricts the sight distance and may also cause premature lift off of the aircraft during the taking off operation. The latter draw-back is observed more in the case of jet and supersonic aircrafts which have high lift-off speeds. The premature lift-off of aircraft will affect the performance of aircraft during its take-off and can also develop structural defects in the aircraft.

Undulations or appreciable changes in slopes located close together along a runway should be avoided. The distance between the points of intersection of two successive curves should not be less than the sum of the absolute numerical values sof the corresponding grade changes multiplied by the appropriate value as follows :

- 3000 m. (1,00,000 ft.) where the runway code letter is A or B;
- 15000 m. (50,000 ft.) where the runway code letter is C;
- 5000 m. (16,500 ft.) where the runway code letter is D or E;

In any case the minimum distance between two successive slope changes should not be less than 45 m.

As an example of how the above mentioned recommendations is applied, consider the case illsutrated in the following profile :

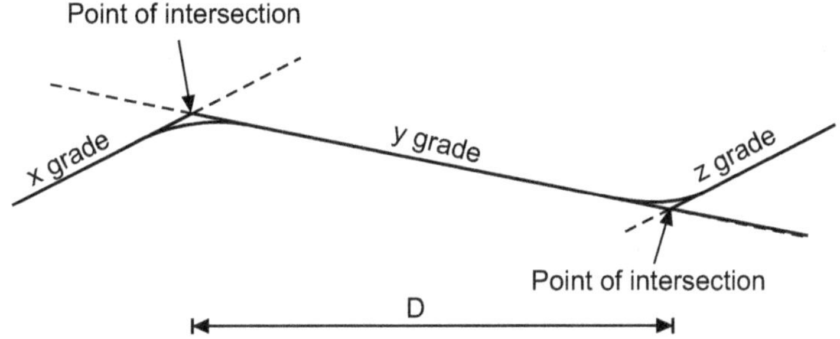

Fig. 12.3 : Profile of centre line of runway

Profile on Centre Line of Runway

D should be at least = 30,000 (/x − y/ + /y − z/) m

/x − y/ being the absolute numerical value of x − y.

y − z/ being the absolute numerical value of y − z.

Assuming

$$x = + 0.01$$
$$y = − 0.005$$
$$z = + 0.005$$

To comply with the specification D should be not less than

30,000 (0.015 + 0.01) m

that is 30,000 × 0.025 = 7.50 m

Where slope changes cannot be avoided, a slope change between two consecutive slopes should not exceed.

- 1.5 per cent where the runway code letter is A, B or C.
- 2 per cent where the runway code letter is D or E.

The transition from one slope to another should be acomplished by a curved surface with a rate of change not exceeding :

- 0.1 percent 30 m (Minimum radius of curvature of 30000 m, 1,00,000 ft.) where the runway code letter is A or B;
- 0.2 percent 30 m (Minimum radius of curvature of 15000 m, 50,000 ft.) where the runway code letter is C;
- 0.4 percent 30 m (Minimum radius of curvature of 7500 m, 25,000 ft.) where the runway code letter is A or B;

(f) Sight Distance :

Where slope changes cannot be avoided, they should be such that there will be an unobstructed line of sight from :

- any point 3 m above the runway to all other points 3 m above the runway within the distance of at least half the length of the runway, where the runway code letter is A, B or C;

- any point 2 m above the runway to all other points 2 m above the runway within the distance of at least half the length of the runway, where the runway code letter is D or E.

12.6.1 Runway Length : Design Objectives

The objectives of the runway length are

- The runway should be long enough to allow for safe arrival and departure of aircrafts likely to be introduced in future.
- The runway length should be compatible with the current equipments at the airport.
- The runway length should be sufficiently long to accommodate.
  - (a) The differences in the skill of pilots.
  - (b) Aircraft types.
  - (c) Landing and take-off operational requirements.

12.6.2 Basic Principle of Runway Design

The basic principle of runway design is the safety of aircraft operations. It takes into account factors such as :

- Take-off and landing characteristics of the most critical aircraft.
- Range of aircraft.
- Altitude of the airport.
- Runway pavement characteristics : Gradients, pavement conditions.
- Weather characteristics and reference to standard atmosphere.

Theoretical methods of determining landing strips are founded on the basis of aerodynamics of aircraft. But experimental data is of great use in the design.

12.6.3 Runway Length Analysis

Following are some terminologies used in analyzing the landing strip requirements :

- **Continued take-off :** When the aircraft continues the take off operation with one or all of its engines in the operating condition is called continued take off.
- **Aborted take-off :** When the aircraft is brought to the stop position within the limits of the paved runway the take off position gets aborted hence it is called aborted take off. The pilot reaction time for decision making after the engine failure is 3 seconds.
- **Take-off distance :** It is the distance travelled by the aircraft from the point of take off to the point which is 10 m above the level of the paved runway centre line.
- **Critical take-off speed :** It is the lowest speed at which pilot can maintain the control of multi engine aircraft in the case one of the engines fails.
- **Balanced field length of the runway and one stop way :** It is the length of the runway which satisfies the length requirements of the critical take off speed (v_{tr}).

12.7 TAXIWAYS

They are the paths on the airfield surface which are designed for taxing of aircraft. They provide the linkage between various parts of the airfield. The speeds of aircraft on taxiways are very less than on the runways. Hence the criteria governing their longitudinal slopes, vertical curves and sight distances are not as stringent as for runways. Their geometric features are governed by F.A.A. and ICAO specifications.

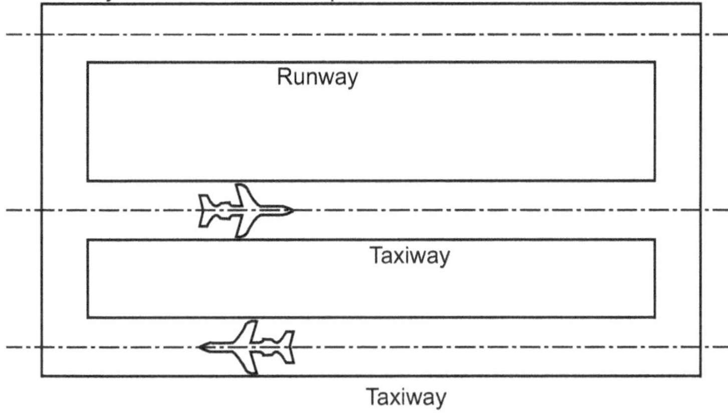

Fig. 12.4 : Runway taxiways

Each taxiway is intended to accommodate only one aircraft at a time. It has not enough space for another aircraft to pass one another. Safe taxing of aircrafts is the objective of taxiway. Various measures taken to ensure safety is passing points, markers, taxiway lights. Taxiways require stronger pavement than runways due to higher loading rate due to aircraft wheels rolling over.

12.7.1 Taxiway Capacity

The runway or gate way capacity falls short of the taxiway capacity. When the taxiway crosses the runway the parameters that decide the taxiway capacity is

- Rate of runway.
- The mix of aircraft type.
- Location (nearness or distantness) of the taxiway with reference to departure end of runway.

FAA has suggested graphical solutions for estimating taxiway capacity.

12.7.2 Design Parameters of Taxiway

The design parameters are affected by density of air-traffic, the configuration of the runway, the location of terminal building and other facilities FAA and ICAO regulations for taxiway design are :

- **Alignment :** It should be direct, straight, simple.

- **Curves :** Large radi should be provided to curves as to ensure minimum taxing speed between the range 30 to 40 Kmph.
- **Instersections :** Speeds are low at intersections. Clear visibility is desired.
- Width of taxiway.
- Pavement widening on curves should be by 5 m with 45 m flare.
- Wing tip clearance (W) on apron taxiway : It is a function of aircraft-type. It varies from 12 m to 25 m.
- Design of longitudinal grade for taxiways.

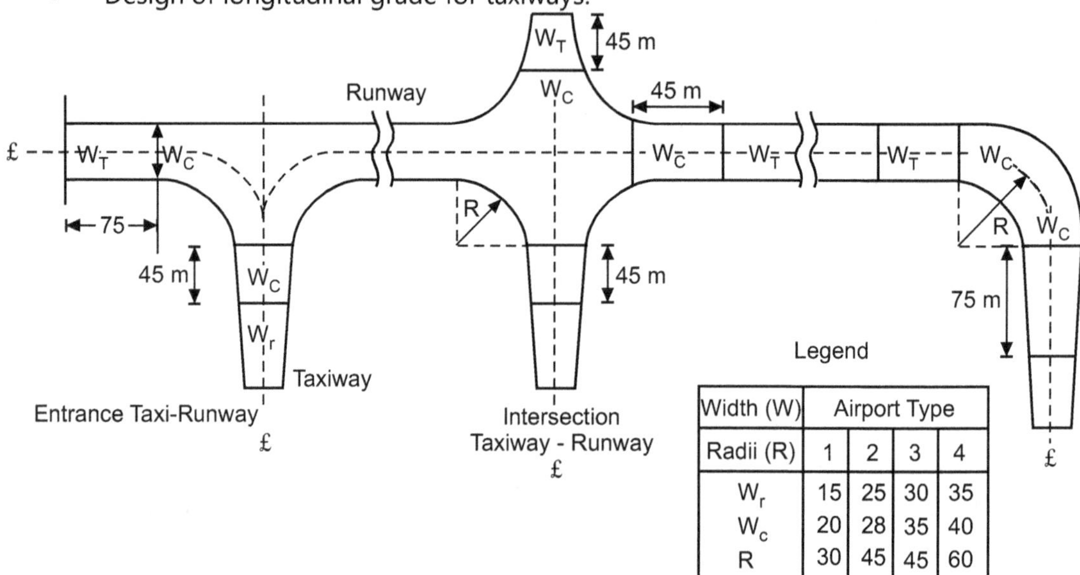

Width (W)	Airport Type			
Radii (R)	1	2	3	4
W_r	15	25	30	35
W_c	20	28	35	40
R	30	45	45	60

Fig. 12.5 : Typical taxi-way

The aircraft speed on the taxiways is less. The precision regarding grades depends on the density of aircraft operations. On taxiways aircraft activities are limited. Therefore, grade regulations are not stringent. In general, grades for runway and corresponding taxiway may be same. For functional airports gradient of 1.5 % is sufficient.

Taxiway vertical curves should be minimum 30 m long for each 1 % grade change. However ICAO relaxation is of 27 m length.

FAA does not point out specific sight requirements for taxiways however where taxiways and runways intersect the analysis of intersection based on the sight distance requirements is suggested.

The gradients of the taxiways should be such that the object 3 m above taxiway should be seen over all the taxiway surface for a distance of not less than 300 m from the object. The actual sight distance requirements will depend on the airport type.

- **Transverse Grade :** The transverse grades for taxiway are similar to that runways.

12.7.3 Types of Taxiways

(1) Exit Taxiway :

Its locations influence the runway capacity. The inclination of taxiway to the runway centre line is determined by the traffic volume during peak period, aircraft type, expected runway occupancy time and desired aircraft maneuverability. The number and location depends on type and mix of aircraft using runway. Generally three exit taxiways are sufficient, one at the centre and two at the ends of the taxiway. Modern runways may have three angled exit taxiways faor each landing direction with several 90° exit taxiways.

The details of common types are given in following figures.

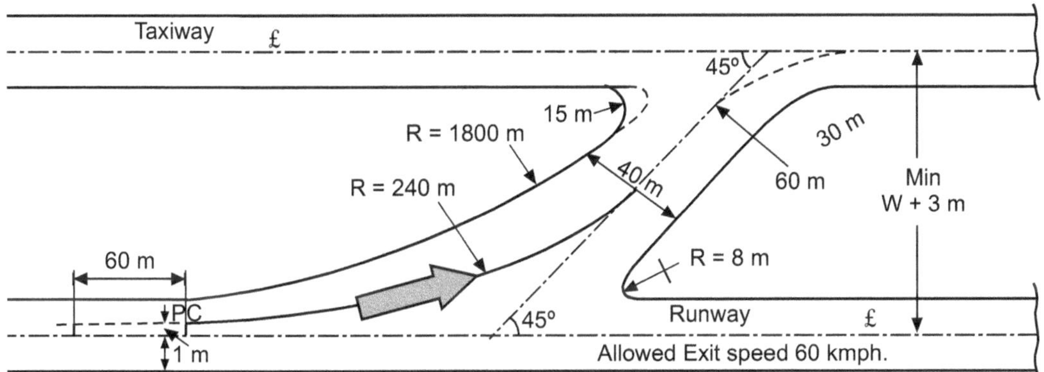

Fig. 12.6 : For Small Aircrafts, 45° Angled Exit Taxiway

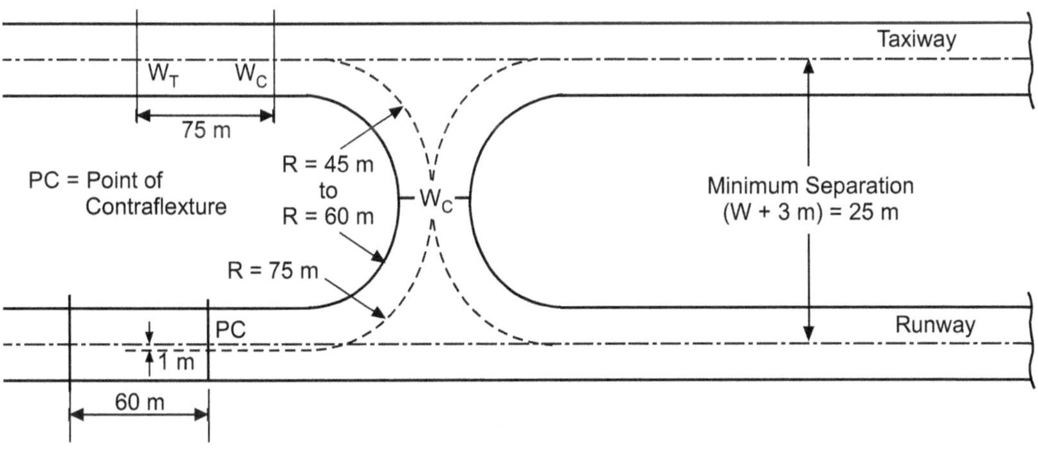

Fig. 12.7 : The 90° Exit Taxiway

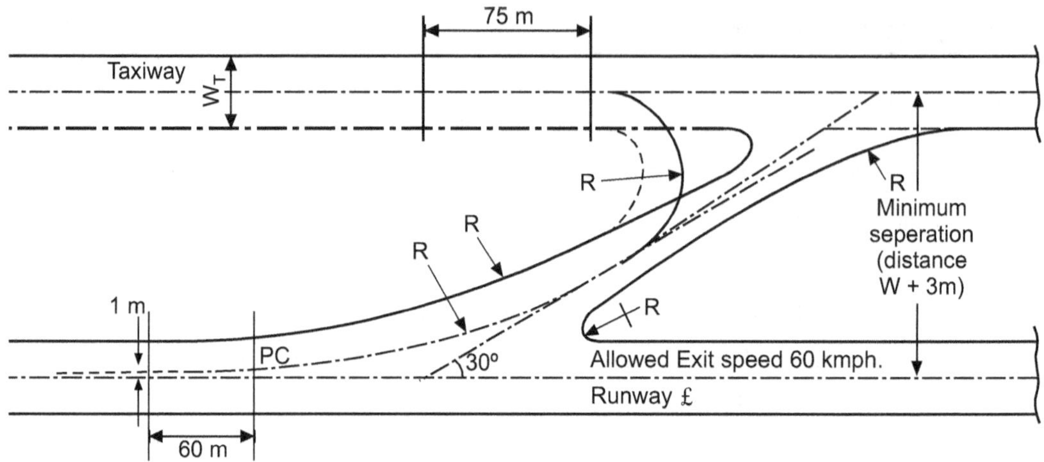

Fig. 12.8 : The 30° Angled Exit for Large Aircrafts

Common types of exit taxiways for large aircrafts

The distance (D) from the threshold to touchdown line for aircraft type and speed ranges from 300 m to 500 m ICAO recommendation of 1.25 m/sec² (4.1/sec and FAA regulation of 13'/sec² for a deceleration rate (a), initial exit speeds are considered while computing the distance from touchdown to ideal exit location. The desired location of high speed taxiway depends on

- Distance from the threshold to touchdown (D).
- Touchdown speed (S_1) 50 m to 75 m/sec.
- Initial exit speed of turn off speed (S_2) (60 kmph).
- Deceleragation rate, (d) 1.3 m/sec².

The distance D is computed using formula.

$$D = \frac{(S_1)^2 - (S_2)^2}{2d}$$

FAA recommends the increase in the distance, D_1 to accommodate increase in airport altitude and temperature. The increase may be 1 % per 100 m of altitude difference over mean sea level 1.5 % per 10°F aobve 59°F.

The distance from threshold in point of contraflex line of the exist curve is generally taken as D + 300 m to 450 m.

(2) Parallel Taxiways :

Three meters margin to minimum wing tip clearance (W) is recommended for parallel taxiways. At high density airports higher speeds and hence larger clearances and separation are desired.

Taxiways interconnect the runway, terminal area and service hangers. Taxiways according to function are classified as return type, branch-type and connecting taxiways, exist taxiways.

The maximum taxing speed range is 30 to 50 Km/hr. for return type and 10 to 20 km/hr for other types. Average declaration/acceleration is limited 1 m/sec^2.

(3) Return Taxiways :

They are aligned parallel to the runway. The separation distance ($L_{r.t}$) is calculated as follows :

$$L_{r.t} = \frac{H_a}{S_{ab}}$$

where, H_a = Height of aircraft.

S_{ab} = Slope of obstruction clearance line for runway shoulders.

The taxiing aircraft should not disturb the gliding path becomes and markers. The center line of the branch, connecting and exit type taxiways may inclined at 30°, 45°, 60° or 90° to the runway center line depending on the turning speed desired.

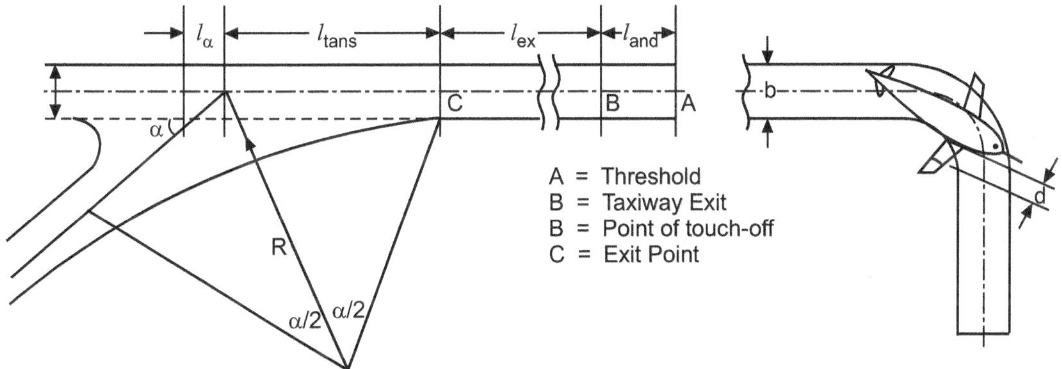

Fig. 12.9 : Return taxiway

The transition curve of clothhoid or cubic parabola is introduced between runway centre line and the circular curve. It controls the centrifugal acceleration. The taxing R_{tax} is calculated by considering taxing speed (V_{tax}), gravitational acceleration (g), banking slope (i) lift of the aircraft wing (Y) and mass of aircraft (m), coefficient of friction (f) as follows.

$$R_{tax} = \frac{V_{tax}^2}{g[i + (1 + Y/m)f]} \qquad \dots \text{(i)}$$

When an aerodynamic lift coefficient for rest condition (C_t) and for landing condition (C_t) and air density if and the velocity of landing $(VI)_t$ wing area S, the taxiing radius is calculated as

$$R_{tax} = \frac{V_{tax}^2}{g\left[i + s\left(\dfrac{C_r V_{tax}^2}{C_1 V_t^2 f}\right)\right]} \qquad \dots \text{(ii)}$$

The taxiing radius is mainly govered by taxiing speed.

The design value of f depends on comfort requirements of the passengers.

12.8 CLASSIFICATION OF AIRPORTS

The classification of airports is necessary for economic planning and efficient design. The airports are classified according to its scale, capacity and functional role.

1. **Function :**
    (a) **Type of Aviation :** General, military, special purpose.
    (b) **Type of Service :** Primary, Commercial, Congestion-relieving airport as an intermediate stage in a flight.
2. **Operation :**
    (a) Level of Service, (b) Range of Flight, (c) All cargo
3. **Region of Operation :**
    (a) International (b) Domestic (c) Intercity Airports
4. **Geographic Destination :**
    Off shore airports, airports at hinter lands, high attitude airports.
5. **Traffic Characteristics :**
    (a) **Traffic Density :** High/medium/Low (scale and capacity) density airports.
    (b) **Nature and Distribution of Airtrips :** (Links to node) Hub airports, non-hub airports.
6. **Facilities Provided :**
    Airports with/without Visual Landing System (VLS) and Instrument Landing System (ILS).
7. **Airport Components :**
    (1) Runway length, (2) Runway pavement surface and type.

Considering the weightages of above factors FAA in 1972 devised a system of classifying airports.

U.S.A. Classification of Airports (1972)

The National Aviation System Plan (NASP) classified airports considering their function and operation. The functional classification takes into account the level of service to the users and capacity defined in terms of traffic density (volume/year) of aircraft operations. The classification of airports in U.S.A. according to activities is done as follows :

Commercial air carrier, general aviation, military airports. Commercial airports have been classified further as Large hub, Medium hub, Small hub, non-hub airports. The classification of airports is shown in Fig. 12.10.

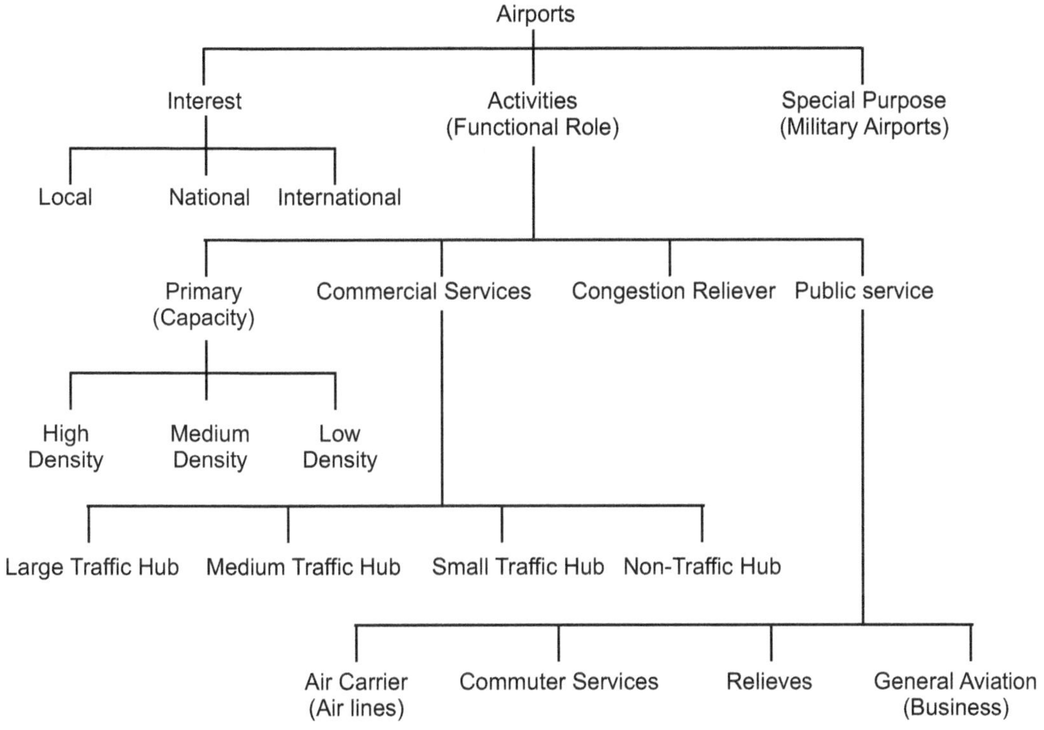

Fig. 12.10 : Classification of Airports in U.S.A.

British Functional Classifications (1978)

In order to develop the airport system in an organised manner airports in U.K. are classified in this way (Fig. 12.11)

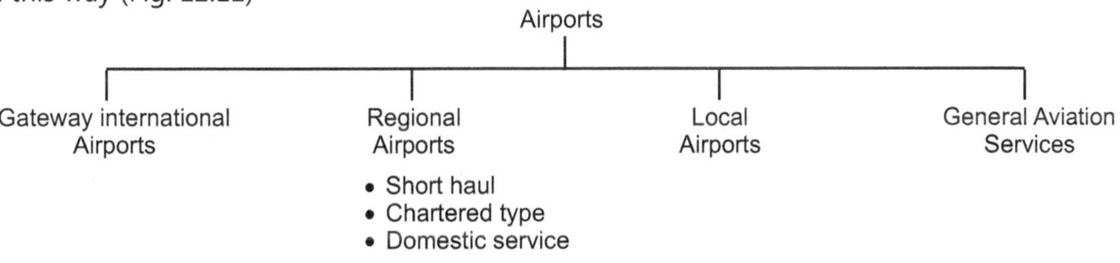

Fig. 12.11 : British (U.K.) Airport Classification

All flights except those by commercial air lines are termed as general aviation service.

Canadian Classification of Airports (1978)

This classification is done as shown in Fig. 12.12

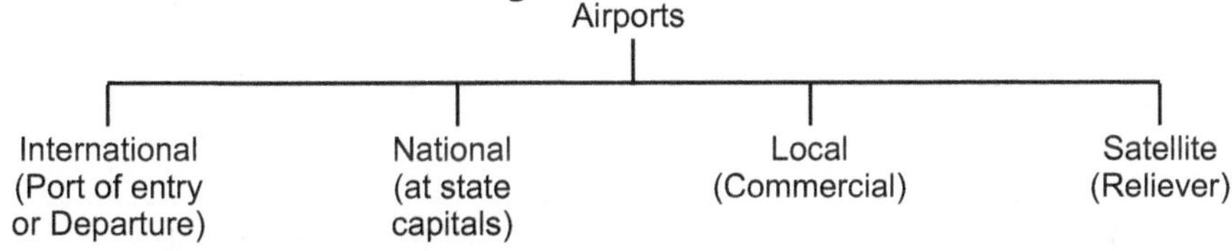

Fig. 12.12 : Classification of Airports in Canada

Soviet System of Airport Classification

Russian classification is based on the volume of traffic per annum as illustrated below :

Table 12.3 Soviet System of Airport Classification

Airport Class	Annual Enplaned Passengers (000)	Shape of various Aircrafts groups in annual Traffic (%)				Annual Aircraft operations (1000) (Arrivals/Departures)
	(00,000)	I	II	III	IV	
I	70-100	10-15	60-65	30-20	-	70-87
II	40-70	5-10	60-75	35-15	-	45-70
III	20-40	-	30-45	45-40	25-15	36-57
IV	5-20	-	0-15	50-55	50-30	20-50
V	1-5	-	-	45-50	55-50	5-20

12.8.1 Airport Classification According to sizes of its Components

International Civil Aviation Organisation (ICAO) and Federal Aviation Administration in U.S.A. (FAA) have adopted different concepts in classifying the airports.

1. ICAO Classification :

With a view to match the aircraft dimensions and aircraft performance characteristics involving, wing span and other main gear wheel span of the aircraft with the length of the runway, the airports are classified. The object of this classification is to make the airport facility compatible with aircraft type.

The airport classification by ICAO based on runway characteristics and wheel load, tyre pressure is shown in the Table 12.4 and 12.5.

Table 12.4 : ICAO Airport Classification based on aircraft and runway characteristics

Airport Type	Basic Runway length (M)		Runway Pavement Width (m)	Longitudinal Gradient (%)	Aircraft Characteristics	
	Desired	Minimum		Maximum	Wing Span (m)	Outer gear wheel base (m)
(1)	(2)	(3)	(4)	(5)	(6)	(7)
A	> 2100	2100	45	1.5	< 15	< 4.5
B	2100	1500	45	1.5	15-24	4.5-6.0
C	1500	900	30	1.5	24-36	6.0-9.0
D	900	750	22.5	2.0	36-52	9.0-14.0
E	750	600	18	2.0	52-60	> 14.0

Table 12.5 ICAO : Airport Classification based on wheel load and tyre pressure

Code No.	Single Isolated Wheel Load (0.000 Kg)	Tyre Pressure Kg/Cm^3
1	45	8.5
2	34	7.0
3	27	7.0
4	20	6.0
5	13	5.0
6	7	2.5
7	2	2.5

2. FAA Classification :

FAA has recommended six categories for the design of airports which may serve the aircrafts having following wing dimensions.

Table 12.6

Airport Design Category	Wing Span (m)
I	< 15
II	15 - 24
III	24 - 36
IV	36 - 52
V	52 - 60
VI	60 - 80

FAA also recommedns the airports to be grouped considering the utility of airports and the size of the population served as follows :

(1) **Basic Utility Group 1 :** Airports which serve small population and have very low activity (scale of operation)

(2) **Basic Utility Group 2 :** Airports serving medium population with major volume of air traffic to be served by small air crafts.

(3) General Utility Airports serving the neighbourhood areas for relatively large population.

12.8.2 Classification of Airports According to the Ownership Form

Different forms of the ownership are :

- Ownership by the Central Government,

- Ownership by the State Government and Quazi Government.

- Ownership by the Public Corporation, Organisations,

- Ownership by the Private Organisations,

- Ownership by the Private Personnels.

Airports can be classified accordingly to the ownership type.

POINTS TO REMEMBER

- Runway orientation.

- Use of wind rose diagrams.

- Taxiways, type of taxiways.

- Classification of airports.

QUESTIONS

1. Explain the steps in the determination of proper orientation for runway.

2. Distinguish between Type I and Type II wind rose diagrams. Explain how the optimum runway orientation is determined.

3. With the aid of a neat suitable sketch, describe the orientation of Runway by wind rose Type - II.

4. Briefly explain the factors to be considered for the geometric design of runways.

5. Summarise the different taxi-way geometrics as recommended by ICAO.

6. Explain with neat sketches the different markings on runway.

7. Give the various geometric standards for different classes of runways and taxiways.

8. Define cross wind component and wind coverage.

9. Give detail classification of Airports.

10. Give detail classification of Airports by ICAO.

11. The length of Runway under standard conditions is 1620 meter. The Airport site has an elevation of 270 meter above mean sea level. Its reference temperature is 32.90°C. If the runway is to be constructed with an effective gradient of 0.20 %. Determine the corrected runway length. Also, carryout the usual checks as per ICAO. Report the correct length to the nearest 10 mtr.

12. The following data refers to the proposed longitudinal section of runway.

End to end of Runway	Gradient
0.0 to 5.0 chains	+ 1.0 %
5.0 to 15.0 chains	- 1.0 %
15.0 to 30.0 chains	+ 0.8 %
30.0 to 40.0 chains	+ 0.2 %

If one metric chain is of 20 mtr. length, determine the effective gradient of runway.

13. Calculate actual length of runway required if basic length obtained is 1000m. The airport is located at an elevation of 120m. Mean of average daily temperature is 38^0 C and the mean of maximum daily temperature is 47^0 C. Longitudinal section details are given below.

End to end of Runway	Gradient
1 to 400	+ 1.0 %
400 to 800	- 0.8 %
800 to 1200	+ 0.6 %

14. The average wind data collected at a particular site is given below. Determine the calm period, the post orientation of runway and the total wind coverage along the direction of EW, and NS by using Wind rose diagram Type II. Permissible cross wind component is 25 kmph.

Wind date		
Wind direction	**Duration of wind**		
	6.4-25 (Kmph)	**25-50 (Kmph)**	**50-75 (kmph)**
N	7.5	2.7	0.2
NNE	5.7	2.1	0.3
NE	3.4	0.9	0.5
ENE	1.2	0.4	0.2
E	0.8	0.2	0.0
ESE	0.3	0.1	0.0
SE	4.3	3	0.0
SSE	5.5	3.2	0.0
S	9.7	4.6	0.0
SSW	6.3	3.2	0.5
SW	3.6	1.8	0.3
WSW	1.0	0.5	0.1
W	0.4	0.1	0.0
WNW	0.2	0.2	0.0
NW	5.3	1.9	0.0
NNW	4.0	1.3	0.3

Chapter 13

INTRODUCTION TO BRIDGE ENGINEERING

13.1 INTRODUCTION

A bridge is an arrangement made to cross obstacle in the form of a low ground or a stream or a river or over a gap without closing the way beneath. The bridges are required for the passages of railways, roadways and footpaths, and even for the carriages of fluids. In short, a bridge is a structure built to span physical obstacles such as a body of water, valley, or road, for the purpose of providing passage over the obstacle. Designs of bridges vary depending on the function of the bridge, the nature of the terrain where the bridge is constructed, the material used to make it and the funds available to build it.

Components of Bridges:

The two basic components of a bridge are:

Substructure: It includes the piers, the abutments and the foundations.

Abutments are the end supports of the superstructure. They also retain the earth of the banks on their back and protect it from falling. Piers are the intermediate supports of the superstructure. They transfer the load from the superstructure to subsoil, through the foundations. They divide the length of the bridge into suitable spans, leading to economy in the design and construction. They, however, obstruct the water, if any, flowing in the vally and cause the heading up of the same.

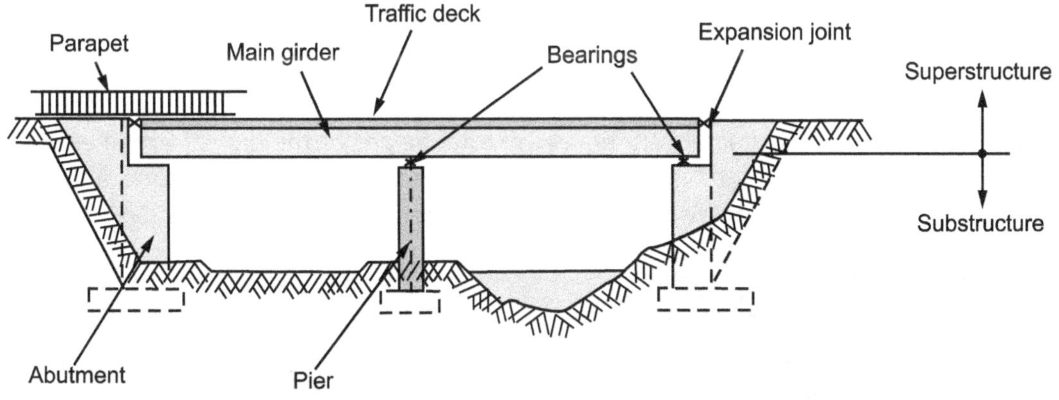

Fig. 13.1: Elevation of typical girder bridge

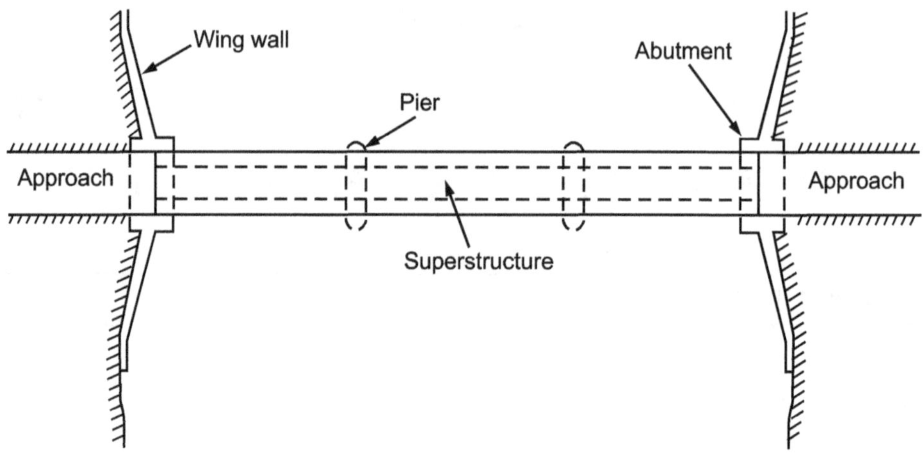

Fig. 13.2: Typical plan of bridge

Superstructure: It consists of the deck structure itself, which supports the direct loads due to traffic and all the other permanent and variable leads to which the structure is subjected.

The connection between the substructure and the superstructure is usually bearings, however, rigid connections between the pier (and sometimes the abutments) may be adopted, particularly in frame bridges with tall (flexible) piers.

Location of Piers and Abutments:

Principles to locate piers and abutments:

- The best use of the foundation conditions available;
- The navigational or aesthetic requirements;
- The minimal number of spans;
- An odd number of spans preferable to even ones;
- Ratio of span to pier or abutment height.

A small bridge with open foundations and solid masonry piers and abutments, the economical span is approximately 1.5 times the total height of the pier or abutments. The span for masonry arch bridges is about 2.0 times the height of the keystone above the foundation. For major bridges with more elaborate foundations, the question has to be examined in greater detail.

13.2 SITE INVESTIGATION

The aim of the investigation is to be select a suitable site at which a bridge can be built economically. Moreover it should satisfy the demands of traffic, the stream, safety etc. before a bridge can be built at a particular site, it is essential to consider many factors, such as need for a bridge stream characteristics, the present and future traffic, sub-soil conditions, cost, alternative sites etc.

Objectives of Site Investigation

The principal objectives for a bridge Site Investigation are as follows :

- **Suitability :** Are the site and surroundings suitable for the bridge site?

- **Design :** Obtain all the design parameters necessary for the works.

- **Construction :** Are there any potential ground or ground water conditions that would affect the construction?

- **Materials :** Are there any materials available on site, what quantity and quality?

- **Effect of Changes :** How will the design affect adjacent properties and the ground water?

- **Identify Alternatives :** Is this the best location?

13.2.1 Field Reconnaissance Survey

For most bridge investigations access and environmental constraints have major influences on cost. It is therefore necessary for a field reconnaissance survey to be conducted as the first stage of a geotechnical investigation. This may be undertaken by concern department or by a consultant specifically engaged for this survey. Information on the following should result :

- Legal and physical aspects of access to site and bridge alignment – both riverbed and adjoining properties.

- Availability of any services or supplies of water, electricity, earthworks plant.

- Buried or overhead services.

- Photographs of surface conditions.

- Traffic control requirements.

- The possible effects of alternative investigation techniques on the environment (for example, ground disturbance, vegetation removal, water discharge, noise etc).

- On-ground survey details.

- Tide, river level or other natural constraints.

- Notes on any exposed geology, for example the presence of boulders, bedrock exposure, swamps etc.

- The physical relationship of the proposed construction to the immediate natural surroundings and any existing developments.

The field reconnaissance survey must be diligently prepared and conducted to allow for reliable cost estimates to be prepared. Experienced and suitably qualified personnel should perform the survey. Further stages of the investigation should be held until the field reconnaissance survey has been completed and reported to department. Cost estimates for the major part of the investigation will be based partly on this reconnaissance survey.

13.2.2 Desk Top Study

Every site investigation should commence with a desk study directed towards collecting, collating and reviewing the following :

- Design drawings from any previous structure at the site.
- Previous site investigation reports, borehole logs, penetrometer results and construction experience e.g. piling records.
- Geological and Topographical maps, survey data and records.
- Hydrological data.
- Aerial photographs.
- Regional seismicity data.
- Survey records, local knowledge and resources.

The collection and collation of the above information, where possible, could be undertaken during the field reconnaissance survey stage. However, further work to fully explore the extent of information available may be required. During the desk study stage, an overview of complexity and risks associated with each geotechnical design should be clearly identified.

13.2.3 Sampling and Testing

This stage of the Geotechnical Investigation is involved with the exploration of subsurface conditions and retrieval of test data for generating geotechnical parameters and geotechnical profiles.

13.2.4 Laboratory Testing

In conducting laboratory testing, procedures to be applied shall be in accordance with Indian Standards, or American Standards (ASTM) and other relevant registered procedures

13.3 SITE SELECTION

The selection of site for a bridge is usually governed by engineering, economic, social and aesthetic considerations. In order to select a least objectionable site, the bridge engineer should consider the following characteristics of an ideal bridge site:

- A well defined and narrow channel.
- A straight reach.
- Good foundation bed at a short depth.
- Suitable high banks.

- Angle of crossing, the axis of steam at bridge site should be crossing at right angles to the centre line of the communication route as far as possible.

- Absence of scouring and silting - It should be free from whirls and cross-currents.

- Location of river tributaries.

- Minimum obstruction to waterway.

- Sound, economical and straight approaches.

- Absence of costly river training work.

- Minimum construction work inside water.

- Proximity to the alignment of communication route.

- Availability of sufficient free board.

- Availability of labour and construction materials.

- Advent of materials / new materials.

- Advances in other branches of science.

- Improvements in constructional methods.

An ideal bridge site is never possible because some ideal conditions are always lacking. Therefore, a least objectionable site is always selected. The best compromise at the time of making selection of a bridge site is a matter of judgement which depends upon the experience of the concerned engineer.

13.4 CLASSIFICATION OF BRIDGES

1. **According to life:**
   (a) Temporary bridges   (b) Permanent bridges

2. **According to loading:**
   (a) Class 'AA' bridges   (b) Class 'A' bridges
   (c) Class 'B' bridges

3. **According to span lengths:**
   (a) Culverts   (b) Minor bridges
   (c) Major bridges   (d) Long-span bridges

4. **According to purpose:**
   (a) Aqueducts   (b) Viaducts
   (c) Grade separations   (d) Foot bridges
   (e) Highway bridges   (f) Railway bridges

5. **According to materials used for constructions:**
   (a) Timber bridges
   (b) Masonry bridges
   (c) Iron and steel bridges
   (d) R.C.C. bridges
   (e) Prestressed concrete bridges

6. **According to structural form:**
   (a) Beam type bridges
   (b) Arch type bridges
   (c) Suspension type bridges

7. **According to alignment:**
   (a) Straight bridges
   (b) Skew bridges

8. **According to level of bridge floor:**
   (a) Deek bridges
   (b) Semi-through bridges
   (c) Through bridges

9. **According to position of high flood level:**
   (a) Submersible bridges
   (b) Non-submersible bridges

10. **According to movement of bridges:**
    (a) Swing bridges
    (b) Traverses bridges
    (c) Bascule bridge
    (d) Transporter bridges
    (e) Lift bridges
    (f) Flying bridges
    (g) Cut boat bridges

13.5 BRIDGE ALIGNMENT

The location of centre line of a communication route to be carried by bridge at the selected site is called bridge alignment.

The following points should be considered while locating the alignment bridges :

- As far as possible centre line of bridge should be at right angle to the axis of river. Such an alignment is known as square alignment and the bridge so constructed is called square bridge. This type of alignment is always preferred because of square bridge is easy to construct and maintain.

- As far as possible, the alignment should not be skew since it is difficult to construct and maintain a skew bridge. Moreover it does not provide smooth entry and exit of water under the bridge.

- As far as possible, the alignment should not be curved since it is difficult to construct and maintain a curved bridge. Moreover, such a bridge is subjected to an additional force due to centrifugal action and there is a greater possibility of traffic accidents.

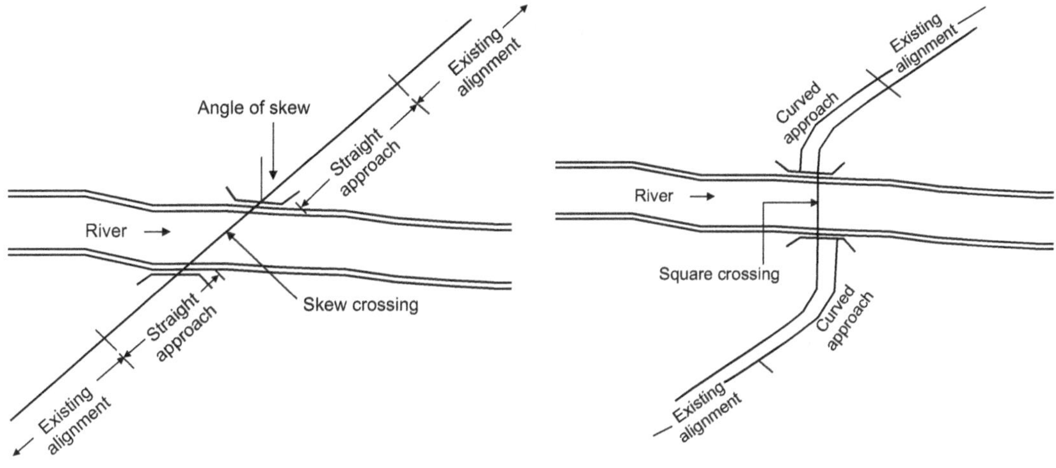

(a) Skew alignment – skew crossing   **(b) Skew alignment – square crossing**

Fig. 13.3 : Skew and square crossing

Despite disadvantages of a curved alignment a bridge may be aligned on a curve to smoothen entries and exists of water. In such a case it is always desirable to arrange piers parallel to the axis of river.

Demerits of skew alignment of a bridge - when the centre line of the bridge is not at right angles to the axis of the river the alignment is called skew alignment and the bridge having such an alignment is known as skew bridge.

(a) The construction and maintenance of a skew bridge is difficult.

(b) The foundation of a skew bridge is more susceptible to scouring action.

(c) The piers of a skew bridge are subjected to excessive water pressure because the passage of water below the bridge superstructure is not smooth and whirls are formed.

13.5.1 Collection of Design Data for a Bridge

- General data:
  - (a) Index map
  - (b) Contour survey map
  - (c) Site plan
  - (d) Cross-section
  - (e) Longitudinal section
- Alternative bridge sites and their typical cross-sections.
- Hydraulic data for the particular selected bridge site.
- Geological data.
- Climatic data.
- Loading and other data.

13.5.2 Determination of Design Discharge

- From the record available, if any of the discharge observed on the stream at the selected bridge site or at any other nearby site.

- From the rainfall and other characteristics of the catchment area by any one of the following methods:

  (a)   By an empirical formula method.

  (b)   By a rational method.

  (c)   By the area velocity method.

  (d)   By unit hydrograph method.

13.5.2.1 Empirical Method

This is an indirect method of determining the maximum flood discharge. in this method, the maximum flood discharge is determined by an empirical formula in which the area of the catchment or basin is mainly considered.

Indirect Method

1. **Dickens formula:** This formula is used almost throughout India.

    According to this formula

$$Q = CM^{3/4}$$

where, Q = Discharge in m^3/sec, M = Area of catchment is sq. km

the value of 'c' in Dickens formula for different regions is given below

Region	Value of 'c'
In area where the annual rainfall is 60 to 120 cm	11 to 14
M.P.	14 to 19
Western ghats	32

2. **Ryve's formula:** Southern India.

$$Q = CM^{2/3}$$

where,   C = 6.8 for area within 25 km from coast

                       = 3.5 within 25 to 160 km

                       = 10.1 for limited hilly areas

3. **Inglis formula:** This formula is used in Maharashtra state only.

$$Q = \frac{4350\,m}{\sqrt{m + 1.04}}$$

where,   m = Catchment area in sq. km.

13.5.2.2 Rational Method

This method is applicable for determination of flood discharge for small culverts only.

$$\text{The runoff, } Q = 0.028 \text{ P.F.A.Ic}$$

where,

Q = Discharge or runoff in m^3/sec

F = Co-efficient

A = Catchment area in hectares

I_c = Critical intensity of rainfall in cm/hour

P = % coefficient of run-off

Direct Method

13.5.2.3 Area Velocity Method

This is direct and an accurate method in determining the maximum flood discharge at the proposed site of a bridge by direct observation. The procedure for determining velocity of flow of a steam water by direct observation is described below:

- Two cables are stretched across the stream at 15 to 30 m apart.

- Then width of stream is divided into suitable number of compartments by hanging pendants as shown in Fig. 13.4.

- After this, the mean velocity of flow of stream water is determined by using any one of the following devices:

(a) A surface float or sub-surface in case of a small river.

(b) A velocity rod or current meter in case of a large river.

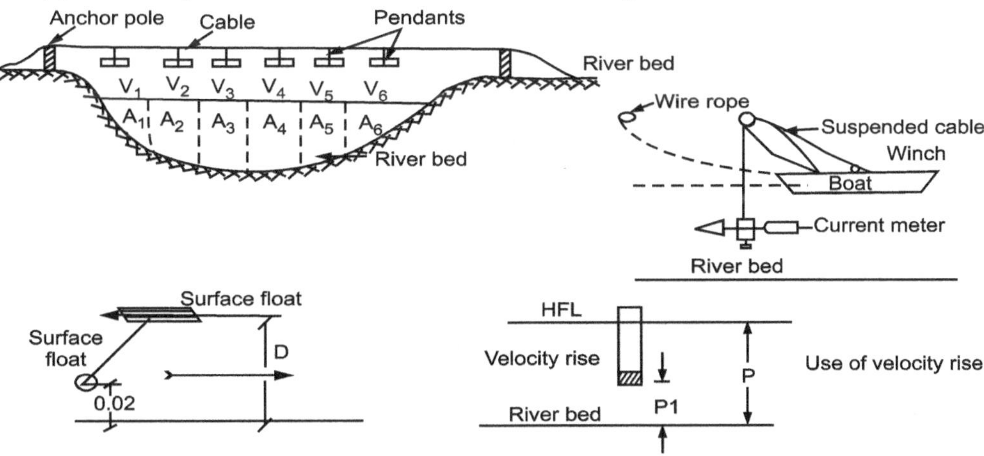

Fig. 13.4

The surface float, sub-surface float or the velocity rod to be used for determining the velocity of flow is allowed to travel from one section to the other in the centre of each compartment and the time taken to cover this distance is noted. Thus, a mean value of the velocity is obtained by taking the average of all the velocities observed in different compartments.

Thus,   mean velocity, v $= \dfrac{v_1 + v_2 + v_3 + v_4 + v_5 + v_6}{6}$

All these devices of measuring velocity of flow of stream water are shown above.

In this case, when surface floats are used, the surface velocity so obtained should be multiplied by a suitable constant to determine the mean velocity of flow as detailed below.

$$\text{Mean velocity } = 4/5 \times \text{Surface velocity}$$

[If surface velocity is less than 0.9 m/sec.]

No correction is required when sub-surface float or velocity rod is used for determining the velocity of flow of stream water.

For determining the velocity of flow by a current meter it is lowered in water from a boat, anchored at the centre of the compartment. Normally, the current meter is kept at a depth of about 0.60 times the depth of water. Then the mean velocity of flow is worked out by the formula supplied by the manufacturer of the meter.

Thus, the maximum flood discharge can be determined from the following relation:

$$\text{Maximum flood discharge, } Q = A.v.$$

where, A = mean cross-sectional area of the steam upto the highest flood level

v = mean velocity of flow of stream water as determined by any of above method

13.5.2.4 By Unit Hydrograph Method

In this method, the continuous discharge of a stream on time base is represented graphically with the aid of a hydrograph.

13.6 CRITERIA FOR FIXING DESIGN DISCHARGE

For fixing design discharge, flood discharge may be determined by as many methods as possible. Then the highest of these values should be taken as the design discharge provided it does not exceed the next highest discharge by more than 50%.

13.7 DETERMINATION OF WATERWAY

The area through which water flows under a bridge structure is known as **waterway.**

While fixing the waterway of a bridge, the following guiding principles must be kept in mind to ensure safety of the bridge structures:

- The increased velocity due to obstructed waterway should not exceed the permissible velocity under the bridge.

- The free board for high level bridges should not be less than 600 mm.
- Sufficient clearance should be allowed according to the navigation requirements.

If 'Q' is maximum flood discharge (design discharge) and 'V' is the permissible velocity of flow under the bridge, then

$$\text{waterway, } a = \frac{Q}{V}$$

The maximum permissible velocity of flow (V) depends upon the nature of the river bed as given in Table 13.1. The velocity of flow of stream or river water should not be more than the values mentioned in this table.

Table 13.1

Sr. No.	Types of Soil	Permissible Velocity
1.	Clay	2.10
2.	Sandy clay	1.50
3.	Very fine sand	0.60 to 1.50
4.	Find sand	0.90 to 1.50
5.	Fine gravel	1.50 to 1.80
6.	Rocky soil	3.00
7.	Rock	4.20 to 6.00

13.8 DETERMINATION OF LINEAR WATERWAY

The linear waterway is the linear measurement of the area way along the bridge. It is equal to the sum of all the clear spans of the bridge.

In the case of large alluvial streams with underlined banks the linear waterway may be determined by the following Lacey's formula i.e.

$$L = C\sqrt{Q}$$

where, L = The linear waterway in metres of regime surface width in m

Q = The maximum design discharge in m^3/sec

C = A constant which is generally taken as 4.8 but for regime channels, it may vary from 4.5 to 6.3 according to the local conditions.

If 'Q' is the design discharge, 'h' is the head or water causing flow and 'ha' is the afflux, then the linear waterway can also be determined from the following relation.

$$\text{Linear waterway, } L = \frac{Q}{\text{Depth of water} \times \sqrt{2g\ (h + ha)}}$$

The linear waterway thus calculated is divided into a number of spans, keeping in view the economy of the bridge.

13.9 DETERMINATION OF AFFLUX

The phenomenon of heading up of water on the upstream site of the bridge is called **afflux.**

When a bridge is constructed, its components like abutments and piers, cause the reduction of the natural waterway. Due to this reduction in natural waterway, the velocity under bridge increases so as to carry the maximum flood discharge. This increased velocity gives rise to a sudden heading up of water on the upstream site of the stream or river. The phenomenon of this heading up water is known as afflux. Thus, greater the afflux greater will be velocity under down stream side of the bridge and greater will be the depth of scour and consequently greater will be the depth of foundation required. Hence, determination of afflux is necessary for the safe design of the bridge.

In view of the above mentioned facts, the afflux should be kept as low as possible due to the following reasons.

- It result in providing shallow foundation of the bridge because lower the afflux, lower will be the velocity under the down stream side of the bridge and lower will be the depth of the scour and thus shallow will be depth of foundation required.

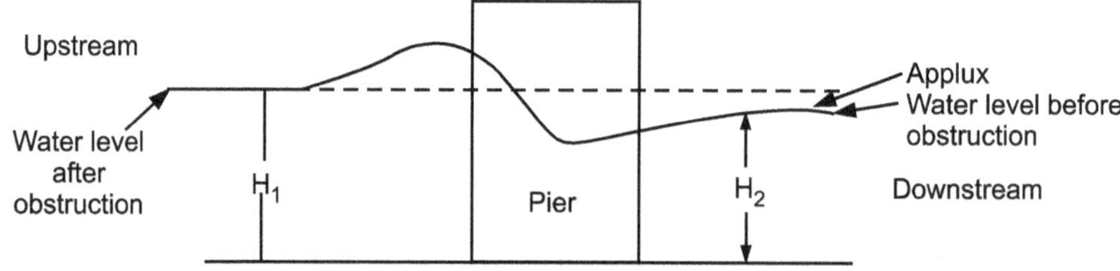

Fig. 13.5

- It helps in deciding the top levels and lengths of guide banks, and flood protection bunds conveniently and economically.

- It facilitates the provision of the bridge at lower level with sufficient free board.

Afflux is determined by using any one of the following two equations:

1. Marriman's equations.

2. Molesworth's equations

1. Marriman's equation: This equation is generally used for determining the values of afflux. According to this equations

$$ha = \frac{Va^2}{2g}\left\{\left(\frac{A}{C.Ac}\right)^2 - \left(\frac{A}{A_1}\right)\right\}$$

where

ha = Afflux in metres

Va = Velocity of approach in m/sec

A = Natural waterway area at this bridge site in m

Ac = Constructed area in m^2

A_1 = The enlarged area upstream of the bridge in m^2

C = Coefficient of discharge which is

$$= 0.75 + 0.35 \left(\frac{Ac}{A}\right) - 0.1 \left(\frac{Ac}{A}\right)^2 \text{ approximately, which may be taken}$$

0.7 for sharp and 0.9 for bell mounted entry.

2. **Molesworth's equations:** According to this equation

$$ha = \left[\frac{Va^2}{17.9} + 0.015\right]\left[\left(\frac{A}{Ac}\right)^2 - 1\right]$$

where Va, A and Ac have the same meanings as used in the Marriman's equation.

Determination of Length of Bridge:

After determining waterway and economic span the length of bridge can be determined by the following relation

$$L = Nl + (N - 1)\, b$$

where

L = Length of the bridge

N = Number of economic span

l = Length of each economic span

b = Thickness of each pier

SOLVED PROBLEMS

Problems 13.1 : A bridge has a liner waterway of 150 m constructed across a stream, whose natural liner waterway is 220 m. If the average floods discharge is 1200 m³/ sec, and average flood depth is 3 m, find Afflux under the bridge.

Solution:

The natural waterway are at the site = A = 220 x 3 = $660 m^2$

Contracted waterway area = Ac = 150 x 3 = 450 m^2

The Velocity of approach = Va = Q/A

Here, Q = Flood discharge = 1200 m^2/ sec

V = 1200/660= 1.818 m/ sec

Using **Molesworth's equations,** the afflux can be given by

$$ha = \left[\frac{Va^2}{17.9} + 0.015\right]\left[\left(\frac{A}{Ac}\right)^2 - 1\right]$$

ha = [(0.184 +0.015) (660/450)^2 -1]

ha = 0.199 x 1.15

ha =0.229m

Afflux under the bridge = 0.229 m

13.10 DETERMINATION OF ECONOMIC SPAN

The economic span is the span for which the overall cost of a bridge will be minimum.

The overall cost of a bridge includes the cost of its substructrure as well as superstructure. The cost of superstructure increases and that of substructure decreases with an increase in span length and vice versa.

Thus, the most economic span length is that for which the cost of the superstructure is equal to that of substructure.

The derivation for economic span can be established on the basis of the following assumptions:

- The bridge has equal span lengths.
- Cost of the supporting system of superstructure varies as the square of the span length.
- Cost of flooring and parapets varies directly as the span.
- Cost of one pier and its foundation is constant.
- Cost of one abutment and its foundation is also constant.

Let, L = Total linear waterway

l = Economic span length

N = The total number of spans = $\dfrac{L}{l}$

C_p = Cost of one pier and its foundation

C_{ap} = Cost of one approach, railing etc.

C_{ab} = Cost of one abutment and its foundation

T_c = Overall cost of the bridge

Now there are $(N - 1)$ number of piers, two abutments and two approaches providing/provided in the proposed bridge.

According to assumptions (2) and (3) cost of one span of superstructure = $(a_1 l^2 + a_2 l)$.

Where a_1 and a_2 are constant of variation for supporting system of superstructure and for flooring and parapets respectively.

Thus, the overall cost of the bridge = Cost of supporting system of the superstructure and that of flooring and parapets for all span + Cost of $(N - 1)$ piers + Cost of two abutments + Cost of two approaches, railings etc.

or $T_C = N\,(a_1 l^2 + a_2 l) + (N - 1)\,C_p + 2C_{ab} + 2C_{ap}$

$$= \frac{L}{l}\left(a_1 l^2 + a_2 l\right) + \left(\frac{L}{l} - 1\right) C_p + 2C_{ab} + 2C_{ap} \qquad \left[\because N = \frac{L}{l}\right]$$

$$\therefore \qquad T_C = a_1 L l + a_2 L + \frac{C_p L}{l} - C_p + 2C_{ab} + 2C_{ap} \qquad \dots (13.1)$$

Differentiating equation (13.1) on w.r.t. l we get

$$\frac{dT_C}{dl} = a_1 L + 0 - \frac{C_p L}{l^2} - 0 + 0 + 0$$

$$= a_1 L - \frac{C_p L}{l^2}$$

Now, for T_C to be minimum $\dfrac{dT_C}{dl} = 0$

$$\therefore \qquad a_1 L = \frac{C_p L}{l^2}$$

$$\therefore \qquad C_p = a_1 l^2$$

or

$$\boxed{\text{Economic span, } l = \sqrt{\frac{C_p}{a_1}}}$$

Hence, for total cost of the bridge to be minimum, the cost of one pier and its foundation should be equal to the cost of supporting system of the superstructure. In other words, for each economical span the cost of substructure is equal to the cost of superstructure.

This equation is suitable for steel girder bridges, truss bridges and arch bridges.

As per I.R.C. recommendation the values of economic span (l) for small culverts and road bridges are as follows:

1. For R.C.C. slab bridges l = 1.5 H
2. For masonry arch type bridges l = 2 H
3. For steel girder bridges l = 1.75 H
4. For steel truss bridges l = 3 H

Problem 13.2 : Following are the costs involved in a uniform multiple span bridge construction

SPAN (m)	5	8	11	14	17
Cost of Girder Rs	2,000	6,000	15,000	22,000	40,000
Cost of Girder Pier and Foundation Rs.	15,000	20,000	25,000	35,000	42,000

Calculate the Economic Span

Solution :

Assuming that the costs of superstructure span various as the square of the span, the constant of variation, a_1 for various values of span is as under:

$$a_1 = \frac{C_p}{l^2}$$

$$\text{For 5 m span, } a_1 = \frac{2000}{25} = 80.00$$

$$\text{For 8 m span, } a_1 = \frac{6000}{64} = 93.75$$

$$\text{For 11 m span, } a_1 = \frac{15000}{121} = 123.96$$

$$\text{For 14 m span, } a_1 = \frac{22000}{196} = 112.24$$

$$\text{For 17 m span, } a_1 = \frac{40000}{289} = 138.40$$

An average valve of $a_1 = 80.00 + 93.75 + 123.96 + 112.24 + 138.40 = 109.67$.

The average cost of sub-structure unit, $= 15000 + 20000 + 25000 + 35000 + 42000 = 27400$

$$\boxed{\text{Economic span, } l = \sqrt{\frac{C_p}{a_1}}}$$

$$\text{Economic span, } l = \sqrt{\frac{27400}{109.47}}$$

$$\text{Economic span, } l = 15.80 \text{ m}$$

13.11 SCOURING

The process of cutting or deeping of river bed due to action of water is called **scouring.**

When the velocity of stream water exceeds the limiting velocity it causes vertical cutting of the river bed, which is known as scouring. It differs from errosions which causes horizontal widening of the river bed.

Determination of Normal Scour Depth:

The normal scour depth is the depth of water in the middle of stream when it is carrying the maximum flood discharge.

1. **Scour depth of alluvial streams:**

Case - I: When linear waterway of the bridge is equal to the regime width: In this case, the normal scour depth is equal to the regime depth given by the following Lacey regime equation.

$$D = 0.473 \left(\frac{Q}{F}\right)^{1/3}$$

where, $\quad$ D = Normal scour depth below H.F.L. for regime section of the channel in m.

$\quad$ Q = The maximum design discharge in m^3/sec

$\quad$ f = Lacey's silt factor which varies from 0.5 to 1.5

Case - II: When linear waterway is less than the regime width:

$$D' = D \left(\frac{W}{L}\right)^{0.61}$$

where, $\quad$ D' = The normal scour depth with constructed waterway in m.

$\quad$ D = The normal scour depth in m when L = W as calculated in the first case

$\quad$ L = Linear waterway provided under the bridge in m

$\quad$ W = The regime width of the stream in m, which can be equal to wetted verimeter P = 4.8 (Q)$^{1/2}$

2. Scour depth for quasi alluvial streams:

In quasi-alluvial streams having rigid banks and erodable beds the normal scour depth, when the stream width is large as compared to depth, can be determined as follows:

Case - I: When velocity is known, we may use the equation

$$D = \frac{Q}{W.V}$$

where, $\quad$ W = The regime or fixed width of the stream in m

$\quad$ V = Velocity of flow

Case - II: When slope is known: We may use the equation

$$Q = 1/n \, W \, S^{1/2} \, D^{5/3}$$

where, $\quad$ n = Manning's coefficient

$\quad$ S = Bed slope

$\quad$ W = The regime or fixed width of the stream in m.

Case - III: When both velocity and slope factors are not known: We may use the equations

$$D = \frac{1.21 \, Q^{0.63}}{F^{0.33} \times W^{0.60}}$$

where, $\quad$ F = Silt factor

Normal scour depth in case of quasi-alluvial streams for constructed waterway can be determined by this equation.

13.12 DETERMINATION OF MAXIMUM SCOUR DEPTH

Maximum scour depth is the depth of water at the round obstruction to the flow of water when the river carries maximum flood discharge.

It usually occurs at bends, pier noses and on the understream noses of guide banks provided for a bridge. Therefore, for the safety of the bridge foundations it becomes essential to estimate the maximum scour depth correctly and design the bridge foundations accordingly.

As per I.P.C. recommendations, the maximum depth of scour may be taken as follows:

- In case of a bridge on a straight reach of the stream having single span, the maximum depth of scour should be taken as 1.5 times the normal scour depth of water.

- For bridge sites on curves or where cross current exists or when the bridge is a multi-span structure, the maximum depth of scour should be taken as 2 times the normal depth of scour.

- In case of bridge causing contraction, the maximum scour depth should not be less than the value obtained by the following equations

$$D_m = D\left(\frac{W}{L}\right)^{1.56}$$

where,
D_m = Maximum scour depth in m

W = Regime width of stream in m

D = Normal scour depth in m

L = Linear waterway in m

13.12.1 Prevention of Scouring

- The site of the bridge should have stream line flow.
- At the site of bridge, the river bed soil should be such as to resist the maximum velocity of water.
- Sufficient waterway should be provided under the bridge so that velocity of water may not exceed the limit after which scouring occurs.
- The shape of the piers should be designed in such a way that it may not cause eddies and currents in water.
- The river bed on upstream side, downstream side and the portion under the bridge should be properly pitched with beams and long stones.
- In the case of sandy beds, sheet piling may be done on understream and downstream sides of the bridge to prevent scouring.
- Piles may also be driven in river bed, where scouring is likely to occur.

13.13 TYPES OF LOADING FOR ROAD BRIDGES

For bridges and culverts, the following loads, forces and stresses should be considered, where applicable. The loads and forces to be considered in designing road bridges and culverts are listed below:

- Dead loads
- Live loads
- Impact effect of the live loads
- Wind loads
- Lateral loads
- Longitudinal forces
- Centrifugal forces due to curvature
- Earthquake forces
  Additional loads for substructure design:
- Forces due to water structures/currents
- Earth pressure
- Buoyancy

In addition to the stress caused by the above loads and forces the following stresses should be taken into account:

- Temperature stresses
- Deformation stresses
- Secondary stresses
- Erection stresses

1. Dead loads: The dead load carried by a bridge member consists of its own weight and the portions of the weight of the superstructure and any fixed loads supported by the member. The dead load can be estimated fairly and accurately during design and can be controlled during construction and service. The dead load is the weight of the structure and the weight of the portion of the superstructure which is supported wholly or in part by the structure. The dead load of the structure depends upon the following factors:

(a) Live load, (b) Type of design, (c) Working stress employed, (d) Length of span (e) Character of the details.

2. Live loads: Live loads are those caused by vehicles which pass over the bridge and are transient in nature. These loads cannot be estimated precisely, and the designer has very little control over them once the bridge is opened to traffic. However hypothetical loadings which are reasonably realistic, need to be evolved and specified to serve as design criteria. Classifications of load are:

- IRC class AA loading,
- IRC class A loading,
- IRC class B loading.

3. Impact effect of live load: The impact is caused due to fact that moving heavy vehicles over rough or uneven surfaces. The provision for impact effect should be made by an increment of live load by an impact allowance expressed as a fraction on a percentage of the applied live load. The magnitude of the impact depends not only on the span but also on the type of smoothness of the road surface, the speed of the vehicle and the type of its tyres. The empirical values suggested in the code are only approximate indications of workable magnitudes.

- Impact effect of class 'A' and class 'B' loading:

    (i)   Impact factor for R.C. bridges $= \dfrac{4.5}{6 + L}$

    (ii)   Impact factor for steel bridges $= \dfrac{9}{13.5 + L}$

    For span between 3 m and 4.5 m

    where, L = Length of span

- Impact effect of class 'AA' loading for road bridge:
    (i)   For spans less than 9 metres.
    (ii) For trucked vehicle = 20% for spans upto 5 m linearity reducing to 10% for spans of 9 m
    (iii) For wheeled vehicles 25%

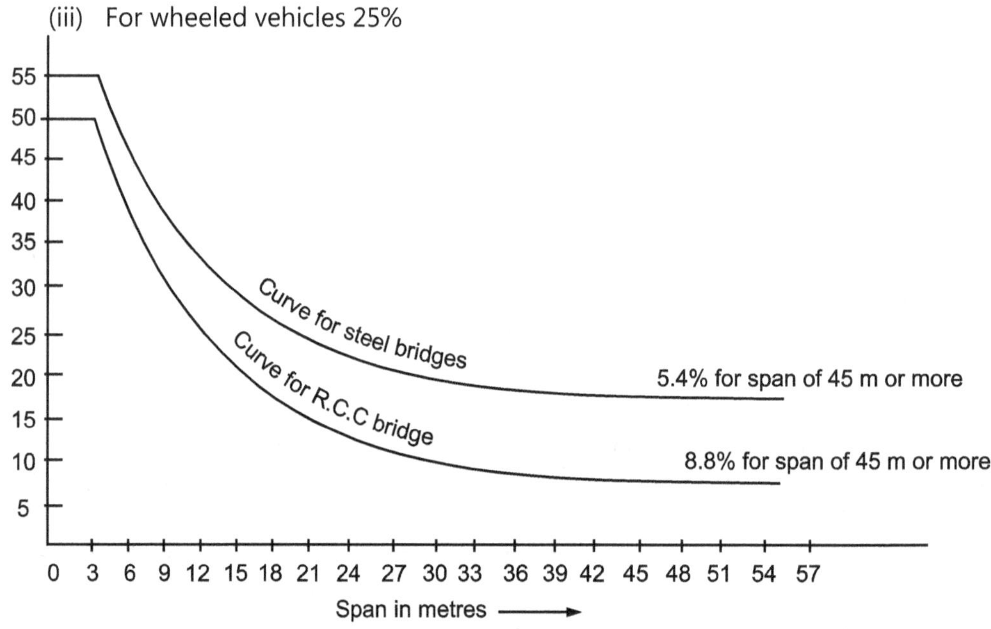

Fig. 13.6: Impact percentage curves for highway bridges for class A and B loadings

4. Wind load: Bridge structures are designed for the following lateral wind forces. These forces should be considered to act horizontally and in such a direction that the resultant stresses in the member under consideration are the maximum.

Wind load depends upon 'H' i.e. average height in metres of the exposed surface above the mean retarding surface.

    V = Horizontal velocity of wind in km/hour at height H and
    P = Horizontal wind pressure in kg/sq. m at height 'H'.

5. **Lateral loading/loads:**
   (a) **Force on railings and parapets** should be designed to resist a lateral horizontal force and vertical force each of 150 kg/m applied simultaneously at the top of the railing or parapet.
   (b) **Force on kerbs:** Kerbs should be designed for lateral loading of 750 kg/m run of kerb applied horizontally at top of the kerb.

6. **Longitudinal forces:** In all road bridges, provision should be made for longitudinal forces arising from any one or more of the following causes:
   - Fractive efforts caused through acceleration of the driving wheels.
   - Braking effects resulting from the application of the brakes to braked wheels. Bracking force is invariably greater than fractive efforts.
   - Frictional resistance offered to the movement of free bearing due to change in temperature or any other cause.

7. **Centrifugal force:** When a road bridge is situated on a curve, all portions of the structure affected by centrifugal action of moving vehicles are designed to carry safely the stress induced by this action in addition to all other stresses to which they may be subjected to:

The centrifugal force should be determined from the following formula:

$$ C = \frac{WV^2}{127\,R} $$

Here
C = Centrifugal force in tonnes
W = Live load
V = Design speed kmph
R = Radius of curvature in metres

8. **Seismic force:** If a bridge is situated in a region subjected to earthquakes allowance should be made in the design for the seismic force.

As per IS 1893-1970 the seismic force to be used in the design of a structure is dependent on may variable factors and therefore it is extremely difficult to determine its correct value. To give broad indications of reasonable values of seismic coefficient for different regions of Indian Standards (IS) has divided the country into five zones designated as zones I to V.

The seismic should be taken as a horizontal force equal to the appropriate function of the weight of the dead and live load acting at the section under consideration.

Zone	Basic Seismic Coefficient
I	0.01
II	0.02
III	0.04
IV	0.05
V	0.08

The vertical seismic coefficient, where applicable may be taken as half of the horizontal seismic coefficient.

$$\text{Earthquake force} = W\frac{\alpha}{g}$$

where α is acceleration due to earthquake from historically available data or $\alpha = \frac{1}{20}g$ to $\frac{1}{10}g$ where g is the gravitational acceleration and W = Weight of structure.

9. Force due to water currents: Any part of a bridge which may be submerged in running water should be designed to sustain safely the horizontal pressure due to the force of the current. In case of piers parallel to the direction of water current, the intensity of pressure should be calculated from the following formula

$$\boxed{P = 52\,KV^2}$$

Here P = Intensity of pressure in kg/m^2 due to the water current

                   K = A constant having the following values for different shapes of the piers

                   V = The velocity of the current in metres/sec.

10. Earth pressure: I.R.C. recommends coulomb's theory of earth pressure with the modification that the height of the centre of pressure above bottom as 0.42 of the height of wall above the base instead of 0.33 of that height.

The distribution of normal pressure on a retaining wall due to a concentrated surface load on the backing can be obtained by using the following spangler's equation.

$$h = \frac{KP\,X^2z}{X^n\,R^5}$$

or $P = \frac{1}{2}\,KaWH^2$

where, $K_a = \dfrac{1 - \sin\phi}{1 + \sin\phi}$

Here h = Normal unit pressure on the wall at any point

                   P = Applied wheel load in kg

                   X = Distance from load to back face of wall in metres subject to a minimum of 150 mm

                   Y = Lateral distance in 'm' from any point on the wall to the normal vertical plain containing the load

                   z = Vertical distance in 'm'.

11. Buoyancy: In case of high level bridge to allow for full buoyancy a reduction should be made in the gross weight of the member affected in the following manner:

- When the member under consideration displace water only, e.g. a shallow pier of abutment pier founded at or near the bed level, the reduction in weight should be equal to that of the volume of the displaced water.

- In case of submersible bridges, the full buoyancy effect on the superstructure, piers and abutments should be taken into consideration.

12. Temperature stresses: All structures tend to change in length with variations in temperature. Temperature stresses are likely to develop if this change in length is fully or partly restrained by fixing the ends.

IRC has recommended the following range of temperature in the design of bridge structures.

(a) **Steel structures:** Moderate climate from minus 18°C to 50°C.

(b) **Concrete structures:**

	Temperature rise	**Temperature fall**
Moderate climate	17°C	17°C
Extreme climate	25°C	25°C

The coefficient of expansion per degree centigrade should be taken as 0.0000177 for steel and reinforced concrete structures and 0.0000108 for plain concrete structure.

13. Deformation stresses: These stresses are considered for steel bridge only. A deformation stress is defined as 'the bending stress in any member of an open web girder or a truss, caused by the vertical deflection of the girder combined with the rigidity of the joints'. All bridges should be designed and erected in such a manner that these stresses are reduced to a minimum. They should in absence of calculation be assumed to be not less than 16% of the dead load and live load stresses. In prestressed girders of steel, deformation stresses may be ignored.

14. Secondary stresses: Secondary stresses are the additional stresses brought into play due to the eccentricity of connections. Floor beam loads applied at intermediate points in a panel, cross girders being connected away from panel points, lateral wind load on the end posts of through girders, movement of the supports, the time yield in concrete, shrinkage of concrete etc. All bridges should be designed and constructed in a manner such that the secondary stresses are reduced to a minimum and they should be allowed for in the design.

For design reinforced concrete members the shrinkage coefficient for purpose of design may be taken as 2×10^{-4}.

15. Erection stress: Erection stresses are the stresses set up in any member during erection. These stresses are different from those occurring when the structure is in position and in actual service. They should be checked. If unsafe, provision should be made for them.

13.14 LOADING FOR RAILWAY BRIDGES

- Dead load

- Live load

- Impact load

- Loads due to curvature of truck

- Loads on parapet

- Wind load

- Racking load

- Longitudinal load

- Seismic load

13.15 BRIDGE LOADING

Road bridges and culvert shall be divided into classes according to the loadings they are designed to carry.

I.R.C. class AA loading: This loading is to be adopted within certain municipal limits in certain existing or contemplated industrial areas, in other specified areas and along certain specified highways. Bridges designed for Class AA loading should be checked for Class A loading also, as under certain conditions, heavier stresses may be obtained under Class A loading.

Note: "Where Class 70-R is specified, it shall be used in place of I.R.C. Class AA loading".

I.R.C. Class A Loading: This loading is to be normally adopted on all roads on which permanent bridges and culverts are constructed.

I.R.C. Class B Loading: This loading is to be normally adopted for temporary structures and for bridges in specified areas. Structures with timber spans are to be regarded as temporary structures for the purpose of this Clause.

Details of I.R.C. Loadings: For bridges classified above, the designed live load shall consist of standard wheeled or tracked vehicles or trains of vehicles as illustrated in Fig. 13.6 to 13.8. The trailers attached to the driving unit are not to be considered as detachable.

Within the kerb to kerb width of the roadway, the standard vehicle or train shall be assumed to travel parallel to the length of the bridge, and to occupy any position which will produce maximum stresses provided that the minimum clearances between a vehicle and the roadway face of kerb and between two passing or crossing vehicles, shown in Fig. 13.7 to Fig. 13.9, are not encroached upon.

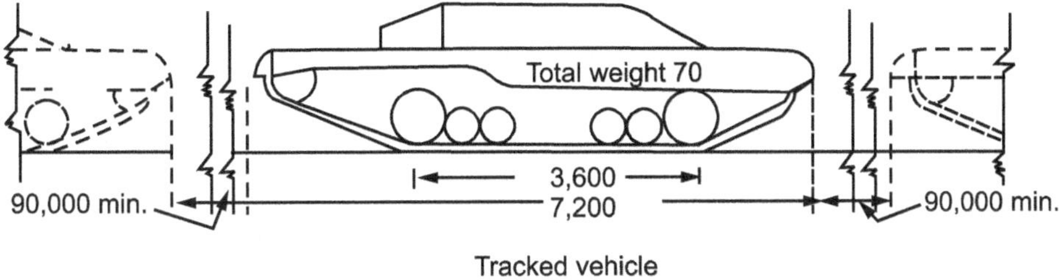

Fig. 13.7: Class AA tracked and wheeled vehicles

Notes:

- The nose to tail spacing between two successive vehicles shall not be less than 90 m.

- For multi-lane bridge and culverts, one train of Class AA tracked or wheeled vehicles whichever creates sever conditions shall be considered for every two traffic land width.

  No other live load shall be considered on any part of the said 2-lane wide carriage-way of the bridge when above mentioned train of vehicles is crossing the bridge.

- The maximum loads for the wheeled vehicle shall be 20 tonnes for a single axle or 40 tonnes for a bogie of two axles spaced not more than 1.2 m centres.

- The minimum clearance, between the road face of the kerb and the outer edge of the wheel or track, C, shall be as under:

Carriageway width	Minimum value of C
Single-Lane Bridges	
3.8 m and above	0.3 m
Multi-Lane Bridges	
Less than 5.5 m	0.6 m
5.5 m or above	1.2 m

- Axle loads in tonne linear dimensions in metre.

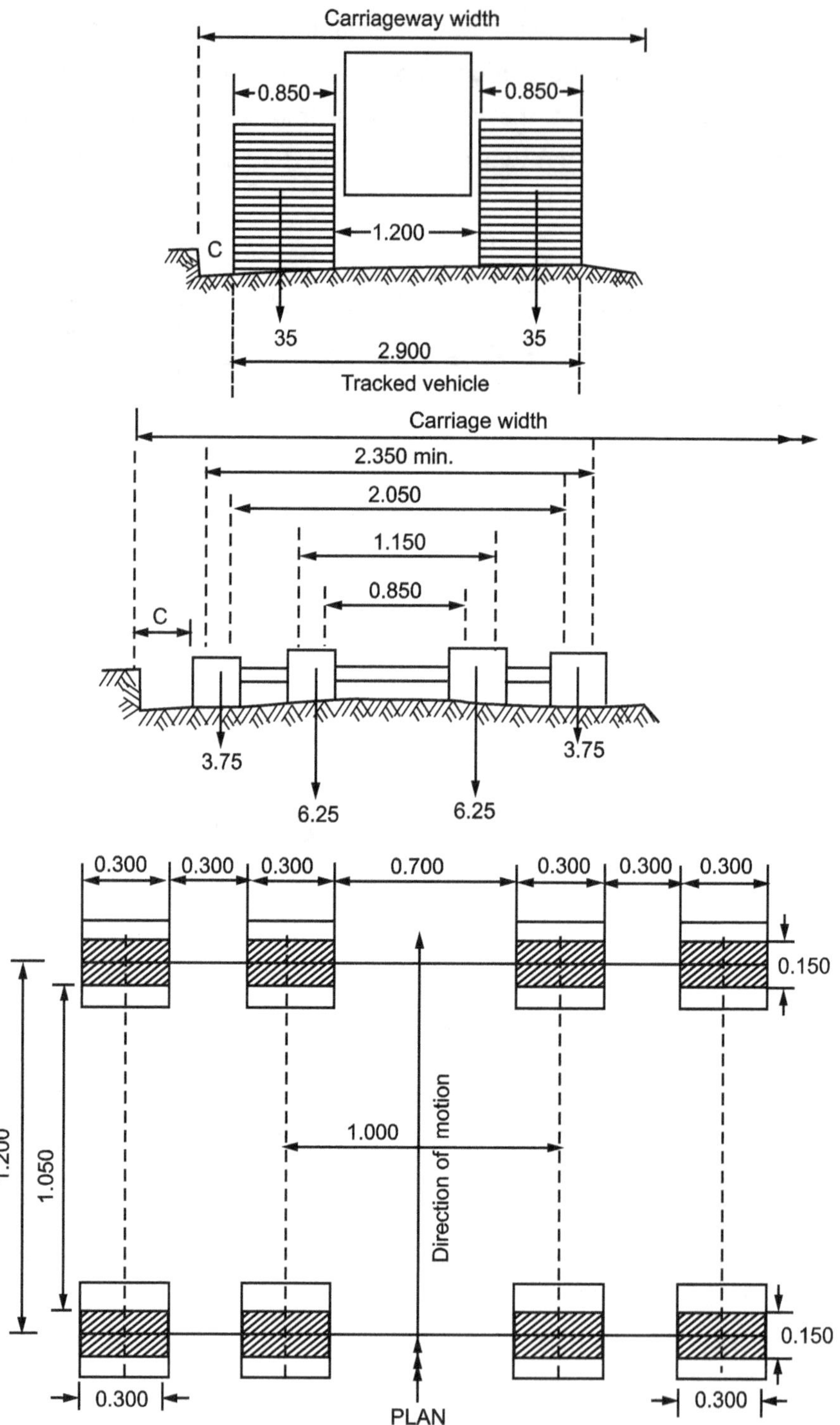

Fig. 13.8: Class A tracked and wheeled vehicles

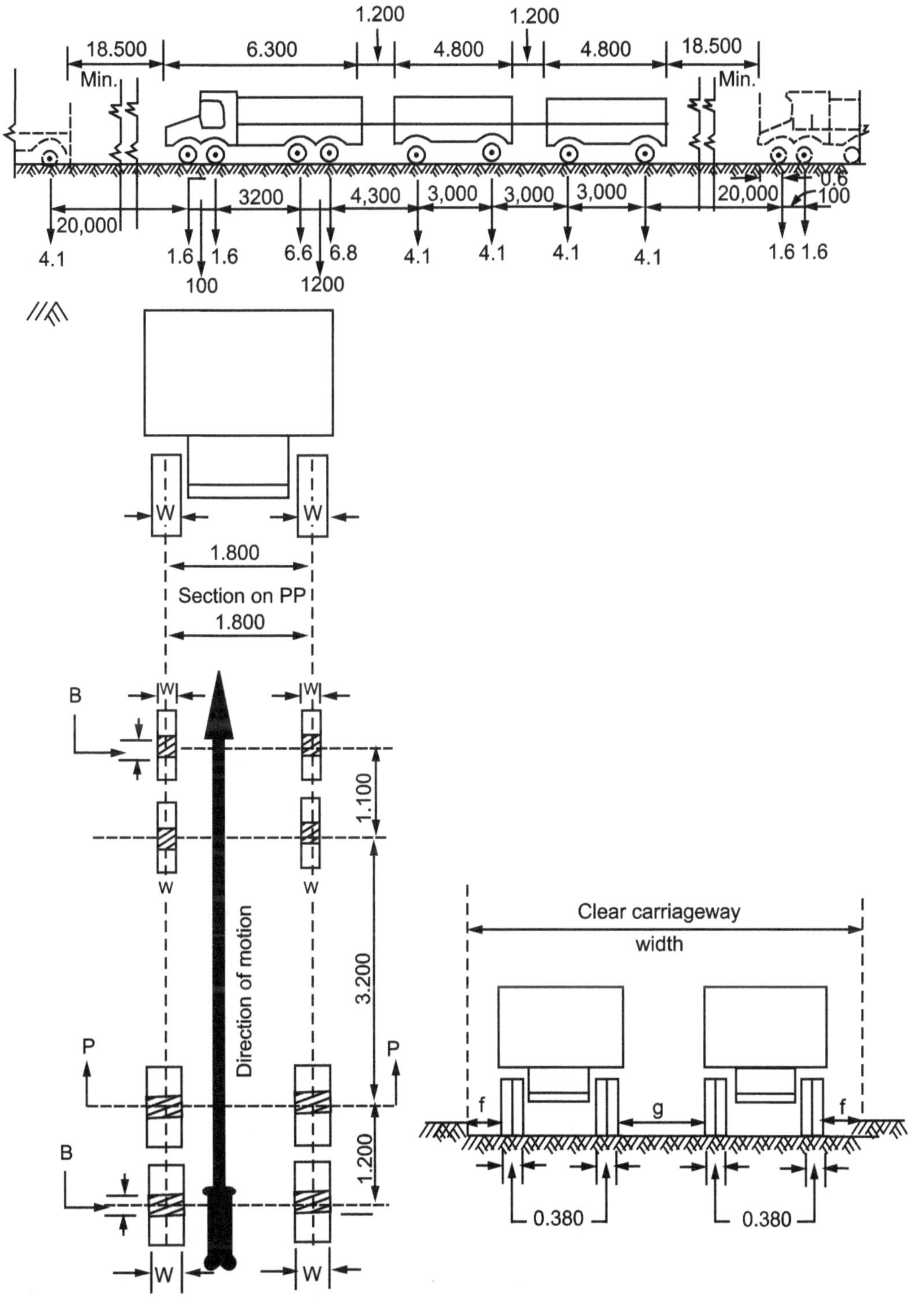

Fig. 13.9: Plan, driving vehicle

Class B Train of Vehicles:

Notes:

1. The nose to tail distance between successive trains shall not be less than 18.4 m.

2. No other live load shall cover any part of the carriageway when a train of vehicles (or trains of vehicles in multi-lane bridge) is crossing the bridge.

3. The ground contact area of the wheels shall be as under:

Axle load tonne	Ground contact area	
	B mm	W mm
6.8	200	380
4.1	150	300
1.6	125	175

4. The minimum clearance, f, between outer edge of the wheel and the roadway face of the kerb and the minimum clearance, g, between the outer edges of passing or crossing vehicles or multi-lane bridges shall be as given below:

Clear carriageway width	g	
5.5 m to 7.5 m	Uniformly increasing from 0.4 to 1.2 m	150 mm for all carriageway widths
Above 7.5 m	1.2 m	

5. Axle loads in tonne linear dimensions in metre.

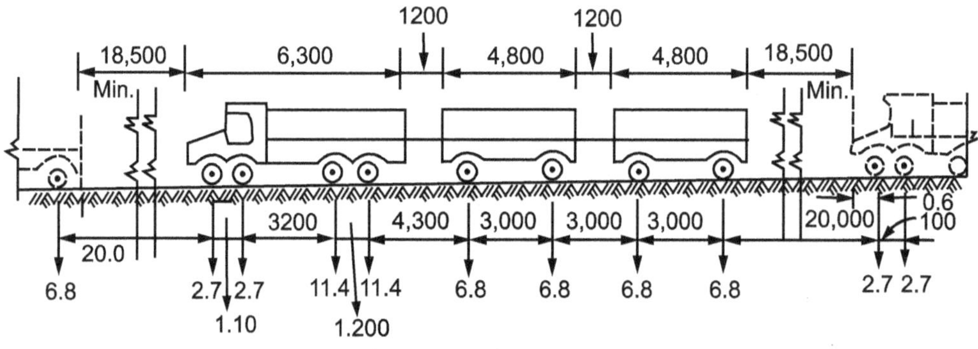

Fig. 13.10: Class A train

Class A Train of Vehicles:

Notes:

1. The nose to tail distance between successive trains shall not be less than 18.4 m.

2. No other live load shall cover any part of the carriageway when a train of vehicles (or trains of vehicles in multi-lane bridge) is crossing the bridge.

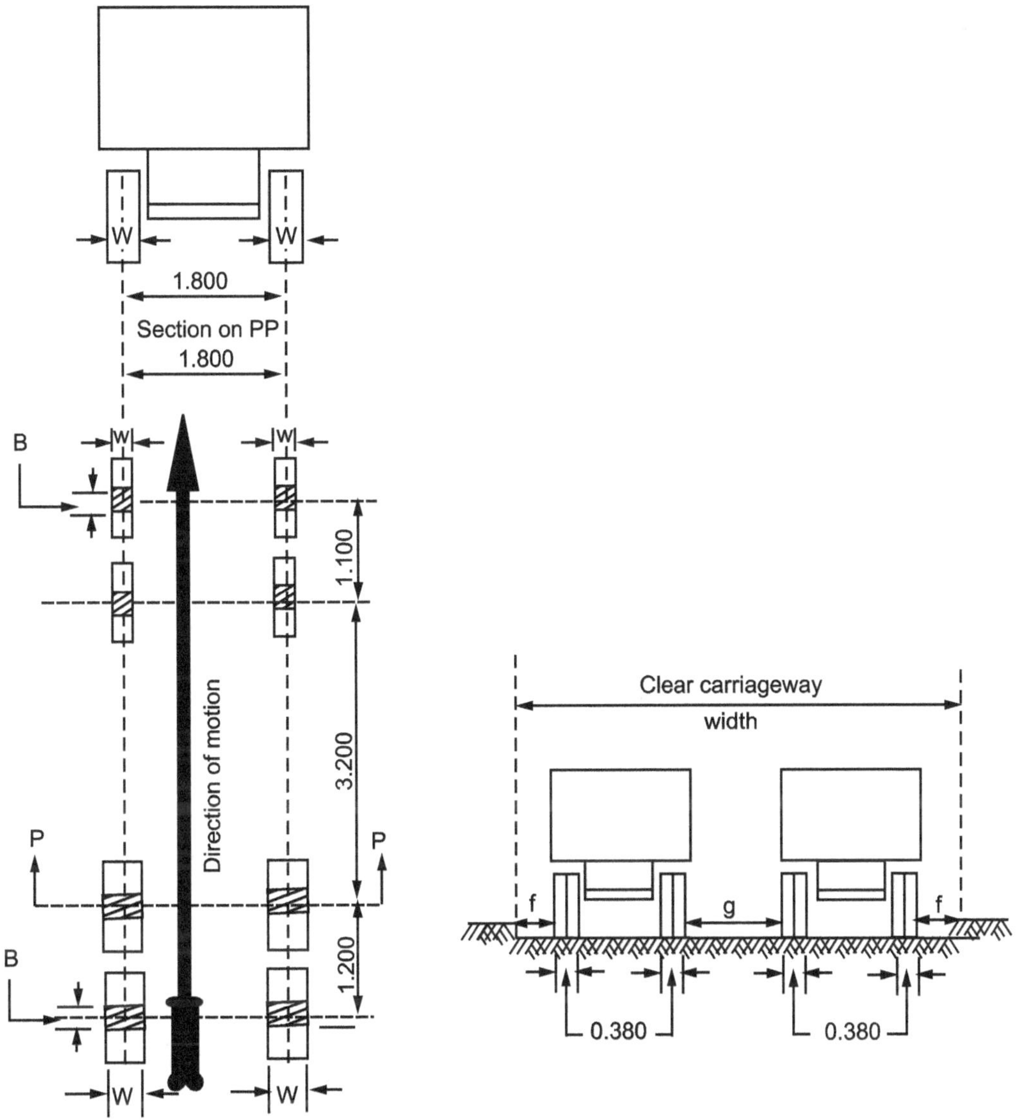

Fig. 13.11: Class 'A' train of vehicles   **Fig. 13.12**

3. The ground contact area of the wheels shall be as under:

Axle load tonne	Ground contact area	
	B mm	**W mm**
11.4	250	500
6.8	200	380
2.7	150	200

4. The minimum clearance, f, between outer edge of the wheel and the roadway face of the kerb and the minimum clearance, g, between the outer edges of passing or crossing vehicles or multi-lane bridges shall be as given below:

13.16 REQUIREMENTS OF TRAFFIC IN THE DESIGN OF HIGHWAY BRIDGE

The following are the requirements of traffic to be considered in the design of highway bridges.

1. Bridge Alignment: The bridge should be so aligned as to fit in with general road alignment. This may entall skew bridges.

2. Roadway Width: For vehicular traffic the following minimum clear widths of roadways are adopted.

Types of Bridge	Roadway Width
Single lane	4.25 m
Two lane	7.50 m
Multi-lane	7.50 m to 3.50 m for every additional line
Pedestrian	2.50 m

Road bridges should provide for either one-lane, two-lanes or multiple of two-lanes. Three-lane bridges should not be constructed. The roadway capacity may be adopted as 1000 vehicles per hr. per lane width of 3.75 m. The roadway width has to be increased by multiples of 3.50 m for every additional 1000 vehicles per hour. The width of roadway over the bridge should be equal to road width on either side.

3. Cycle Track Width: In urban areas when the number of the cycles exceed 500 per hour, separate cycle tracks are provided. The minimum width at 2.0 m upto 2000 cycle per hour. The width has increased by multiple of 1 m for every additional 1000 cycles per hour.

4. Safety Kerbs: A safety kerb of 600 × 225 mm should be provided on either side of a roadway. The road site kerb will have a slope line for 200 m height and curved edge with a radius of 25 mm at the top.

5. Footpath: Foothpaths are provided where the traffic is heavy and at the same time to avoid accidents and to permit the vehicular traffic at greater speed. The width generally vary between 1.5 m and 3.90 m depending upon the volume and importance of pedestrians.

6. Segregation of Traffic: Segregation is separation of traffic in the interest of safety and flow.

7. Bridge Lighting: The bridge lighting should be so aligned along railing so as to become an active element of expression. It must be tastefully designed.

8. Sight Distance: The minimum sight distance available on highway should be of sufficient length to stop without collision. The minimum sight distance is in other words, equal to the stopping sight distance. The stopping distance for bridges on different class of roads for design speeds is given below.

Classification of Roads	Design Speed in km/h	Stopping Sight Distance in m
NH and SH	100	150
MDR	80	110
ODR	65	80
VR	50	60

In case of underpasses it should be ensured that sight distance is not reduced below the distance by piers, abutments or shrubs in verges.

13.17 SUBSTRUCTURES

13.17.1 Abutments

Abutment of bridge is one of the important and vital structural parts. An abutment is the substructure on which rests one end of the superstructure of the bridge. The abutment has following purposes to serve:

- Supporting one end of the bridge.

- Laterally supporting the embankment which serves as an approach to the bridge.

- Protecting embankment from scour.

- Withstanding lateral pressure of the backfill.

- The abutments establish the connection between the bridge superstructure and the embankments.

- They are designed to support the loads due to the superstructure which are transmitted through the bearings and to the pressures of the soil contained by the abutment.

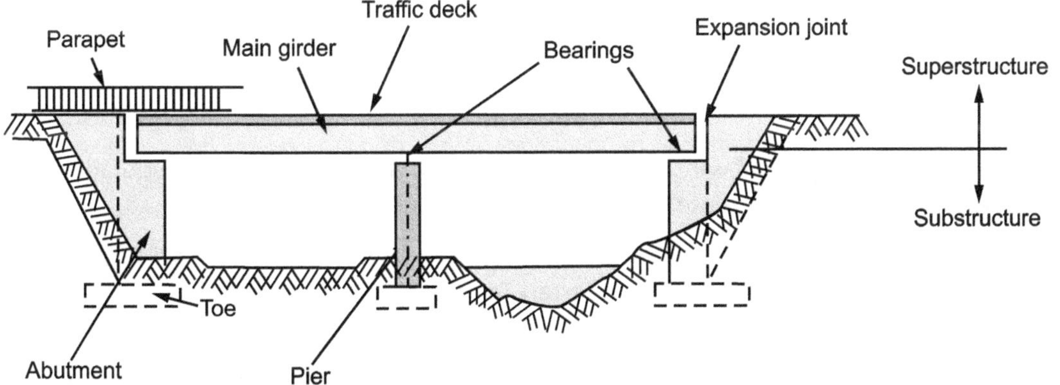

Fig. 13.13

A two spanned bridge has two abutments and one pier and four-spanned bridge has two abutments and three piers. For a bridge or culvert with more than one span, there are intermediate supports which called pier. The function of the abutment is to transmit the load from the bridge superstructure to foundation, to give final formation to the bridge and to retain the earthwork of the embankment of the approaches. The abutment serves both as pier and as a retaining wall. Abutments can be of brick masonry, stone masonry, and concrete or of pre-cast concrete blocks. An abutment consists of the breast, which supports dead load and live load of the superstructure, wings and extension of breast and furnish no support for the superstructure but act as retaining walls for the material deposited behind the abutment and back or parapet wall which prevents the material in back of the abutment from flowing onto the bridge. It is necessary to provide weep holes in abutment and wing walls of the height of the course and two inches wide packed with spalls for draining the embankment.

Types of Abutments:

1. **Stub or straight without wings:** The earth fill flows around the ends of abutment and flow water may wash the fill away and the banks are damaged.

2. **Abutment with straight wing wall:** Suitable for a railway bridge over a roadway or a street crossing another street at a lower level. Not suitable over a water way as water may flow immediately behind the wing wall and damage the embankment.

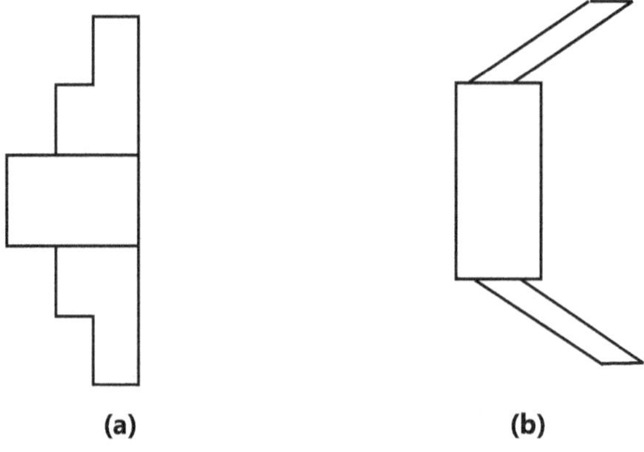

(a)   (b)

Fig. 13.14

3. **Abutment with splayed wing walls:** The wing walls are straight but splayed at an angle of 45° to 35° with the face of the abutment.

4. **Abutment with wings shaped convex or concave facing the flow of water:** The latter type form eddies; the former is preferred for the smooth flow of water although the latter is more.

5. **Abutment with wing walls at right angle to it i.e. U abutment:** The wings are tied together by old rails. The wing walls run back into fill, which flows down infront of the wings; the wings are parallel to the roadway, suitable where rock slopes make it possible to step up the wing wall footing.

6. **T abutment:** The head of T supports the bridge and the stem carries the roadway. Was widely used in early rail road construction. The stem carried the railway track and had to be wide enough. The quantity of masonry in its construction is larger than in any other type.

7. **Pulpit abutment:** It is a variation of U abutment, the arms of U being made short; adopted for high abutments. The returned wings are only of sufficient length to prevent the retaining material from flowing on bridge seat.

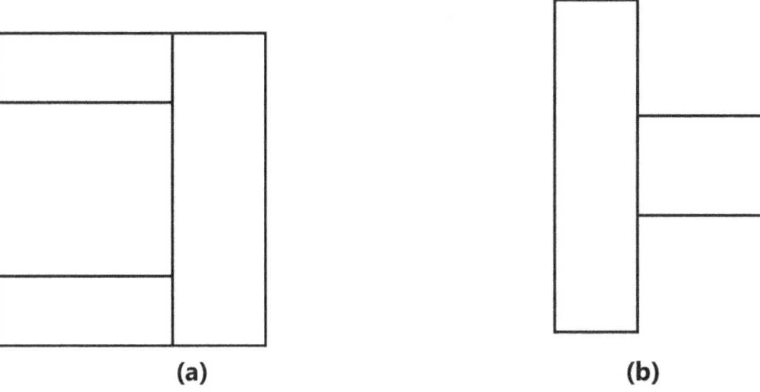

Fig. 13.15

8. **Buried abutment:** Instead of placing the abutment at the edge of the stream, it is set back in the embankment and the latter spills out in front of the bridge seat. Here the earth pressure at the back is balanced by that in the front and so less massive abutment is required, but this involves greater length for the superstructure. Sometimes a pier is placed at the toe embankment.

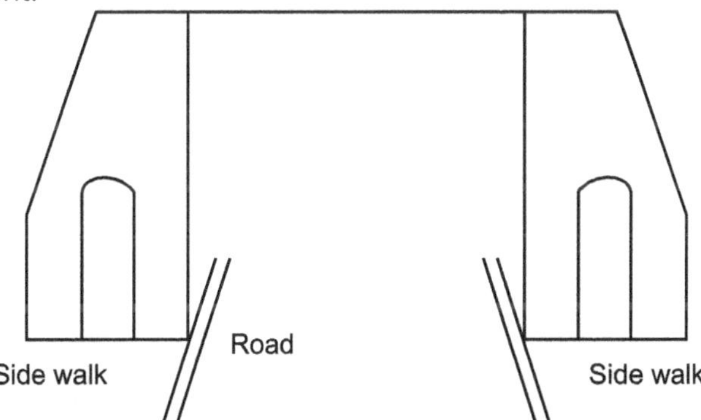

Fig. 13.16

9. **Hollow or Arch abutment or Box type abutment:** This abutment is adopted where a rail road crosses a highway having sidewalks.

10. **Abutment with flying wing walls:** The wings extend a sufficient depth into the embankment to prevent spewing out beneath them.

There are two types of abutments:

- Gravity type abutments
- Counter-fort type abutments

Comparison between Counter-fort type abutment and Gravity type abutment:

Though counter-fort requires complicated design and skilled labours, still it has advantages over the gravity type in many aspect. Counterfort requires less labour, material, time for construction and therefore is economical in comparison with the gravity type abutment.

In the gravity abutment, there may exist few limitations such as the height increases, there is a variable and drastic increase in cost, which is undesirable. The gravity type abutment is advantageous in some aspects such as the design procedures are simple and hence easily approachable. The construction work requires less skilled labours, i.e. more unskilled labour force can be utilized. The counterfort type is uneconomical upto the height of abutment upto 7 metre, so gravity type is preferred.

The counterfort type also has higher material availability. As it uses hi-technology, reliability is higher as compared to the gravity type abutment. It is always advantageous to use ready formwork of the other structural member making no major alteration in it. Therefore versatility and ready use of formwork helps in saving cost and thus counterfort is preferred to gravity type abutment.

From the including design and estimation one can easily conclude that, counterfort type abutment is much more preferable to gravity type abutment.

13.18 PIERS

I. Piers for Girder Bridges:

The piers may be of solid or open type. One type piers are composed of beams, columns and bracings. Solid piers have a solid section in elevation, plan or end views.

(a) Solid Piers:

They are classified as follows: (i) Masonry piers.   (ii) R.C.C. piers.

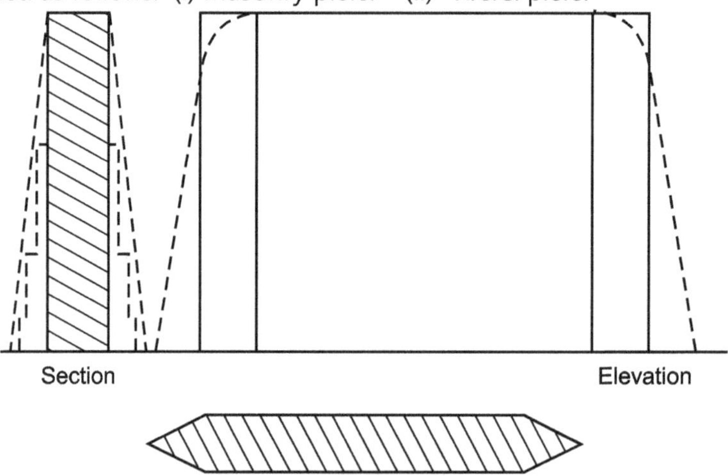

Fig. 13.17: A masonry pier

Masonry piers may be constructed of brick, stone, plain cement concrete or plum concrete. Plain cement concrete may be used cast-in-situ or pre-cast in blocks. Sometimes, hollow cells of masonry are filled with moorum, sand etc. to form a solid pier.

(i) Masonry Piers:

The cross-section of a masonry pier is shown in Fig. 13.17. Its top is in level and may carry a cement concrete block of a richer mix, called the *bed block*. Sometimes, for small spans, a stone slab may also serve the purpose. The sides of a masonry pier may be vertical, uniformly or varyingly battered or stepped. The alternative treatments are shown in the Fig. 13.17 by dotted lines. In elevation, the pier has its ends vertical or slightly battered. In plan, the ends are given any of the shapes shown in Fig. 13.18. The end on the upstream side is known as the cutwater and that on the downstream side is known as the *easewater*. They are shaped for easy passage of water. Both ends may be similarly or differently shaped according to the design. The cutwaters are usually triangular in shape, making an angle of 30° to 60°. The easewaters are generally semi-circular or consist of two parabolic arches.

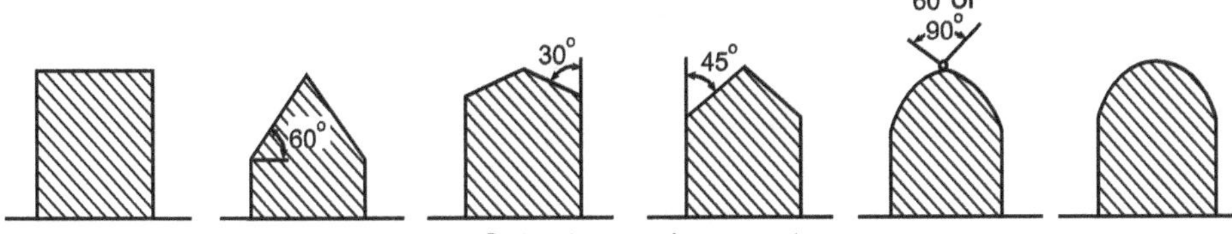

Fig. 13.18: Cutwaters and easewaters

(ii) R.C.C. Piers:

They are generally rectangular in cross-section. They too are provided with easewaters and cutwaters. They do not need bed blocks. The main reinforcement is vertical and secondary reinforcement is provided horizontally along the length, binding the main reinforcement.

Dumbbell Pier is a special type of R.C.C. pier. It consists of R.C.C. columns connected by thin reinforced concrete web, all along their height, in a direction transverse to the bridge (See Fig. 13.19). The columns here may have a variety of shapes and may be stepped, if exceptionally high.

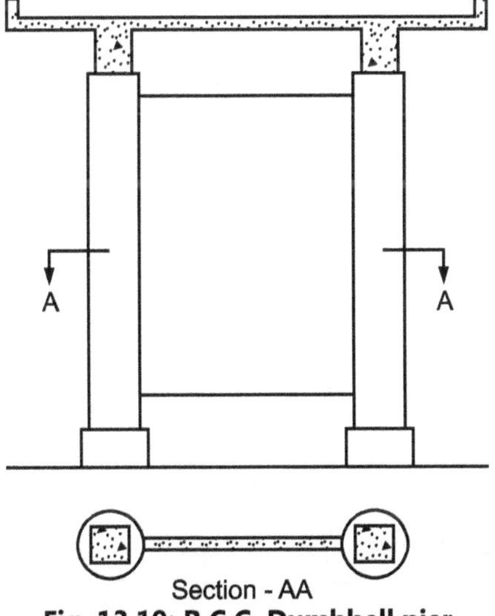

Fig. 13.19: R.C.C. Dumbbell pier

(b) Open Piers:

They are classified as follows:

    (i) Cylindrical piers.   (ii) Column bents.

    (iii) Pile bents.   (iv) Trestle bents.

(i) Cylindrical Piers:

Here, mild steel cylinders, filled with concrete, are constructed to support the main girders. They are connected by steel frame work. They are many times, extended below ground level and are connected to steel cylinder caisson.

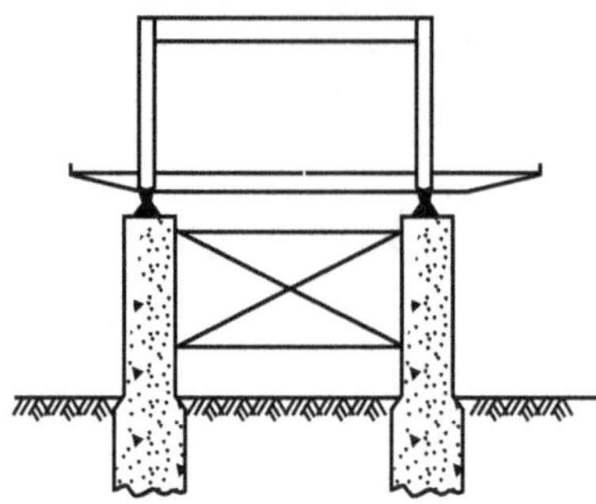

Fig. 13.20: A cylindrical pier

(ii) Column bents:

Here, two or more columns are constructed to support the main girders and are connected laterally by beams and braces or short diaphragms. Fig. 13.21 shows an R.C.C. column bent of two R.C.C. pillars with a beam, brace and a diaphragm, to connect them. The columns may be uniform in cross-section or may have varying section.

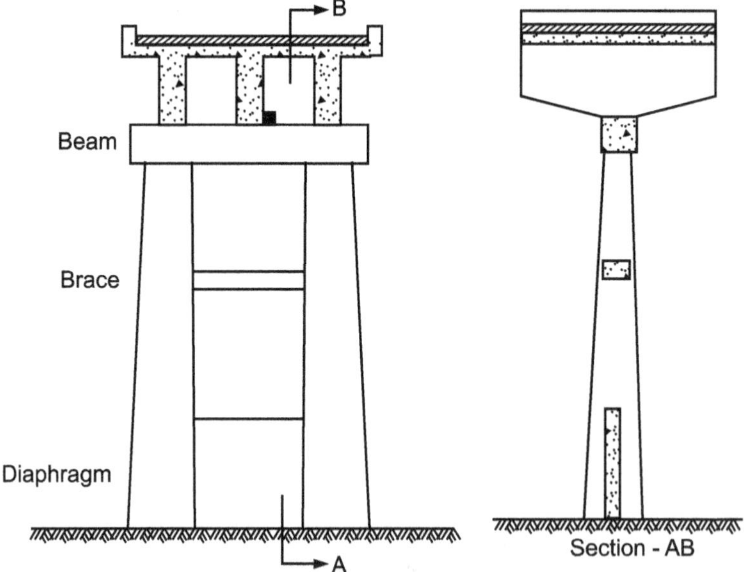

Fig. 13.21: An R.C.C. column bent

(iii) Pile Bents:

The piles may be used to support the main girders over their caps. They are laterally connected by frames of steel or R.C.C. The piles may be R.C.C. or steel or screw or disc type. They extend below the bed level to form the foundation. Wooden piles will not be used for substructure of a permanent bridge.

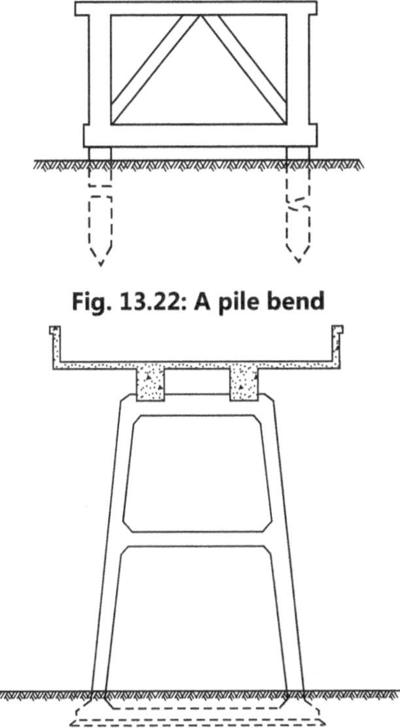

Fig. 13.22: A pile bend

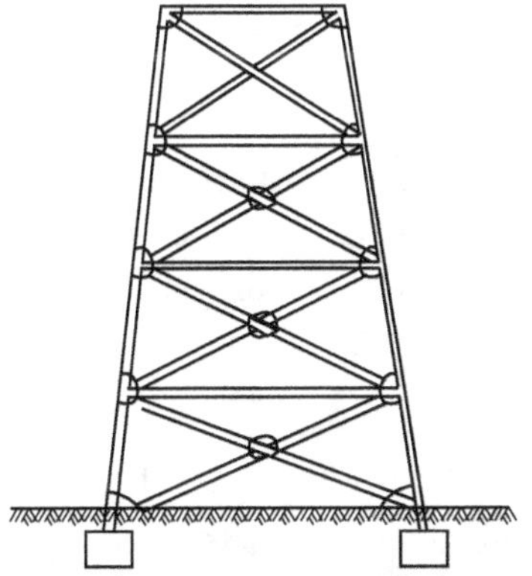

Fig. 13.23: An R.C.C. trestle bent

(iv) Trestle Bents:

An R.C.C. trestle bent is shown in Fig. 13.23 and a steel trestle bent is shown in Fig. 13.24.

Fig. 13.24: A steel trestle bent

All the members are square or rectangular in section. A steel trestle may have bracings of the type shown in Fig. 13.24. The connections of the steel trestle bent may be riveted or welded.

II. Piers for Arch Bridges:

The piers or abutment piers for an arch bridge are always solid. In cross-section, at the top their sides are splayed to receive the arch rings or their bearings normally (see Fig. 13.25). Other details are similar to those of solid piers of girder bridges.

If the bridge consists of a number of arches, every fourth or fifth pier is made of thicker cross-section and strong enough to resist the horizontal thrust of the arch on each side. Such abutment piers reduce the cost of centering because the arches ay then be constructed in set between abutment piers. They also localize damage caused by failure of an arch under adverse conditions.

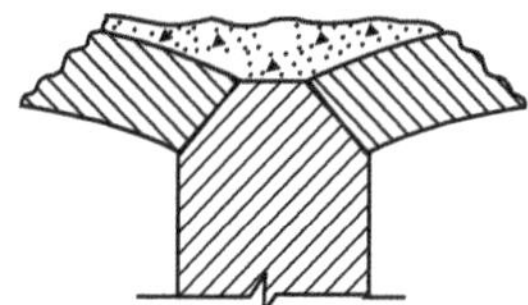

Fig. 13.25: A pier of an arch bridge

III. Piers for Suspension Bridges:

Piers for big suspension bridges are sometimes, called *towers*. They are either of masonry or more generally, of steel. If masonry is used, the pier may consist of shafts springing from a solid common base below the flooring. These shafts are connected together at the top by arches. If steel is used, the pier consists of two pier legs braced together by cross girders and bracings or by arched portals. Steel pier columns are made of built-up sections.

For high piers, individual legs may be made of braced construction, each leg consisting of four columns spreading apart towards the base and cross braced.

IV. Piers for Rigid Frame Bridges:

Here a pier is not provided as a separate structural pait, but the intermediate legs of the frames may be loosely called *piers*.

13.19 WING WALL

The abutment can be either buried or its front face can be left exposed. In the latter case, the walls constructed on either side of an abutment to support and protect the embankment are known as the *wing walls*.

Functions of Wing Walls:

A wing wall has mainly to perform the following two function:

- To provide a smooth entry into the bridge site; and
- To support and protect the embankment.

Types of Wings Walls:

According to their functions there are three types of wing walls

- Straight wing walls
- Splayed wing walls
- Return wing walls

    Please refer Figs. 13.13 to 13.15.

According to their materials used for construction there are two types of wing walls

- Masonry wing walls
- R.C.C. wing walls

QUESTIONS

1. Give detail classification of bridges stating clearly on which these depend?

2. Define the following: Waterway, Effective linear waterway, Afflux, HFL, Scour depth.

3. Discuss how the design flood discharge can be estimated by direct method.

4. What are different methods of determining flood discharge?

5. What are preliminary data required for investigation of site for bridges.

6. What is height of afflux? State also its importance and hence calculate the height of afflux from the following particulars.

7. Derive the expression for economical span and the factor affecting on it.

8. Preventive measures to minimize the effect of scour.

9. Enlist factor affecting the choice of bridge superstructure.

10. What is height of afflux? State also its importance and hence calculate the height of afflux from the following particulars.

    (i) Normal velocity of flow in a river is 1.50 m/sec.

    (ii) The normal and artificial waterway under the bridge and enlarged area upstream of the bridge are respectively 8000 m^2, 7000 m^2 and 10,000 m^2. Assume g = 9.81 m/sec^2. Use Merriman's formula. Also find increase in velocity.

11. Discuss the various forces coming over bridge pier and also state the conditions of stability.

12. Make a list of any eight and briefly discuss any four loads that are acting simultaneously on bridge structure.

13. Sketch the different types of abutments.

14. Sketch the different types of wing walls.

15. Sketch the different types of piers.

16. Describe the various types of foundations to piers and abutments.

17. Mention the different types of wing walls and explain them with neat sketches.

18. Enlist and explain Requirement of various data of traffic in the design of highway bridges.

19. Enumerate various forces, loads and stresses which are to be considered in the design of a bridge.

20. Give sketches of IRC Class AA Loading

21. **Example:** Following are the costs involved in a uniform multiple span bridge construction

SPAN (m)	5	10	15	20
Cost of Girder Rs	4000	13000	26000	45000
Cost of Girder Pier and Foundation Rs.	16000	18000	22000	250000

Calculate the Economic Span

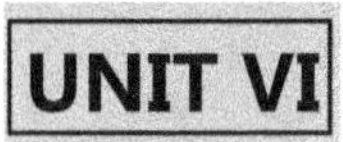

Chapter 14
TYPES OF BRIDGES

14.1 INTRODUCTION OF CULVERTS

There are many instances when road has to cross small nalas and rivulets or even canals. If the road is crossing these water courses in flat country, there is every likelihood that the span to be so bridged between the faces of the abutment or extreme ventways boundaries measured right angles there to is 6 metres or less, in that case the structure to bridge such gap will be called as **culvert**. It is very clear that since the gap to be catered for is somewhat small the culvert is intended for comparatively less design flood discharge. Based on the type of construction the culverts could be classified.

14.2 CLASSIFICATION OF CULVERTS

14.2.1 Pipe Culvert

In this case, by suitably providing nala training works the flood discharge is carried by the non pressure reinforced concrete pipes and the road over this pipe. (See Fig. 14.1)

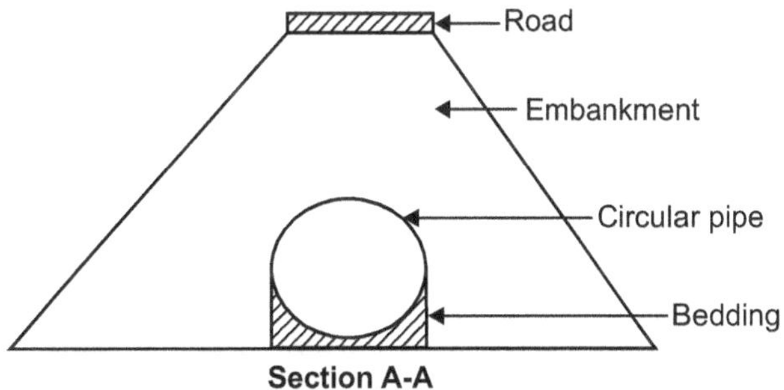

Fig. 14.1 : General picturization of pipe culvert

Naturally the road is in embankment and the pipe should be strong enough to withstand the load of the earth above it and should be capable of carrying out the flood discharge when running full. The diameter of the pipe line when serving as culvert should be minimum 600 mm so that easy inside cleaning should be possible and the pipe line should not be choked.

14.2.2 Reinforced Concrete Box Culvert

In this case the place of circular pipe is taken by square or rectangular box of about 3 meter height. Box culvert may be useful for gaps upto 4 meters to 6 meters. Generally the top slab of the box serves as a rock deck.

Reinforced Concrete Box Culvert :

With the advent of reinforced concrete, R.C.C. box culvert are now becoming more and more popular. It consists of R.C.C. box of square or rectangular opening with span of 4 meter. The top of the box section can be at the road level or it may be at a depth below road level, if the road is in embankment. The r.c.c. box also contain wing walls splayed at 45° to retain the embankments and to guide the flow of water into and out of barrel. The pictorial view of R.C.C. box culvert is shown in Fig. 14.2. If the design discharge is small only one box may be sufficient. If the design discharge is considerable erecting one single box to pass this discharge will be uneconomical due to higher thickness of top slab and the walls. In such a case, more than one boxes kept side by side and monolithically cast called multiple box culvert is the answer. Multtiple box bridges are very economical and these are new replacing single box culverts.

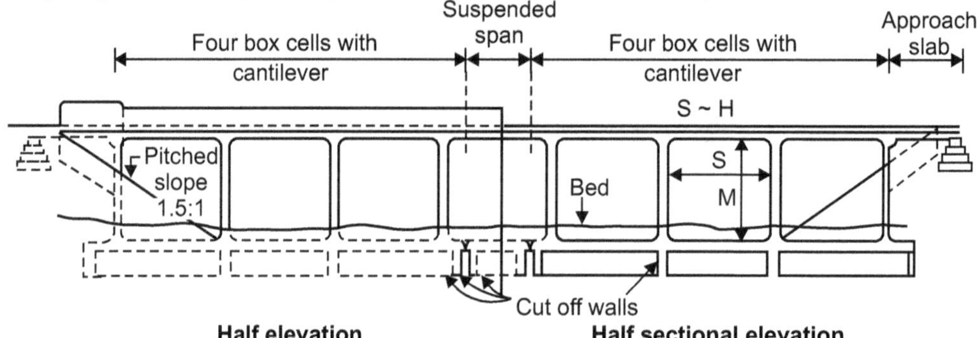

Fig. 14.2 : Multiple units (here two units) box bridge with seven cells

14.2.3 Reinforced Concrete Slab Culvert

The construction is useful about 8 meters gap and is virtually a small bridge with deck slab abutments and wing walls with foundations etc. It is essentially a small bridge except the fact that since spans are comparatively shorter, provision of T beams etc. is not required. The structural performance of reinforced concrete culvert may therefore be grouped along with reinforced concrete bridges.

14.2.4 Stone Arch Culvert

In this case the weight of deck slab which in turn is supporting the road traffic is borne by the stone arch which rests on abutment (See Fig. 14.3). When the span is shorter, you need not have pier in between and with only one arch the gap can be closed. Most of the old cross drainage work in India is stone arch type. Some of the stone arch culverts in Roman times are still existing. The stone arch culvert is pleasing in appearance.

It should be noted that the pipe culvert will generally be in embankment i.e., the road level will be higher than the pipe level but in the case of reinforced concrete box culvert or reinforced concrete slab culvert, it is economical and convenient that top of the slab in both the cases serve road deck. Thus the road level and top of the slab level is more or less the same.

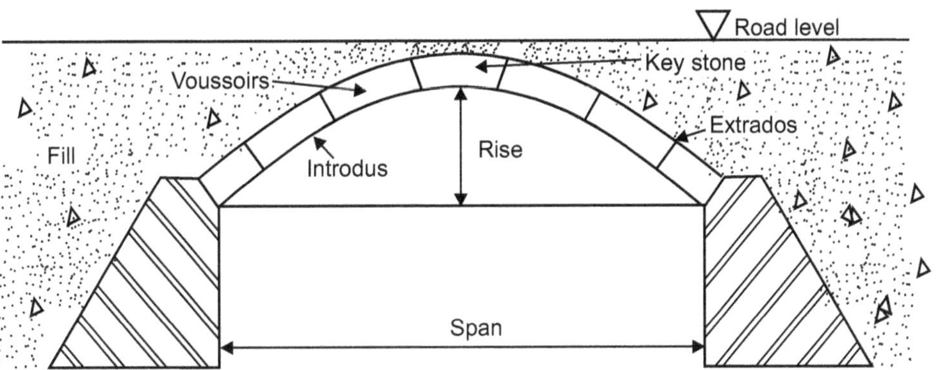

Fig. 14.3 : Single arch stone culvert

14.3 INTRODUCTION AND TYPES

Depending upon the amount of money available the life span of the superstructure and length of the span to be bridged, we can plan different types of bridge superstructures. While one bridge superstructure is useful and apt for one location it may serve the useful purpose at another location. These superstructures are :

(a) Temporary Bridge Superstructures :

1.   **Military bridges :** (a) Fixed bridges, (b) Floating bridges which consists of boat, raft or pantoon bridges.

2.   **Other temporary bridge superstructures :** (a) Flying bridges which may be with the use : (1) Supension cables, (2) Anchors and swing cables, (3) Cable with rollers. (b) Cut boat bridges.

3.   **Causeways :** (a) Flush causeway, (b) Low level causeways.

4.   **Timber bridges which may be :** (a) Timber trestle bridge, (b) Bridge with pile bents, (c) With cribs, (d) With crates, (e) Cantilever, (f) Suspension, (g) Trestle suspension, (h) Sling, (i) Ramp.

Temporary Bridge / Superstructures

The temporary bridge superstructure does not necessarily mean low cost structures or short duration life span structures. Temporary bridge superstructure means that the bridge has been erected for a specific purpose and after that purpose is served it is possible, to dismantle the bridge in short time and the material used elsewhere. The necessity of constructing temporary bridges arises when :

•   In military campaigns, when in short time you want to construct the bridge for the passage of foot soldiers, tanks, armored vehicles etc. and once this material is transported, you want to unwind the bridge so that material can be reused.

•   There is shortage of funds and time.

•   There is shortage of resource and skill.

- Repairs are to be carried out to the permanent bridge.
- Due to requirement of another bridge to facilitate the construction of permanent bridge.
- Due to requirement of some sort of arrangement to span the river during the construction of permanent bridge, i.e. Diversion Bridge.
- Due to requirement of soundings in the river.

Advantages of Temporary Bridges

- These bridges are easy in construction
- They are cheap in construction
- Their structural from is simple, therefore be easily designed
- Less skill labour is required
- Cost of repair and maintenance is less
- Require less time for construction
- Temporary bridges are most suitable in case of emergency.

Disadvantages of Temporary Bridges

- Temporary bridges are not suitable for heavy traffic
- Useful life of these bridges is less up to 10 years
- Not suitable for every purposes

14.3.1 Classification of Temporary Bridges

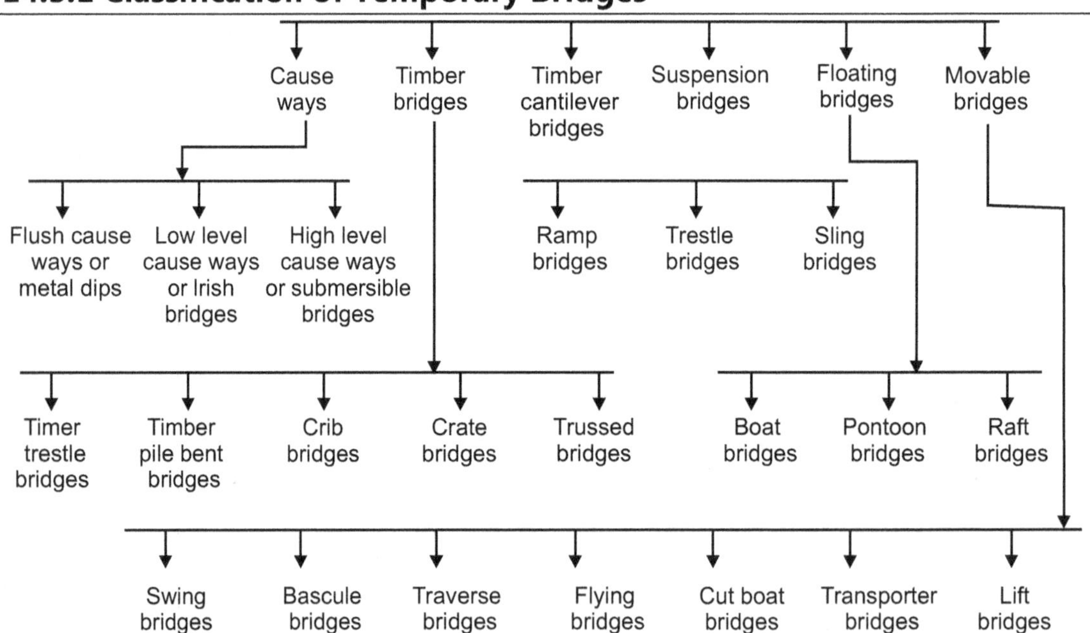

(B) Permanent Bridges :

1. **High level causeways.**

2. **Masonary bridges which may be :** (a) Filled spandrel, (b) Open spandrel arch bridge.

3. **Reinforced concrete bridges which may be :** (a) R.C.C. slab bridge, (b) T-beam and slab bridge, (c) R.C.C. girder bridge, (d) Parapet girder bridge, (e) T-beam girder bridge, (f) Hallow girder bridges, (g) R.C.C. rigid frame bridge, (h) R.C.C. multiple span portal frame bride, (i) R.C.C. balanced cantilever bridge, (j) R.C.C. continuous bridge, (k) R.C.C. arch bridge fixed or two hinged or three hinged, with filled or open spandrel, (*l*) Bow string girder bridge.

4. **Prestressed concrete bridges :** Cable stayed bridges.

5. **Iron and steel bridges which may be :** (a) Steel trough plate brides, (b) Steel girder bridge, (c) Steel arch bridge, (d) Steel truss bridges which may be bow string girder type, (e) Steel rigid frame bridge, (f) Continuous steel bridge, (j) Steel suspension bridge, (k) Steel cantilever bridge.

6. **Movable steel bridges which may be :** (a) Swing, (b) Transverse, (c) Transporter, (d) Bascule, (e) Lift.

14.3.2 Temporary Bridge Superstructures

The temporary bridge superstructure does not necessarily mean low cost structures or short duration life span structures. Temporary bridge superstructure means that the bridge has been ereced for a specific purpose and after that purpose is served it is possible, to dismantle the bridge in short time and the material used else where. The necessity of constructing temporary bridges arises when :

- In military campaigns, when in short time you want to construct the bridge for the passage of foot soldiers, tanks, armoured vehicles etc. and once this material is transported, you want to unwind the bridge so that material can be reused.
- There is shortage of funds and time.
- There is shortage of resource and skill.
- Repairs are to be carried out to the permanent bridge.
- You require another bridge to facilitate the construction of permanent bridge.
- You require some sort of arrangement to span the river during the construction of permanent bridge, i.e. diversion bridge.
- You require soundings in the river.

14.4 MILITARY BRIDGES

Introduction :

During the military campaign, the army engineers, the army engineers have to erect structures to bridge either river or dry gaps or may be glaciers so that movement of troop and material is facilitated. During large religious gathering such "Kumbha Mela" also these types of bridges are constructed since these can be constructed at a short notice and are sufficiently strong.

The India army is very old and army engineers have constructed the bridges is very odd circumstances such as very high altitude bridges, glacier bridges etc. Recently in 1982 army engineers constructed a bridge on ice body at a very high altitude and this feat was mentioned in Guinness Book of Records.

The road Leh-Chalunka passes over Khardugla at an altitude of 18380 feet. The alignment of the road near Khardungla passes over an ice body which an obstacle to vehicular traffic and resulted in road capacity of only 10-12 vehicles per day in 1982. Glaciologists and experts had opined that the ice body was in a state of flow; accordingly a realignment of a portion of the road had been proposed for completion over a period of 2 to 3 years at a cost of about Rs. 45 lakhs to remove this traffic bottleneck. However, in August 1982 Lieutenant Colonel (now Colonel) S. G. Vombatkere in command of 16 Border Road Task Force planned, designed and constructed a 90 ft. Bailey bridge on the ice body against expert opinion. The construction of the bridge was done in 4 days at a cost of about Rs. 25 lakhs removed the traffic bottleneck and the vital road link was made immediately available for full traffic. It also permitted the road to be kept open during the winters. This bridge through only 90 ft. in length, has the following unique distinctions :

- It is the World's highest altitude motorable bridge.

- It is a semi-permanent bridge across an ice body.

- It is founded upon the ice body.

14.4.1 The Types of Military Bridges

The types of military bridges are (1) fixed bridges for narrow streams and dry gaps. (2) floating bridges where a roadway is laid on floating supports, here we many have boat bridge, pontoon bridge or raft bridge.

(A) Fixed Type Bridges :

This bride essentially consists of light prefabricated modular units which are to be transported at the site of works and then assembled so that full bridge designed by Sir Donald Bailey and extensively used in World War II. The typical details are shown in Fig. 14.4 (a), (b). It consists of standard truss panel, bracing frames, transforms, stringers, bearings, slinks and pin. The roadway consists of wooden chases laid over stringers which rest on transforms supported on trusses on the two sides of the roadway. Each truss composes of a number of panels pined together. The Bailey Bridge can be assembled by man power alone, can carry upto 100 t overspans of 9 to 67 meters. Depending upon span length and load the bridge may have one or more trusses and one or more storeys of panels.

Generally the bridge is constructed by cantilever launching with the aid of launching nose. Framework of panels is corrected on rollers on the near bank for suitable length of nose and the first bay is added. After constructing additional bays, the entire bridge is pushed forward on rollers across the gap. When leading end of nose reaches the far bank, it is to be guided on rollers on that bank. When the first bay comes and settles on the other bank, the launching nose can be dismantled and end posts are attached. The bridge is to be jacked off the rollers one end and one roller at a time and lowered on to the stable bearing. The bridge can be opened to the military traffic by adding end ramps. The military bridge class is denoted by number 8, 9, 40, 70 etc. i.e., 70 class carry 70 ton vehicle i.e., a centurian tank with trailer. Army engineers and their research organizations are now trying to use light, strong durable alloys for Bailey bridges, so that weight is lessenced and assembling can occur in short time.

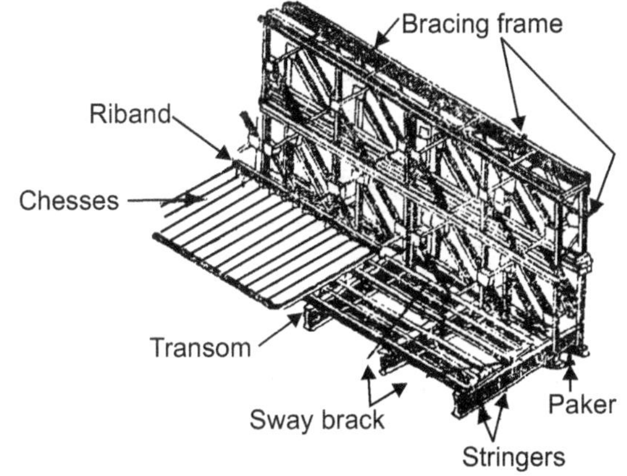

Fig. 14.4 (a) : Out away view showing components

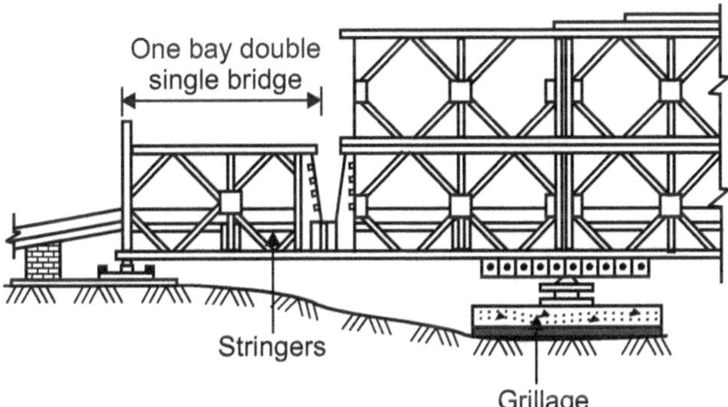

Fig. 14.4 (b) : Elevation at bank end

(B) Floating Bridges :

Foating bridges i.e., the boat bridge or pantoon bridge or the raft bridges have been used in wars in historical times and even now. Alxeander has been credited to pass the mighty Sindhu with the help of boat bride during night. The major advantages over the fixed bridge are

- Quicker to construct.
- Capital can be constructed where firm ground for locating the rollers of Bailery is not available for example marshy ground.

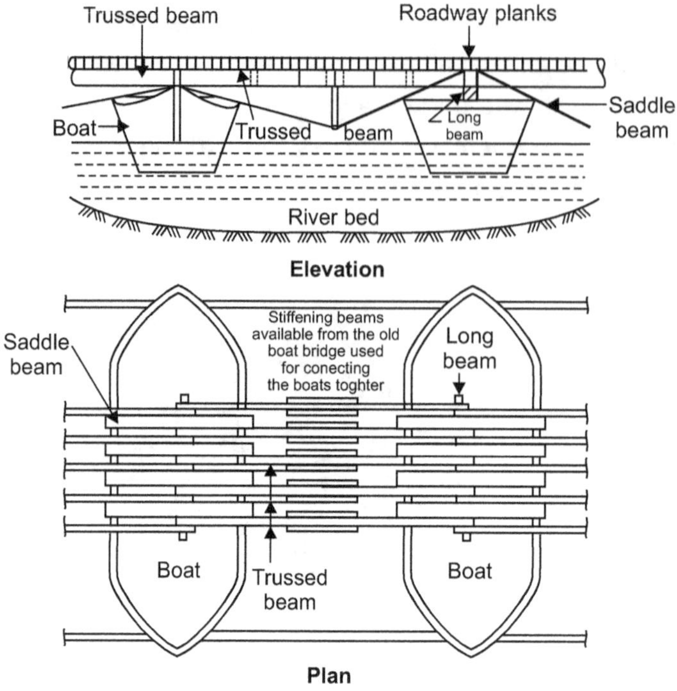

Fig. 14.5 : Boat bridge

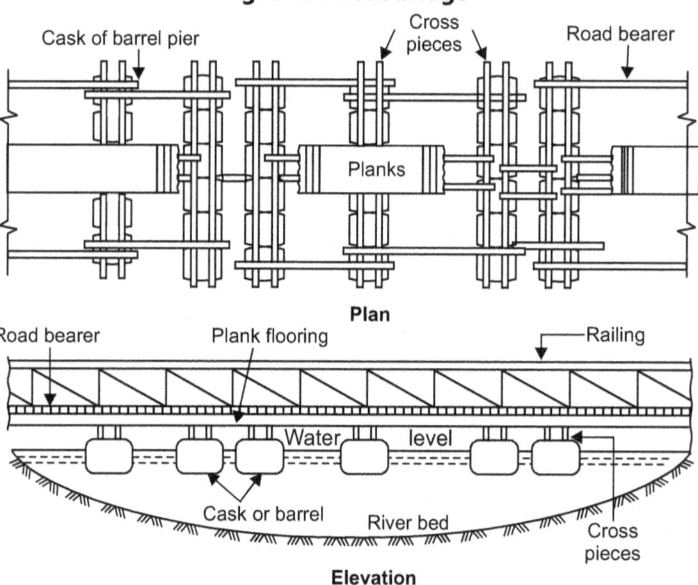

Fig. 14.6 : Raft bridge

- They can be constructed and used during night and after use dismantled before sun rise such that enemy may not spot it. A schematic diagram of a boat bridge is shown in Fig. 14.5 and the pantoon bridge is shown in Fig. 14.6 whereas the raft bridge is shown in Fig. 14.7.

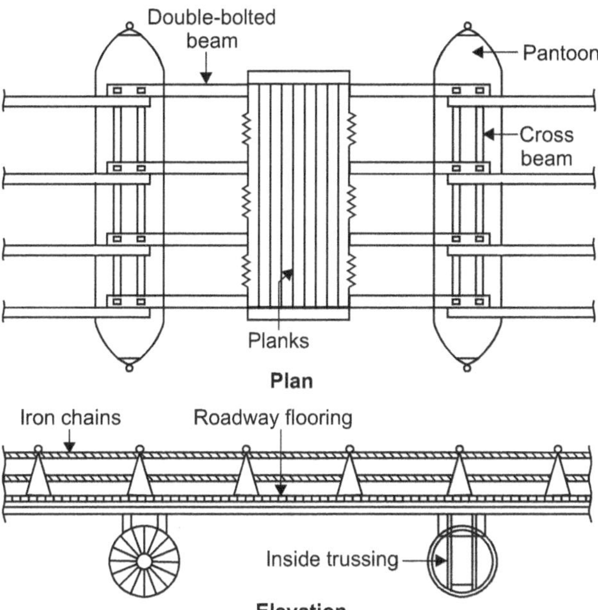

Fig. 14.7 : Pantoon bridge

The floating bridge consists of floating pantoons/boats main axis parallel to current of river. The pantoons/boat may be flat bottomed, decked large or pneumatic, pneumatic ones are now preferred. In between superstructure and the float, saddle is placed for seating purposes. Float has number of air pockets, so that damage to one or few air pockets due to enemy fire will not cause distress to the bridge. The superstructure could be that of Bailey bridge, the superstructure is designed as one continuous member, so that load on one span will be carried by a number of pantoons on either side. This facilitates the design of pantoons. The spacing of pantoons is such that floating matter in the river should pass without causing damage, wider spacing of boats or pantoons make the bridge superstructure heavy and difficult to assemble. The pantoons or the boats must be anchored together so that alignment is maintained. Throughout the world army engineers are now opting for Krup-man brides made out of aluminium alloy section for transporting heavy fighting military equipment. A defense establishment at Ambazhari in Maharashtra is scheduled to manufacture these components.

(C) Raft bridges are not favoured by army engineers. The substructure consists of floating piers made of casks or barrels lashed together by spars i.e. by long pieces of wood-laid cross at top. These acts as gunwales to support the road bearers that support the floating.

14.5 OTHER TEMPORARY BRIDGE SUPERSTRUCTURES/BRIDGES

It is not only the army which is required to construct temporary bridges. This may be due to paucity of funds or as a short term measure. We have over here the following types.

(A) Flying Bridges :

In this case a boat or a raft is used as a ferry. The ferry boats which either rowed or pulled across are termed as flying bridges. We can guide the ferry by the following three methods.

1. Suspension Cable :

Here a cable is suspended on the river. Cable is supported on two vertical towers tone on each bank such that cable will be above H.F.L. Cable carries a traveler which in term is attached to a boat by two cables. The length of these two cables is such that the boat makes an angle of 45° to the river current. the traveler is to be pulled by which or manpower from either bank thus transporting the ferry from one bank to the other. See Fig. 14.8.

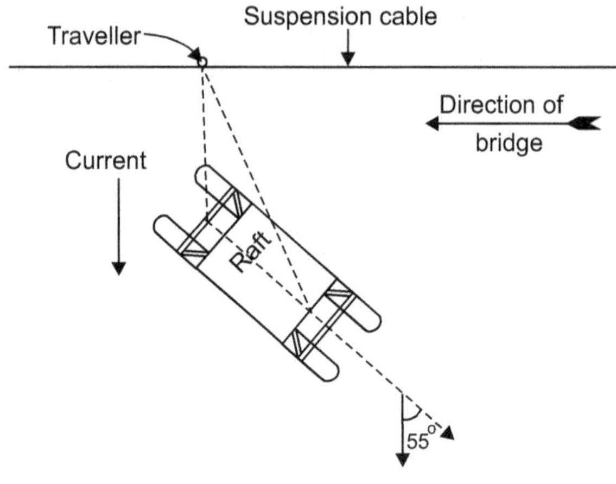

Fig. 14.8

2. Using Anchors and Switching Cables :

In this case a cable in the centre of bridge and along the river line is laid. One end of the cable is supported on a float or casks and is anchored to the river bed. The other end is connected to the ferry in such a way that ferry always makes an angle of 45° to the river current. The cable is slack between ferry and the anchorage and is about $1\frac{1}{2}$ times the breadth of river. In this method the men in the boat actually row the boat from one bank to the other and the use of cable is to keep the angle around 55° and give extra support. See Fig. 14.9.

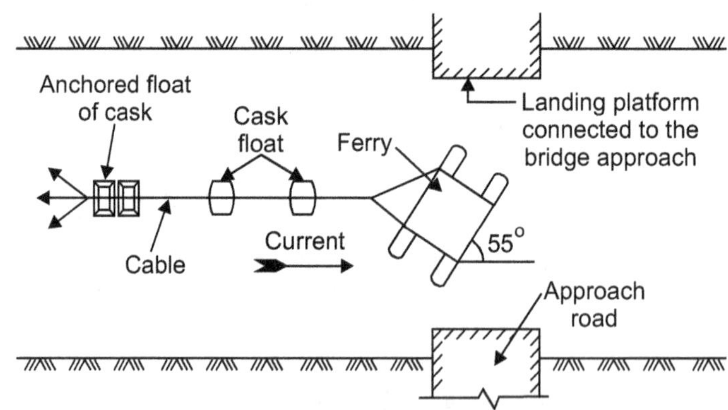

Fig. 14.9 : Drying bridge with anchors and swinging cables

3. Using a Warp or Cable with Rollers :

In this method cable is erected on two vertical towers one on each bank. Instead of the traveler in the first method we have here rollers fixed on the raft and the cable moves through the rollers. By moving the roller from the bank to the other, transportation is achieved.

(B) Cut-Boat Bridges :

the cut-boat is also a type of floating bridge. It is employed when you want some portion of river navigable, to allow the boat traffic to pass. Therefore, one or more bays of the floating bridge are made movable. The movable bays are to be constructed into an independent raft which is allowed to float downstream during the time river is used for navigation purposes. See Fig. 14.10.

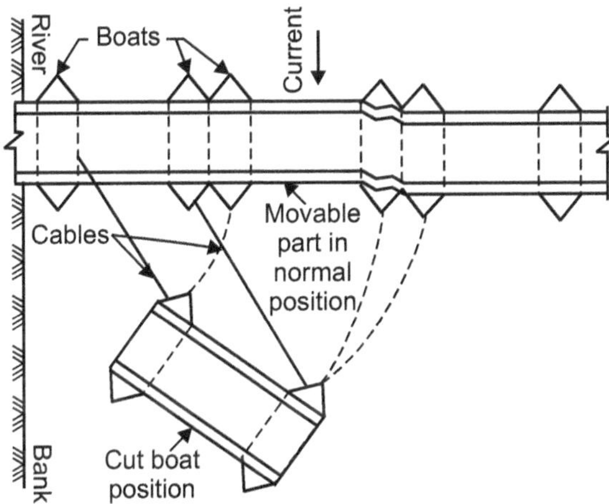

Fig. 14.10 : Cut-boat bridge

(C) Cause Ways :

Bridges constructed with their decks flush or little above the bed of river are known as **causeways**, i.e. arish bridges or metal dips. These can be made in R.C.C. masonary and can carry light traffic even small amount of flood passes over the deck since its level is slightly above the bed stream. When the traffic on the communication route increases these have to be replaced by permanent bridges.

Circumstances for Causeways : These are :

- Unimportant road and the crossing carrying practically no or little water for major part of year.

- The floods if and when they occur are of small duration (3 days in a year).

- Pauncity of funds.

- Hilly region when many small streams have to be crossed.

- Natural width of stream considerable.

Classification of Causeways : These are classified as :

- High level causeway or vented causeway.
- Low level causeway or Irish bridges.
- Flush causeway or metal dips.

Whereas the high level causeway is a sort of permanent bridge the later two falls in the category of temporary bridges due to this comparative short life.

Flush Causeway :

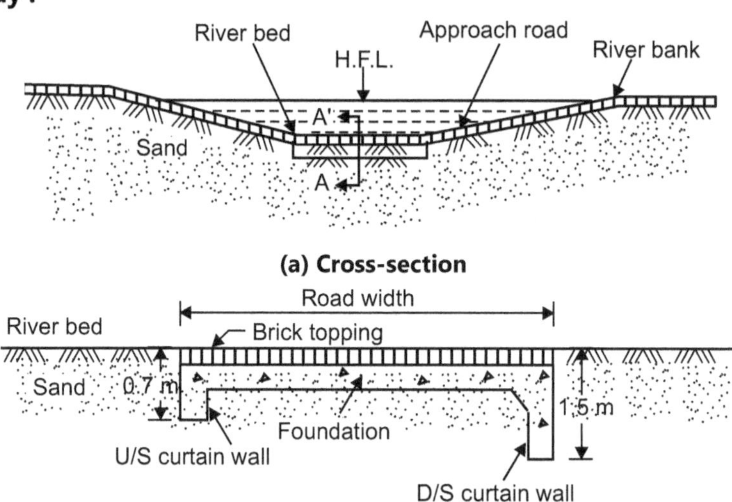

Fig. 14.11 : Flush causeways

In these structure, the bank of the stream is tailored to a gentle slope, and stream is paved for sufficient width on both sides of the causeway. The floor is flush with bed of the stream with no vents. In the most crude form it may be in the form of bundles of grass held in position by stakes across the sandy bed. When the floor is metallied, it is known as the **metal dip**. Sometimes R.C.C. slab may be provided in the stream bed for providing smooth surface Fig. 14.11 shows pictorial view of flush causeway. Many times curtain walls are constructed to prevent distress of causeway slab due to scour. Downstream side curtain wall may be 0.8 m deep than that u/s curtain wall which may be 0.7 m deep. The metal dips are good for non-perenial streams in hilly roads where flood duration is short and the river or stream water level in food is about 1.7 m.

See Fig. 14.12. low level causeway the those in which one or two vents are provided under the roadway slab so that small discharge may pass in dry reason and road deck is free of water. These causeway are called as **Irish bridges**. The level of the roadway near the stream bed is raised and 30-40 cm vents provided below roadway slab. During moderate discharge traffic is therefore undisturbed by flood of course high flood cannot be catered by Irish brides. Socur can be prevented by u/s and D/s curtain walls and an apron on D/s. Road pavement leading to Irish bridges are required to the made stable if bank to river bed slope is steep and approaches long. In such case cross dwarf walls are provided as shown. The low level causeways are good for shallow perennial rivers having a discharge depth of 30 to 45 cm depth for major part of the year and heavy discharge for only rainy season for a few hours only.

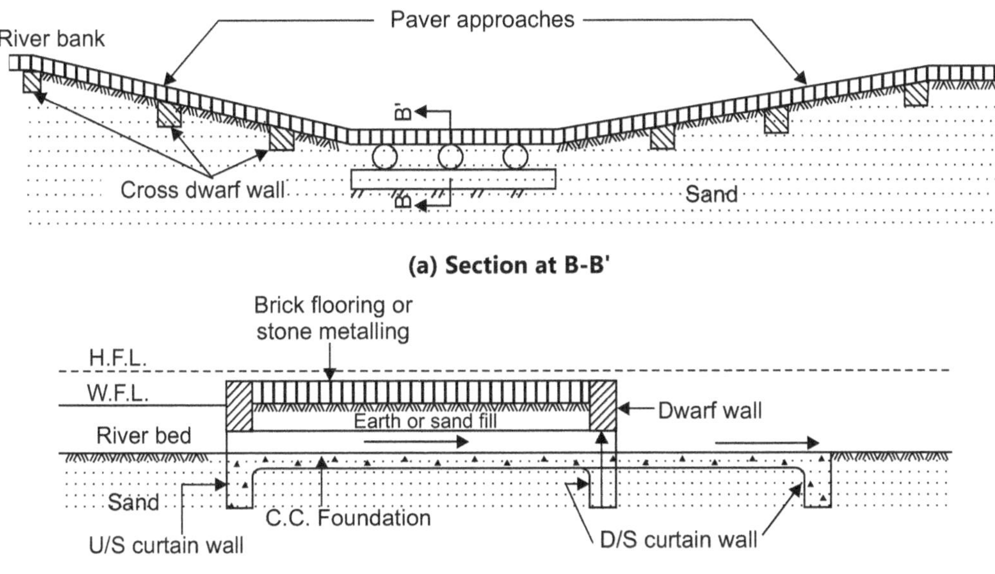

(a) Section at B-B'

(b) Enlarged section at B-B'

Fig. 14.12 : Low level causeway or Irish bridge

14.6 TIMBER BRIDGES

When the substructure and superstructure of a bridge made out of timber it may be called timber brides. Life of timber bridge may be 10-15 years even when painted.

14.6.1 Suitability and Limitations

In hilly areas where timber is plentry and cheap timber bridges may be adopted as a short term measure. During the time of constructing permanent bridge it may be used as diversion. At the most it can be used for B loading with no impact. Evidently these brides are not popular. Reasons are :

- The present high cost of timber.

- Ease with which timber can catch fire.

- Non-uniform strength of timber.

- Effect of environment on timber and the decay and disintegration caused by it and as such the short life associated with it.

14.6.2 Superstructure of Timber Bridges

The typical superstructure of the timber bridge is shown in Fig. 14.13. The floating would be 30 cm wide planks on longitudinal beams called bearers. If the span is more than 6 m, we have to use wood trusses in place of bearers. The details of wooden truss is also shown in the figure.

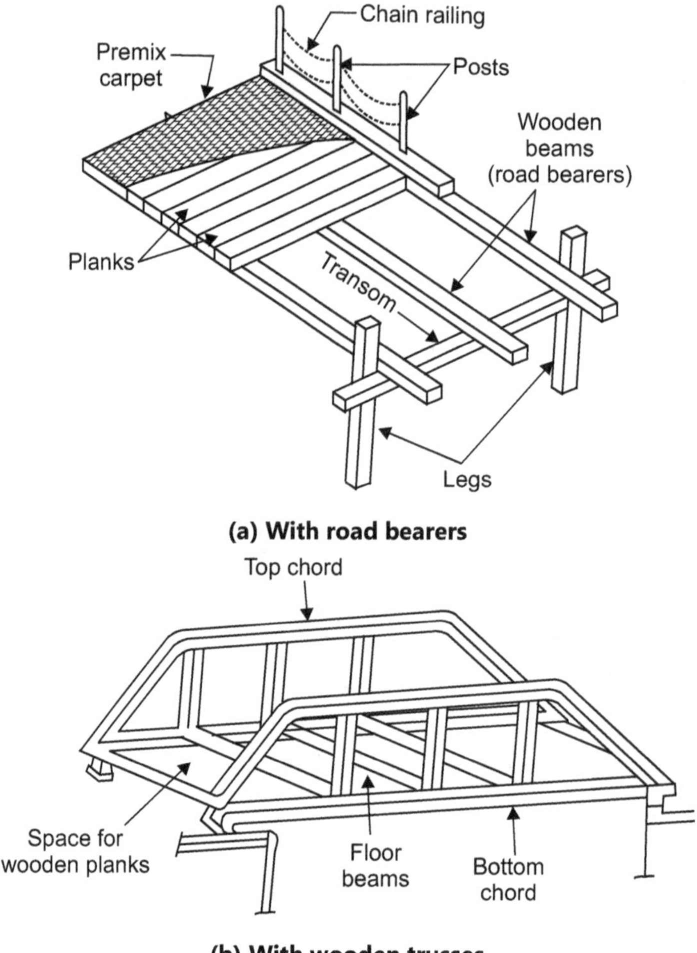

(a) With road bearers

(b) With wooden trusses

Fig. 14.13 : Superstructure of a timber

14.6.3 Substructure of Timber Bridges

In timber bridges the pairs and abutments also to be made out of timber. The piers and abutments could be timber pile-bent, timber crib or timber crate. The bridges are named accordingly.

(a) Timber Trestle Bridge :

These trestles are shown in Fig. 14.14. They could be of square or round sections the spikes and nails being used to bind square section and ropes and steel wires being used to bind round sections. Two legged, three legged and four legged trestle are shown in Fig. 14.14.

When trestles an be used when the stream bed is hard and the velocity of water is not much.

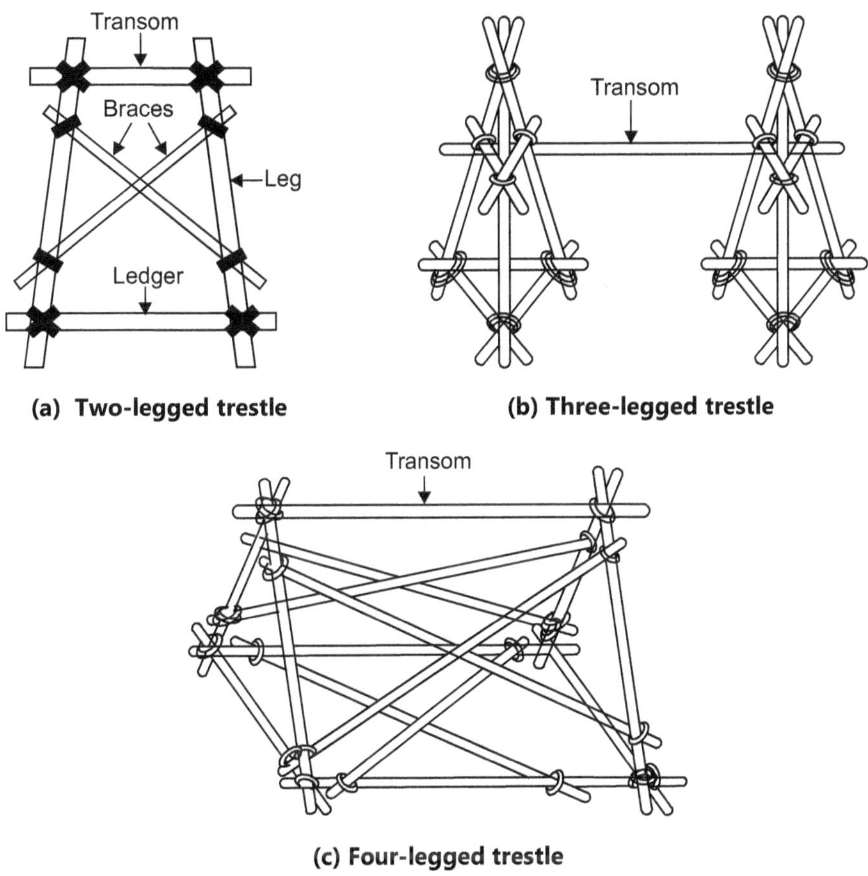

(a) Two-legged trestle   **(b) Three-legged trestle**

(c) Four-legged trestle

Fig. 14.14 : Different types of timber trestles

(b) Pile Bents :

In this case two or three wood piles are driven vertically in a line about 1.2 meters away parallel to the axis of the stream. Piles are connected together at top by horizontal member called transom or capsill and braced together by diagonal members called braces. Pile may be kept in position by connecting their lower portion by a member called ledger. Older bridges had these pile bents. A typical bent is shown in Fig. 14.15. The bents may used for muddy streams.

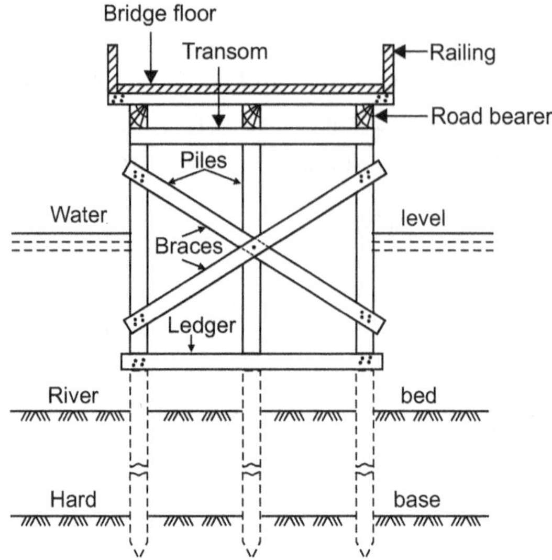

Fig. 14.15 : Pile bent

(c) Cribs :

Wooden sleepers placed in transverse direction alternatively in layers fastened together with ropes and bikes constitute crib. Different wood sections as are available at site may be used. Crib is construcuted on bank tower to the site and sunk by filling stones in the interior places, such that it is sufficiently heavy so as not to be washed away by running water. A typical crib is shown in Fig. 14.16. These could be used as piers and abutments.

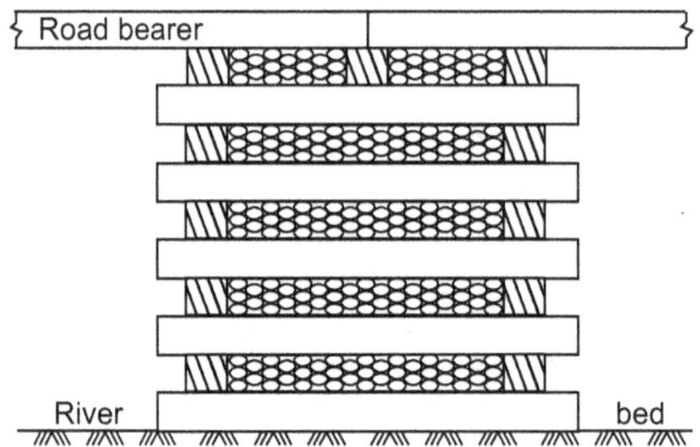

Fig. 14.16 : Crib pier

(d) Crates :

Crates are generally used for piers. Each pier would consist of four vertical stout wood members called uprights connected to top and bottom as shown in the figure. The bottom is generally planked for ease of towing. We may add an inclined pole to form cutwater. Figure 14.17 shows the general arrangement. Crate is prepared on the bank towed to site of pier and sunk by filling the inter space by brushwood and stones. Crates an take heavy load.

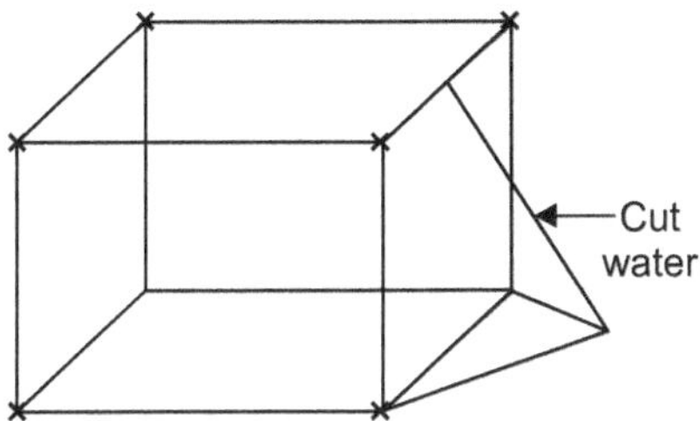

Fig. 14.17 : Crate pier

14.6.4 Timber Cantilever Bridges

These bridges generally are made of timber logs laid in layers projecting beyond the underlying layer from each bank. Fig. 14.18 illustrates these bridges. Each timber section projects around 1.5 m to 3 m beyond the underlying layer. The middle gap of about 4-6 meter is bridged by the road bearer and then the flooring is completed. All timber sections are anchored together by spikes and buried in dry stone masonary of the abutment. Wire stays can be provided to this bridge to carry moderate traffic. The bridge is suitable when foundation condition of the river bed is poor so that testle bents can not be erected. These bridges are O.K. when velocity of running water is high since there is no obstruction to the river flow in these of bridges. In hilly regions where timber logs are somewhat spans upto 50 m have bridged by this type of bridges.

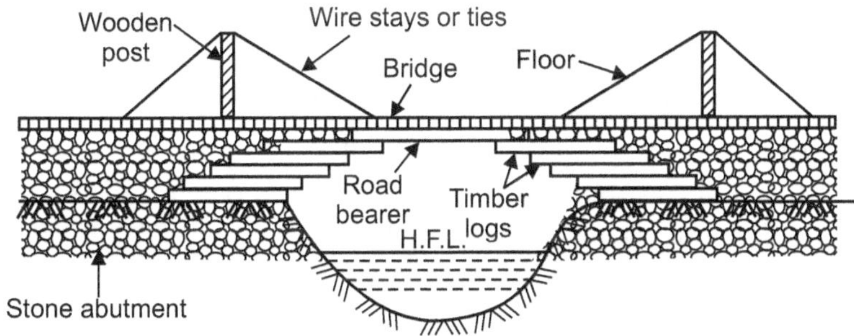

Fig. 14.18 : Cantilever bridge

14.6.5 Suspension Bridges

When two or more cables hang in space and support the roadway it is a suspension bridge. The suspension bridge could be of the following types :

(a) Trestle Suspension Bridge :

See Fig. 14.19. In this case, the roadway is supported on trestles which in turn in supported by cable which are well anchored. Compared to the sway of suspension bridge, this type less sway, but it is very heavy and costly.

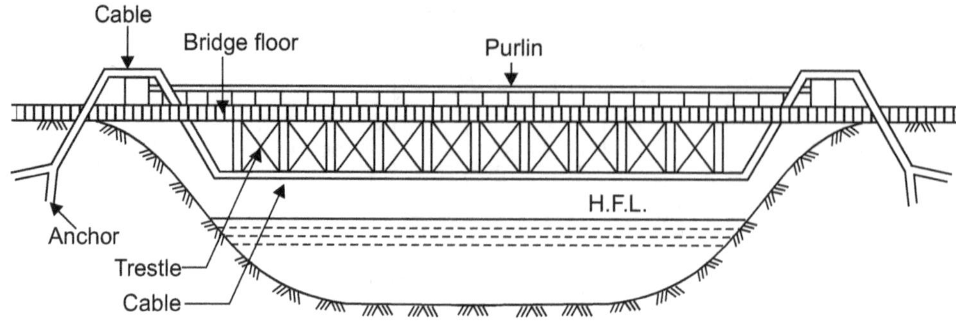

Fig. 14.19 : Trestle suspension bridge

(b) Sling Bridge :

See Fig. 14.20. It consists of two sets of cables which carry the roadway through suspenders known as slings.

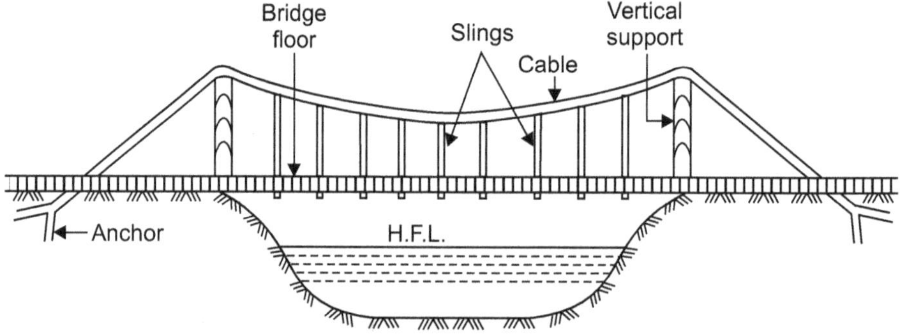

Fig. 14.20 : Sling type suspension bridge

The roadway may be wooden planks connected at ends to the wooden transom beams hung by suspenders from the cables or ropes. The cables generally pass over the vertical towers and then these are safely anchored in the bed.

(c) Ramp Bridge :

See Fig. 14.21. This bridge requires less quantity of material and can be constructed in short duration. Here the roadway would be generally wooden planks directly laid on rectangular pattern of cables. The longitudinal cable is supported on two vertical posts erected on each bank. Naturally with the movement of traffic the roadway is distorted and suffers sway.

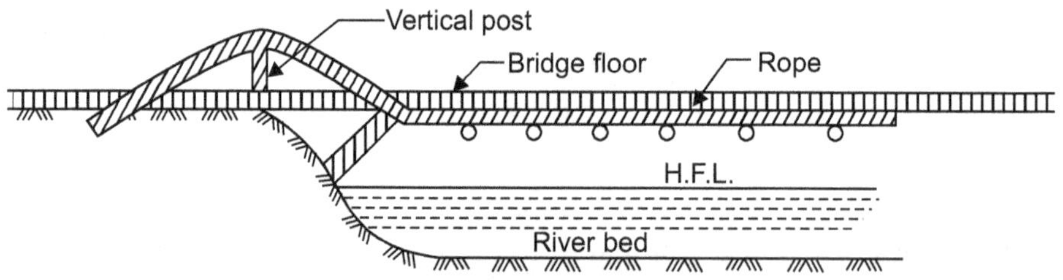

Fig. 14.21 : Ramp suspension bridge

14.7 PERMANENT BRIDGES

The permanent bridges are those which with usual maintenance and up keep can last at least 50 years. This is its design life. There are many bridges in our country which are at least century old. When the permanent bridge becomes this old, it is generally discorded and new bridge is constructed. Because in such case, actually bridge may last for a couple years more but it's life becomes uncertain and can collapse without giving warning, hence new bridge is constructed. Design life of temporary bridge is about 5 years, between life span can be lengthened by proper maintenance to 8 years.

14.7.1 Comparison between Permanent and Temporary Bridge

- Temporary bridges have short (5 years to 3 years) life whereas permanent bridge have long design life (50 years).
- Temporary bridges are for light loads have limited use and take less construction time, permanent bridges are to carry heavy loads, have wide use and consume more time of construction.
- Structurally temporary bridges are easy to analyze require less skill of construction and less machinery, where as the permanent bridges can be complex structural forms, require higher skilled labour heavy machinery.
- Made of timber and steel wire, temporary bridge costs less whereas the permanent bride which is generally brick, stone, steel R.C.C. are costly.

Generally classification of permanent bridges have already been dealt with. Now we shall consider details.

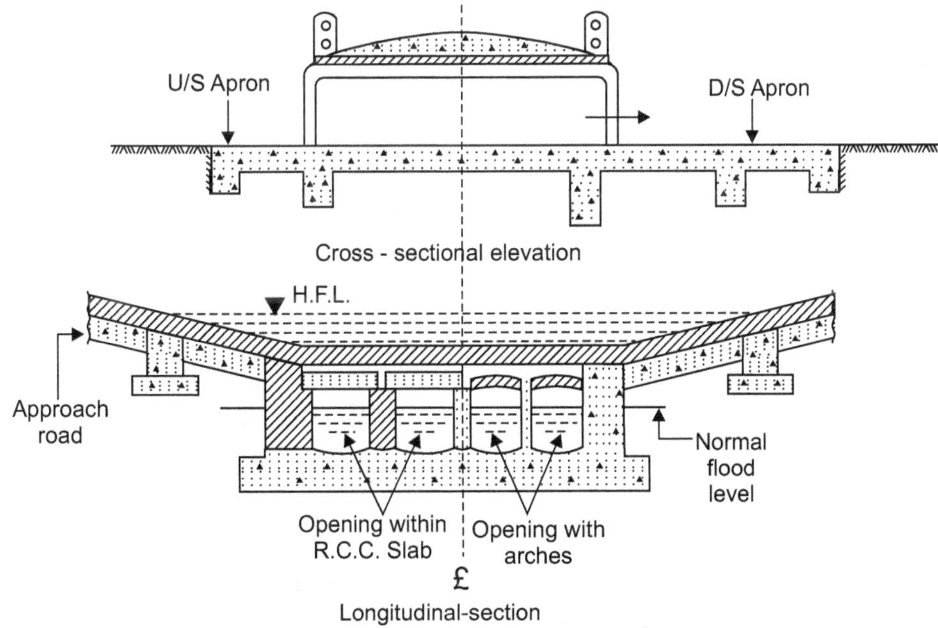

Fig. 14.22 : High level causeway

14.7.2 High Level Causeway

Refer Fig. 14.22. High level causeway or vented causeway has a number of openings to allow the normal flood discharge to pass but does not cater for high flood discharge. In case of later it acts as submersible bridge. These are suitable fro non-perenial streams of great width and is generally a masonry structure. Openings are provided with small arches or slab spans over masonary piers or big pipes with a layer of concrete underneath. Downstream curtain wall is generally provided for these types.

14.7.3 Masonary Bridges

Depending upon the way the arch supports the road decks, here we have two types : (1) Filled spandrel arch bride, (2) Open spandrel arch bridge.

14.7.4 Filled Spandrel Arch Bridge

See Fig. 14.23. Here the side walls are constructed along the side of the arch and the space between walls filled with earth, murum, sand, brick masonary (generally brick masonary is employed) to bring the horizontal level at the top over which the roadway is laid. When approaches are infilling, this is a good alternative. In such case, segmental or semi-circular arches are employed.

Fig. 14.23 : Filled spandrel arch bridge

14.7.5 Open Spandrel Arch Bridge

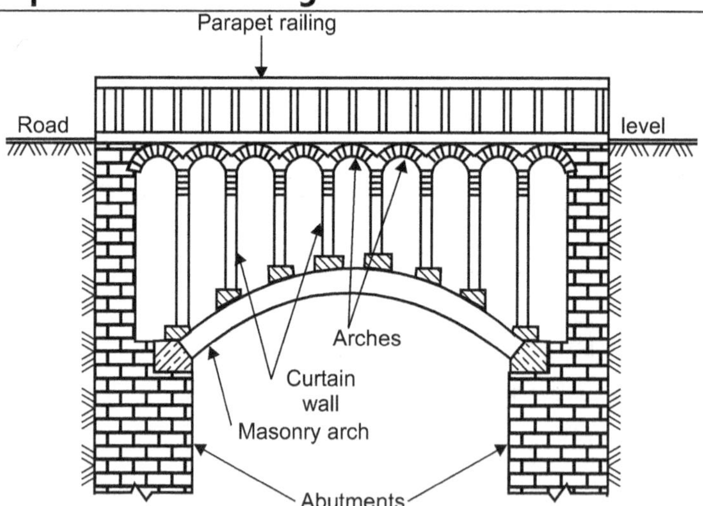

Fig. 14.24 : Open spandrel arch bridge

See Fig. 14.24. In this case the main arch rib supports the vertical walls which in turn supports the roadway which may be r.c.c. slab. In this case instead of filled spandrel we have vertical walls, hence there is less load on arch. Aesthetically the bridge looks good. Where the approaches are in cutting through hard rock, it is a good alternative..

14.8 REINFORCED CONCRETE BRIDGES

Here we have

14.8.1 R.C.C. Slab Bridge

See Fig. 14.25. This is suitable for culverts and submersible bridge for span upto 8 m. The R.C.C. slab form the road deck to carry the traffic.

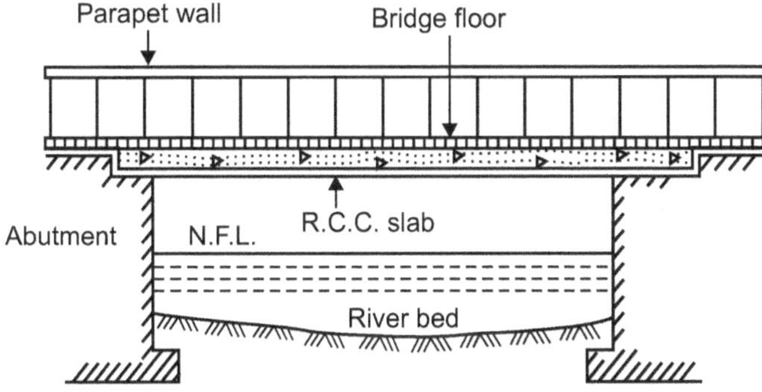

Fig. 14.25 : R.C.C. slab bridge

See Fig. 14.25. Here we have R.C.C. T-beam and slab construction supporting the road deck-T beams are to be cast monolithically with slab, but these T beams are generally treated as simply supported over abutments and piers T beam provision economises the concrete in the slab and are suitable upto 30 meter span.

14.8.2 R.C.C. Girder Bridge

In this types, road deck is supported by R.C.C. girders which in turn are supported on abutments and piers. Depending upon the form of superstructure we have here.

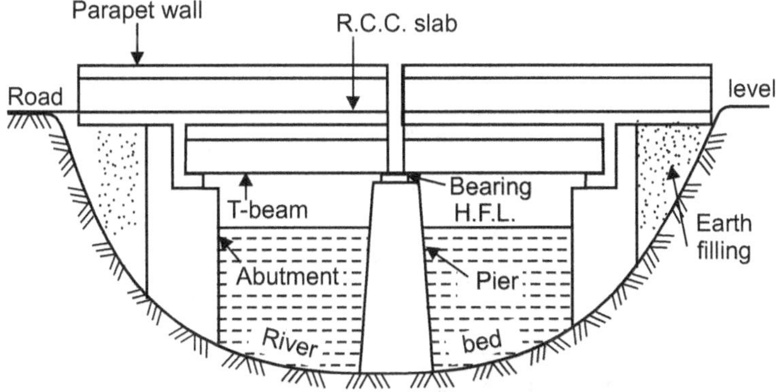

Fig. 14.26 : R.C.C. T-beam and Slab bridge

14.8.3 Parapet Girder Bridge

See Fig. 14.27. Here parapet girders are main supporting members with thick R.C.C. slab or transverse beams with thinner slabs of course cast monolithically with girders at their bottom as their structural system. For bridges of narrow width the bridge is suitable.

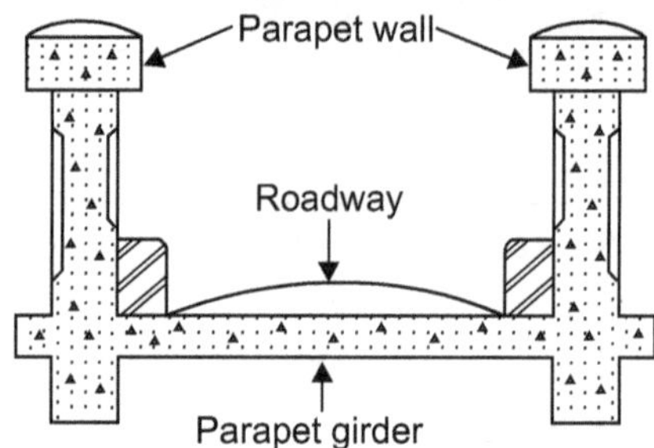

Fig. 14.27 : Paper girder type bridge

14.8.4 T-Beam Bridge

Here the main girders are in the form of 'T'. 'T' beams themselves may be simply supported, continuous balanced cantilevers etc.

If the roadway width is side more number of 'T' beams are employed as longitudinal girders with or without transverse beam.

14.8.5 Hollow Girder Bridge

See Fig. 14.28. The only difference from the former is employing closed box section girder width could be made multicellular of rectangular or trapezoidal shaped cells. In this case tension reinforcement is spread over large area on base slab and as such for spans of 20-30 meters the arrangement become more economical.

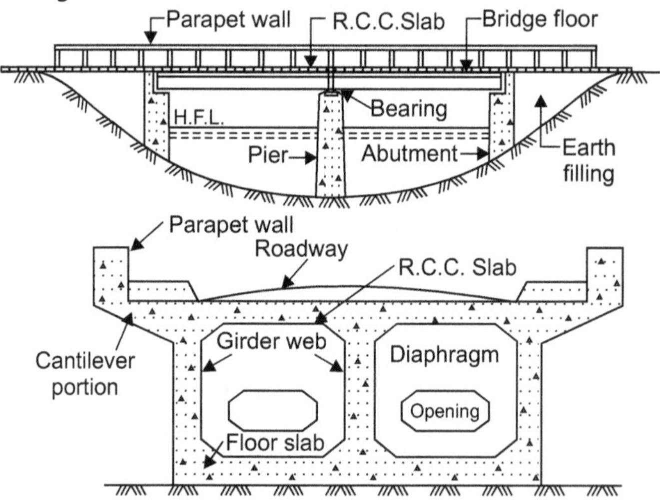

Fig. 14.28 : Hollow girder type bridge

14.8.6 R.C.C. Rigid Frame Bridge

See Fig. 14.29. This bridge is essentially a portal frame of deck slabs cast monolithically with abutments. Abutment therefore is a part of this frame. The bride road deck can be suitably constructed over the slab of the portal frame. The bridge is uneconomical for spans upto 10 meters due to large fixed end moments but can be considered upto 20 meter span.

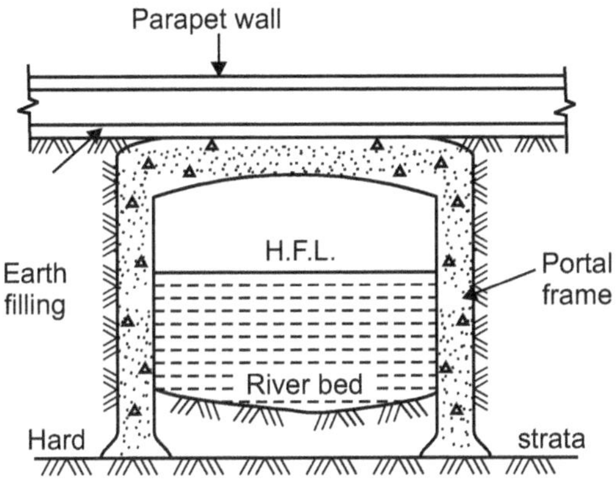

Fig. 14.29 : R.C.C. rigid frame bridge

14.8.7 R.C.C. Multiple Span Portal Frame Bridge

See Fig. 14.30. Here we have more than two portals. Generally the width of the portal frame is equal to the width of roadway. The top portion of rigid portals which carry the bridge floor may be solid ribbed or cellular. The section used are elegant and much clearance can be achieved under the bridge super-structure so that navigational ease can be given. The construction of this bridge is suitable for unyielding foundations since portal frame requires rigid foundation bed.

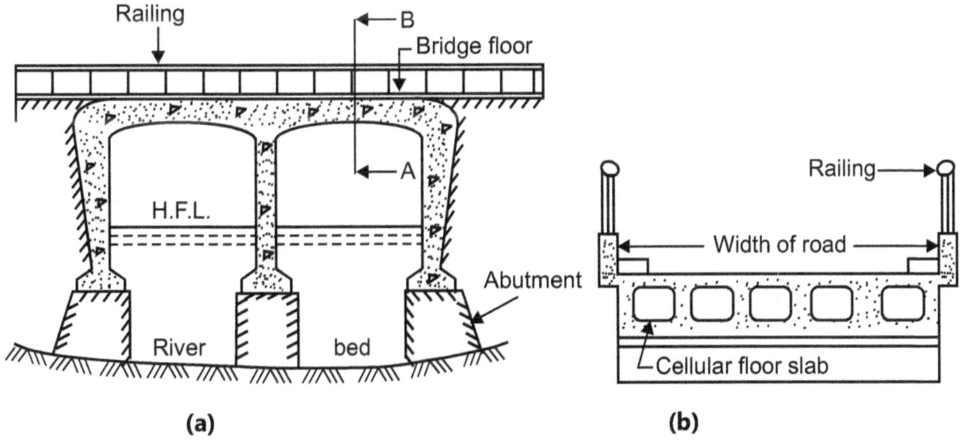

Fig. 14.30 : R.C.C. multiple span portal frame bridge

14.8.8 R.C.C. Balanced Cantilever Bridges

Here we have balanced cantilever beams may be 'T' or hollow girder which support the bridge floor. The bridge is generally suitable for 30-60 meter span and is economical to construct because of less form work and some what lessened quantities of cement and aggregate. For each pier only one bearing is required and hence top width of pier can be less than that of simply supported girder bridges which require two bearings at every support.

14.8.9 R.C.C. Continuous Bridges

When the bridge superstructure is continuous over more than one span consisting R.C.C. continuous beams or girder, it is called as R.C.C. continuous bridge. As with balanaced cantilever it requires one bearing per pier and has less expansion joints. Economical to construct and maintain, continuous bridges are susceptible to foundation settlement. Even small settlement of foundation can lead to failure, but otherwise the bridge is useful in spanning long spans.

14.8.10 R.C.C. Arch Bridge

If instead of brick masonary, R.C.C. is used to construct the arch, then it is R.C.C. arch bridge. Here we have

1. R.C.C. Fixed Arch :

See Fig. 14.31. The arches resting on abutments or piers have fixity and therefore suitable for unyielding type foundation.

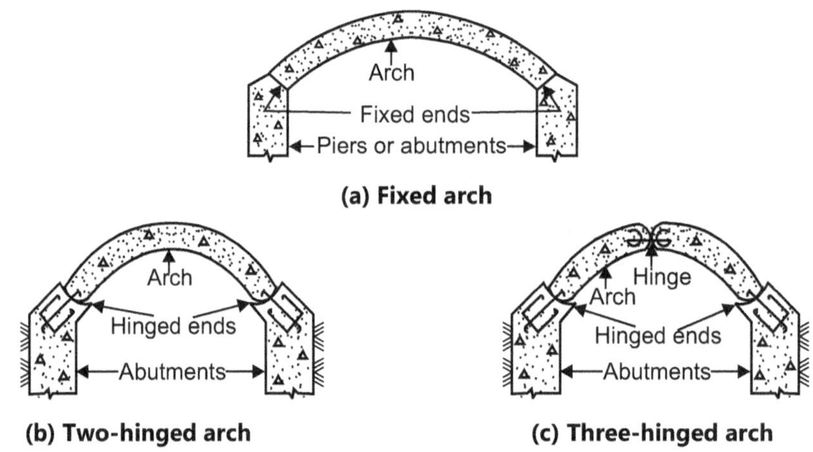

Fig. 14.31 : Types of R.C.C. arches

2. R.C.C. Two Hinged Arch :

See Fig. 14.31. In this case, resting point of arch with the abutment or pier is a hinge and as such only reactions are transmitted to the supports but no bending moment in the arch at the springing point. Even when the foundation bed is yielding type, the arrangement can therefore be employed.

3. R.C.C. Three Hinged Arch :

In this case, in addition to the two hinges at spring point, one hinge is constructed at the crown point see Fig. 14.31. One disadvantage of this arrangement is that even small movement of one foundation pier relative to the other can cause distress. One advantage is that one can span longer opening with only arch. For deep gorges in hilly areas, the arrangement is aesthetically good. Depending upon the method of supporting the roadway over the arch as in the case of masonary arch bridge, the r.c.c. bridge can be further classified as :

14.8.10.1 R.C.C. Filed Spandrel Arch

See Fig. 14.32. A solid barrel type arch ring in between the two abutments supports front as well as back walls, space between these walls being filled with sand, soil, masonary, upto desired level for laying the roadway. This type is suitable for spans upto 70 meters. The arch employed is a moderate one, with ratio of rise to span of arch being small.

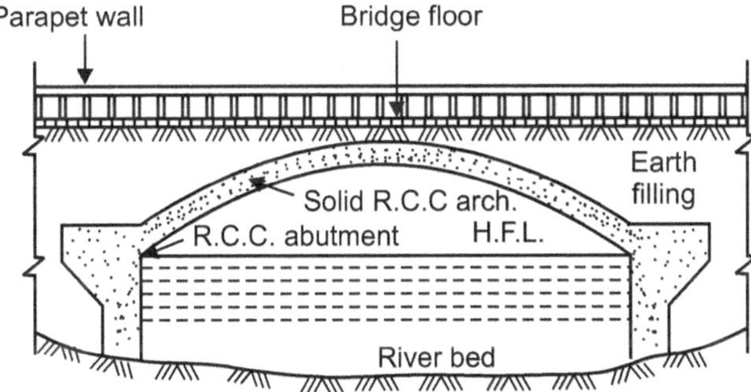

Fig. 14.32 : R.C.C. filled spandrel or barrel type arch bridge

14.8.10.2 R.C.C. Open Spandrel Arch Bridge

Just as in the case of it's brother masonary open spandrel arch bridge, here the arch ring which itself may be fixed or hinged support a number of vertical columns or walls. Which in turn support the roadway. See Fig. 14.33. In between columns, we may have small arches or slabs to support the road deck. As in the case of masonary arch, there is less load on the arch and the design can therefore be made economical. Higher rise to span ratio arches can be employed and the bridge is aesthetically nice. The arrangement is suitable for span upto 250 meters.

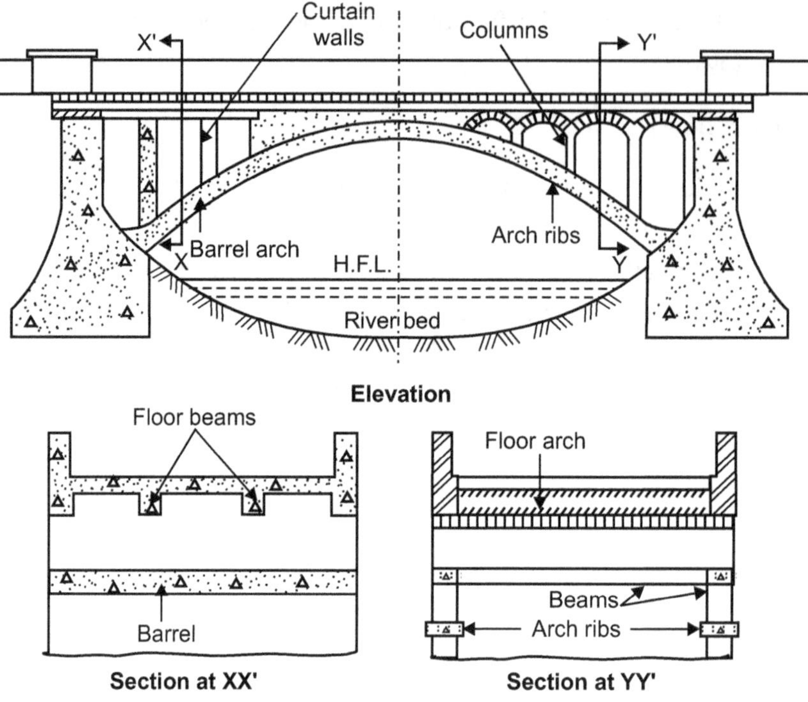

Fig. 14.33 : R.C.C. open spandrel or RIB type arch bridge

14.8.11 R.C.C. Bow String Girder Bridge

See Fig. 14.34. Here the main components is a set of R.C.C. Bow string girder carrying the bridge floor on their ties. In this case, the horizontal thrust is taken by the lower horizontal member called the tie of the girder and abutment is called upon to take only vertical thrust. The weight of the floor is taken by vertical members called suspenders which in turn spring from arch. For bridges requiring more head room, this type of bridge is suitable. Commonly adopted for span upto 200 m, the bridge is nice to look at due to appearance of bow.

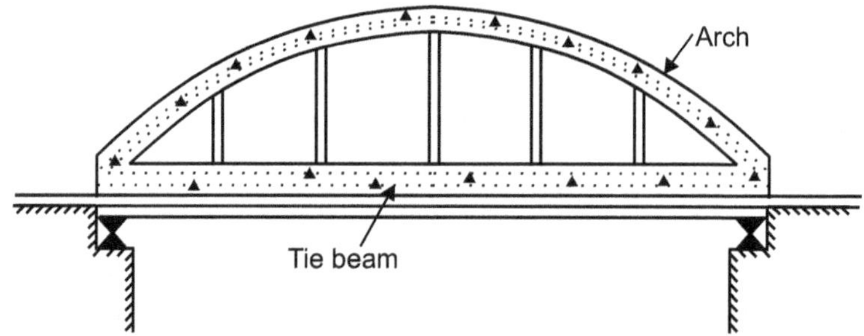

Fig. 14.34 : R.C.C. now string girder bridge

14.9 PRESTRESSED CONCRETE BRIDGES

If any member of the bridge superstructure is prestressed either pre or post tensioned, then it is a prestressed concrete bridge. The principle of prestressing though initiated by Jackson in 1886 and Daehring in 1888, the actual use in bridge started in 1926. The technique of prestressing allows thin members to be used in bridges, compared to R.C.C. bridges and thus economy in bridge building can be achieved. Gifted with higher load carrying capacity and less deflection for the same cross-section, the construction can become light and economical. Prestressed members have less expansion joints due to allowable long length. The resistance to fatigue is also better and with less joints the road deck is smooth and gives better riding comfort. The disadvantage if they could be called as disadvantage is requirement of careful supervision.

One of the longest prestresed bridge in Asia is in India on "Dehrion sone" river in Bihar. It is about 3013 m long, 93 spans of about 32.4 m each and completed in 1865.

Proper cover of concrete is a must for these bridges. Of late some of the prestressed bridges have shown corrosion of reinforcement bars and great care should be employed when constructing these brides in humid or sea climate.

The prestressed concrete bridge can have (1) Precast I beams with an insitu reinforced concrete deck (2) Continuous in situ solid post tensioned slabs spanning upto 35 m or (3) Continuous hollow box girder bride.

The future era of bridges is that of prestressed concrete.

14.10 IRON AND STEEL BRIDGES

Here we have the following types :

14.10.1 Steel Trough Plate Bridges

See Fig. 14.35. These bridges are suitable for very short spans of about 1.5 metres. Suitable sizes of iron or steel troughs which will span the opening in the required width of road are laid and tied together by means of steel bars or lap joints. At the ends steel troughs are rigidly fastened to bearing plates, which are then fixed over abutment or piers. Concrete is laid in the roughs and concrete wearing coat is then added for bridges.

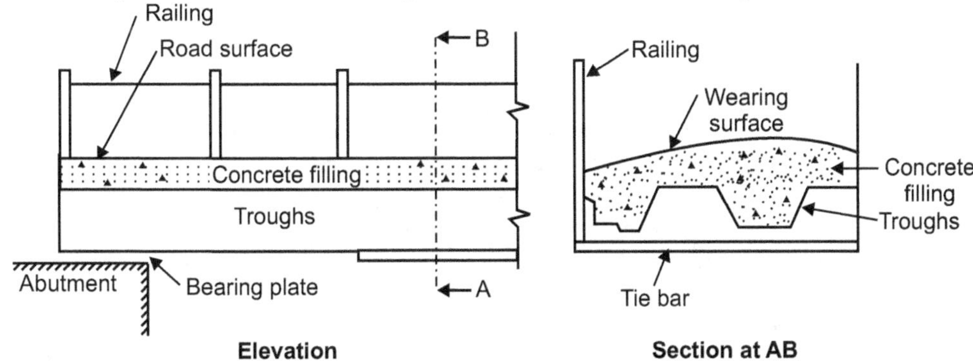

Fig. 14.35 : Steel trough plate bridge

14.10.2 Steel Girder Bridge

Depending upon the girder used for steel girder bridge we may classify the bridge further as (1) Rolled just bridges, (2) Plate girder bridges, (3) Tubular or Box girder bridges. These girders are shown in Fig. 14.36. In all these types, it is the steel girder and transverse steel beam which carry the bridge floor which is used for plying the traffic. In the first type called steel I beams with or without cover plates is used as main beam. In the second type the plate girder which is the fabricated girder is used as main girder, whereas in the third type a tabular or box girder which essentially is nothing but two plate girders joined together by viveted plates and angles is used.

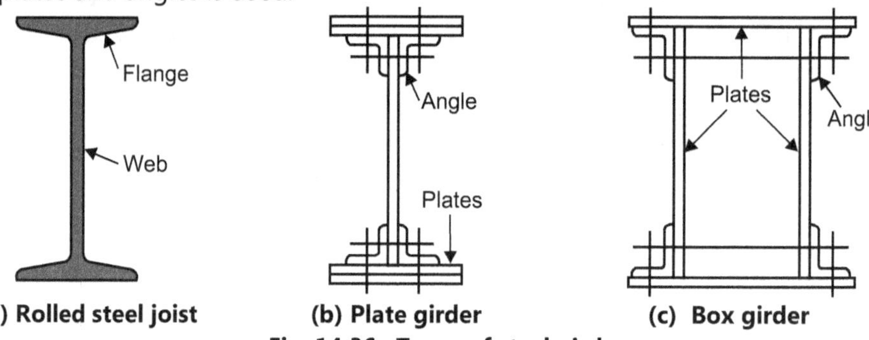

(a) Rolled steel joist   **(b) Plate girder**   **(c) Box girder**

Fig. 14.36 : Types of steel girder

14.10.3 Steel Arch Bridge

When the superstructure is a steel arch to carry bridge floor, it is a steel arch bridge. These are illustrated in Fig. 14.37 and 14.38. The deck type steel arch bridge can be compared to filled spandrel arch bridge since the arrangement is essentially the same. Through and semi through arch bridge could be compared to R.C.C. bow string arch since the arrangement is similar.

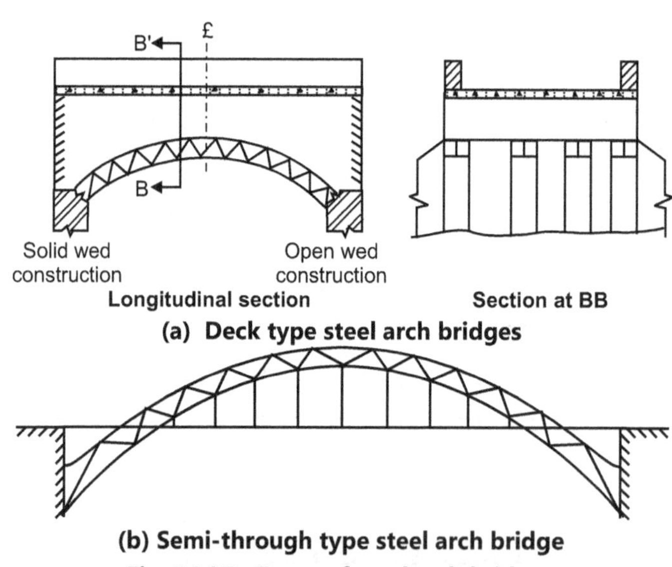

(a) Deck type steel arch bridges

(b) Semi-through type steel arch bridge

Fig. 14.37 : Types of steel arch bridges

The steel arches could be further truss type or braced type and the truss type arch can be further three hinged two hinged etc. The depth of truss is 1/6 of the span. The bridge will serve as a good alternative river bed conditions are poor in foundations and construction of intermediate pier is difficult. This may be sometimes due to high velocity of river water so that construction of pier with it's associated cofferdam construction is uneconomical. The bridge is good for large span where there are navigational requirements. The various steel arches are shown in Fig. 14.38.

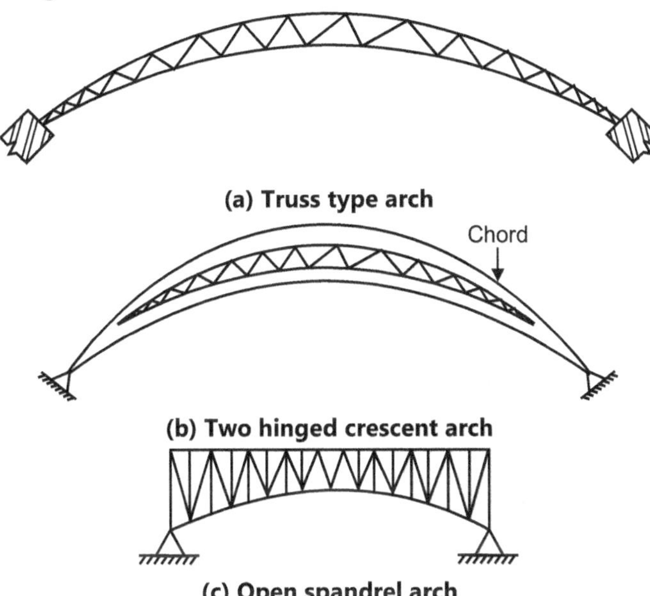

(a) Truss type arch

(b) Two hinged crescent arch

(c) Open spandrel arch

Fig. 14.38 : Various steel arches used for steel arch bridges

14.10.4 Steel Truss Bridge

Here the steel truss carry the bridge floor and hence these serve as main girders. For spans greater than 30 meter the bridge is economical, for spans from 40 to 375 m the truss bridge can be adopted. This bridge will be called deck bridge if its floor is supported at the top of truss. Naturally the bridge is suitable where the vertical clearance between H.F.L. and ground level of approaches is sufficient to accommodate the superstructure with a suitable free board. When the approaches are in cutting the bridge is suitable.

The bridge with it's rock deck supported at some intermediate level of the superstructure is called as semi through bridge. When the vertical distance between H.F.L. and ground level of the approach is not sufficient to have free board, this bridge is suggested.

The bridge is called as through bridge when its deck is either suspended or supported at the bottom of the superstructure. When the approaches are in filling or when the vertical distance between H.F.L. and ground level of approaches is not sufficient to accommodate the superstructure with a free board, this structure is suitable. The various trusses that are used for steel truss bridge are shown in Fig. 14.39.

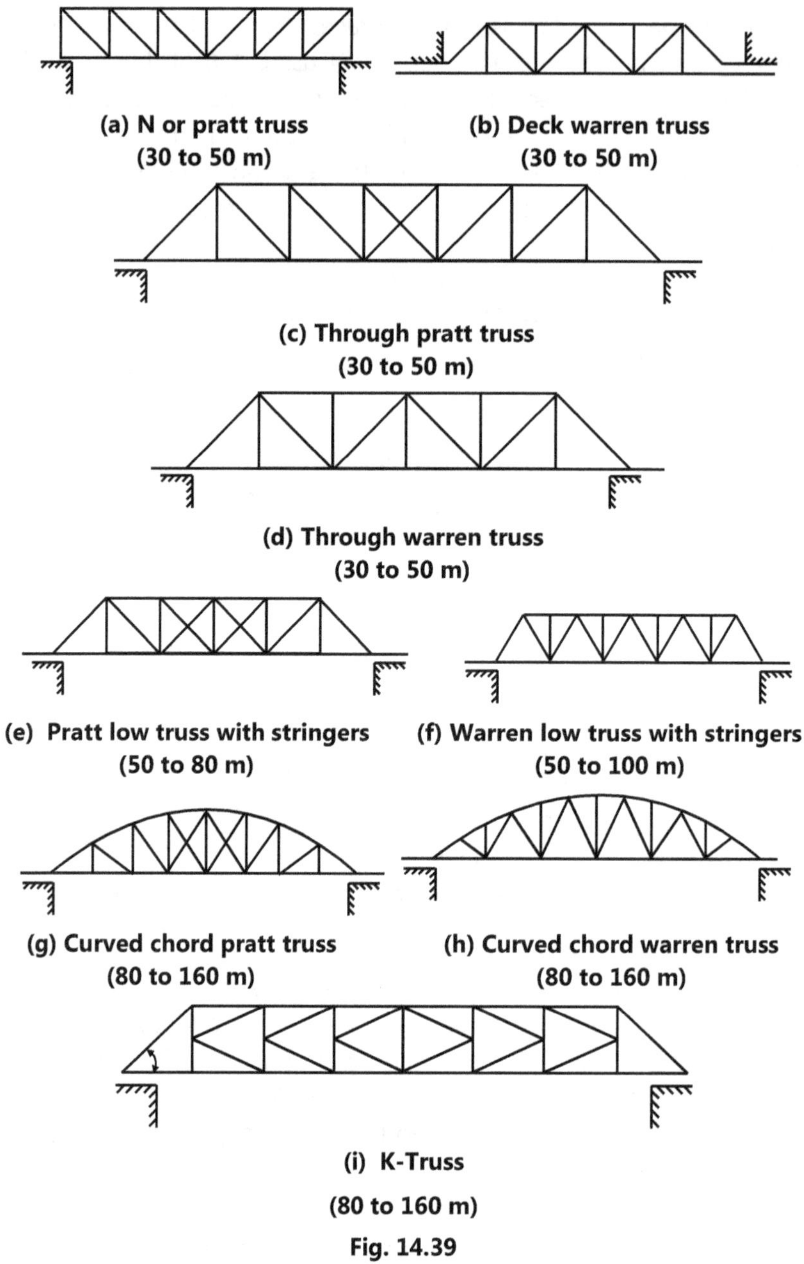

Fig. 14.39

The steel truss bridge can be further classed as :

14.10.4.1 Bow String Girder Bridge

When the superstructure is a steel bow string girder the deck being carried on their transverse ties it is known as how string steel girder bridge. See Fig. 14.40. In these type of bridges, tie of the bow string girder takes the horizontal thrust relieving the abutment of this thrust.

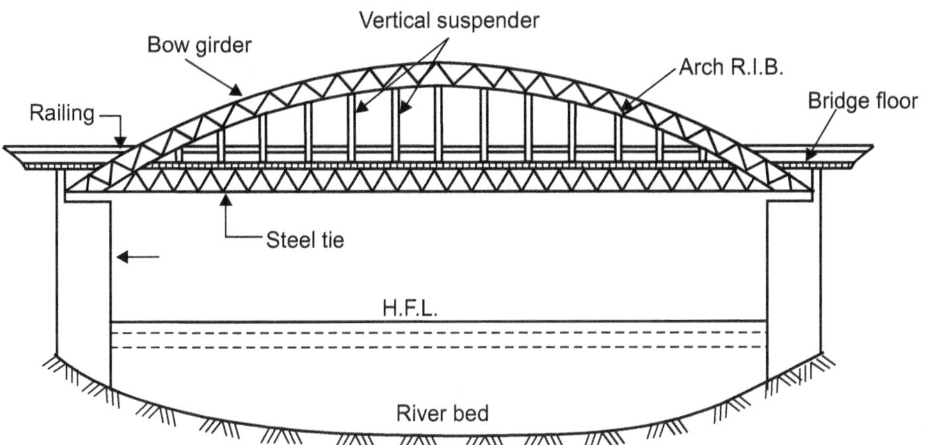

Fig. 14.40 : Bow string steel girder bridge

The bridge abutment, carries only the vertical thrust transferred from the superstructure in addition to lateral thrust that might be transferred from earth backfill. The roadway in such bridges is usually suspended from arch by means of vertical rods called suspenders. Suitable for large span of about 250 m, now-a-days these bridges are rarely used.

14.10.4.2 Steel Rigid Frame Bridge

The principle is that of R.C.C. rigid frame bridge see Fig. 14.41. Here we have a portal frame made of plate girders which carry the bridge floor. Naturally the size and number of and design of portal frame would depend upon the load on the bridge and the width of road. The corners of the portal frames are generally stiffened for rigidity and their legs are either fixed or hinged to the foundations. When more clearance for the navigational purposes is required and when the cost of excavations for bridge abutment is high, the bridge is suitable. Since these do not require strong abutment and bearings, the roadway for such bridges carried over the top of portals.

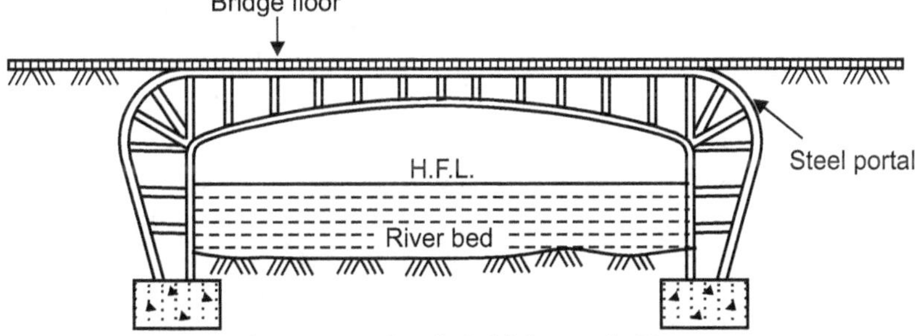

Fig. 14.41 : Steel rigid frame bridge

14.10.4.3 Continuous Steel Bridge

When the superstructure (like double track in the case of railways) span continuous, through type steel truss supports the bridge floor, it is a continuous steel bridge. The truss may be supported on R.C.C. piers. The bridge has certain advantages such as elimination of expensive hinge details, less stress variation under traffic and facility for errection with one or more span without false work and economy of material.

14.10.4.4 Steel Suspension Bridge

See Fig. 14.42 when the superstructure is one or two sets of cables carrying the bridge floor by suspenders it is steel suspension bridge. There are saddler provided on top of side piers which carry these cables. The cables are securely anchored to the bank. The road deck is suspended from these cables by suspenders. Here also we can further classify the bridge. Fig. 14.42 shows a suspension bridge which is not stiffened and is called as simple suspension bride which can be used for light loads. A stiffened suspension bridge which can be used for light loads. A stiffened suspension bridge is also shown in Fig. 14.42, which may be used for heavy loads. The stiffening trusses which are provided at the four level prevent the distortion of the bridge. Suspension bridges can be constructed in short time without false work, are light and the components required for the bridge can be transported at site. They are using higher tensile ropes. Light and heavy traffic can be made to pass on these bridges and can be used even for spans of 600 to 1200 meters. The bridge also looks good.

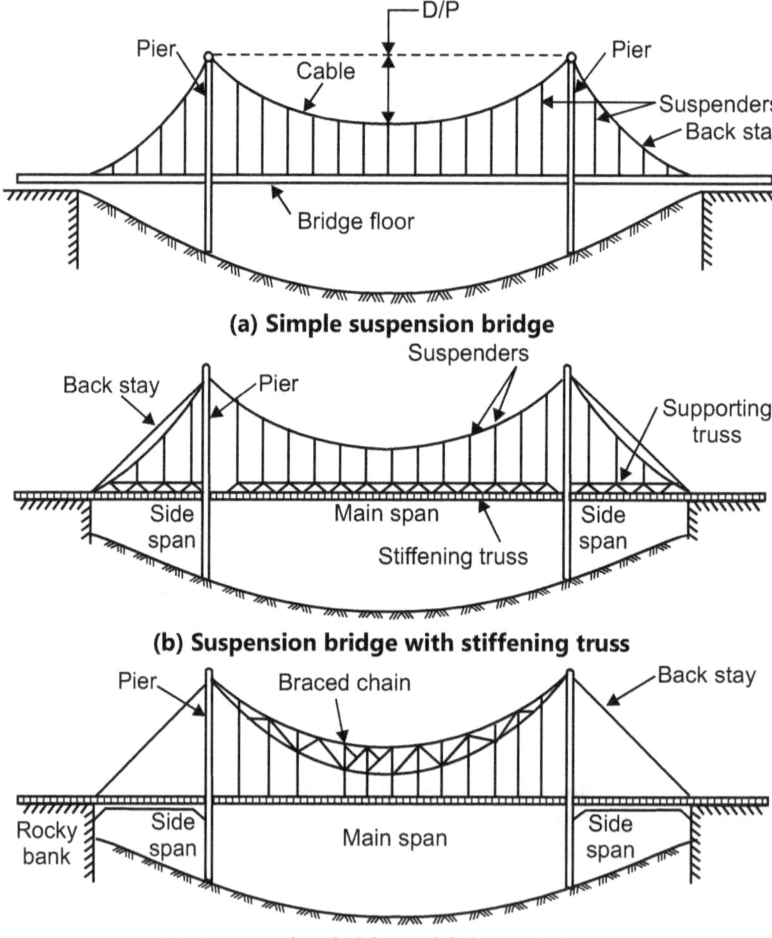

(a) Simple suspension bridge

(b) Suspension bridge with stiffening truss

(c) Suspension bridge with braced chains

Fig. 14.42 : Various forms of suspension bridges

It might be mentioned here that the days of steel truss bridge as road bridges are now past since these do not give rise aesthetic appearance in urban areas but steel suspension bridge will be continued to be used as road bridge since, these are quite good aesthetically. Laxman Jhulla at Haridwar is a steel suspension bridge.

14.10.4.5 Steel Cantilever Bridge

If the superstructure is a cantilever truss carrying the bridge floor, it is a steel cantilever bridge. The labour and the material required are large and the days of steel cantilever bridge as road bridge are now a past history. The howrash bridge is cantilever since it permits long span. The place of such bridge is now slowly taken by cable stayed bridge.

14.10.4.6 Cable Stayed Bridges

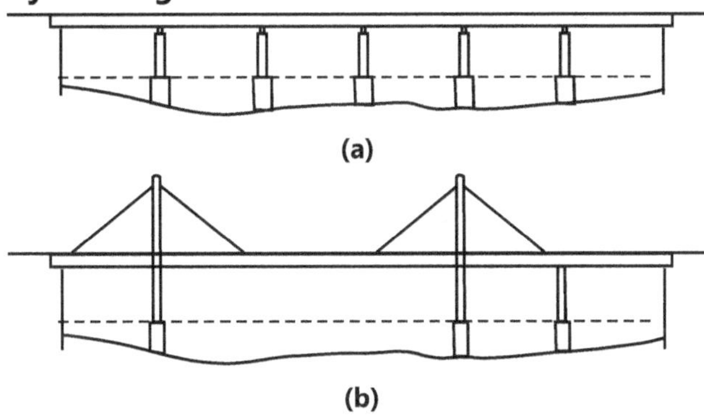

(a)

(b)

Fig. 14.43 : Layout of cable stayed bridge

See Fig. 14.43. It is a via media between continuous box girder bridge and the stiffened suspension cable bridge. The development was mainly in West Germany as an aftermath of World War II, in an effort to save steel which was then in short supply. In the simple way the bridge could described as a deck which is supported by a bunch of cables which in turn are connected to the mighty towers. The placement of tower may be on either bank or it may be intermediate to the banks. Large width for navigation is thus mad available. cables are to be deigned and prestressed in such a manner that on the whole the bhaviour of the bridge is like a continuous beam on rigid support. Because of he dampening effect of inclined cables, these bridges are some what less prone to wind induced oscillations than suspension bridges.

14.11 MOVABLE STEEL BRIDGES

It is not always possible to construct the bridge superstructure at such a level that navigational ships can pass below bridge superstructure during high floods. On such rivers, bridge might the designed so that one or two spans of the superstructure can be moved out of position whenever required for passage of ships, steamers or boats. Movable steel bridges can be classified as temporary bridges, because these can be put out of use whenever required. But it must be remembered that the life span of movable steel bridge is considerable. These bridges may be

14.11.1 Swing Bridges

In this type of bridge superstructure, it can be rotated in a horizontal plane on vertical axis. It is generally a balanced girder carrying the flooring supported at its ends on abutment tops, and in the centre on an intermediate pier, provided usually with disc bearing. The schematic diagram is in Fig. 14.32. When the steamer wants to navigate the river, the superstructure is rotated through an angle of 90° by means of mechanical or electrical power which is provided on the intermediate pier, where the disc bearing is located. When the ship has passed, the bridge is brought back to its original position to allow the traffic to pass on it.

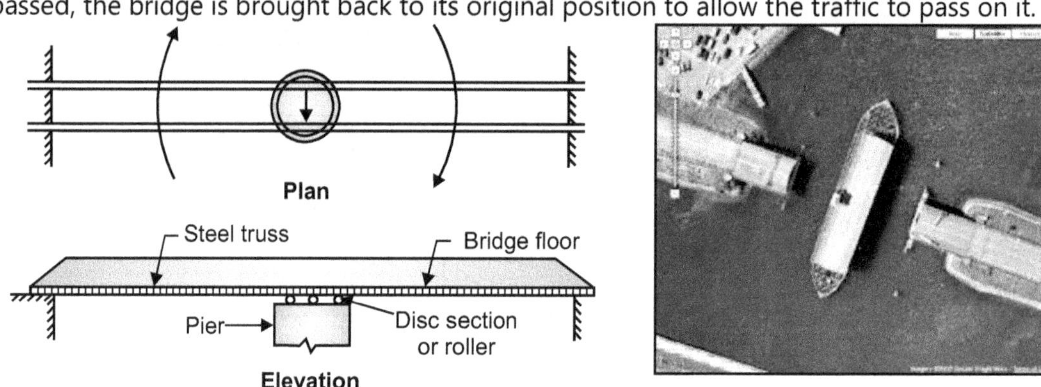

Fig. 14.44 : Swing bridge

14.11.2 Traverser Bridge (See Fig. 14.45)

In this type the superstructure is a balanced framework in the form of steel truss which carries the bridge floor on its bottom chord. The superstructure can be rolled back wards and forwards a cross the opening so that sufficient gap can be created for the ship to pass unobstructured. Rollers are provided under the bridge superstructure on one of the banks for this purpose. The movement of the bridge is by manual means of electrical power.

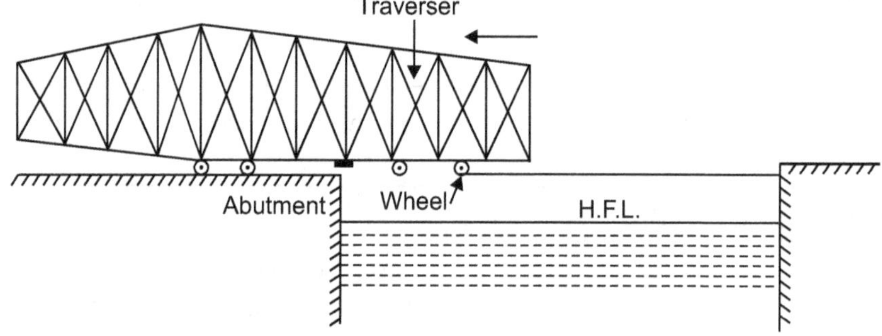

Fig. 14.45 : Traverser bridge

14.11.3 Transporter Bridge (See Fig. 14.46)

Here we have solid or open type steel girder resting on top of two high towers which are provided on each bank. The girder supports the travelling cage or cradle through suspension cables as shown. The travelling cage can move from one bank to the other generally through the use of electrical power. This type of bridge is for transportation of materials rather than men since the capacity of cage has to be limited.

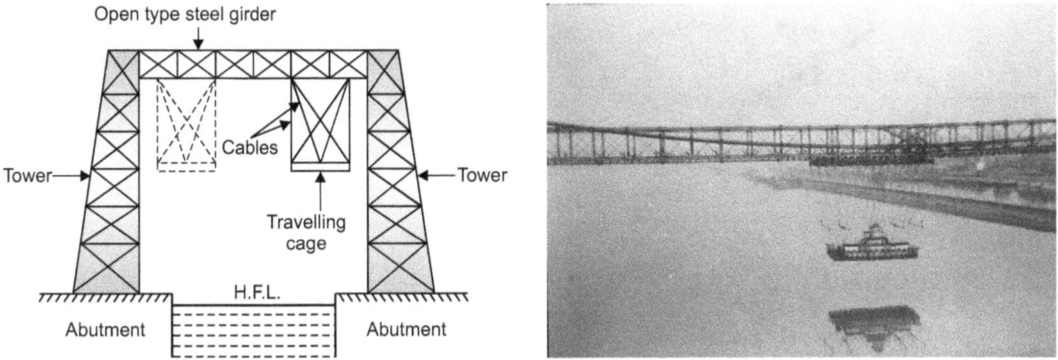

Fig. 14.46 : Transporter bridge

14.11.4 Bascule Bridge

In this type, the superstructure can be moved vertically on a horizontal hinge. See Fig. 14.47. The hinge is provided on the abutment. The bridge could be called single leaf or double leaf, according to the span of the bridge. For short span of the bridge. For short span single leaf bridge and for long spans double leaf bascule Leaf Bridge is commended. The arrangement may be such that the bridge can be countered weighted at ends and raised or lowered by rack and pinion arrangement shown in Fig. 14.47. When the bridge is lowered, the counter weights provided lowers into the pit called bascule chamber.

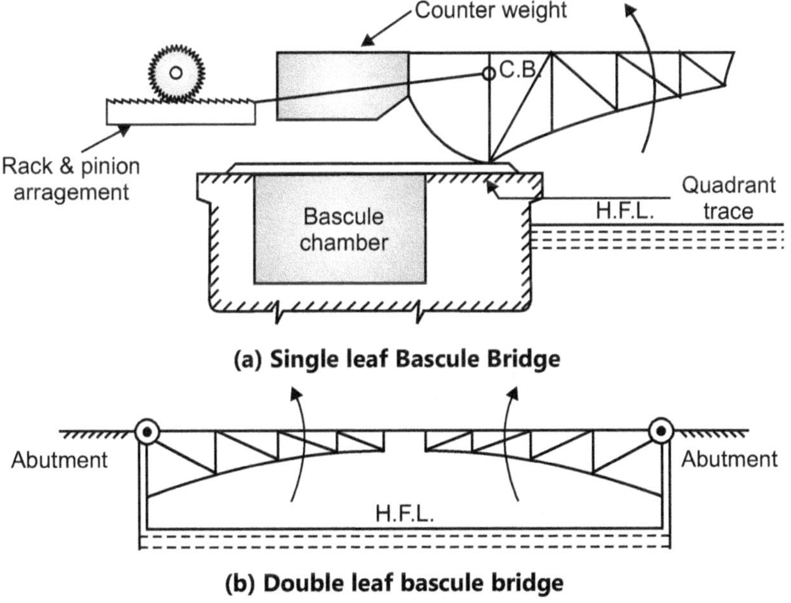

Fig. 14.47 : Types of bascule bridge

Fig. 14.48 : Single leaf bascule bridge

Fig. 14.49 : Double leaf bascule bridge

14.11.5 Life Bridge

There are two towers on each bank. The tops of towers are connected by overhead span. This gives more rigidity to the structure. In between the two towers a main span carrying the bridge floor is provided. This main span can be lifted by means of cables which pass over sheaves fixed on the towers, when the ship is to be passed across. Lift bridge is generally not recommended.

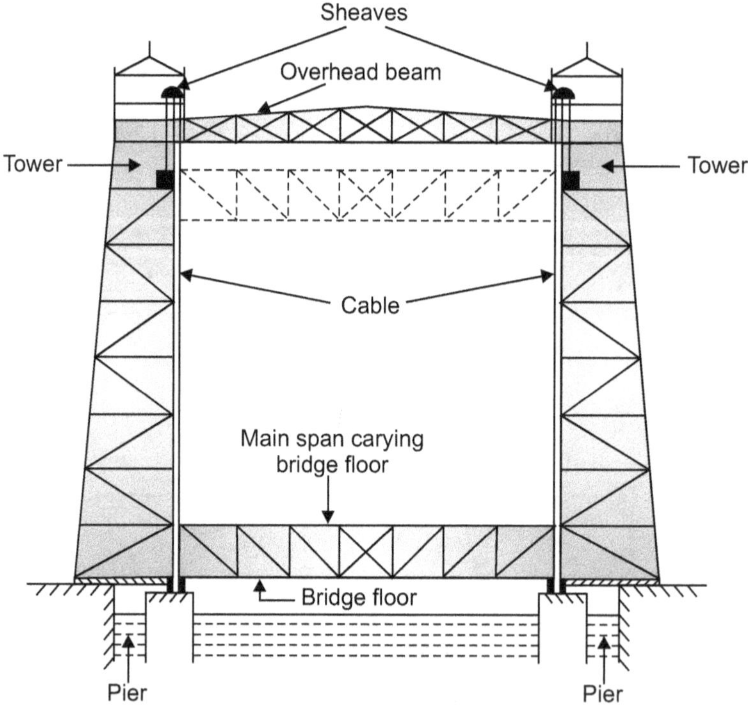

Fig. 14.50 : Lift bridge

POINTS TO BE REMEMBER

- Types of culvert and its types :

  (a) Pipe convert

  (b) Reinforced concrete box culvert.

  (c) Reinforced concrete slab culvert.

  (d) Stone arch culvert.

- Types of superstructures : (a) Temporary bridge superstructure, (b) Permanent bridges.

- Different types of temporary bridge : (a) Military bridges, (b) Cause ways, (c) Timber bridges, (d) Other temporary bridges.

- Types of permanent bridges : (a) High level cause way, (b) Masonry bridges, (c) R.C.C. bridges.

- Types of military bridges : (a) Fixed bridges, (b) Floating bridges with advantages.

- Circumstances for cause-ways with points.

- Different types of causeway : (a) Low level causeway, (b) Flush causeway.

- Types of substructure of timber bridges : (a) Timber trestle bridge, (b) Pile bents, (c) Cribs, (d) Crates.

- Comparison between permanent and temporary bridge.

- Different types of suspension bridges : (a) Suspension trestle bridge, (b) Sling bridge, (c) Ramp bridge.

- Types of R.C.C. bridges : (a) R.C.C. slab bridge, (b) R.C. T-beam and slab bridge, (c) Parapet grider bridge, (d) T-beam bridge, (e) Hollow girder bridge, (f) Continuous bridges, (g) Multiple span portal frame bridge, (h) R.C.C. arch bridges, (i) Pre-stressed concrete brides.

- Different types of iron and steel brides with types : (a) Steel trough plate bridge, (b) Steel girder bridge, (c) Steel arch bridge, (d) Steel truss bridge.

- Different types of movable steel bridges : (a) Swing bridges, (b) Transverse bridge, (c) Transporter bridge, (d) Bascule bridge, (e) Lift bridge.

QUESTIONS

1. What is culvert ? How many types of culvert are there ?
2. Describe the method of installation of pipe culvert.
3. Discuss the various types of culverts w.r.t. their suitability of use in the field.
4. Explain with neat sketches slab culverts, pipe culverts and box girder bridges.
5. Give details classification of bridge.
6. State relative merits and demerits of the following type of bridges :
   (a) Arch bridge.
   (b) Suspension bridge.
   (c) Temporary bridge.
   (d) Permanent bridge.
   (e) R.C.C. balanced cantilever.
   (f) R.C.C. bow string girder.
7. Differentiate between :
   (i) Cantilever bridges and Bascule bridges.
   (ii) Movable span and Fixed span bridges.
   (iii) Temporary bridge and permanent bridge.
8. Draw an illustrative sketch of the following :
   (i) Cable stayed bridges.
   (ii) Cut boat bridges.
   (iii) Knuckle bearings.
   (iv) Bascule bridges.
   (v) Flying bridges.
9. Discuss the various types of movable span superstructure with respect to their suitability only.
10. Draw plan and elevation of R.C.C. slab bridge showing all the components.
11. Explain the situations where through, semi-through and deck type bridges are preferred.
12. Under what circumstances mobile steel bridge are used. Explain lift bridge.
13. Describe with sketch, the importance of cantilever bridges.

Chapter 15
BEARINGS

15.1 INTRODUCTION

The devices which are provided over the supports of bridge to accommodate the changes in the main girders due to deflection, temperature, vertical movement due to sinking of the supports, shrinkage, prestressing creep etc. and to transmit the load from the superstructure to the substructure are within permissible limits are known as the bearings. Thus, the bearings are provided for the distribution of the load evenly over the s
ubstructure material which may not have sufficient bearing strength to bear or take-up the load of superstructure directly.

In this chapter, some of the salient features of this important component of the bridge structure will be discussed.

15.2 FUNCTIONS OF BEARINGS

- To allow for the longitudinal movement of the bridge deck and the girder due to variation in temperature. This movement takes place in steel R.C.C. or prestressed bridges and it is the job of bearings to allow for it.

- Rotation at supports due to breaking. The knowledge of applied mechanism tells us that under the action of load, the bridge girder deflects and this results in angular movement over the supports. The bearings which are provided at the end must alos rotates so that there is uniform distribution of bearing pressure.

- Transference of horizontal forces. The application of breaking force induces a horizontal force which can be transmitted to the substructure by the use of bearings.

- To allow some vertical movement due to sinking of foundations.

15.2.1 Purposes of Bearings

Following are the purposes or objects of providing bearings in a bridge:

- To absorb movements of girder,

- To allow for angular movements of girder due to deflection under the load,

- To allow for longitudinal expansion or contraction due to changes in the temperature,

- To distribute the load on a large area,

- To keep the compressive stress within safe limits,

- To make movements of girder harmless,

- To rotate at supports to accommodate the deflection of a simply supported girder under load,

- To simplify the procedure in design.

- To take up the vertical movement due to sinking of the support,

- To transfer horizontal forces developed due to application of brakes to the vehicles etc.

15.2.2 Importance of Bearings

It should be remembered that the successful functioning of a bridge primarily depends on the design of its bearings. It is observed that faulty design or improper working of the bearings in the main cause of failure of many bridges that have collapsed. The design of bearing to be adopted for a particular bridge will mainly depend on the type of supports, length of the span and the type of superstructure.

The bearings form an important component of a bridge and hence, extreme care and skill should be exercised in its design, execution and maintenance. For major bridges, the cost of bearings roughly works out to about 10 to 15 per cent of the total cost of the bridge. Hence, there is ample scope of achieving economy by designing the bearings properly and carefully.

15.3 WHY ONE BEARINGS IS FIXED AND THE OTHER FREE

Generally for each span, one end of the supporting girder is kept fixed and the other free. The reason is the free end of the girder allows movement in the longitudinal direction. This movement may be due to temperature, tractive force etc. If this is not done internal excessive stresses will be generated in the girder.

15.4 BEARING FOR STEEL GIRDER BRIDGES

These are (1) Fixed bearing, (2) Expansion bearings.

15.5 FIXED BEARINGS

Here we have :

(a) **Shallow or fixed plate bearing :** Her in between the lower flange of the girder and the pier or abutment we have flat rectangular steel plate which is anchored to the girder on one hand and to the bridge pier on another hand through two anchor bolts. See Fig. 15.1 (a). Suitable upto 12 m span.

(b) **Deep cast base bearing :** Here instead of shallow plate, we have deep cast base on one hand attached to the bridge girder and on other hand anchored to pier. Because of the depth of bearing, stress concentration is less and suitable for 12 to 16 m span. See Fig. 15.1 (b).

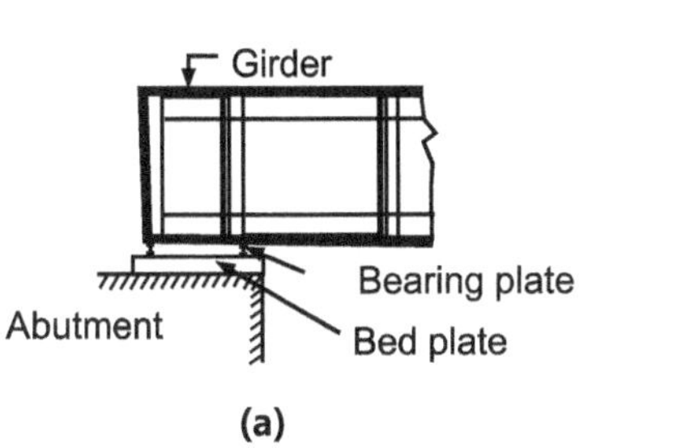

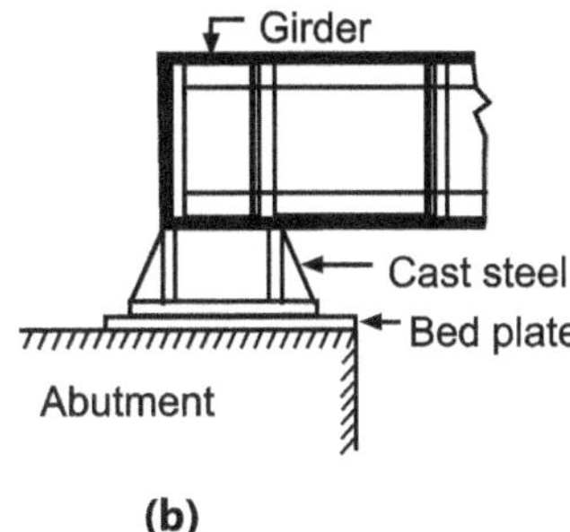

Fig. 15.1

(c) Rocker bearing : Here the steel girder had a top inverted shoe and the abutment or pier has a depression shoe. In between these, rocker pin is inserted, with the deflection of the girder, the top inverted, shoe rotates, over the pin and this allows free angular movement of girder. See Fig. 15.2 (a).

(d) Knuckle bearing : In this case, there is no rocker pin. The bottom shoe which is anchored to the pier or abutment is formed in the shape of hemisphere on which top shoe can rotates. Thus there is no rocker pin. Bearing is good for 20 m to 30 m. See Fig. 15.2 (b).

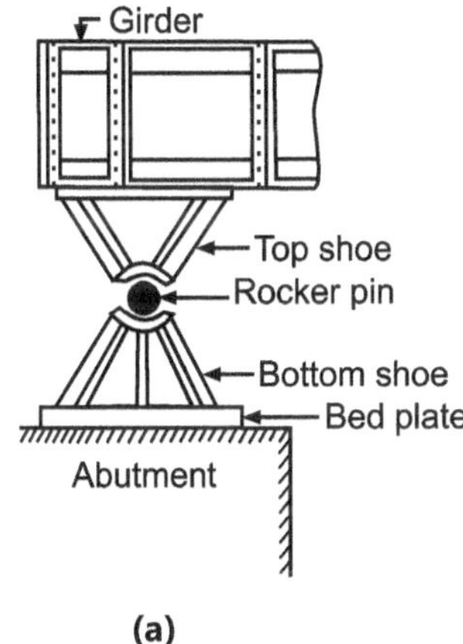

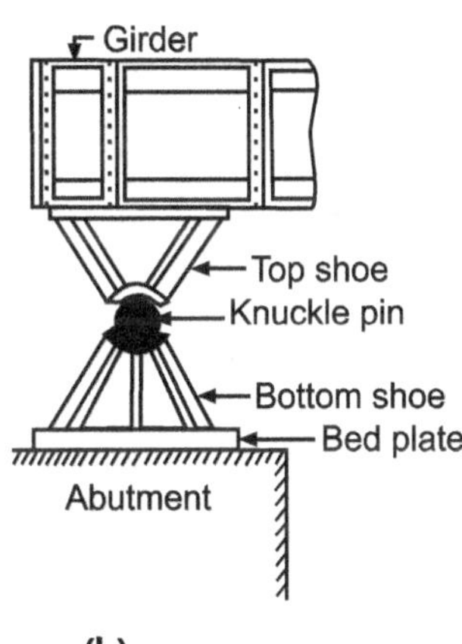

Fig. 15.2

15.6 EXPANSION BEARINGS

These bearings allow longitudinal movement of the bridge girder and hence are called as expansion or free bearing. The general practice is to give one fixed bearing at one end of the bridge, the other end of the bridge girder being provided with expansion bearing so that the expansion or the contraction of the bridge girder due to variations in temperatures in allowed for. These bearings could be

- Sliding plate bearing.
- Deep cast base curved plate bearing.

- Rocker bearing with curved base.

- Rocker and roller bearing.

(a) Sliding plate bearing : In this case, there is a slotted plate which is attached to underside of the girder. The slotted plate rests on bed plate which is anchored to the pier or abutment. The joint between bed plate and slotted plate is through iron bolts which are well anchored to the bed plate and go through the slots of sliding slotted plate. Because of the gap thus provided by slots the horizontal movement of girder is possible. Suitable for 12 to 20 m span. See Fig. 15.3 (a).

(b) Deep cast base with curved plate bearing : In this case, deep case base with curved bed plate is anchored to the bridge pier/abutment as shown. The sole plate which is anchored to the underside of the girder rests on this deep cast base curved base plate. Because of the spherical shape of the curved bed plate, the girder is allowed some longitudinal and some rotational movement. See Fig. 15.3 (b). The bearing may be O.K. for 12 to 20 m.

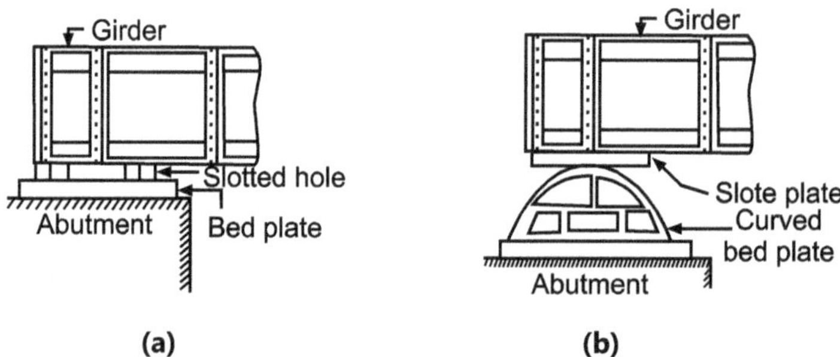

Fig. 15.3

(c) Rocker bearing with curved bottom base : See Fig. 15.4 (a). In this case the bottom shoe is provided with curved bottom. Thus offering lessened resistance to the longitudinal movement of the girder. The horizontal force generated because of the restraint put on this movement is thus lessened. This bearing was suitable for 12 to 20 m span.

(d) Rocker and roller bearing : See Fig. 15.4 (b). This is essentially a rocker bearing with bottom shoe resting on number of steel rollers which in turn roll on honey combed bed plate (i.e. bed plate which is not very smooth). This bed plate is anchored to pier to abutment. Free longitudinal and rotational movement is thus allowed for. The general practice is to install rocker bearing one end and rocker and roller bearing on the other end of the bridge girder. In such case the bearing can be used for spans more than 20 m.

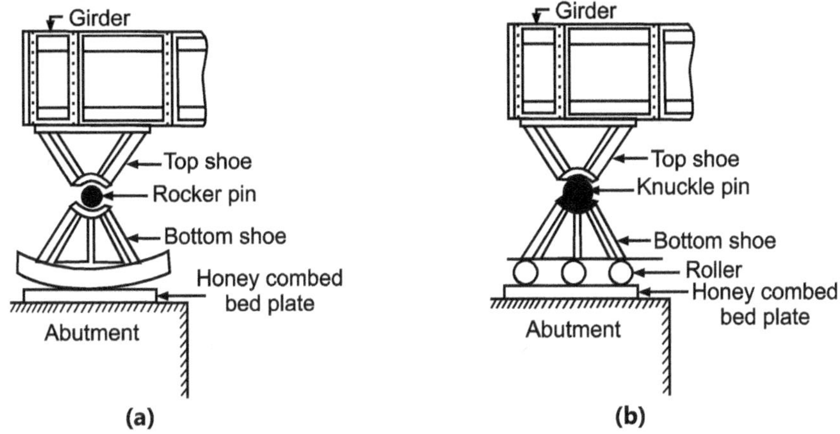

Fig. 15.4

(e) Bearings for each and suspension bridge : Arch and suspension bridge require inclined bearings. These are illustrated in (Fig. 15.5).

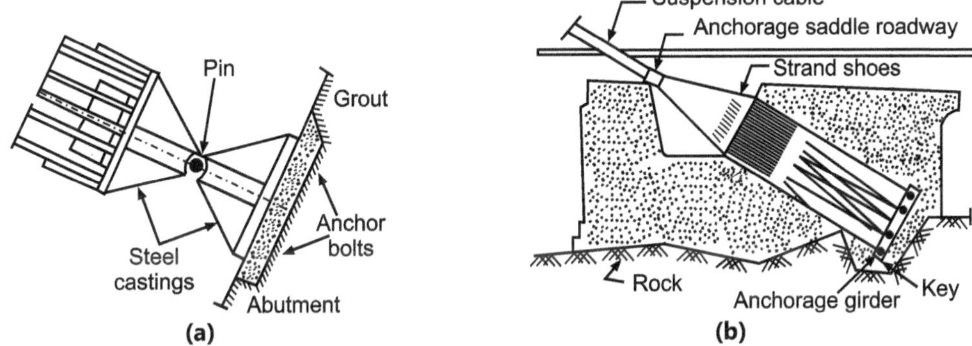

Fig. 15.5

15.7 EMPLOYMENT OF METALLIC BEARINGS

For different span lengths, different bearings are generally recommended for steel bridges. The following guidelines may be followed in such a case.

- Simply supported spans less than 8 m, only a bituminous layer or paper (which should be impregnated with tar and bitumen) may be interposed between the supporting member and the superstructure.
- Simply supported spans 8 to 16 m and for floating spans resting on abutments/piers, sliding plate bearing at free end and fixed plate bearing with curvature in the top plate could be recommended.
- Simply supported span 16 to 24 m and for suspended units of balanced cantilever construction of spans not more than 16 m, rocker roller bearing and free end and fixed plate bearing with curvature in the top plate at the fixed support.
- Simply supported spans more than 24 m and suspended units of balanced cantilever construction spans more than 16 m, rocker roller bearings at the expansion support (free end) and rocker or knuckle bearings at the fixed support.

15.8 BEARINGS FOR CONCRETE BRIDGES

Here we have the following types of bearings :

15.8.1 Bearings for Slab Bridges

See (15.6). Here we have several layers of tar paper placed between bridge slab and the capping slab of pier or abutment. The provision of paper is to prevent bending between abutment and slab. The abutment or pier or the capping slab of the abutment or pier is rounded so that slight rotational movement of bridge girder is possible. For spans upto 8 m the bearings function nicely. For such bridges, one support of the slab has to be dowelled and the other end is to be kept free. For single span, slab bridges, downelling has to be dowelled at abutments, but for pipe no dowelling need be done. While the case of multispan bridge dowelling be done to abutment and alternate piers and bearings on the remaining piers be kept undowelled.

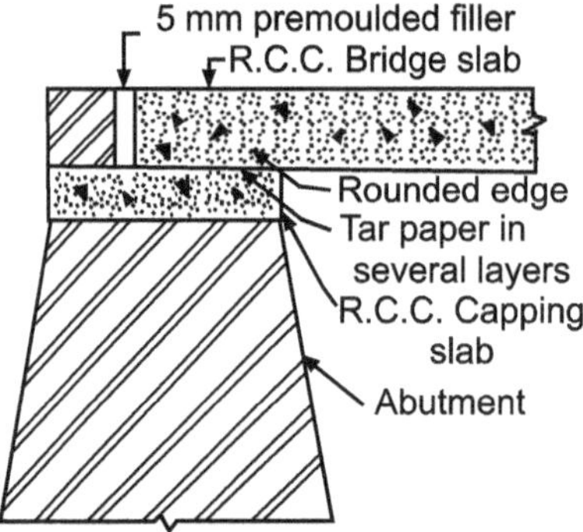

Fig. 15.6

The bearings for the slab may be classed as fixed end and free end bearing. These details are shown in Fig. 15.7 (a) and (b). The bearings which restrain expansion but permit rotation are fixed end bearings. These are shown in Fig. 15.7 (a). Here we provide a lead sheet of 3 mm thickness. Due to deformation of lead sheet, rotation movement is possible but not free expansion. For concrete bridges more than 8 m span, there is considerable rotational movement and these bearings are good for such cases.

Free end bearing allow for free movement, these are shown in Fig. 15.7 (b) and suitable upto 8 m span.

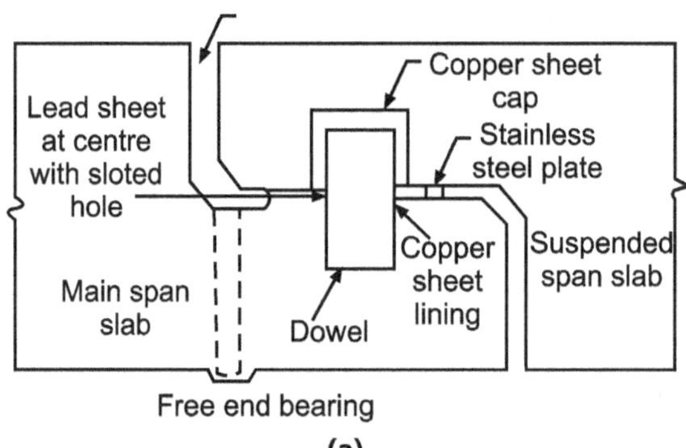

(a)

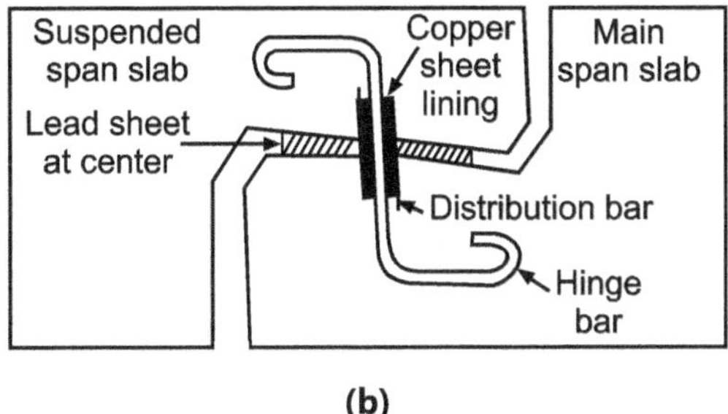

(b)

Fig. 15.7

15.8.2 Bearings for Concrete Girder Bridge

Here we have

(a) **Fixed plate bearing :** See Fig. 15.8 (a). Here we have two mild steel plates bearing on one another with flat machined surfaces, the top plate being anchored to the girder and the bottom plate being anchored to the pier through capping slab. Generally a few mild steel rods are provided as shown for dowelling the girder to the capping slab after cutting through top mild steel plate. There may be lead sheet between two m.s. plaes which equalize the bearing pressure and allows may be slight rotation. For spans of 8 to 16 m, these bearings can transmit to the substructure the lateral force that might be induced due to variation in temperature and the tractive force.

(b) **Sliding plate bearing :** See (Fig. 15.8 (b)). These are essentially expansion bearings. Here we have the slope plate attached to the underside of the girder which can slide over another plate which is well anchored to the capping slab of abutment or pier. A thin lead sheet can be provided in between the two m.s. plate to improve the efficiency of bearing. These bearings allow free expansion or contraction of girders due to temperature variation and can also allow slight rotation, good for spans of 8 m to 16 m.

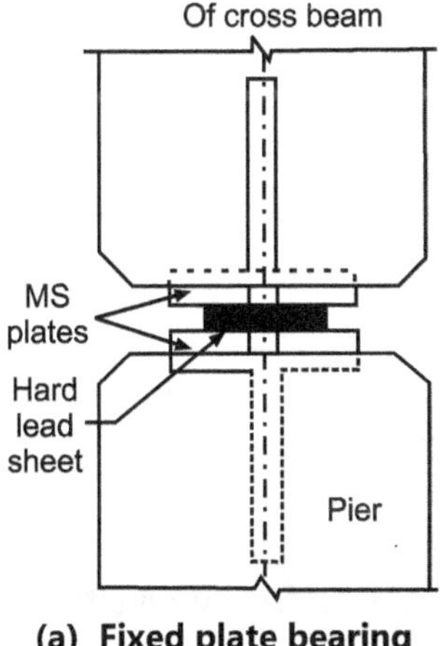

(a) Fixed plate bearing

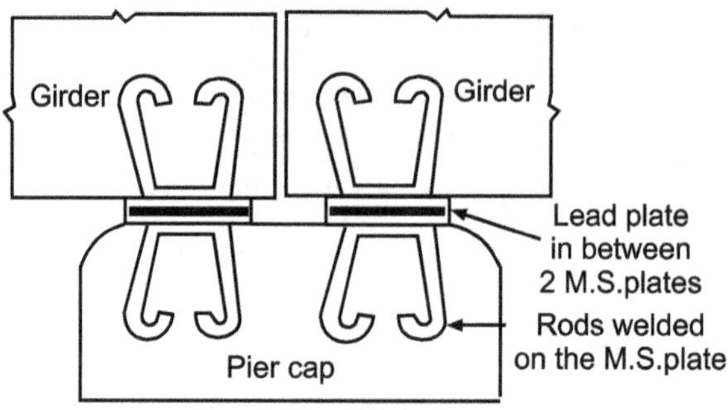

(b) Sliding plate bearing

Fig. 15.8

(c) **Sliding plate bearing with curved top plate :** Here we have curved sole plate attached to the underside plate to allow longitudinal and rotational movement. The constructional details are same as sliding plate bearing as above. Good for 8 m to 20 m span.

(d) **Free bearings :** These are essentially roller bearing with a Kunckle pin or a rocker pin as discussed for steel bridges. Instead of steel girder we have concrete girder here. Rollers could be case or mild steel the latter is preferable. Good for span of 20 to 27 m.

15.9 BEARINGS FOR SUBMERSIBLE BRIDGES

In case of bearings provided in the submersible bridges, these bearing get submerged when the river is in spate. There is also a possibility that due to the velocity of flowing water, or due to the impact of objects floating in the river, the bridge may slide, specially since bridge slab weight is not very heavy.

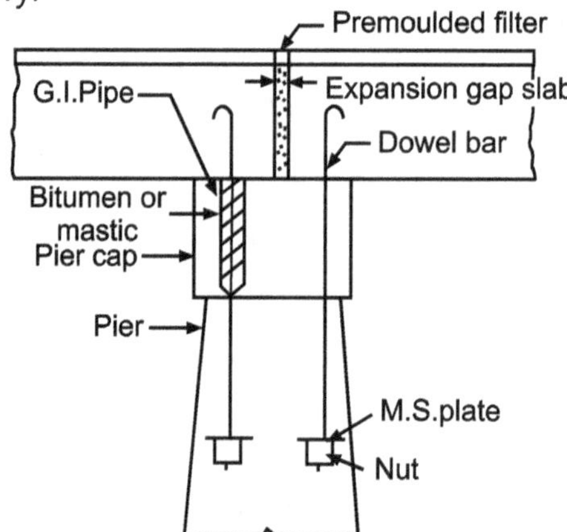

Fig. 15.9 : Bearing for a submersible bridge

Therefore, in the case of submerisible bridges which are generally minor bridges of small span the slab should be anchored to the sub-structure below. For such provision, when the slab is anchored, the longitudional expansion or contraction of the bridge slab due to temperature variation should be catered for by inserting a dowel bar through a pipe filled with bitumen or mastic as shown in the Fig. 15.9.

For small submerisible bridges, two plate sliding bearing at the free end and two plate bearing at the fixed end be provided. In order that rusting should not take place, the material of the bearing should be copper alloy or stainless steel.

15.10 BEARINGS FOR CONTINUOUS SPAN BRIDGES

When the total length of continuous span does not increase 14 m no bearings need to given. Between the supporting member i.e. pier and the superstructure several leavers of tar paper or a laver of bearing may be as in Fig. 15.10. For this arrangement AC is the span which is maximum affected by temperature charge. The following guidelines may help in installing bearing for continuous bridges.

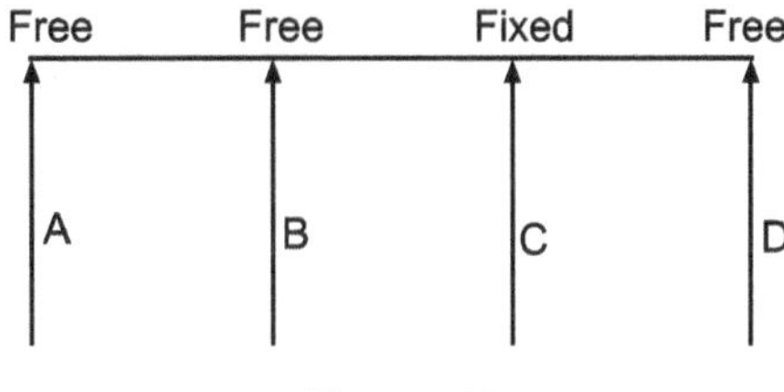

Fig. 15.10

1. **Continuous span 7 to 26 m :** Sliding plate bearing on free support and fixed plate bearing with curvature in the top plate at the fixed support.

2. **16 m to 24 m continuous spans :** Metallic roller bearings over the free supports and fixed plate bearings with curvature in the top plate at fixed supports.

3. **Spans more than 24 m :** Metallic roller bearings at free support and metallic rocker bearings at the fixed support.

15.11 THE I.R.C. PROVISIONS FOR BEARINGS

The bridges code classifies the bearings as metallic and elastomeric.

15.12 METALLIC BEARINGS

These could be :

1. **Sliding bearing :** A type of bearing where sliding movement is permitted between two surfaces. Fig. 15.11.

2. **Rocker bearing :** A type of bearing where no sliding movement is permitted but which allows rotational movement. Fig. 15.12.

3. **Sliding-cum rocker bearing :** A type of bearing where, in addition to the sliding movement either the top or bottom plate is provided with suitable curvature to permit rotation.

4. **Roller cum-rocker bearing :** A type of bearing which permits longitudinal movement by rolling and simultaneously allows rotational movement. See Figs. 15.13 and 15.14.

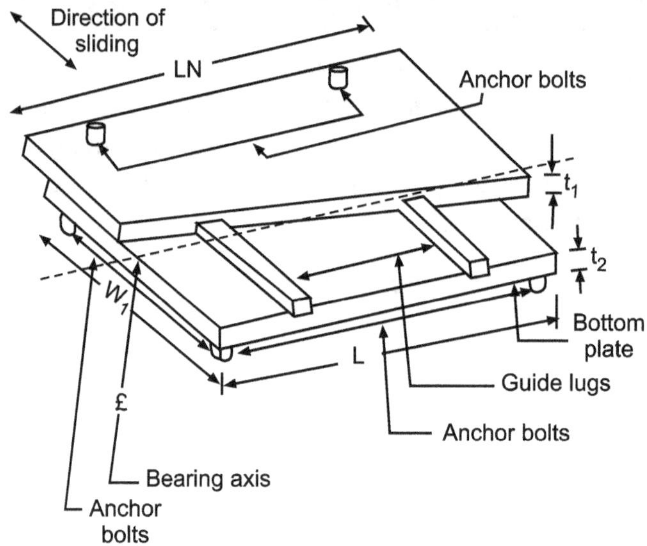

Fig. 15.11 : Sliding bearing

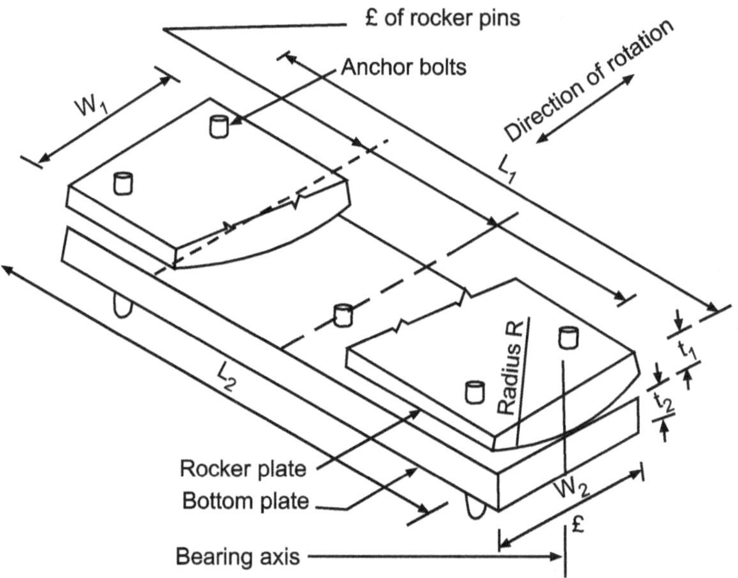

Fig. 15.12

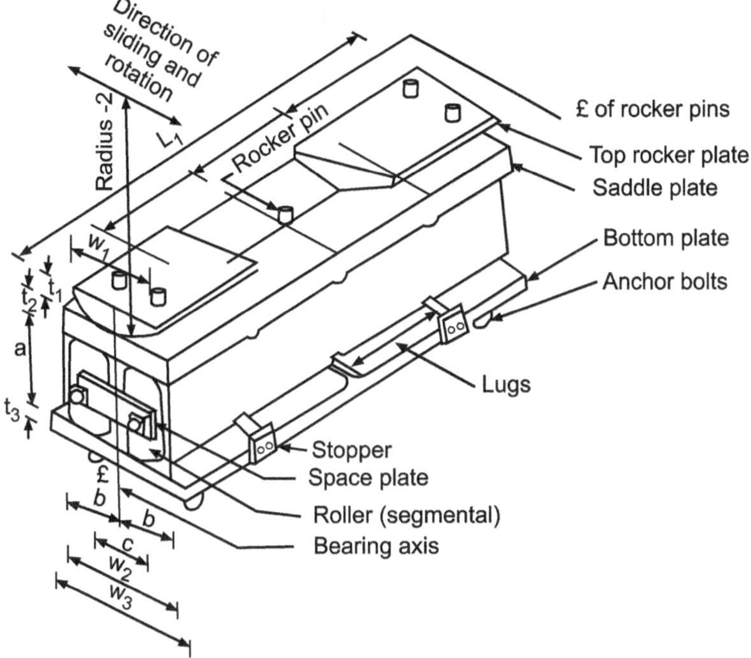

Fig. 15.13 : Roller rocker bearing (with segmental roller)

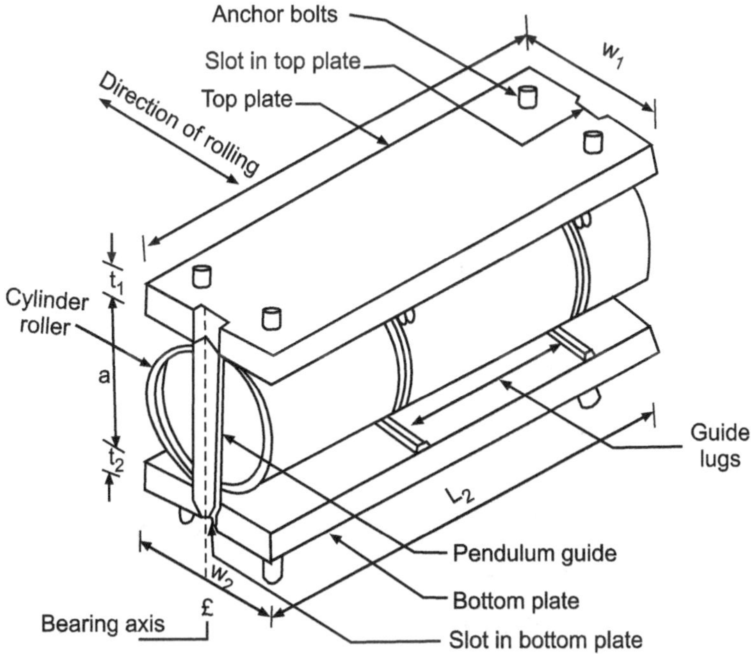

Fig. 15.14 : Roller-cum-rocker bearing with slots to guide movement of roller

15.13 PARTS OF METALLIC BEARING

These are :

1. **Top plate :** A plate which is attached to the underside of the structure and which transmits all the forces from it to the other members of the bearing.

2. **Saddle plate :** A plate which is positioned between the top plate and the rollers.

3. **Roller :** A part of bearing which rolls between a top plate and a bottom plate or between a saddle plate and a bottom plate. The roller may either cylinder or segmental.

4. **Bottom plate :** A plate which rests on the supporting structure and transmits forces from the baring to the supporting structure.

5. **Kunckle pin :** A cylindrical pin provided between recesses of the top and bottom parts of a bearing for arresting relative sliding movement of the top and bottom parts without restriction rotational movement.

6. **Knuckle :** A recess in the surface of the bottom/saddle plate or top plate housing a knuckle pin preventing relative movement between two plates without restricting rotational movement.

7. **Rocker pin :** A lug on the surface of the bottom plate or saddle plate which fit into corresponding clear recess made in the top plate to prevent relative movement of the two plates without restricting rotational movement. Fig. 15.13.

8. **Guide :** A projection on the surface of bottom plate, top plate or saddle plate, which fits into a corresponding clear recess made in the rollers, to maintain their alignment.

9. **Stopper :** A projection provided in the bottom plate, to arrest the roller from moving beyond the bottom plate.

10. **Anchor bolts :** A rag bolt or ordinary bolt anchoring the top and bottom plates to the structure.

11. **Spacer bar :** A bar loosely fixed at each end of a roller assembly for connecting the individual rollers in a nest and to facilitate movement of rollers in unison.

12. **Free support/Free bearings :** A support/bearing which permits the free relative movement of the parts of the structure.

13. Fixed support/Fixed bearing : A support/bearing which prevents the translational movement of the relative parts of the structure.

14. Bearing axis : The symmetrical axis of the bearing.

15. Effective displacement : The total relative movement between the structures in contact with the bearing.

15.14 ROCKER AND ROLLER-CUM-ROCKER BEARINGS

- **Top, saddle and bottom plates** be symmetrical to the bearing axis.

- The width of plates shall not be less than either of the following :

  (i)   100 mm or

  (ii)   The distance between the centre to centre distance of outermost rollers (where applicable) plus twice the effective displacement during service or twice the thickness of the plate plus 10 mm as margin for error in sitting. (The centre to centre distance of outermost rollers if these are two or more. For single roller bearing shall be taken as zero). See Fig. 15.15.

- The thickness of the plate shall not be less than (i) 20 mm or (ii) $1/4^{th}$ the distance between consecutive lines of contact, whichever is higher.

- The thickness of the plate shall also be checked, based on the contact stresses arrived at accounting for the actual width of the plate provided, to satisfy the requirements of structural design and permissible stresses as laid down in code.

- **Rollers :** The minimum diameter of roller shall be 75 mm.

- The ratio of the length of the roller to its diameter shall normally not be more than 6 but not more than 10 m any case.

- The effective contact length with the plate shall be used for arriving at the length of the rollers to be used in the formula given.

- The gap between the rollers shall not be less than 5 mm in case of multiple full rollers.

- Preferably cylindrical rollers shall be used. In case segmental rollers are used, diameter for such rollers shall exceed 250 mm.

- The width of segmental rollers shall be at least half the diameter of the roller or four times the effective displacement of the bearings, whichever is more.

- The gap between the segmental rollers shall not be less than 0.1 d, where 'd' is the diameter of the roller.

- Wherever single segmental roller is used, it shall be provided with vertical guide plate. When two or more segmental rollers are used, necessary shall be made to ensure positive.

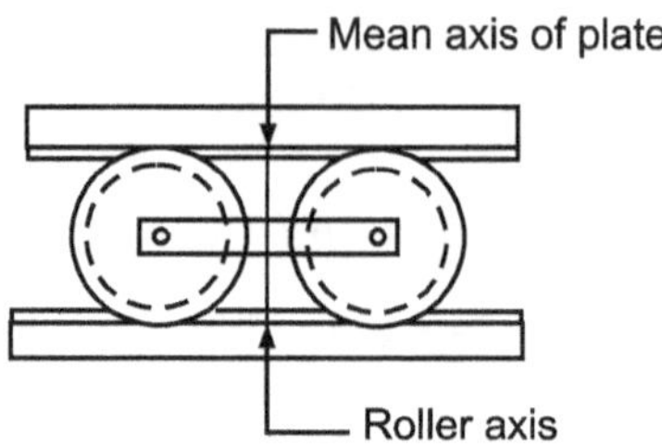

Fig. 15.15

15.15 SLIDING BEARINGS

- Sliding plate bearings alongwith their components shall be composed of one metal or a combination of different metals which are not likely to result in electrolytic action. However sliding bearings with mild steel contact shall be avoided.

- The top plates shall project on all sides over the bottom plate by at least 10 mm for any extreme position of the bearing.

- The thickness of the plate shall satisfy the requirements of structural design and permissible stresses laid down in but shall not be less than 12 mm.

15.16 ELASTOMERIC BEARINGS

Now-a-days there is more emphasis to provide elastomeric bearings. These do not rust.

Laminated rectangular free elastomeric bearings as shown in Fig. 15.16 are in common use in road bridges. These should satisfy the following requirements.

- Internal layers of elastomer should be of equal thickness having elastomer cover on top, bottom and sides and the entire bearing vulcanized as single homogeneous block.

- Top and bottom of elastomer should bear directly on structure face. There should be no adhesive or other external and choring device in between.

- No dowel holes in elastomer and laminate be provided including those filled in subsequently.

- In general, special elastomeric bearings to be used for subzero temperature.

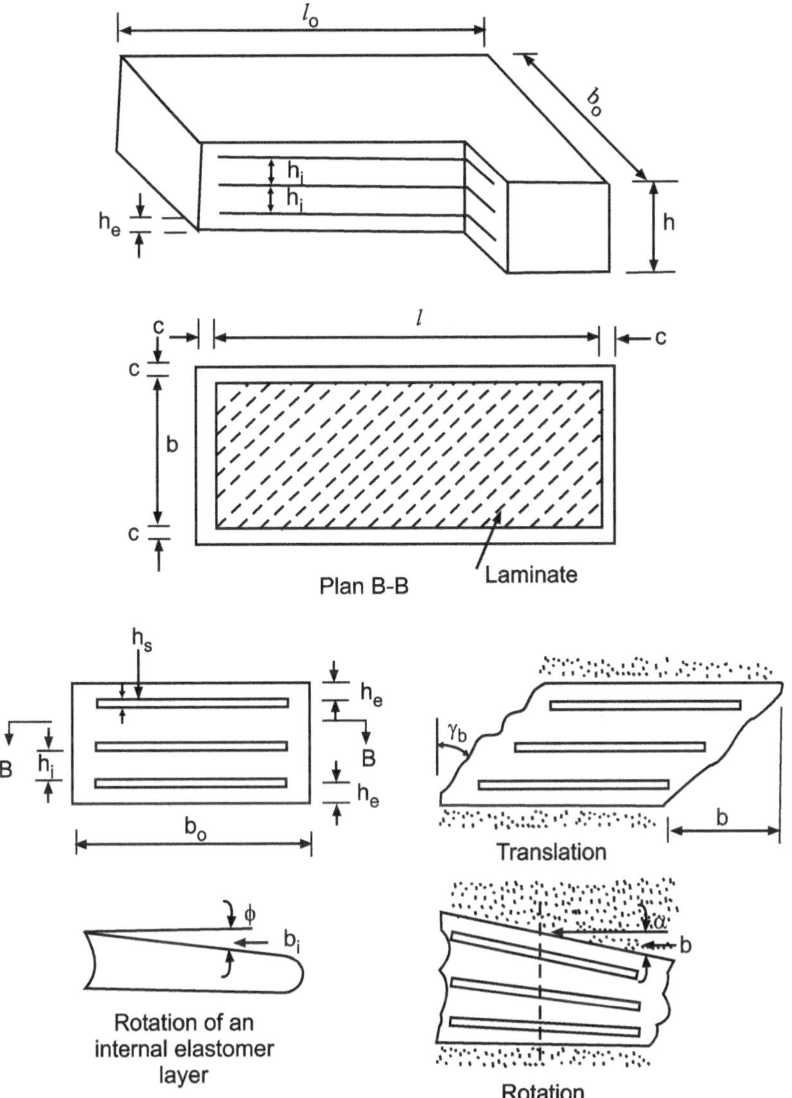

Fig. 15.16 : Elastomeric bearing general features

15.17 MAINTENANCE OF BEARINGS

- The bearings shall be subjected to planned maintenance care.

- The exposed bearing surface shall be maintained clean and free iron contamination with grease or oil etc.

- Annual routine maintenance inspection or special maintenance inspection of all bearings shall be made to check for any surface cracking or signs of damage, deterioration or distress.

- Damaged bearings shall be replaced immediately. To avoid differences in stiffness all adjacent bearings on the same lines of support shall also be replaced.

- Arrangement for insertion of jacks to lift the bridge deck shall be made in detailing of the structure.

The lifting of a cast-in-place post-tensioned bridge deck for relieving time dependent deformation shortly after installation of bearings should be avoided. In case such lifting is unavoidable, the lifting arrangement, proper seating of the girder on the bearing etc. shall be rigidly controlled to avoid any risk of misalignment.

15.18 DEFECTS IN THE BEARINGS

In a bridge, bearings are provided between the superstructure and the substructure to cater for movements resulting from elongation of shortening, bending of the deck. The superstructure system is subjected to two types of movements viz (i) expansion and contraction this may be due to change in temperature of the area from time to time are due to creep and shrinkage in concrete etc. (ii) rotational movement at the support due to deflection in the girder on account of its own weight or due to superimposed load etc.

As per IRC Bridge Code for concrete structures, provision shall be made for movements resulting from variations in temperature of $\pm$ 17°C for moderate climate and $\pm$ 25°C for extreme climate. Collection of climate data giving the variation in temperature for different areas is an essential prerequisite in the temperature variation to be catered for it with reference to the normal temperature. Calculations for the initial set of the bearings should take into considerations the normal temperature, the temperature at the time of placement of bearing, time dependent deformations the creep and shrinkage in concrete etc.

Some instances have come to notice where metallic bridge bearings of road bridges have tilted excessively resulting in the girder ends jamming and hitting against the dirt walls. Some of the possible causes for such a phenomenon are.

- Inaccurate alignment and positioning of bearings at the time of construction due to lack of proper supervision.

- Wrong initial set of rollers.

- Rotation of the foundation and substructure even by a fraction of a degree.

In case suitable measures are not taken to prevent excessive movement or to reset the bearings in time when excessive movement occurs, the bridge may be put out of commission.

15.19 MEASURES TO AVOID EXCESSIVE MOVEMENT IN BEARINGS

- IRC Bridge Code Section V(RC-24-1967) specifies that in seismic areas where seismic coefficient exceeding G/20 is taken, segmental rollers shall not be permitted. Even in other areas, it is suggested that cut rollers should be avoided both in respect to large spans where excessive movement is expected and also in respect of cases where settlement and or tilting of abutment is anticipated due to poor soil supporting the abutment or in cases where high abutment are provided.

- Where cut rollers are provided, the width of the cut roller should be such that even with the maximum anticipated movement, 50 per cent of the rolling margin is still left. The top and bottom plates should also be made larger.
- In order to cater for any possible relative undue movement between the superstructure and the dirt wall over the abutment resulting in the girder ends jamming and hitting against the dirt walls, a bigger gap (say 150 mm) could be provided between the girder end and the dirt wall.
- The back filling upto the abutment cap level should be done before the superstructure is constructed so that most of the tilting of the abutment, if any, due to the earth pressure can take place before the superstructure is in position, thus facilitating the placing of the bearings in their correct positions.
- Adequate soil investigations should be carried out for the foundations so that cut rollers can be avoided in cases where soil is likely to yield.
- Regarding back filling of the abutments, the specifications for material and construction of backfill laid down should be fully complied with. It should be ensured that heavy rolling is not resorted to behind the abutments.
- Initial reverse tilt to be given for the cast in situ prestressed concrete bridges should be very carefully worked out. It may even to desirable to reset the bearings after completion of prestressing and back filling particularly for long spans (greater than 30 m). The temperature at the time of erection shall be taken into account in placing the rocker/rollers and the top bearing plates. The rocker or rollers shall be adjusted (or set) at the time of placement in such a way that if any computed or anticipated movement of the bridge seat (due to creep, strinkage and temporary effects) takes place after they have been set, the line of the bearing will be centred on the bearing plates at the normal temperature adopted in the design.
- The bearings shall be protected while concreting the decking in-situ that there is no flow of mortar or any other such matter into the bearing assembly and particularly on to the bearing surfaces. The protection shall be such that it can be dismantled after the construction is over without disturbing the bearing assembly.
- Special attention should be given to the temporary fixtures to be provided for the bearings during the concreting of superstructure in order to ensure that they do not get displaced during the initial installation itself.
- The behaviour of the bearings right from the time of installation should be watched at regular intervals and observations recorded in a systematic way so that corrective action could be taken in time. In particular there should be a thorough examination of the bearings just before the expiry of the defect liability period so that the

- excessive movement if any, could be got rectified through the contractor who has constructed the bridge.
- Provision should be made for jacking up to superstructure, so as to facilitate resetting of bearings in case abnormal movement is noticed in spite of the above precautions.
- Adequate investigations, design expertise and competent supervision all go a long way to avoid the problem.

15.20 BRIDGE ERECTION

The method selected depends very much on the type of bridge construction, span, height above ground or water etc.

Commonly used methods for the erection of bridges:

- In-situ - assembly of bridge components on temporary falsework.
- Lifting - e.g. (a) beams and trusses - placing of individual beams or a complete deck by crane (b) suspension bridges - lifting of pre-fabricated deck modules which are then hung from the deck hangers connected to the previously installed main cables, slung between the main towers and anchorages.
- Launching - sequential construction (on rollers or tracks) of a continuous deck at one end of the bridge. As each new section is added the whole deck is pushed or pulled out (usually over multiple spans).
- Sliding or rolling - construction of a complete new bridge (usually alongside a busy existing bridge) which is then jacked into place over a few hours or days, to replace the existing structure.
- Cantilevering - (a) for arches - successive construction from the two springing points which is temporarily tied back until the two halves can be joined at midspan (b) for cable-stayed bridges - successive cantilevering out from the pylons of deck units suspended from the stay cables.

15.21 FACTORS TO BE CONSIDERED WHILE ERECTING A BRIDGE

The following factors should be considered while making the choice between method of bridge construction:

- The site conditions.
- Type of the bridge structure to be constructed.
- Depth and current of the river water at the site.
- Standards of material and layout available.
- The equipment available.
- Type of foundation bed available at the site.
- Scheduled period of construction.
- Sequence of construction.

15.21.1 Problems During Erection of Bridge

- Passing of existing traffic during construction of the bridge.
- Transportation of the materials and machinery required for construction of the bridge.
- Storage of the material.
- Space required for placing equipment and machinery.
- Diversion of the river course.
- Time pattern in which the bridge is to be completed.

15.21.2 Erection of Steel Girder Bridges

- Erection by assembling the girders on the river bed.
- Erection by use of staging.
- Erection by floating the girders.
- Erection by rolling out girders.
- Erection by launching of single girder span.

15.21.3 Erection of Suspension Bridges

- Erection of tower.
- Erection of suspension.
- Erection of stiffening trusses.
- Erection of flooring system.

- **Erection of Tower :** The main towers of a suspension bridge are erected first with the help of floating crane or derrick. The successive towers are erected with the help of a creeper traveler.

- **Erection of Catwalk :** Catwalk are working platforms which help in the over ropes placed concentric with the main cables. A tramway system is then installed from anchorage to anchorage along the catwalk for pulling the bridge wire. At each anchorage a wheel called spinning wheel is attached to the tramway system.

  The bridge wire ends are fastened to anchorage end and then looped over the spinning wheels. The wheels are then pulled along the catwalk and over the towers to the opposite anchorage, the wires are attached to the anchorage and the procedure is repeated.

- **Erection of Suspender :** Cable bands are placed around the cable to grip it at each-point of suspension of the roadway. Suspenders are attached to the cable bands to receive the roadway.

- **Erection of Flooring System :** The flooring system is provided over the stiffening trusses and the roadway surface is placed over it.

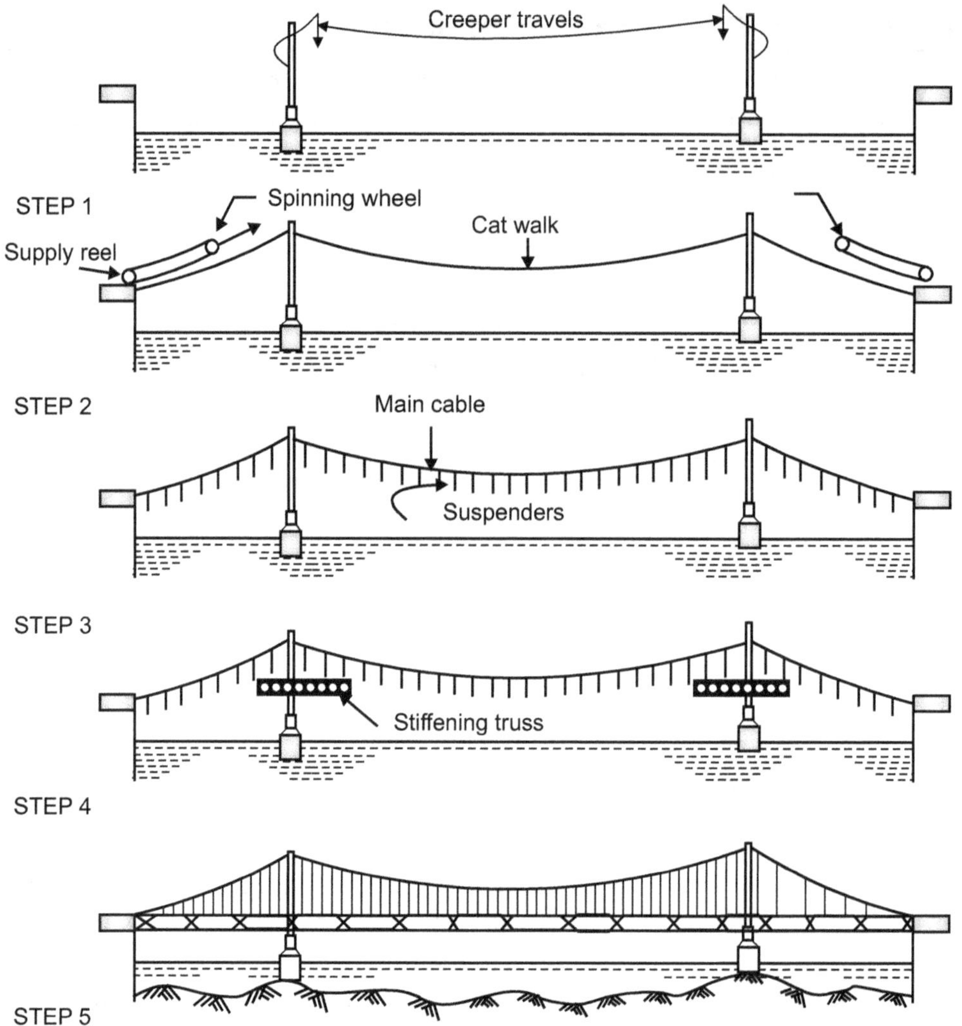

Fig. 15.17 : Erection of suspension bridge (parallel wire type)

15.21.4 R.C.C. and Prestressed Concrete Bridges

In these types of bridges the main work is Form work and placing of steel reinforcement in-position. Normally the work is done cast in-situ.

After completing form work and placing reinforcement, the concrete (1 : 2 : 4) is poured. Then curing is done. After 21 days generally form work is removed.

The construction of prestressed concrete super-structure is carried out in the following stages :

• Casting of beams in casting yard.

• Transport of the beams from the casting yard to the nearest abutment.

• Transporting beam to the span where it is to be placed.

- Casting of the deck and other details.

Note : For transporting the beams from casting yard to the abutments a rail-track is laid. Two trolleys one caring the rear and the other the front end of the girder are used to move on this track. Placing is done by using a block of rollers under the beam and a polley-block.

15.22 MAINTENANCE OF BRIDGES

The maintenance details vary with the materials of construction. Steel must be painted at regular intervals. R.C.C. works must be inspected for the cracks and if any cracks are found, they should be sealed as soon as possible. Masonry works must be kept well-plastered or pointed.

The regular inspection of bridges is a matter of great importance, since the early detection of trouble and the prompt attention may well obviate costly repairs which may be needed, if defects are allowed to develop too far.

The matters required regular attention are as follows :

- The proper functioning of weep holes and other drainage devices.
- The free action of expansion joints and drainage.
- Examination of bridge superstructures and sub-structures.
- Clearing of obstructions in channels tending to cause scour.
- Detection and tracing of water leakage through decks.
- Maintenance of water-proofing coats.
- Signs of movement of foundations, especially on clay, as evidenced by cracks in the structure or the road surface over it.
- The careful examination of steel structures for corrosion, especially in parts where moist or polluted air may be partially trapped.

It is well to systematize inspection and to record the results so that a full history of each bridge, including any trouble which may have been encountered during construction, is readily available.

15.23 STRENGTHENING OF BRIDGES

In the past, live load carried by a bridge was very light as compared to the dead load. There has been a tremendous increase in the carrying capacities of our transport vehicles. The road system however, has not sufficiently developed to cater for such increase in payloads. There is a dire need for improvement of the old and out of service bridges on our roads.

Strengthening of Bridge Substructure: The substructure is strengthened in following different ways:

1. Masonry substructure: In case of old masonry substructure showing signs of disintegrations, the entire loose material all around the structure is removed to find out the defect. If it is found that masonry has large cavities, then they should be filled with cement concrete. Later a wire netting should be stretched around the entire masonry and fastened there to with spikes. Finally a coat of cement mortar is forced by a gun.

2. **Strengthening of bridge pier:**

- In order to strengthen an old pier a cofferdam is constructed around the piers. A thick concrete casing is provided all around the pier after pumping out the water.

- In case of foundation showing unequal settlements it is necessary to underpin the base of pier in deep and running water. This is done by sinking a pneumatic caisson near the pier.

15.24 STRENGTHENING OF BRIDGE SUPERSTRUCTURE

Method of strengthening a bridge superstructure depends upon the type of the bridge. The following methods for different types of bridge are in vogue:

- To fill large voids in honey combed concrete by cement grouting so that quality of concrete is improved and cover to reinforcement is obtained.
- Sealing of cracks and voids by epoxy grouting.
- To impact extra shear strength to girders when shear cracks appear on the girder, by providing shear plates.
- Providing I-beams on sides.

(a) Grouting: High pressure grouts are not useful for strengthening of R.C.C. bridges. Therefore grouting should be done by hand operated pump with low pressure operations for cracks more than 0.25 mm in any bad concrete, we may employ solid suspension grout such as cement water or cement sand water with water cement ratio 0.47 to 0.52. For finer cracks, we may employ chemical grout as epoxy grout.

For thin cracks and pressure, epoxy should be used under pressure.

(b) I-Beams: R.C.C. beam and slab bridge - In this type, the beams are strengthened by providing steel I-beam on each side of the existing beams. In case of longer spans the load from the existing beams are directly taken away by steel cross girders supported on steel built-up girders.

If an existing bridge in sound condition is proposed to be widened by adding additional beams. It is preferable to do the entire widening on one side, from considerations of lateral stability provided the geometrics of the road alignments permits it.

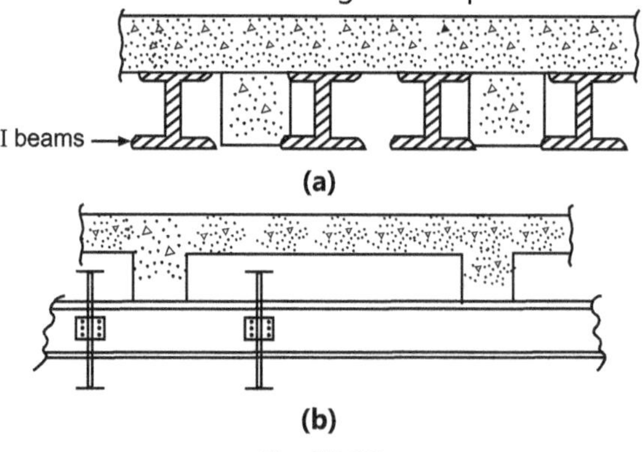

Fig. 15.18

(c) Masonry Arch Bridges: They are usually strengthened by first removing the filling above the arch and then casting R.C.C. arch slab on the top of the roughened extrudes. the slab is securely keyed into the abutments.

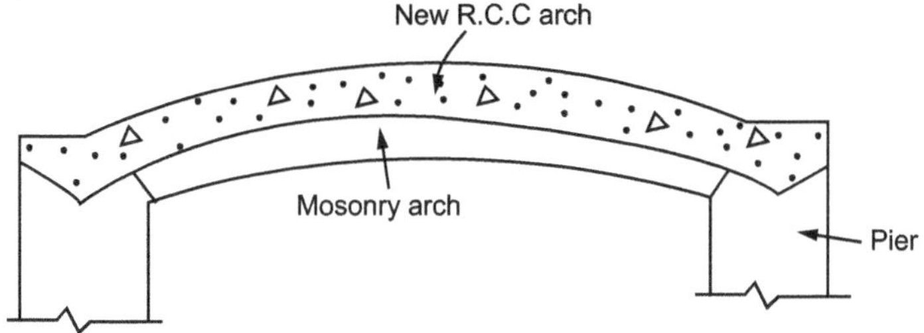

Fig. 15.19 (a)

When the arch is too weak to hear loud more than its own weight, then a new R.C.C. arch must be built several centimeters above existing extrudes with the help of removable shuttering.

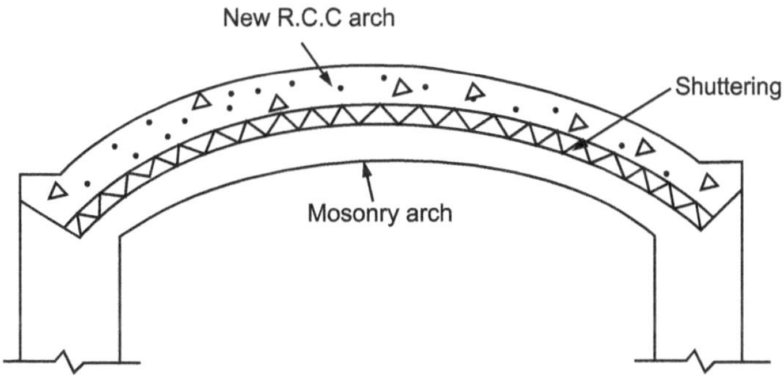

Fig. 15.19 (b)

(d) Continuous Bridge: They are strengthened by methods similar to that of single span care should be taken that when a span is being strengthened the adjacent span is not weakened.

(e) Steel Bridge: They are strengthened by providing extra steel plates or angles or concrete encasements.

(f) Suspension Bridge: They are usually strengthened by providing additional cables with fasteners.

(g) Shear Plates: When girder shows shear cracks, external shear reinforcement in the form of shear plate could be provided in end portion of girder where generally, these cracks are observed. These plates are to be bounded to the sides of ribs by cutting groove and bounding them with epoxy. Edges of plate are to be sealed with epoxy. Mortar and epoxy injected through inlets to achieve good bond with concrete proper anchorage with bond plate is necessary. For this, mild steel bars in the inverted U fashion are welded to bond plate and embedded in the concrete.

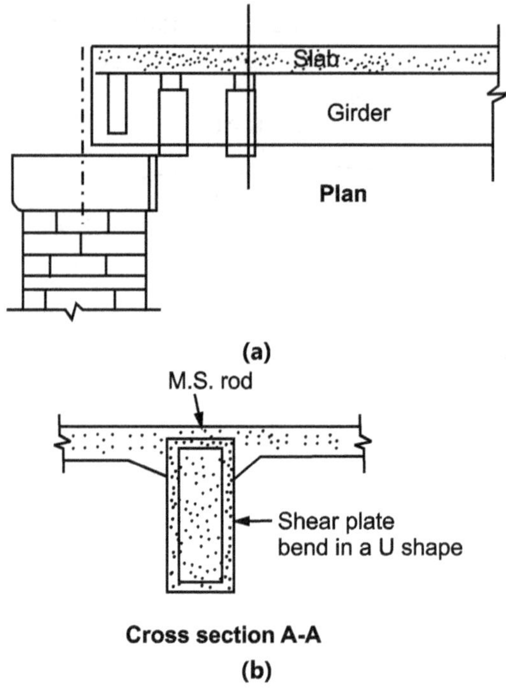

Fig. 15.20

QUESTIONS

1. What are bridge bearings ? Explain the procedure of design of elastomeric bearing.
2. State various functions of bearings for bridges.
3. Explain various part of metallic bearing.
4. What are bridge bearings ? Explain with the neat sketches.
5. Write a detail note on maintenance of bridge bearings.
6. Draw a neat sketch of the following and label the parts.
   (a) Knuckle bearing
   (b) Roller cum rocker bearing
   (c) Elastomeric bearing.
7. Differntiate between :
   (a) Rocker and Roller bearing and Expansion bearing.
   (b) Fixed bearing and free bearing.
8. What are different techniques of errection of bridge superstructures.
9. Why maintenance of bridges required.

Sample Question Paper for
In-Semester Examination

Marks: 30   **Time: 1 Hour**

---

1. (a) What are the various methods of classification of roads? Briefly explain classification as per Nagpur Road Plan. **[6 M]**

(b) Write an explanatory note on Highway planning Survey's. **[4 M]**

OR

2. (a) Discuss how different road patterns are gainfully employed in the metropolitan cities of India. **[6 M]**

(b) Discuss the need for off-street parting. How it can be arranged ? What are the relative merits and demerits of this system ? **[4 M]**

OR

3. (a) How road improvement decision can be based on the level of service ? **[6 M]**

(b) What is Arboriculture? What role does it play in highway environment? Discuss any specific case. **[4 M]**

OR

4. (a) Explain the concept of super-elevation. Why some curves may not require super-elevation? What part friction between tyre and road plays in determining super-elevation? **[6 M]**

(b) What is meant by alignment of roads? What are the points to be kept in mind while aligning a road? **[4 M]**

OR

5. (a) What are various test carried out on soil? Explain any one briefly? **[6 M]**

(b) How do we calculate traffic intensity as per I.R.C. method of design of rigid pavements and how traffic is classified in it? **[4 M]**

OR

6. (a) Explain the details the contraction procedures for water Bound Macadam Road construction. **[6 M]**

(b) Explain the detial about marshal stability teal. with neat diagram. **[4 M]**

Sample Question Paper for
End-Semester Examination

Marks: 70   **Time: 2:30 Hour**

---

1. (a) Discuss in details the road development plan of 1981 – 2001. **[4 M]**

   (b) What guiding principles should be kept in mind while making a route selection for highway? **[8 M]**

   (c) Define terms (i) Flakiness Index (ii) Elongation Index, and also state the importance of that. **[8M]**

OR

2. (a) Discuss the need for off-street parting. How it can be arranged ? What are the relative merits and demerits of this system ? **[8 M]**

   (b) Explain the concept of super-elevation. Why some curves may not require super-elevation? What part friction between tyre and road plays in determining super-elevation? **[4 M]**

   (c) Draw the neat sketches for the cross-section of Flexible and Rigid pavements. Mention in detail about the materials used, their properties, merits and demerits and failure of the pavements in Rainy Season. **[8 M]**

3. (a) What are the facilities to be provided in the terminal building of an international airport ? **[8 M]**

   (b) What are the different control surfaces at an airport ? Explain the concepts of airport zoning with the help of sketches. **[4 M]**

   (c) Distinguish between Type I and Type II wind rose diagrams. Explain how the optimum runway orientation is determined **[4 M]**

OR

4. (a) What are advantages and limitation of air transportation ? **[4 M]**

   (b) Write notes on

      (i) Aprons

      (ii) Hangers

      (iii) Wind Rose Diagram

      (iv) Runway Configuration

      (v) Airport Obstruction   **[4 M]**

   (c) The average wind data collected at a particular site is given below. Determine the calm period, the post orientation of runway and the total wind coverage along the direction of EW, and NS by using Wind rose diagram Type II. Permissible cross wind component is 25 kmph.   **[8 M]**

5. (a) Discuss the various forces coming over bridge pier and also state the conditions of stability.   **[8 M]**

   (b) Describe the various types of foundations to piers and abutments.   **[4 M]**

   (c) What is height of afflux? State also its importance and hence calculate the height of afflux from the following particulars.   **[4 M]**

OR

6. (a) Enumerate various forces, loads and stresses which are to be considered in the design of a bridge.   **[4 M]**

   (b) What is height of afflux? State also its importance and hence calculate the height of afflux from the following particulars.

      (i) Normal velocity of flow in a river is 1.50 m/sec.

      (ii) The normal and artificial waterway under the bridge and enlarged area upstream of the bridge are respectively 8000 m^2, 7000 m^2 and 10,000 m^2.

      Assume g = 9.81 m/sec^2. Use Merriman's formula. Also find increase in velocity. **[8 M]**

   (c) Give detail classification of bridges stating clearly on which these depend?   **[4 M]**

7. (a) Differentiate between :   **[6 M]**

      (i) Cantilever bridges and Bascule bridges.

      (ii) Movable span and Fixed span bridges.

   (b) Discuss the various types of movable span superstructure with respect to their suitability only. **[6 M]**

   (c) Explain with neat sketches slab culverts, pipe culverts and box girder bridges. **[6 M]**

OR

8. (a) What are different techniques of errection of bridge superstructures **[6 M]**

   (b) What are bridge bearings ? Explain the procedure of design of elastomeric bearing. **[6 M]**

   (c) Write a detail note on maintenance of bridge bearings **[6 M]**